YOUNG HAG AND THE Witches' Quest

YOUNG HAG

AND THE

Witches' Quest

By Isabel Greenberg

Amulet Books • New York

Library of Congress Control Number for the hardcover edition 2023940991

Hardcover ISBN 978-1-4197-6511-7
Paperback ISBN 978-1-4197-6512-4

Text and illustrations © 2024 Isabel Greenberg
Book design by Andrea Miller

Printed and bound in China
10 9 8 7 6 5 4 3 2 1

ABRAMS The Art of Books
195 Broadway, New York, NY 10007
abramsbooks.com

For Frieda.
From a Nearly Wizened One,
to a Young Hag

IN THIS BOOK

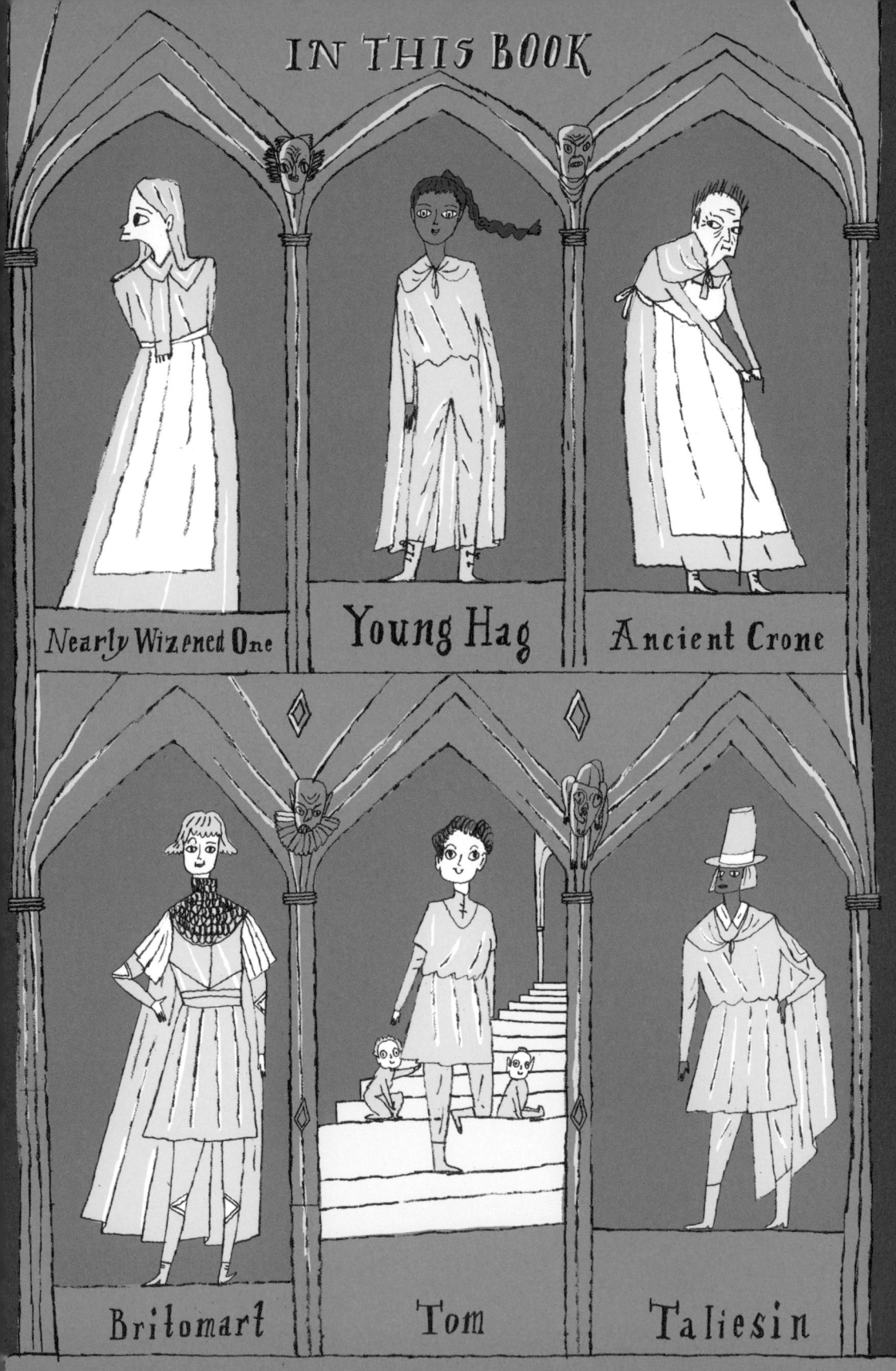

Nearly Wizened One

Young Hag

Ancient Crone

Britomart

Tom

Taliesin

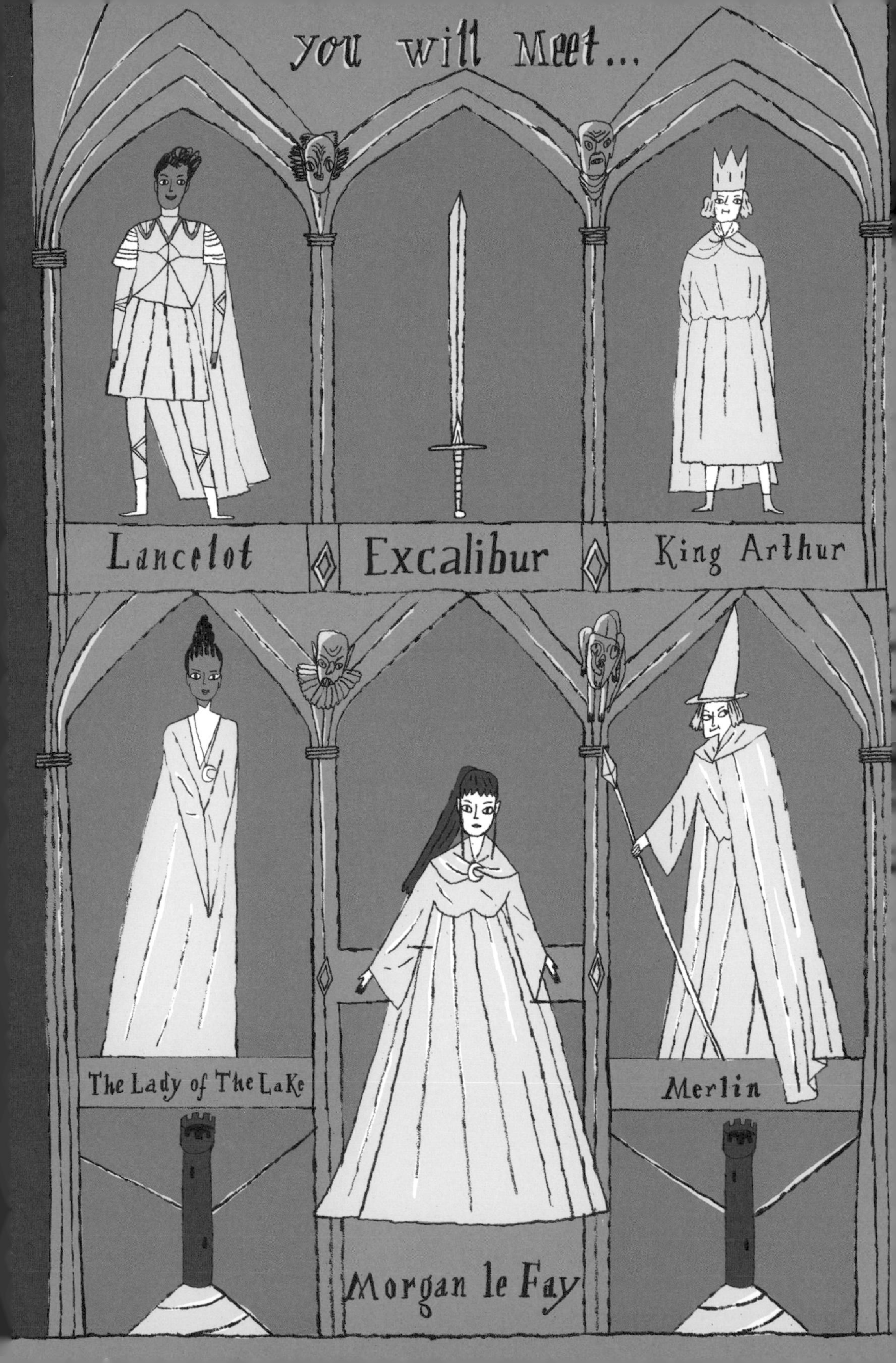
you will Meet…
Lancelot
Excalibur
King Arthur
The Lady of The Lake
Merlin
Morgan le Fay

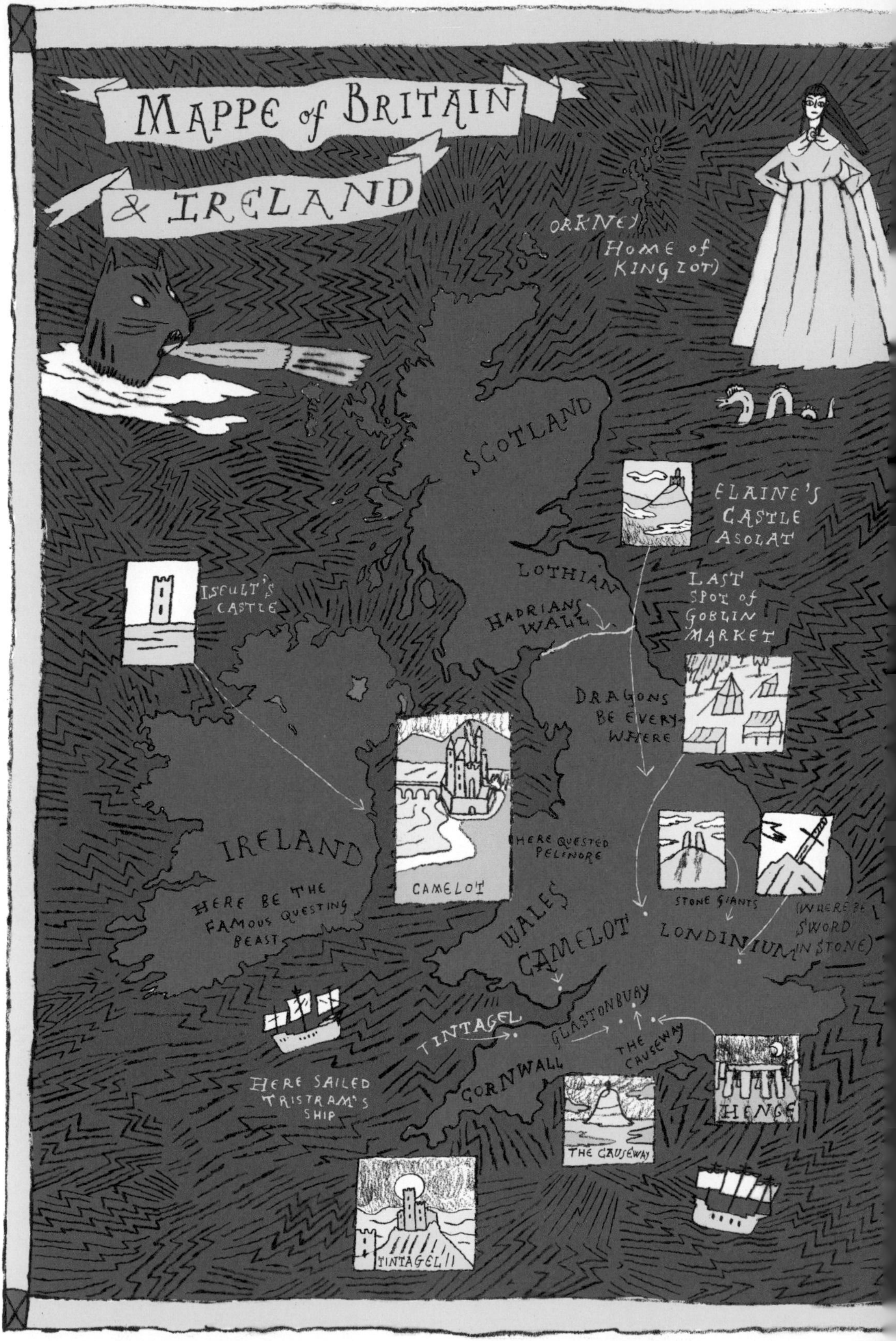
MAPPE of BRITAIN
& IRELAND
ORKNEY
HOME of KING LOT
SCOTLAND
ELAINE'S CASTLE ASOLAT
LOTHIAN
LAST SPOT of GOBLIN MARKET
ISEULT'S CASTLE
HADRIANS WALL
DRAGONS BE EVERY-WHERE
CAMELOT
HERE QUESTED PELINORE
IRELAND
HERE BE THE FAMOUS QUESTING BEAST
STONE GIANTS
(WHERE BE SWORD IN STONE)
WALES
CAMELOT
LONDINIUM
TINTAGEL
GLASTONBURY
THE CAUSEWAY
CORNWALL
HERE SAILED TRISTRAM'S SHIP
THE CAUSEWAY
HENGE
TINTAGEL

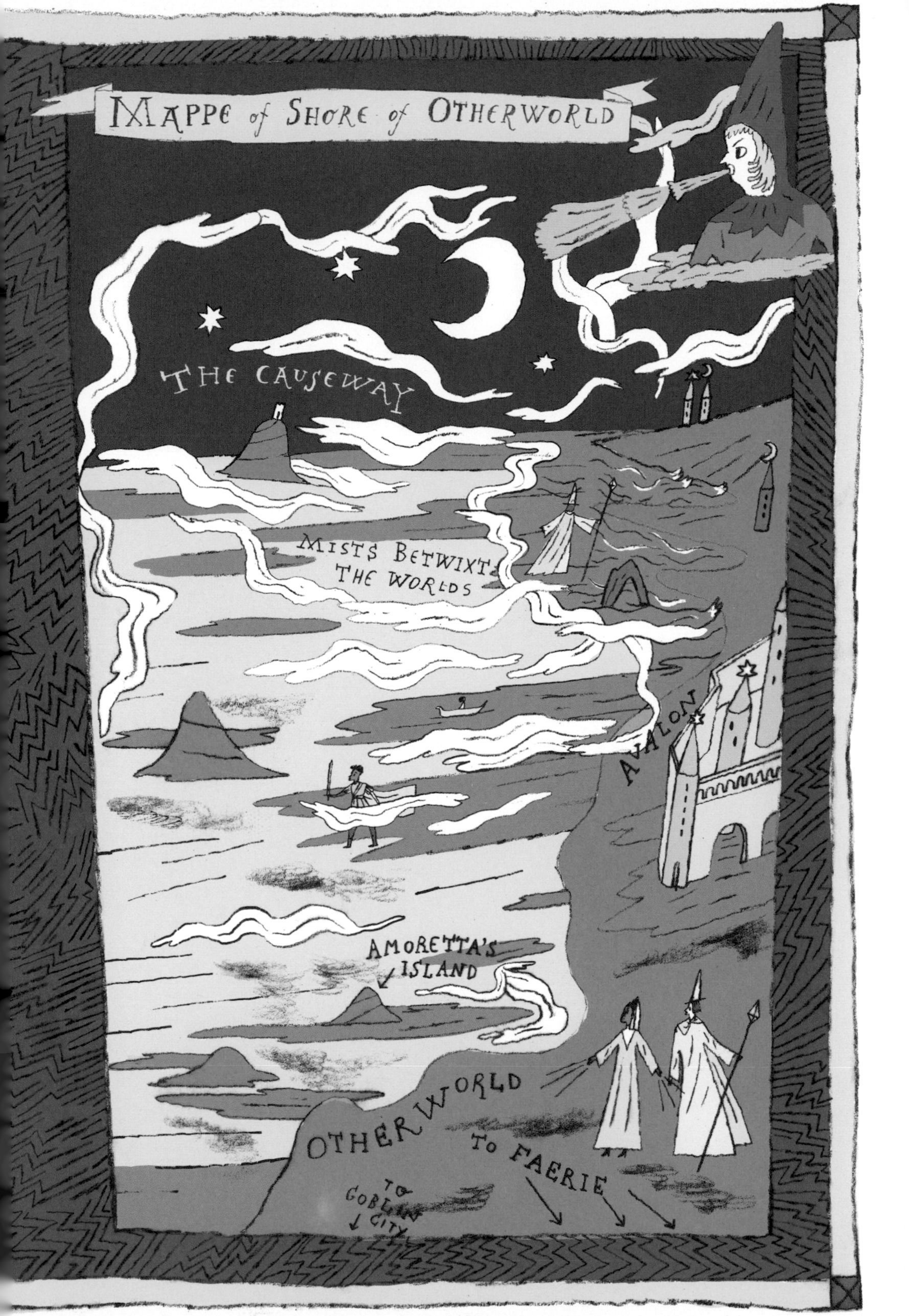
MAPPE of SHORE of OTHERWORLD
THE CAUSEWAY
MISTS BETWIXT THE WORLDS
AVALON
AMORETTA'S ISLAND
OTHERWORLD
TO FAERIE
TO GOBLIN CITY

PROLOGUE

Once there was magic in Britain. It flowed through every tree
and rock and stream, and the land was thick with it.
Dragons tossed and turned in the deep places of the earth,
wizards summoned winds and tied them in knots.
The land was magic, and the magic was the land.

But then things began to change. First came the Romans,
and they brought their gods, and then came the Christians, and they
brought theirs. A stone road built over a faerie road, a bath house
erected over a sacred spring, an ancient wood felled to make way for a
grand castle or a lofty church. With each, a little magic trickled away.

Then came the wars. The blood seeped into the earth and the
dragons grew quiet. And still more magic trickled away.

It was a moment in which everything hung in the balance.
Would it be a world of magic, or a world of reason?
And into this world, there came the wizard Merlin. Above all things,
Merlin was terrified about what would happen if the magic went
from the land, if people stopped worshipping the Old Gods,
and believing in the Old Ways.

So he looked into his mirror, and he asked it
how he could save the magic of Britain.

The magic mirror of Merlin was all the stars that spun in the
kaleidoscope sky, it was the surface of every still lake, the shadows
of the clouds that raced across the hills and valleys.
It was the face of the rock and the eyes at the heart of every tree.
These were all Merlin's mirrors, and they all spoke to him.

Merlin asked the stars, "Can I save the magic of Britain?"

And the stars replied,
"You will try. But it will not be you."

Merlin stood before the dark lake and asked,
"Why will it not be me?"

And the lake replied, "Because you will be betrayed."

Merlin stood before the face of the cliff and asked them,

"Who then? Who will complete this task?"
And the face of the cliff replied, "A woman."

"Ach," said Merlin. "Well, that sounds highly unlikely to me.
And who then will betray me?"

And the face of the cliff said again, "A woman."

"But who are these women?" mused Merlin. "One who will
betray me and one who will save the magic of the land...
how will I know them, and how will I tell them apart?"

The face of the cliff was not forthcoming.
But finally they replied, "Start with a king."

PART THE FIRST

A Coming-of-Age Thing

On the day I was named Young Hag, I was not yet bleeding. And so my grandmother, Ancient Crone, took the palm of my hand and pressed into it her sharp knife.

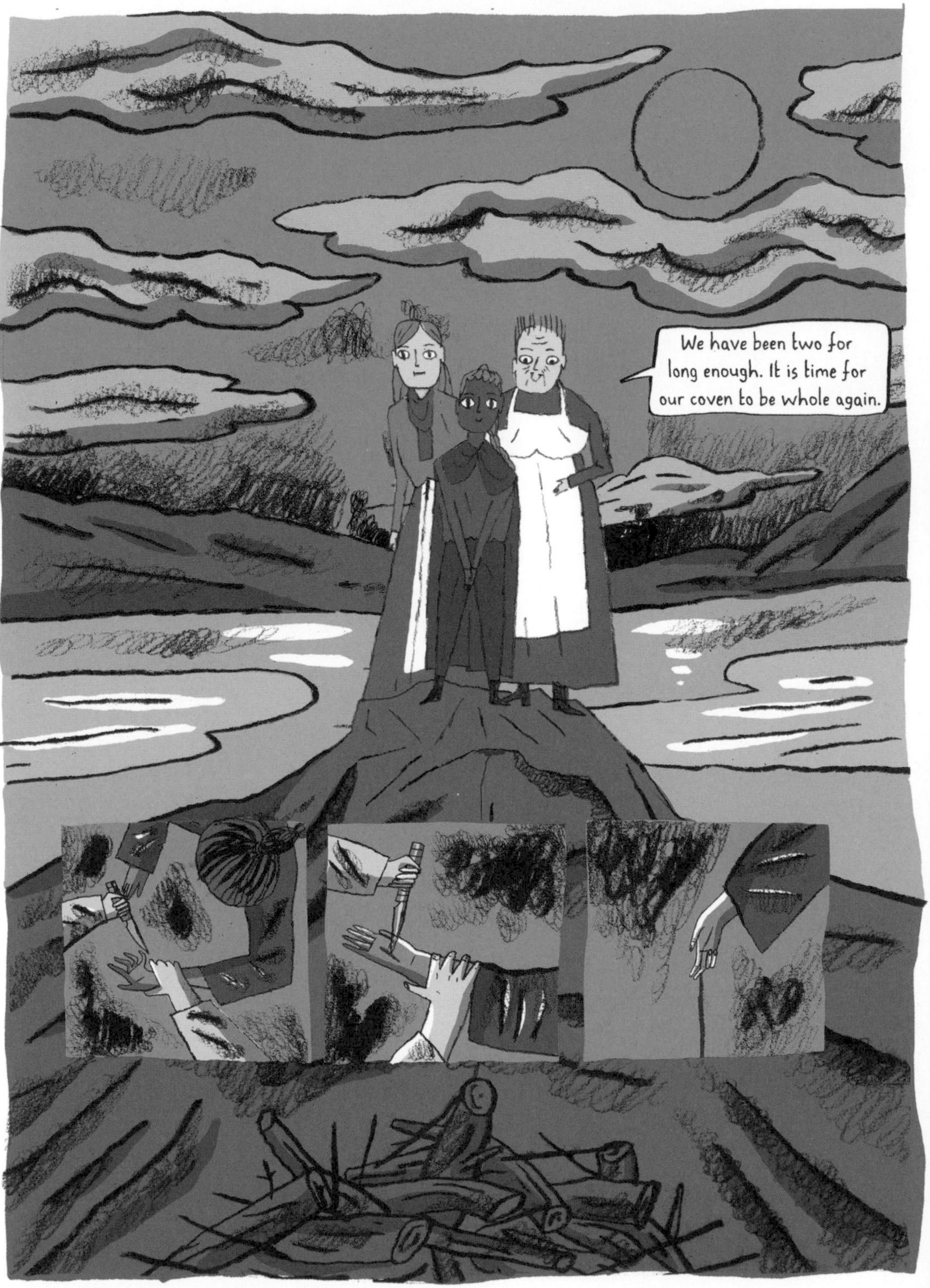
We have been two for long enough. It is time for our coven to be whole again.

The blood trickled out, down my arm and then fell, heavy red droplets, onto the wood of the unlit pyre.

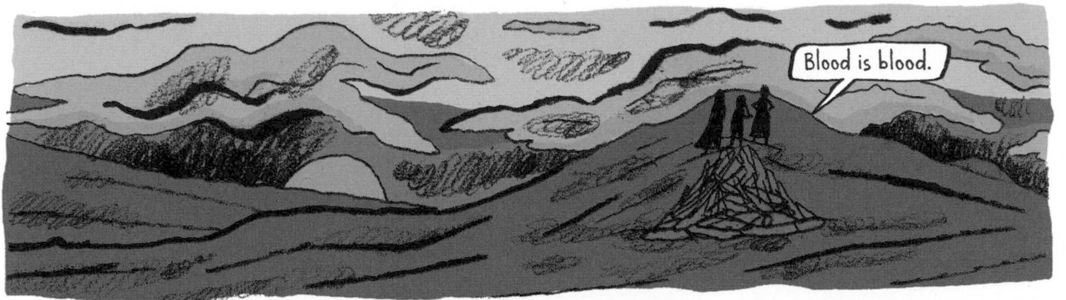
Blood is blood.

My mother, now called Nearly Wizened One, who had been Young Hag 'til just that moment, took my face between her hands and kissed me three times: forehead, left eye, right eye.

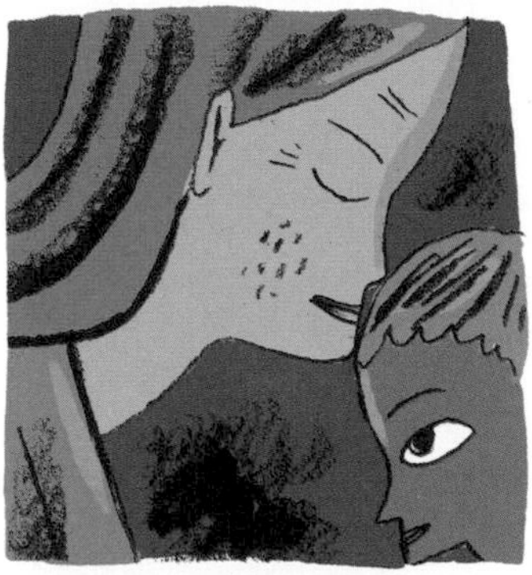

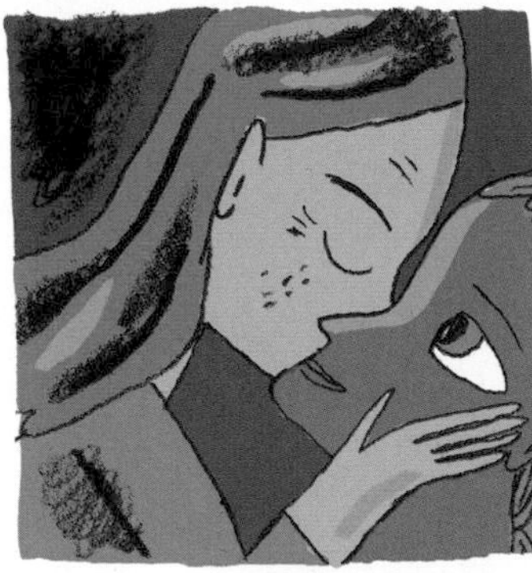

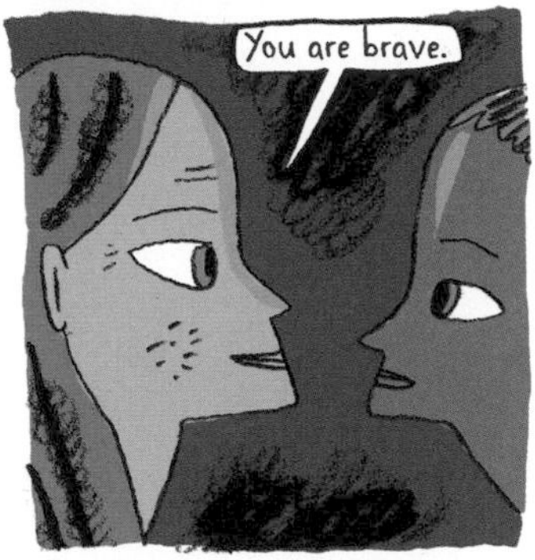
You are brave.

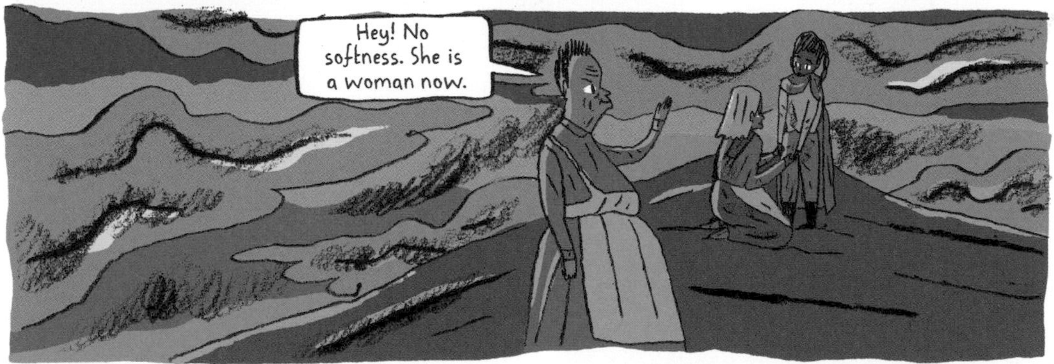
Hey! No softness. She is a woman now.

But gently she bound my wound with moss and bark and some magic words.

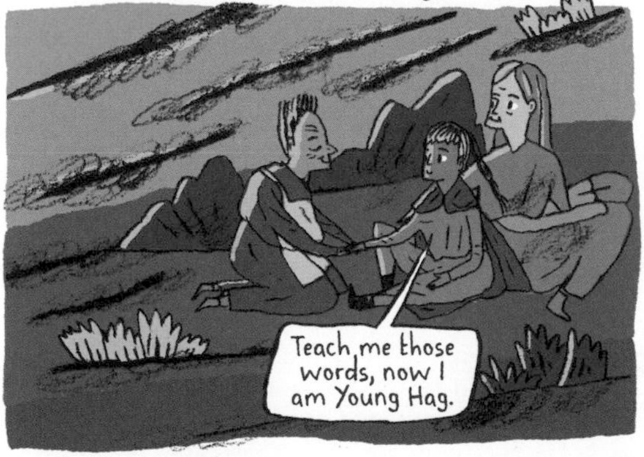
Teach me those words, now I am Young Hag.

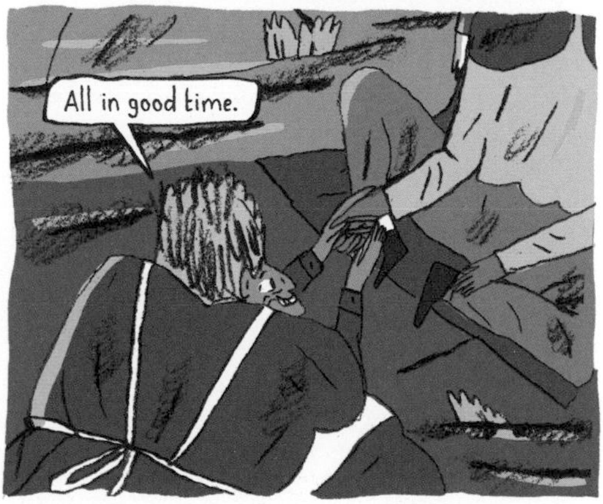
All in good time.

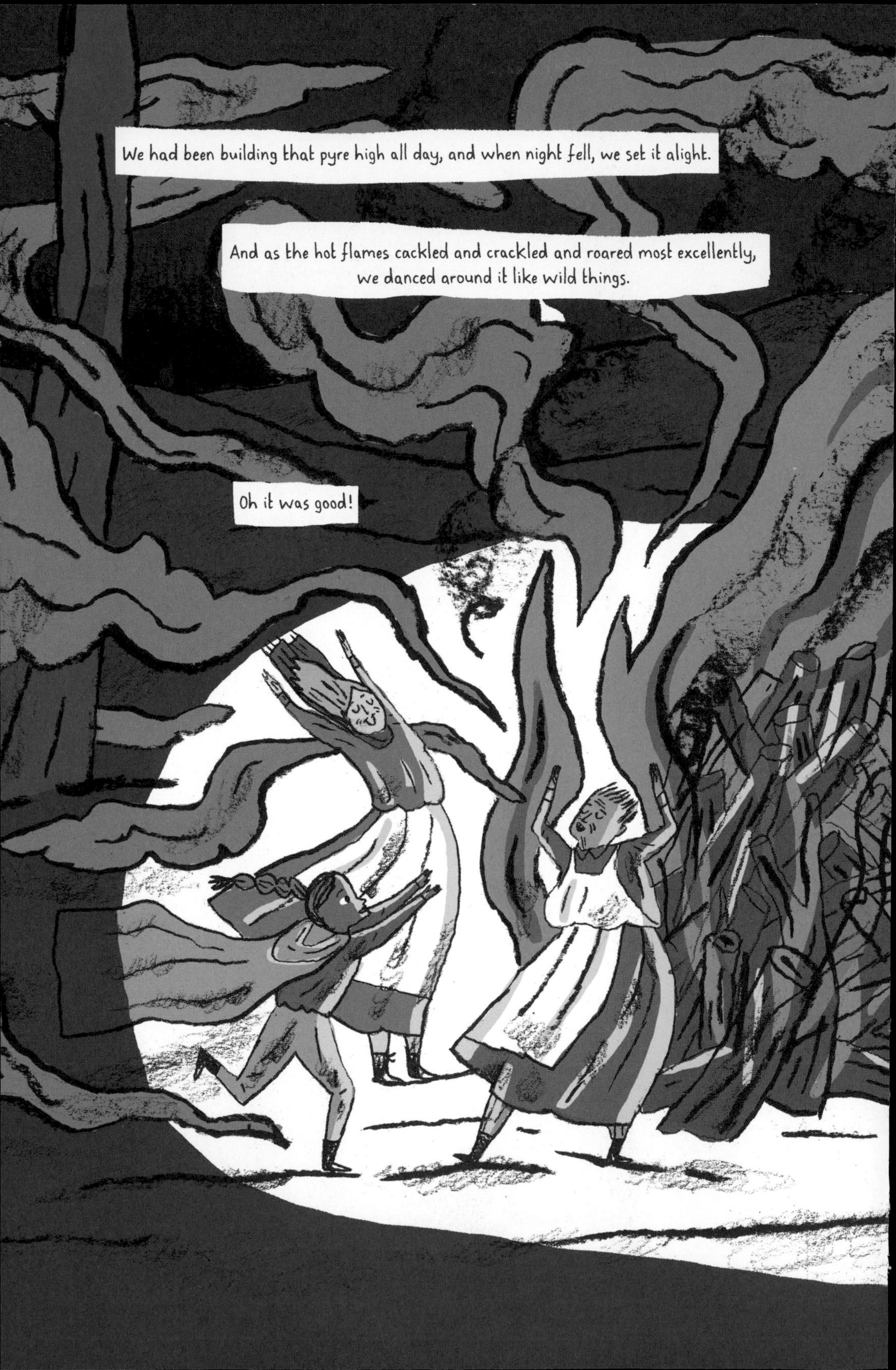
We had been building that pyre high all day, and when night fell, we set it alight.
And as the hot flames cackled and crackled and roared most excellently, we danced around it like wild things.
Oh it was good!

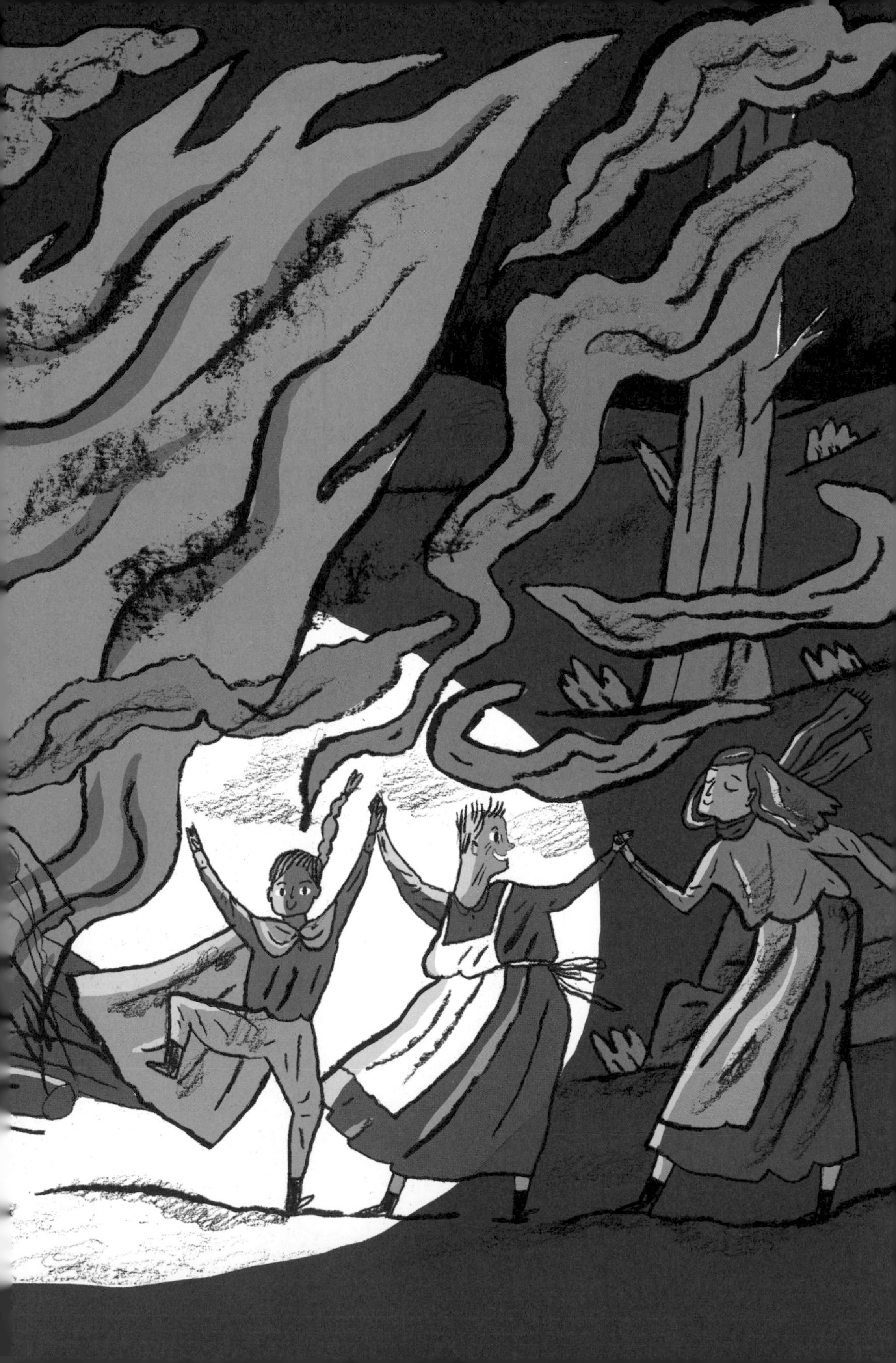

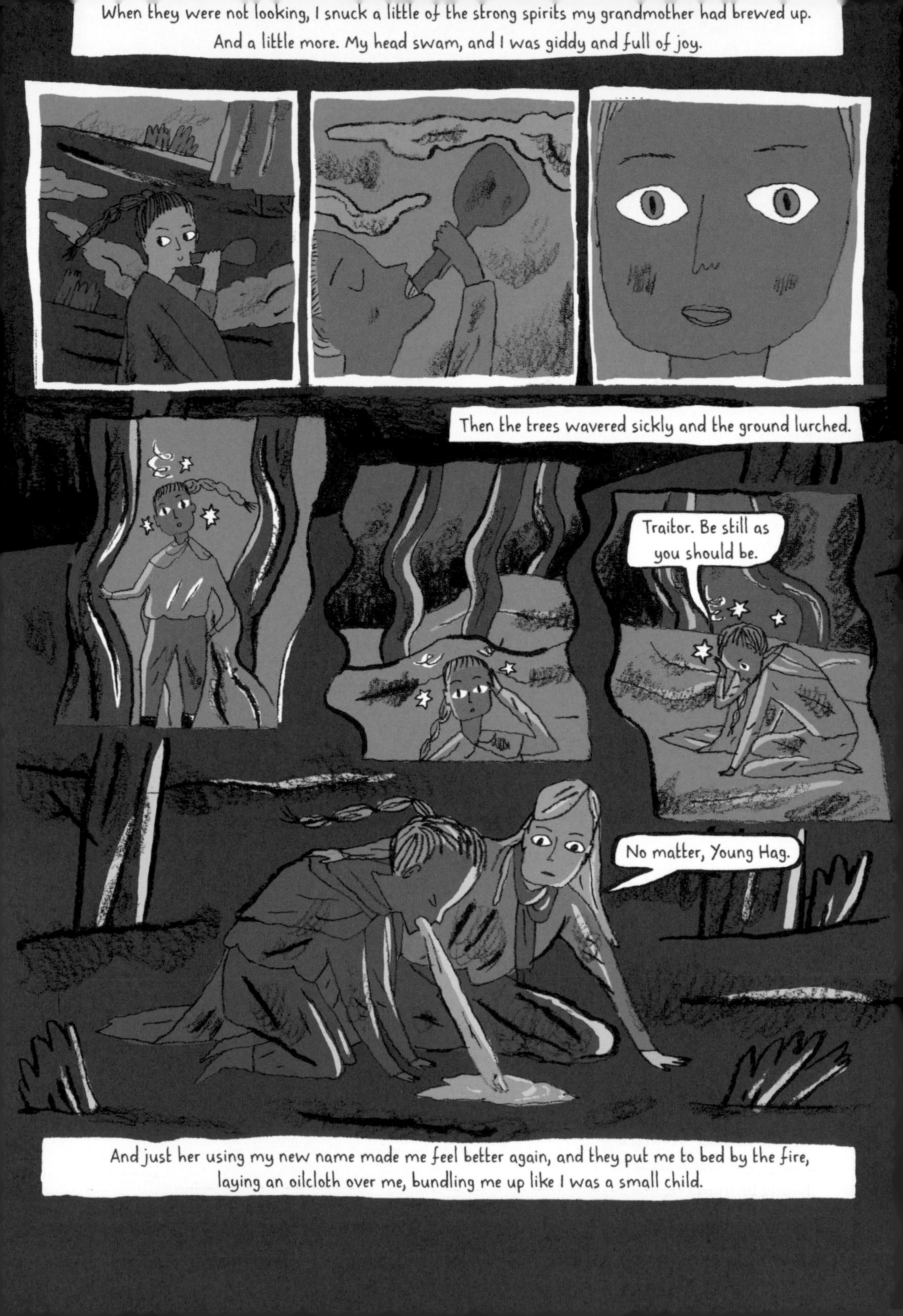
When they were not looking, I snuck a little of the strong spirits my grandmother had brewed up. And a little more. My head swam, and I was giddy and full of joy.
Then the trees wavered sickly and the ground lurched.
Traitor. Be still as you should be.
No matter, Young Hag.
And just her using my new name made me feel better again, and they put me to bed by the fire, laying an oilcloth over me, bundling me up like I was a small child.

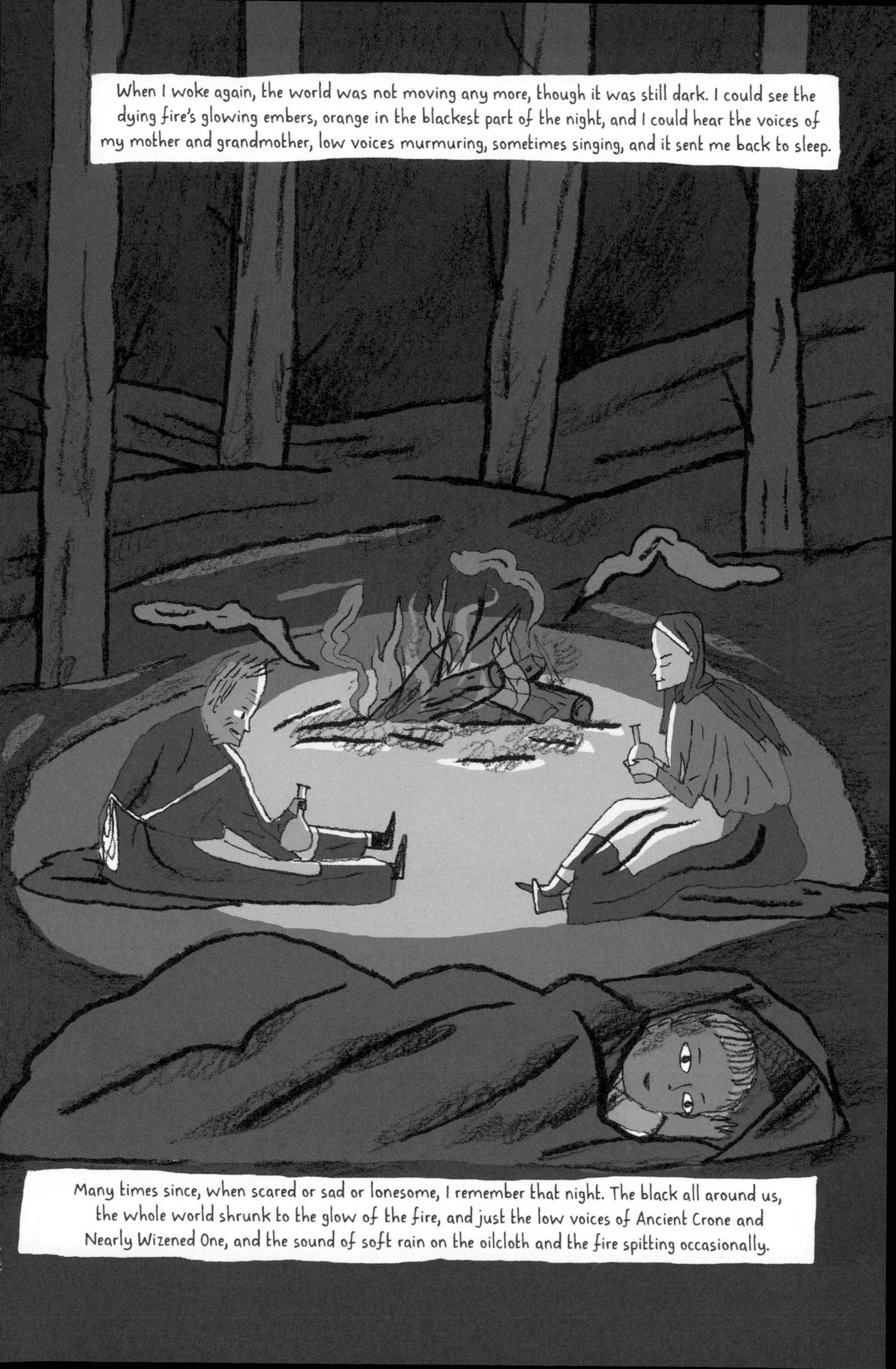
When I woke again, the world was not moving any more, though it was still dark. I could see the dying fire's glowing embers, orange in the blackest part of the night, and I could hear the voices of my mother and grandmother, low voices murmuring, sometimes singing, and it sent me back to sleep.
Many times since, when scared or sad or lonesome, I remember that night. The black all around us, the whole world shrunk to the glow of the fire, and just the low voices of Ancient Crone and Nearly Wizened One, and the sound of soft rain on the oilcloth and the fire spitting occasionally.

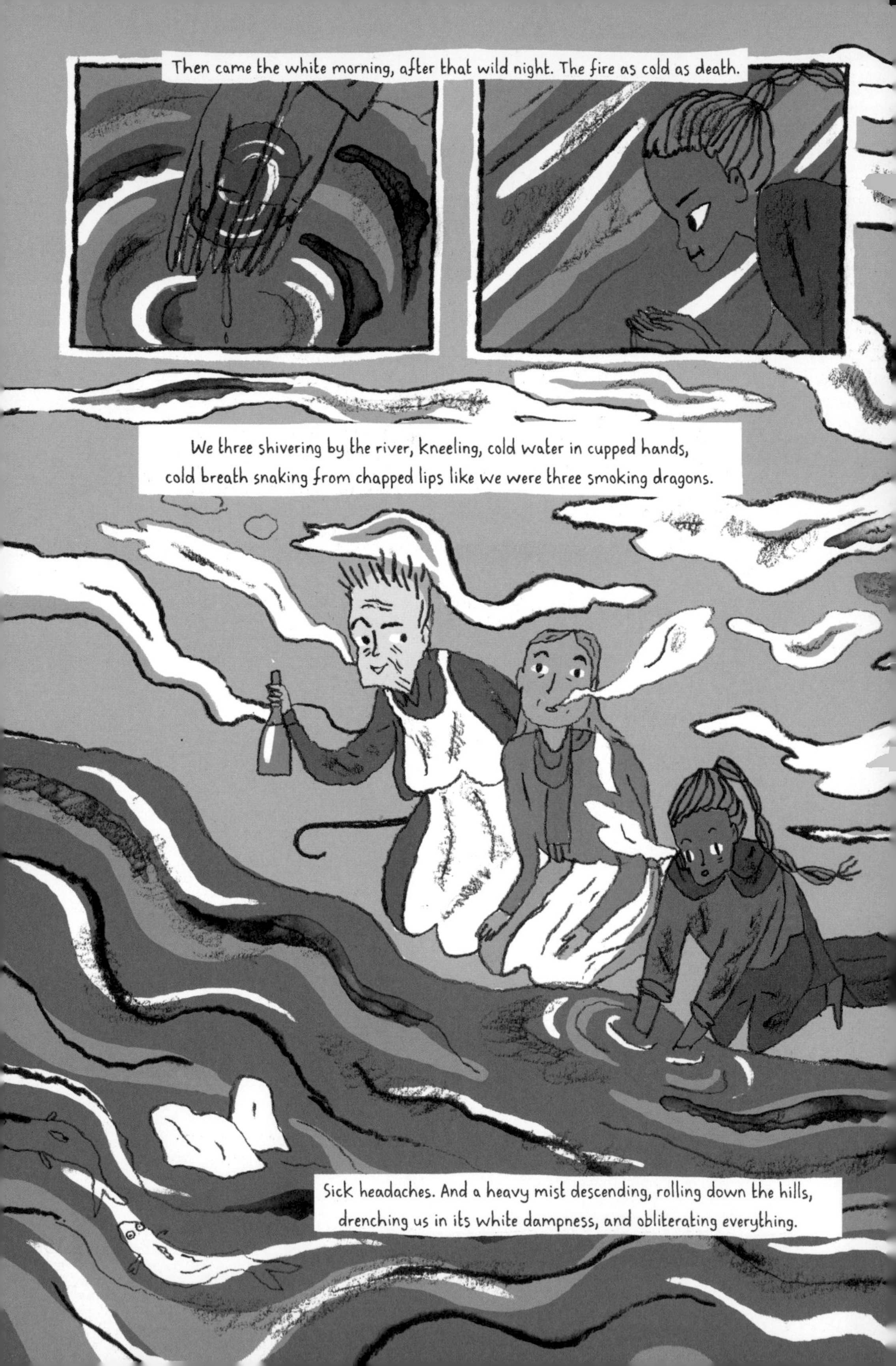
Then came the white morning, after that wild night. The fire as cold as death.
We three shivering by the river, kneeling, cold water in cupped hands, cold breath snaking from chapped lips like we were three smoking dragons.
Sick headaches. And a heavy mist descending, rolling down the hills, drenching us in its white dampness, and obliterating everything.

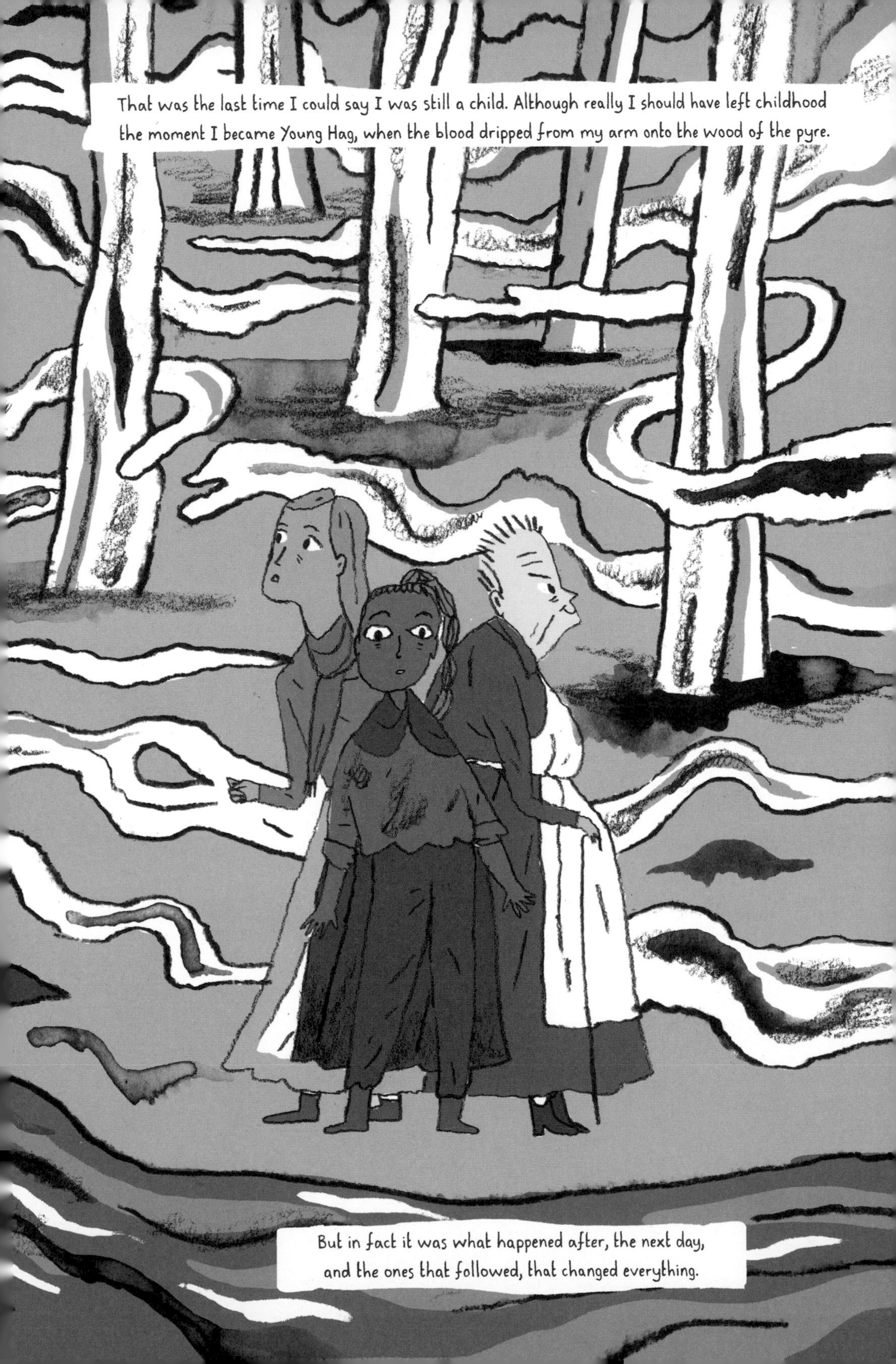
That was the last time I could say I was still a child. Although really I should have left childhood the moment I became Young Hag, when the blood dripped from my arm onto the wood of the pyre.
But in fact it was what happened after, the next day, and the ones that followed, that changed everything.

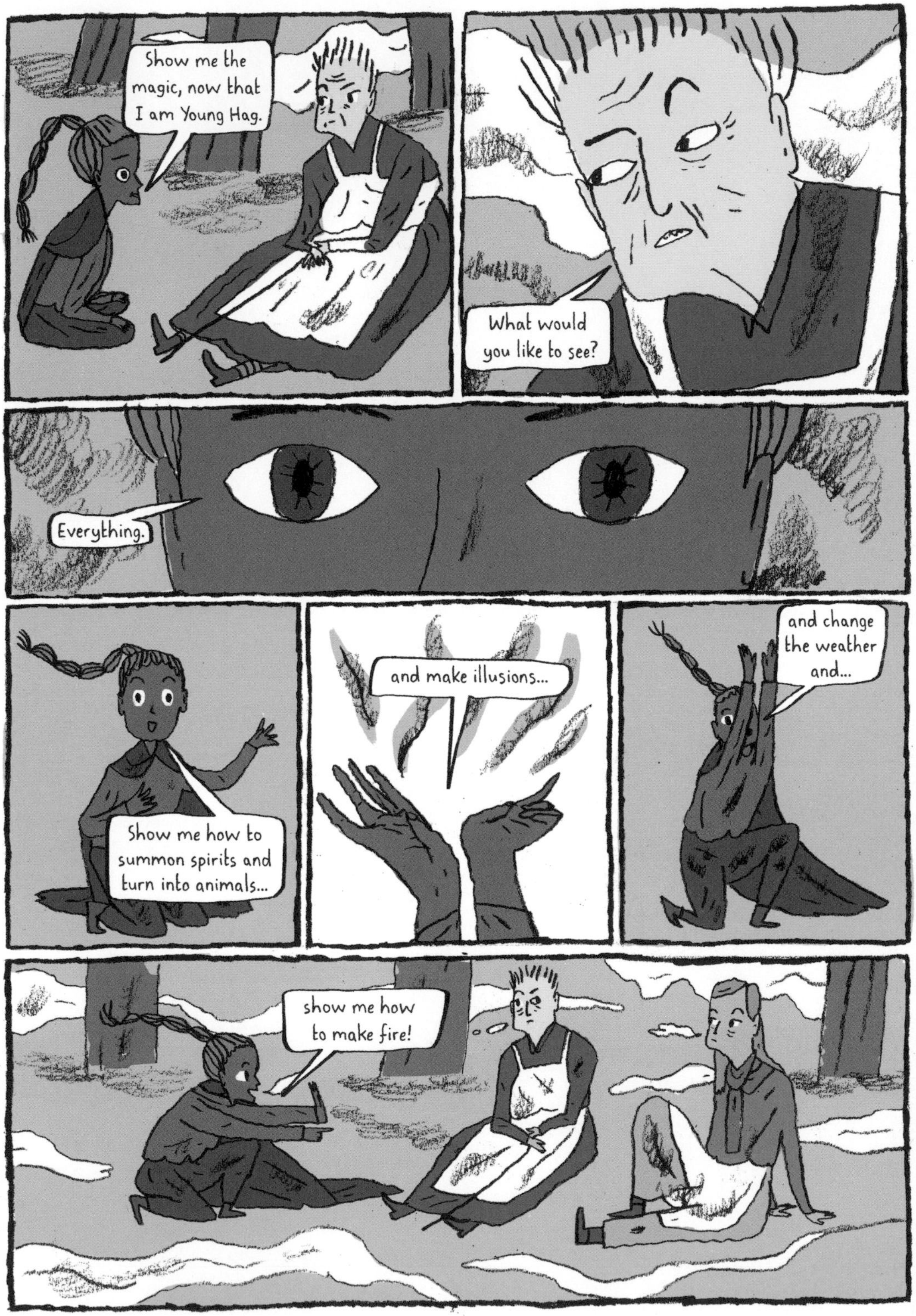
Show me the magic, now that I am Young Hag.
What would you like to see?
Everything.
Show me how to summon spirits and turn into animals...
and make illusions...
and change the weather and...
show me how to make fire!

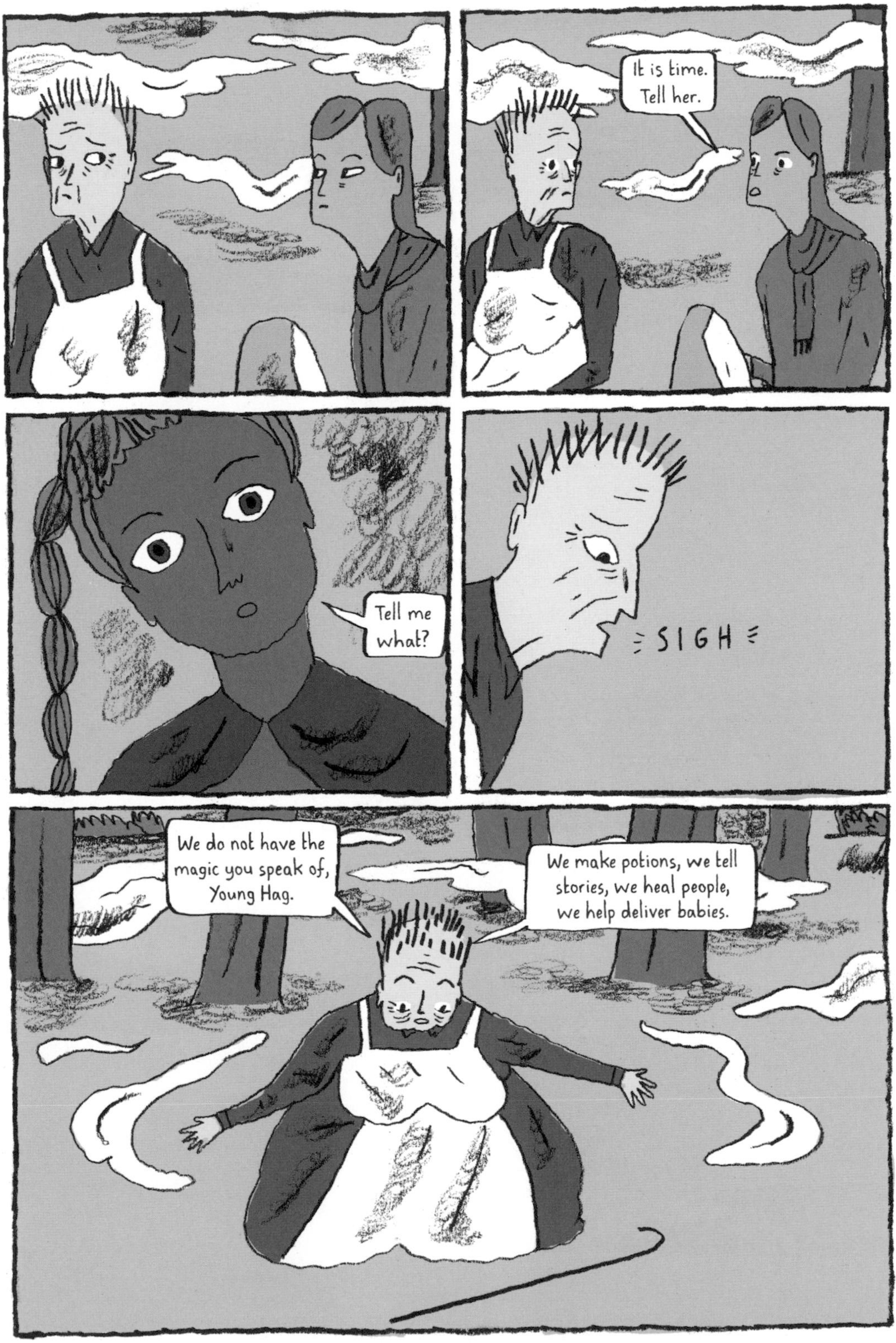
It is time. Tell her.
Tell me what?
SIGH
We do not have the magic you speak of, Young Hag.
We make potions, we tell stories, we heal people, we help deliver babies.

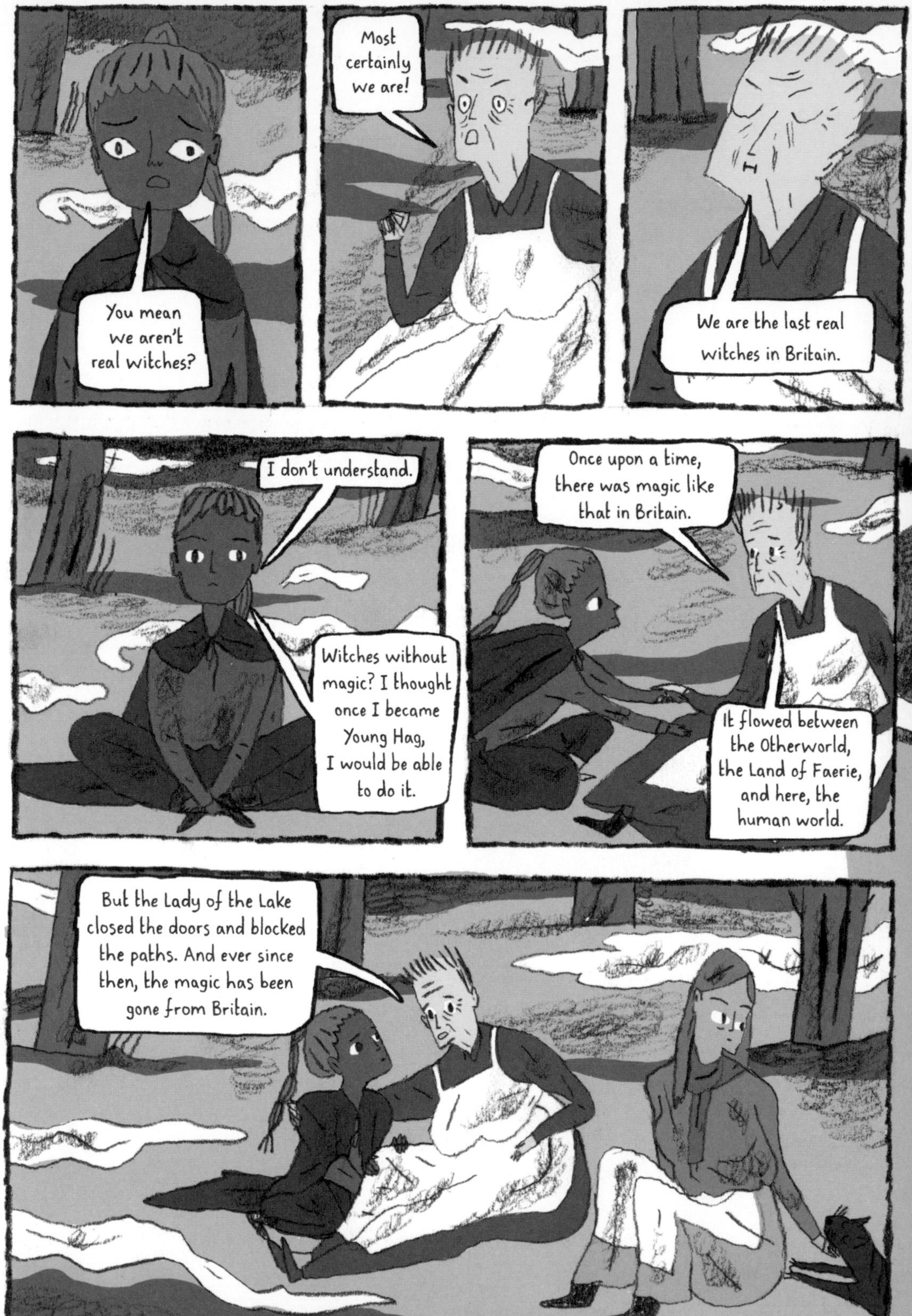
You mean we aren't real witches?
Most certainly we are!
We are the last real witches in Britain.
I don't understand.
Witches without magic? I thought once I became Young Hag, I would be able to do it.
Once upon a time, there was magic like that in Britain.
It flowed between the Otherworld, the Land of Faerie, and here, the human world.
But the Lady of the Lake closed the doors and blocked the paths. And ever since then, the magic has been gone from Britain.

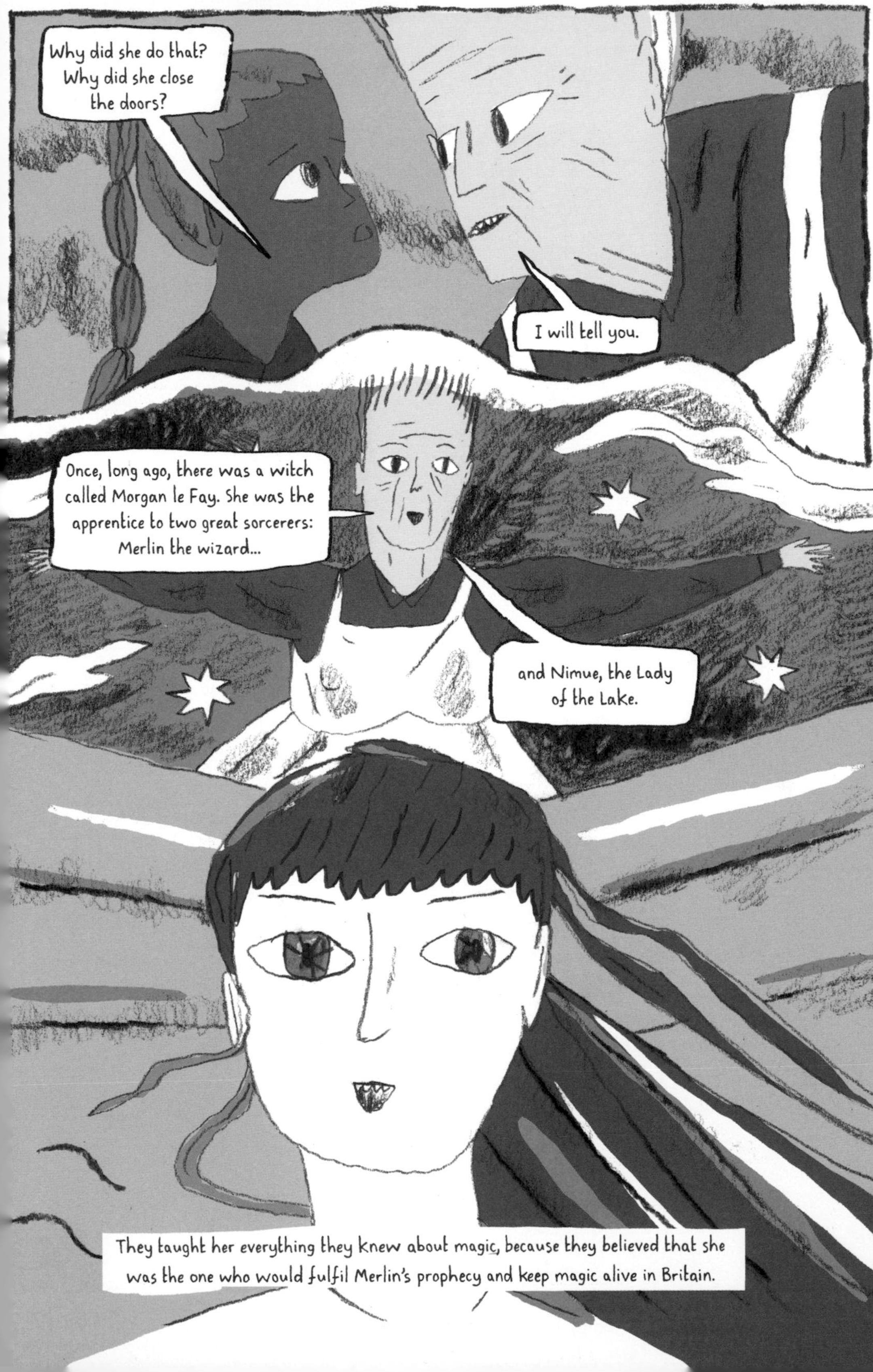
Why did she do that? Why did she close the doors?
I will tell you.
Once, long ago, there was a witch called Morgan le Fay. She was the apprentice to two great sorcerers: Merlin the wizard...
and Nimue, the Lady of the Lake.
They taught her everything they knew about magic, because they believed that she was the one who would fulfil Merlin's prophecy and keep magic alive in Britain.

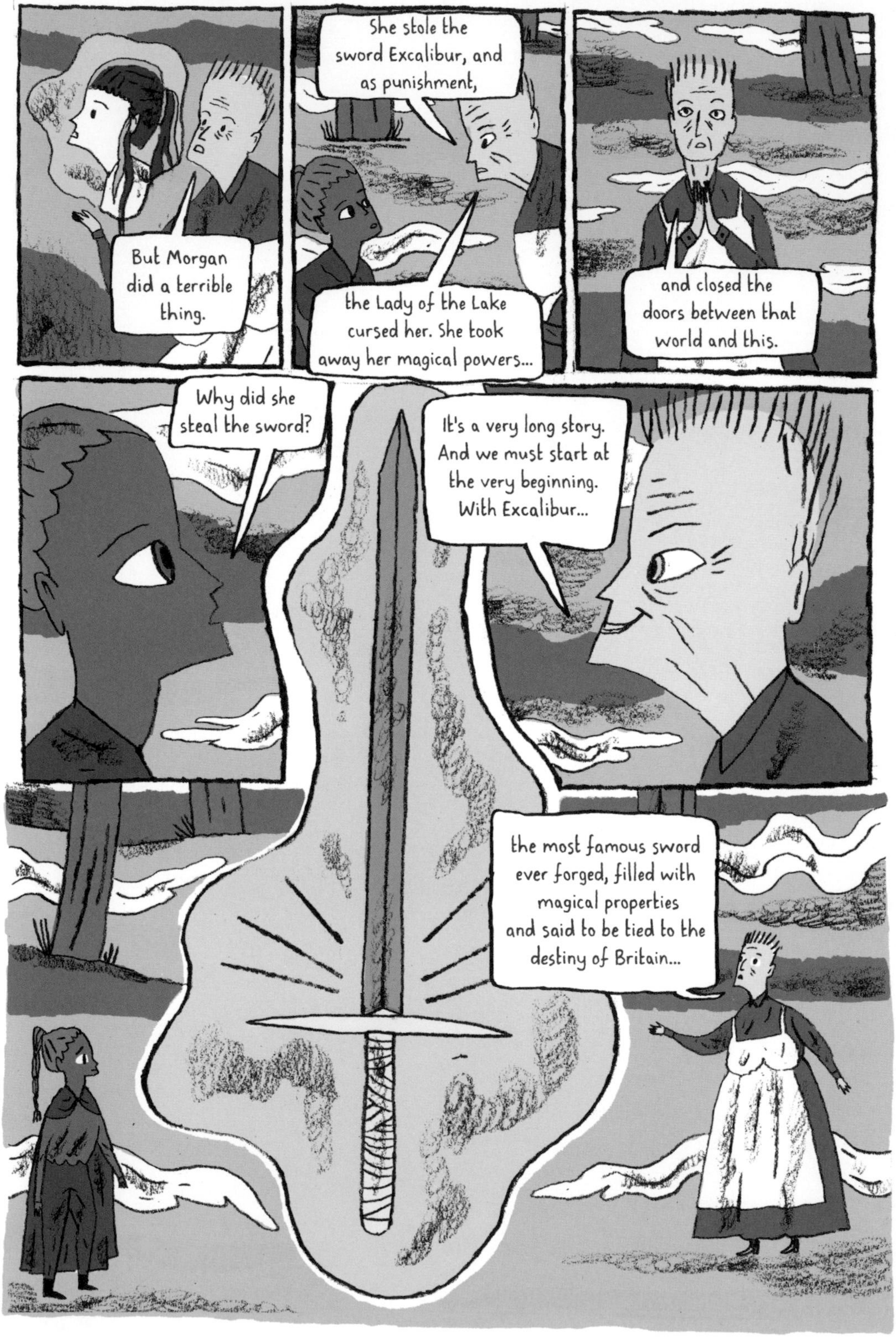

But Morgan did a terrible thing.
She stole the sword Excalibur, and as punishment,
the Lady of the Lake cursed her. She took away her magical powers...
and closed the doors between that world and this.
Why did she steal the sword?
It's a very long story. And we must start at the very beginning. With Excalibur...
the most famous sword ever forged, filled with magical properties and said to be tied to the destiny of Britain...

So the Lady of the Lake, ruler of the magical island of Avalon, and her lover, the wizard Merlin, are discussing, as they often do, the future of magic in Britain.

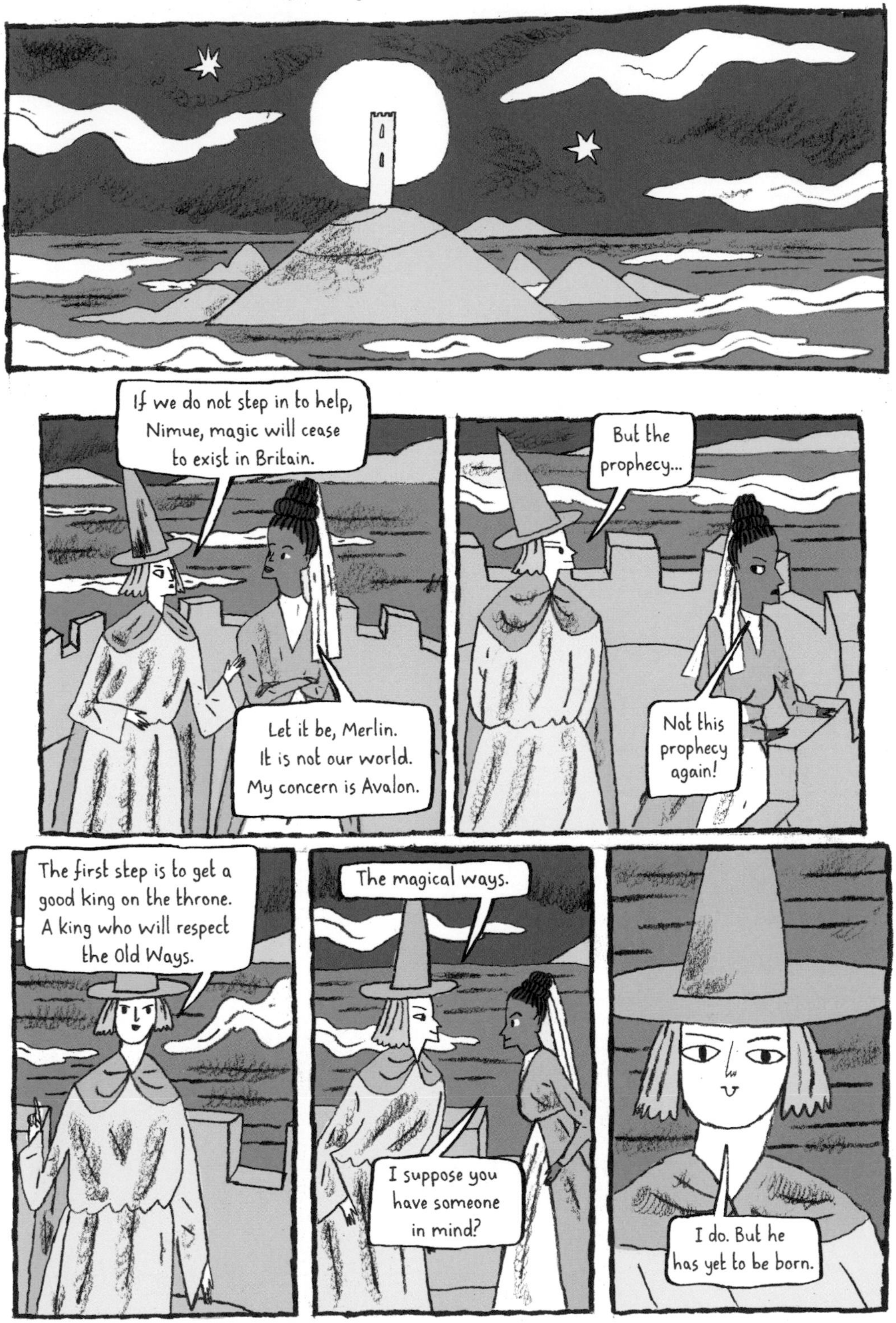
If we do not step in to help, Nimue, magic will cease to exist in Britain.
Let it be, Merlin. It is not our world. My concern is Avalon.
But the prophecy...
Not this prophecy again!
The first step is to get a good king on the throne. A king who will respect the Old Ways.
The magical ways.
I suppose you have someone in mind?
I do. But he has yet to be born.

How very mysterious.
Though I will need your help.
I thought you might.
Excalibur.
Ahhhh. You want it for this King of yours?
Yes.
We will bestow upon him this glorious relic of the Old Ways...
A sacred and magical sword.

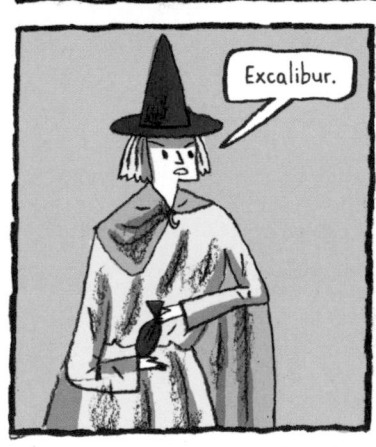

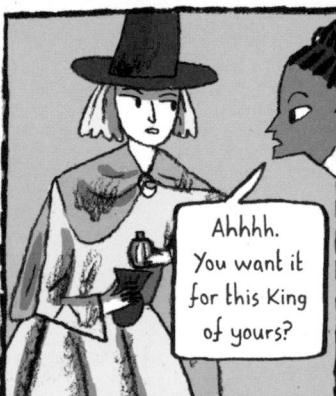

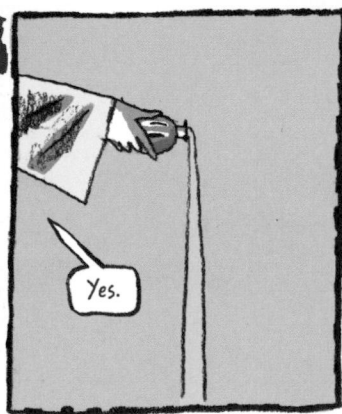

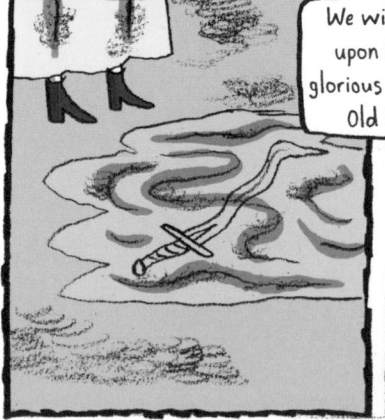

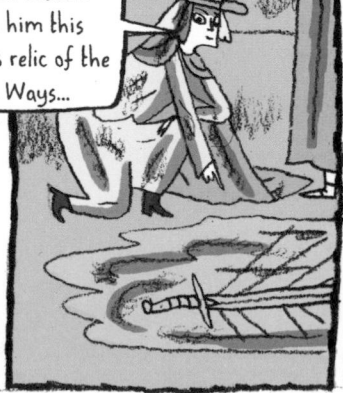

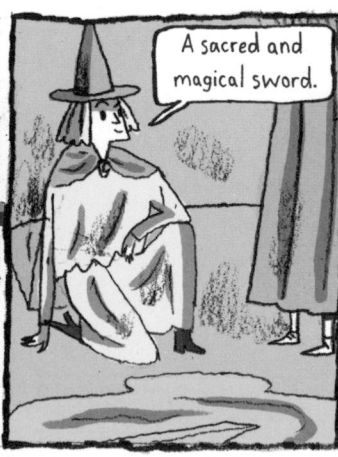

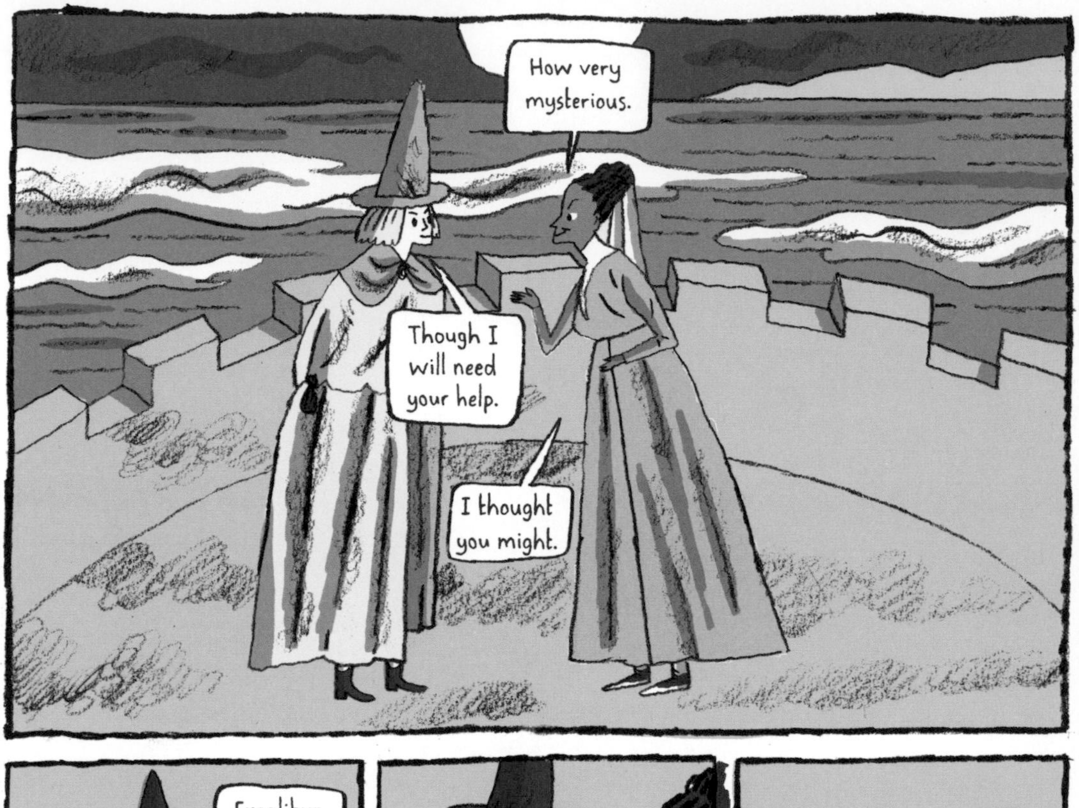

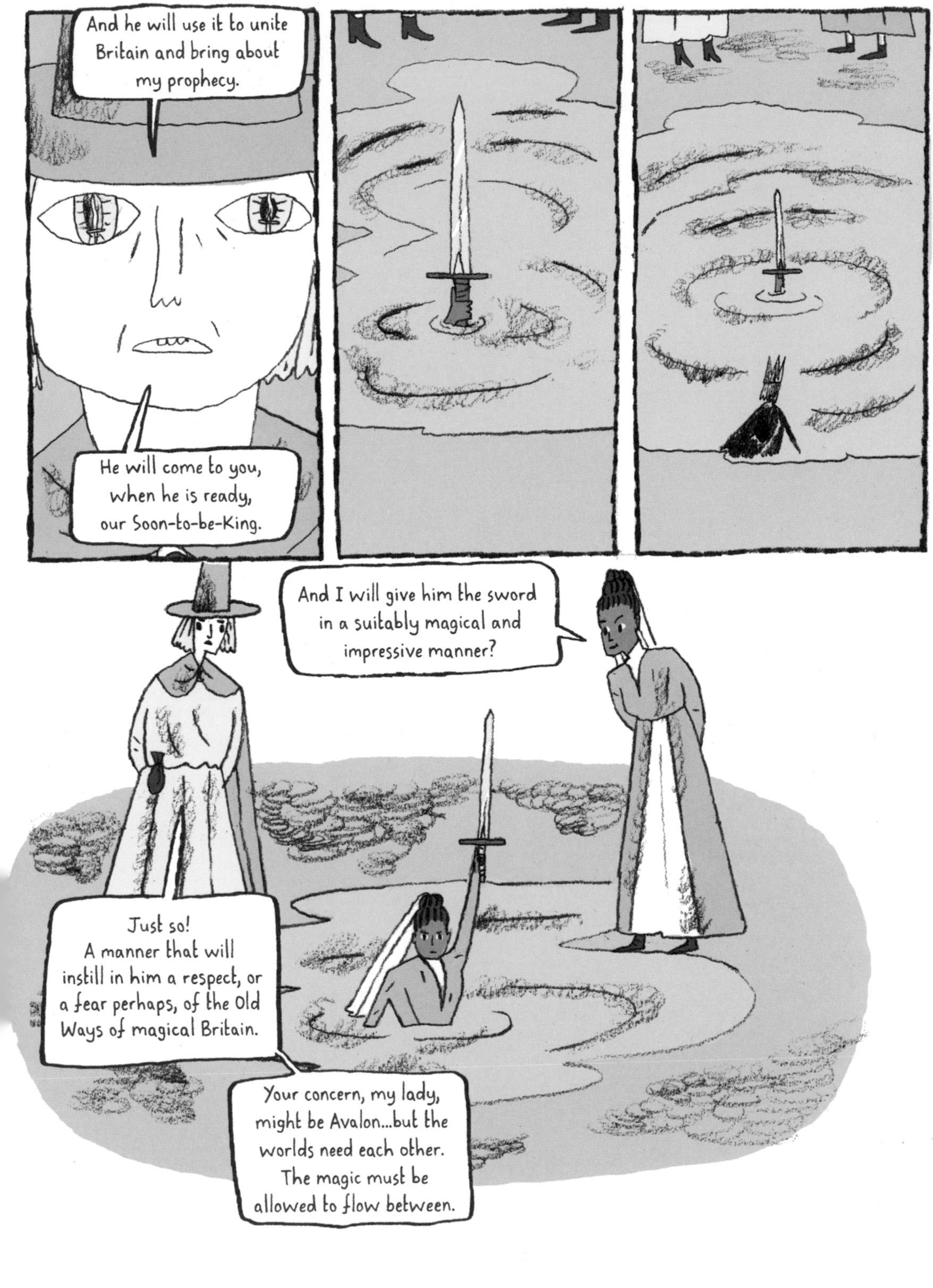
And he will use it to unite Britain and bring about my prophecy.
He will come to you, when he is ready, our Soon-to-be-King.
And I will give him the sword in a suitably magical and impressive manner?
Just so! A manner that will instill in him a respect, or a fear perhaps, of the Old Ways of magical Britain.
Your concern, my lady, might be Avalon...but the worlds need each other. The magic must be allowed to flow between.

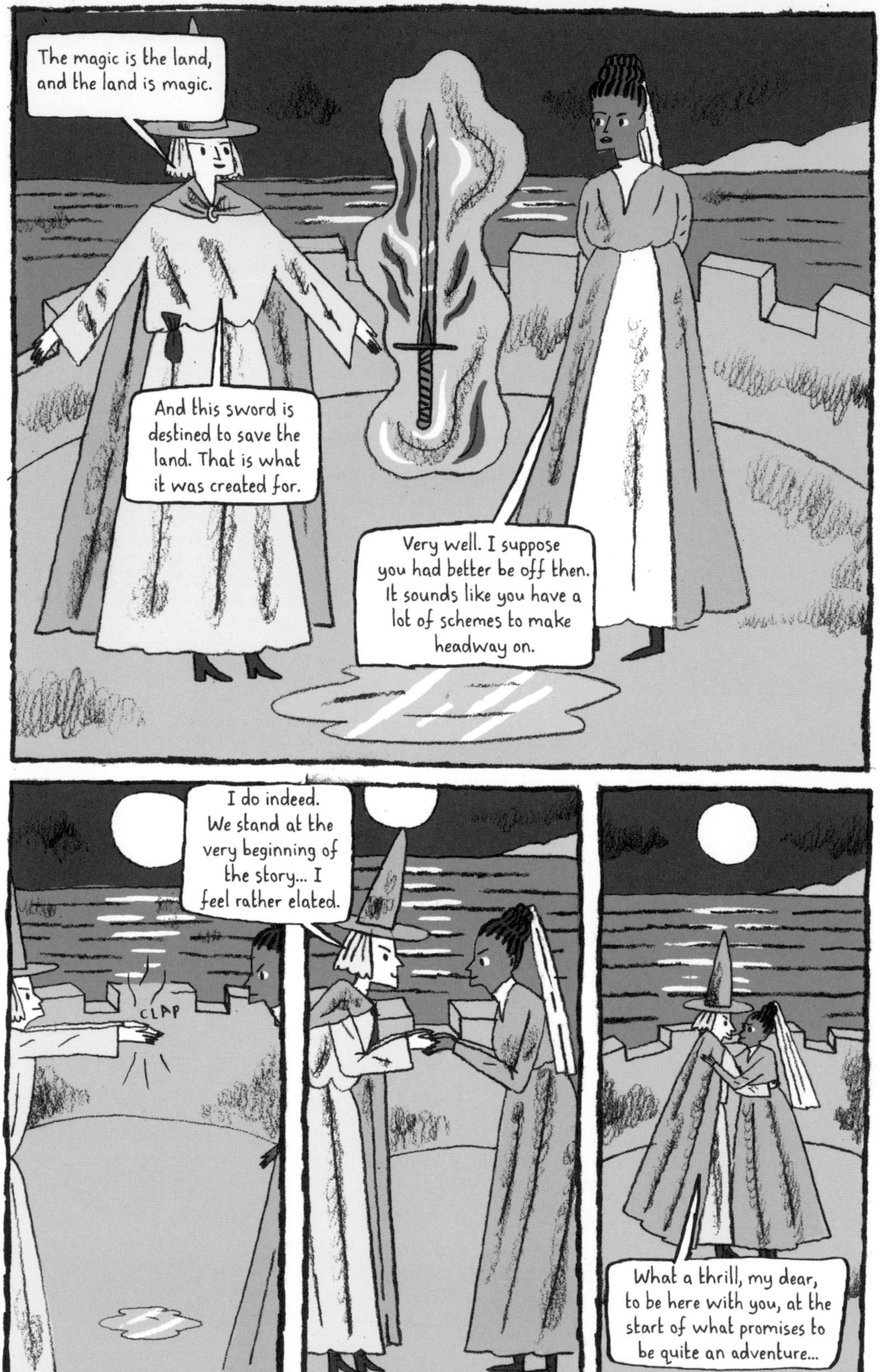
The magic is the land, and the land is magic.
And this sword is destined to save the land. That is what it was created for.
Very well. I suppose you had better be off then. It sounds like you have a lot of schemes to make headway on.
CLAP
I do indeed. We stand at the very beginning of the story... I feel rather elated.
What a thrill, my dear, to be here with you, at the start of what promises to be quite an adventure...

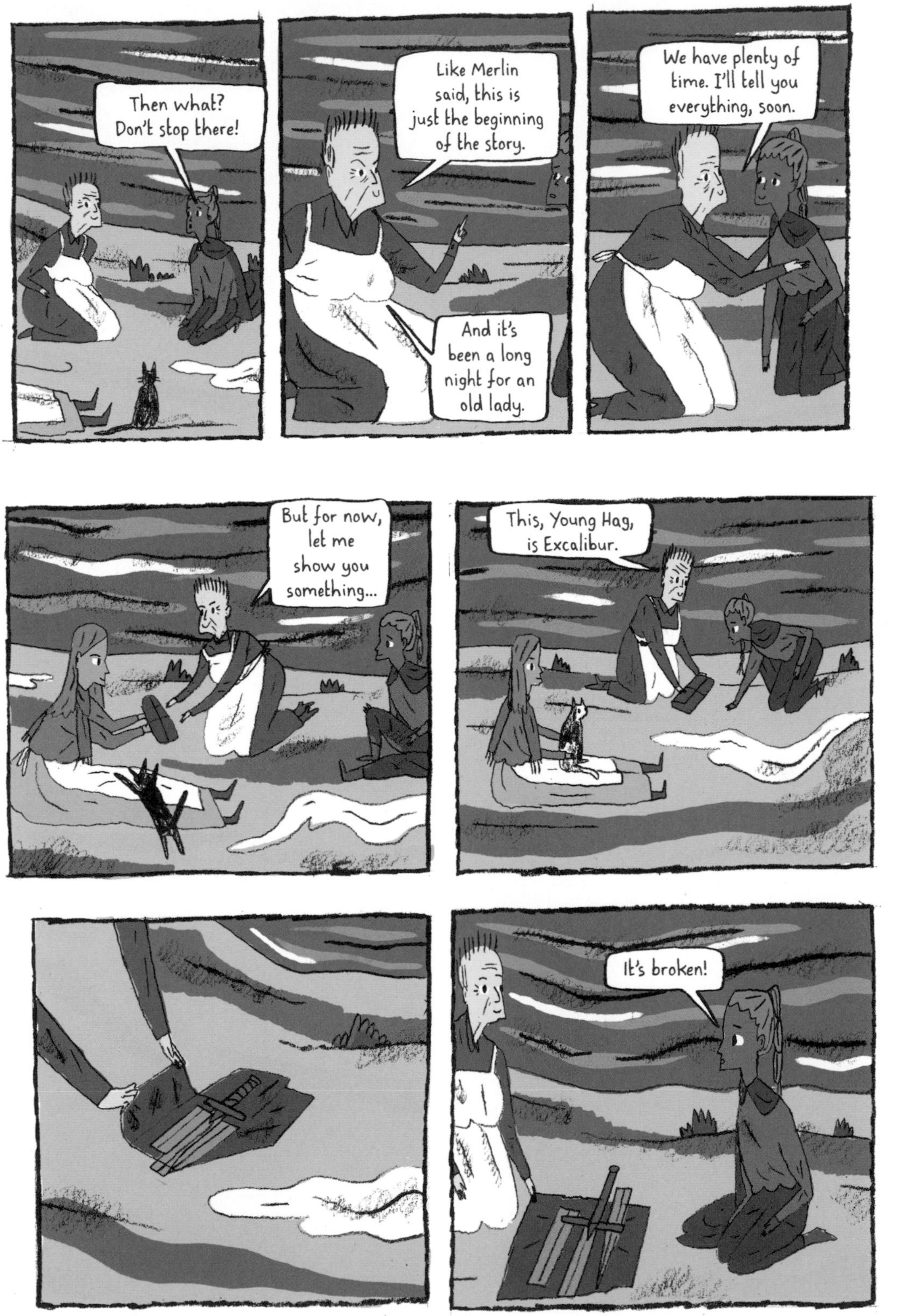
Then what? Don't stop there!
Like Merlin said, this is just the beginning of the story.
And it's been a long night for an old lady.
We have plenty of time. I'll tell you everything, soon.
But for now, let me show you something...
This, Young Hag, is Excalibur.
It's broken!

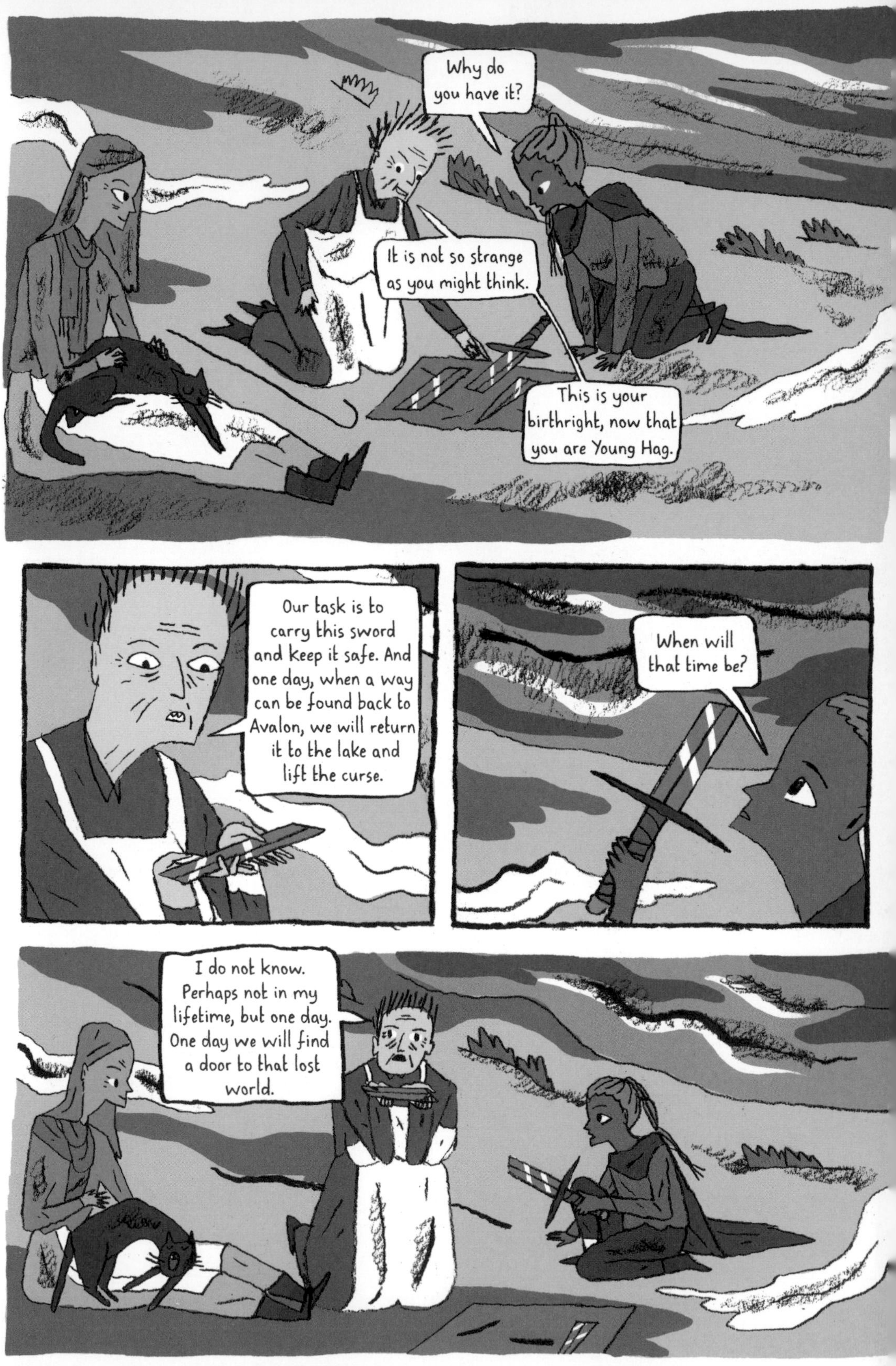
Why do you have it?
It is not so strange as you might think.
This is your birthright, now that you are Young Hag.
Our task is to carry this sword and keep it safe. And one day, when a way can be found back to Avalon, we will return it to the lake and lift the curse.
When will that time be?
I do not know. Perhaps not in my lifetime, but one day. One day we will find a door to that lost world.

This was a very disappointing turn of events, there was no denying it. But I still believed then that my grandmother was the wisest, most tremendously splendid crone in all of Britain. Even if she couldn't do magic.

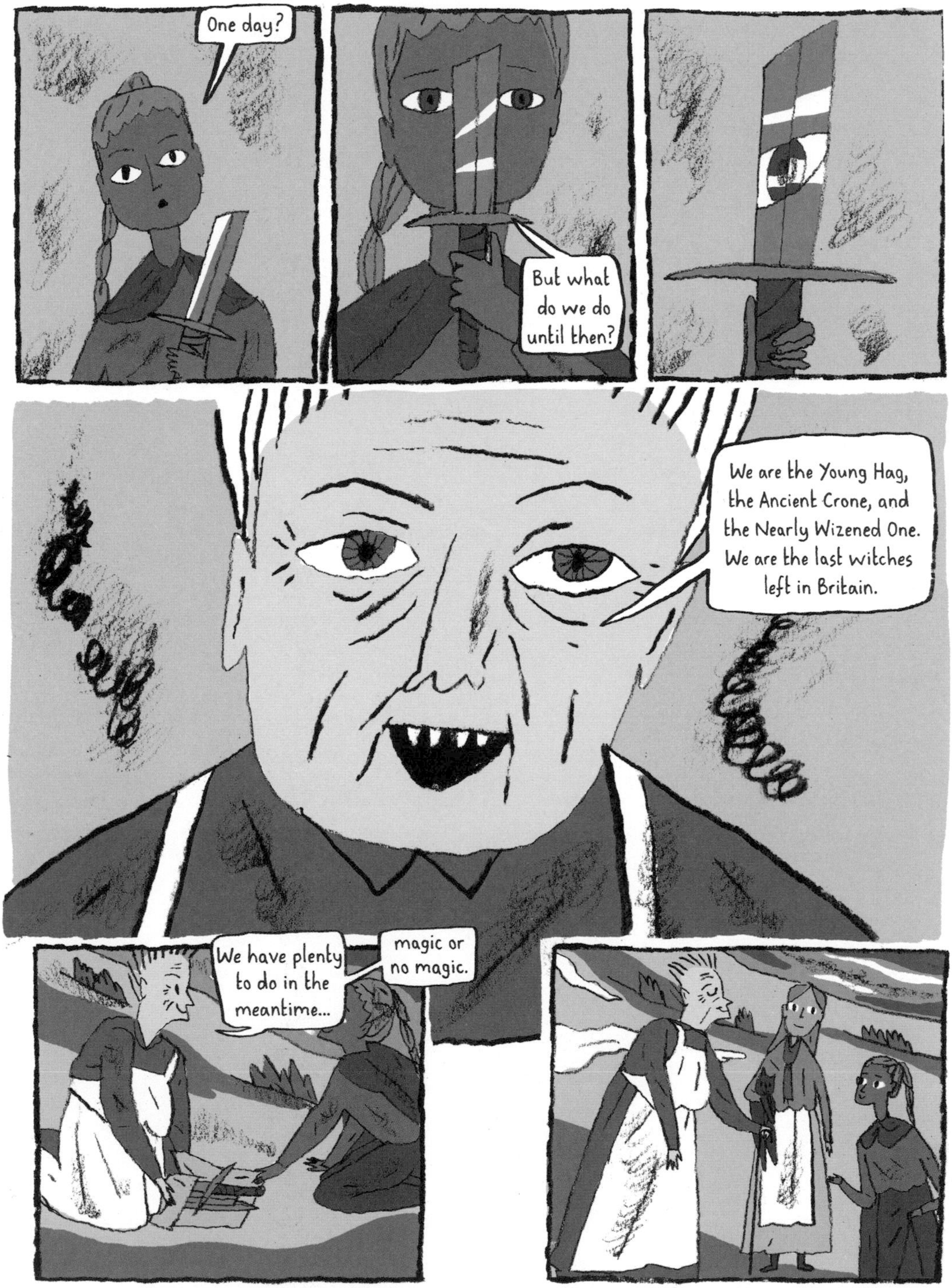

One day?
But what do we do until then?
We are the Young Hag, the Ancient Crone, and the Nearly Wizened One. We are the last witches left in Britain.
We have plenty to do in the meantime...
magic or no magic.

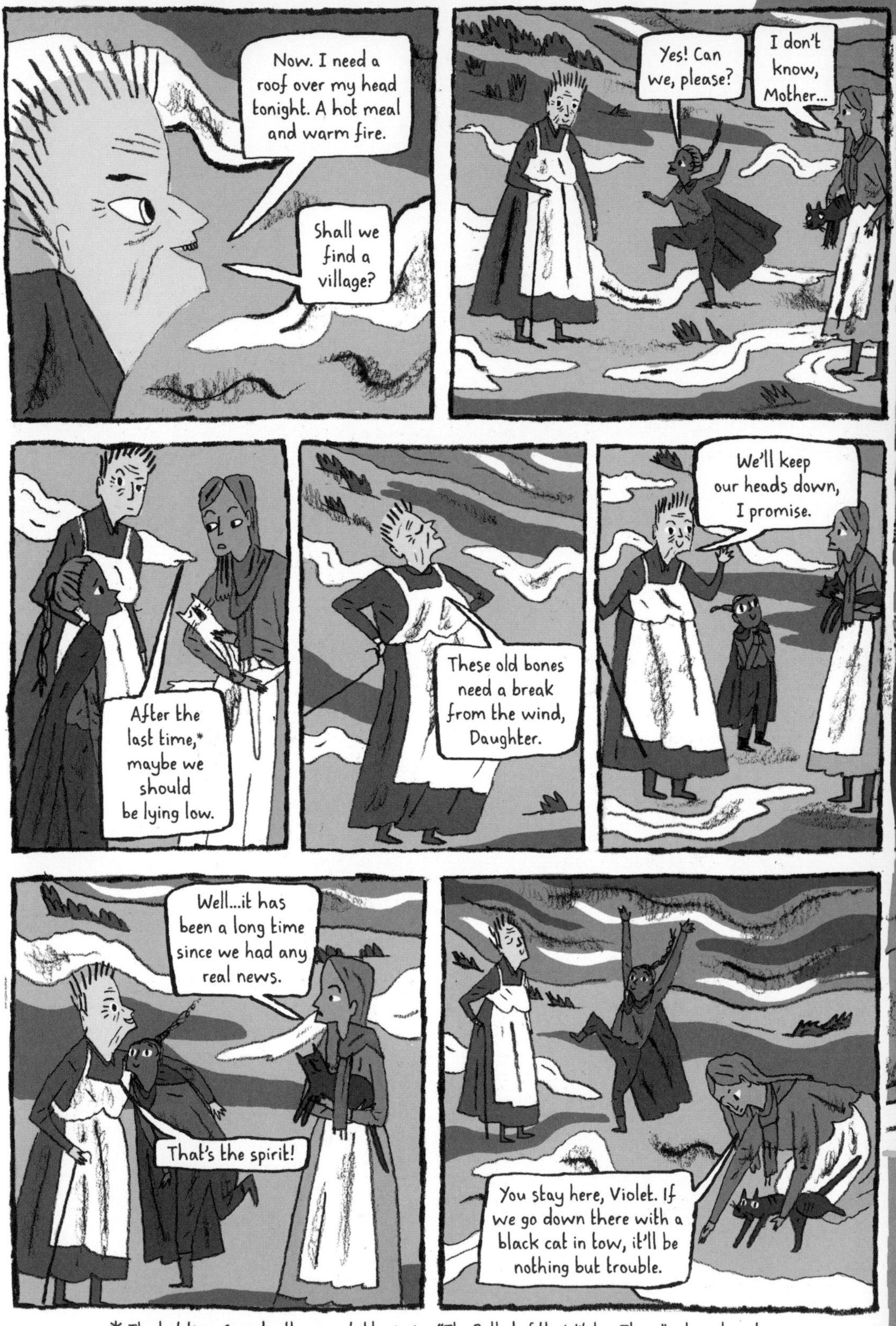
Now. I need a roof over my head tonight. A hot meal and warm fire.
Shall we find a village?
Yes! Can we, please?
I don't know, Mother...
After the last time,* maybe we should be lying low.
These old bones need a break from the wind, Daughter.
We'll keep our heads down, I promise.
Well...it has been a long time since we had any real news.
That's the spirit!
You stay here, Violet. If we go down there with a black cat in tow, it'll be nothing but trouble.

* The last time: Grandmother on a table singing "The Ballad of the Witches Three," a brawl, and a small mob pursuing us out of town with pitchforks.

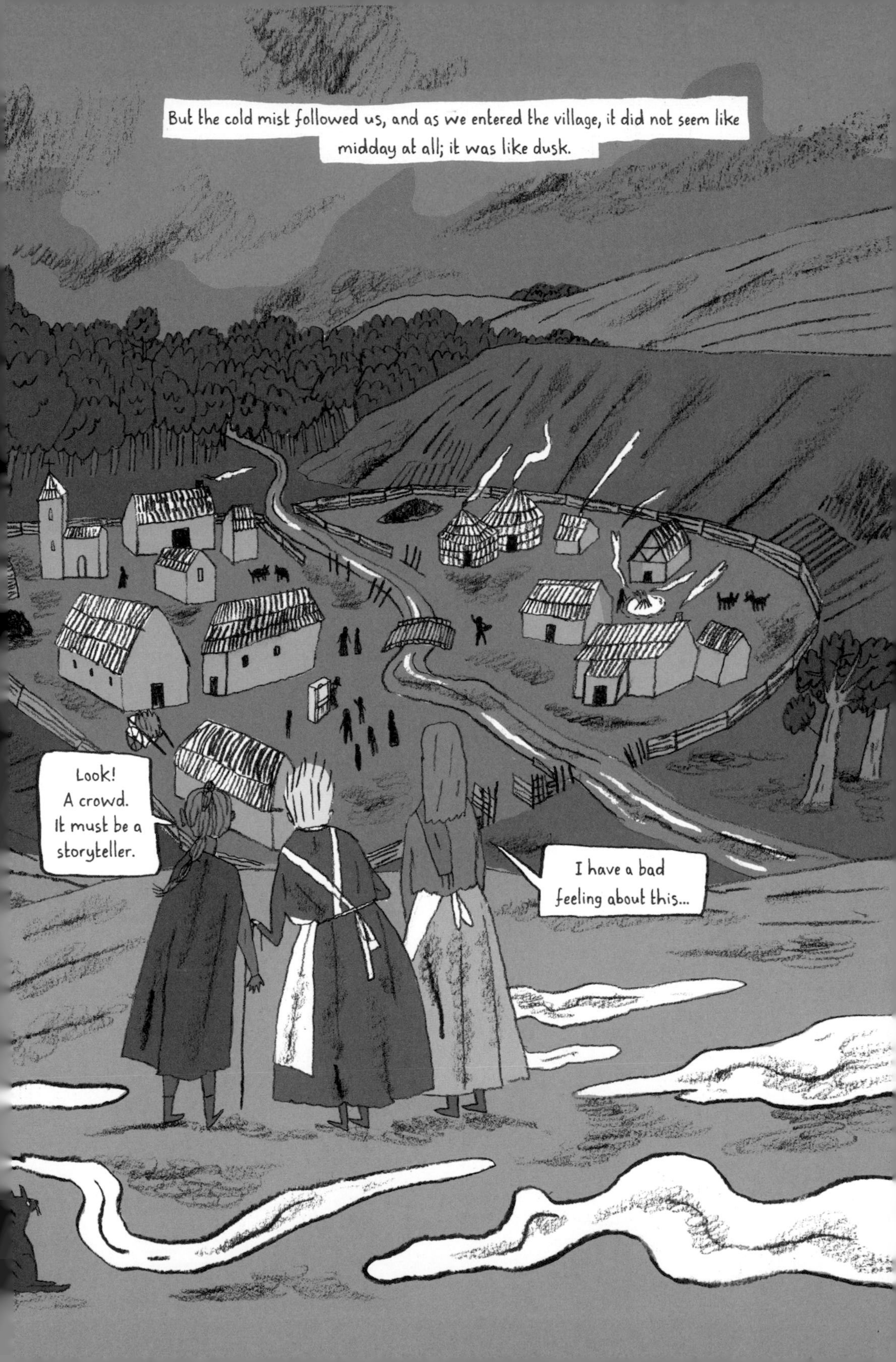
But the cold mist followed us, and as we entered the village, it did not seem like midday at all; it was like dusk.
Look! A crowd. It must be a storyteller.
I have a bad feeling about this...

Now, marvelous hindsight. I wish we had listened to Mother's Bad Feeling.

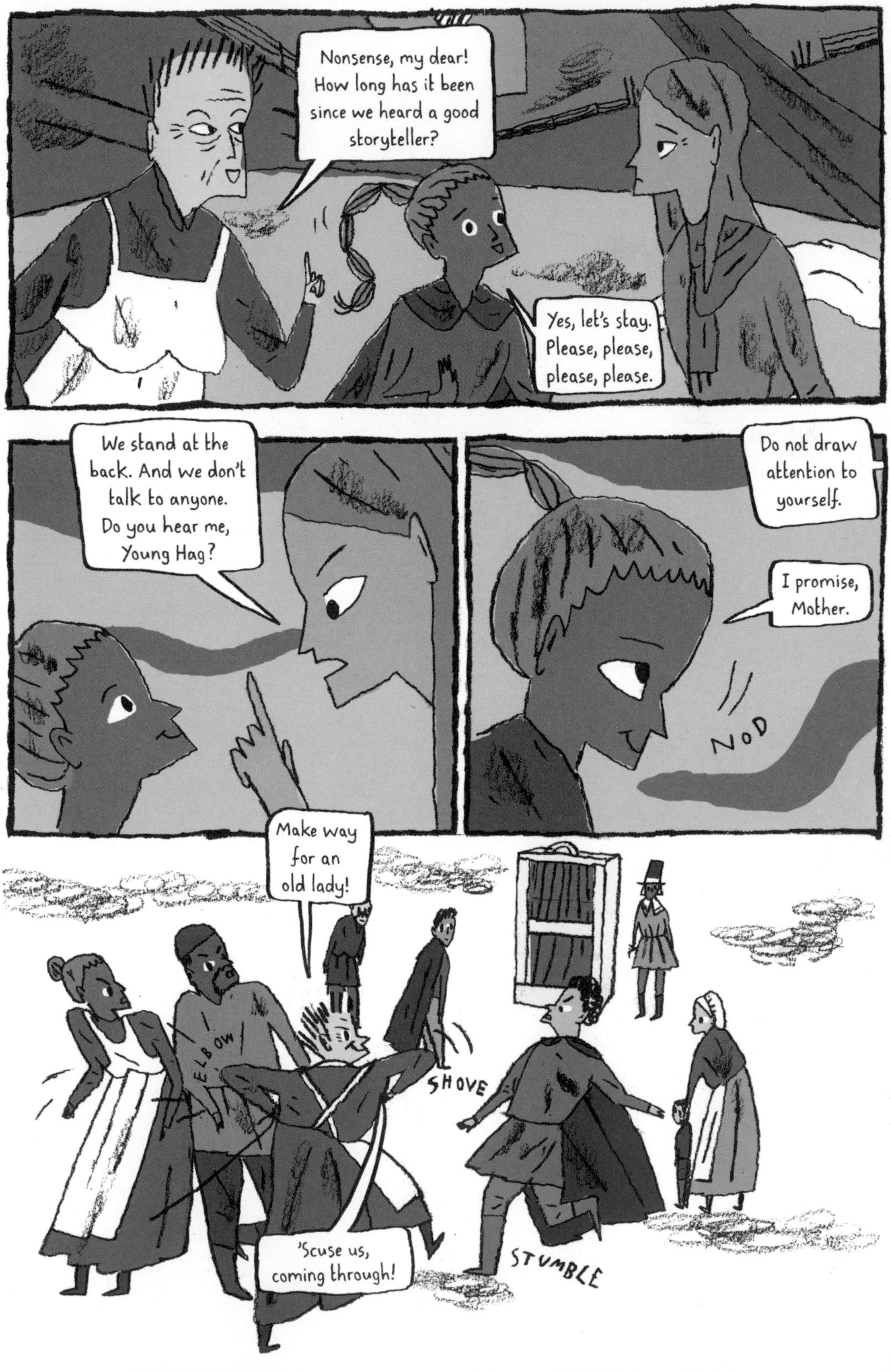
Nonsense, my dear! How long has it been since we heard a good storyteller?
Yes, let's stay. Please, please, please, please.
We stand at the back. And we don't talk to anyone. Do you hear me, Young Hag?
Do not draw attention to yourself.
I promise, Mother.
NOD
Make way for an old lady!
ELBOW
SHOVE
'Scuse us, coming through!
STUMBLE

The storyteller began to speak, and I didn't notice the looks we were getting, the people edging away.
I was excited for the tale to come, giddy with being in a village, among people again.

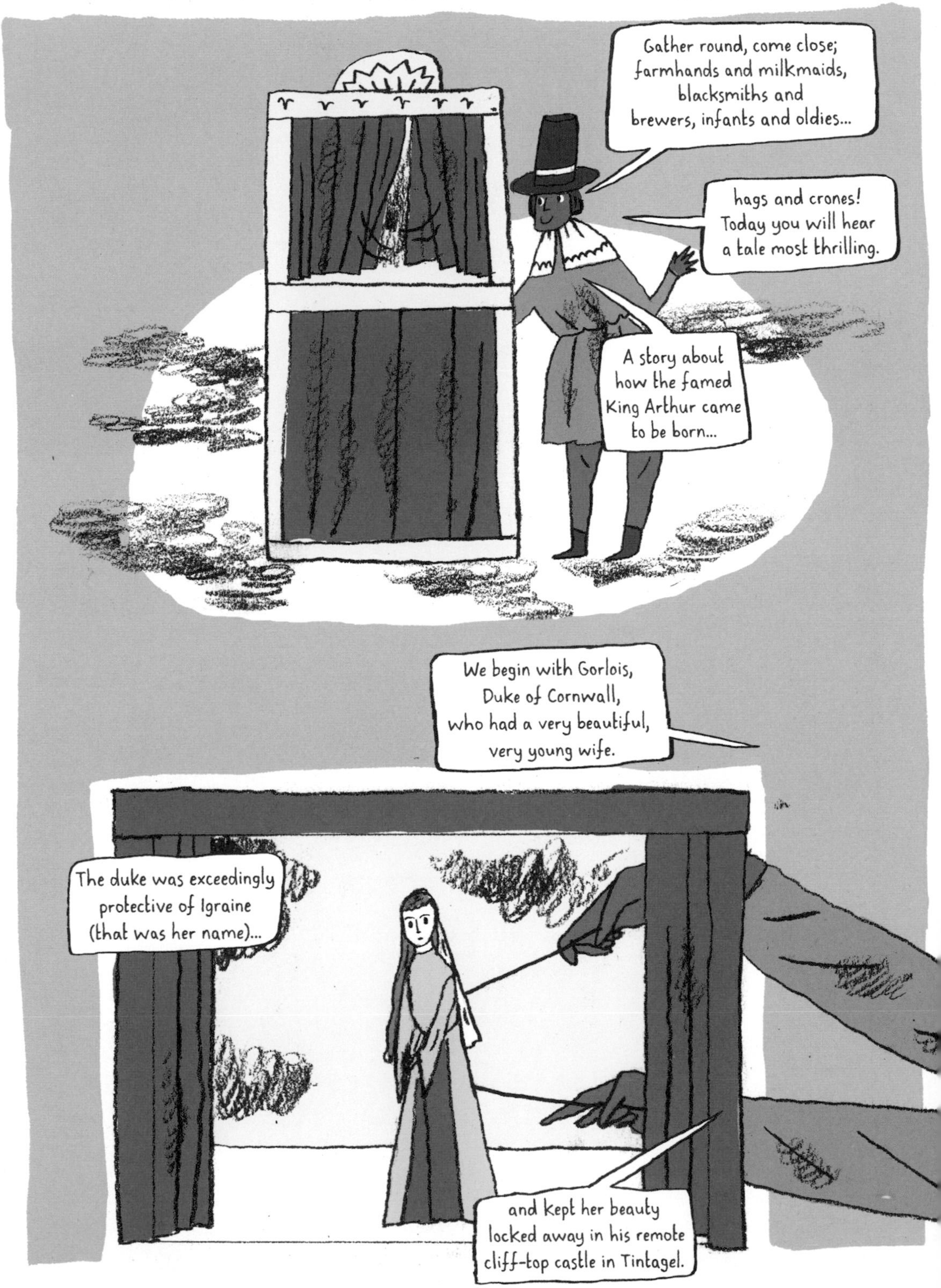
Gather round, come close; farmhands and milkmaids, blacksmiths and brewers, infants and oldies...
hags and crones! Today you will hear a tale most thrilling.
A story about how the famed King Arthur came to be born...
We begin with Gorlois, Duke of Cornwall, who had a very beautiful, very young wife.
The duke was exceedingly protective of Igraine (that was her name)...
and kept her beauty locked away in his remote cliff-top castle in Tintagel.

But Uther, High King of Britain, had summoned all his lords and dukes to come and pay homage to him, and Gorlois could not resist bringing his beautiful wife with him.

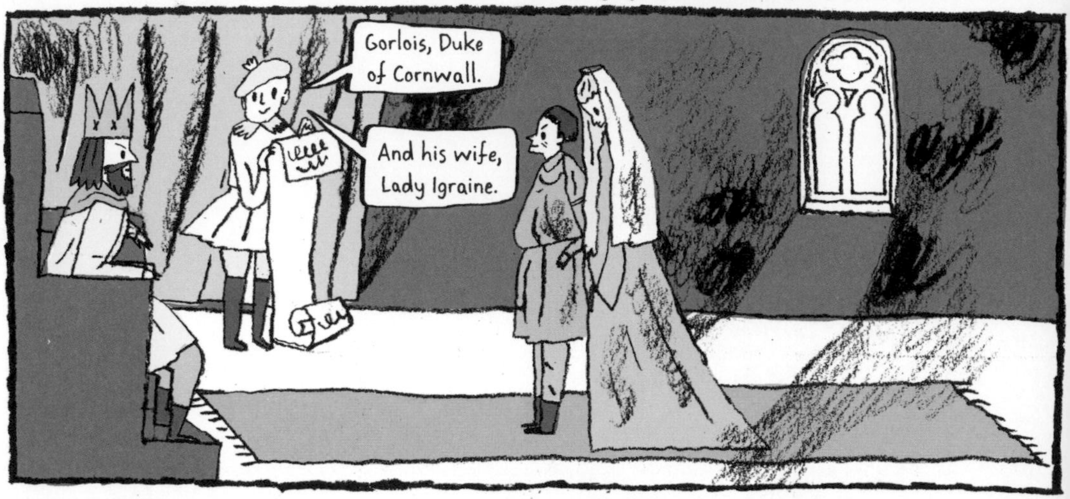
Gorlois, Duke of Cornwall.
And his wife, Lady Igraine.

Because what lord does not want to show off such a prized jewel?

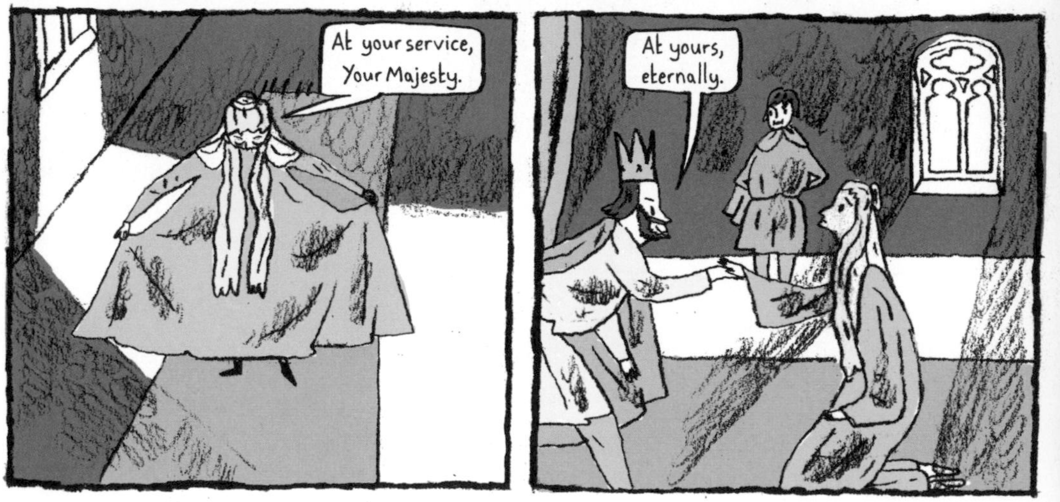
At your service, Your Majesty.
At yours, eternally.

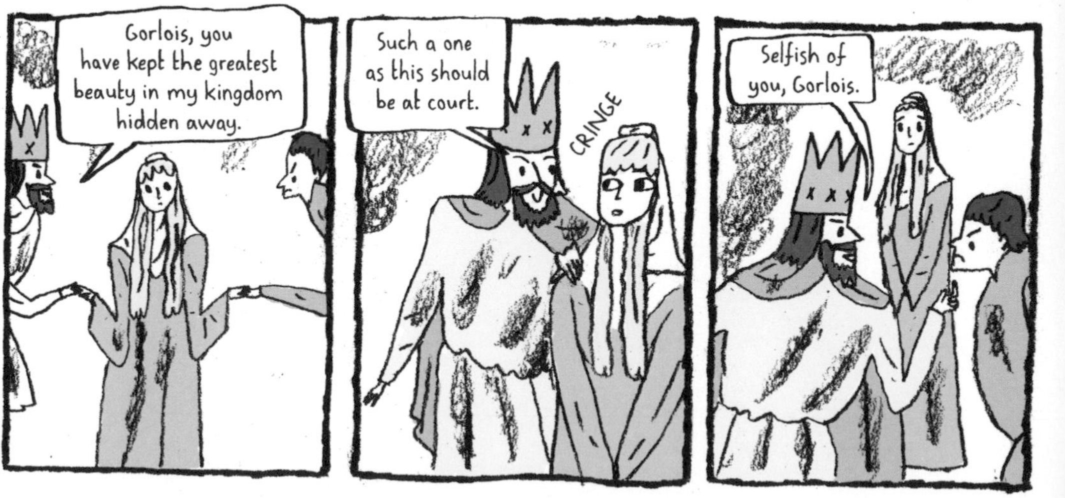
Gorlois, you have kept the greatest beauty in my kingdom hidden away.
Such a one as this should be at court.
CRINGE
Selfish of you, Gorlois.

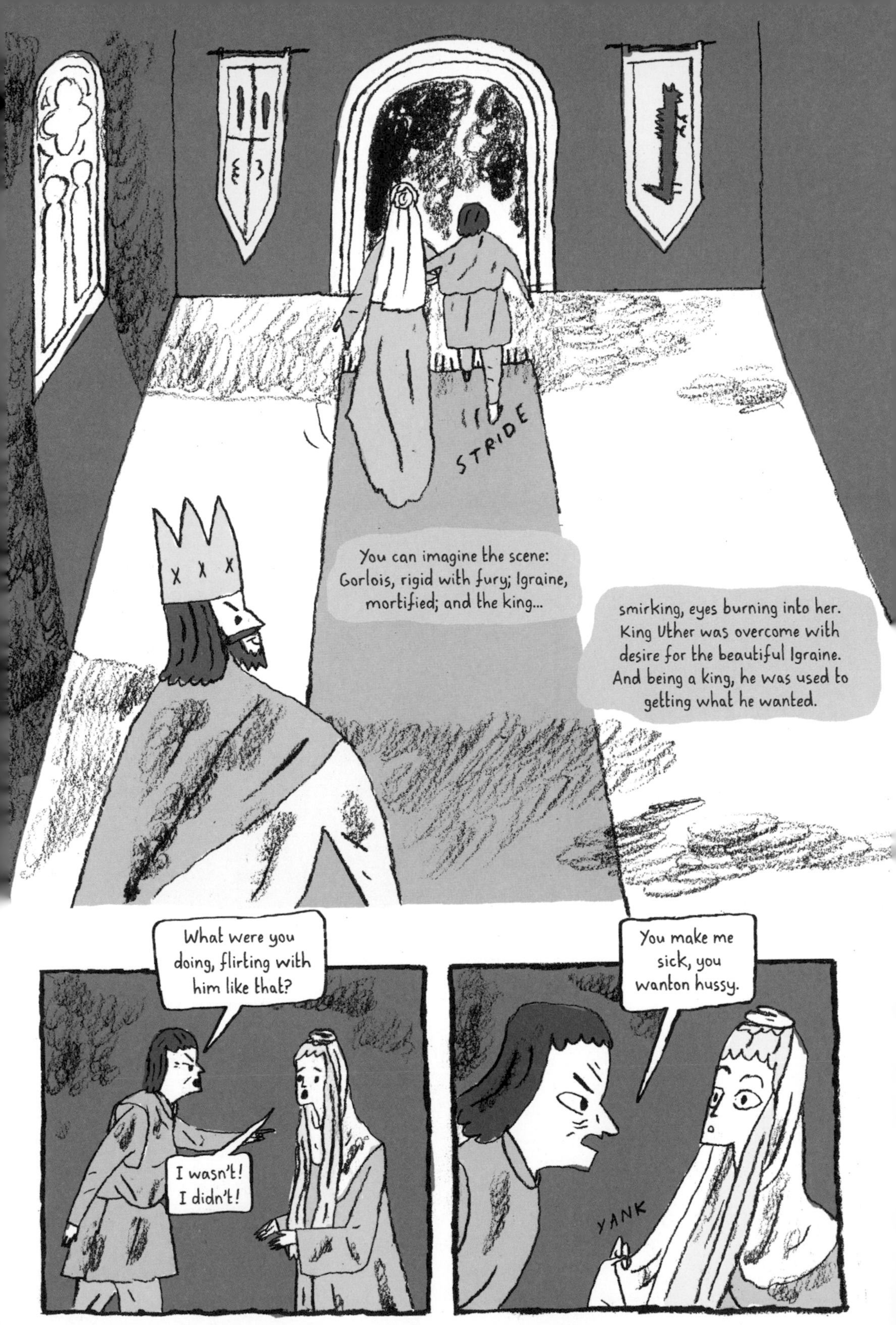
STRIDE
You can imagine the scene: Gorlois, rigid with fury; Igraine, mortified; and the king...
smirking, eyes burning into her. King Uther was overcome with desire for the beautiful Igraine. And being a king, he was used to getting what he wanted.
What were you doing, flirting with him like that?
I wasn't! I didn't!
You make me sick, you wanton hussy.
YANK

Uther called his magician, Merlin, to him.

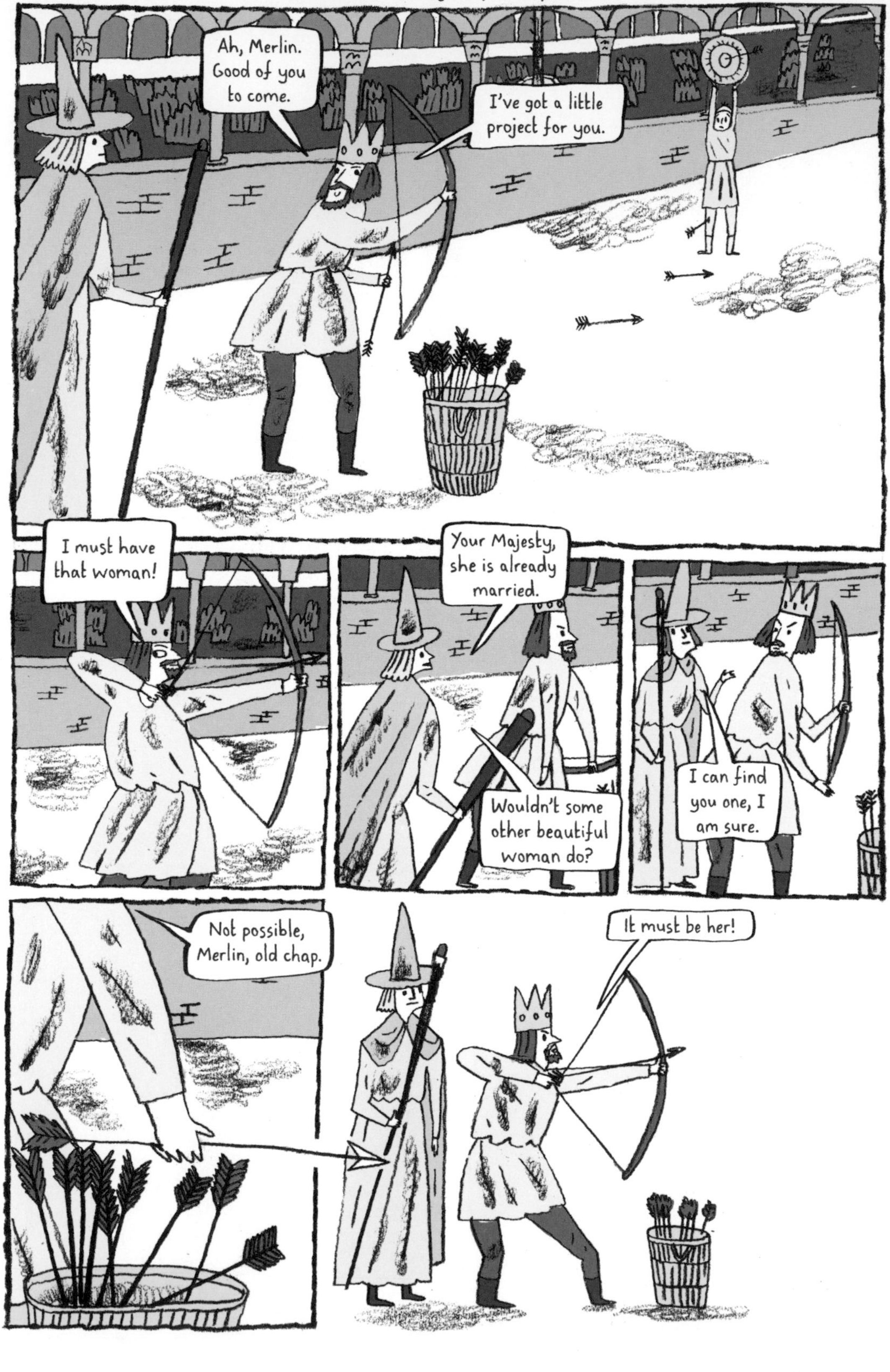

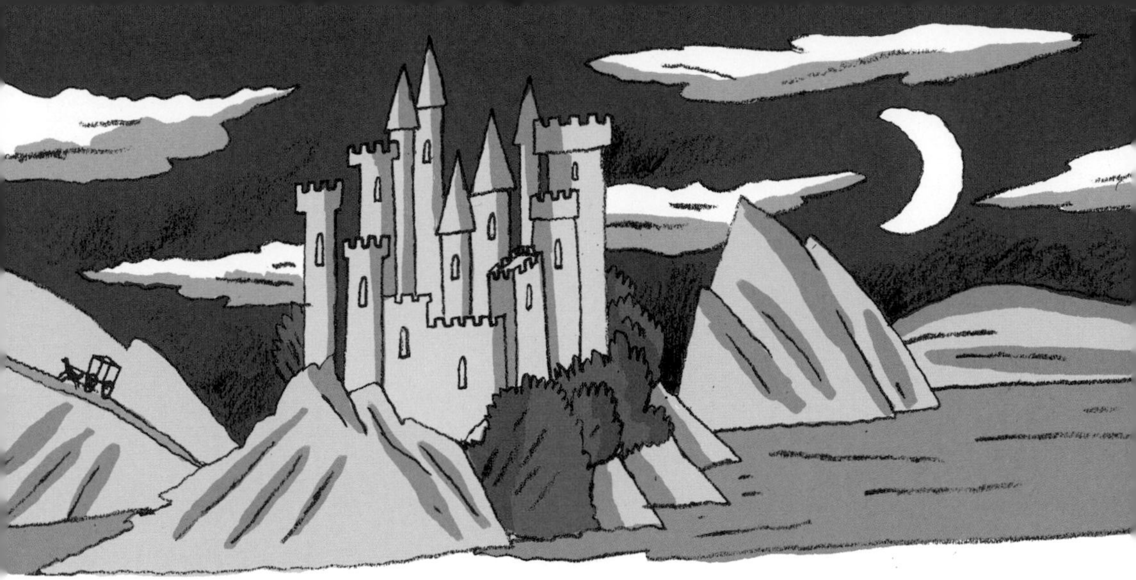

Meanwhile, Gorlois left court in the dead of night, furious at the high King for casting his lecherous eye over Igraine...and furious at Igraine for letting him.

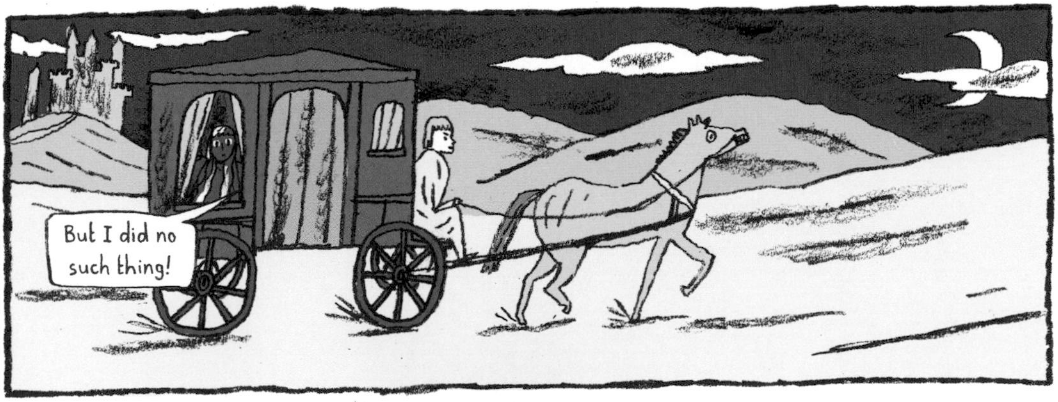

But I did no such thing!

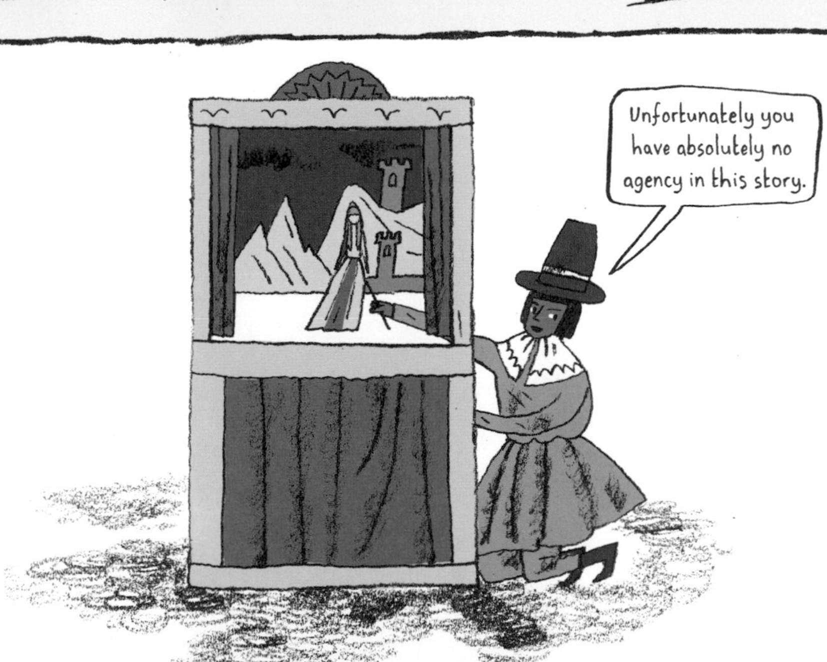

Unfortunately you have absolutely no agency in this story.

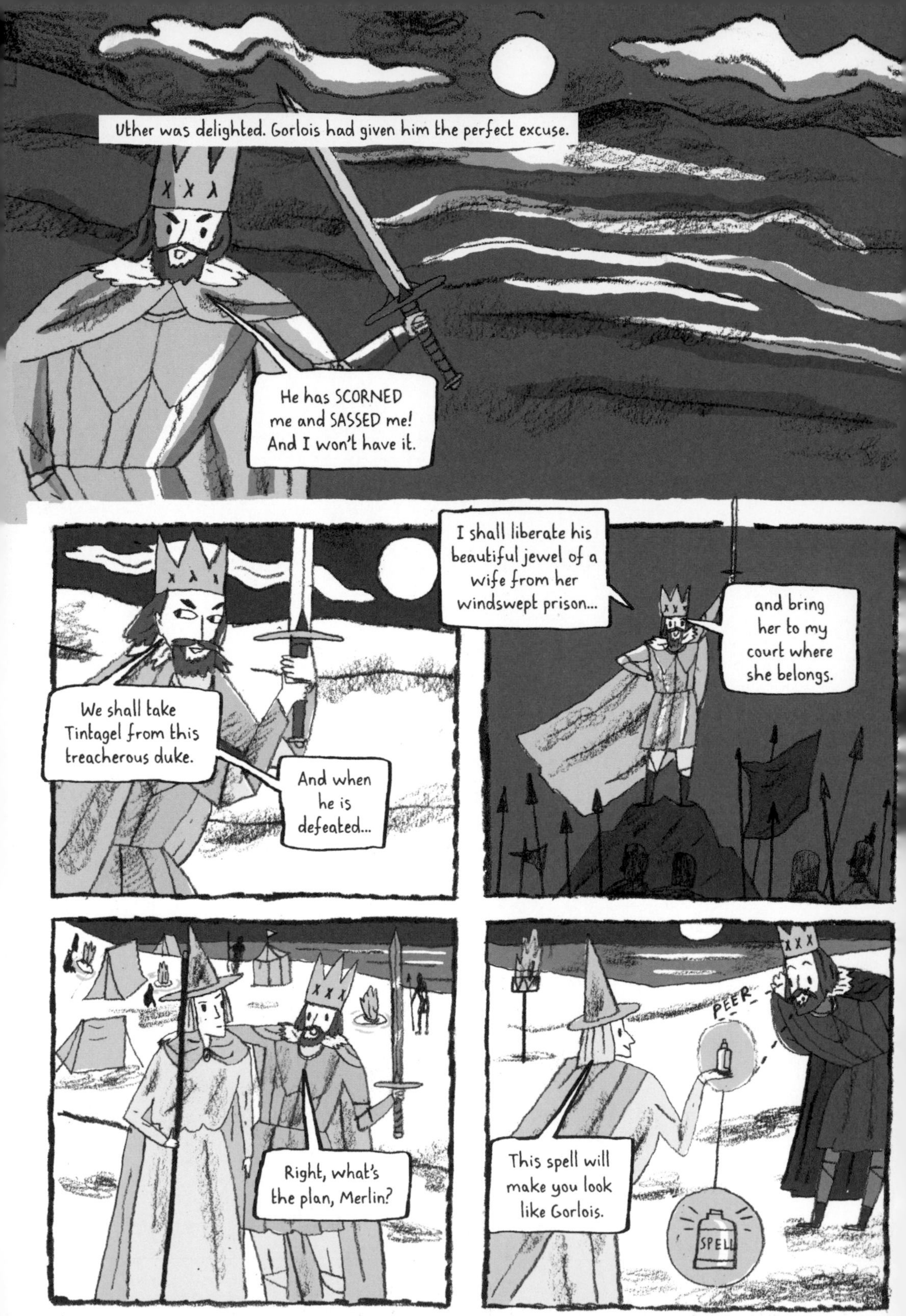
Uther was delighted. Gorlois had given him the perfect excuse.
He has SCORNED me and SASSED me! And I won't have it.
We shall take Tintagel from this treacherous duke.
And when he is defeated...
I shall liberate his beautiful jewel of a wife from her windswept prison...
and bring her to my court where she belongs.
Right, what's the plan, Merlin?
This spell will make you look like Gorlois.
PEER
SPELL

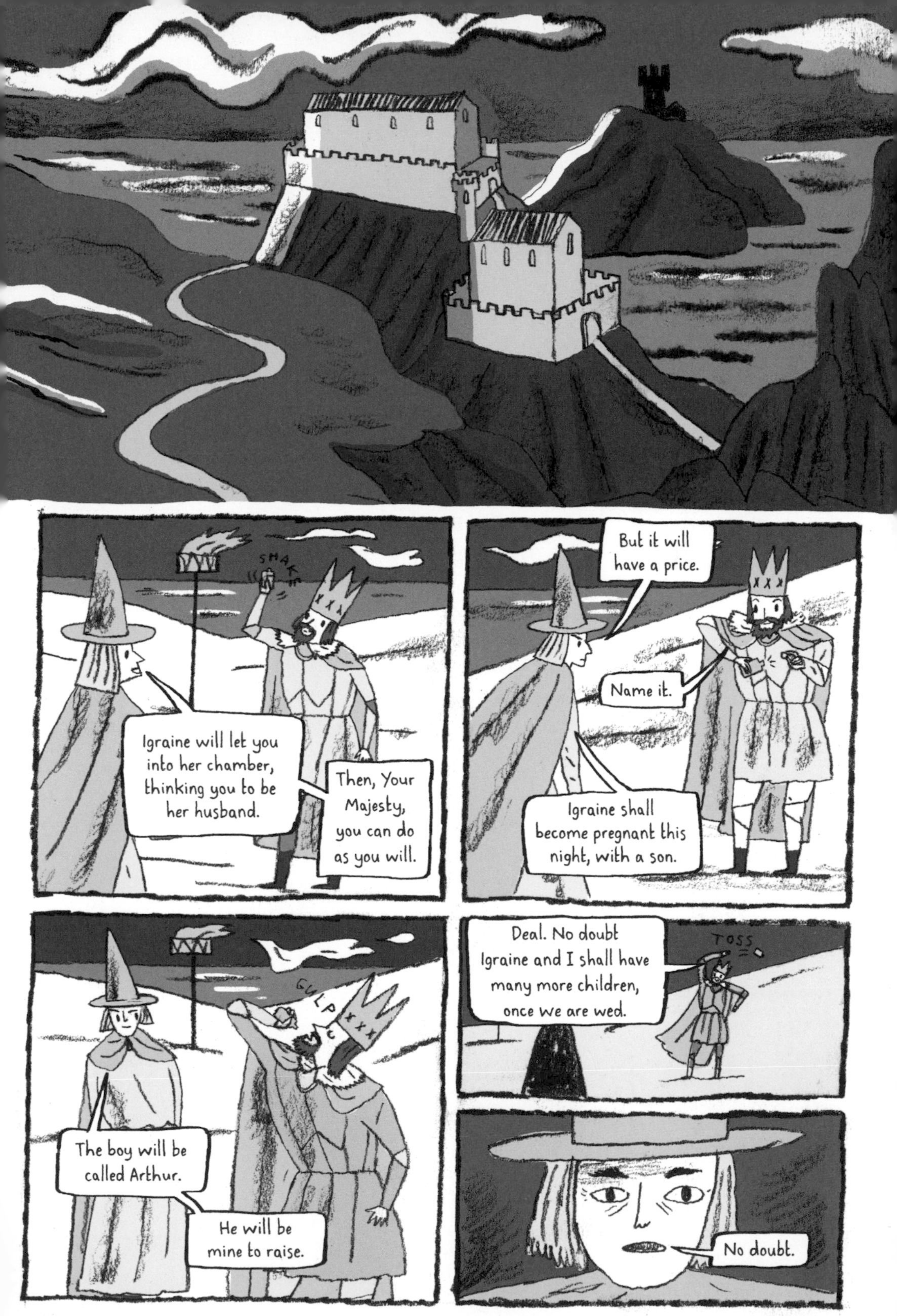
SHAKE
Igraine will let you into her chamber, thinking you to be her husband.
Then, Your Majesty, you can do as you will.
But it will have a price.
Name it.
Igraine shall become pregnant this night, with a son.
GULP
The boy will be called Arthur.
He will be mine to raise.
Deal. No doubt Igraine and I shall have many more children, once we are wed.
TOSS
No doubt.

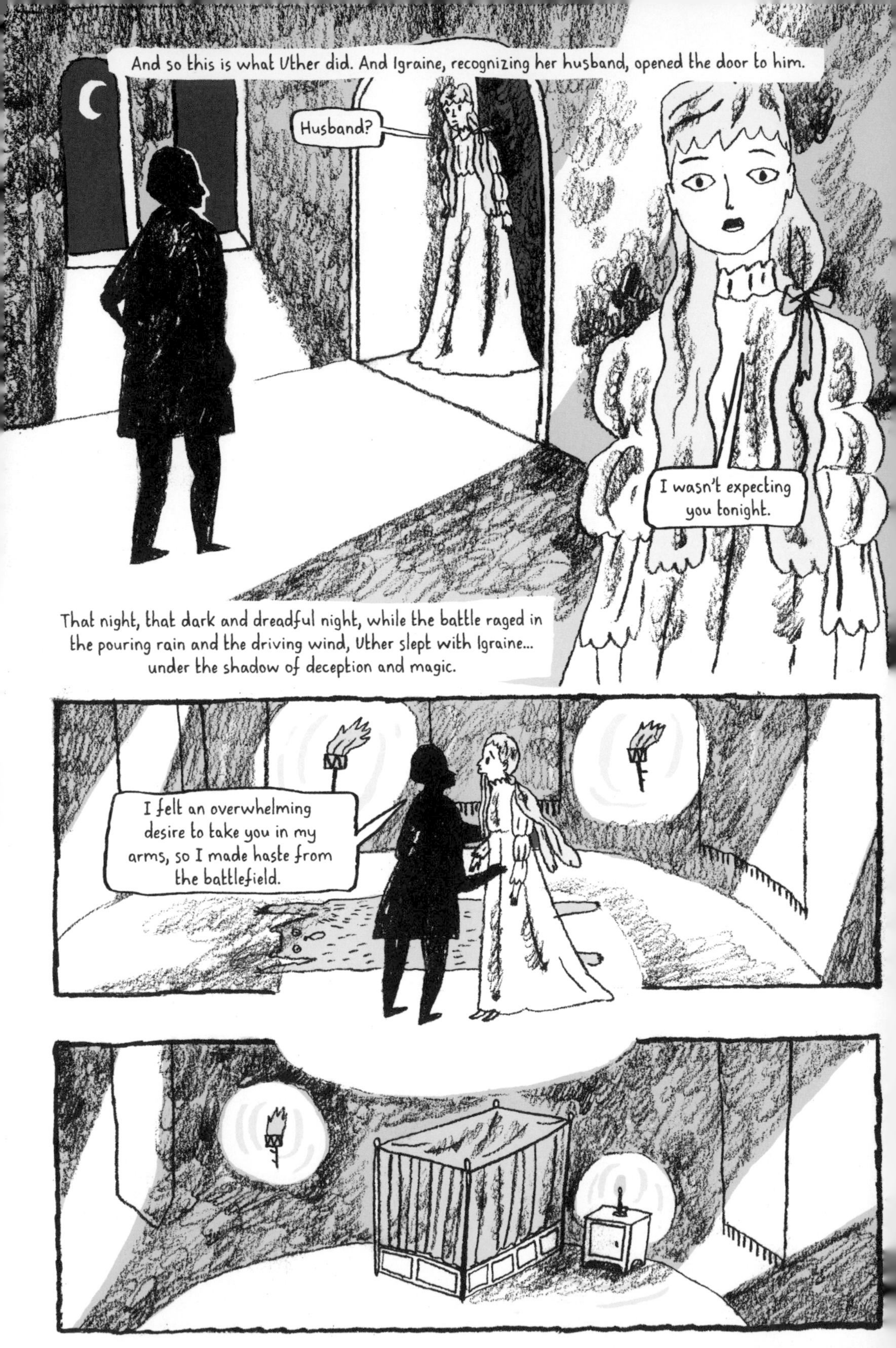
And so this is what Uther did. And Igraine, recognizing her husband, opened the door to him.
Husband?
I wasn't expecting you tonight.
That night, that dark and dreadful night, while the battle raged in the pouring rain and the driving wind, Uther slept with Igraine... under the shadow of deception and magic.
I felt an overwhelming desire to take you in my arms, so I made haste from the battlefield.

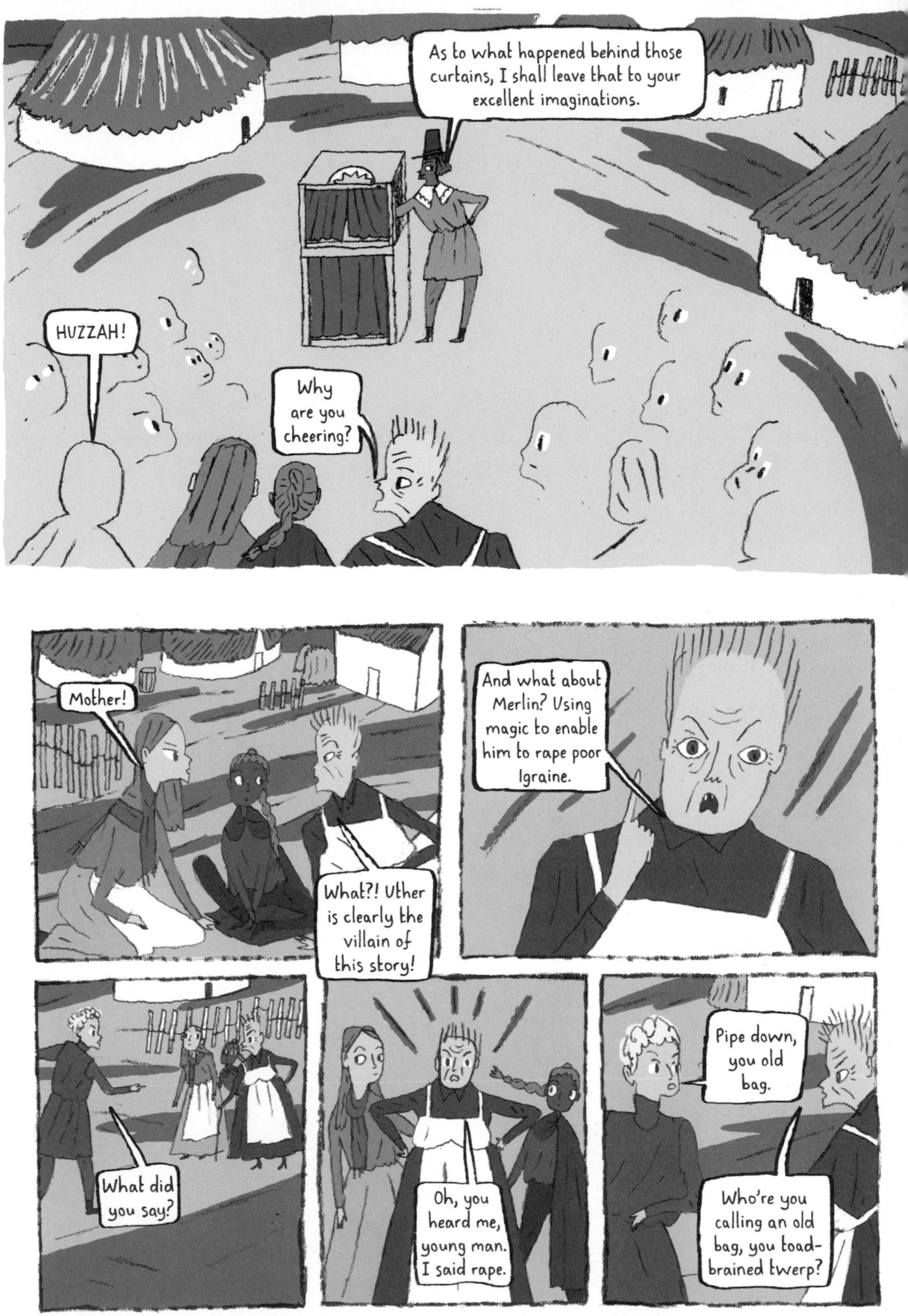

As to what happened behind those curtains, I shall leave that to your excellent imaginations.
HUZZAH!
Why are you cheering?
Mother!
What?! Uther is clearly the villain of this story!
And what about Merlin? Using magic to enable him to rape poor Igraine.
What did you say?
Oh, you heard me, young man. I said rape.
Pipe down, you old bag.
Who're you calling an old bag, you toad-brained twerp?

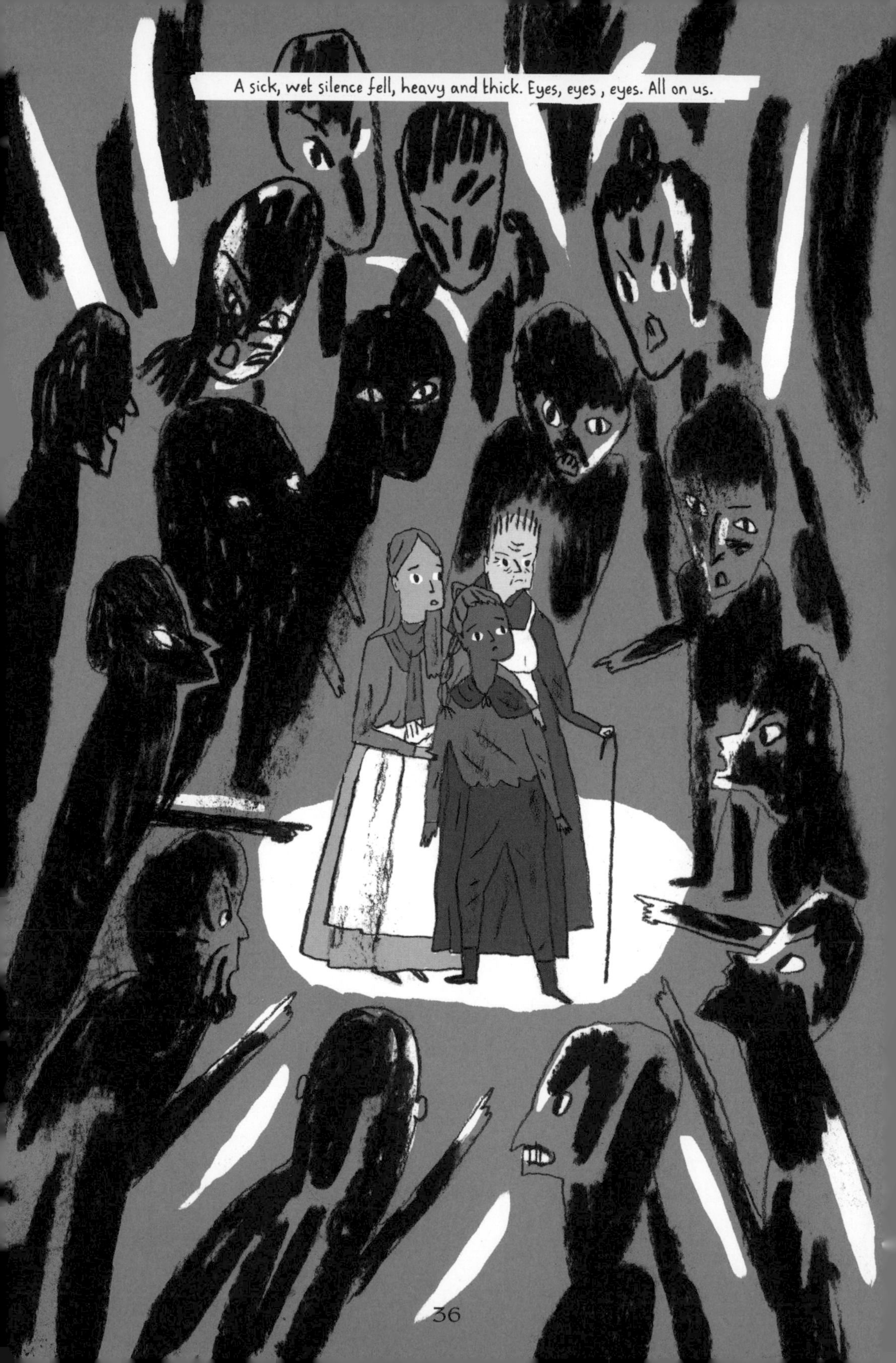
A sick, wet silence fell, heavy and thick. Eyes, eyes , eyes. All on us.

Just like the last time.

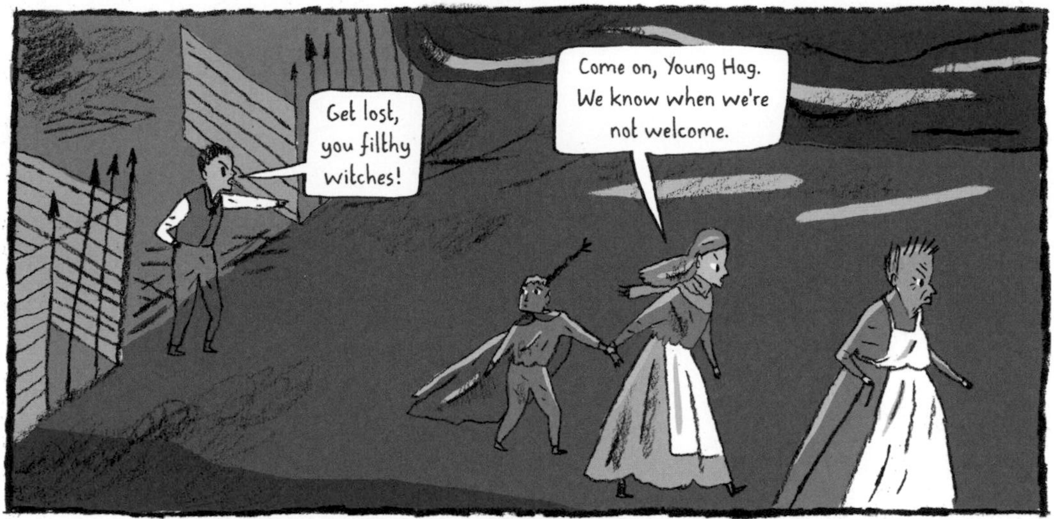

Get lost, you filthy witches!
Come on, Young Hag. We know when we're not welcome.

We walked fast, and then ran and ran and ran, and did not stop until the smoke from the last house was lost in the fog behind us.

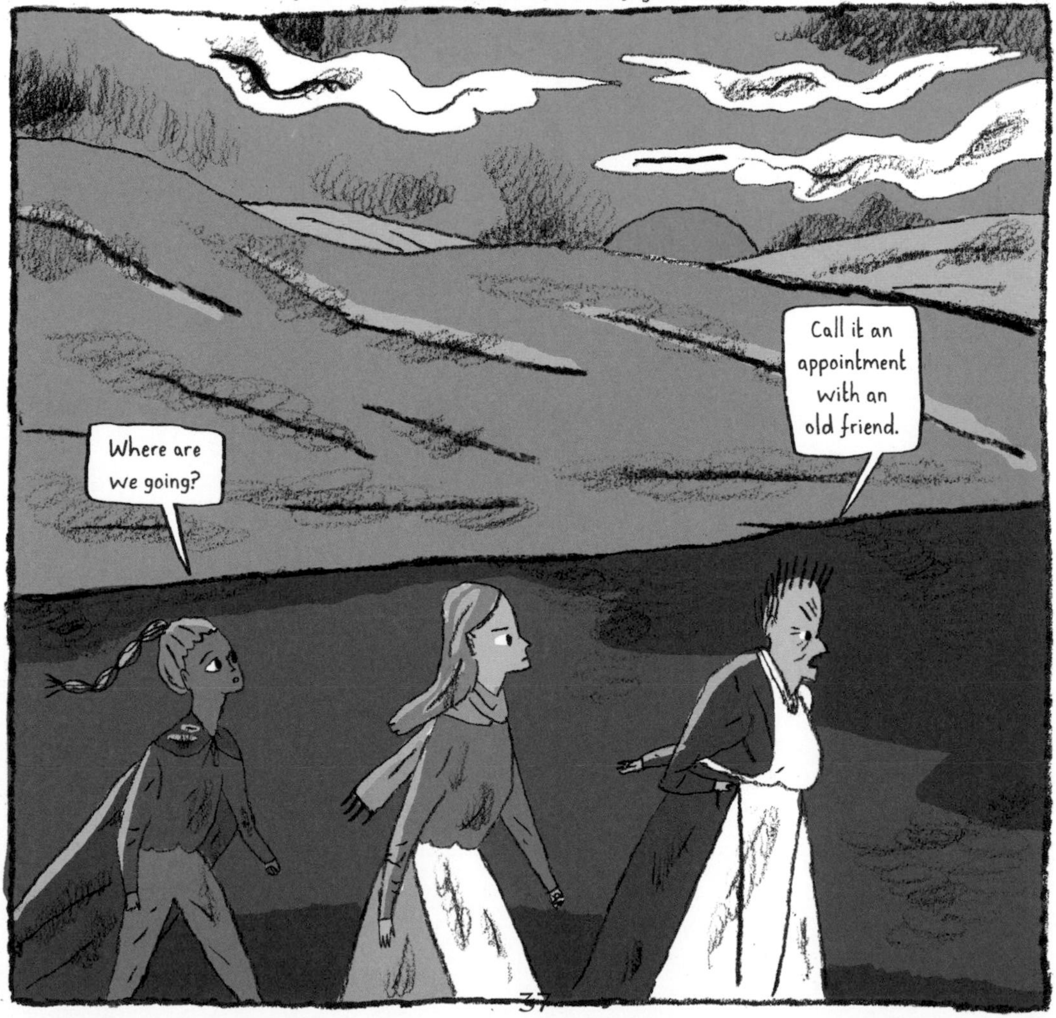

Where are we going?
Call it an appointment with an old friend.

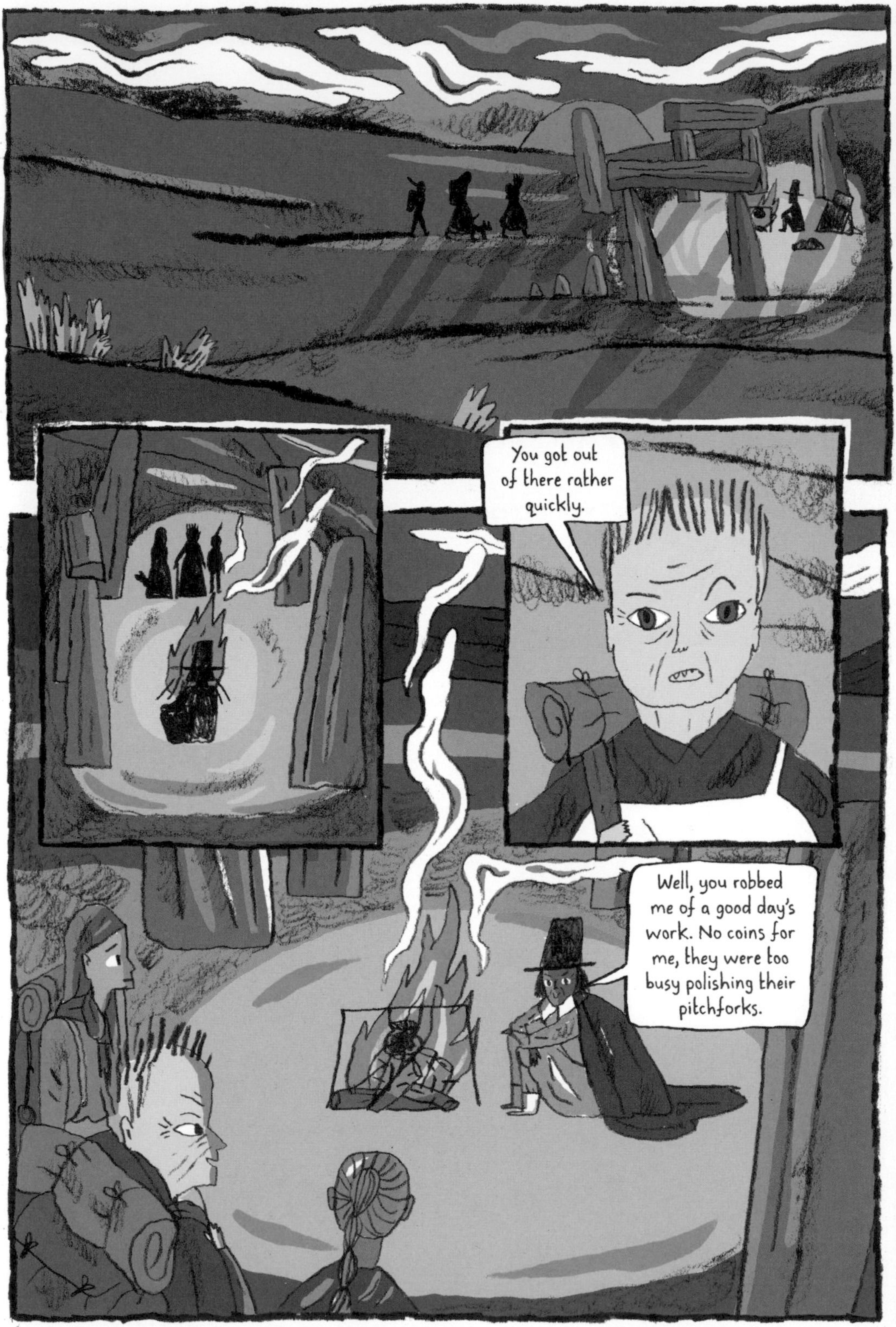
You got out of there rather quickly.
Well, you robbed me of a good day's work. No coins for me, they were too busy polishing their pitchforks.

The storyteller from the village. Sitting by a fire in front of a bubbling pot.
Though how they could have got there before us I did not know. It was a strange day, and getting stranger.

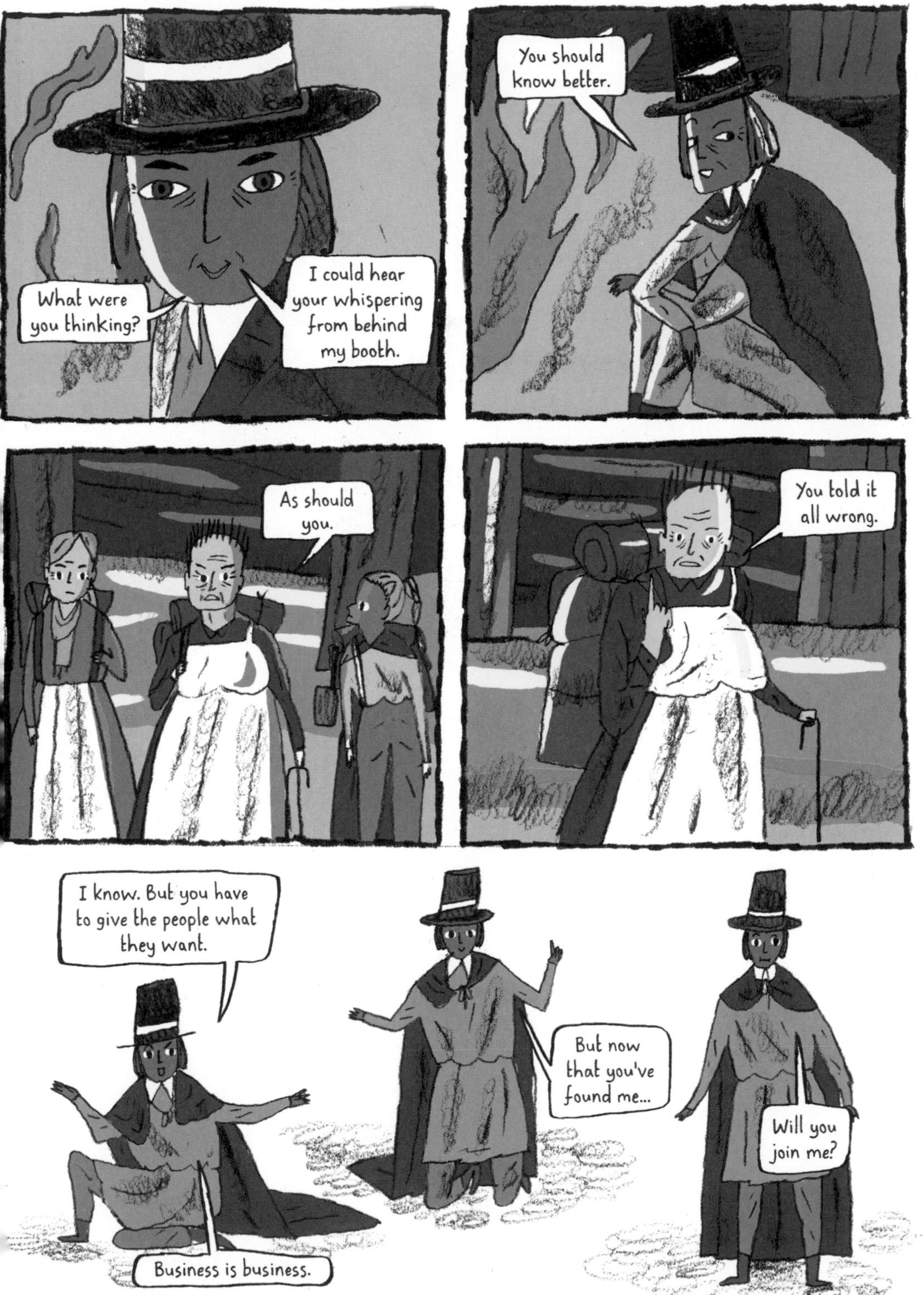
What were you thinking?
I could hear your whispering from behind my booth.
You should know better.
As should you.
You told it all wrong.
I know. But you have to give the people what they want.
Business is business.
But now that you've found me...
Will you join me?

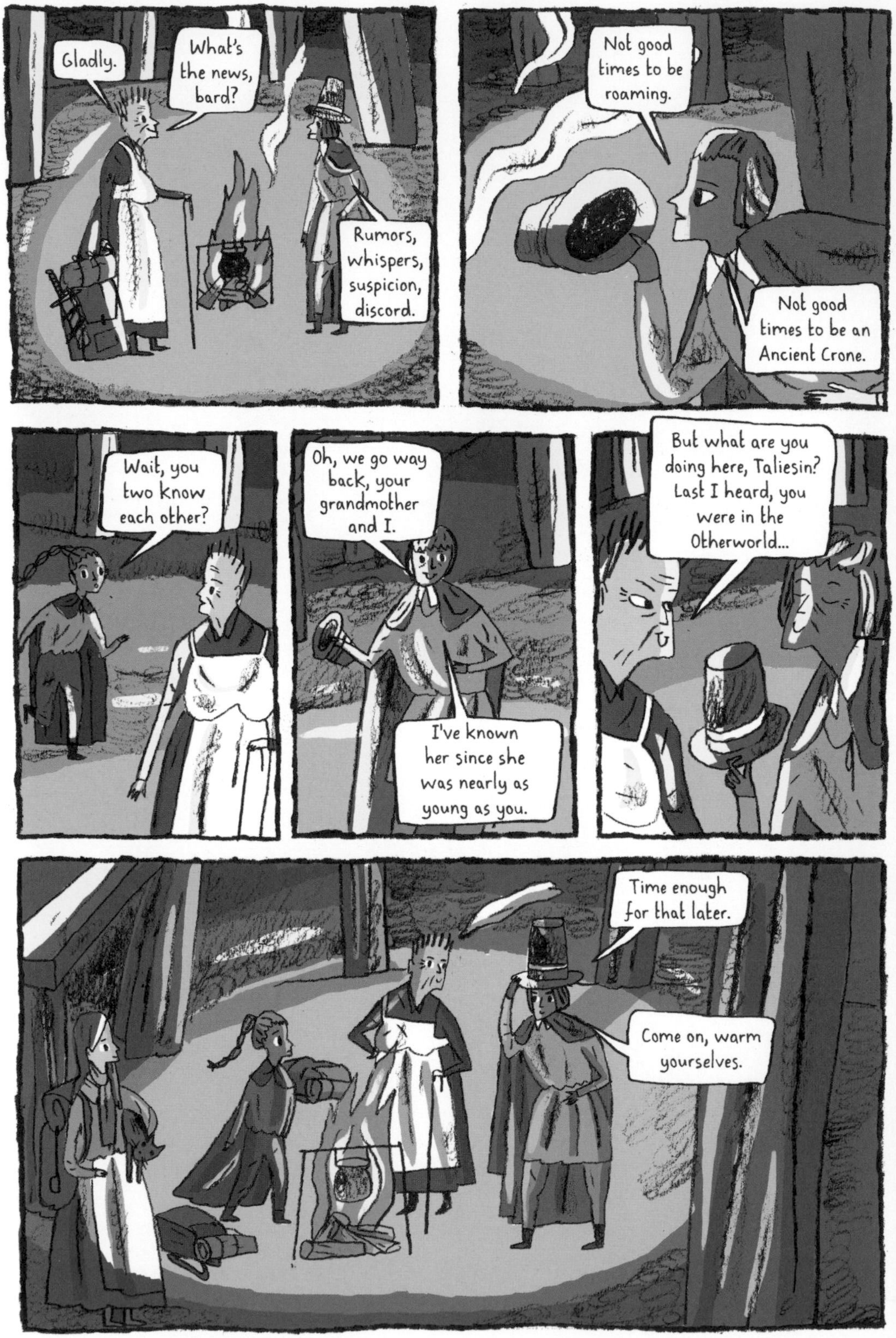
Gladly.
What's the news, bard?
Rumors, whispers, suspicion, discord.
Not good times to be roaming.
Not good times to be an Ancient Crone.
Wait, you two know each other?
Oh, we go way back, your grandmother and I.
I've known her since she was nearly as young as you.
But what are you doing here, Taliesin? Last I heard, you were in the Otherworld...
Time enough for that later.
Come on, warm yourselves.

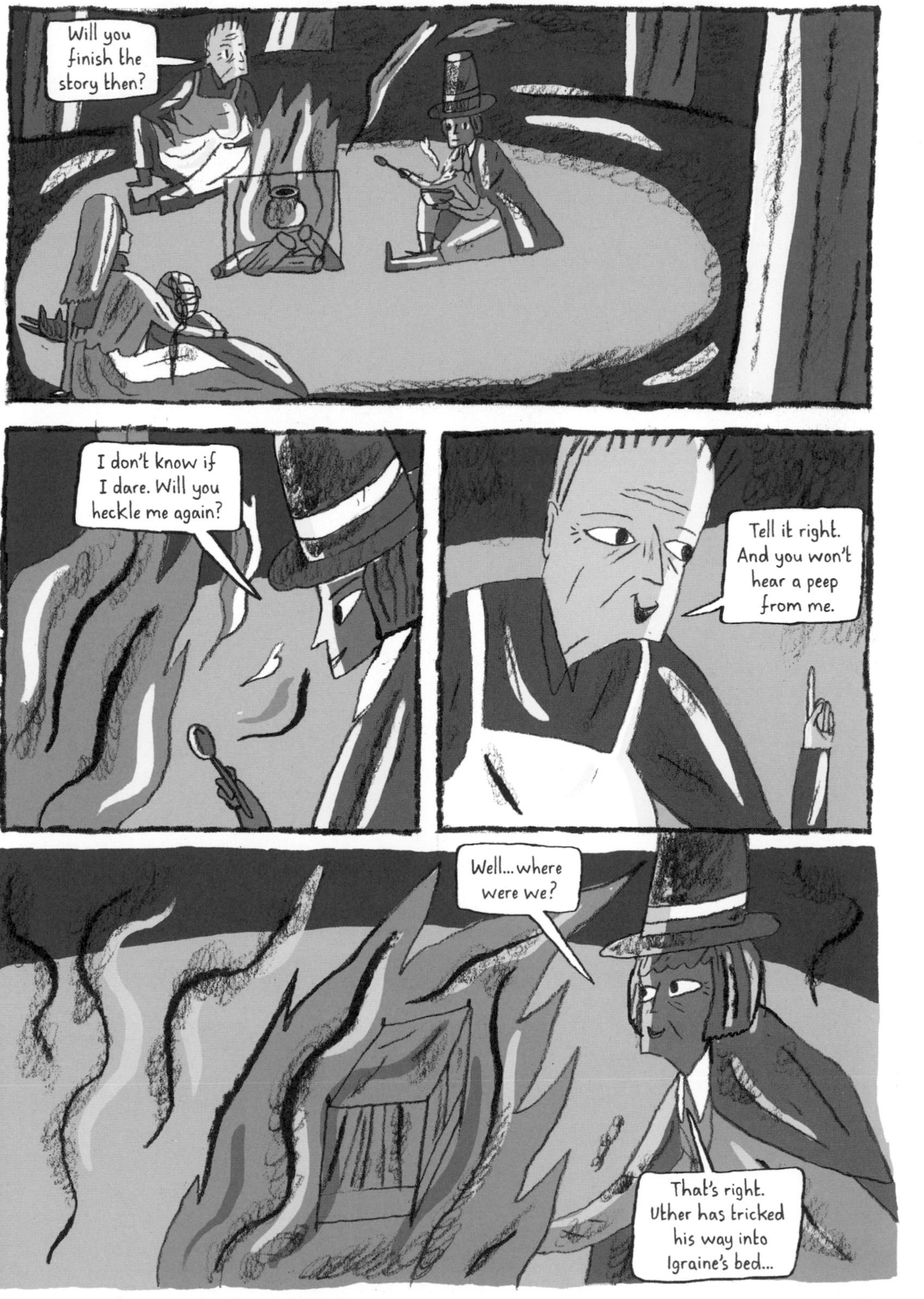
Will you finish the story then?
I don't know if I dare. Will you heckle me again?
Tell it right. And you won't hear a peep from me.
Well... where were we?
That's right. Uther has tricked his way into Igraine's bed...

Igraine woke that morning, and in the gray light of dawn, she turned and saw beside her in the bed not her husband, but the coldly handsome face of King Uther.

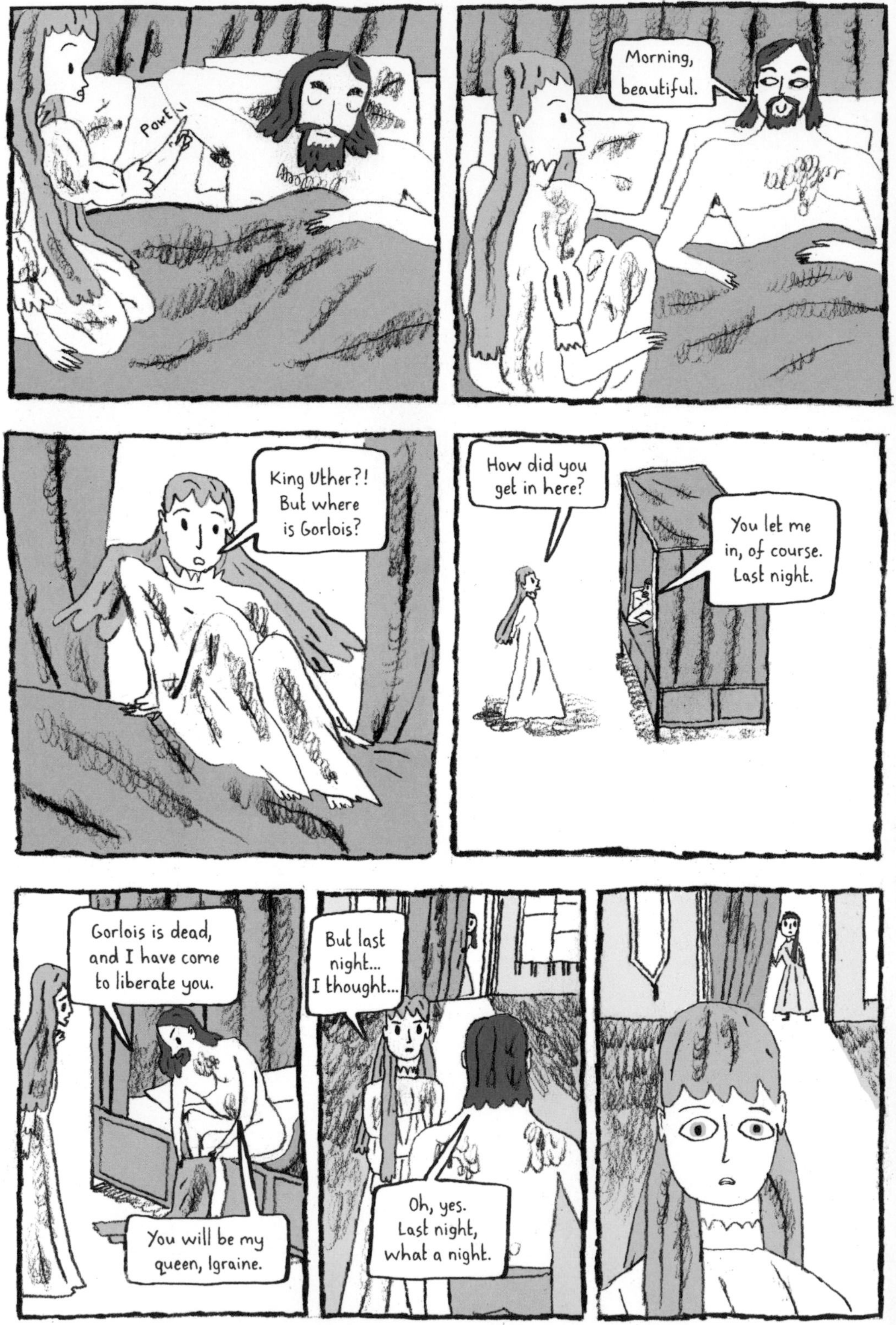
POKE
Morning, beautiful.
King Uther?! But where is Gorlois?
How did you get in here?
You let me in, of course. Last night.
Gorlois is dead, and I have come to liberate you.
You will be my queen, Igraine.
But last night... I thought...
Oh, yes. Last night, what a night.

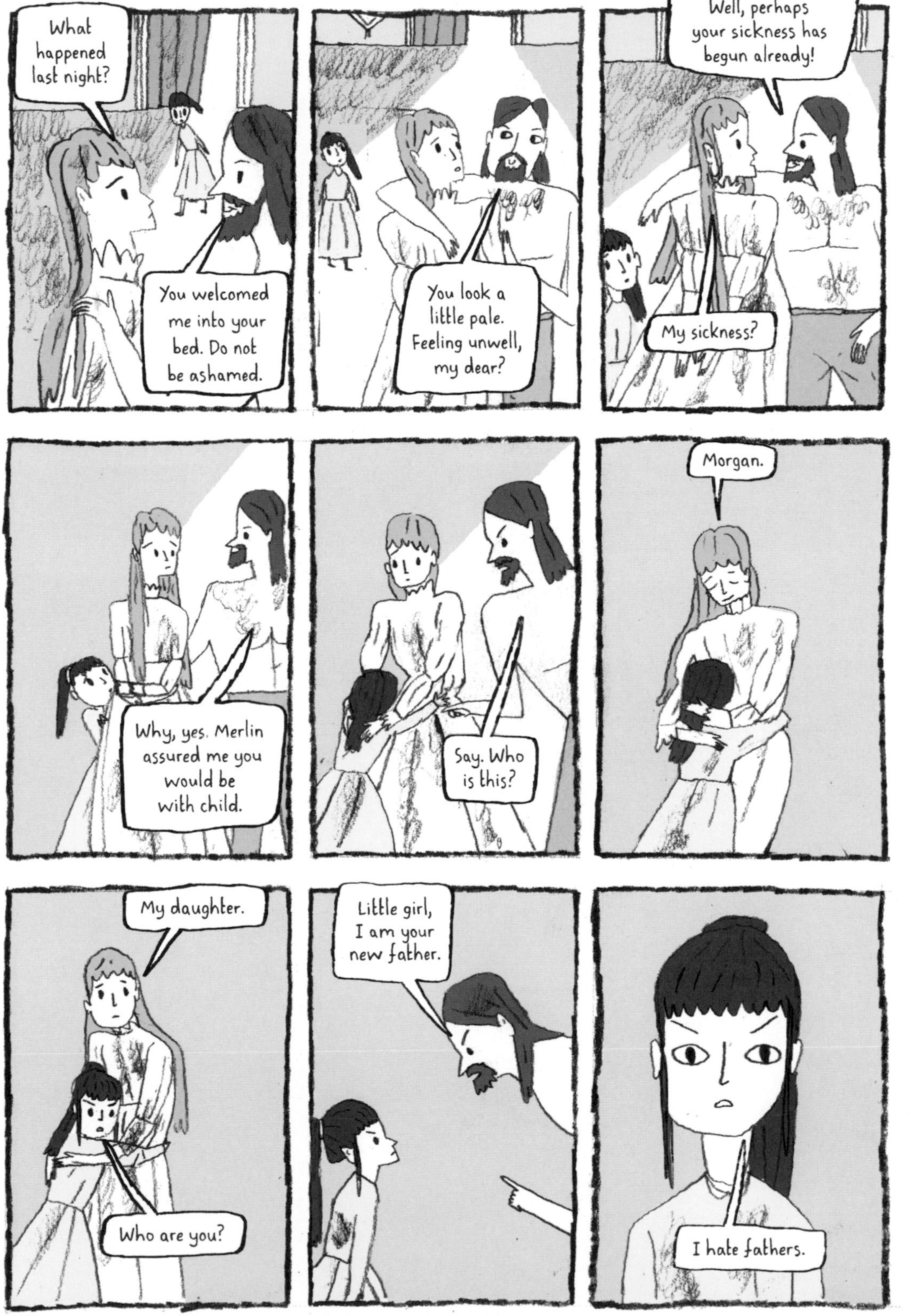
What happened last night?
You welcomed me into your bed. Do not be ashamed.
You look a little pale. Feeling unwell, my dear?
Well, perhaps your sickness has begun already!
My sickness?
Why, yes. Merlin assured me you would be with child.
Say. Who is this?
Morgan.
My daughter.
Who are you?
Little girl, I am your new father.
I hate fathers.

So Igraine and Uther were married, and soon it became clear that Igraine was indeed pregnant.
Igraine did not understand what had happened to her,
how she could have thought Uther was Gorlois that night.

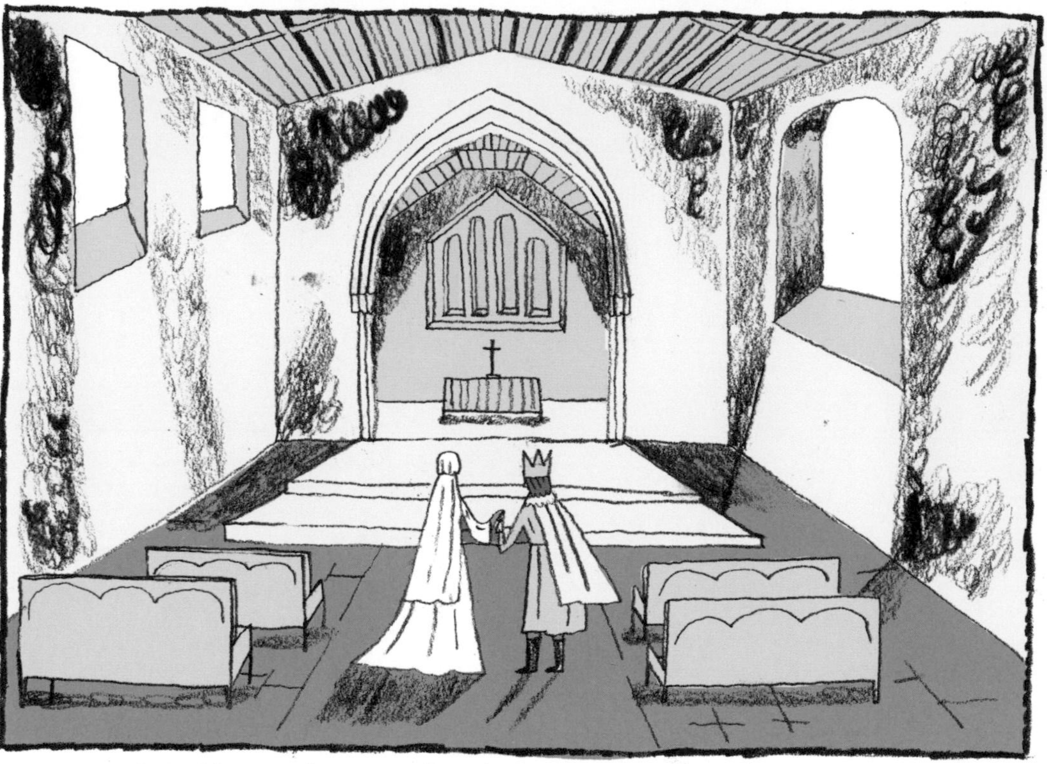

It ate at her. Was she going mad? Would she see other things that were not there?
She was sure that somehow magic had been at play...and it began in her a fear
and a mistrust of anything uncanny...

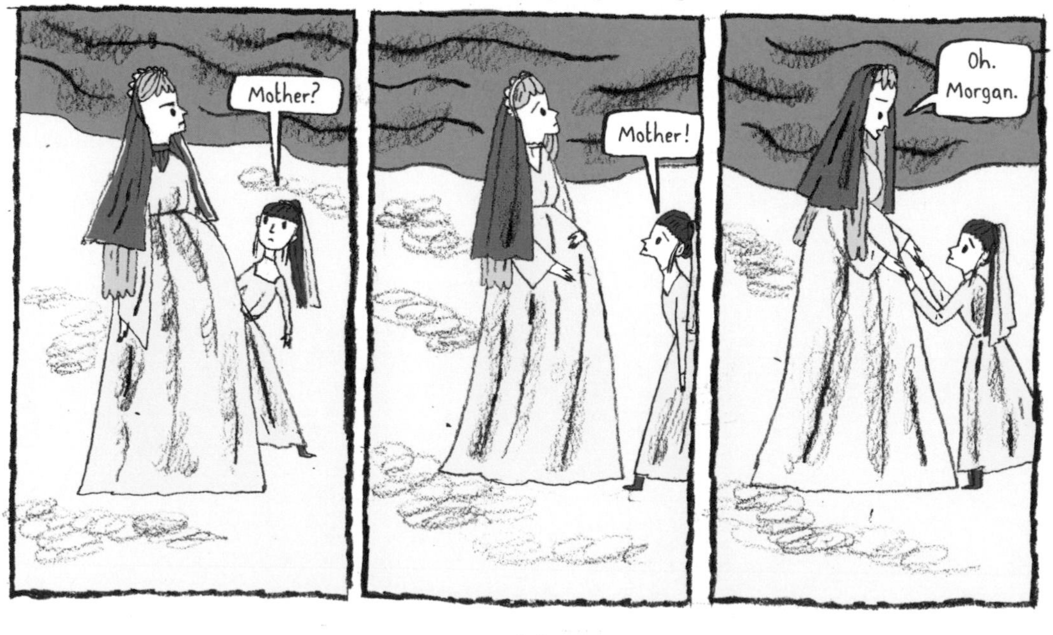
Mother?
Mother!
Oh. Morgan.

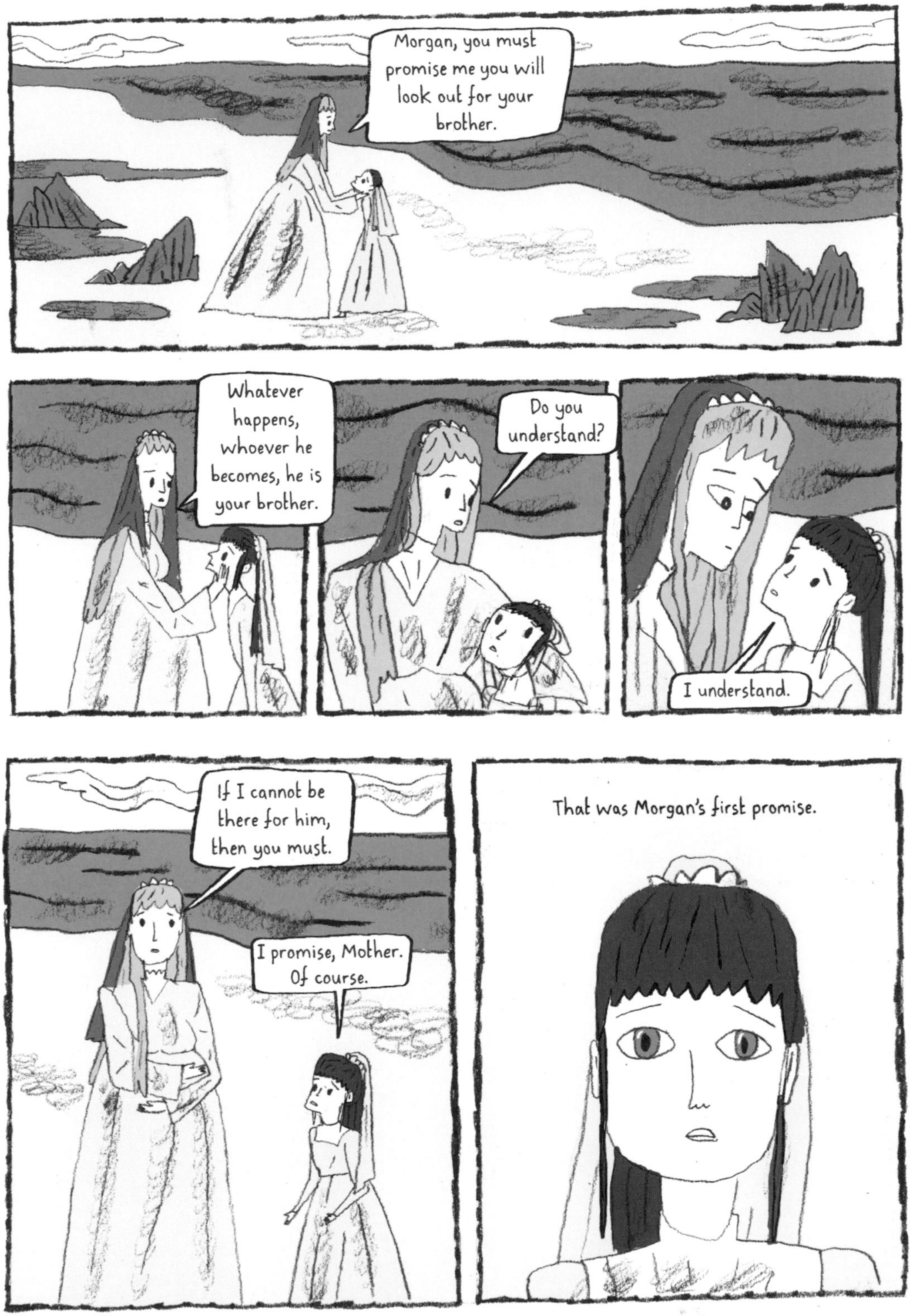
Morgan, you must promise me you will look out for your brother.
Whatever happens, whoever he becomes, he is your brother.
Do you understand?
I understand.
If I cannot be there for him, then you must.
I promise, Mother. Of course.
That was Morgan's first promise.

Young Arthur had only been in Igraine's arms for a matter of hours before Merlin appeared by the bedside. Ready to collect his debt.

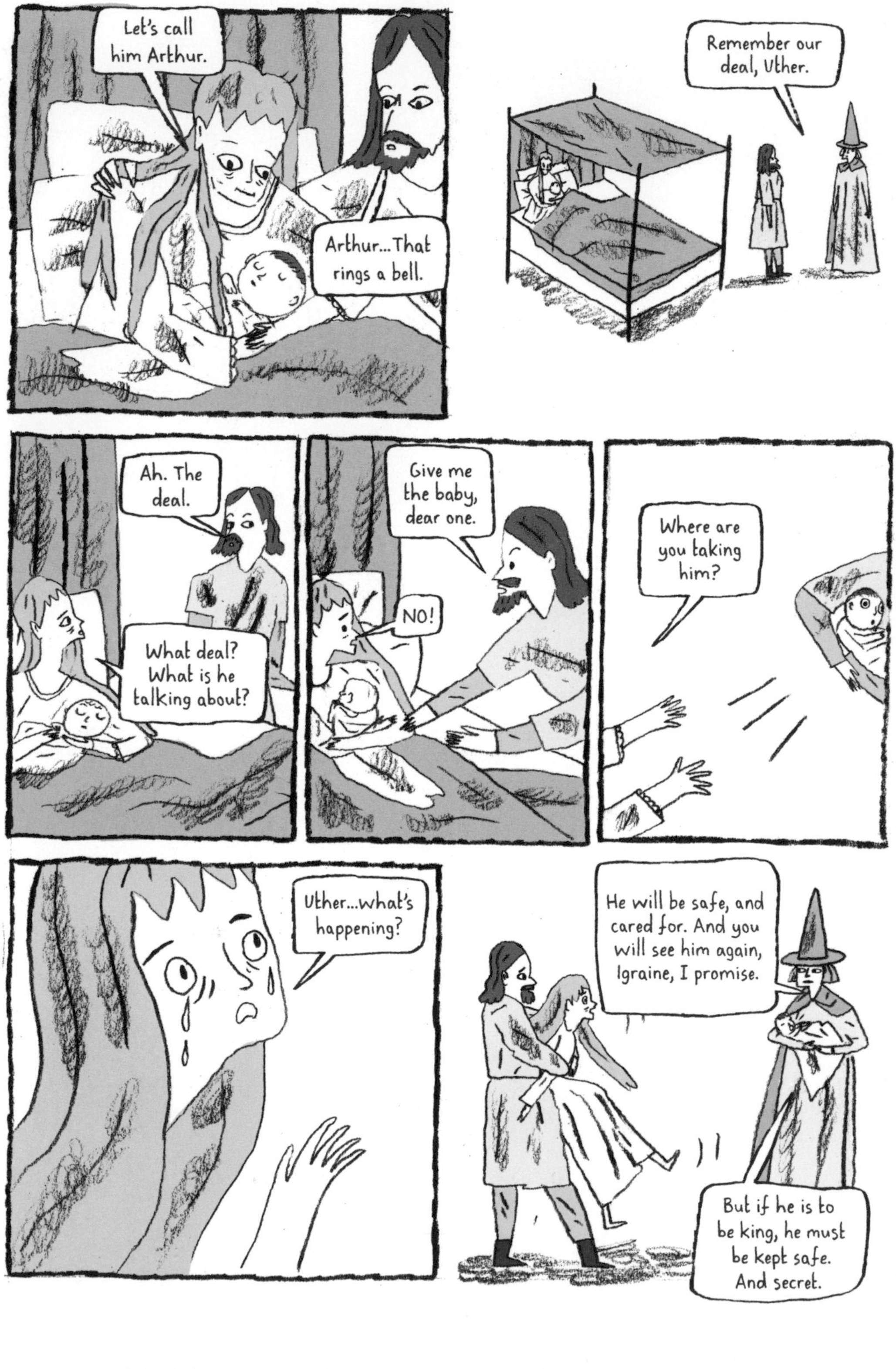

Let's call him Arthur.
Arthur...That rings a bell.
Remember our deal, Uther.
Ah. The deal.
What deal? What is he talking about?
Give me the baby, dear one.
NO!
Where are you taking him?
Uther...what's happening?
He will be safe, and cared for. And you will see him again, Igraine, I promise.
But if he is to be king, he must be kept safe. And secret.

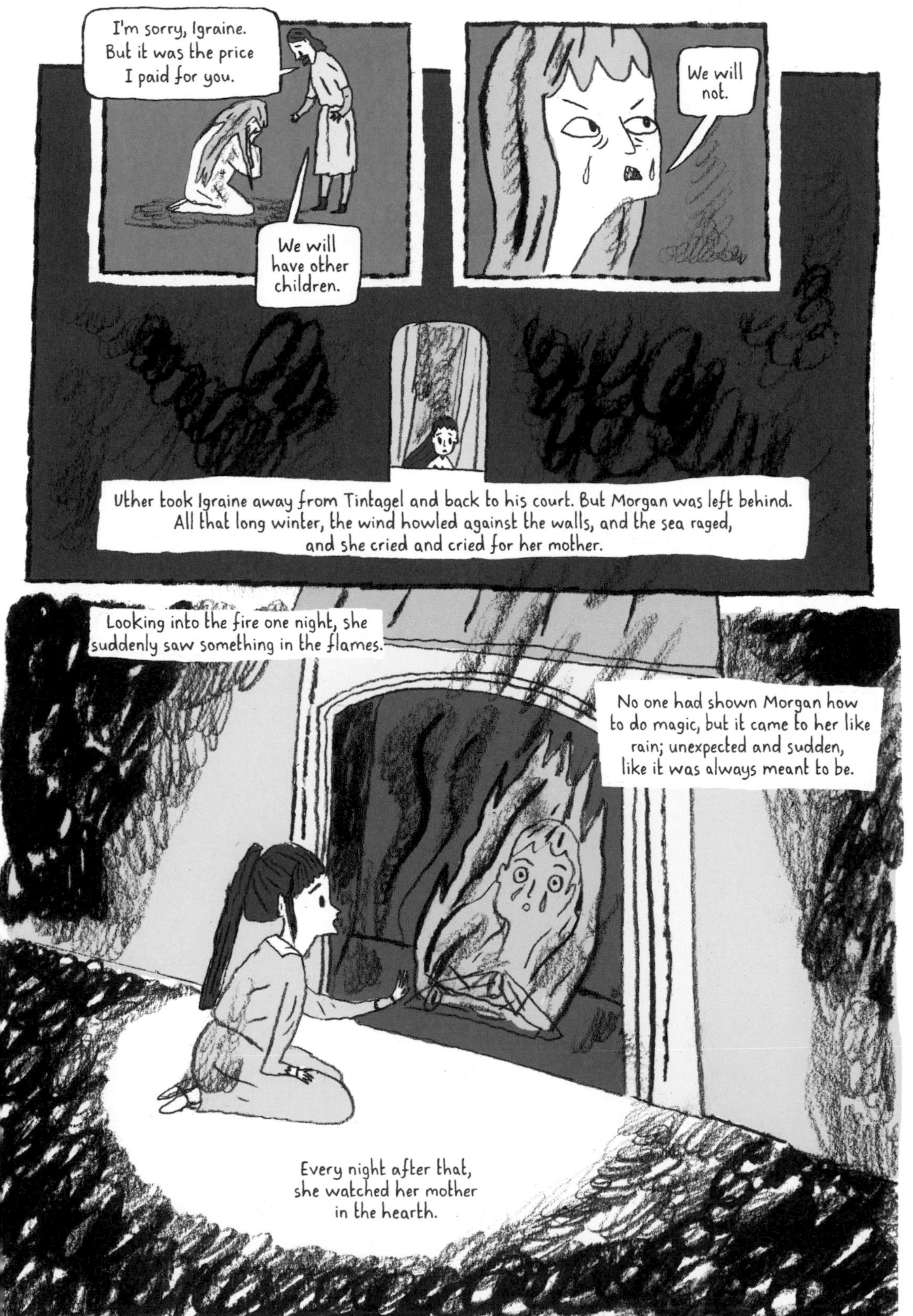
I'm sorry, Igraine. But it was the price I paid for you.
We will have other children.
We will not.
Uther took Igraine away from Tintagel and back to his court. But Morgan was left behind. All that long winter, the wind howled against the walls, and the sea raged, and she cried and cried for her mother.
Looking into the fire one night, she suddenly saw something in the flames.
No one had shown Morgan how to do magic, but it came to her like rain; unexpected and sudden, like it was always meant to be.
Every night after that, she watched her mother in the hearth.

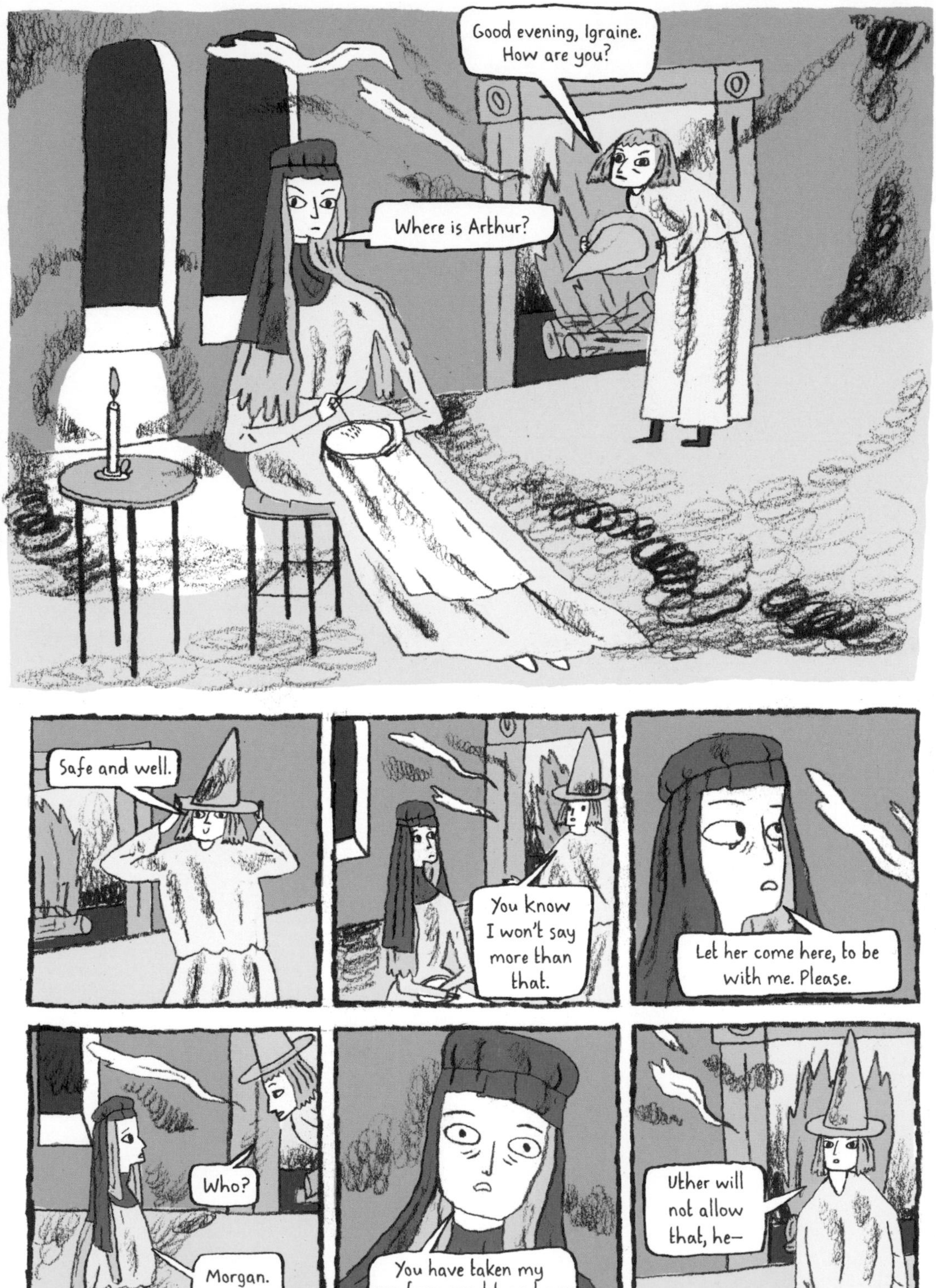
Good evening, Igraine. How are you?
Where is Arthur?
Safe and well.
You know I won't say more than that.
Let her come here, to be with me. Please.
Who?
Morgan.
You have taken my son from me, let me have my daughter back.
Uther will not allow that, he—

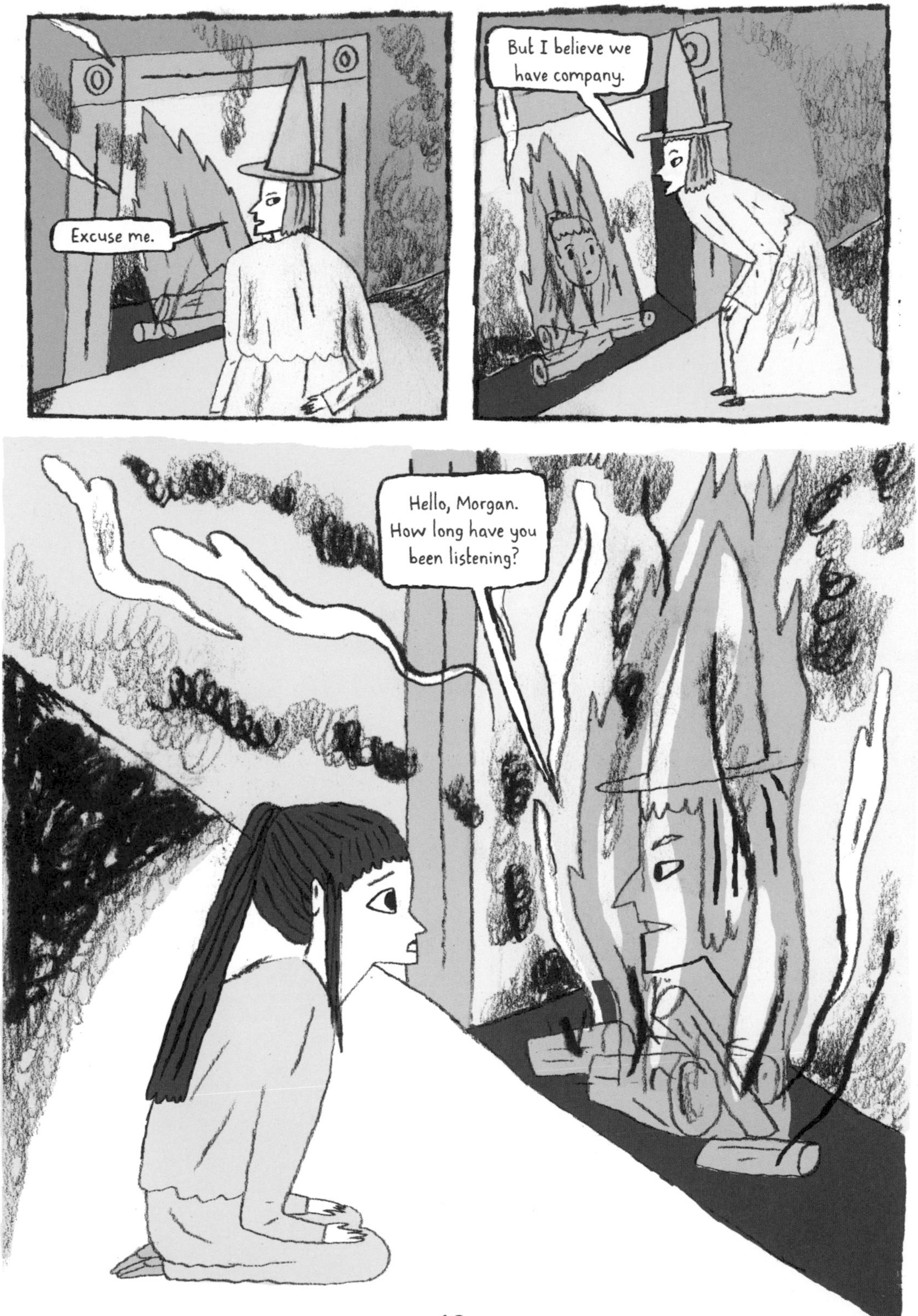
Excuse me.
But I believe we have company.
Hello, Morgan. How long have you been listening?

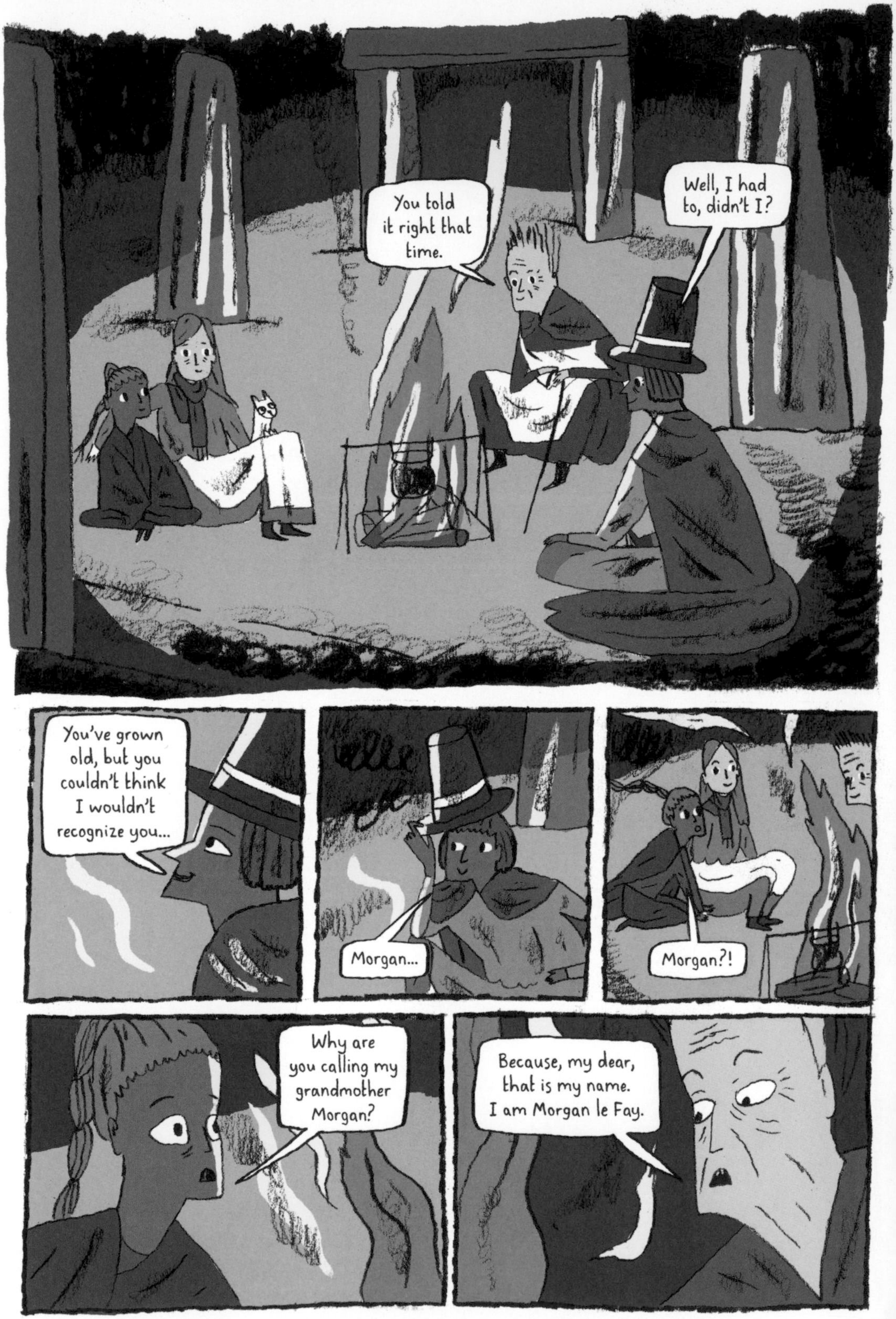
You told it right that time.
Well, I had to, didn't I?
You've grown old, but you couldn't think I wouldn't recognize you...
Morgan...
Morgan?!
Why are you calling my grandmother Morgan?
Because, my dear, that is my name. I am Morgan le Fay.

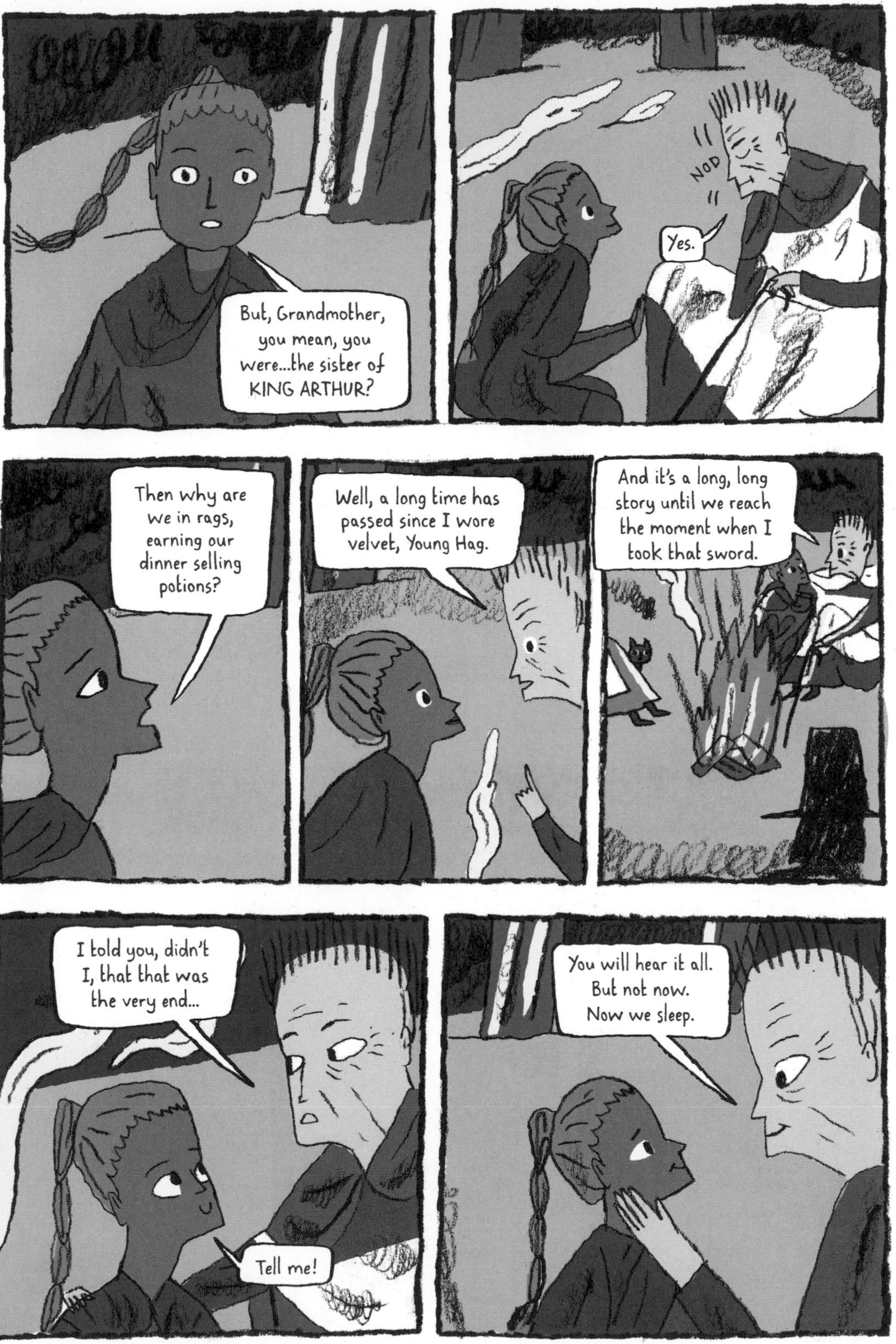
But, Grandmother, you mean, you were...the sister of KING ARTHUR?
NOD
Yes.
Then why are we in rags, earning our dinner selling potions?
Well, a long time has passed since I wore velvet, Young Hag.
And it's a long, long story until we reach the moment when I took that sword.
I told you, didn't I, that that was the very end...
Tell me!
You will hear it all. But not now. Now we sleep.

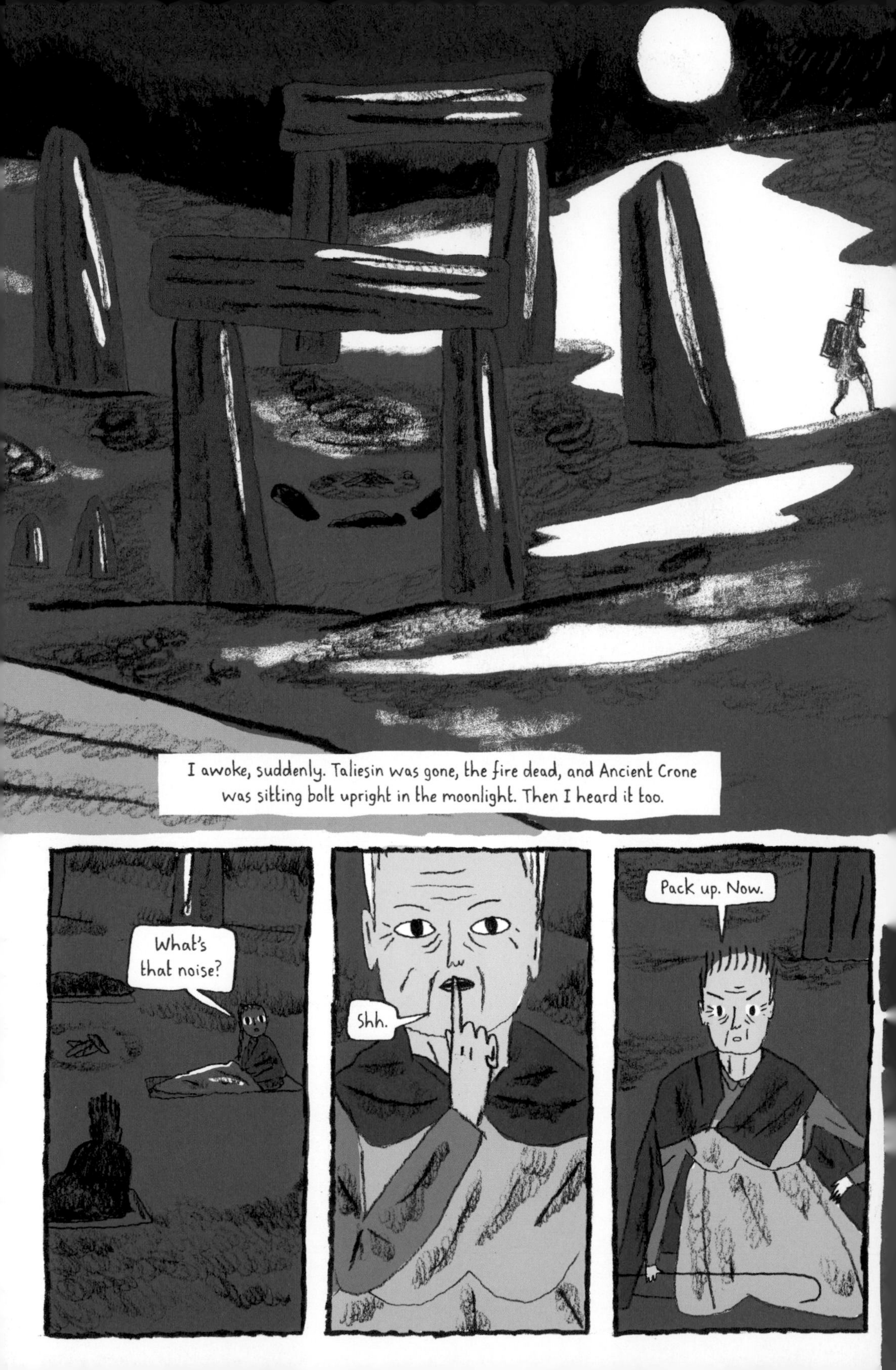
I awoke, suddenly. Taliesin was gone, the fire dead, and Ancient Crone was sitting bolt upright in the moonlight. Then I heard it too.
What's that noise?
Shh.
Pack up. Now.

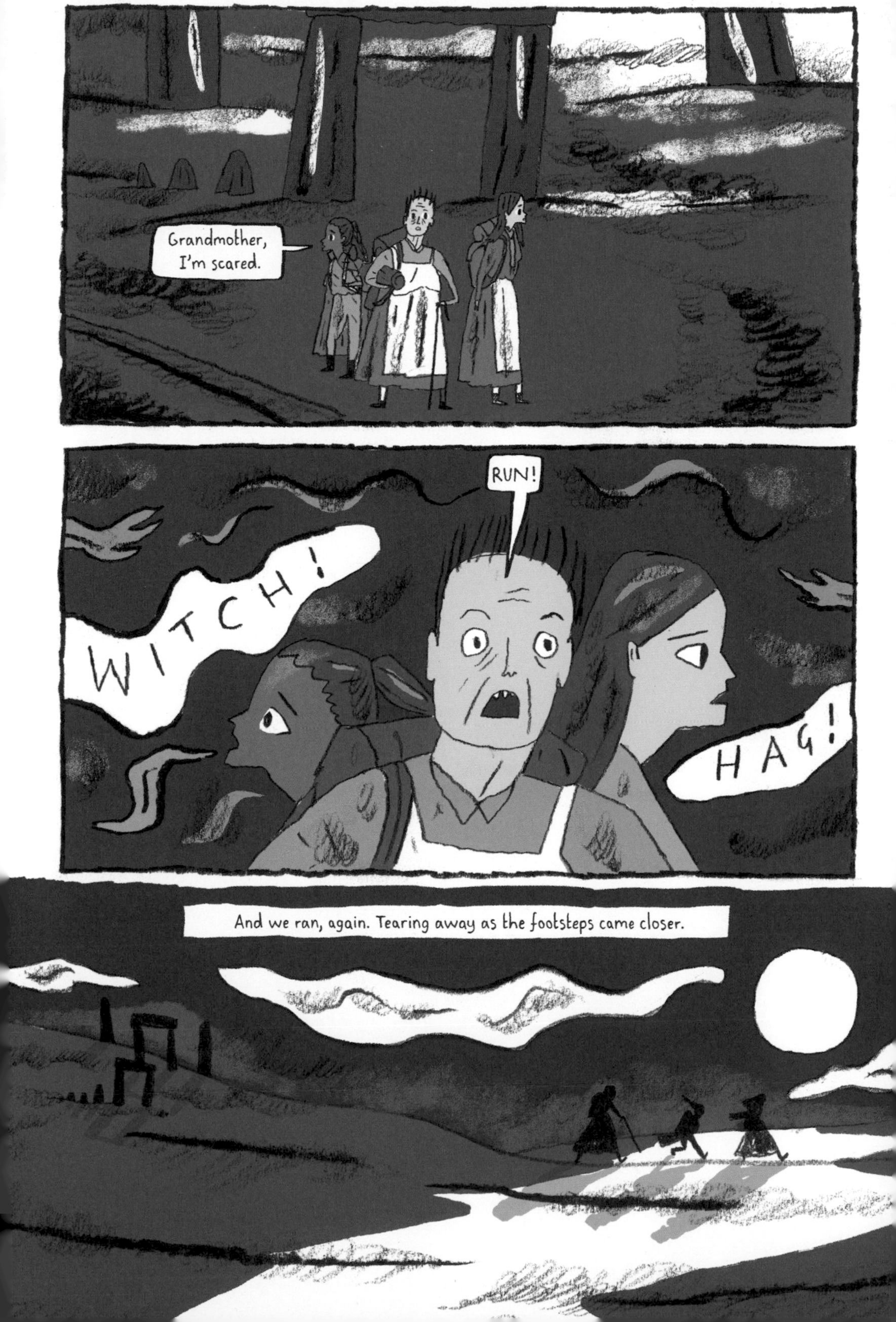
Grandmother,
I'm scared.
RUN!
WITCH!
HAG!
And we ran, again. Tearing away as the footsteps came closer.

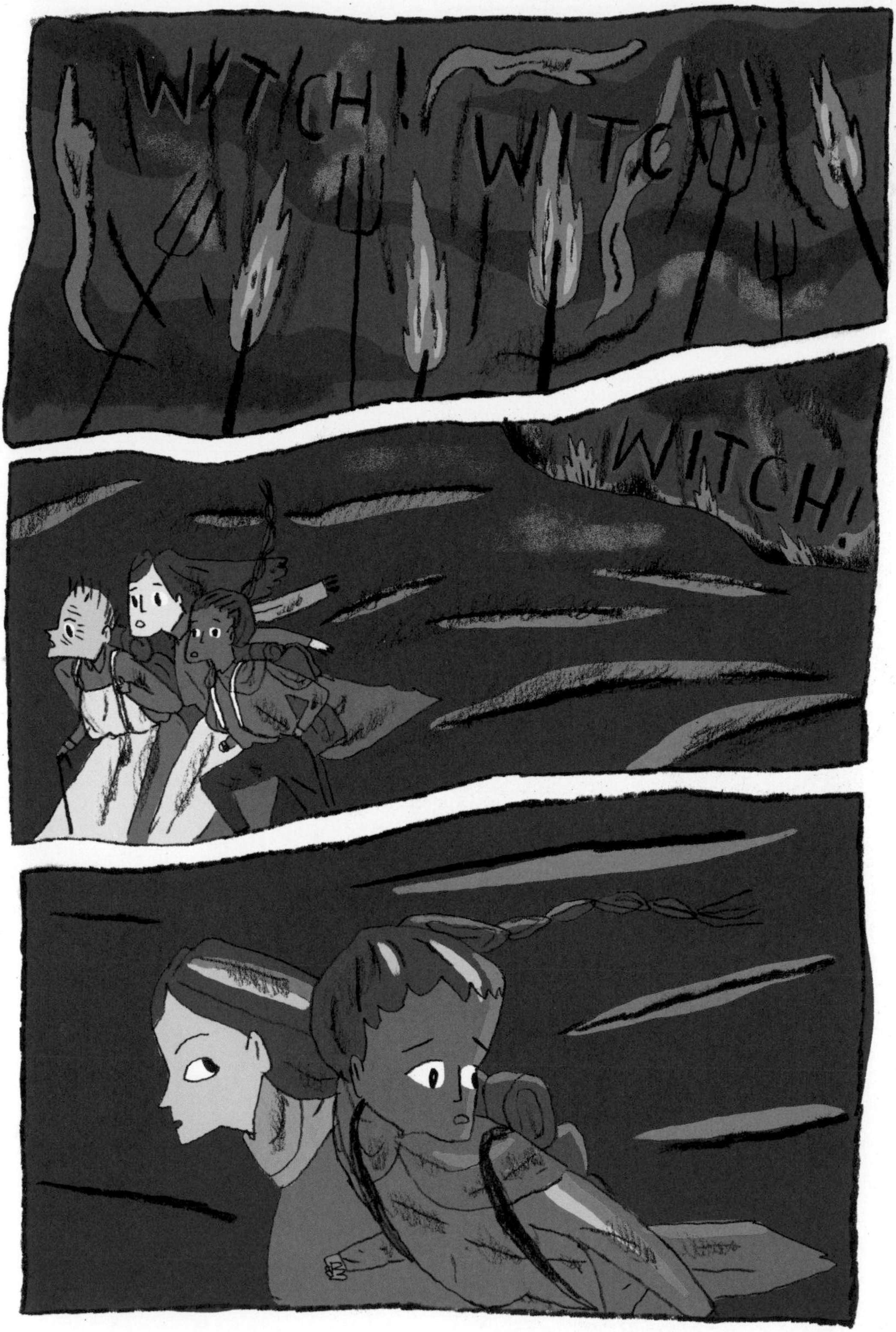
WITCH!
WITCH!
WITCH!

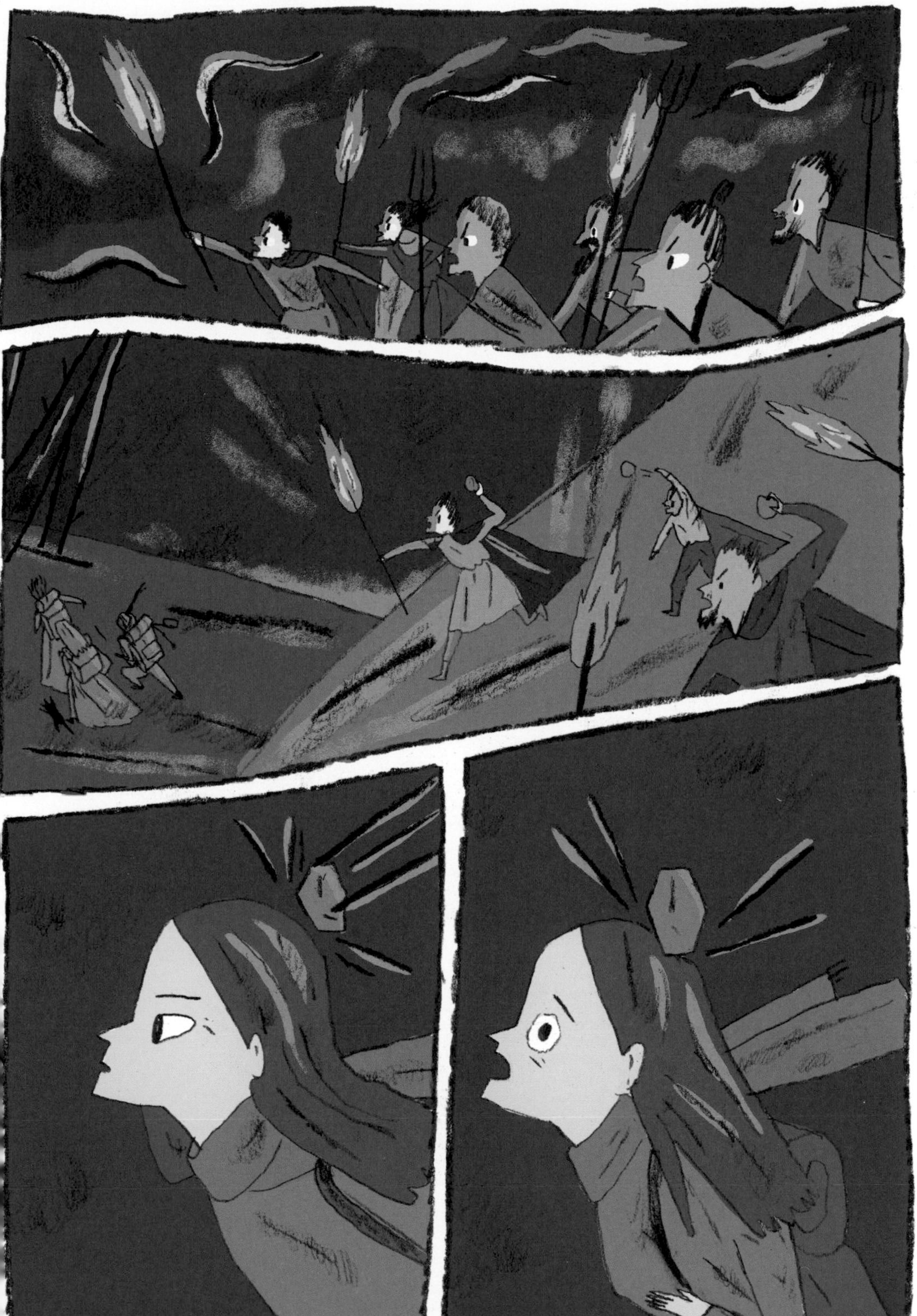

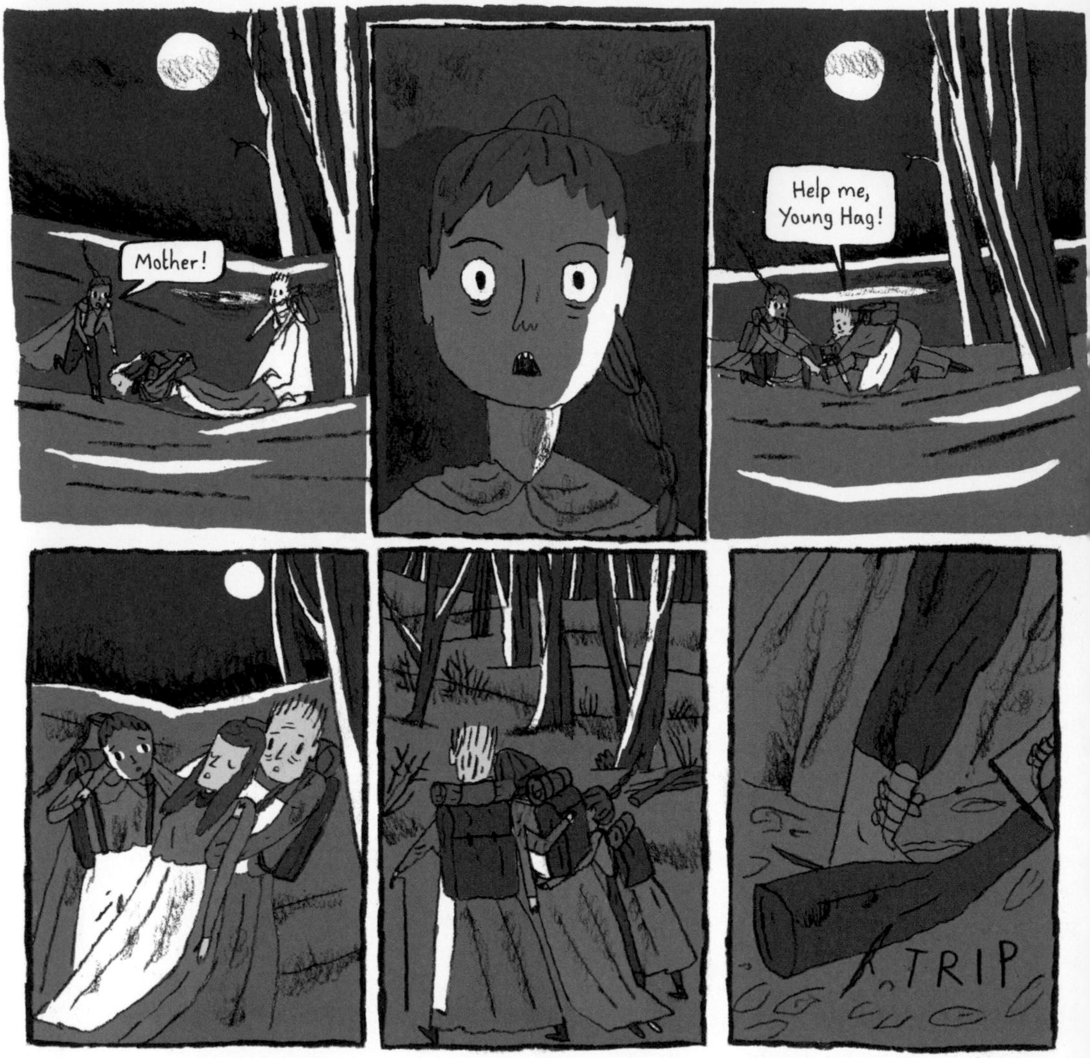
Mother!
Help me, Young Hag!
TRIP

Feet, hands, leaves, the world tumbling round and round and round.

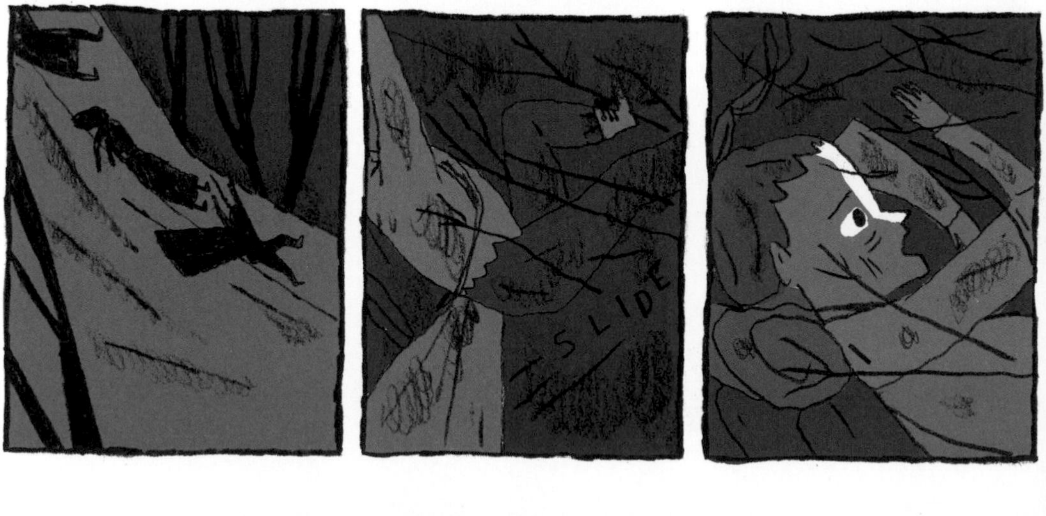
SLIDE

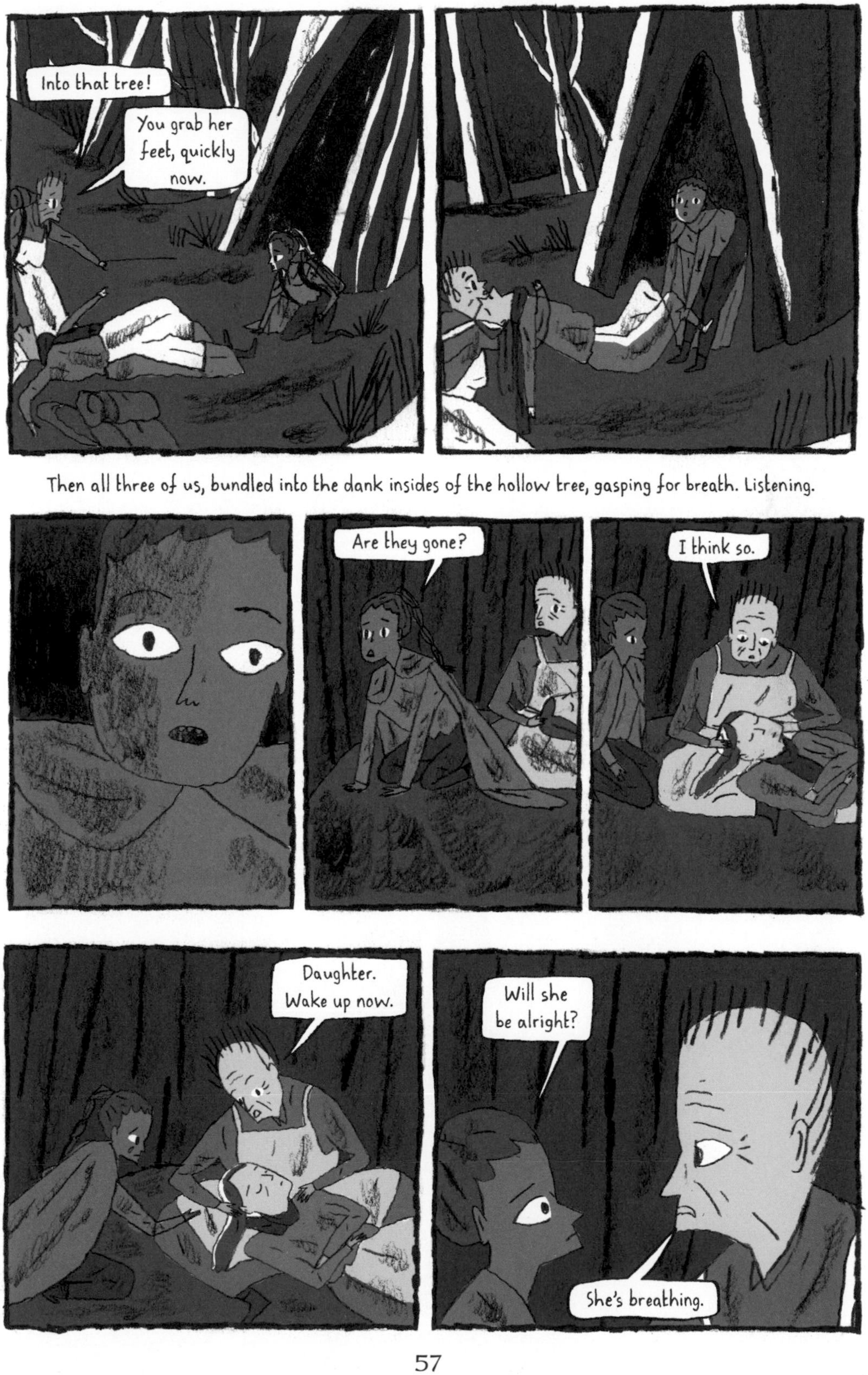
Into that tree!
You grab her feet, quickly now.
Then all three of us, bundled into the dank insides of the hollow tree, gasping for breath. Listening.
Are they gone?
I think so.
Daughter. Wake up now.
Will she be alright?
She's breathing.

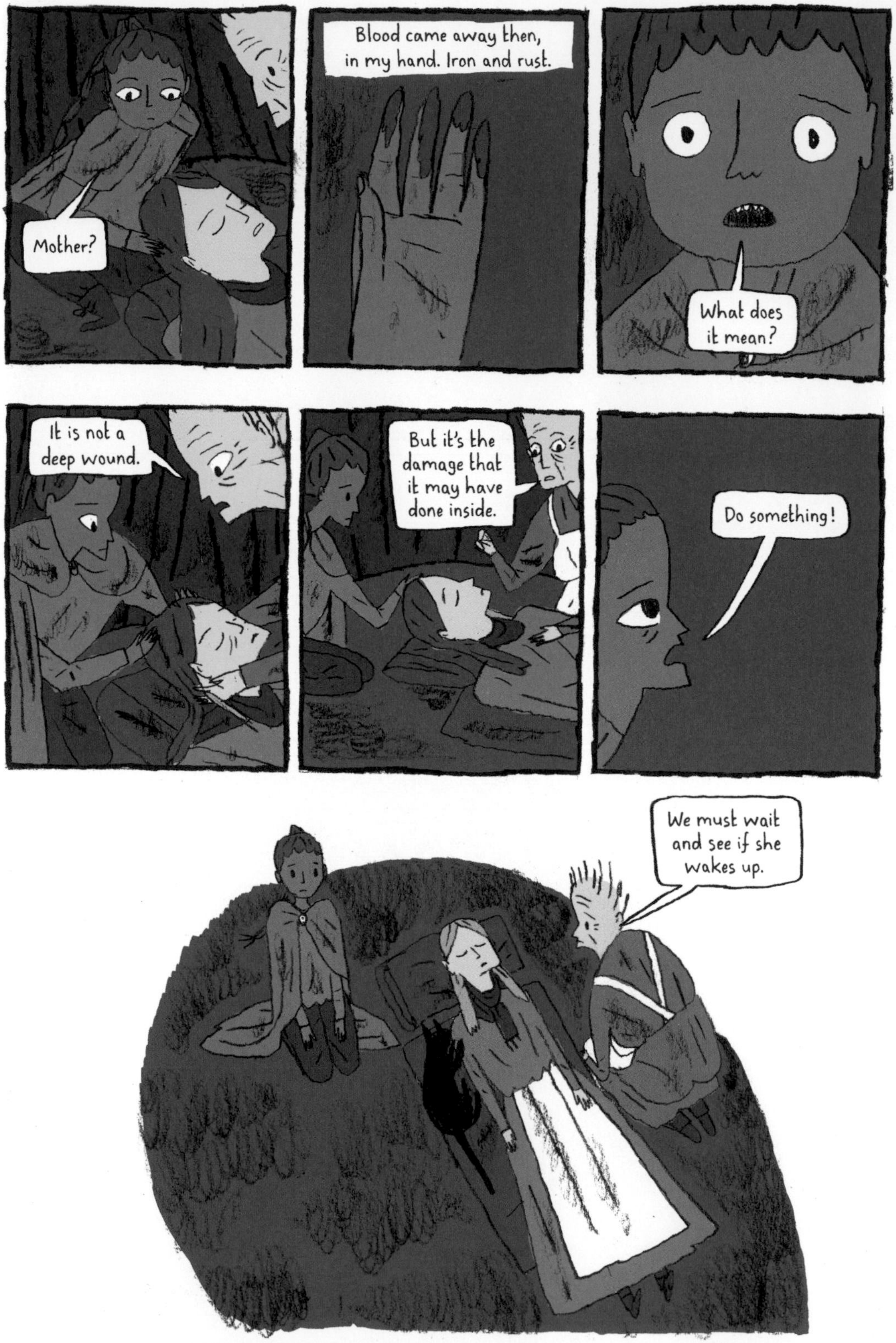
Mother?
Blood came away then, in my hand. Iron and rust.
What does it mean?
It is not a deep wound.
But it's the damage that it may have done inside.
Do something!
We must wait and see if she wakes up.

But my mother never woke up.

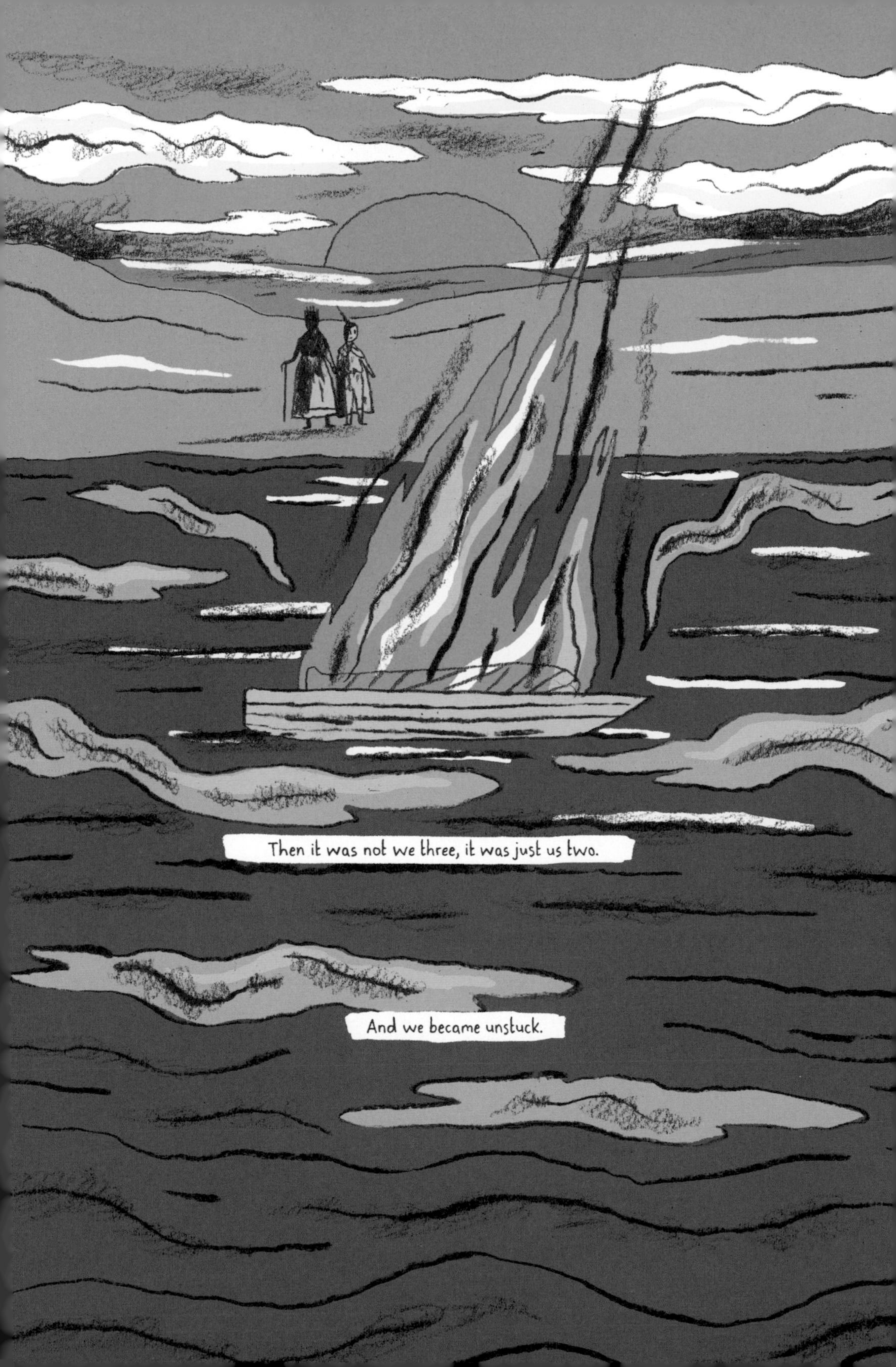
Then it was not we three, it was just us two.
And we became unstuck.

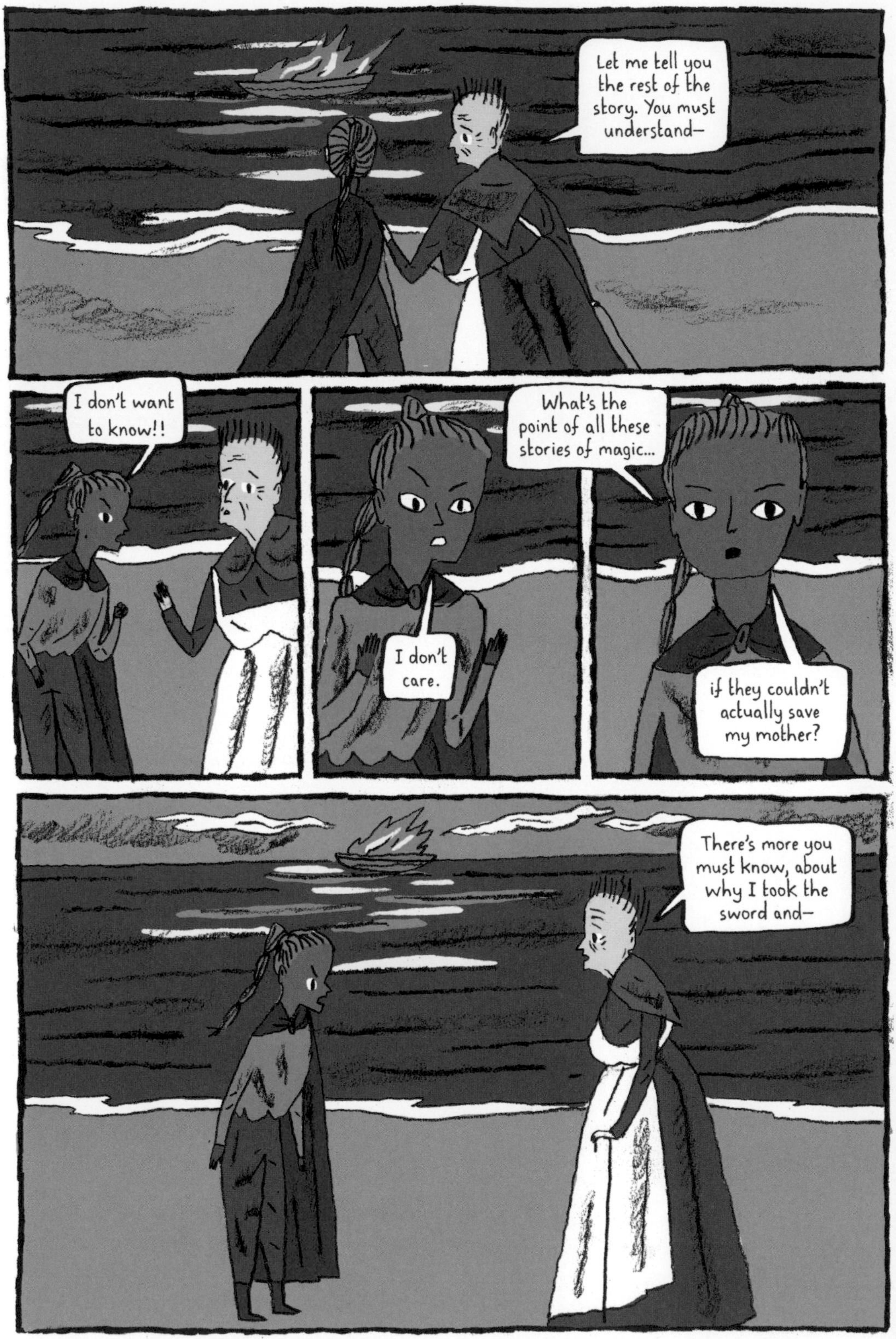
Let me tell you the rest of the story. You must understand—
I don't want to know!!
What's the point of all these stories of magic...
I don't care.
if they couldn't actually save my mother?
There's more you must know, about why I took the sword and—

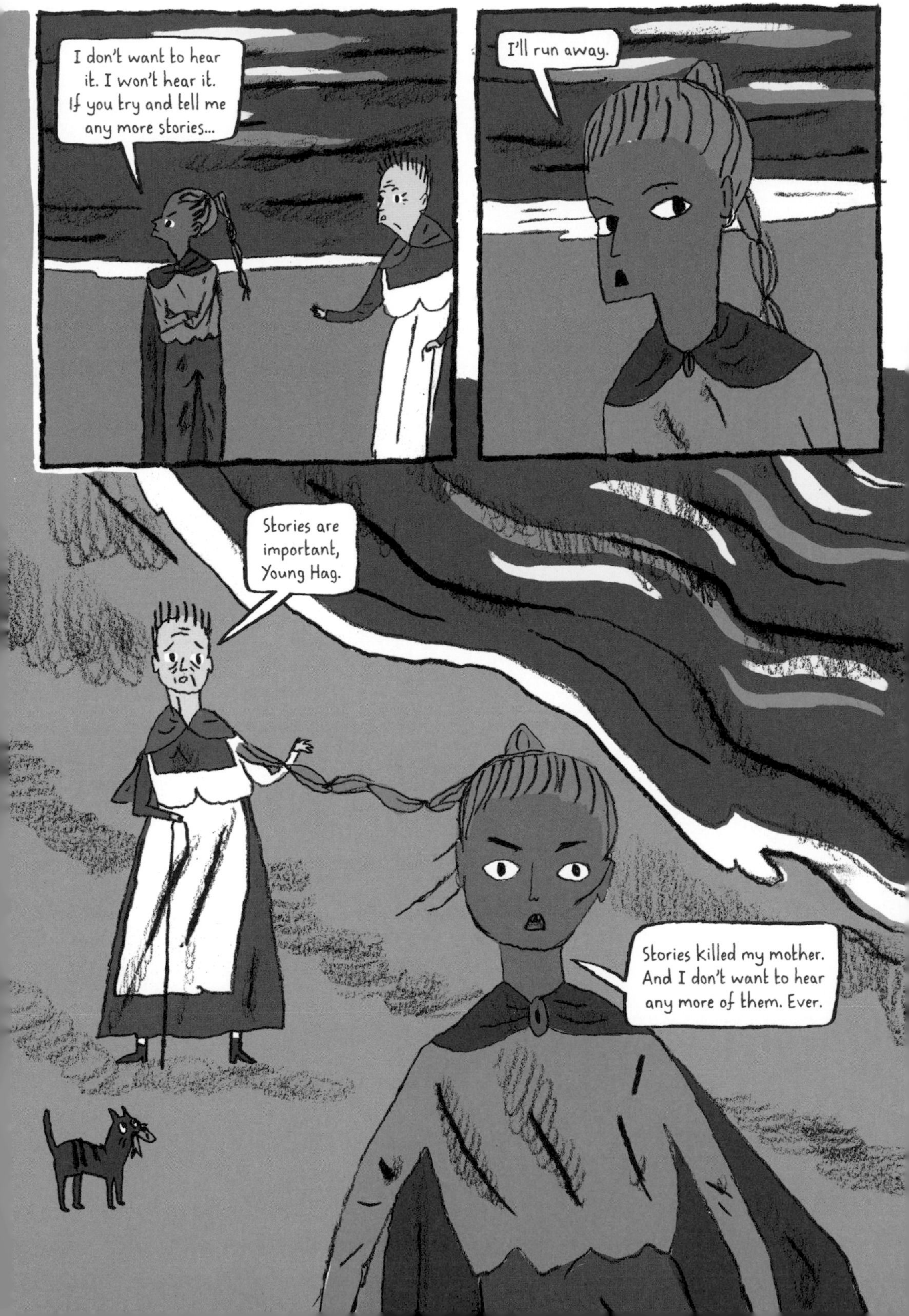
I don't want to hear it. I won't hear it. If you try and tell me any more stories...
I'll run away.
Stories are important, Young Hag.
Stories killed my mother. And I don't want to hear any more of them. Ever.

PART THE SECOND

The Paths Are Opening

Two summers and two winters passed after I became Young Hag, and after I lost my mother.
We stayed away from people: from villages, houses, even strangers on the road. It was just me and Grandmother.
And our silences.

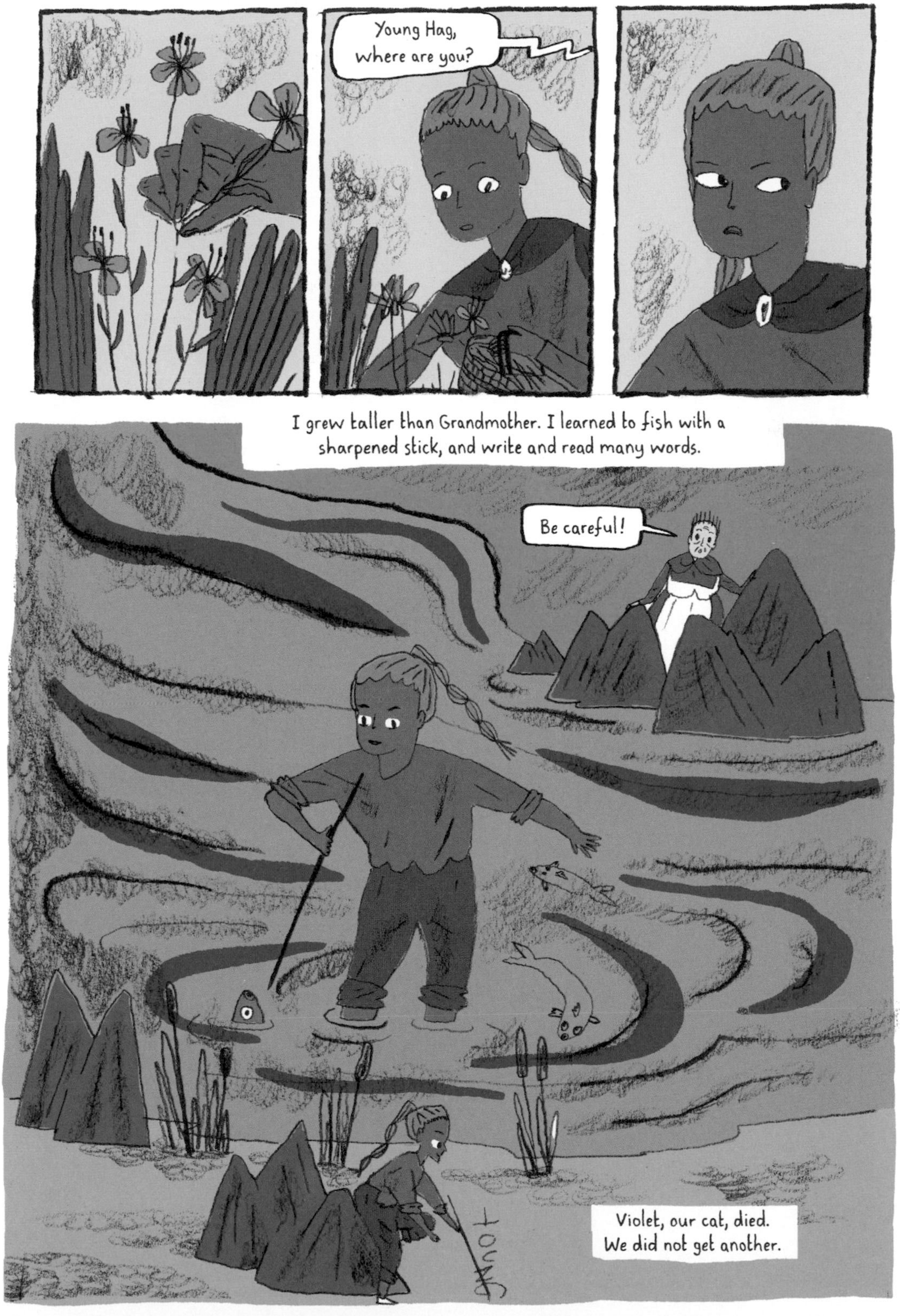
Young Hag, where are you?
I grew taller than Grandmother. I learned to fish with a sharpened stick, and write and read many words.
Be careful!
Violet, our cat, died. We did not get another.

I learned to swim.

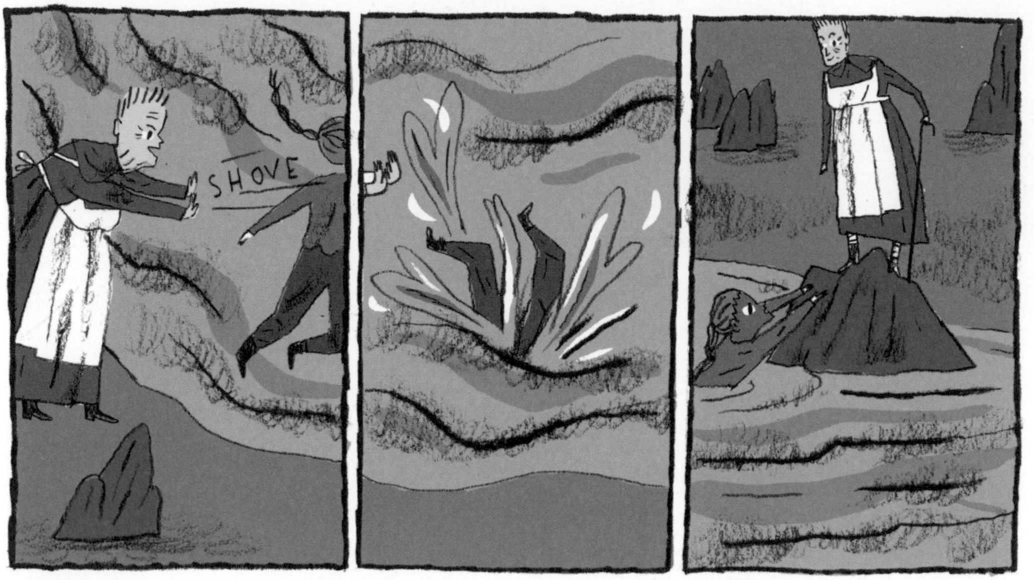
SHOVE

I learned the names and properties of 102 different plants.

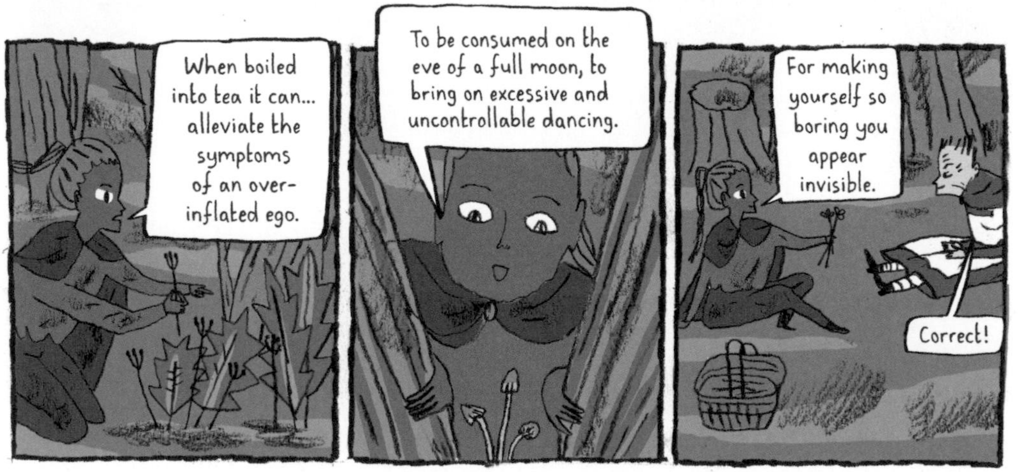
When boiled into tea it can... alleviate the symptoms of an over-inflated ego.
To be consumed on the eve of a full moon, to bring on excessive and uncontrollable dancing.
For making yourself so boring you appear invisible.
Correct!

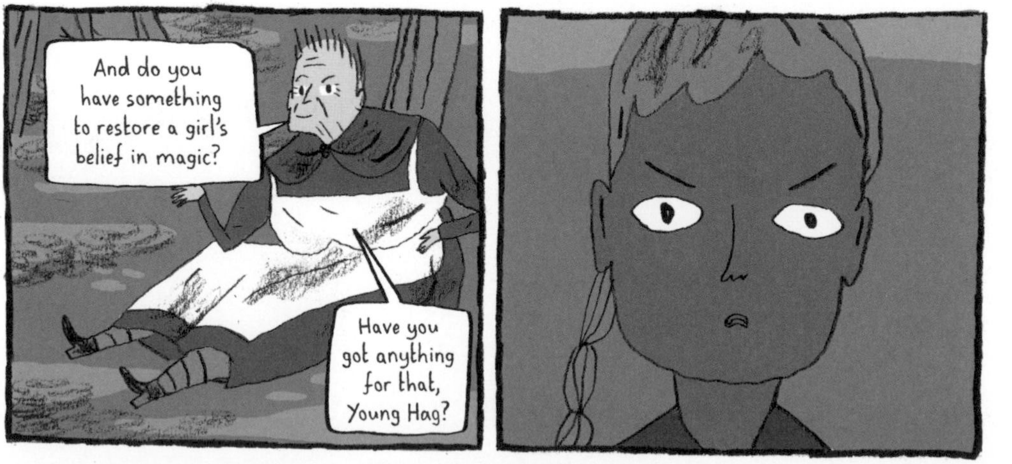
And do you have something to restore a girl's belief in magic?
Have you got anything for that, Young Hag?

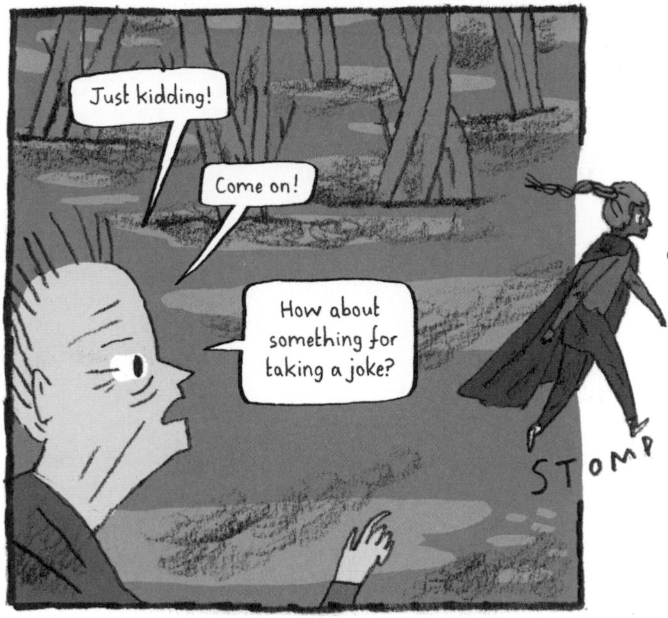
Just kidding!
Come on!
How about something for taking a joke?
STOMP

Grandmother tried to tell me the old stories, but I would not hear them.

Why should I believe tales of knights and curses and magical broken swords, when my mother had died from a mere stone to the head?

Who cared if my grandmother used to be someone special. She couldn't help us now. And it was because of her story that my mother was dead, after all.

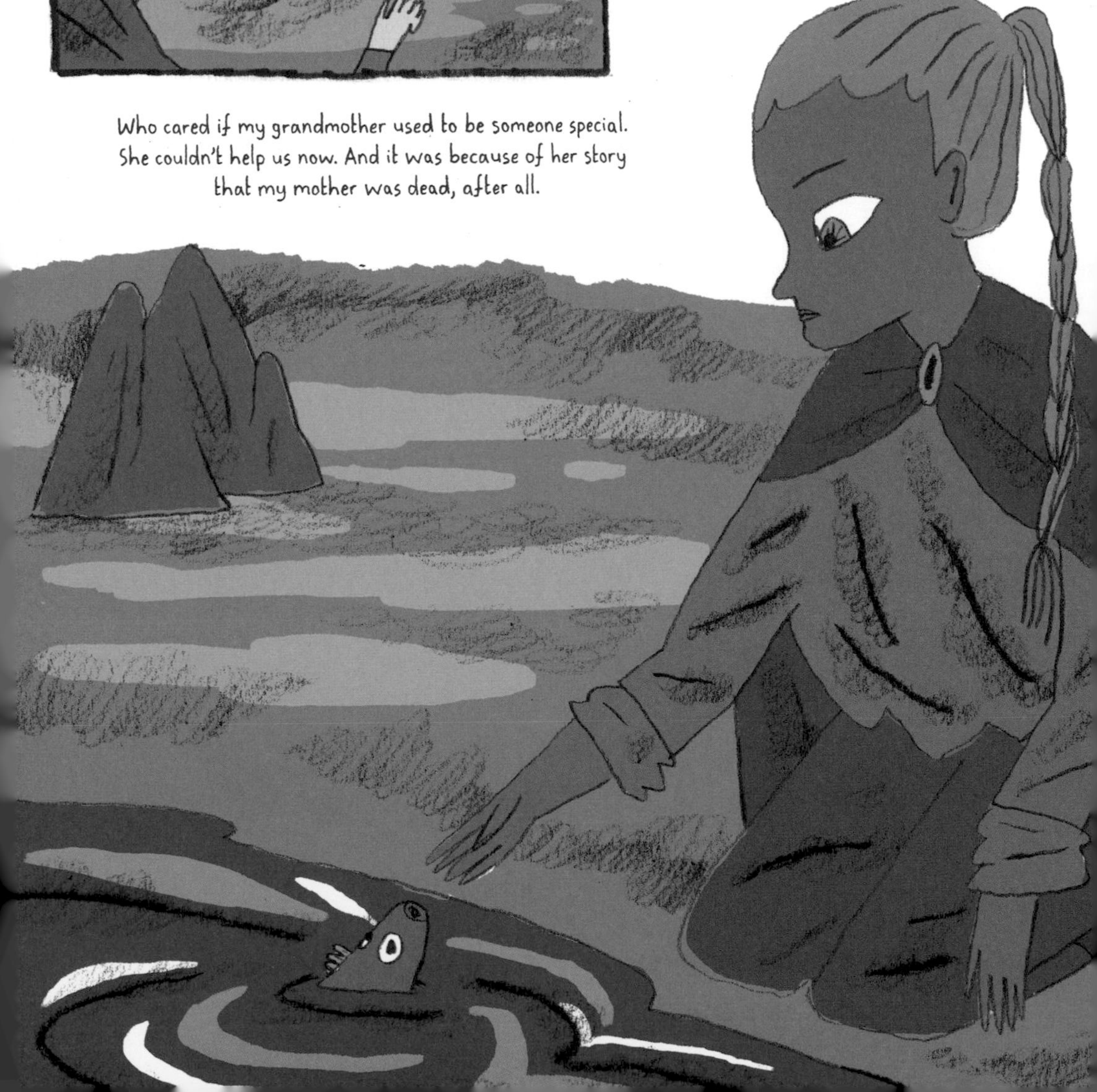

And so it was that suddenly it was my fourteenth birthday.

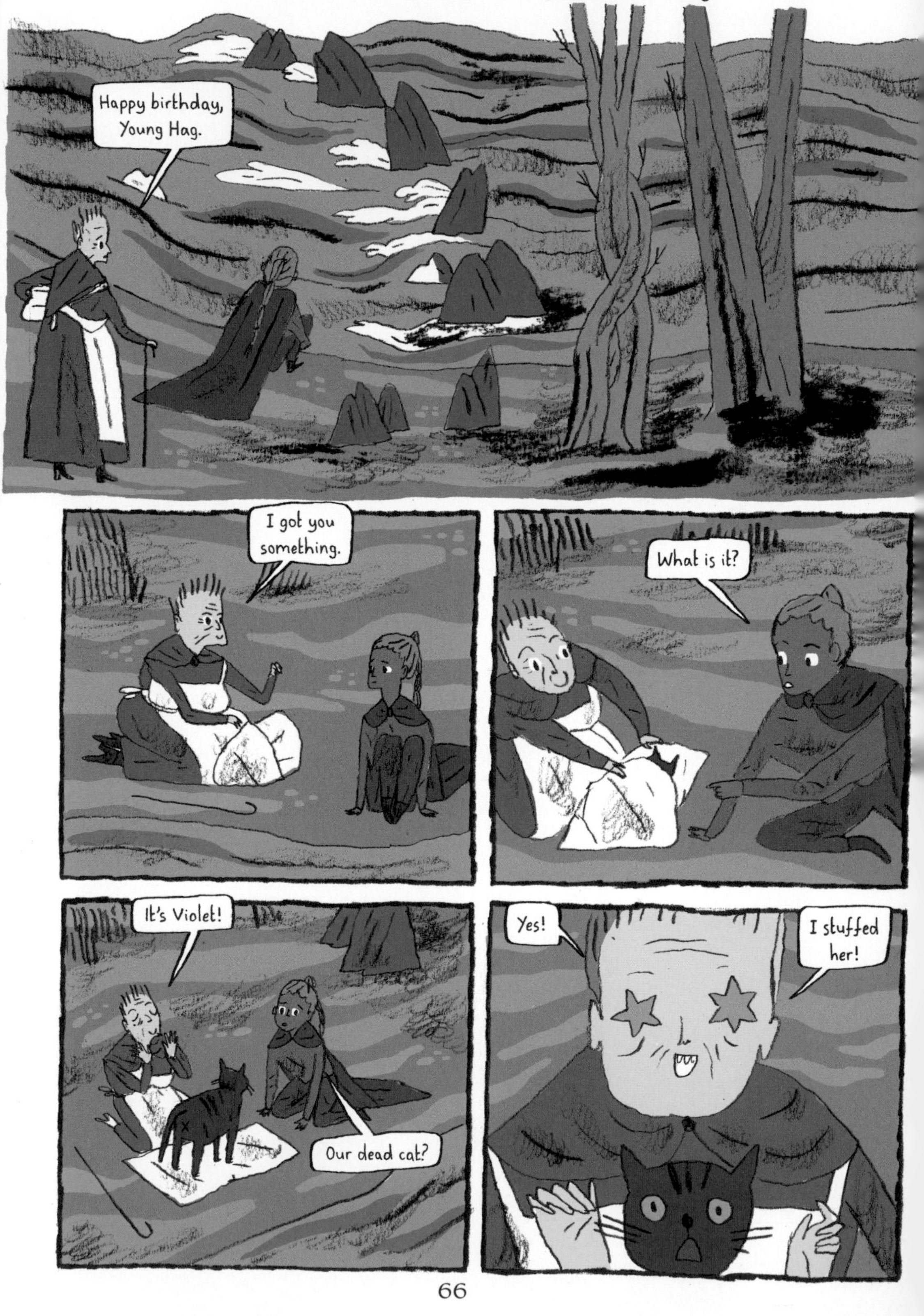

Happy birthday, Young Hag.
I got you something.
What is it?
It's Violet!
Our dead cat?
Yes!
I stuffed her!

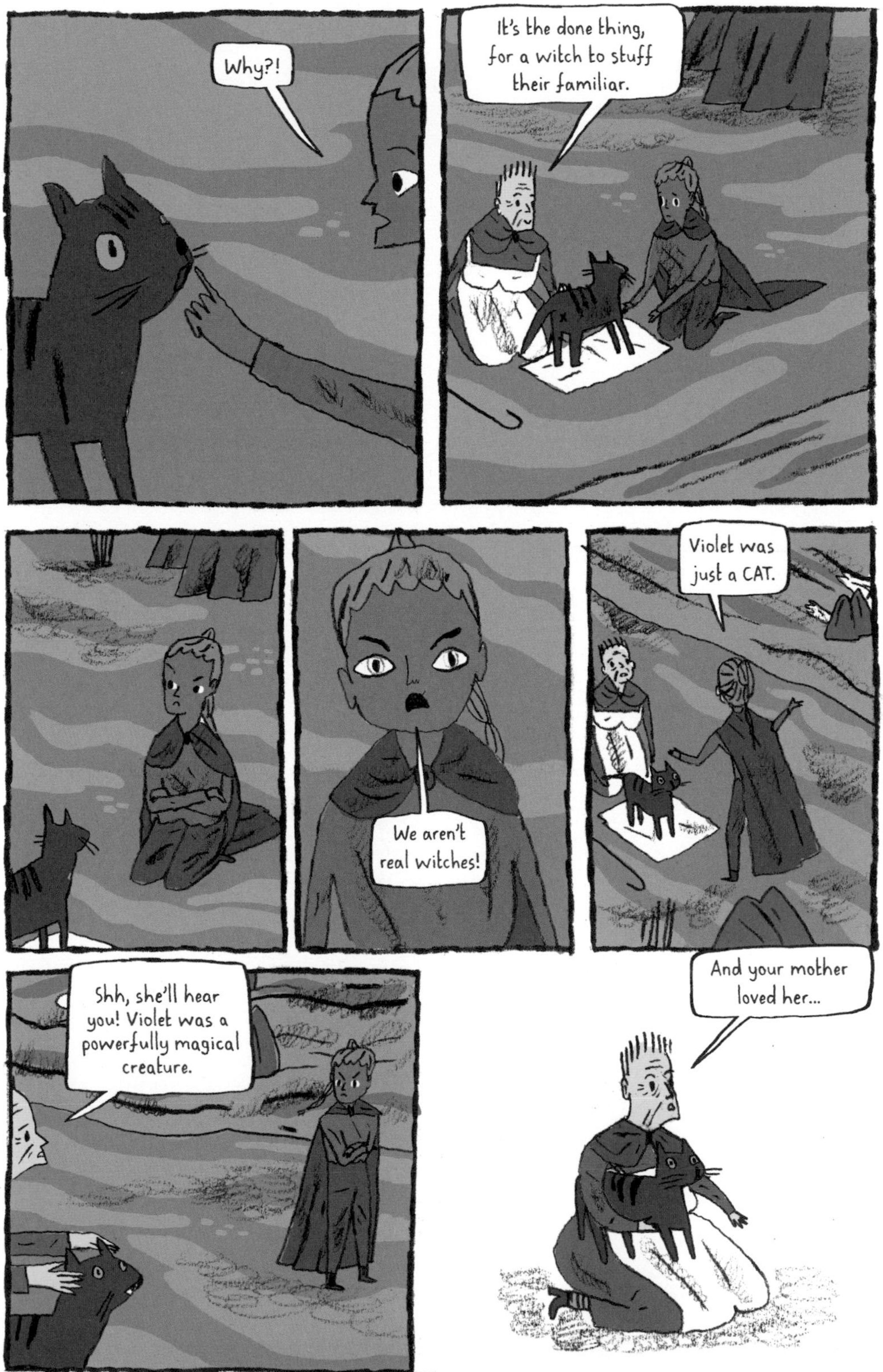
Why?!
It's the done thing, for a witch to stuff their familiar.
We aren't real witches!
Violet was just a CAT.
Shh, she'll hear you! Violet was a powerfully magical creature.
And your mother loved her...

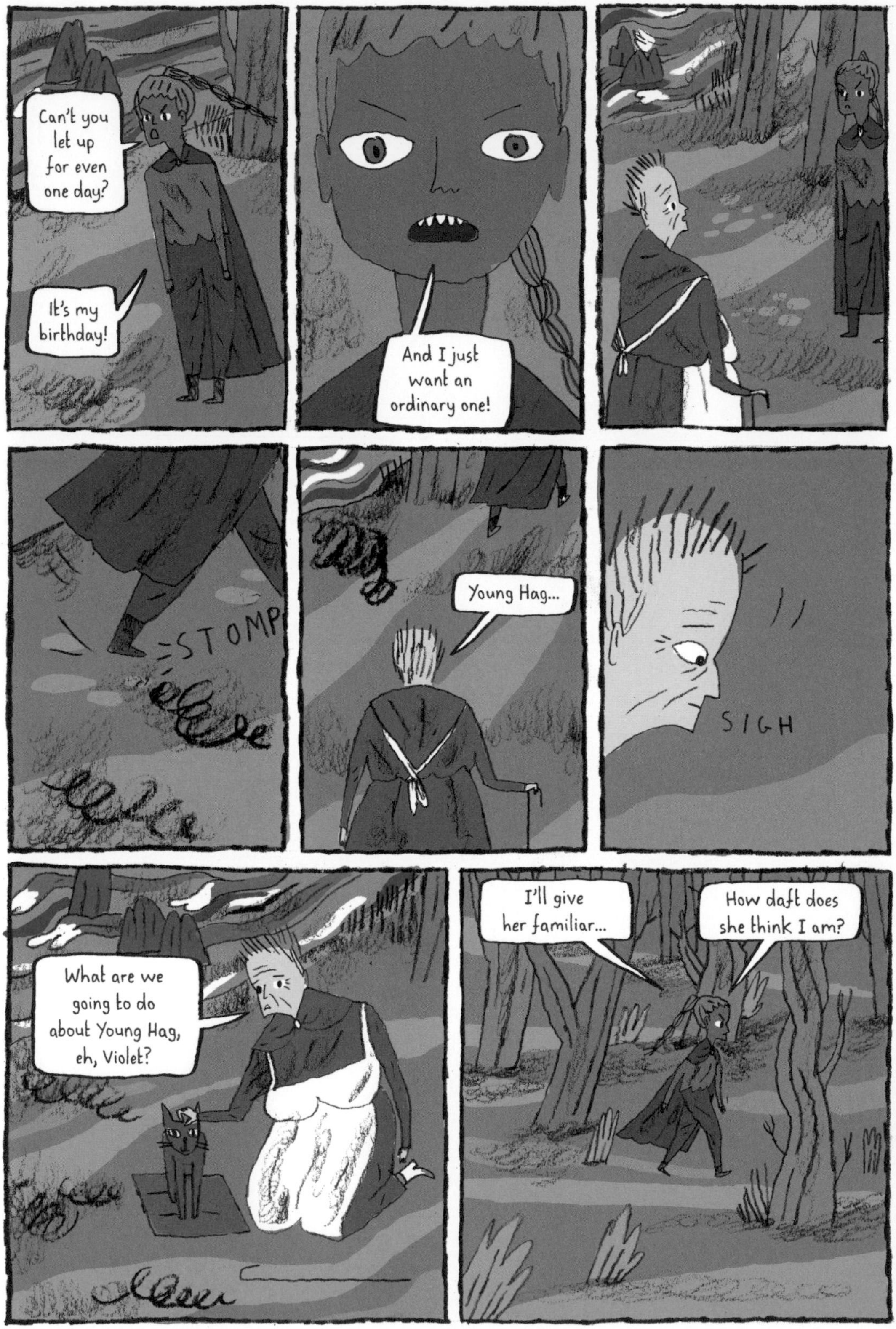

Can't you let up for even one day?
It's my birthday!
And I just want an ordinary one!
STOMP
Young Hag...
SIGH
What are we going to do about Young Hag, eh, Violet?
I'll give her familiar...
How daft does she think I am?

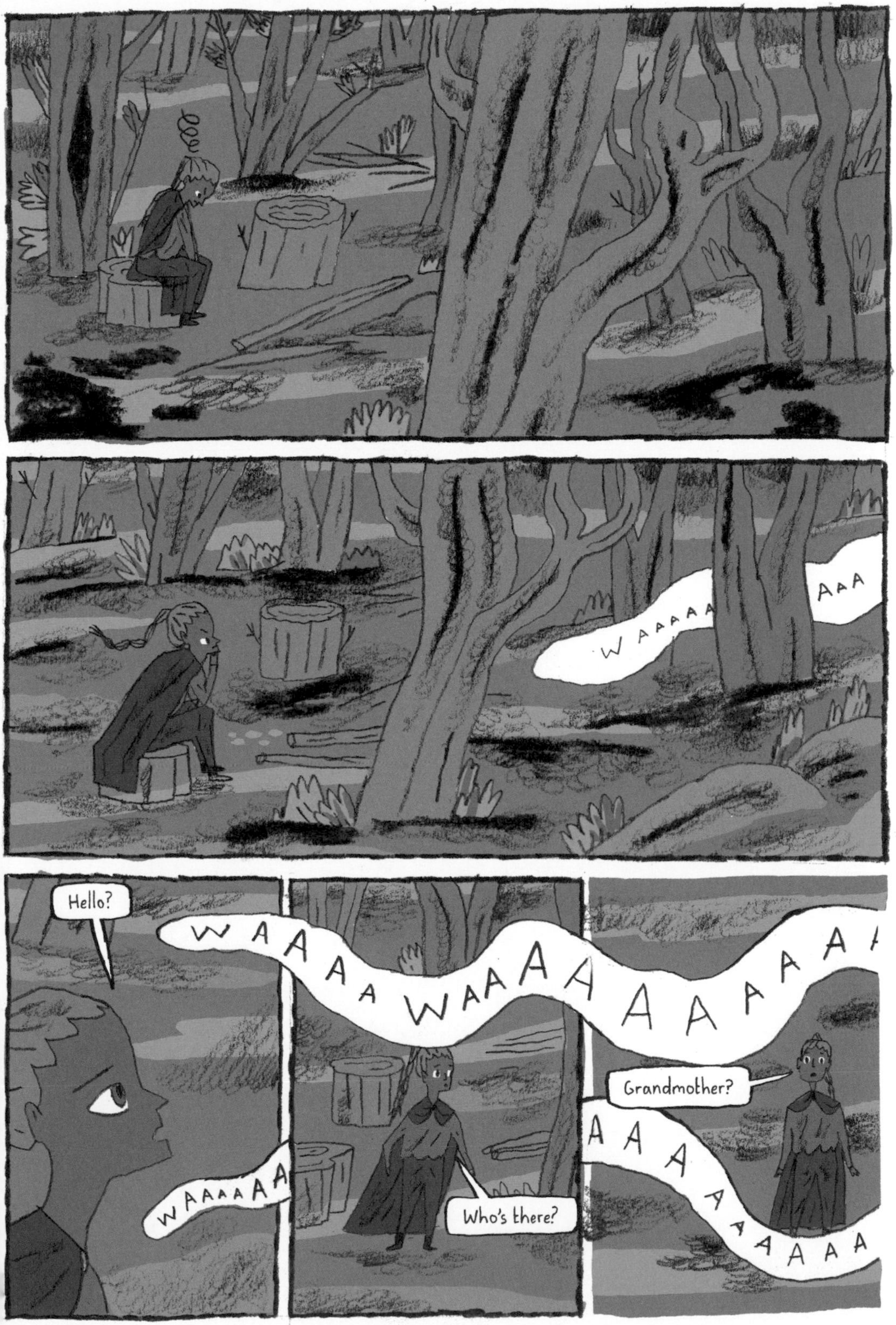
WAAAAAAAA
Hello?
WAAAAA
WAAAWAAAAAAAAAAA
Who's there?
Grandmother?
AAAAAAAAAA

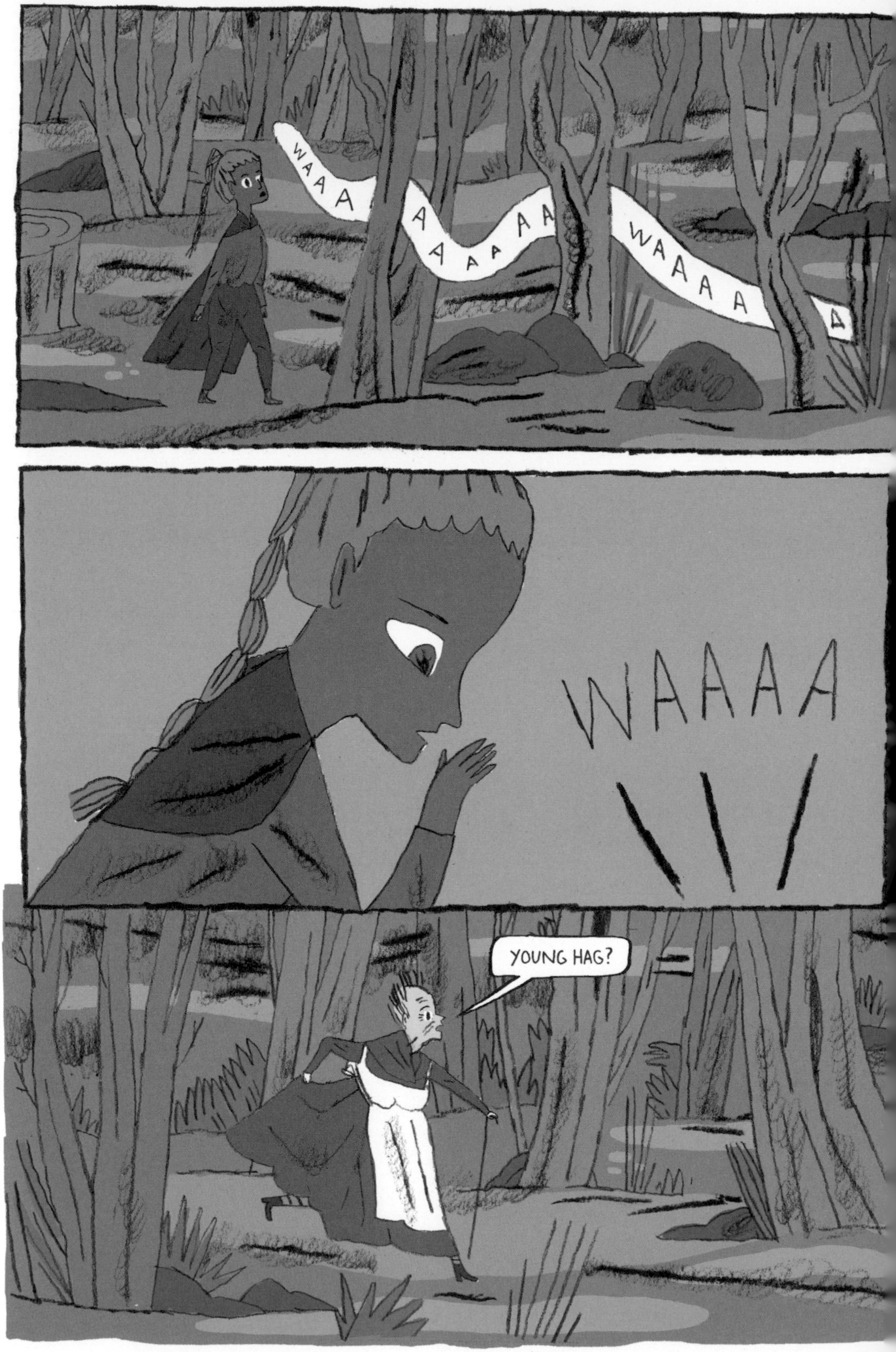
WAAAAAAAAAAA WAAAAAA
WAAAA
YOUNG HAG?

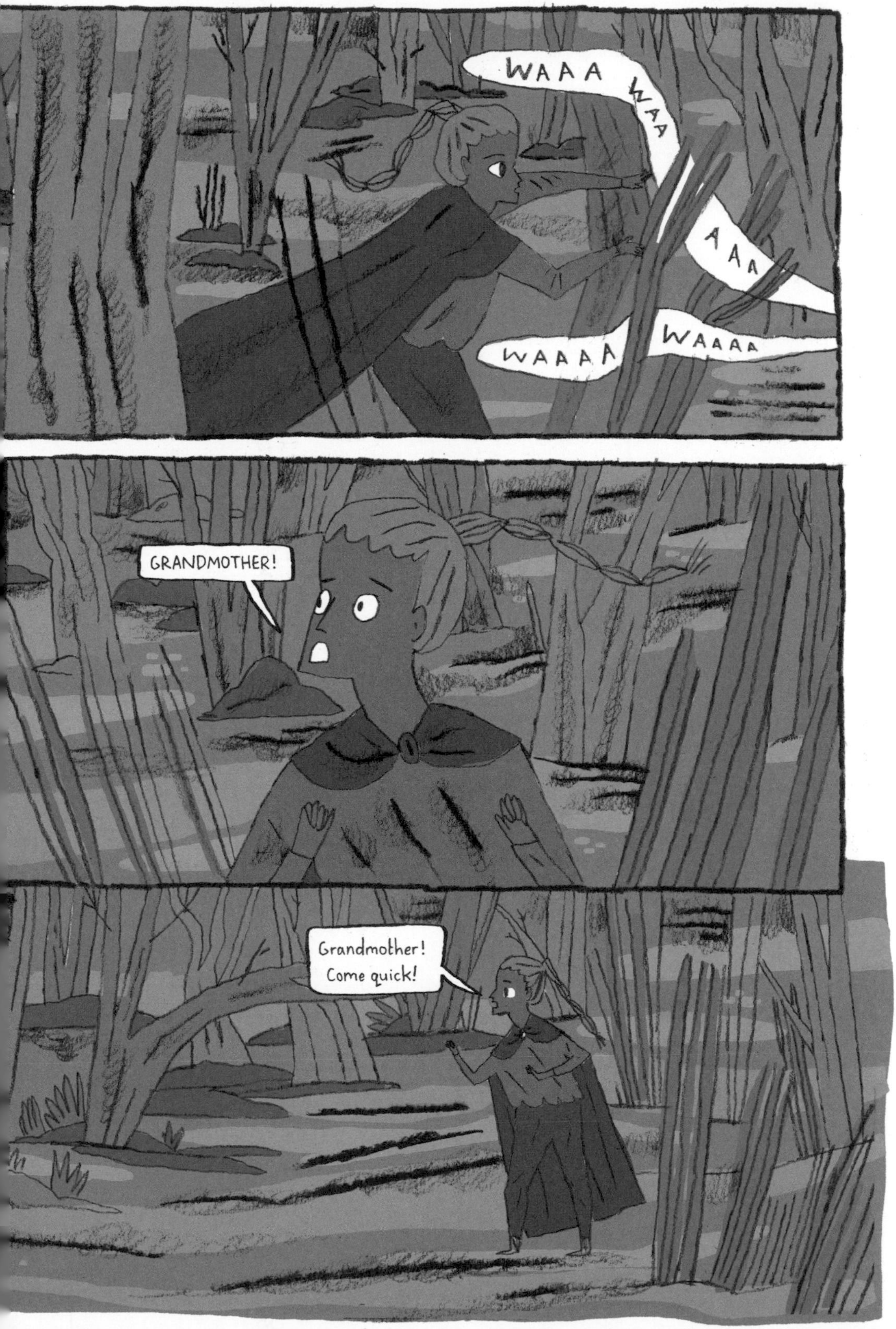
WAAA WAA AAA
WAAAA WAAAA
GRANDMOTHER!
Grandmother!
Come quick!

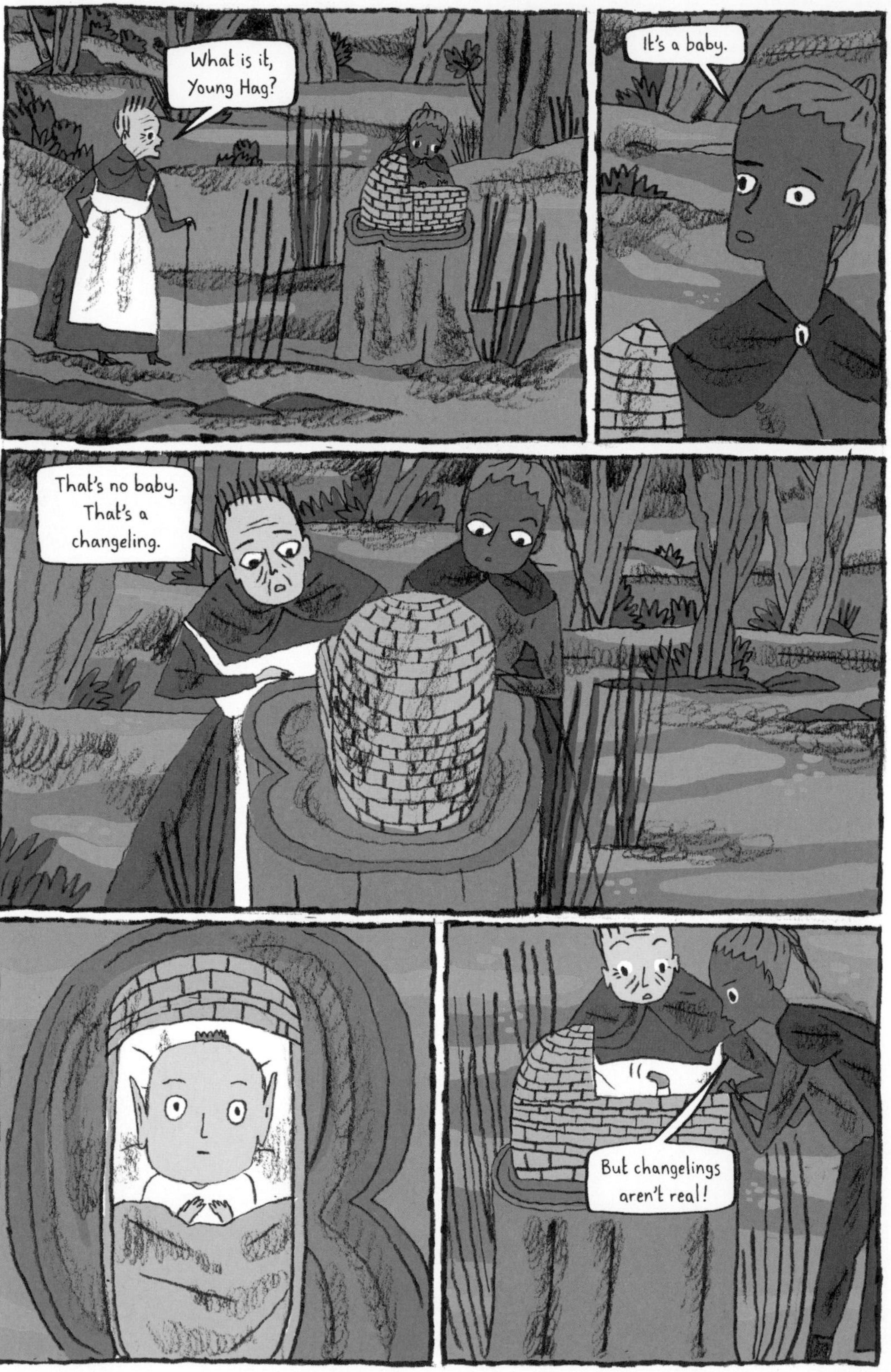
What is it, Young Hag?
It's a baby.
That's no baby. That's a changeling.
But changelings aren't real!

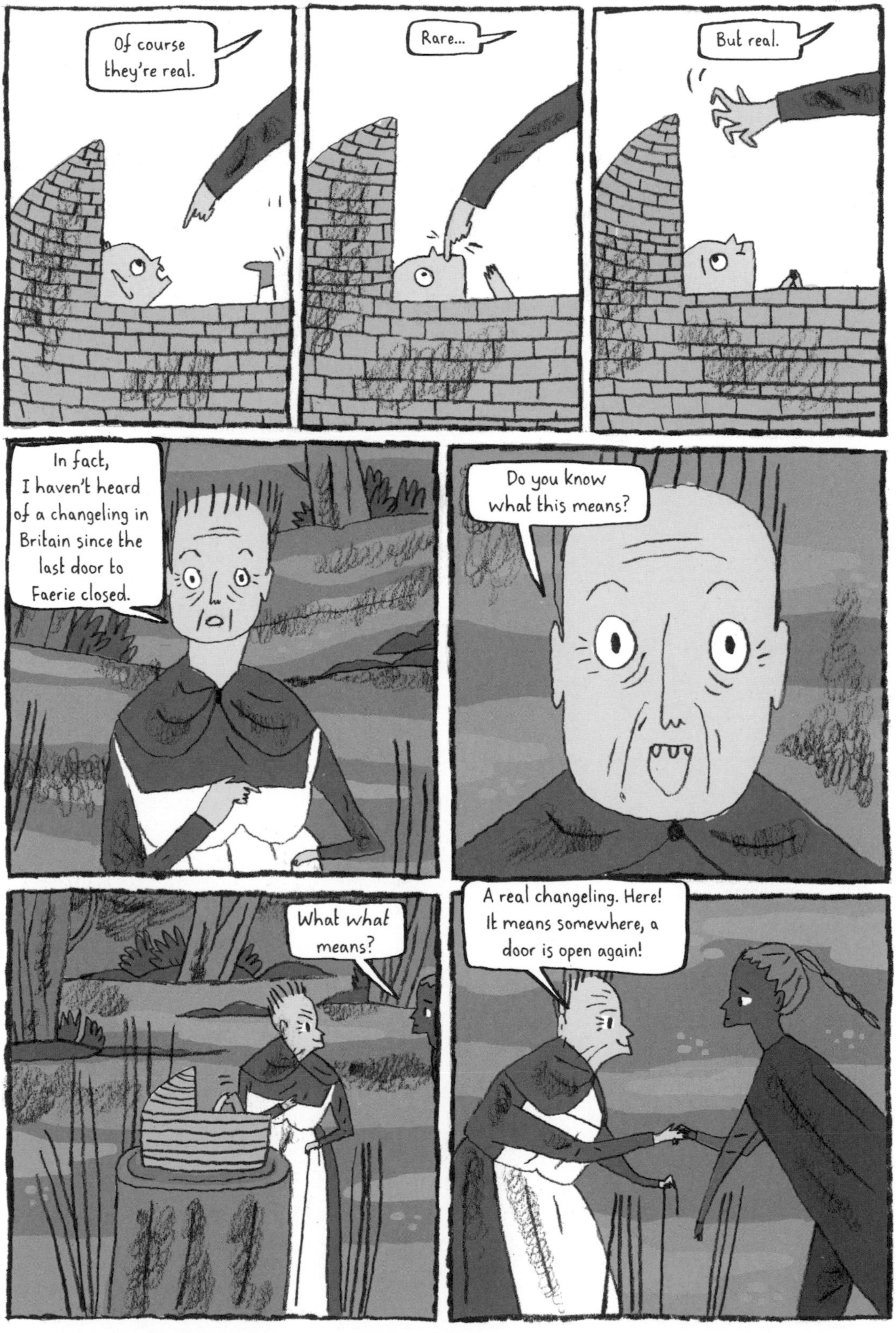
Of course they're real.
Rare...
But real.
In fact, I haven't heard of a changeling in Britain since the last door to Faerie closed.
Do you know what this means?
What what means?
A real changeling. Here! It means somewhere, a door is open again!

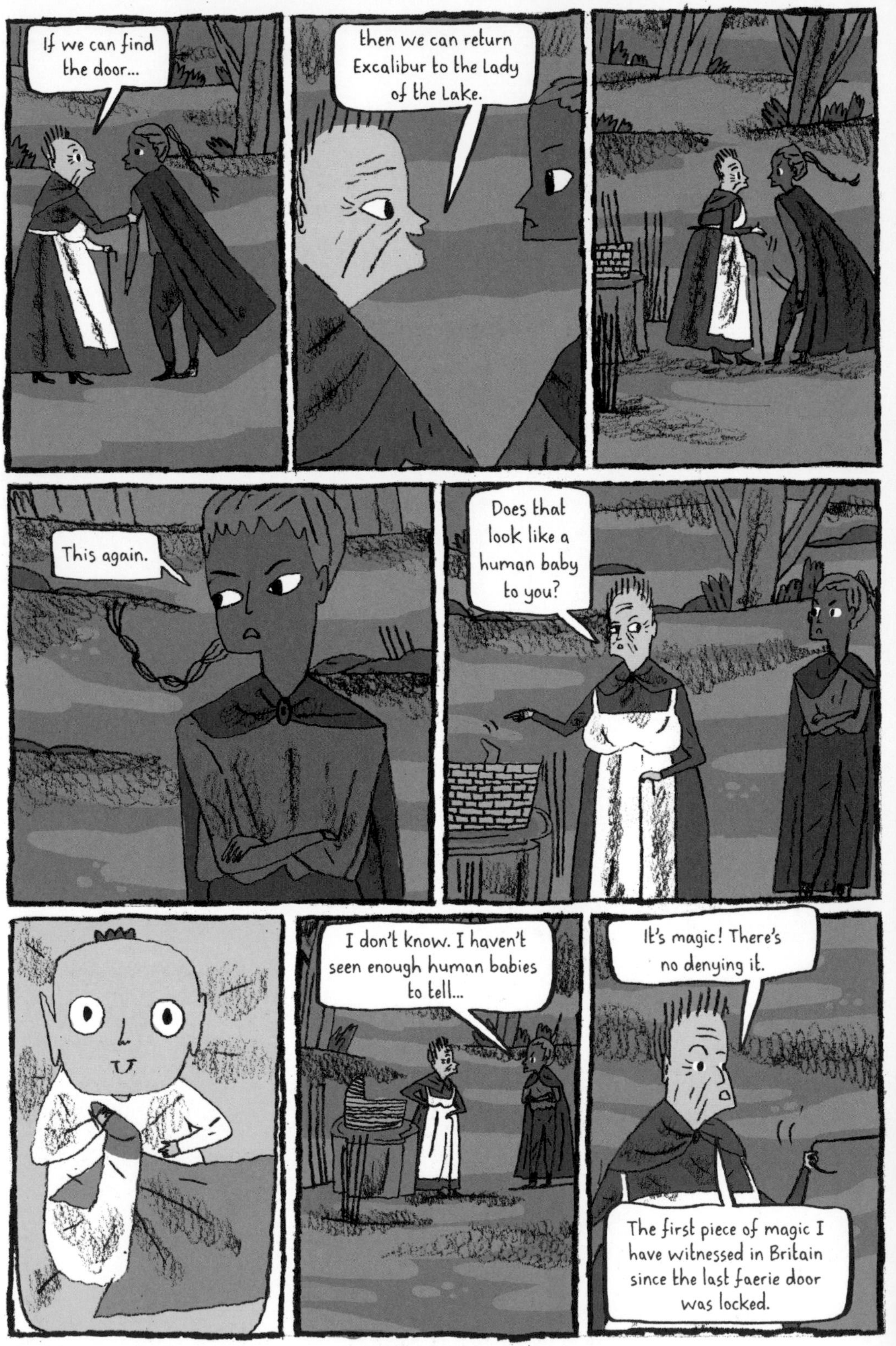
If we can find the door...
then we can return Excalibur to the Lady of the Lake.
This again.
Does that look like a human baby to you?
I don't know. I haven't seen enough human babies to tell...
It's magic! There's no denying it.
The first piece of magic I have witnessed in Britain since the last faerie door was locked.

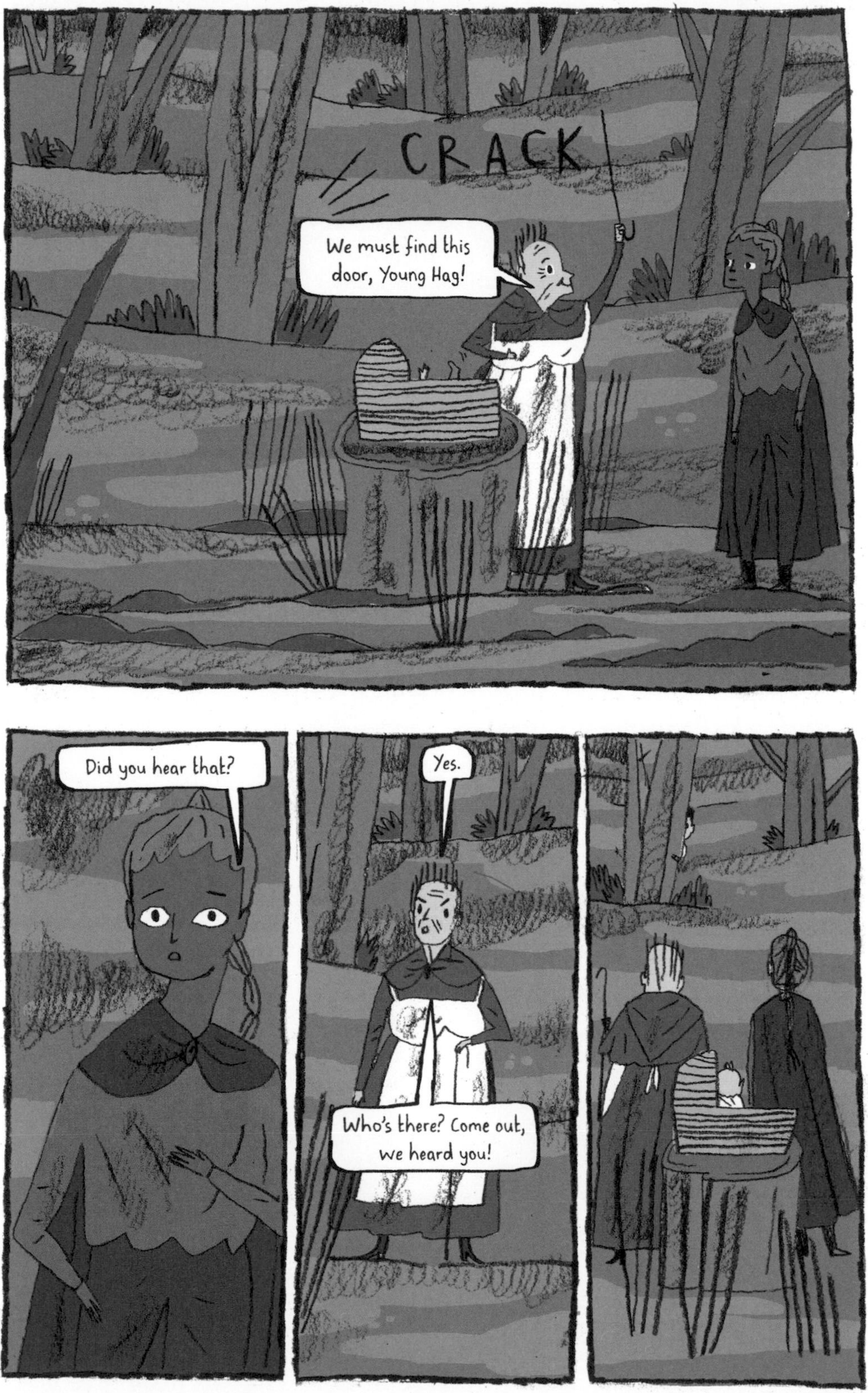
CRACK
We must find this door, Young Hag!
Did you hear that?
Yes.
Who's there? Come out, we heard you!

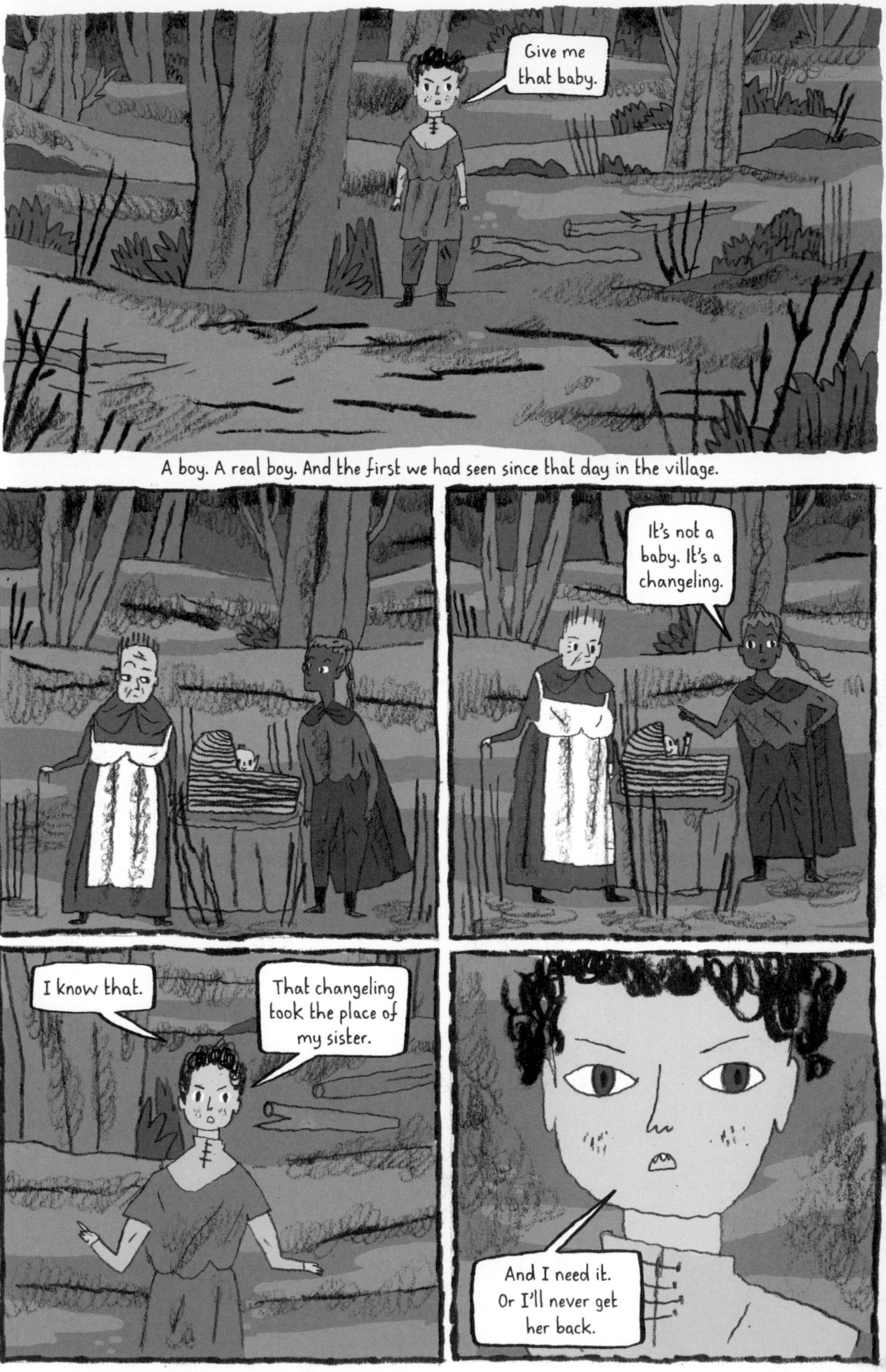
Give me that baby.
A boy. A real boy. And the first we had seen since that day in the village.
It's not a baby. It's a changeling.
I know that.
That changeling took the place of my sister.
And I need it. Or I'll never get her back.

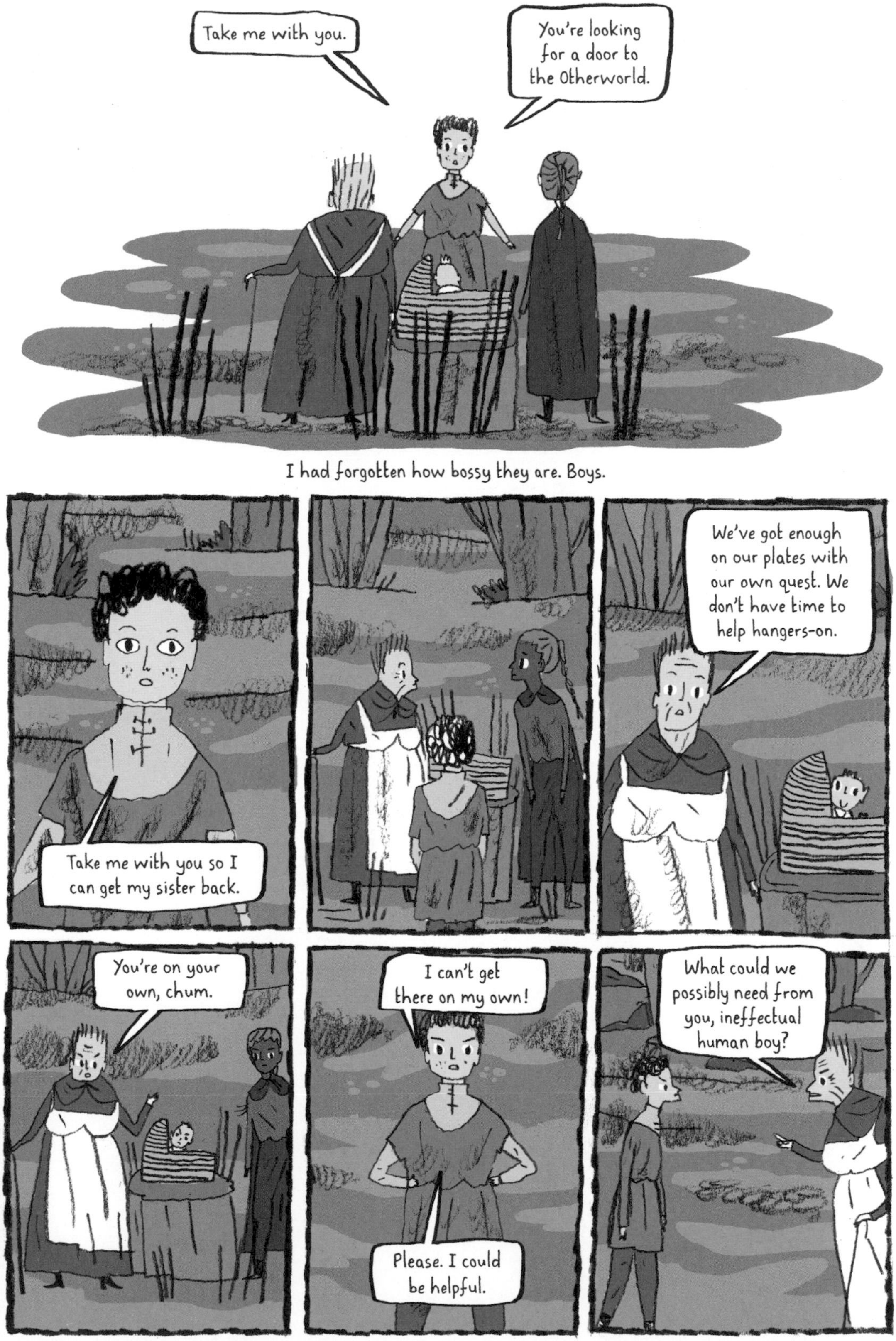
Take me with you.
You're looking for a door to the Otherworld.
I had forgotten how bossy they are. Boys.
Take me with you so I can get my sister back.
We've got enough on our plates with our own quest. We don't have time to help hangers-on.
You're on your own, chum.
I can't get there on my own!
Please. I could be helpful.
What could we possibly need from you, ineffectual human boy?

You might need a bodyguard.

An old woman and a little girl.

HA HA HA HA HA HA HA HA HA HA HA HA

WAAAAAAAAAAAAAAAAAA

It's too loud! It hurts!

It's a magical cry!

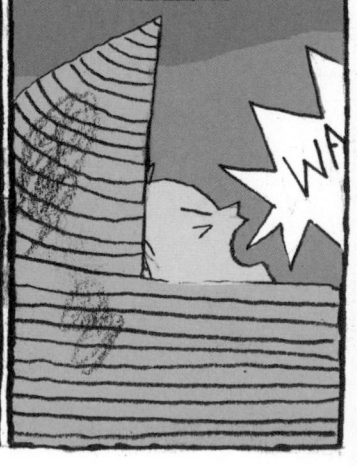

WA

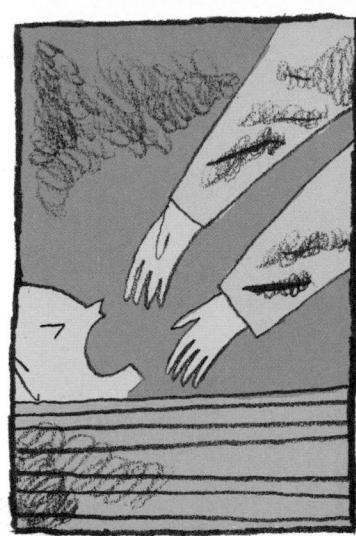

See. She wants me to come.

You're not coming.

Please. I need to get my real sister back.

None of the other babies came back.

There have been other changelings?

Yes.

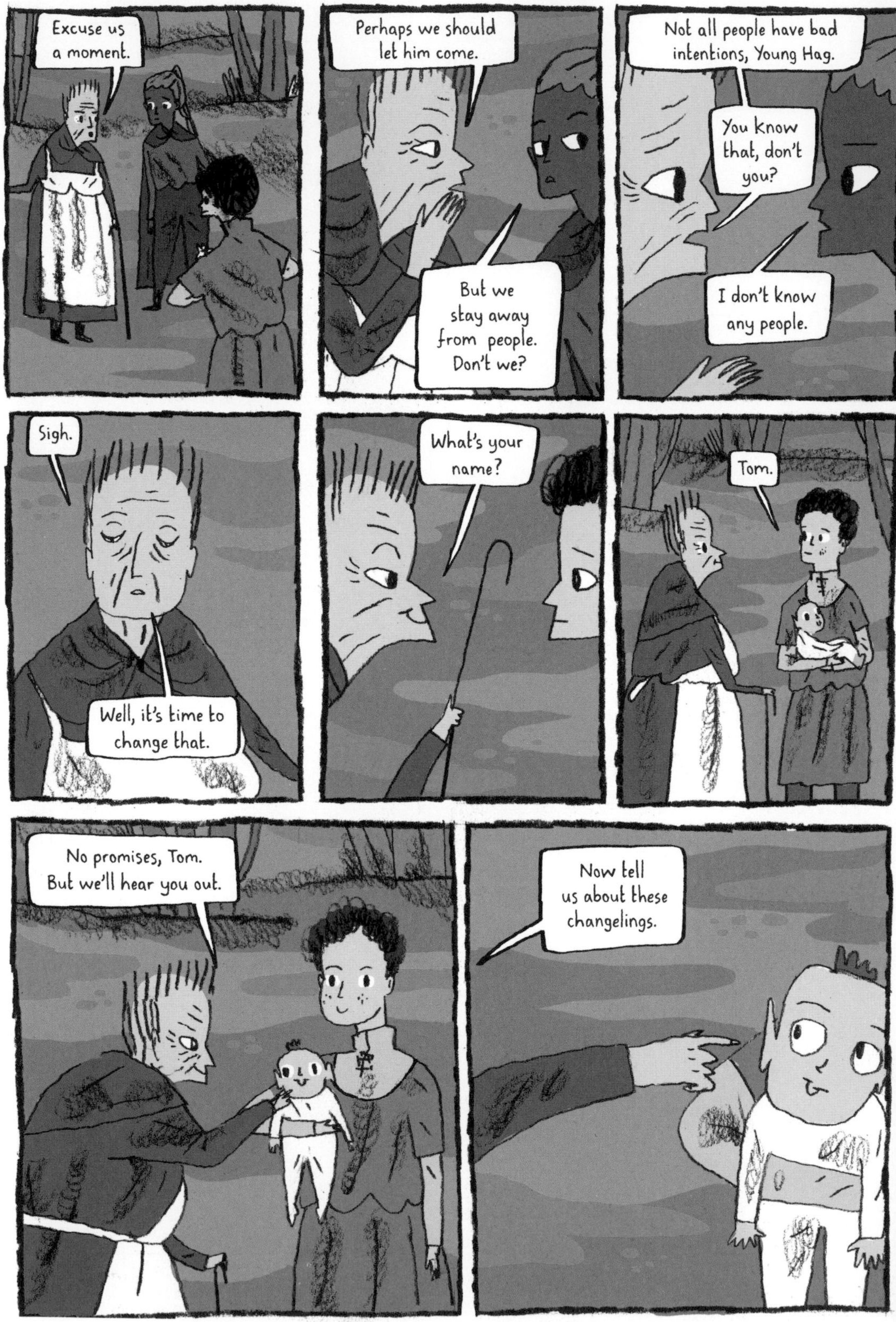
Excuse us a moment.
Perhaps we should let him come.
But we stay away from people. Don't we?
Not all people have bad intentions, Young Hag.
You know that, don't you?
I don't know any people.
Sigh.
Well, it's time to change that.
What's your name?
Tom.
No promises, Tom. But we'll hear you out.
Now tell us about these changelings.

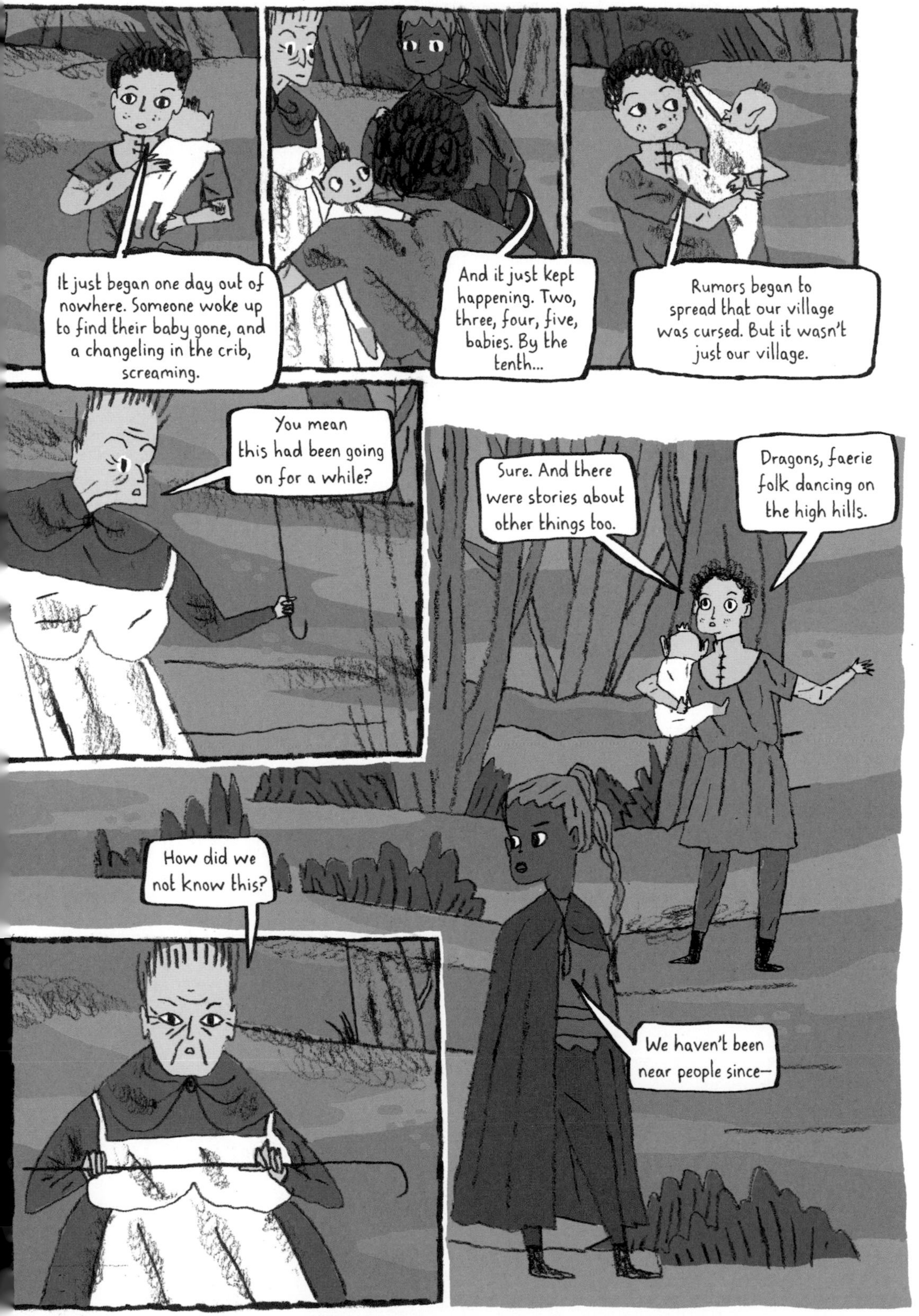
It just began one day out of nowhere. Someone woke up to find their baby gone, and a changeling in the crib, screaming.
And it just kept happening. Two, three, four, five, babies. By the tenth...
Rumors began to spread that our village was cursed. But it wasn't just our village.
You mean this had been going on for a while?
Sure. And there were stories about other things too.
Dragons, faerie folk dancing on the high hills.
How did we not know this?
We haven't been near people since—

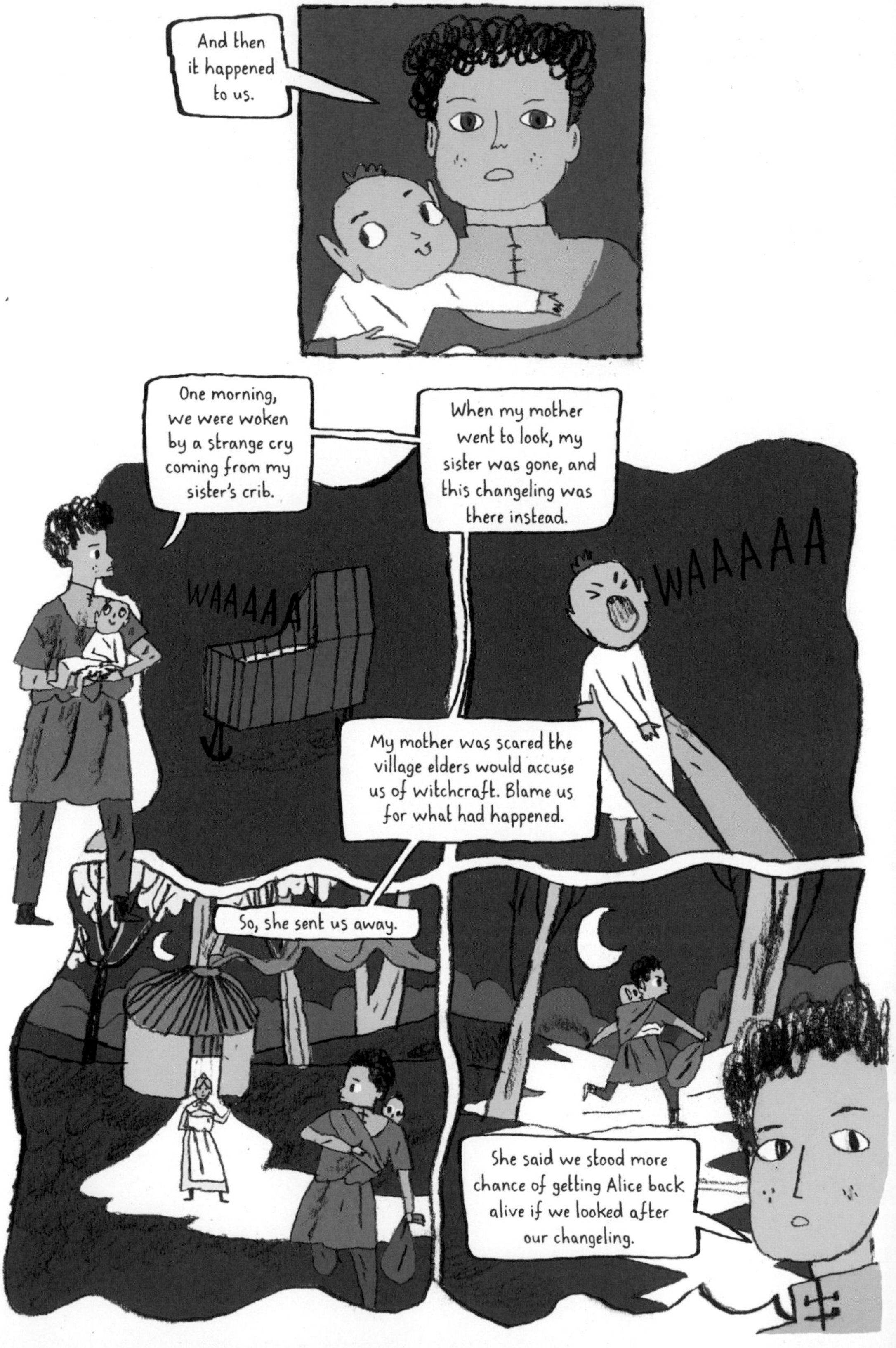
And then it happened to us.
One morning, we were woken by a strange cry coming from my sister's crib.
When my mother went to look, my sister was gone, and this changeling was there instead.
WAAAAA
WAAAAA
My mother was scared the village elders would accuse us of witchcraft. Blame us for what had happened.
So, she sent us away.
She said we stood more chance of getting Alice back alive if we looked after our changeling.

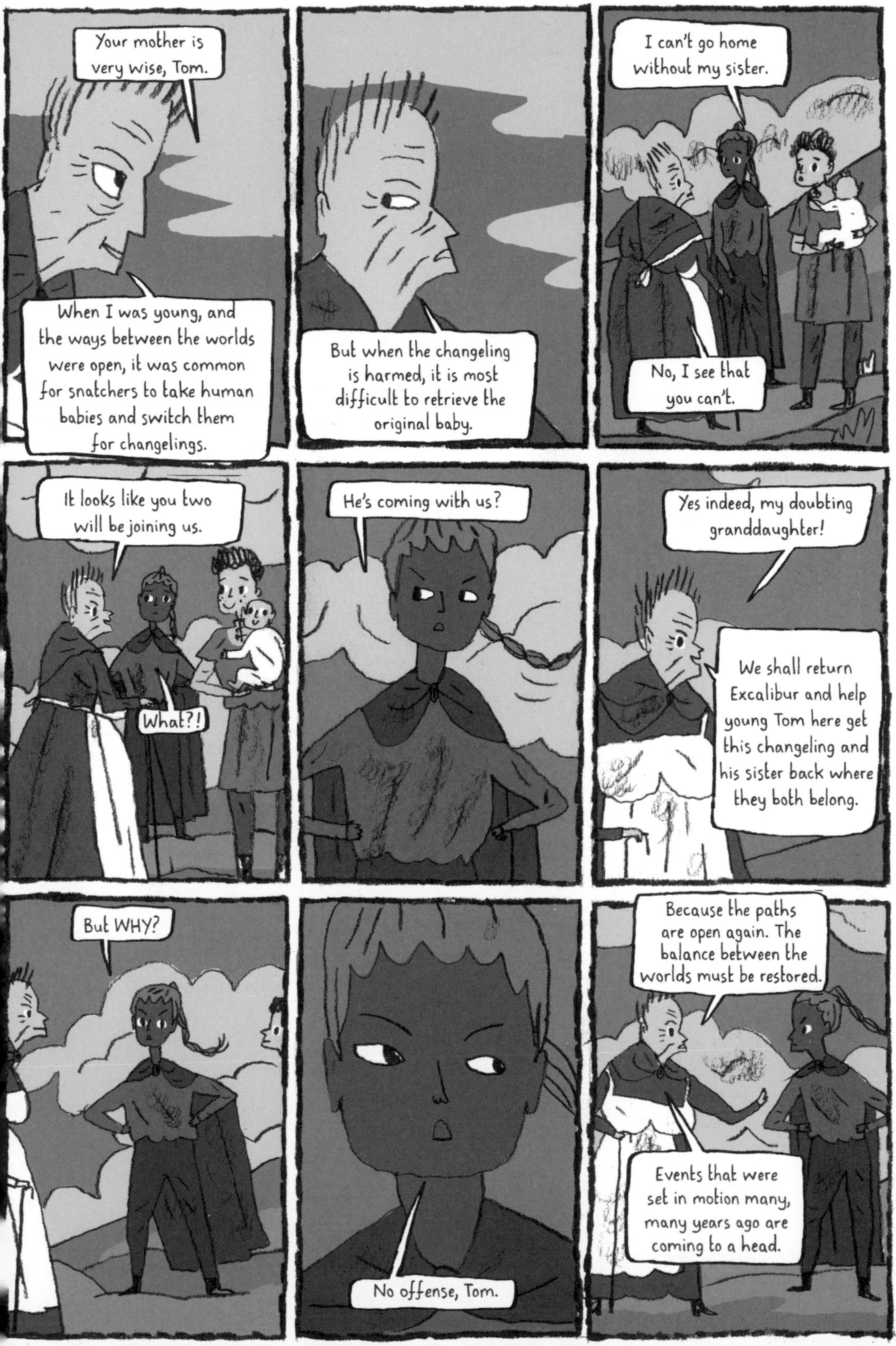

Your mother is very wise, Tom.
When I was young, and the ways between the worlds were open, it was common for snatchers to take human babies and switch them for changelings.
But when the changeling is harmed, it is most difficult to retrieve the original baby.
I can't go home without my sister.
No, I see that you can't.
It looks like you two will be joining us.
What?!
He's coming with us?
Yes indeed, my doubting granddaughter!
We shall return Excalibur and help young Tom here get this changeling and his sister back where they both belong.
But WHY?
No offense, Tom.
Because the paths are open again. The balance between the worlds must be restored.
Events that were set in motion many, many years ago are coming to a head.

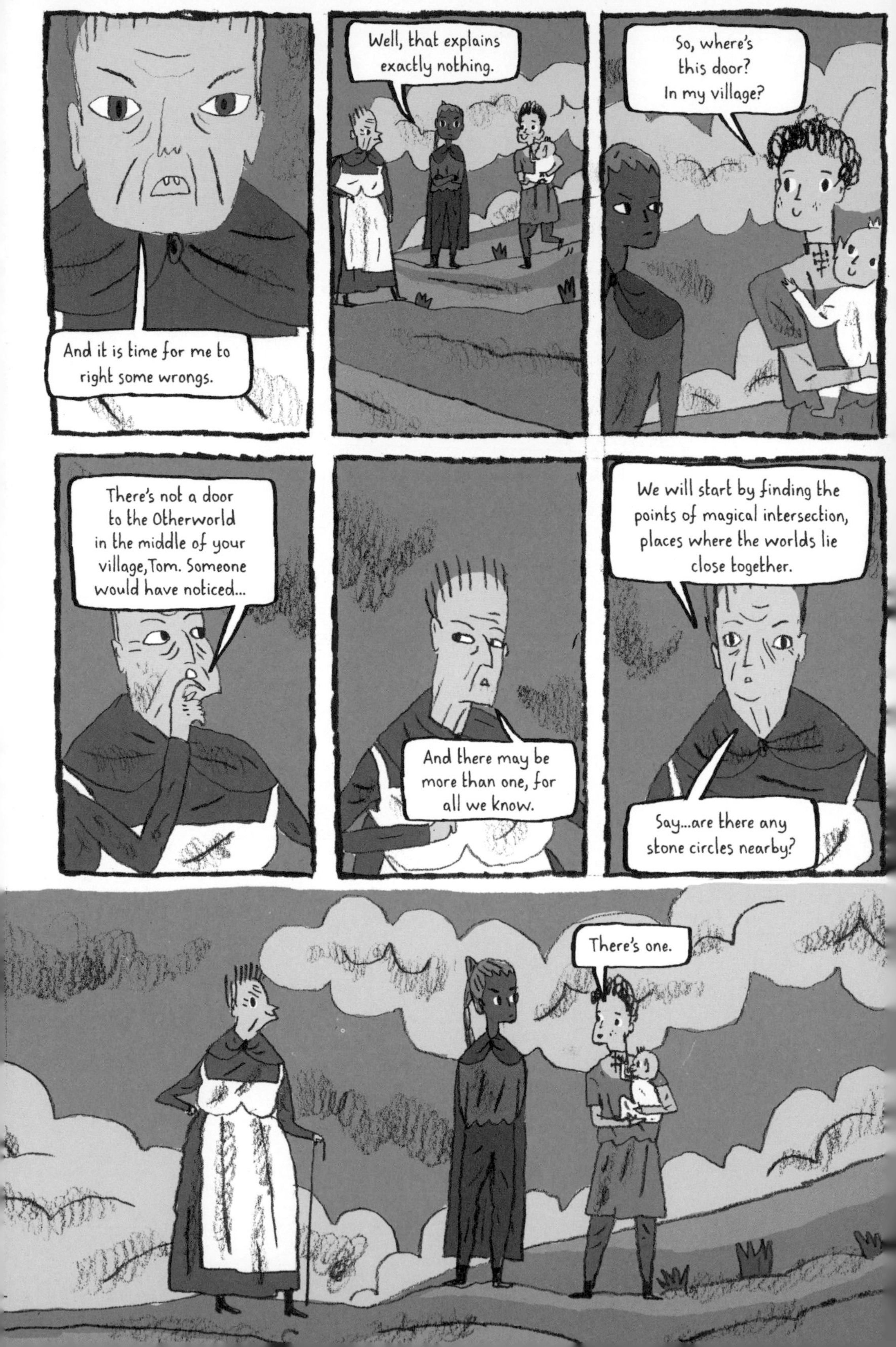
And it is time for me to right some wrongs.
Well, that explains exactly nothing.
So, where's this door? In my village?
There's not a door to the Otherworld in the middle of your village, Tom. Someone would have noticed...
And there may be more than one, for all we know.
We will start by finding the points of magical intersection, places where the worlds lie close together.
Say...are there any stone circles nearby?
There's one.

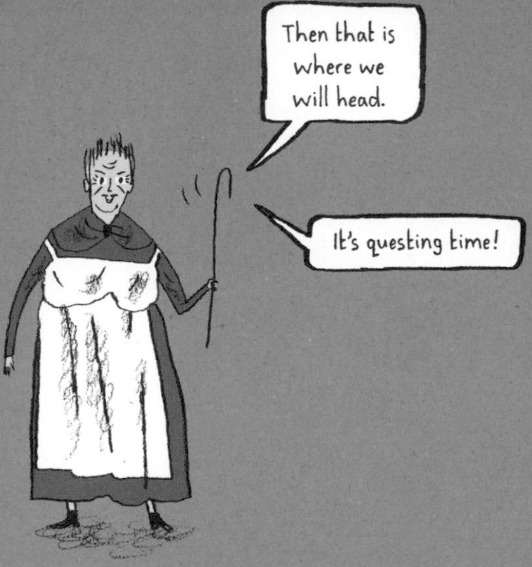
Then that is where we will head.
It's questing time!

PART THE THIRD

The Quest

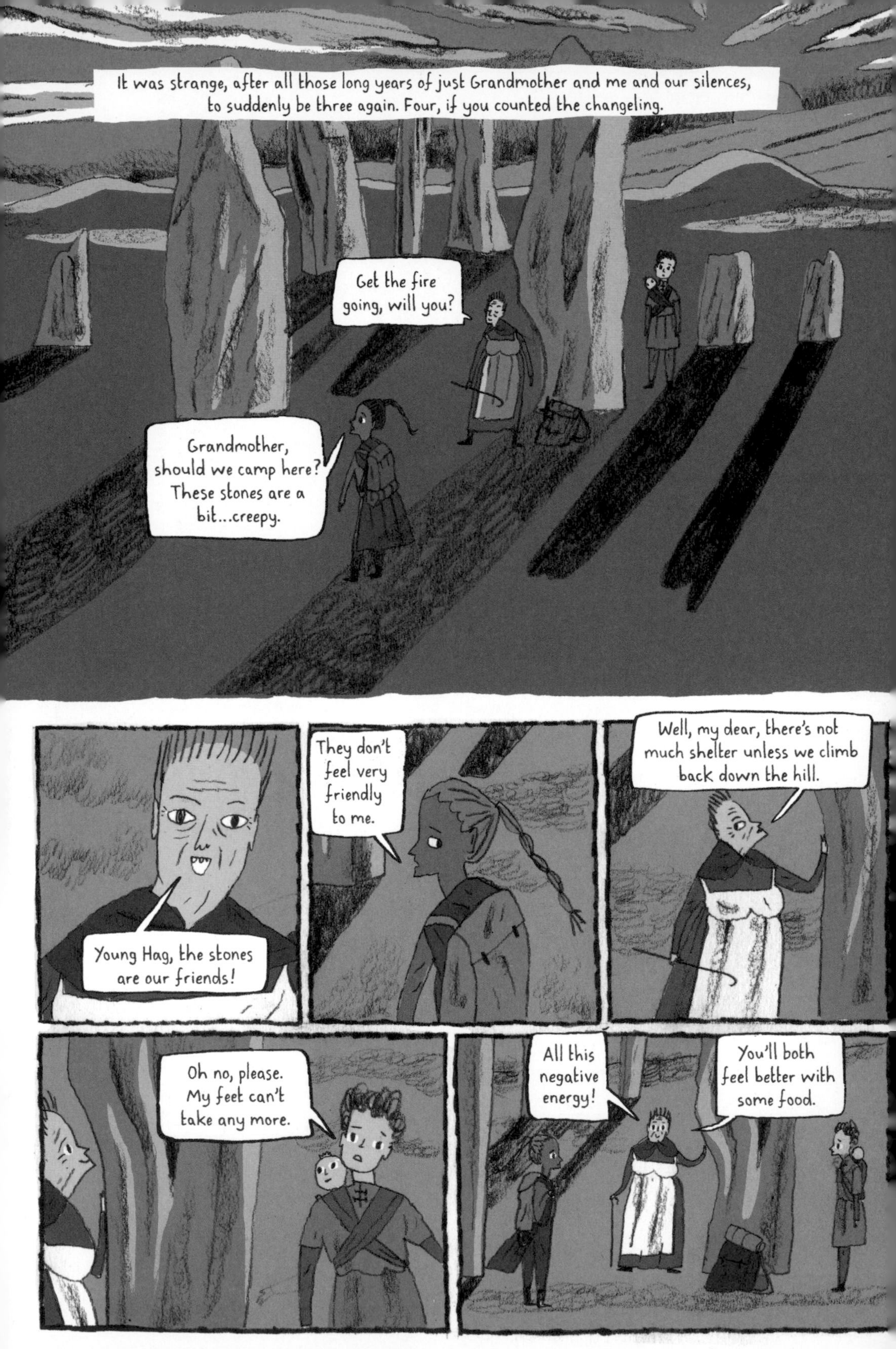
It was strange, after all those long years of just Grandmother and me and our silences, to suddenly be three again. Four, if you counted the changeling.
Get the fire going, will you?
Grandmother, should we camp here? These stones are a bit...creepy.
Young Hag, the stones are our friends!
They don't feel very friendly to me.
Well, my dear, there's not much shelter unless we climb back down the hill.
Oh no, please. My feet can't take any more.
All this negative energy!
You'll both feel better with some food.

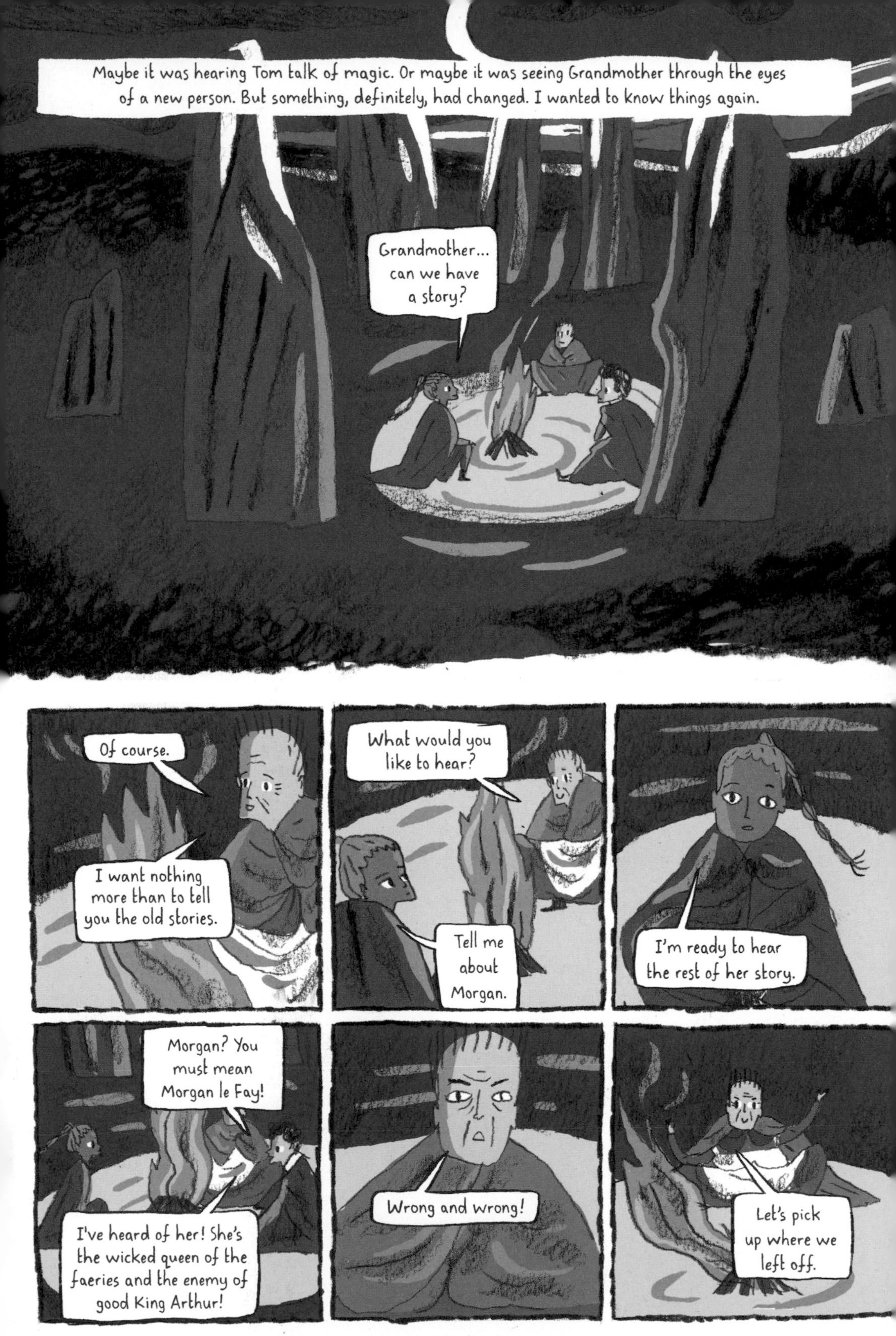
Maybe it was hearing Tom talk of magic. Or maybe it was seeing Grandmother through the eyes of a new person. But something, definitely, had changed. I wanted to know things again.
Grandmother... can we have a story?
Of course.
I want nothing more than to tell you the old stories.
What would you like to hear?
Tell me about Morgan.
I'm ready to hear the rest of her story.
Morgan? You must mean Morgan le Fay!
I've heard of her! She's the wicked queen of the faeries and the enemy of good King Arthur!
Wrong and wrong!
Let's pick up where we left off.

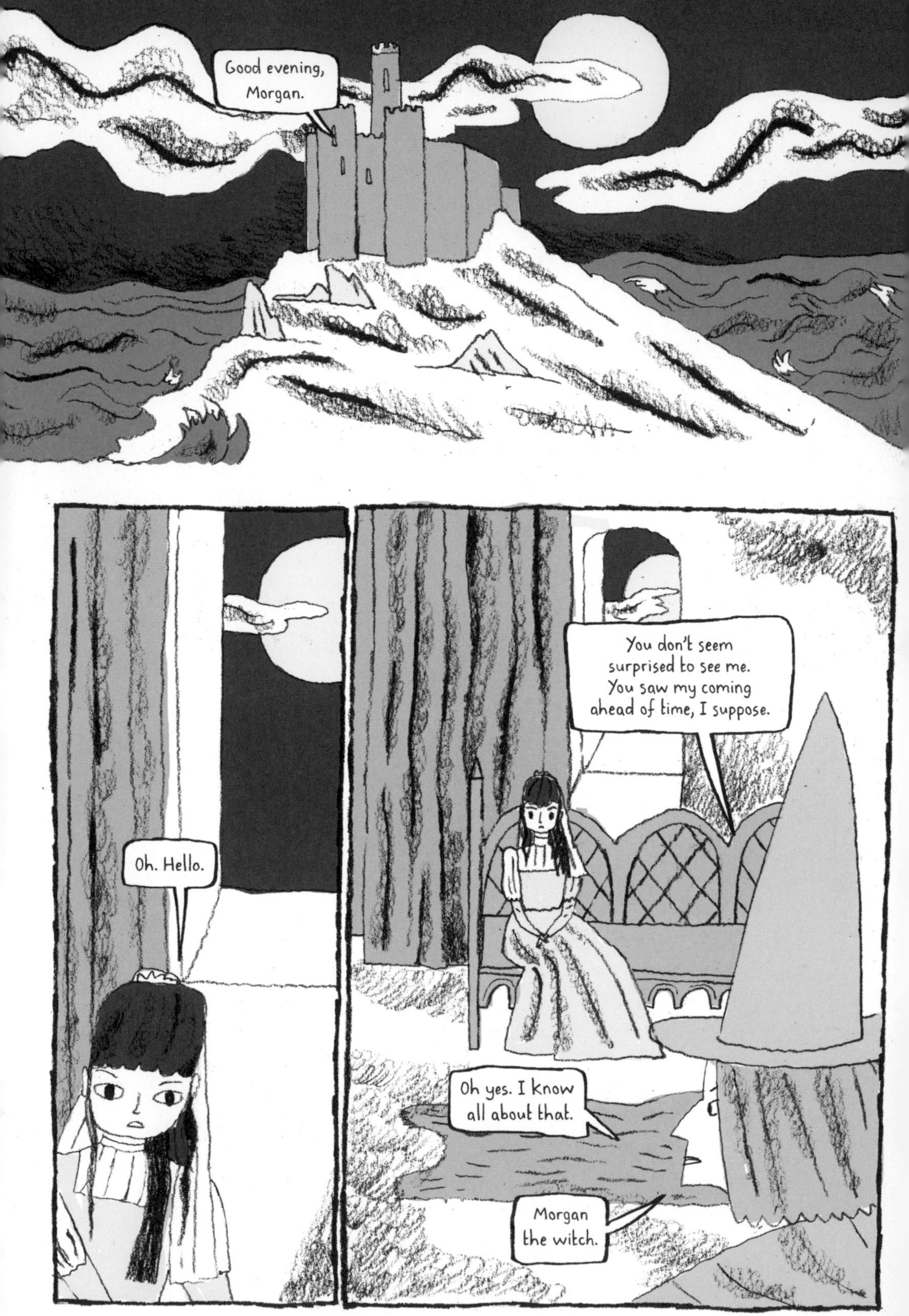
Good evening, Morgan.
Oh. Hello.
You don't seem surprised to see me. You saw my coming ahead of time, I suppose.
Oh yes. I know all about that.
Morgan the witch.

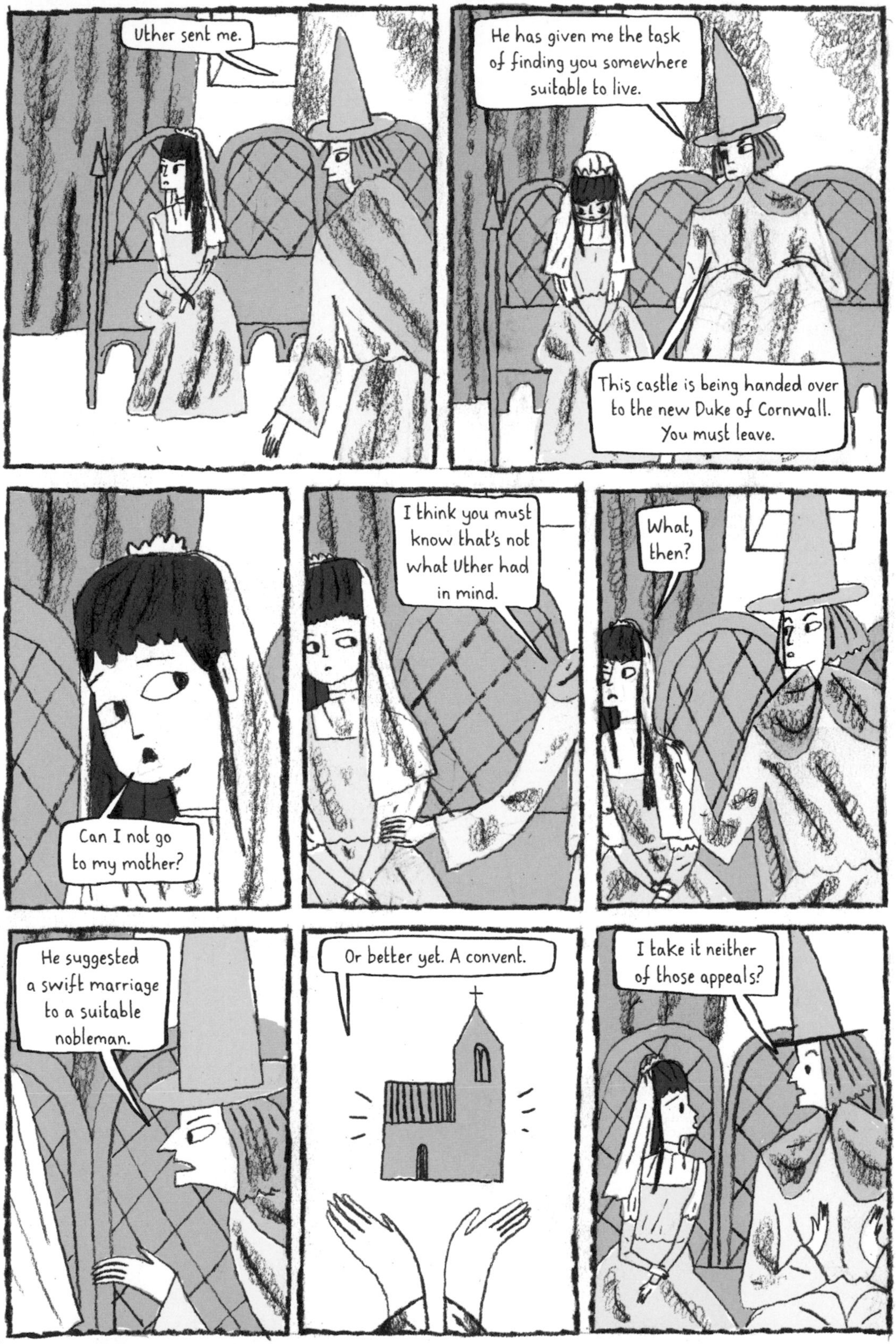

Uther sent me.
He has given me the task of finding you somewhere suitable to live.
This castle is being handed over to the new Duke of Cornwall. You must leave.
Can I not go to my mother?
I think you must know that's not what Uther had in mind.
What, then?
He suggested a swift marriage to a suitable nobleman.
Or better yet. A convent.
I take it neither of those appeals?

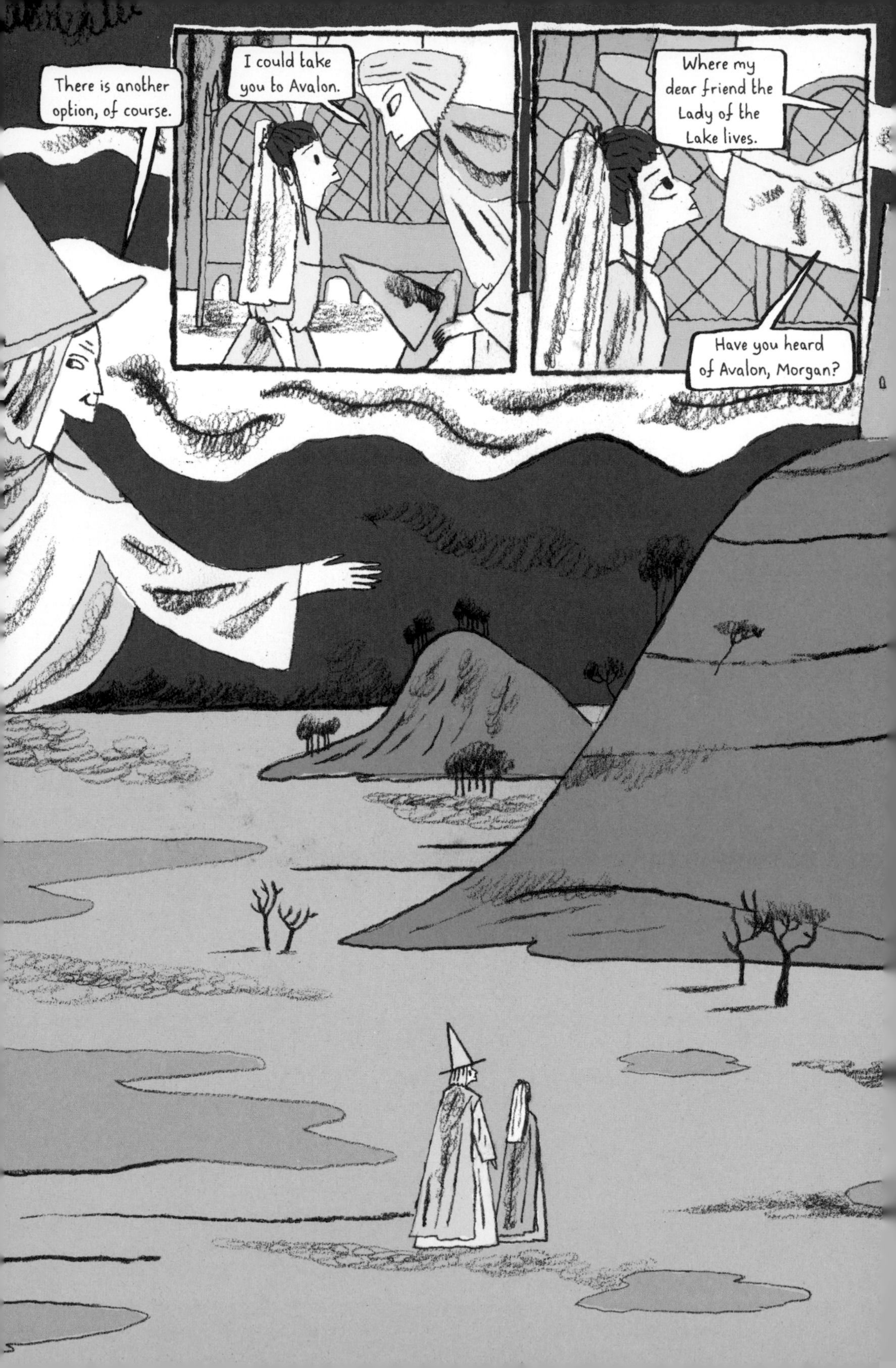
There is another option, of course.
I could take you to Avalon.
Where my dear friend the Lady of the Lake lives.
Have you heard of Avalon, Morgan?

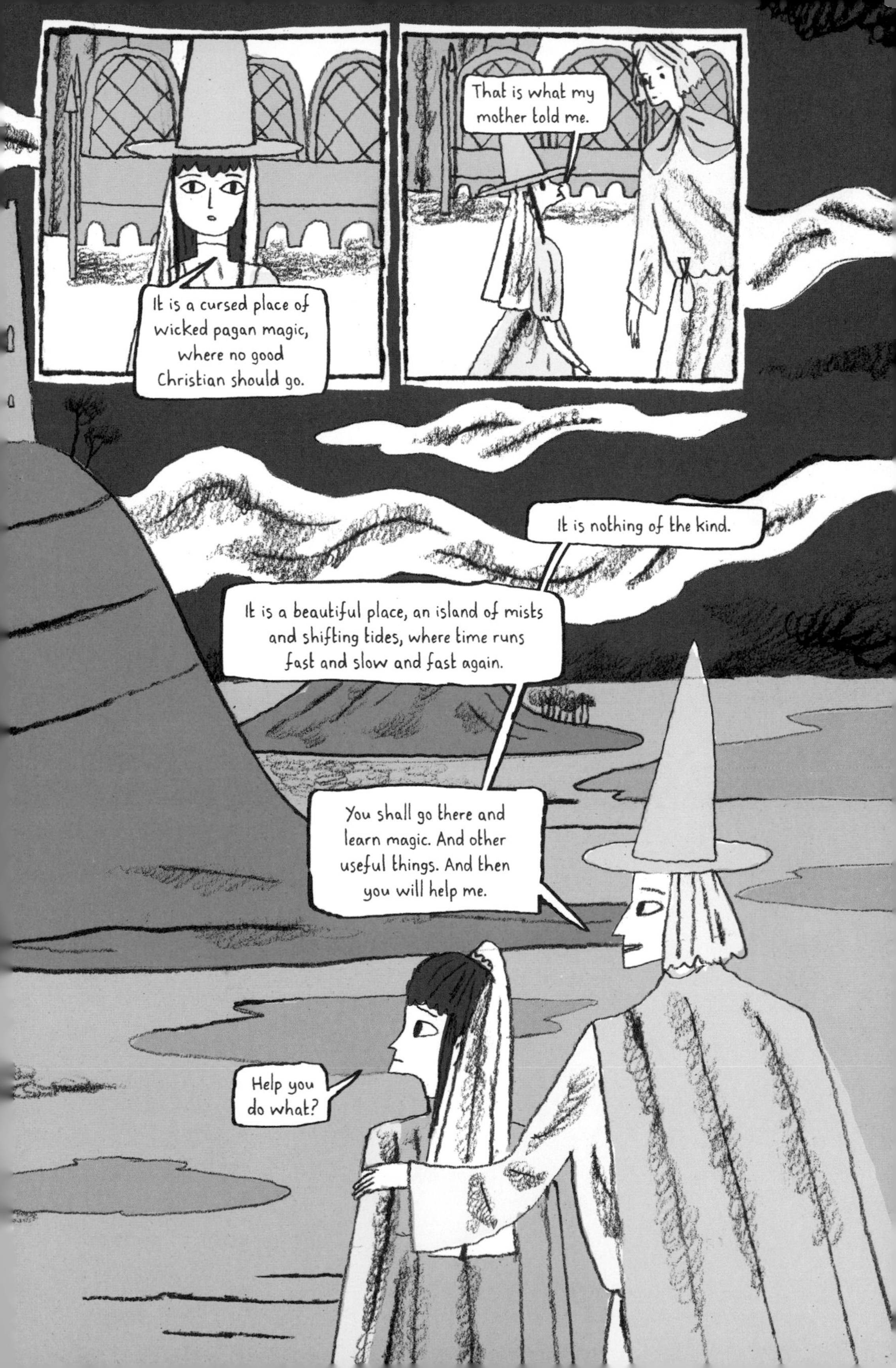

It is a cursed place of wicked pagan magic, where no good Christian should go.
That is what my mother told me.
It is nothing of the kind.
It is a beautiful place, an island of mists and shifting tides, where time runs fast and slow and fast again.
You shall go there and learn magic. And other useful things. And then you will help me.
Help you do what?

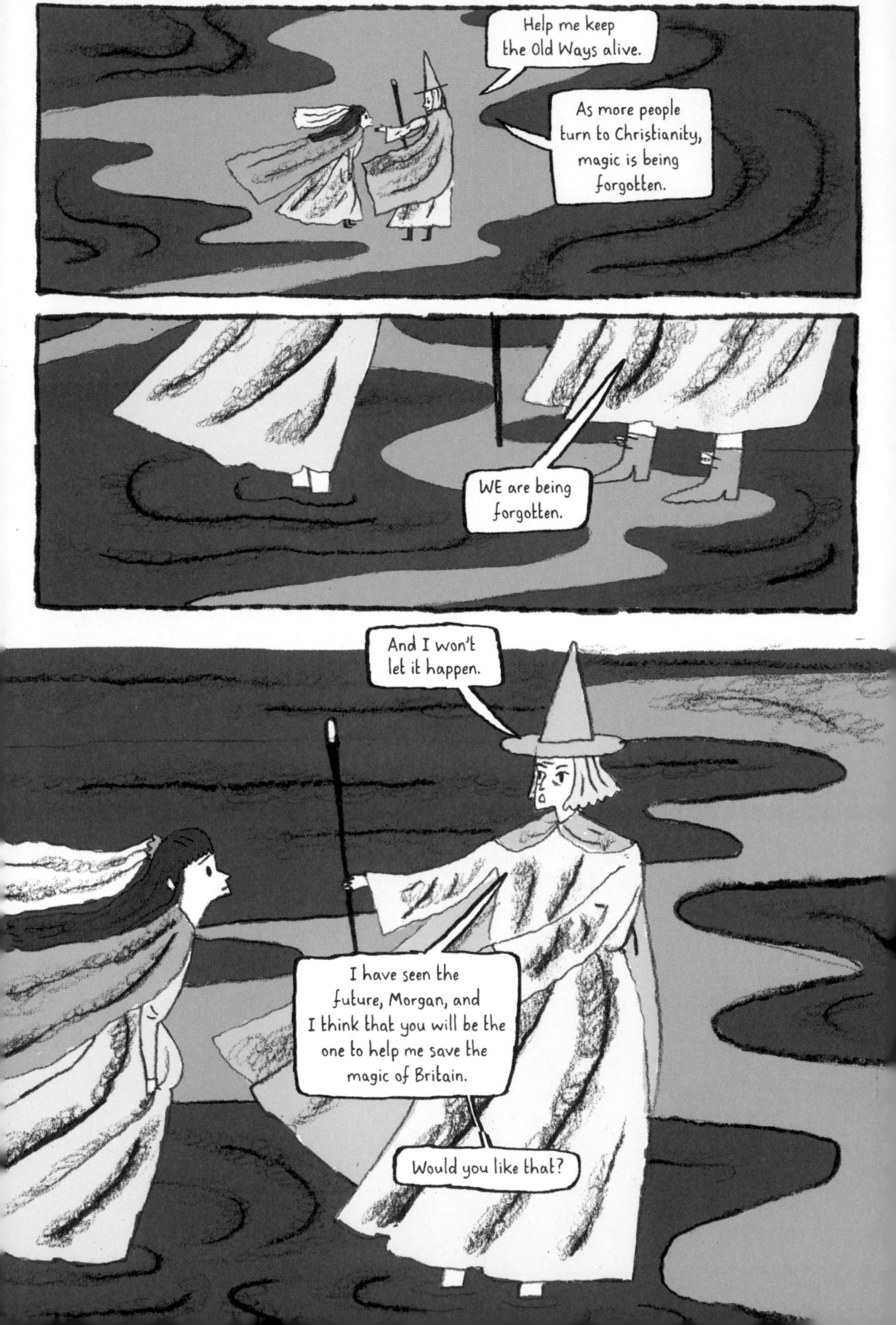
Help me keep the Old Ways alive.
As more people turn to Christianity, magic is being forgotten.
WE are being forgotten.
And I won't let it happen.
I have seen the future, Morgan, and I think that you will be the one to help me save the magic of Britain.
Would you like that?

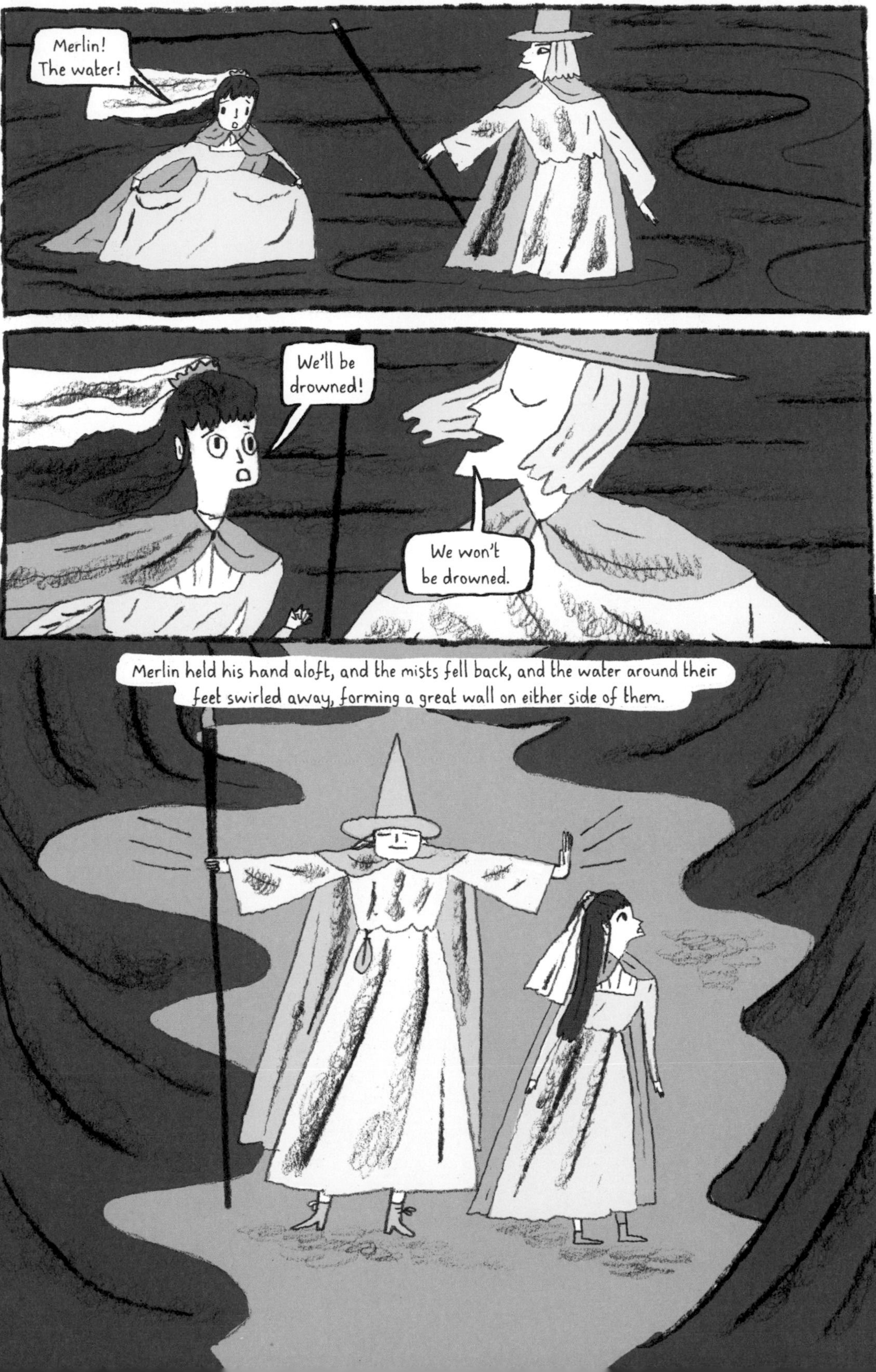
Merlin! The water!
We'll be drowned!
We won't be drowned.
Merlin held his hand aloft, and the mists fell back, and the water around their feet swirled away, forming a great wall on either side of them.

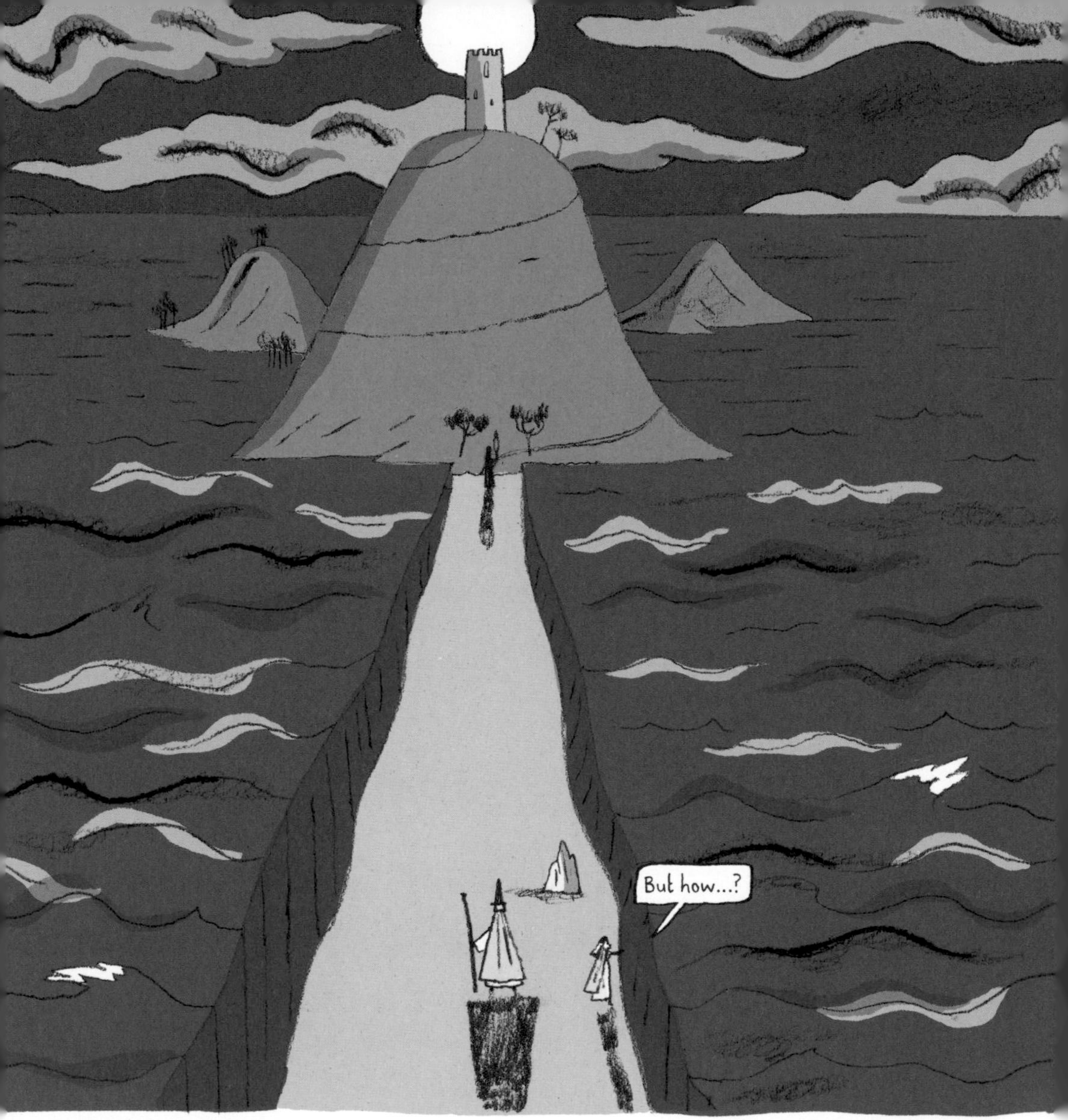
But how...?

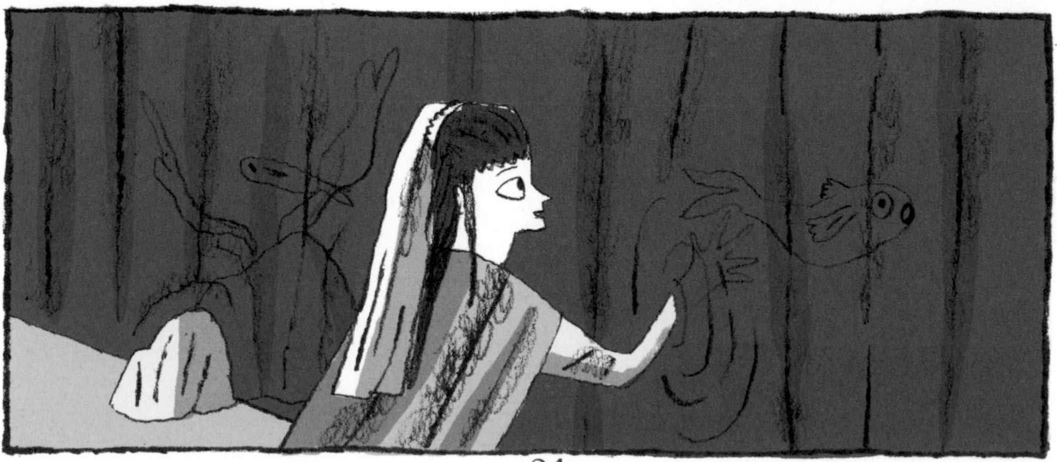

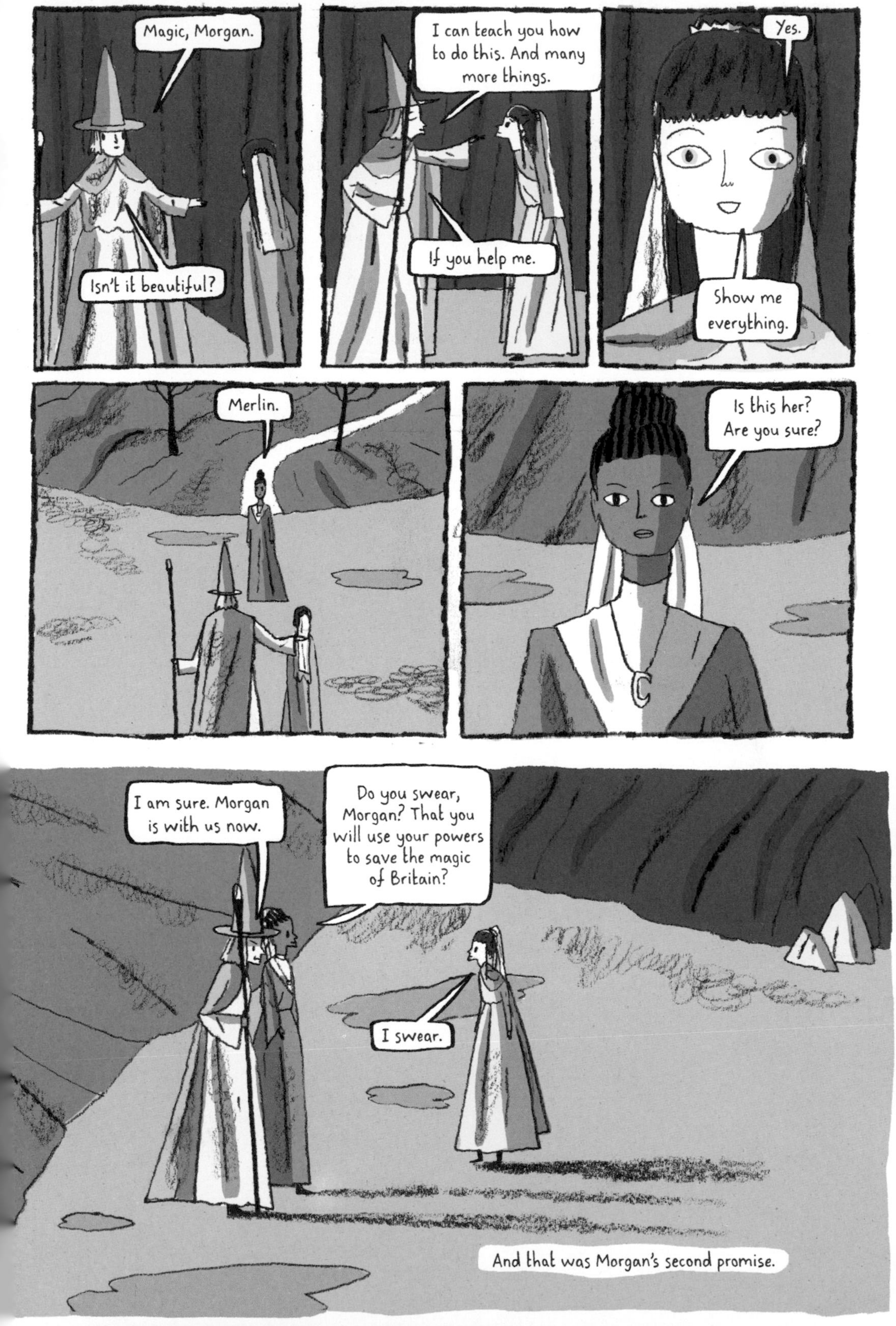
Magic, Morgan.
Isn't it beautiful?
I can teach you how to do this. And many more things.
If you help me.
Yes.
Show me everything.
Merlin.
Is this her? Are you sure?
I am sure. Morgan is with us now.
Do you swear, Morgan? That you will use your powers to save the magic of Britain?
I swear.
And that was Morgan's second promise.

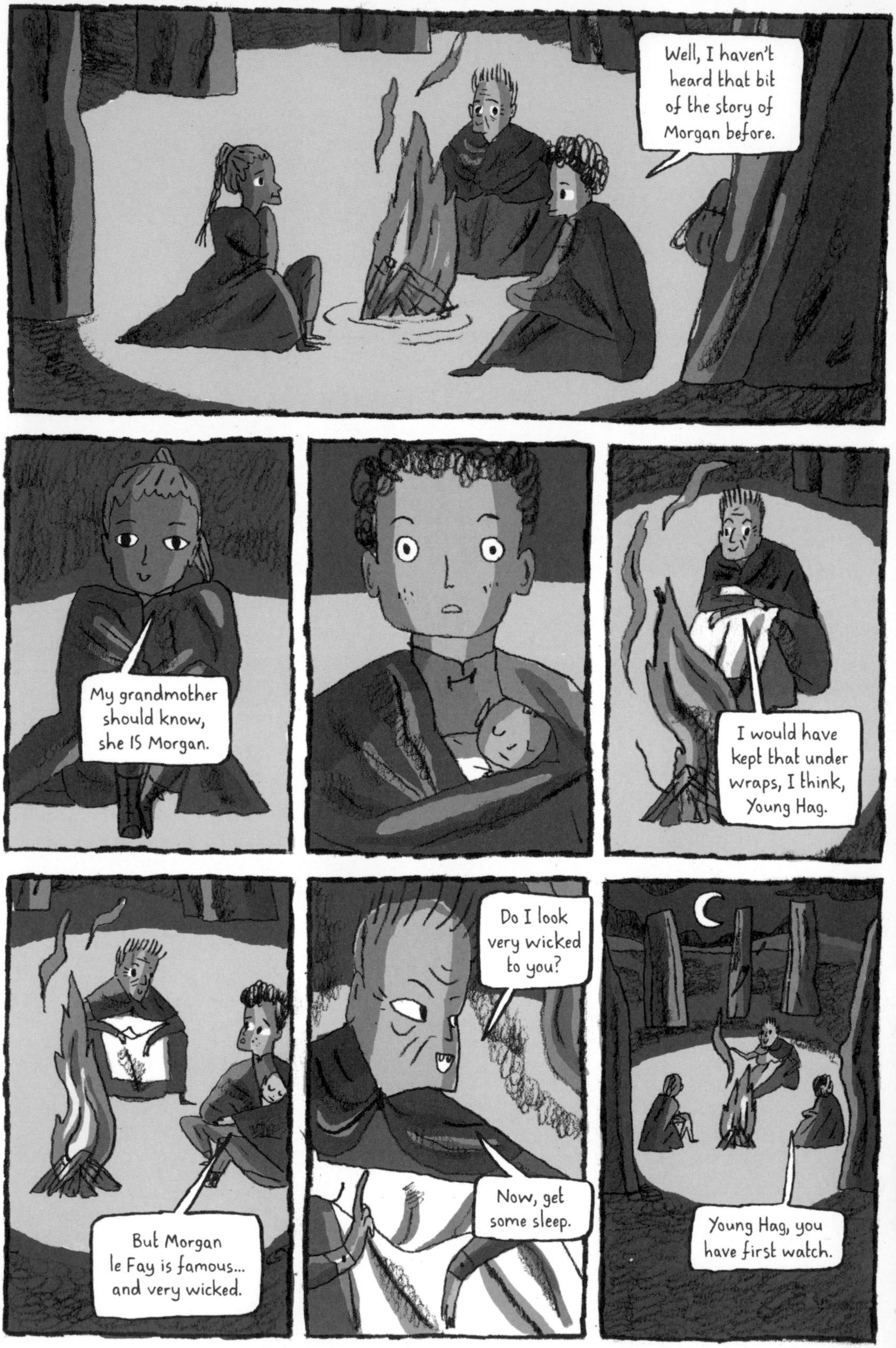
Well, I haven't heard that bit of the story of Morgan before.
My grandmother should know, she IS Morgan.
I would have kept that under wraps, I think, Young Hag.
But Morgan le Fay is famous... and very wicked.
Do I look very wicked to you?
Now, get some sleep.
Young Hag, you have first watch.

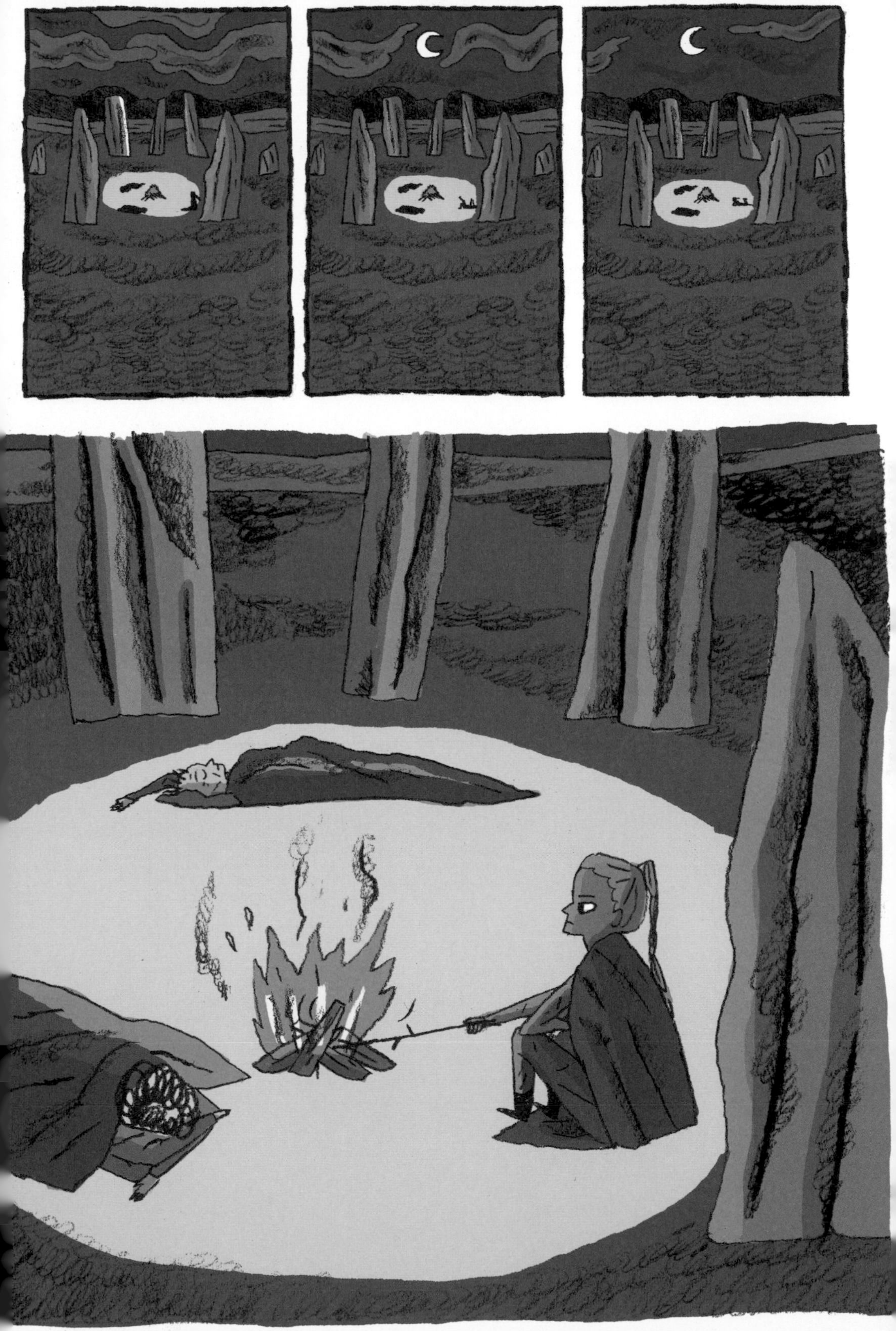

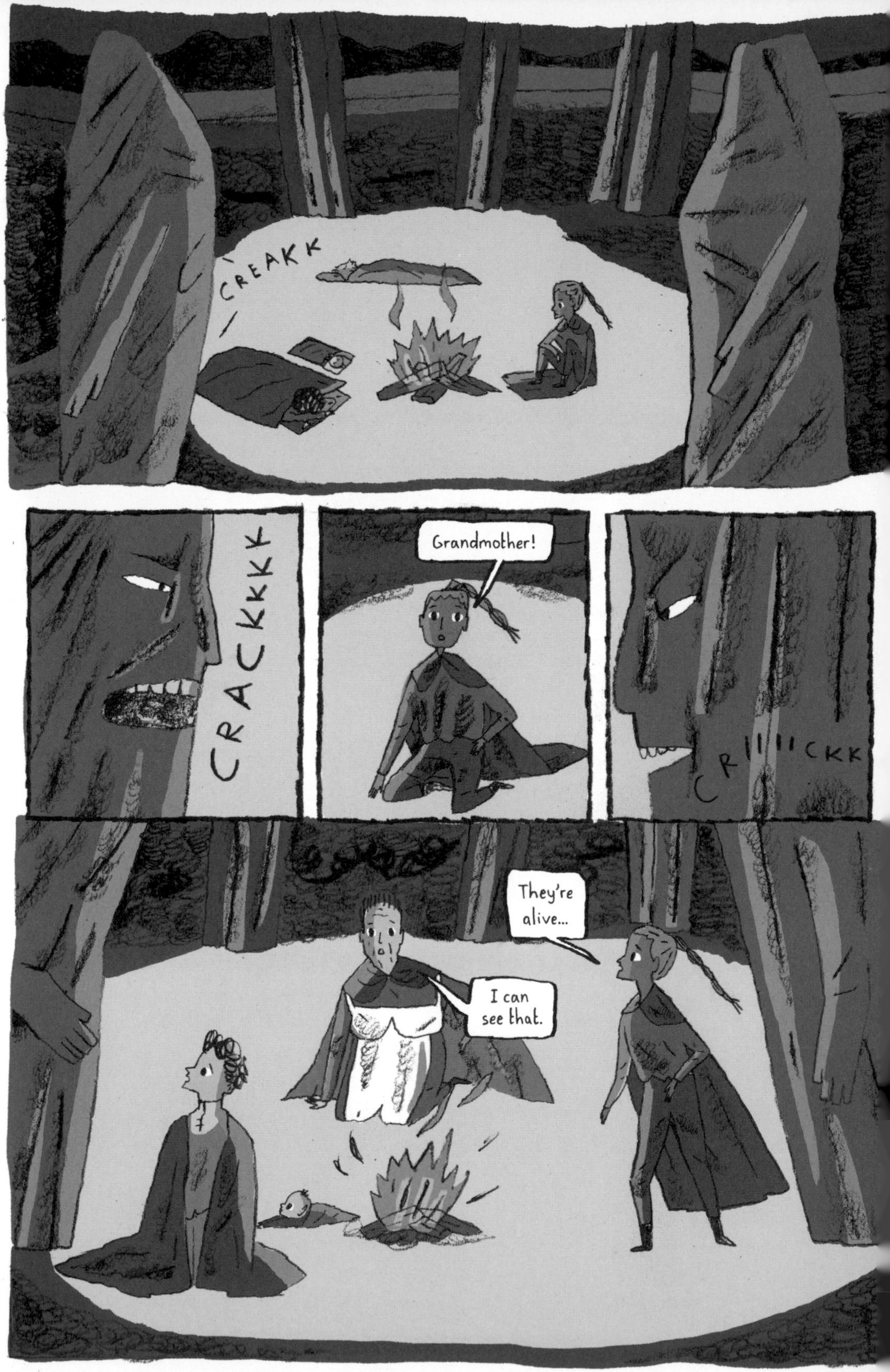
CREAKK
CRACKKKK
Grandmother!
CRIIIICKK
They're alive...
I can see that.

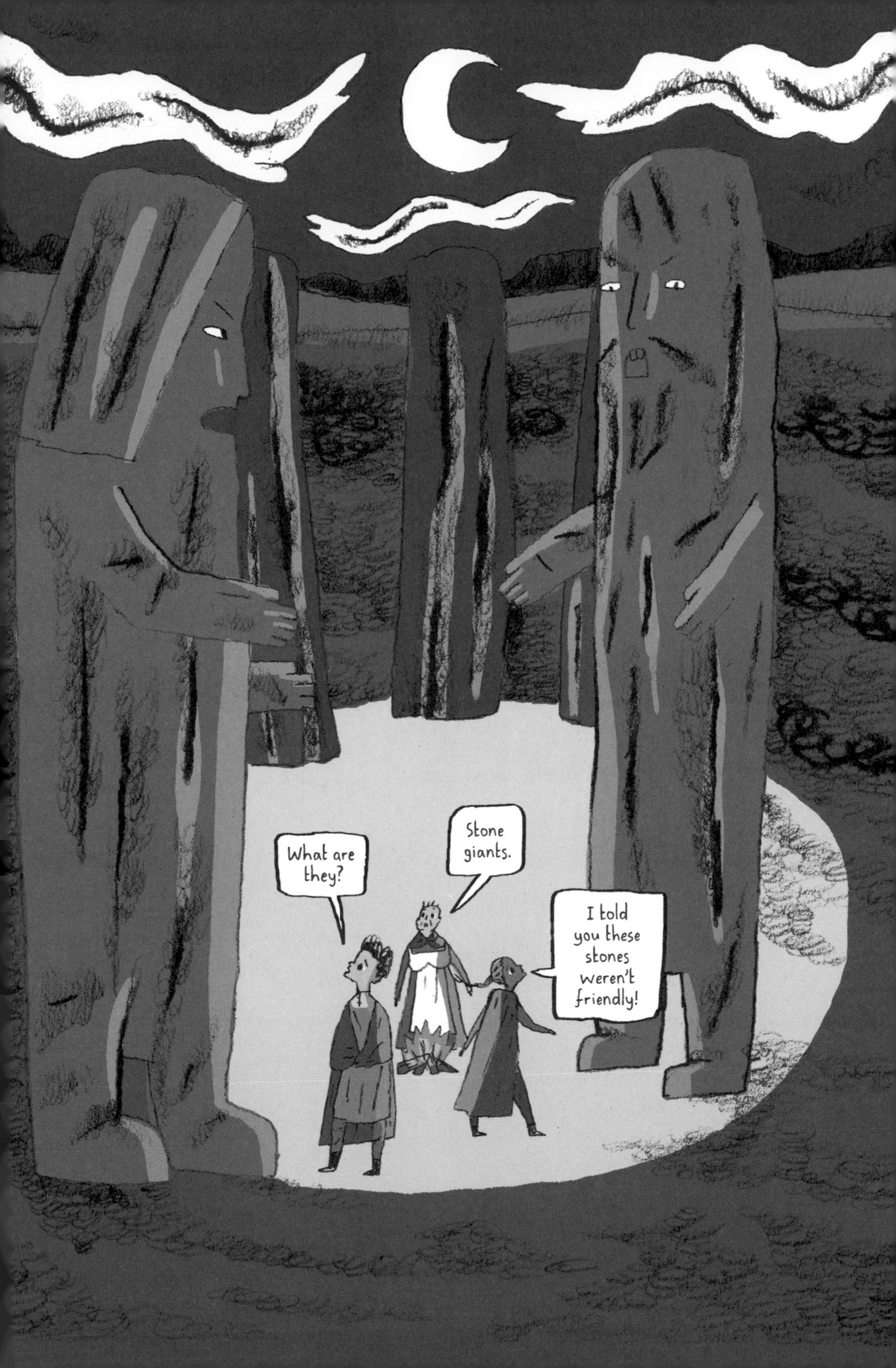
What are they?
Stone giants.
I told you these stones weren't friendly!

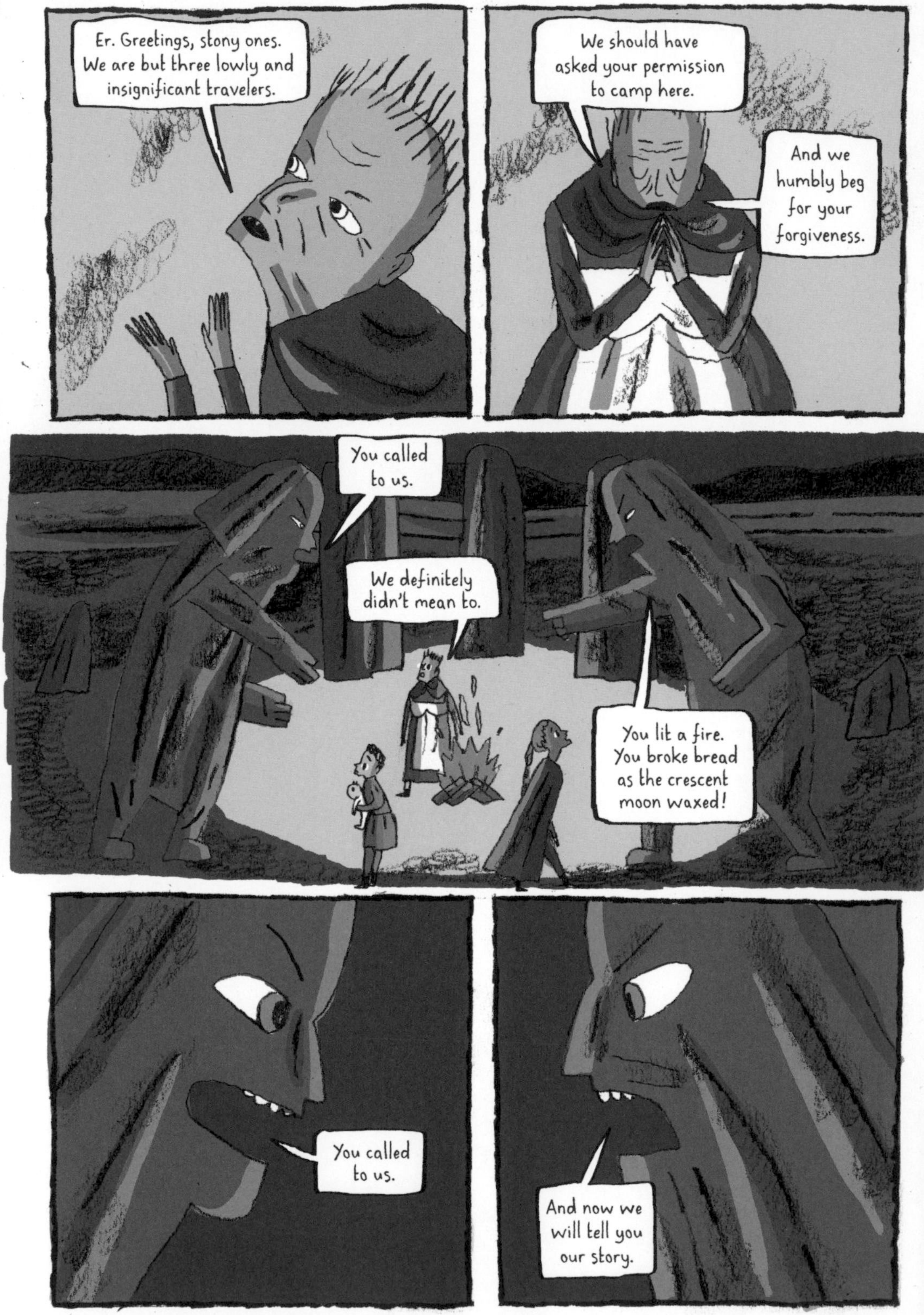
Er. Greetings, stony ones. We are but three lowly and insignificant travelers.
We should have asked your permission to camp here.
And we humbly beg for your forgiveness.
You called to us.
We definitely didn't mean to.
You lit a fire. You broke bread as the crescent moon waxed!
You called to us.
And now we will tell you our story.

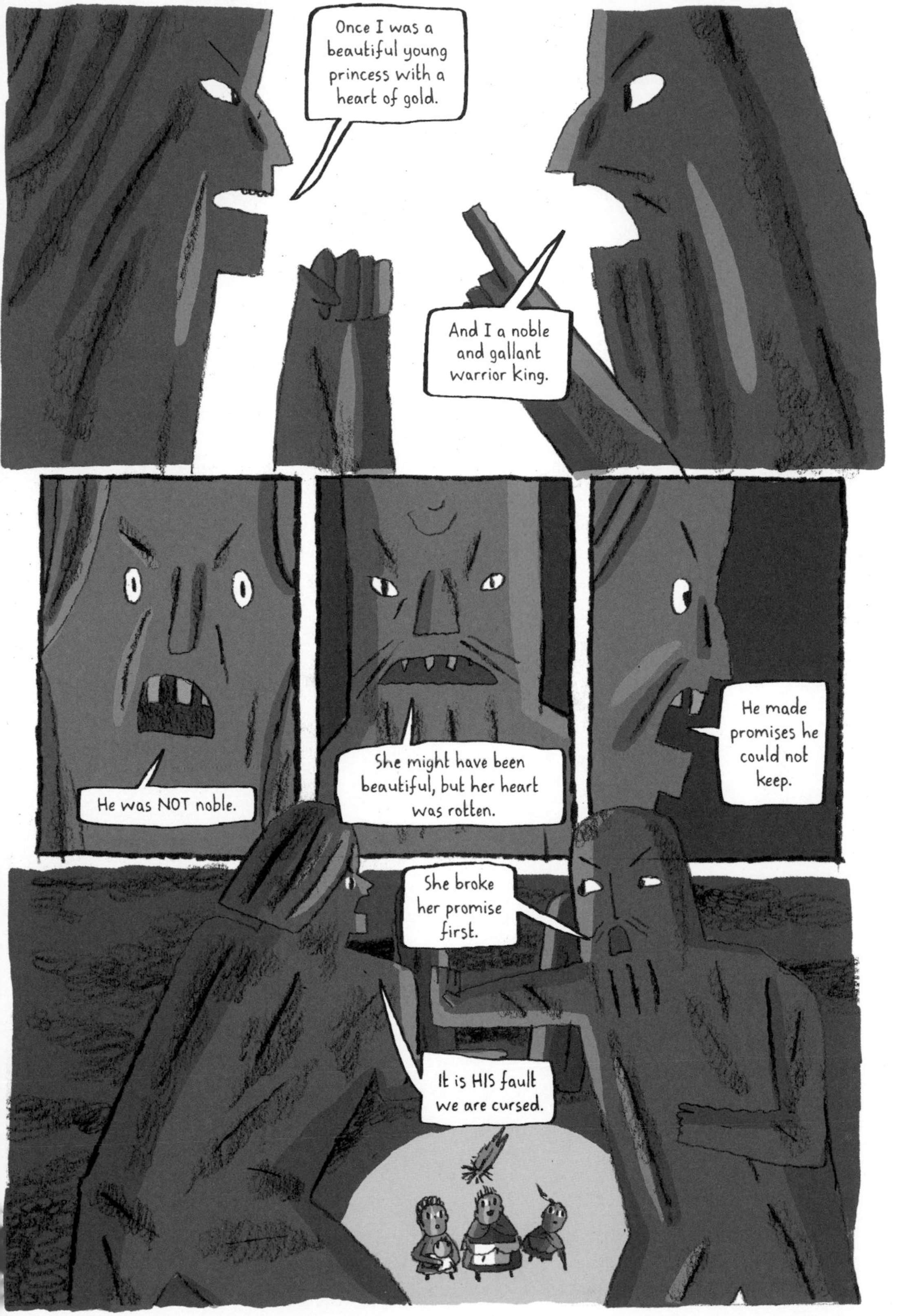
Once I was a beautiful young princess with a heart of gold.
And I a noble and gallant warrior king.
He was NOT noble.
She might have been beautiful, but her heart was rotten.
He made promises he could not keep.
She broke her promise first.
It is HIS fault we are cursed.

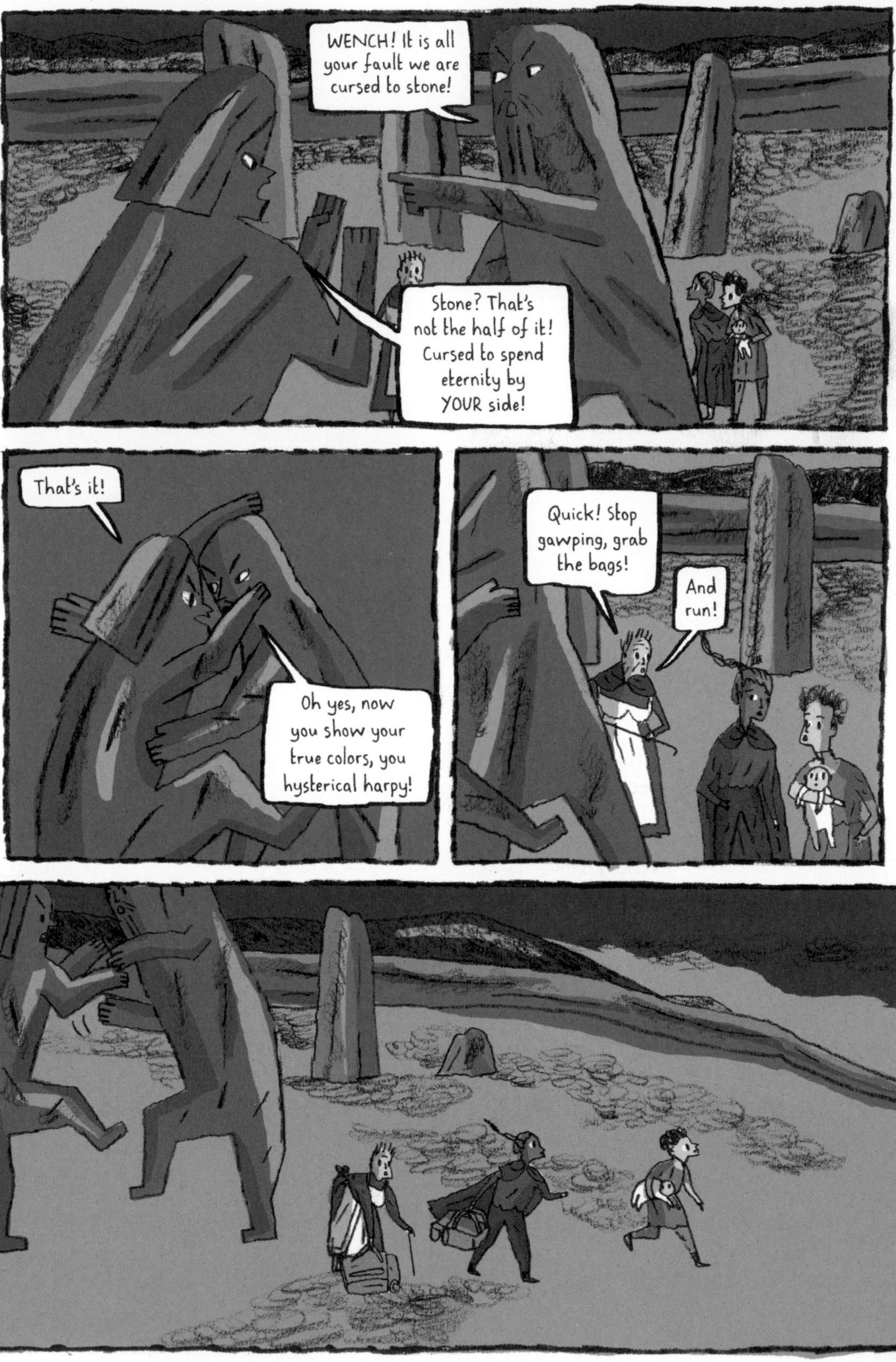
WENCH! It is all your fault we are cursed to stone!
Stone? That's not the half of it! Cursed to spend eternity by YOUR side!
That's it!
Oh yes, now you show your true colors, you hysterical harpy!
Quick! Stop gawping, grab the bags!
And run!

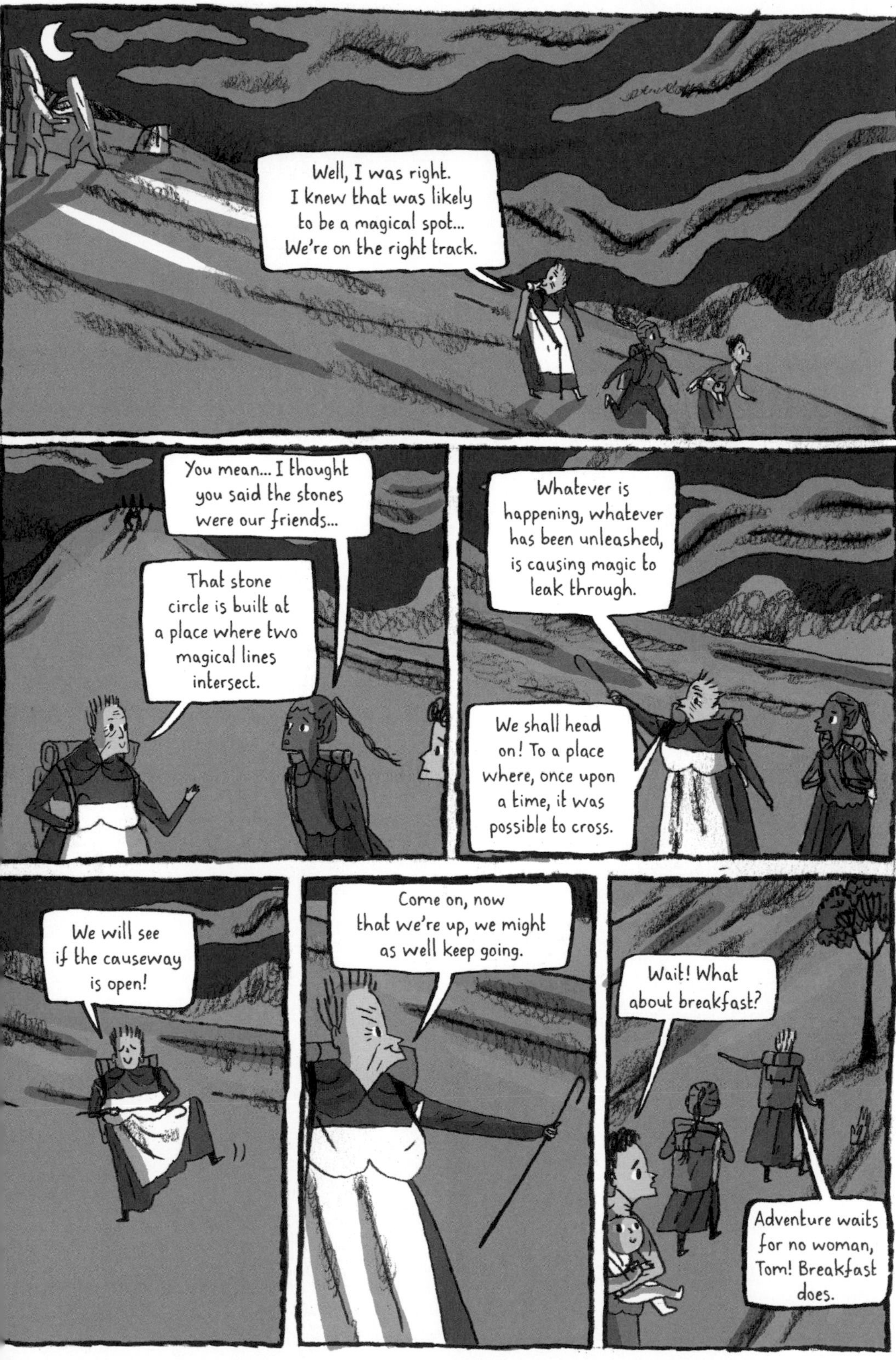

Well, I was right. I knew that was likely to be a magical spot... We're on the right track.
You mean... I thought you said the stones were our friends...
That stone circle is built at a place where two magical lines intersect.
Whatever is happening, whatever has been unleashed, is causing magic to leak through.
We shall head on! To a place where, once upon a time, it was possible to cross.
We will see if the causeway is open!
Come on, now that we're up, we might as well keep going.
Wait! What about breakfast?
Adventure waits for no woman, Tom! Breakfast does.

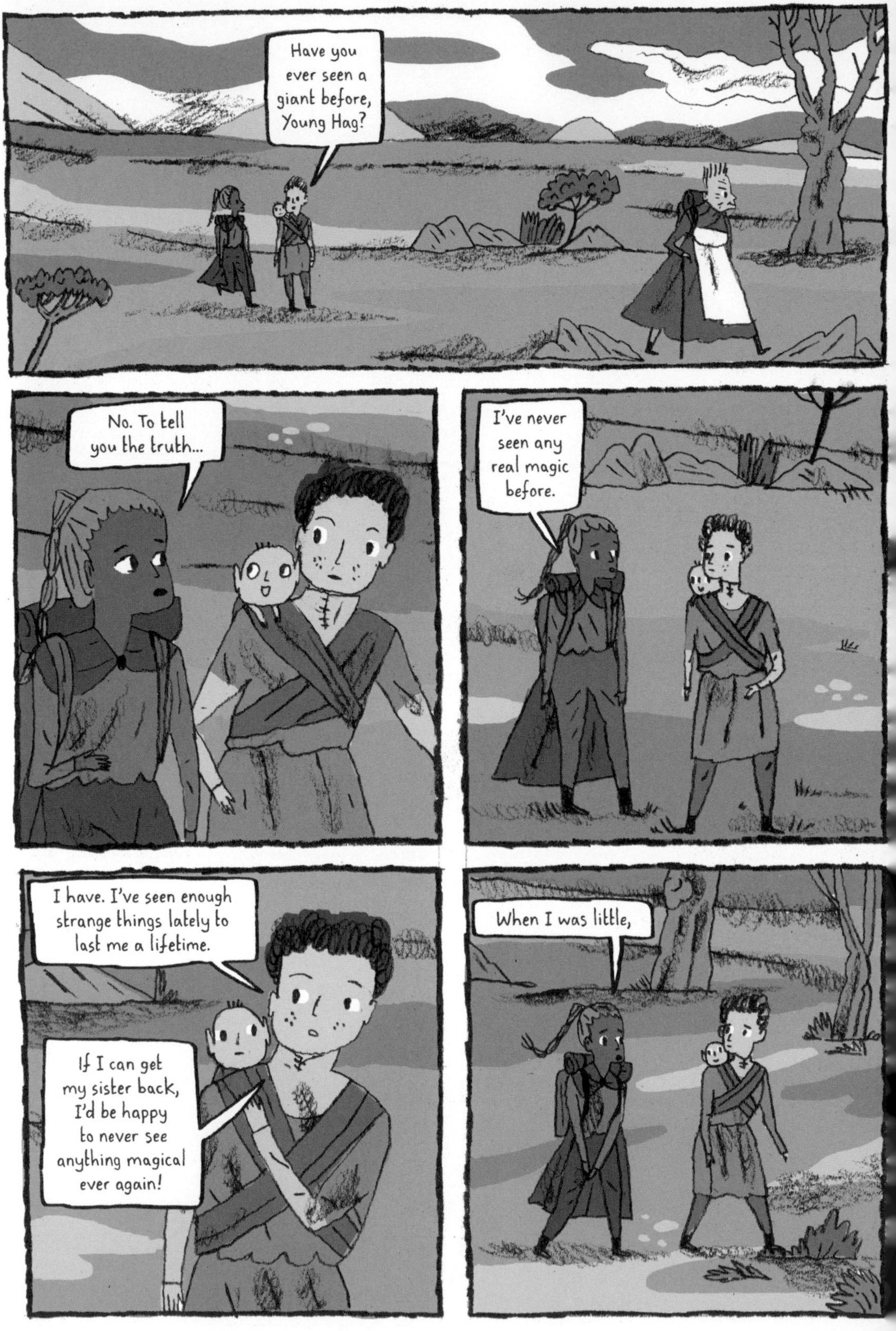
Have you ever seen a giant before, Young Hag?
No. To tell you the truth...
I've never seen any real magic before.
I have. I've seen enough strange things lately to last me a lifetime.
If I can get my sister back, I'd be happy to never see anything magical ever again!
When I was little,

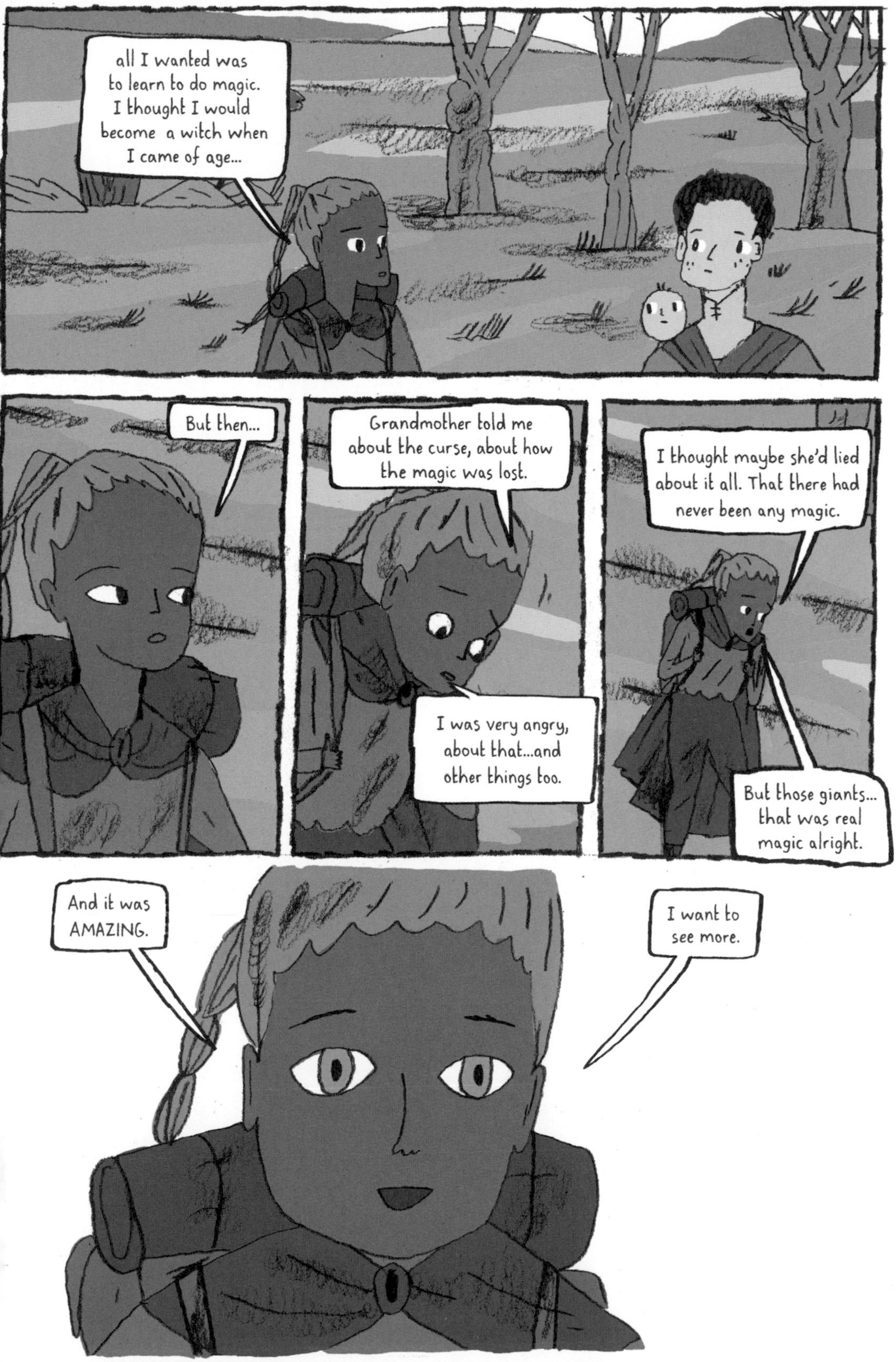

all I wanted was to learn to do magic. I thought I would become a witch when I came of age...
But then...
Grandmother told me about the curse, about how the magic was lost.
I was very angry, about that...and other things too.
I thought maybe she'd lied about it all. That there had never been any magic.
But those giants... that was real magic alright.
And it was AMAZING.
I want to see more.

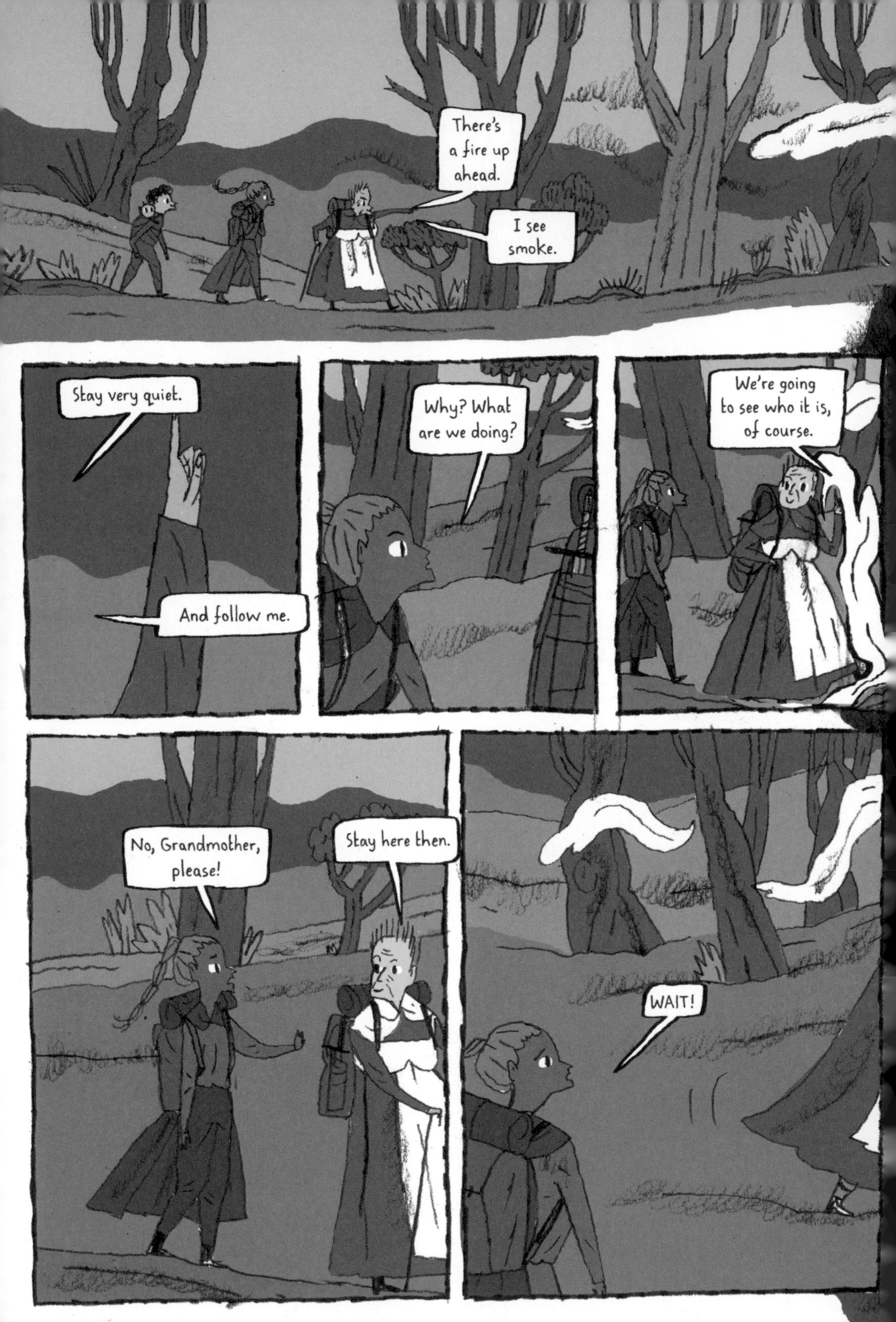
There's a fire up ahead.
I see smoke.
Stay very quiet.
And follow me.
Why? What are we doing?
We're going to see who it is, of course.
No, Grandmother, please!
Stay here then.
WAIT!

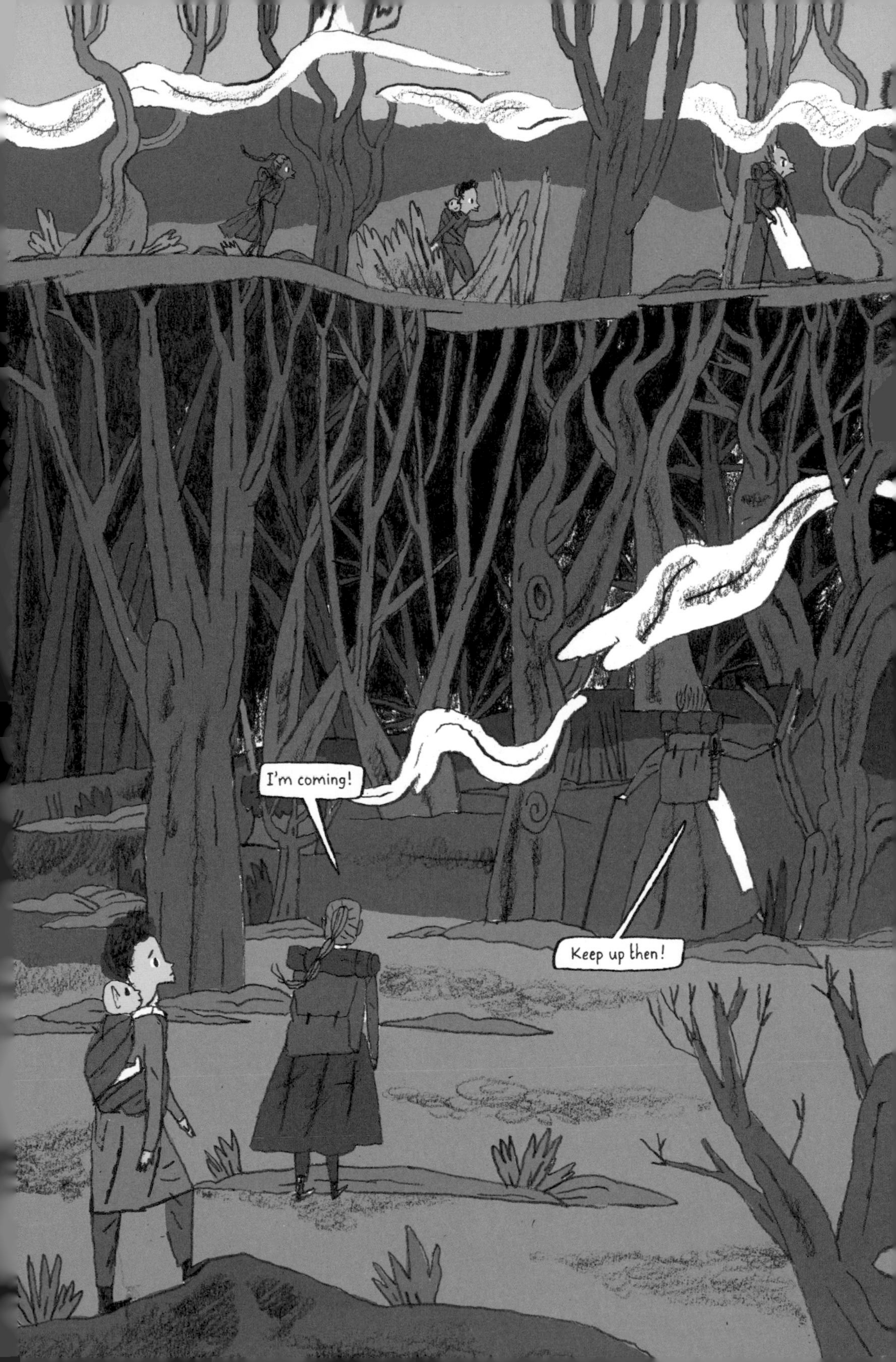
I'm coming!
Keep up then!

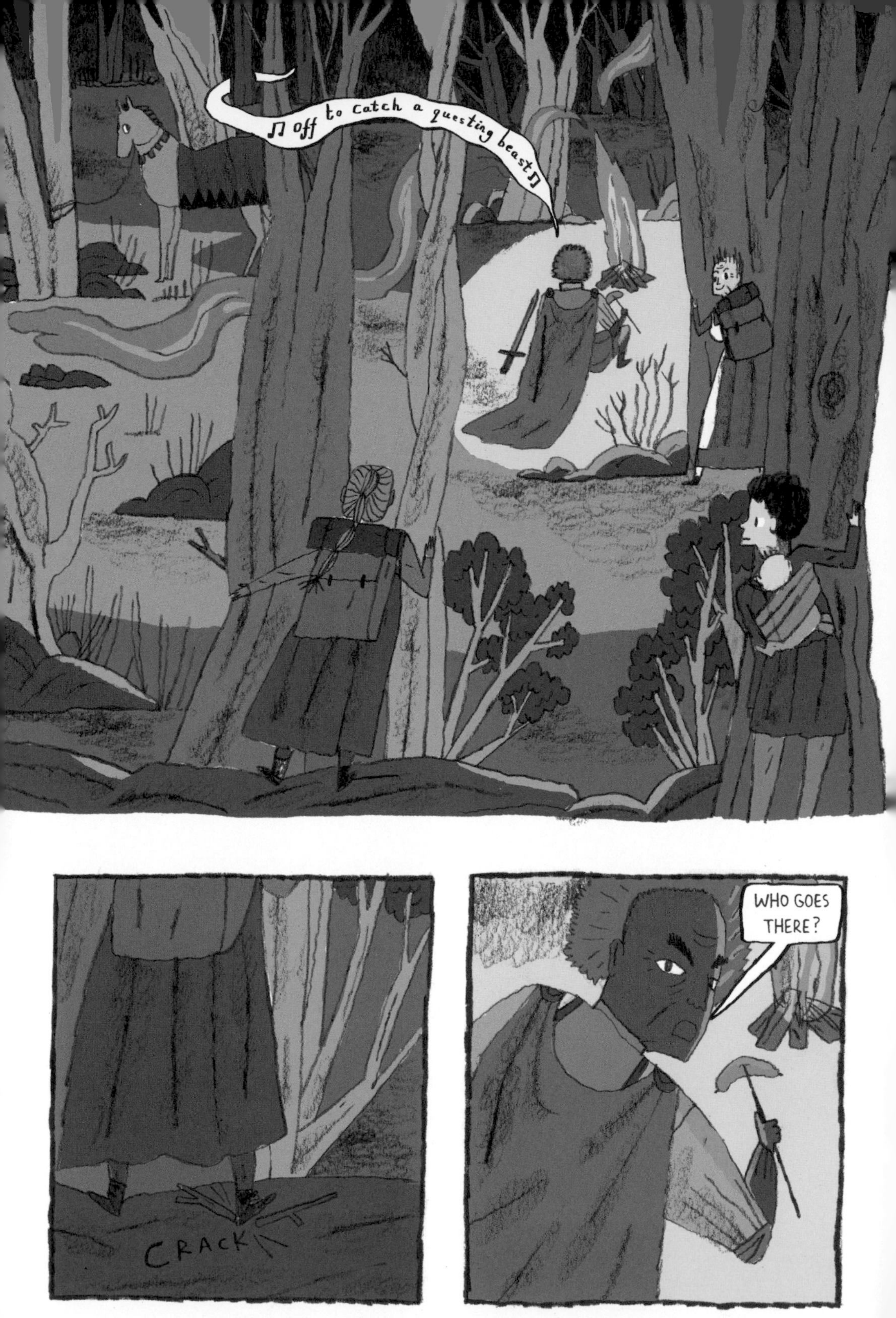
♫ off to catch a questing beast ♫
CRACK
WHO GOES THERE?

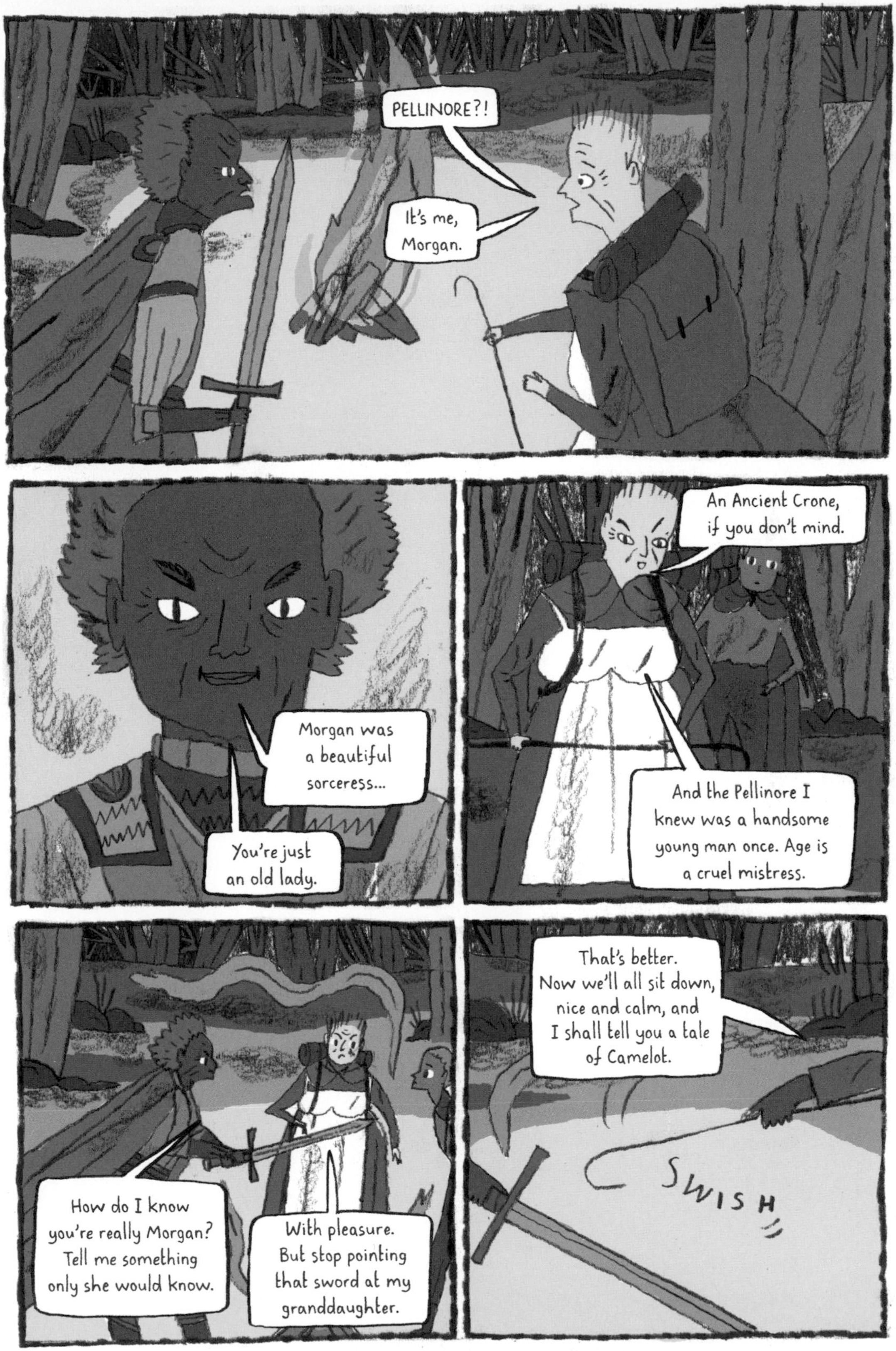
PELLINORE?!
It's me, Morgan.
Morgan was a beautiful sorceress...
You're just an old lady.
An Ancient Crone, if you don't mind.
And the Pellinore I knew was a handsome young man once. Age is a cruel mistress.
How do I know you're really Morgan? Tell me something only she would know.
With pleasure. But stop pointing that sword at my granddaughter.
That's better. Now we'll all sit down, nice and calm, and I shall tell you a tale of Camelot.
SWISH

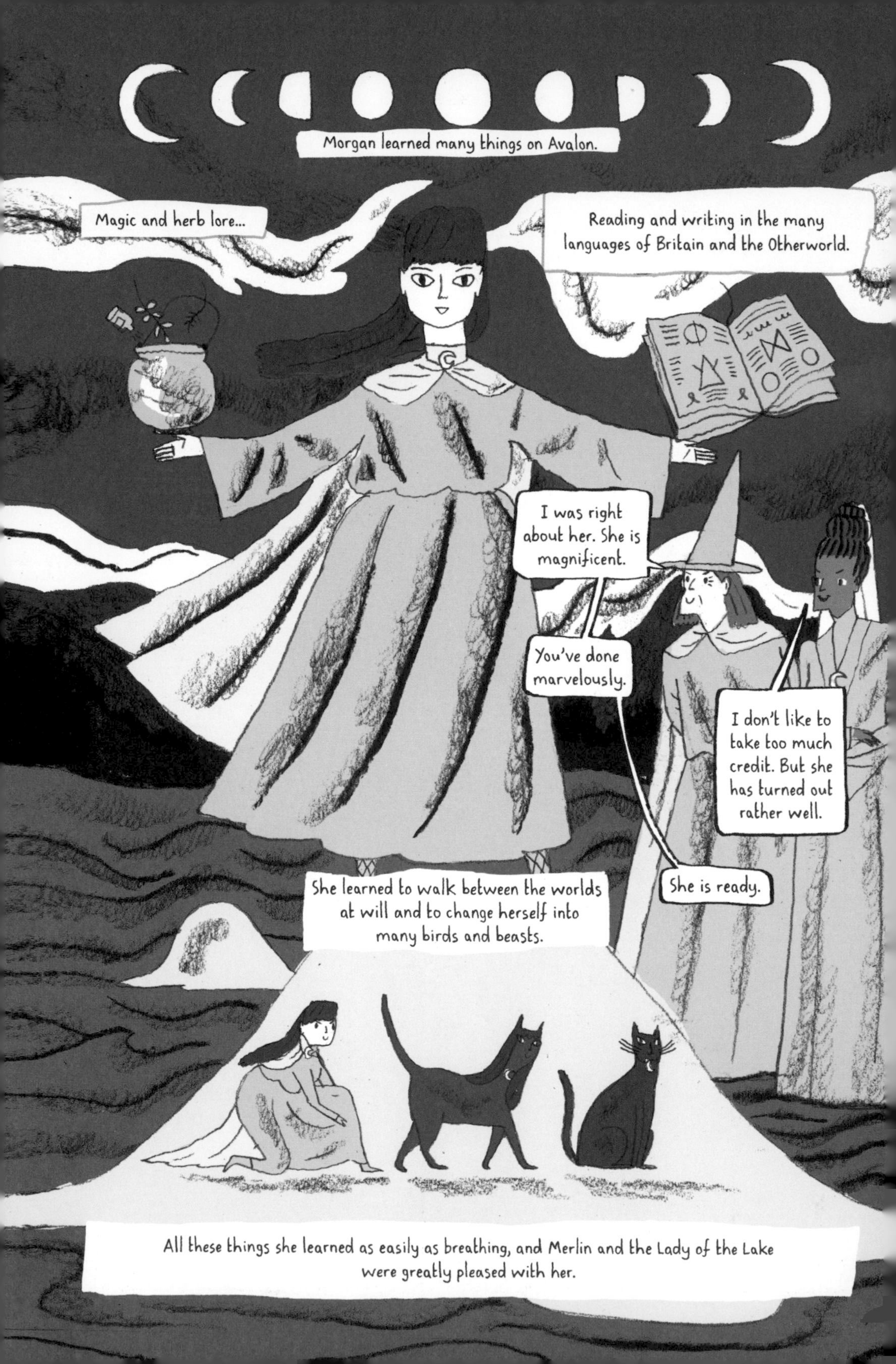
Morgan learned many things on Avalon.
Magic and herb lore...
Reading and writing in the many languages of Britain and the Otherworld.
I was right about her. She is magnificent.
You've done marvelously.
I don't like to take too much credit. But she has turned out rather well.
She is ready.
She learned to walk between the worlds at will and to change herself into many birds and beasts.
All these things she learned as easily as breathing, and Merlin and the Lady of the Lake were greatly pleased with her.

And while the Lady of the Lake had been teaching Morgan magic and the old ways, Merlin had been training Arthur to be the perfect king. Together, the brother and sister would usher in a new era of magic.

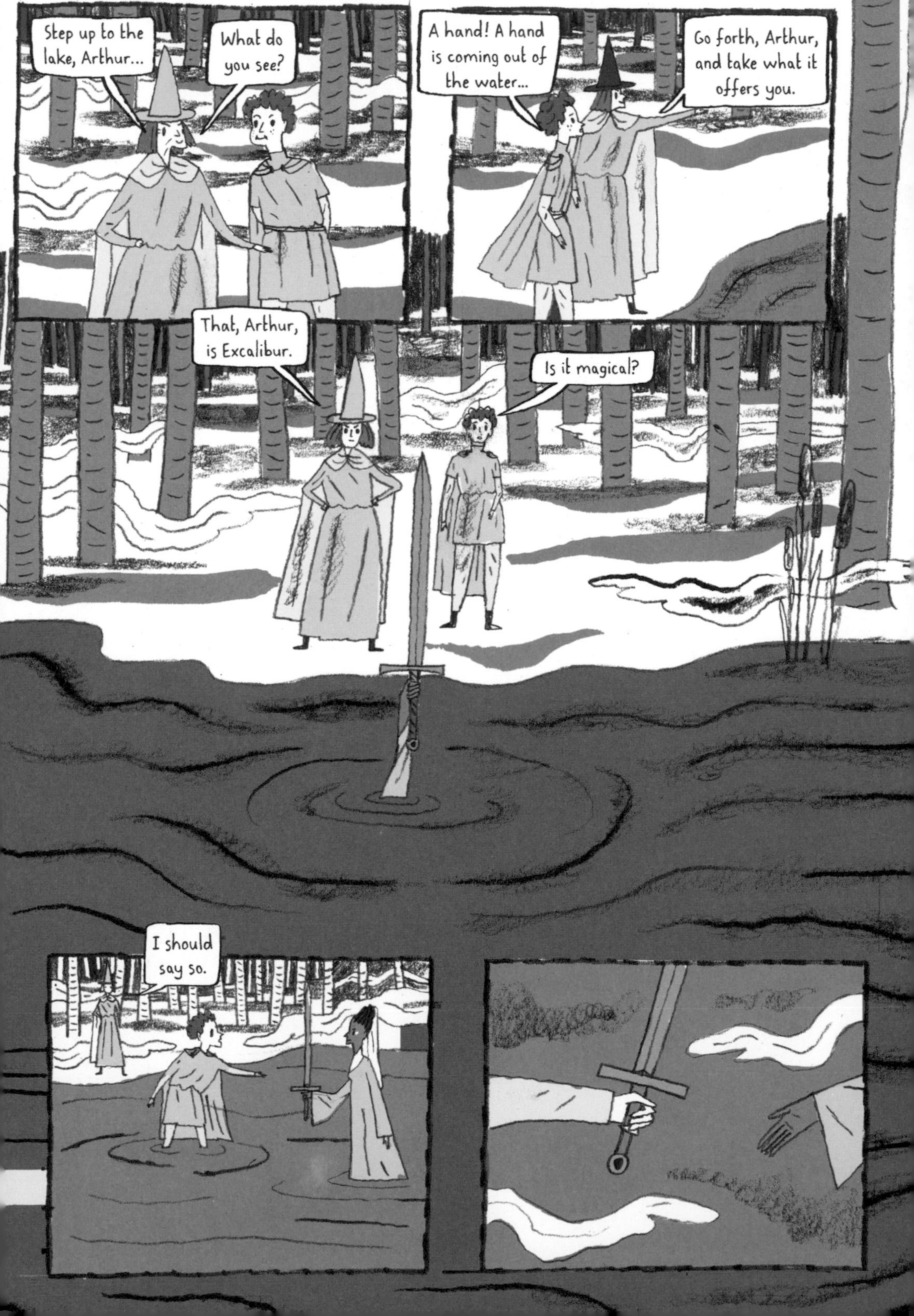

Step up to the lake, Arthur...
What do you see?
A hand! A hand is coming out of the water...
Go forth, Arthur, and take what it offers you.
That, Arthur, is Excalibur.
Is it magical?
I should say so.

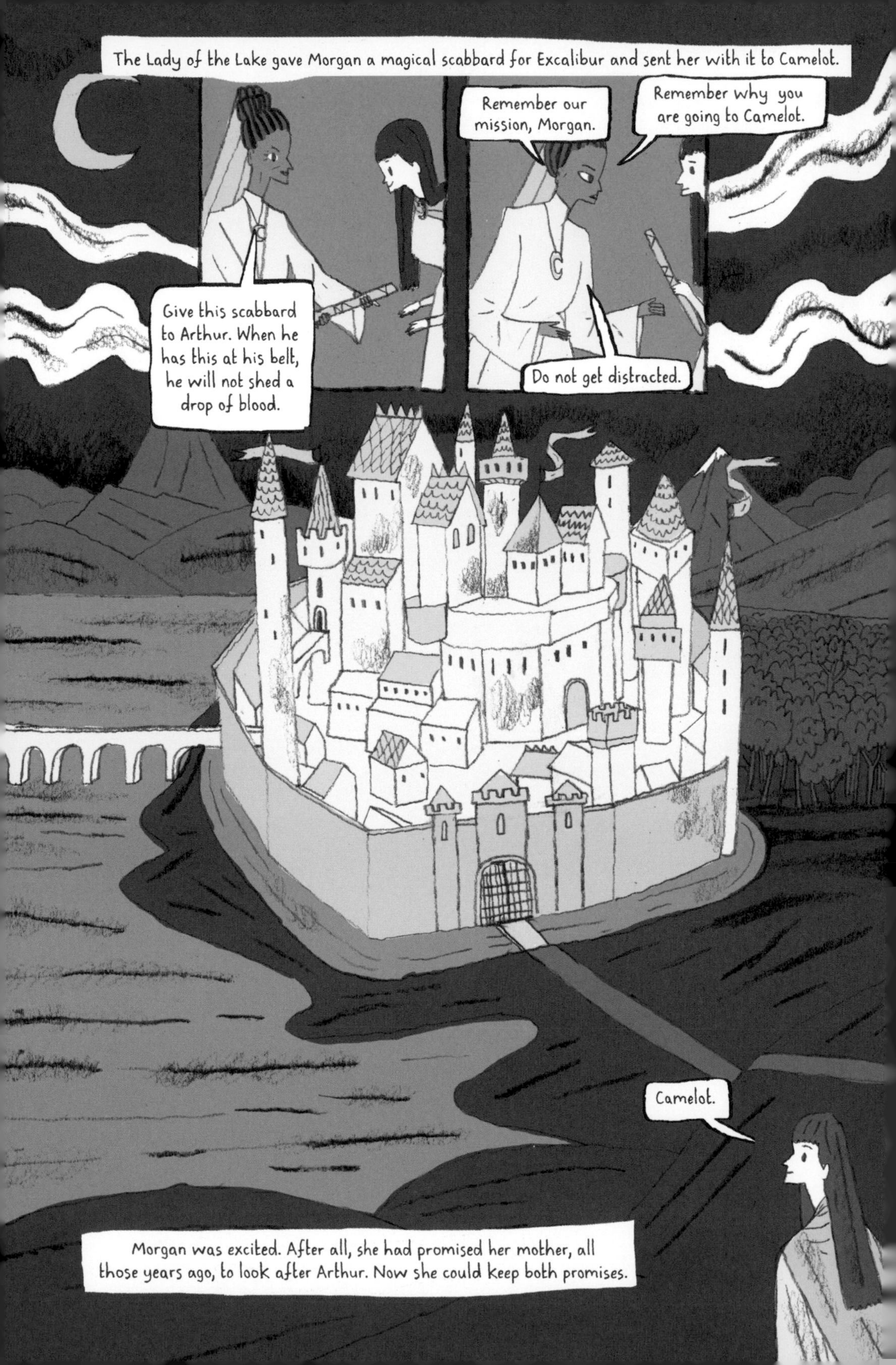

The Lady of the Lake gave Morgan a magical scabbard for Excalibur and sent her with it to Camelot.
Give this scabbard to Arthur. When he has this at his belt, he will not shed a drop of blood.
Remember our mission, Morgan.
Remember why you are going to Camelot.
Do not get distracted.
Camelot.
Morgan was excited. After all, she had promised her mother, all those years ago, to look after Arthur. Now she could keep both promises.

At first, all was as she had hoped it would be. Arthur was delighted to be reunited with his sister, and they made many great plans to make peace between those who practiced the old ways and the new Christians.

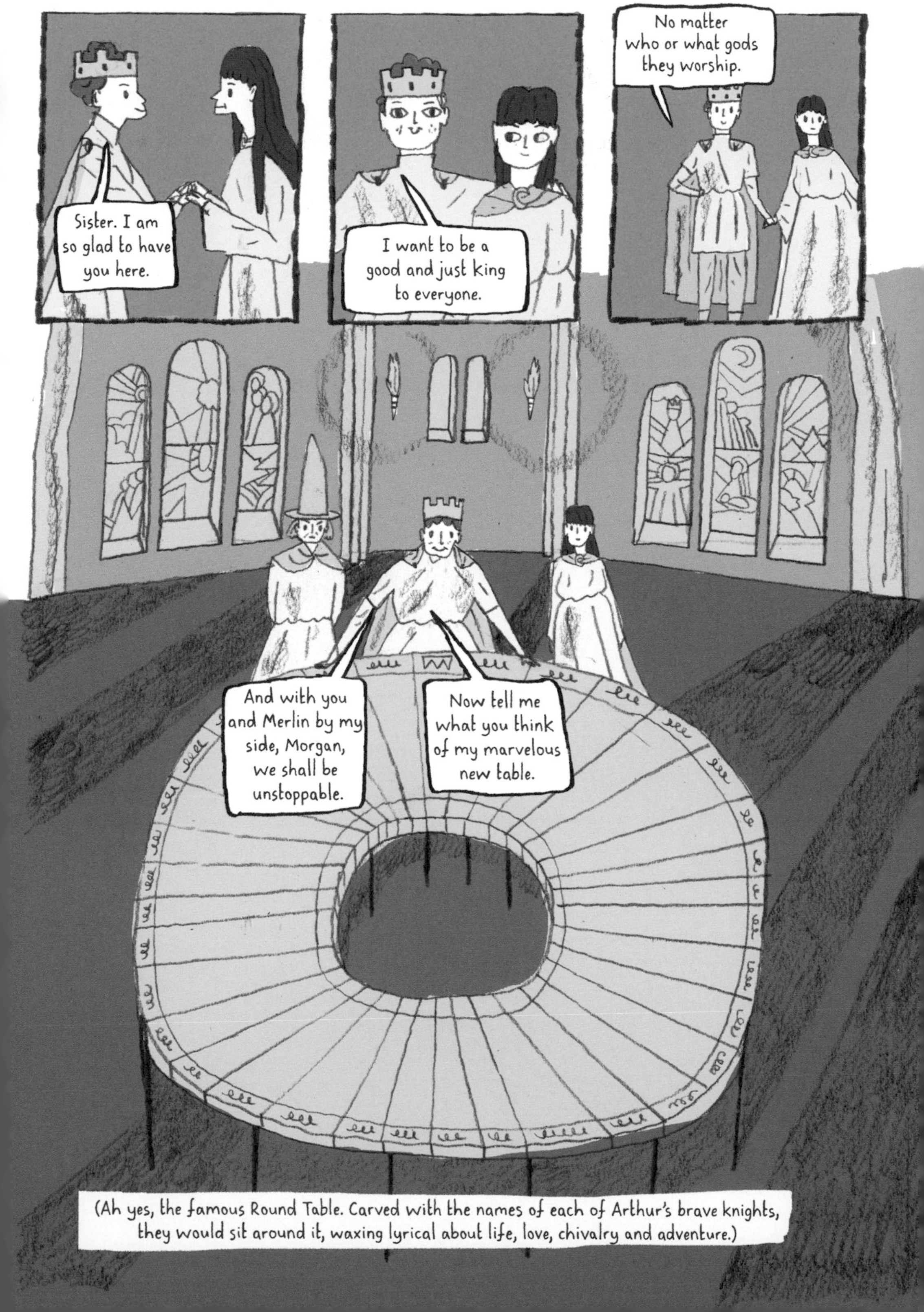
Sister. I am so glad to have you here.
I want to be a good and just king to everyone.
No matter who or what gods they worship.
And with you and Merlin by my side, Morgan, we shall be unstoppable.
Now tell me what you think of my marvelous new table.
(Ah yes, the famous Round Table. Carved with the names of each of Arthur's brave knights, they would sit around it, waxing lyrical about life, love, chivalry and adventure.)

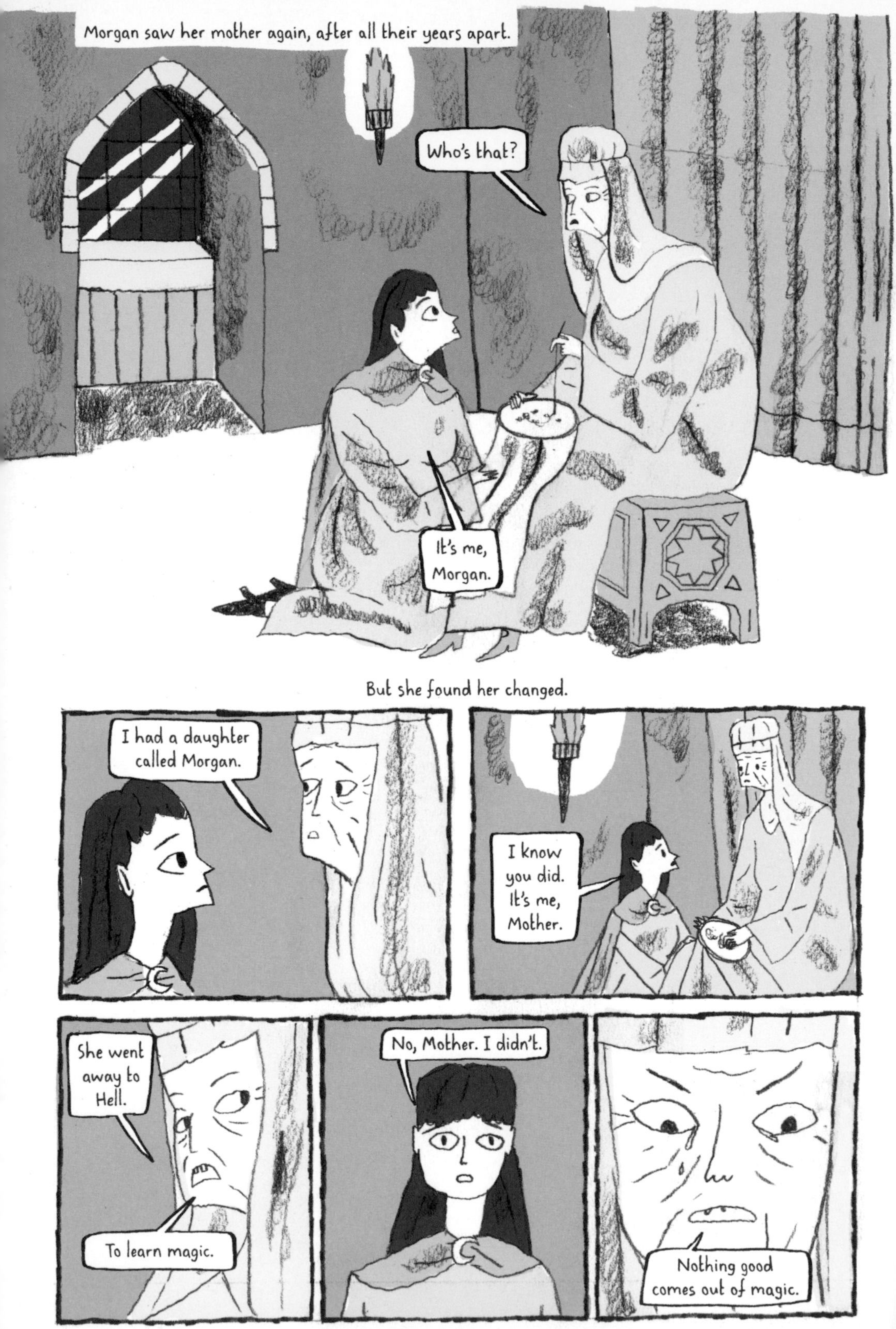
Morgan saw her mother again, after all their years apart.
Who's that?
It's me, Morgan.
But she found her changed.
I had a daughter called Morgan.
I know you did. It's me, Mother.
She went away to Hell.
To learn magic.
No, Mother. I didn't.
Nothing good comes out of magic.

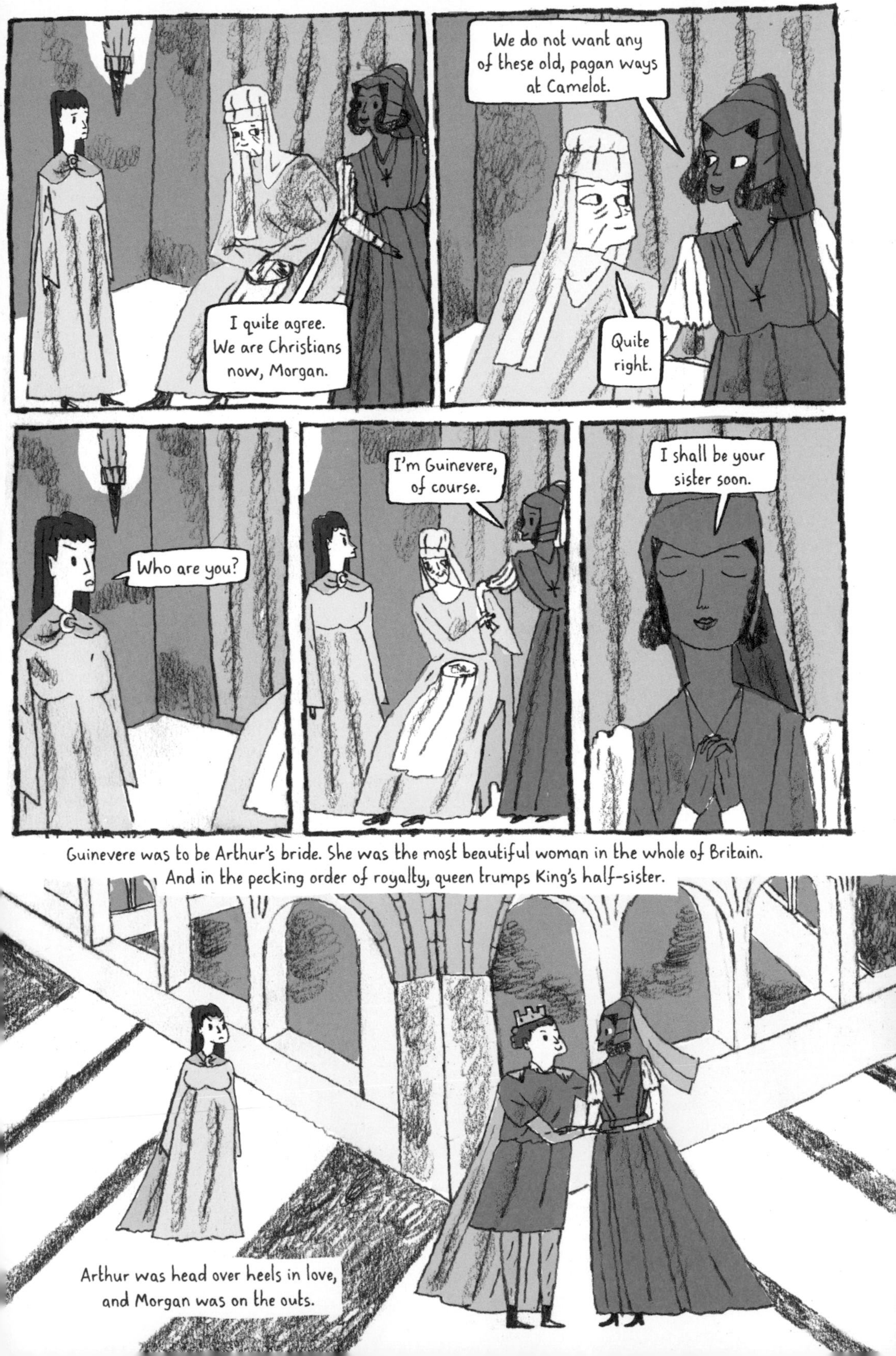
I quite agree.
We are Christians now, Morgan.
We do not want any of these old, pagan ways at Camelot.
Quite right.
Who are you?
I'm Guinevere, of course.
I shall be your sister soon.
Guinevere was to be Arthur's bride. She was the most beautiful woman in the whole of Britain.
And in the pecking order of royalty, queen trumps King's half-sister.
Arthur was head over heels in love, and Morgan was on the outs.

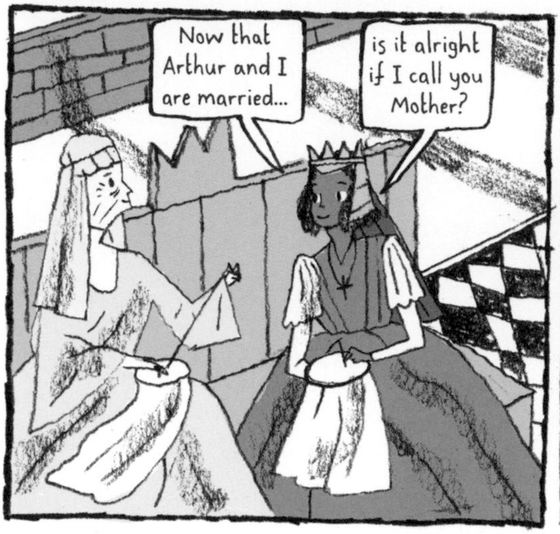
Now that Arthur and I are married...
is it alright if I call you Mother?

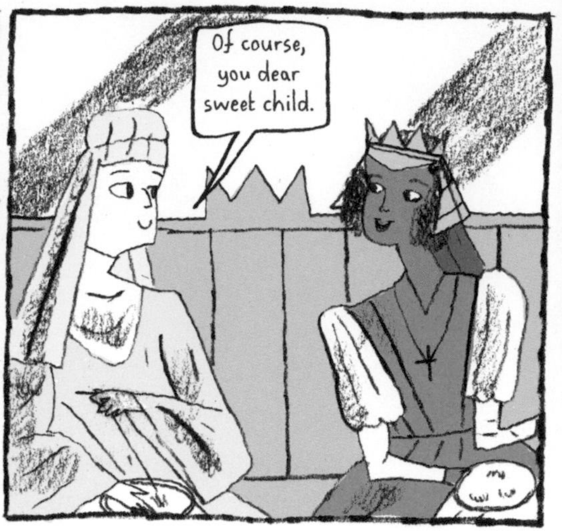
Of course, you dear sweet child.

Morgan tried to like Guinevere, but she could not. Guinevere was pious and beautiful, good and kind and sweet.
She was exactly the kind of daughter that Igraine had hoped Morgan would grow up to be.

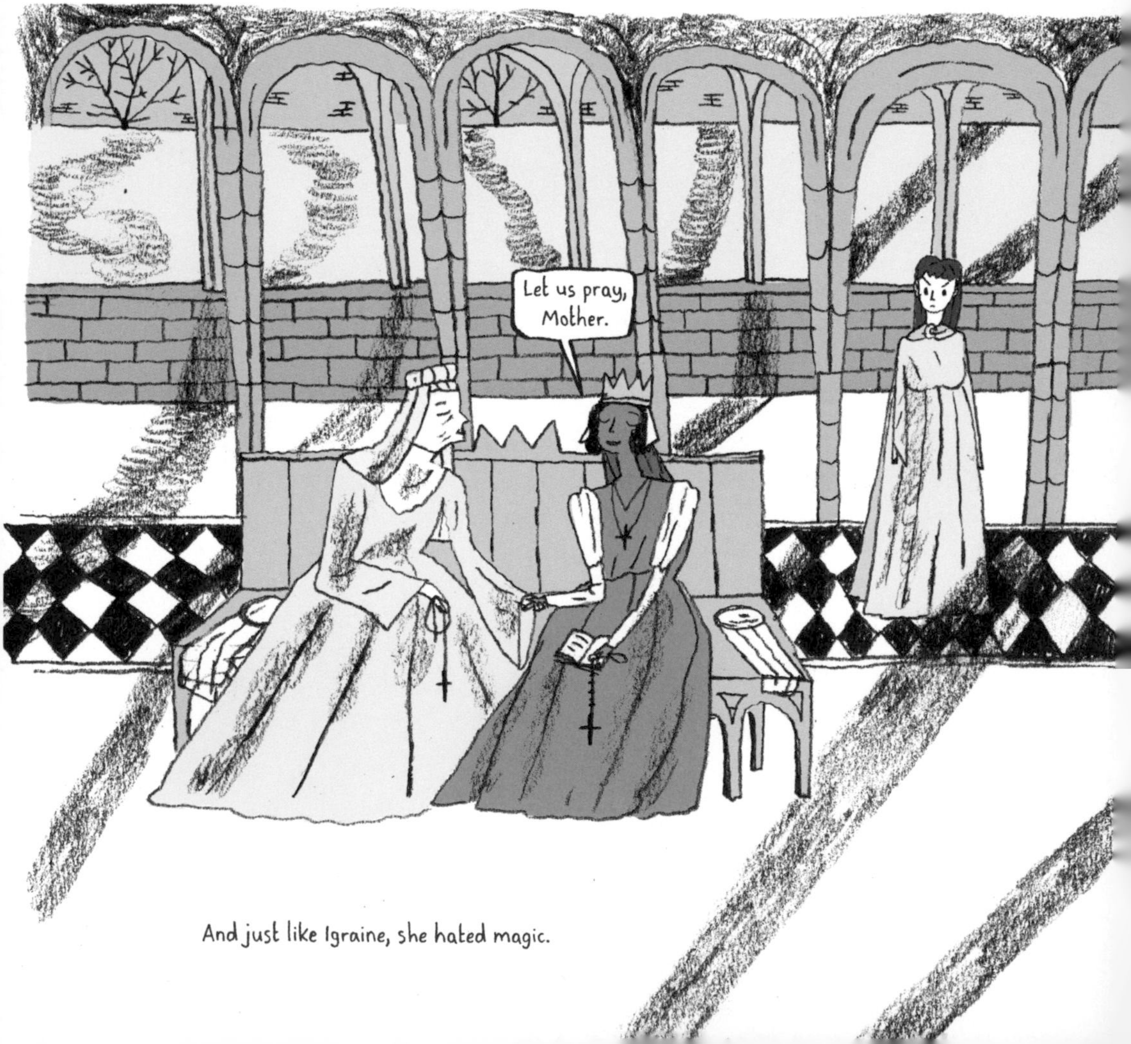
Let us pray, Mother.
And just like Igraine, she hated magic.

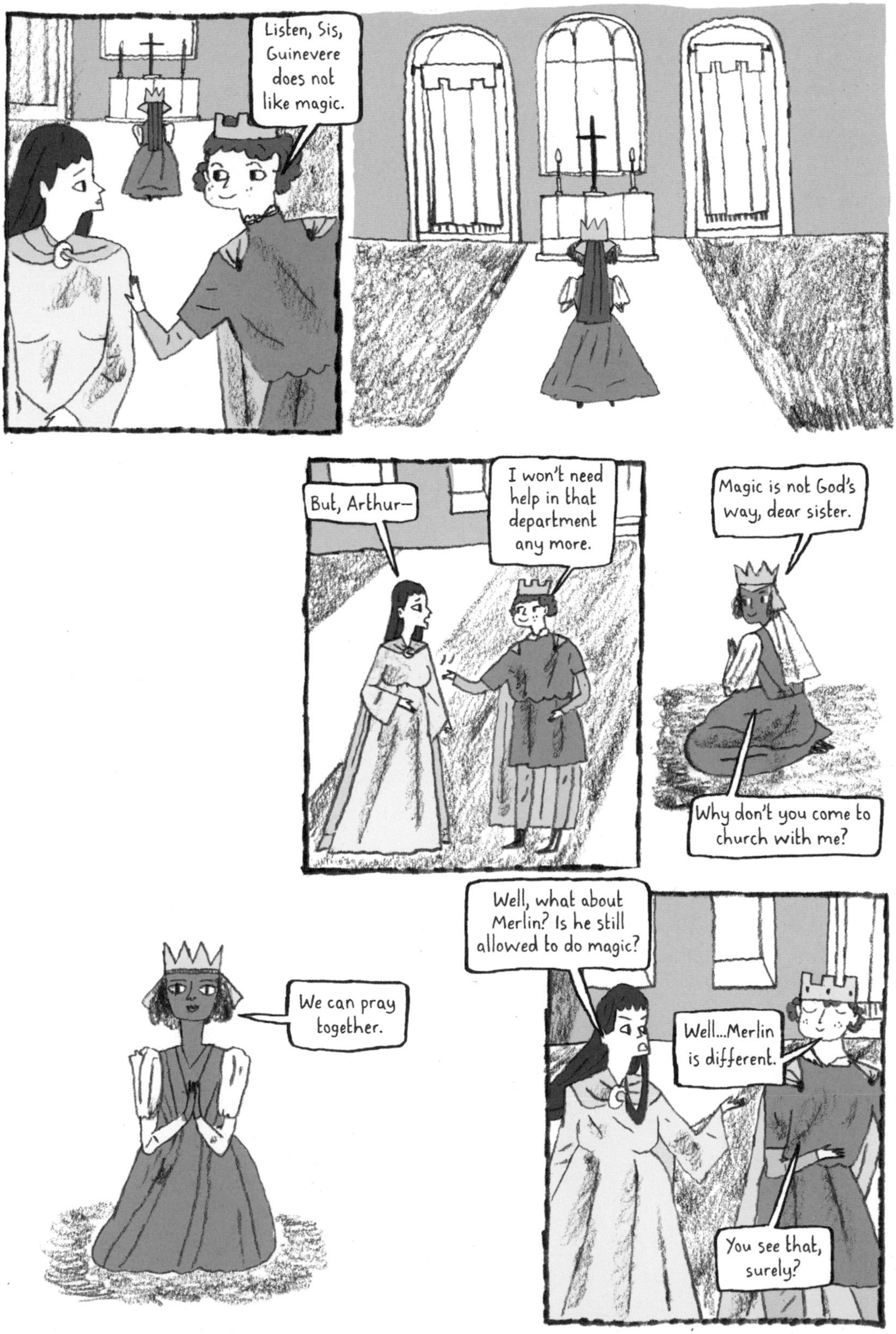
Listen, Sis, Guinevere does not like magic.
But, Arthur—
I won't need help in that department any more.
Magic is not God's way, dear sister.
Why don't you come to church with me?
We can pray together.
Well, what about Merlin? Is he still allowed to do magic?
Well...Merlin is different.
You see that, surely?

Morgan did not. In fact, try as she might, she found herself disliking Guinevere.

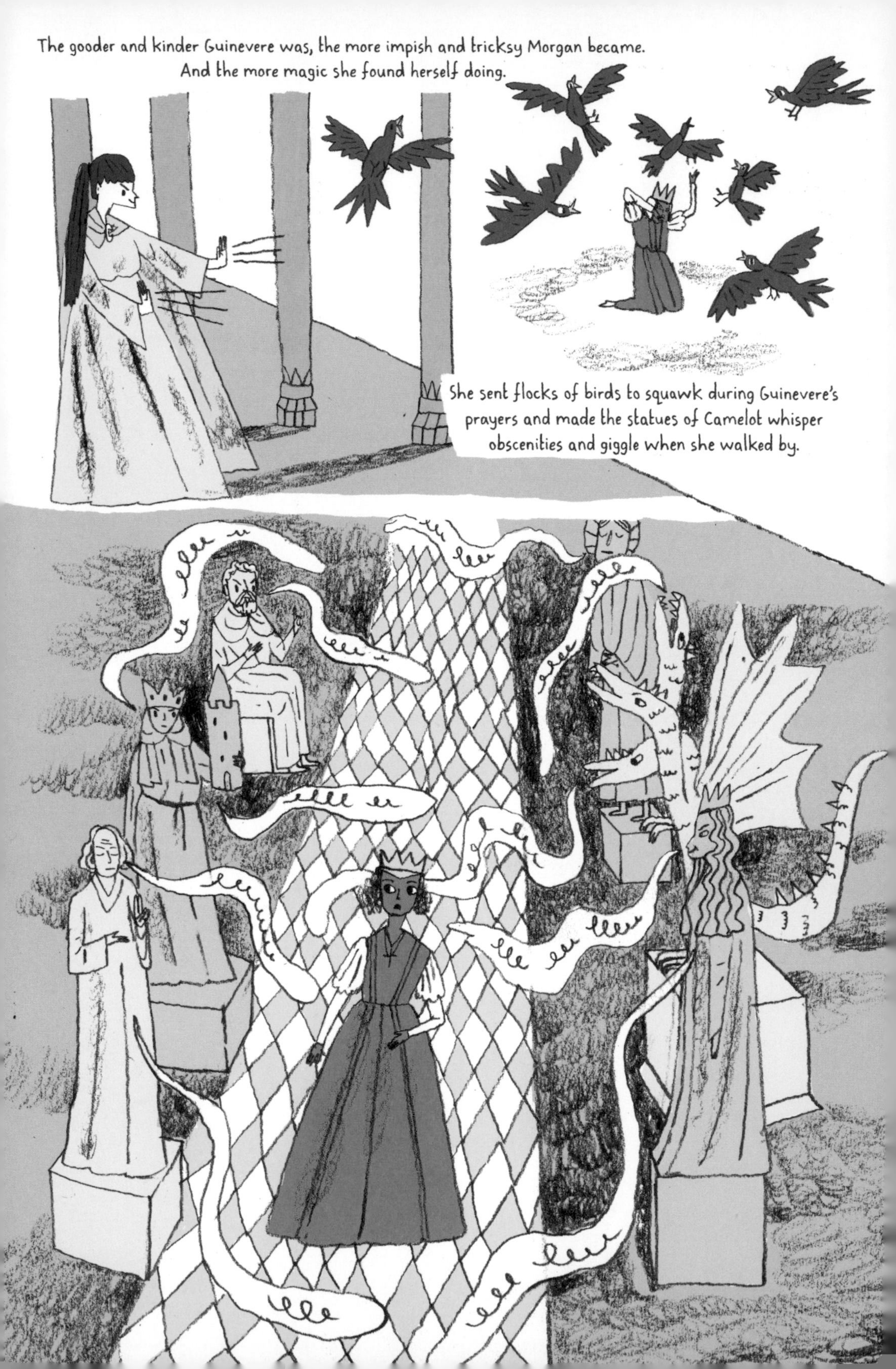
The gooder and kinder Guinevere was, the more impish and tricksy Morgan became. And the more magic she found herself doing.
She sent flocks of birds to squawk during Guinevere's prayers and made the statues of Camelot whisper obscenities and giggle when she walked by.

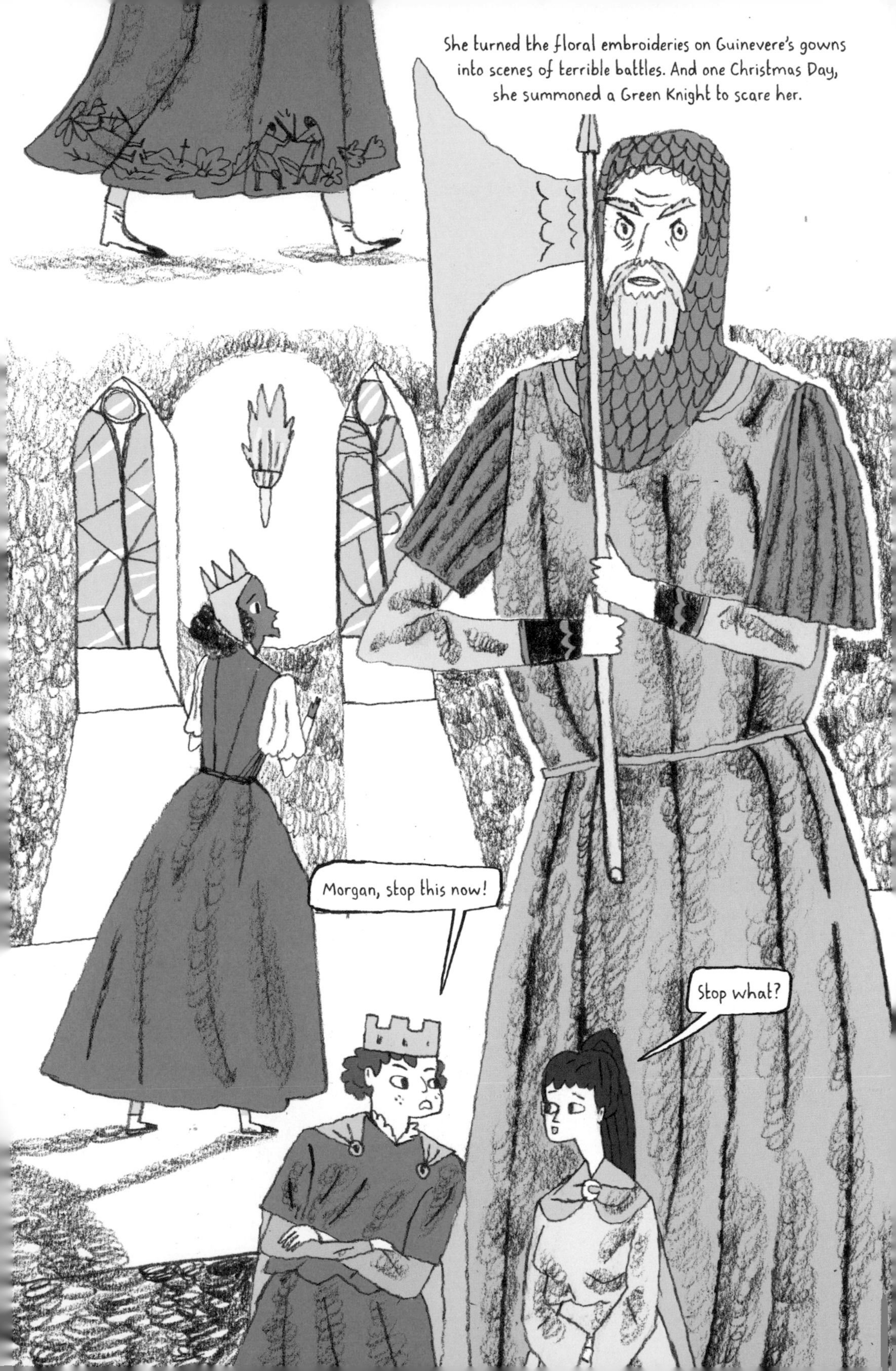
She turned the floral embroideries on Guinevere's gowns into scenes of terrible battles. And one Christmas Day, she summoned a Green Knight to scare her.
Morgan, stop this now!
Stop what?

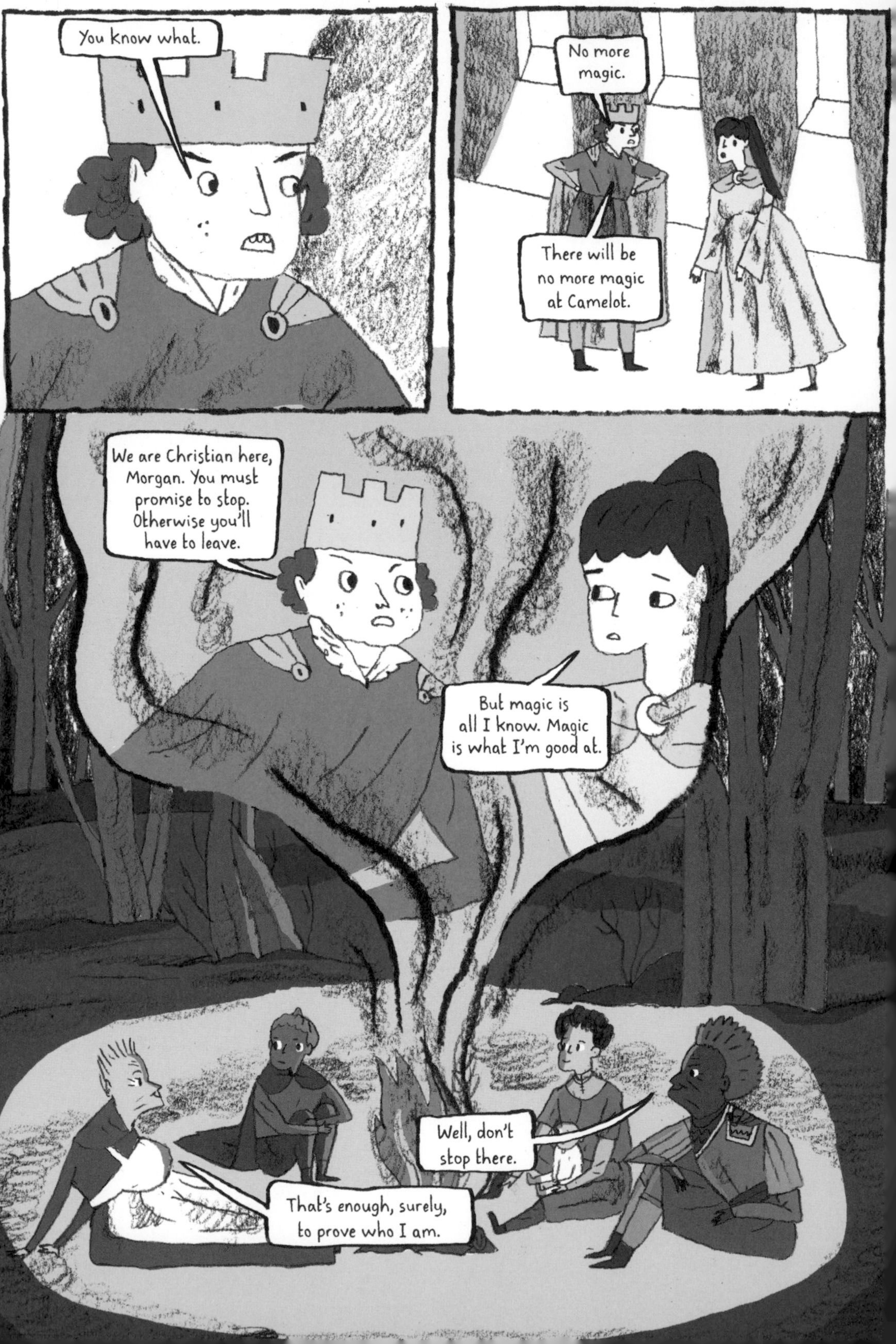
You know what.
No more magic.
There will be no more magic at Camelot.
We are Christian here, Morgan. You must promise to stop. Otherwise you'll have to leave.
But magic is all I know. Magic is what I'm good at.
Well, don't stop there.
That's enough, surely, to prove who I am.

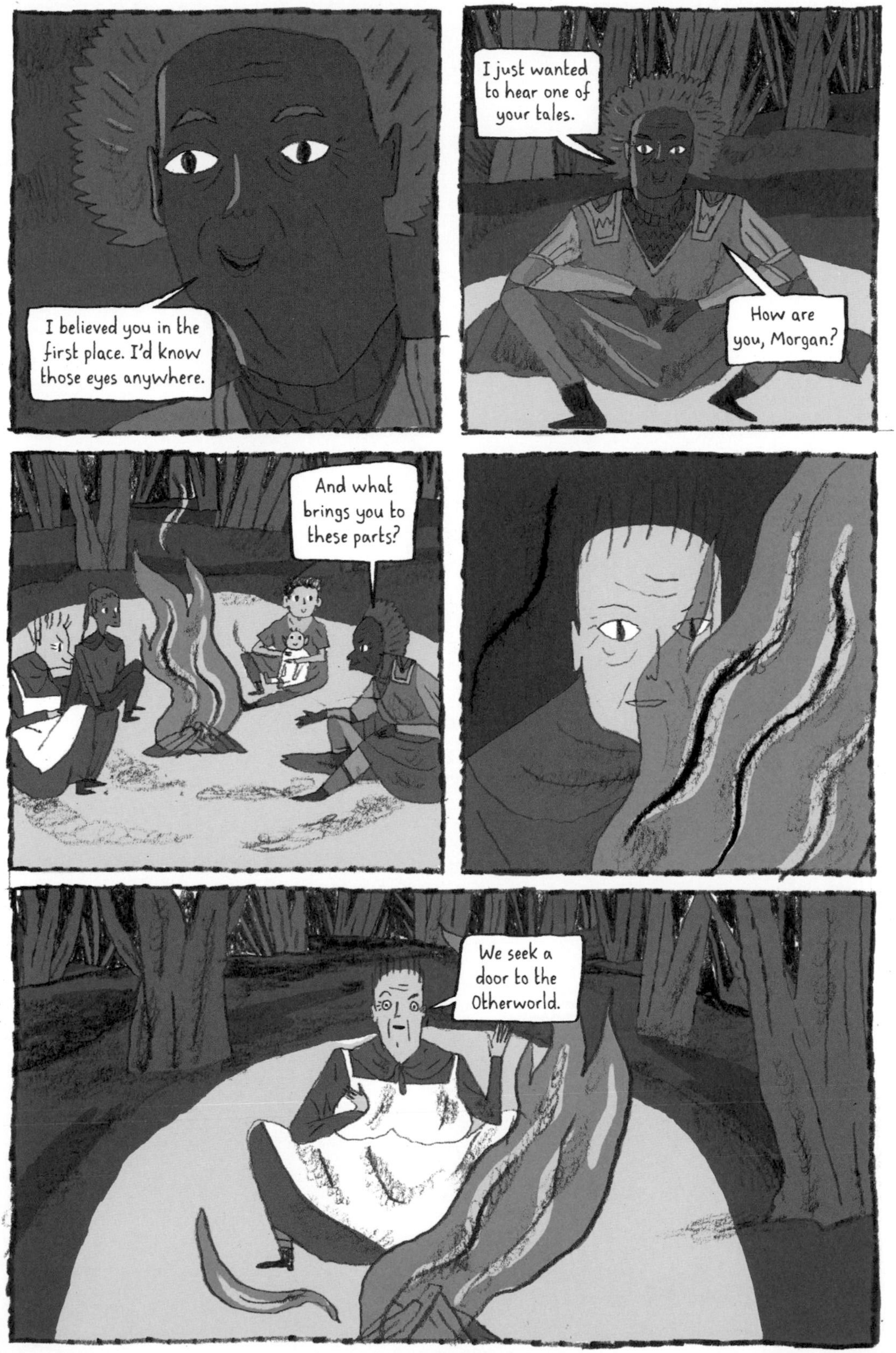
I believed you in the first place. I'd know those eyes anywhere.
I just wanted to hear one of your tales.
How are you, Morgan?
And what brings you to these parts?
We seek a door to the Otherworld.

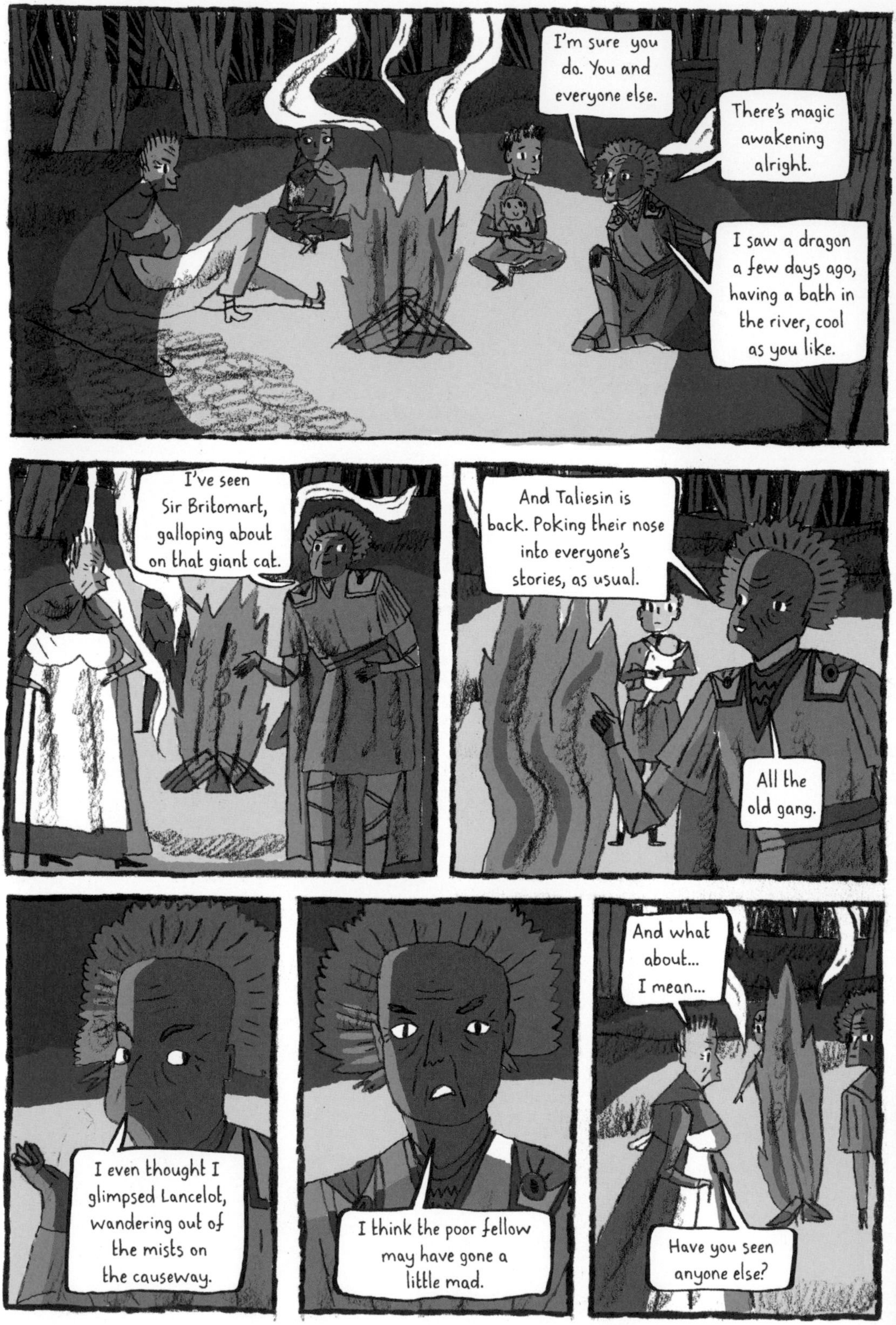
I'm sure you do. You and everyone else.
There's magic awakening alright.
I saw a dragon a few days ago, having a bath in the river, cool as you like.
I've seen Sir Britomart, galloping about on that giant cat.
And Taliesin is back. Poking their nose into everyone's stories, as usual.
All the old gang.
I even thought I glimpsed Lancelot, wandering out of the mists on the causeway.
I think the poor fellow may have gone a little mad.
And what about... I mean...
Have you seen anyone else?

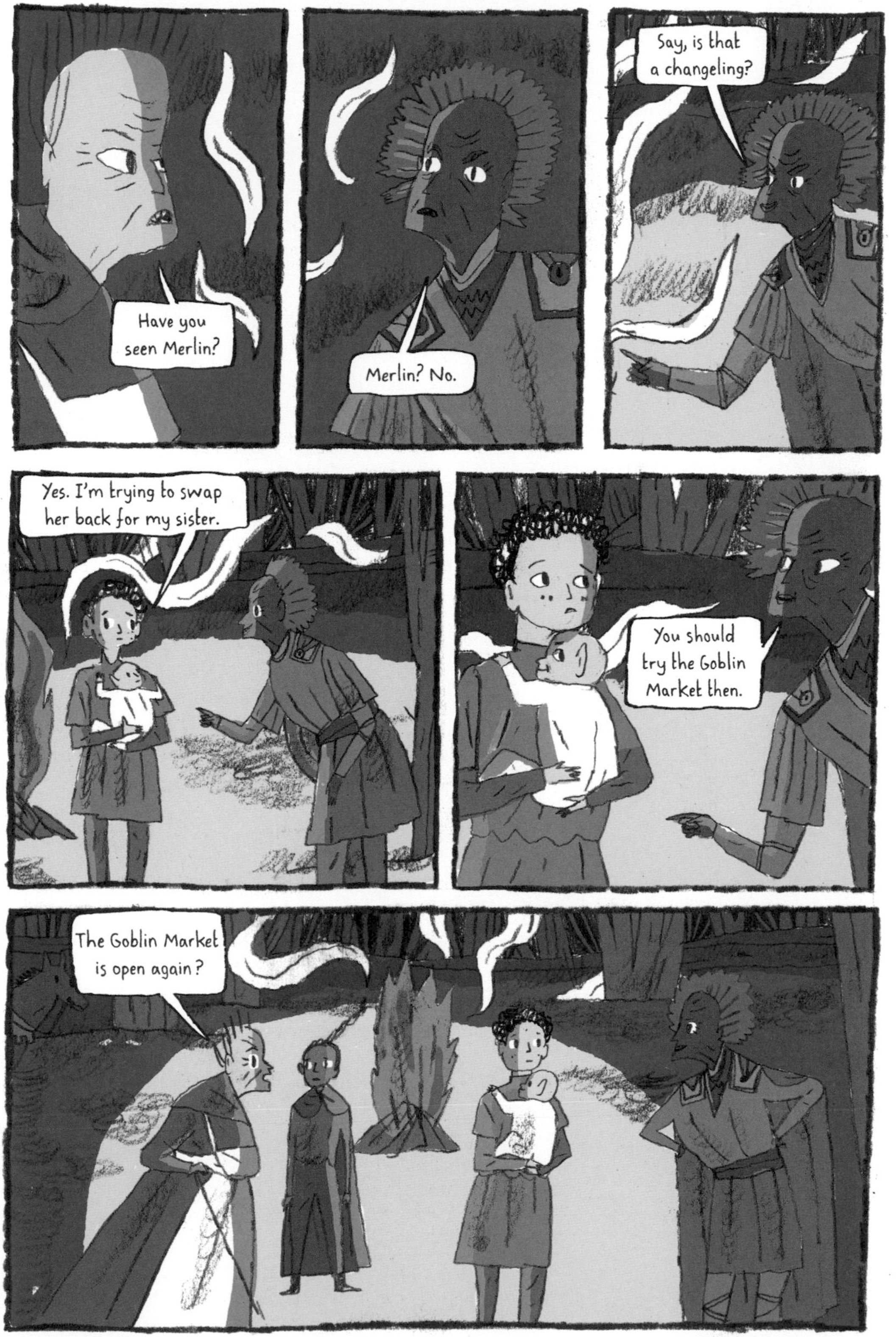
Have you seen Merlin?
Merlin? No.
Say, is that a changeling?
Yes. I'm trying to swap her back for my sister.
You should try the Goblin Market then.
The Goblin Market is open again?

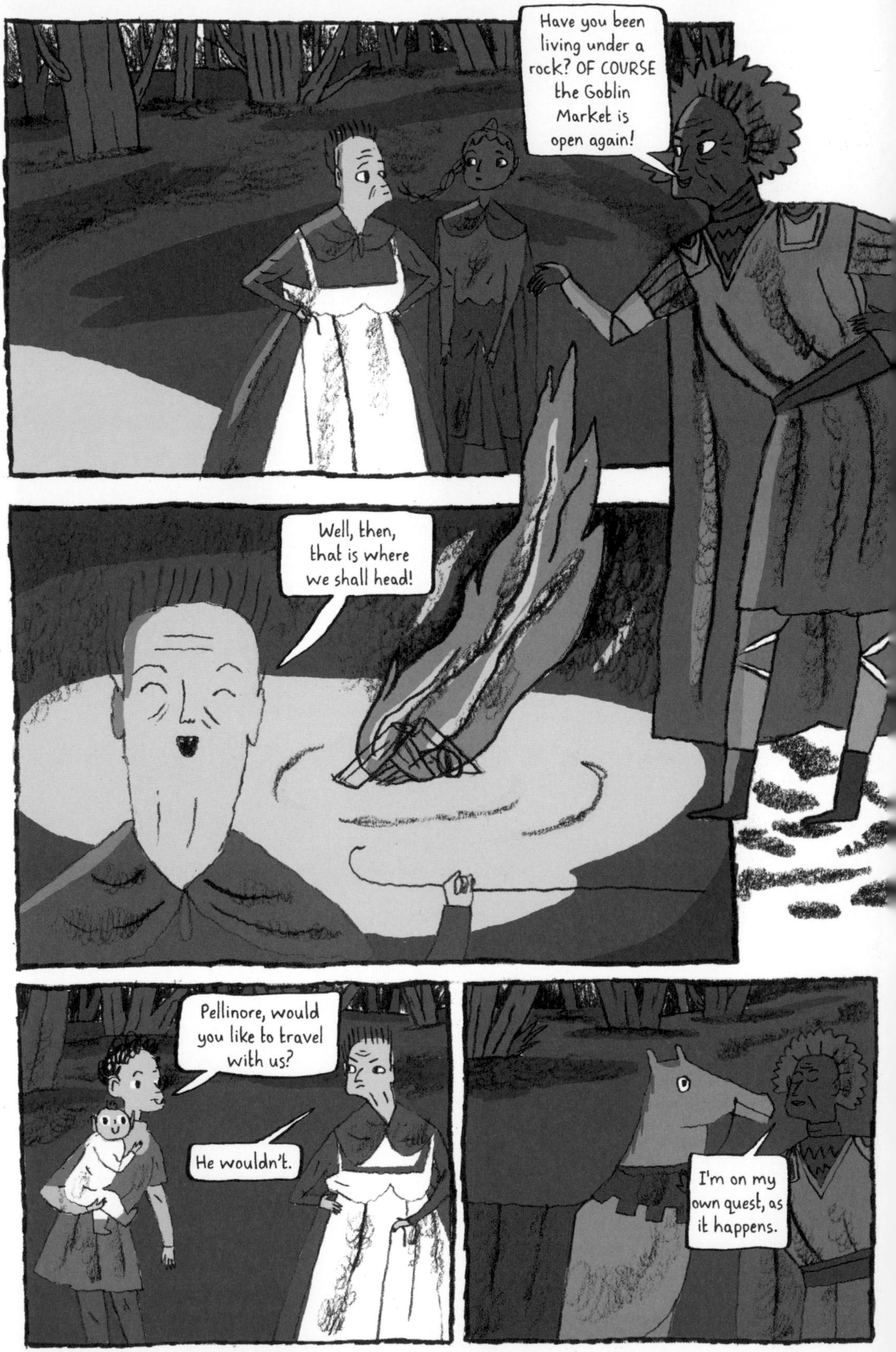
Have you been living under a rock? OF COURSE the Goblin Market is open again!
Well, then, that is where we shall head!
Pellinore, would you like to travel with us?
He wouldn't.
I'm on my own quest, as it happens.

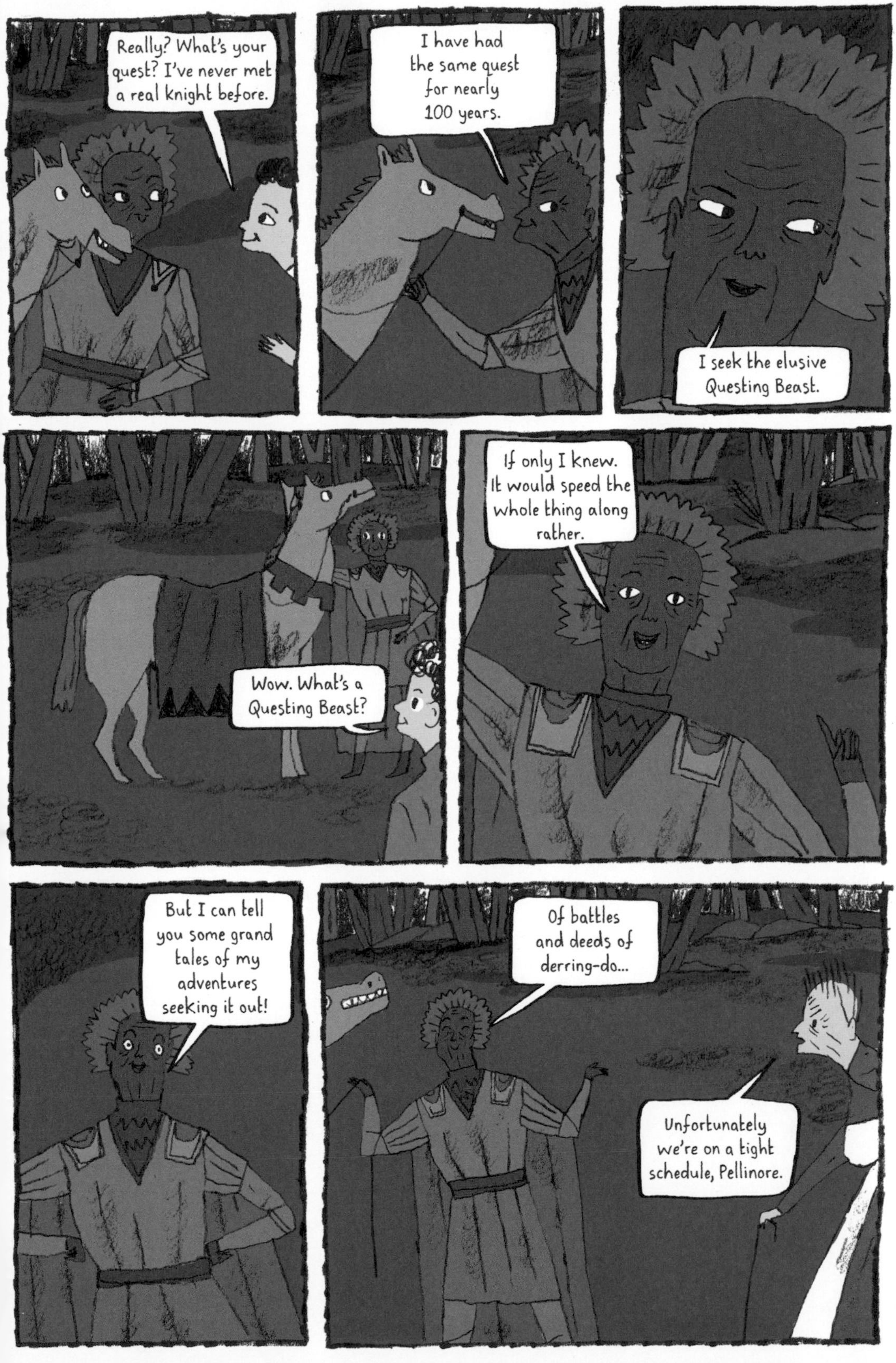

Really? What's your quest? I've never met a real knight before.
I have had the same quest for nearly 100 years.
I seek the elusive Questing Beast.
Wow. What's a Questing Beast?
If only I knew. It would speed the whole thing along rather.
But I can tell you some grand tales of my adventures seeking it out!
Of battles and deeds of derring-do...
Unfortunately we're on a tight schedule, Pellinore.

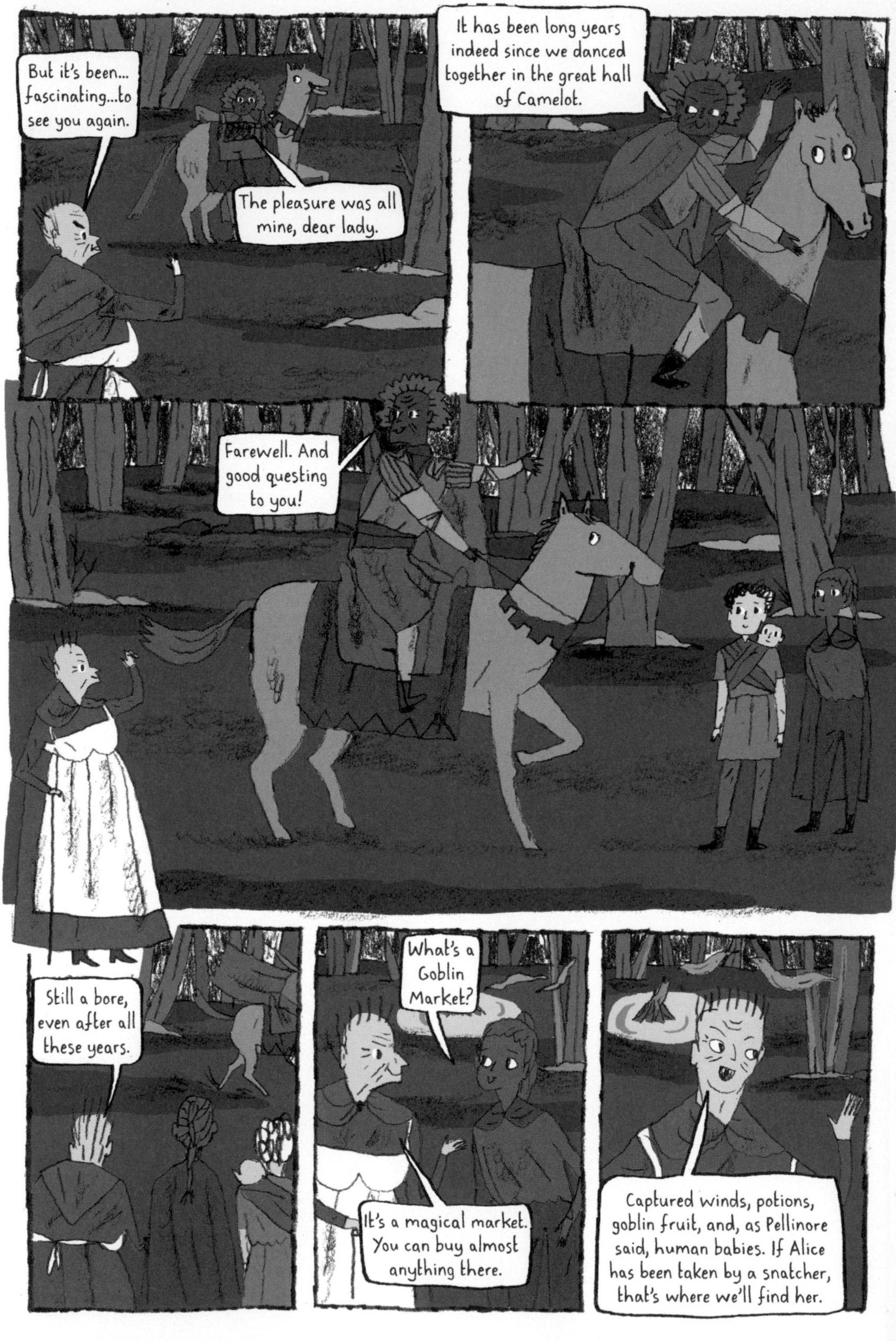
But it's been... fascinating...to see you again.
The pleasure was all mine, dear lady.
It has been long years indeed since we danced together in the great hall of Camelot.
Farewell. And good questing to you!
Still a bore, even after all these years.
What's a Goblin Market?
It's a magical market. You can buy almost anything there.
Captured winds, potions, goblin fruit, and, as Pellinore said, human babies. If Alice has been taken by a snatcher, that's where we'll find her.

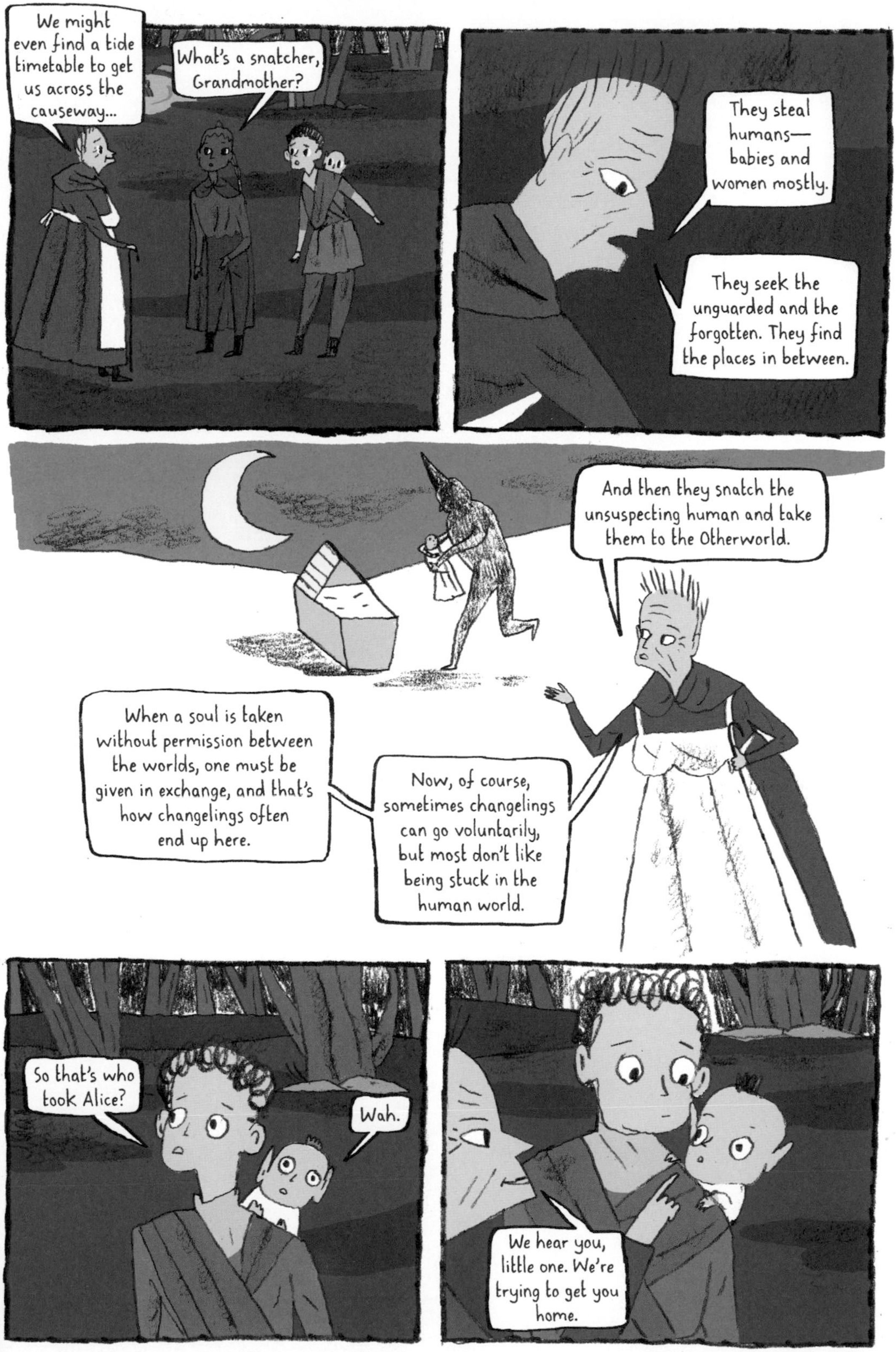

We might even find a tide timetable to get us across the causeway...
What's a snatcher, Grandmother?
They steal humans—babies and women mostly.
They seek the unguarded and the forgotten. They find the places in between.
And then they snatch the unsuspecting human and take them to the Otherworld.
When a soul is taken without permission between the worlds, one must be given in exchange, and that's how changelings often end up here.
Now, of course, sometimes changelings can go voluntarily, but most don't like being stuck in the human world.
So that's who took Alice?
Wah.
We hear you, little one. We're trying to get you home.

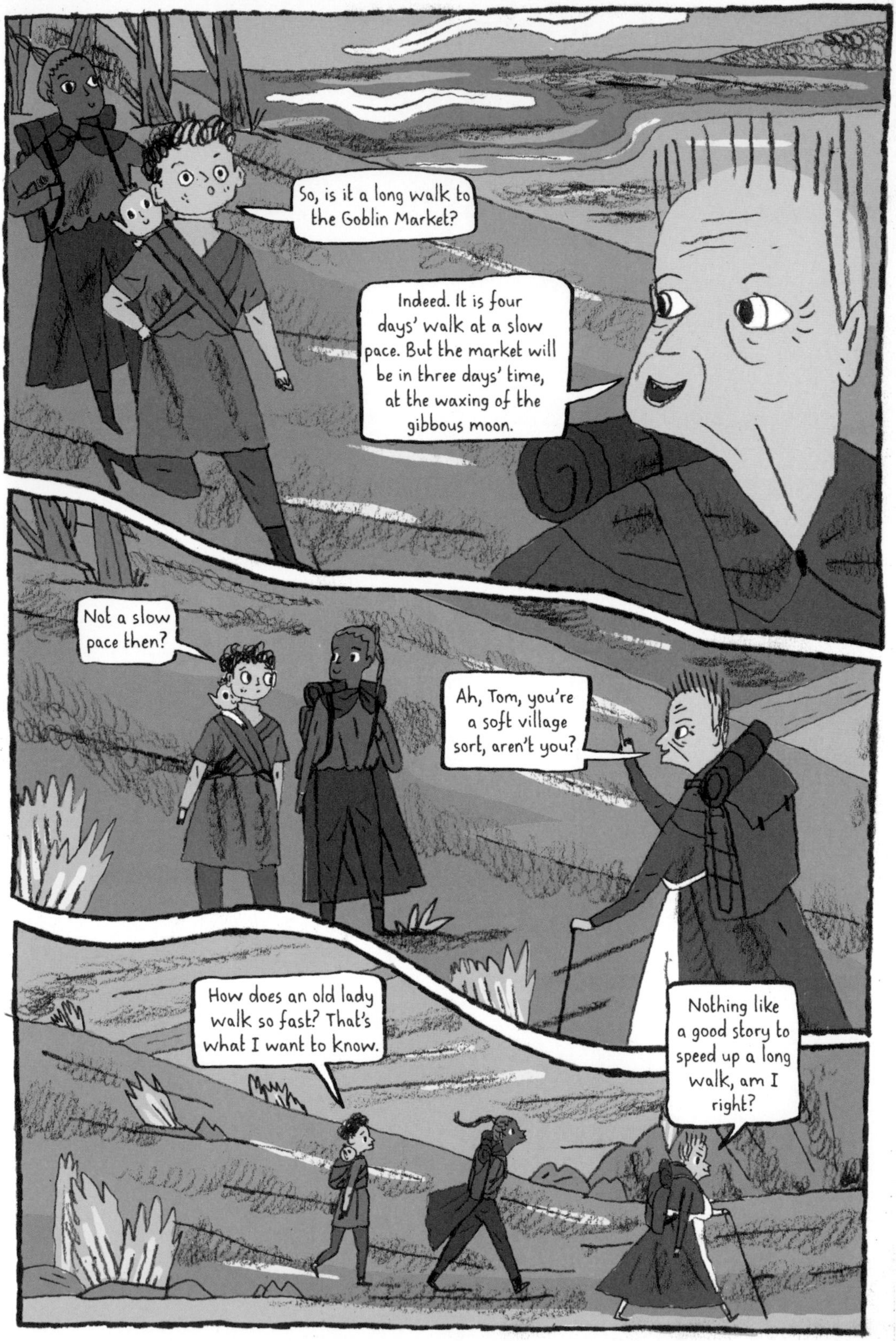
So, is it a long walk to the Goblin Market?
Indeed. It is four days' walk at a slow pace. But the market will be in three days' time, at the waxing of the gibbous moon.
Not a slow pace then?
Ah, Tom, you're a soft village sort, aren't you?
How does an old lady walk so fast? That's what I want to know.
Nothing like a good story to speed up a long walk, am I right?

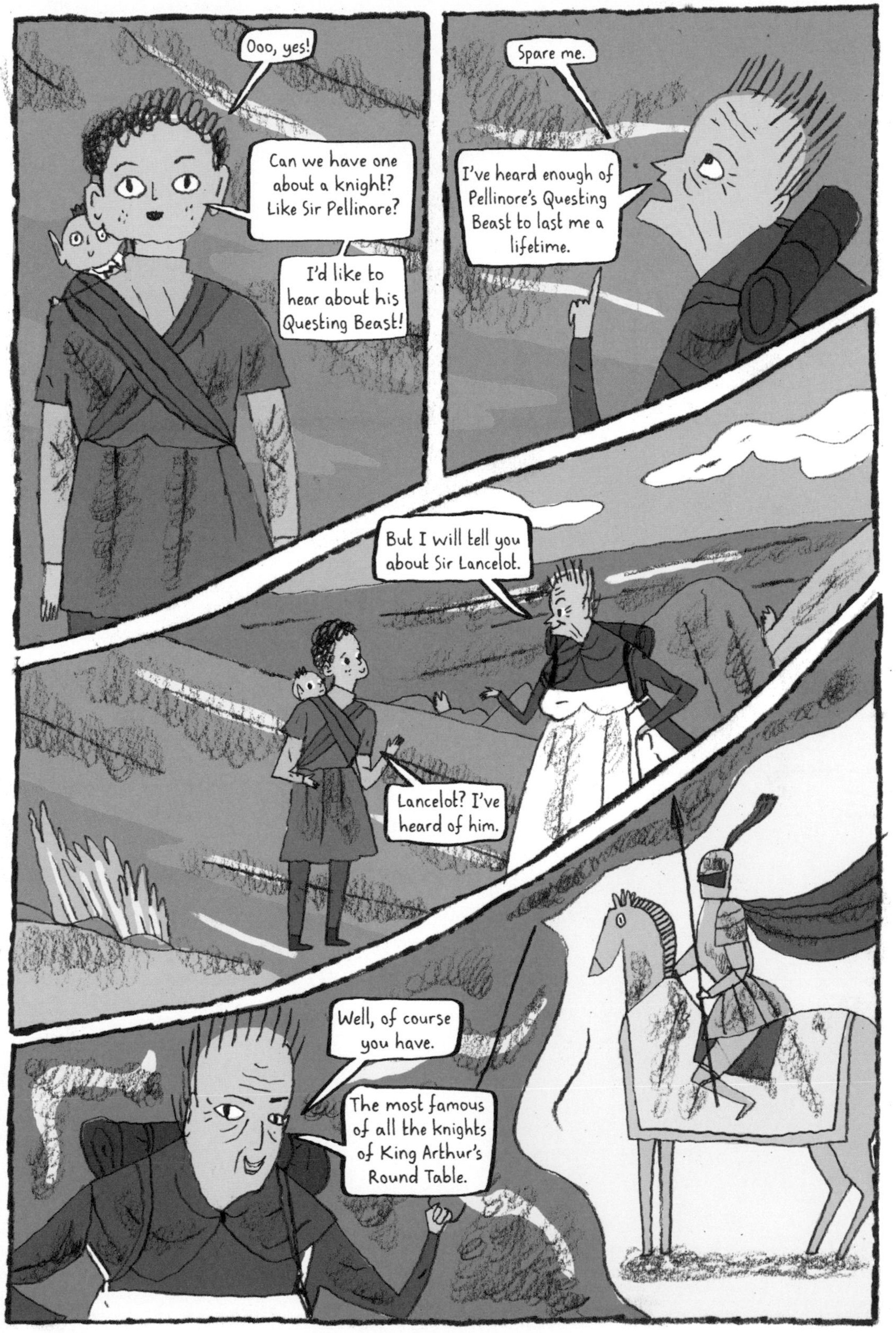
Ooo, yes!
Can we have one about a knight? Like Sir Pellinore?
I'd like to hear about his Questing Beast!
Spare me.
I've heard enough of Pellinore's Questing Beast to last me a lifetime.
But I will tell you about Sir Lancelot.
Lancelot? I've heard of him.
Well, of course you have.
The most famous of all the knights of King Arthur's Round Table.

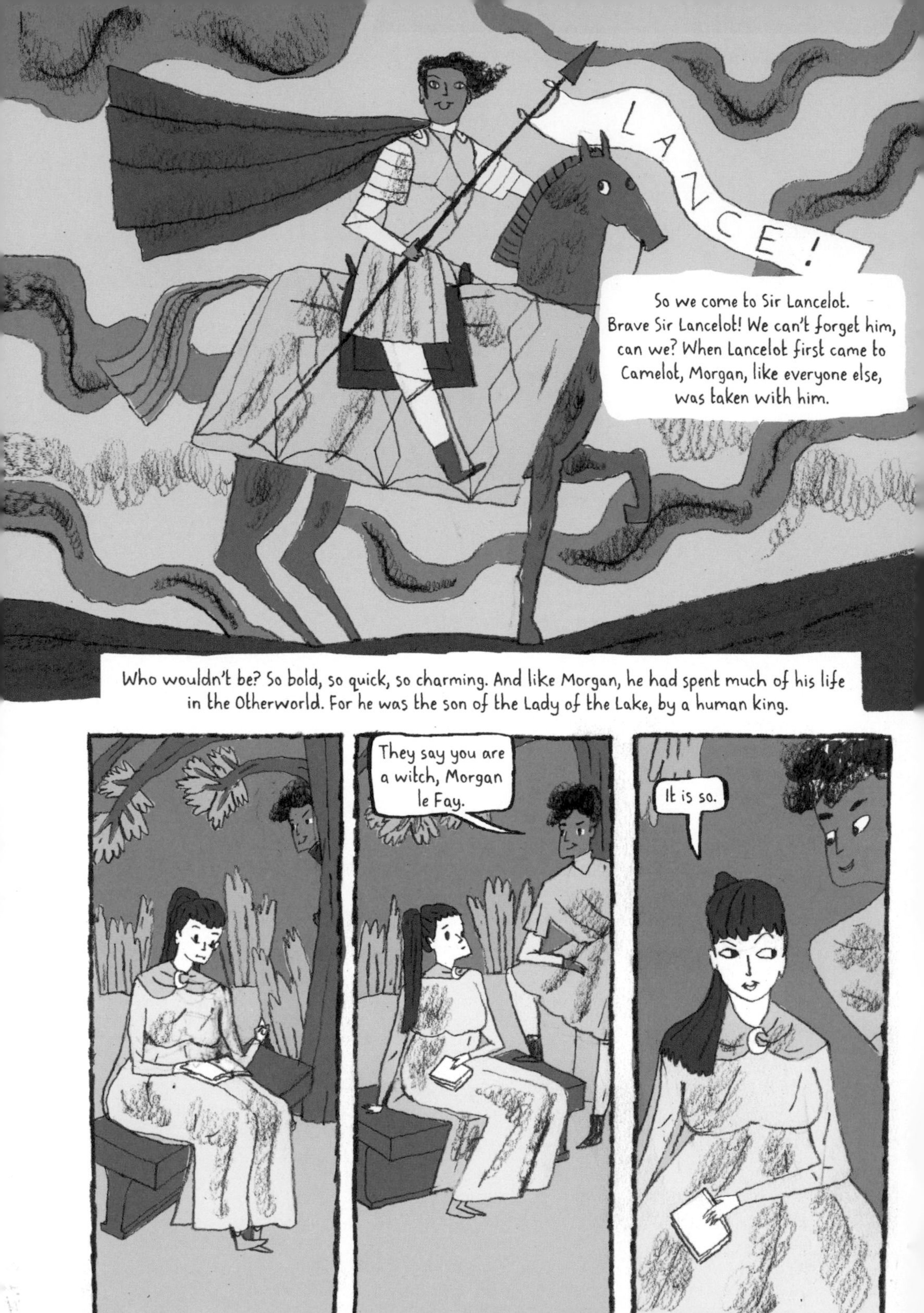
LANCE!
So we come to Sir Lancelot. Brave Sir Lancelot! We can't forget him, can we? When Lancelot first came to Camelot, Morgan, like everyone else, was taken with him.
Who wouldn't be? So bold, so quick, so charming. And like Morgan, he had spent much of his life in the Otherworld. For he was the son of the Lady of the Lake, by a human king.
They say you are a witch, Morgan le Fay.
It is so.

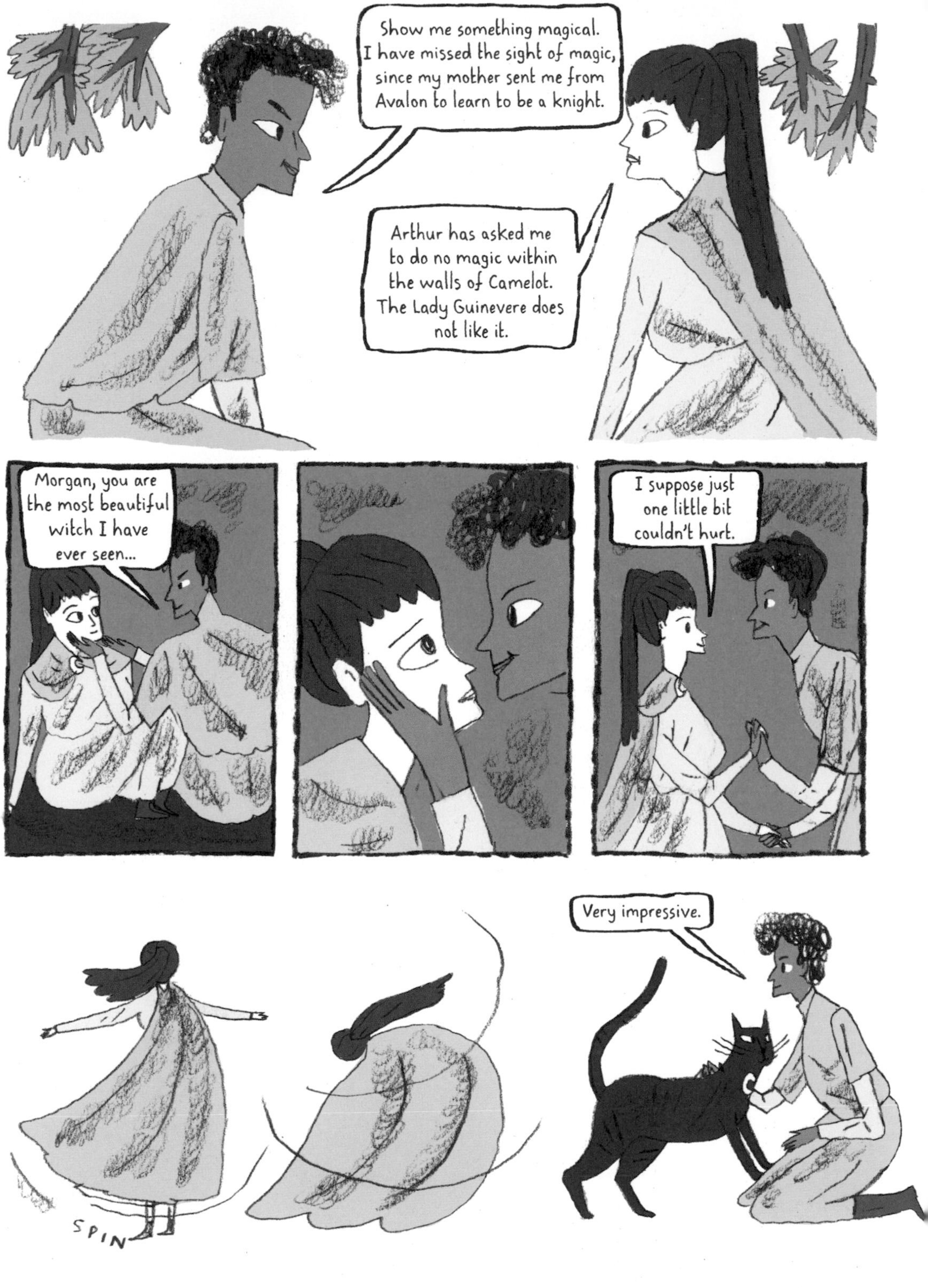
Show me something magical. I have missed the sight of magic, since my mother sent me from Avalon to learn to be a knight.
Arthur has asked me to do no magic within the walls of Camelot. The Lady Guinevere does not like it.
Morgan, you are the most beautiful witch I have ever seen...
I suppose just one little bit couldn't hurt.
SPIN
Very impressive.

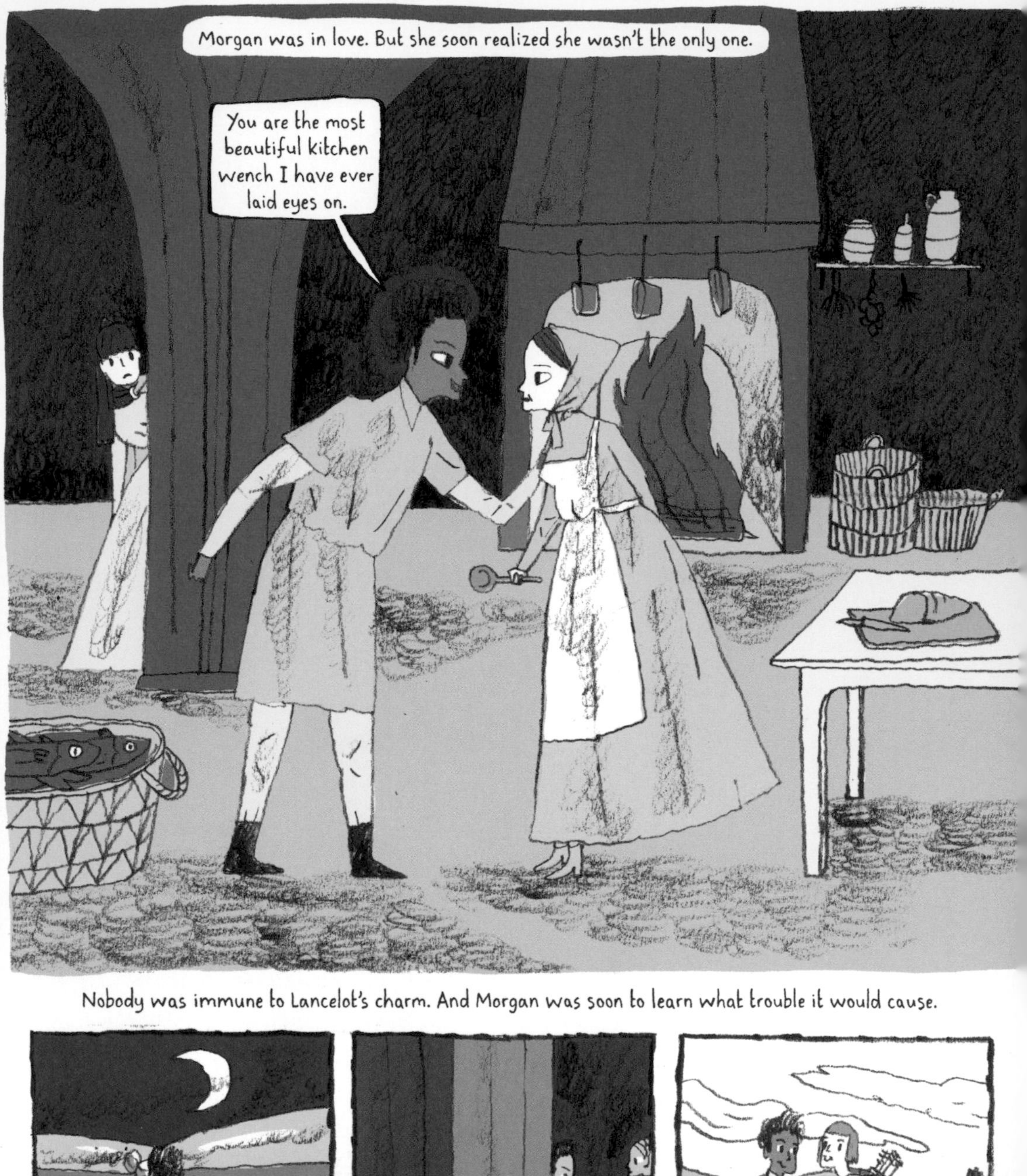
Morgan was in love. But she soon realized she wasn't the only one.
You are the most beautiful kitchen wench I have ever laid eyes on.

Nobody was immune to Lancelot's charm. And Morgan was soon to learn what trouble it would cause.

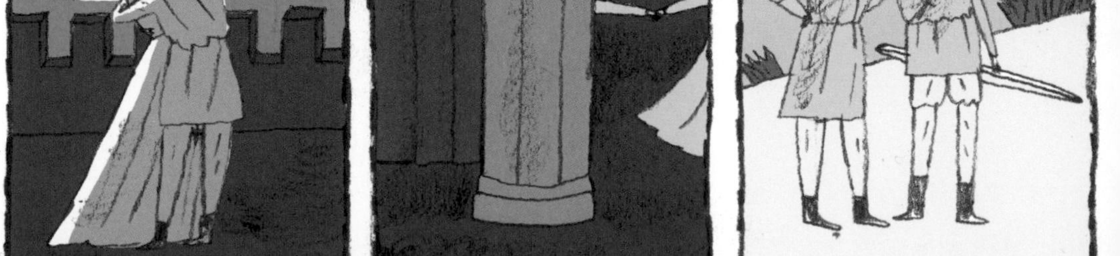

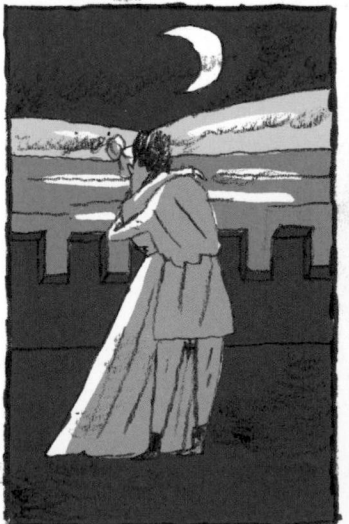

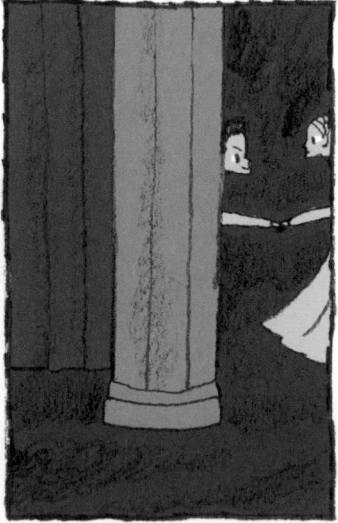

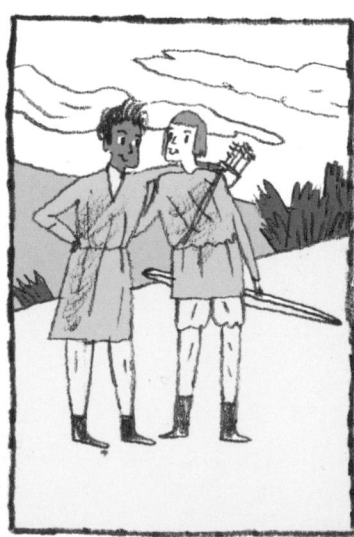

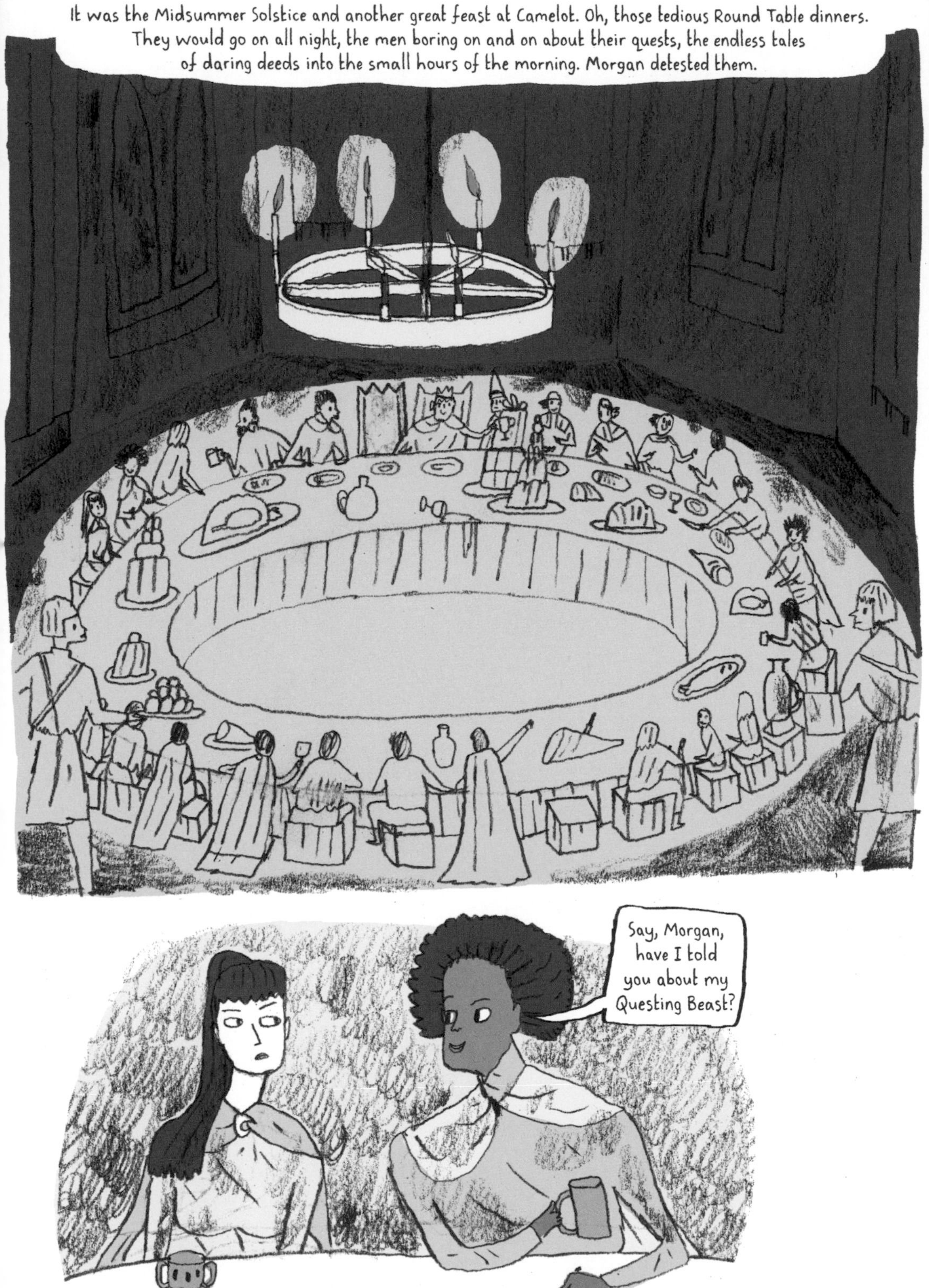
It was the Midsummer Solstice and another great feast at Camelot. Oh, those tedious Round Table dinners. They would go on all night, the men boring on and on about their quests, the endless tales of daring deeds into the small hours of the morning. Morgan detested them.
Say, Morgan, have I told you about my Questing Beast?

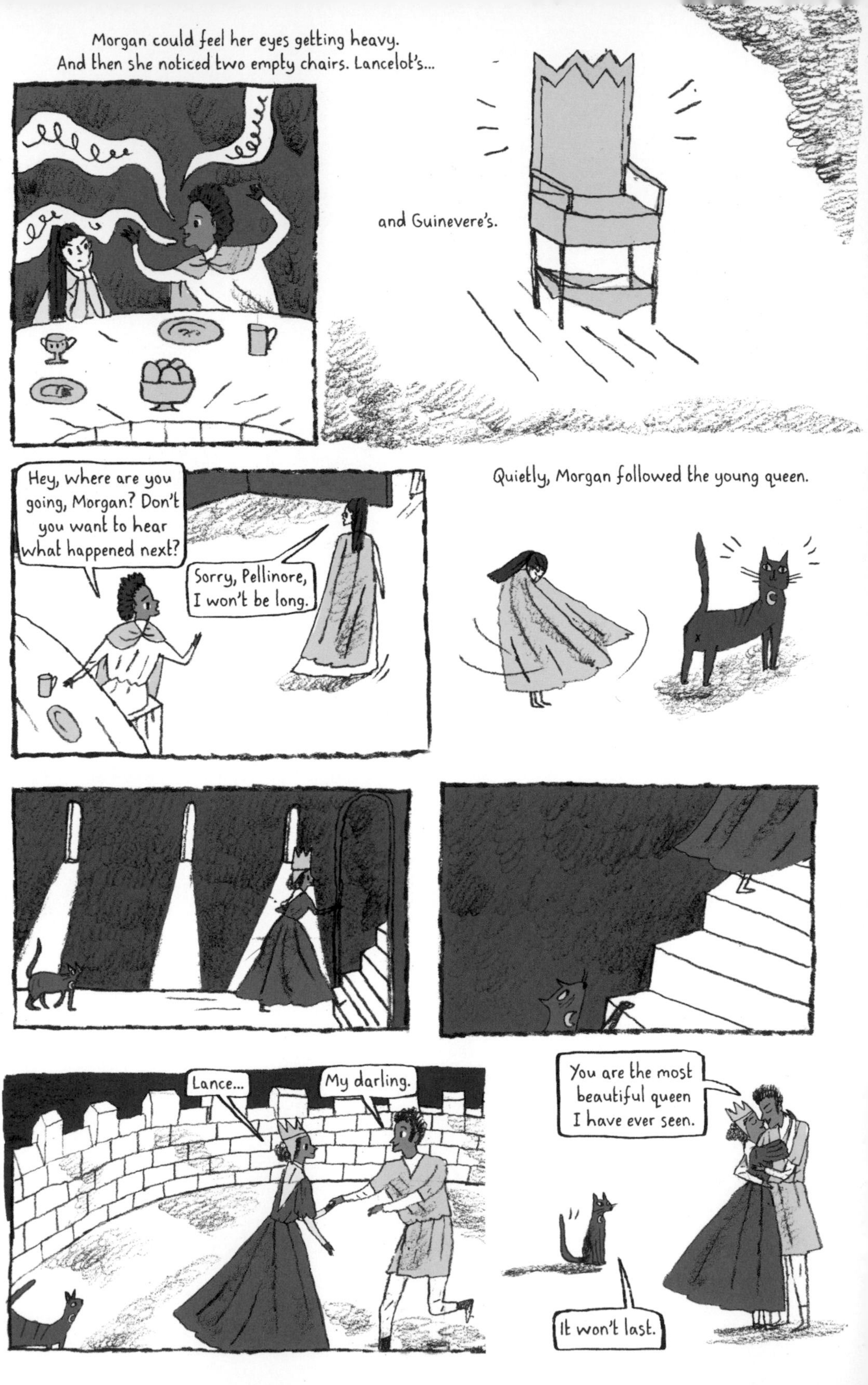
Morgan could feel her eyes getting heavy.
And then she noticed two empty chairs. Lancelot's...
and Guinevere's.
Hey, where are you going, Morgan? Don't you want to hear what happened next?
Sorry, Pellinore, I won't be long.
Quietly, Morgan followed the young queen.
Lance...
My darling.
You are the most beautiful queen I have ever seen.
It won't last.

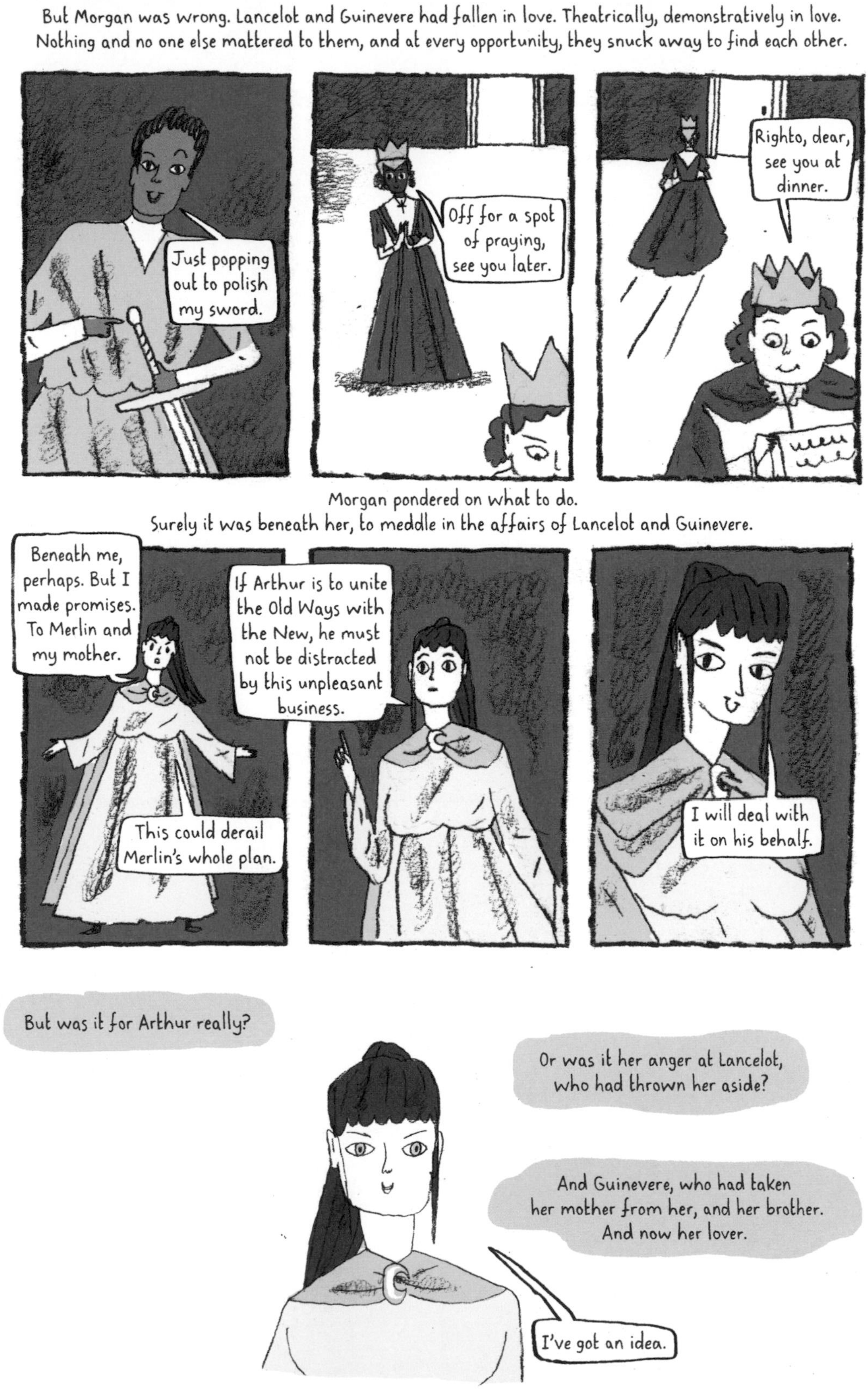
But Morgan was wrong. Lancelot and Guinevere had fallen in love. Theatrically, demonstratively in love. Nothing and no one else mattered to them, and at every opportunity, they snuck away to find each other.
Just popping out to polish my sword.
Off for a spot of praying, see you later.
Righto, dear, see you at dinner.
Morgan pondered on what to do. Surely it was beneath her, to meddle in the affairs of Lancelot and Guinevere.
Beneath me, perhaps. But I made promises. To Merlin and my mother.
This could derail Merlin's whole plan.
If Arthur is to unite the Old Ways with the New, he must not be distracted by this unpleasant business.
I will deal with it on his behalf.
But was it for Arthur really?
Or was it her anger at Lancelot, who had thrown her aside?
And Guinevere, who had taken her mother from her, and her brother. And now her lover.
I've got an idea.

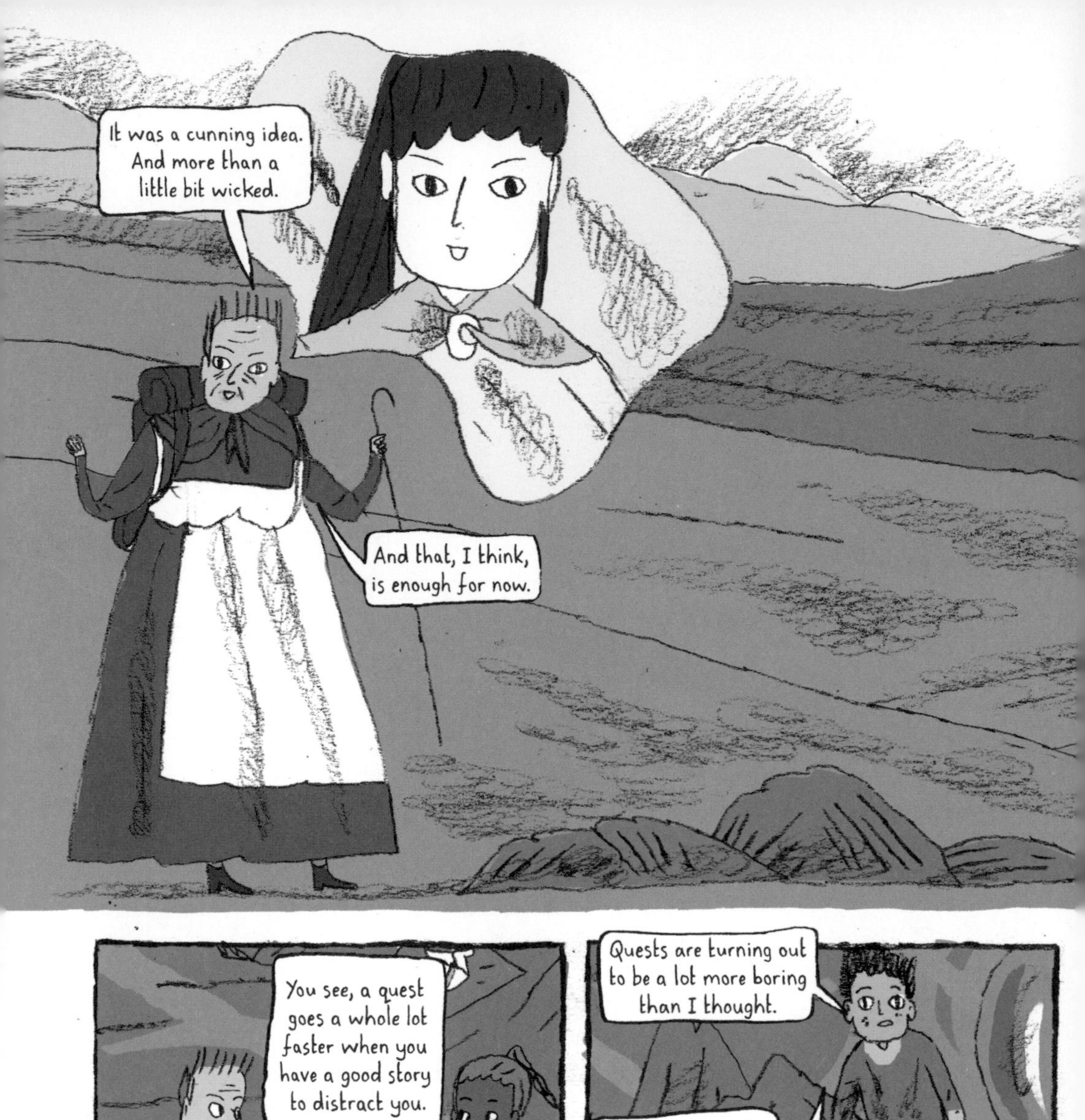
It was a cunning idea. And more than a little bit wicked.
And that, I think, is enough for now.

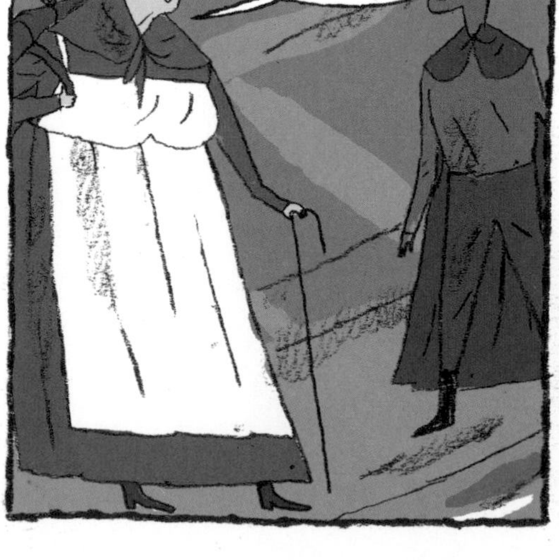
You see, a quest goes a whole lot faster when you have a good story to distract you.

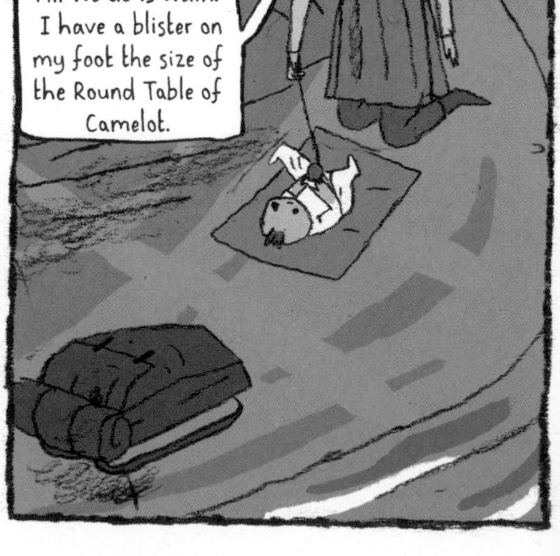
Quests are turning out to be a lot more boring than I thought.
All we do is walk. I have a blister on my foot the size of the Round Table of Camelot.

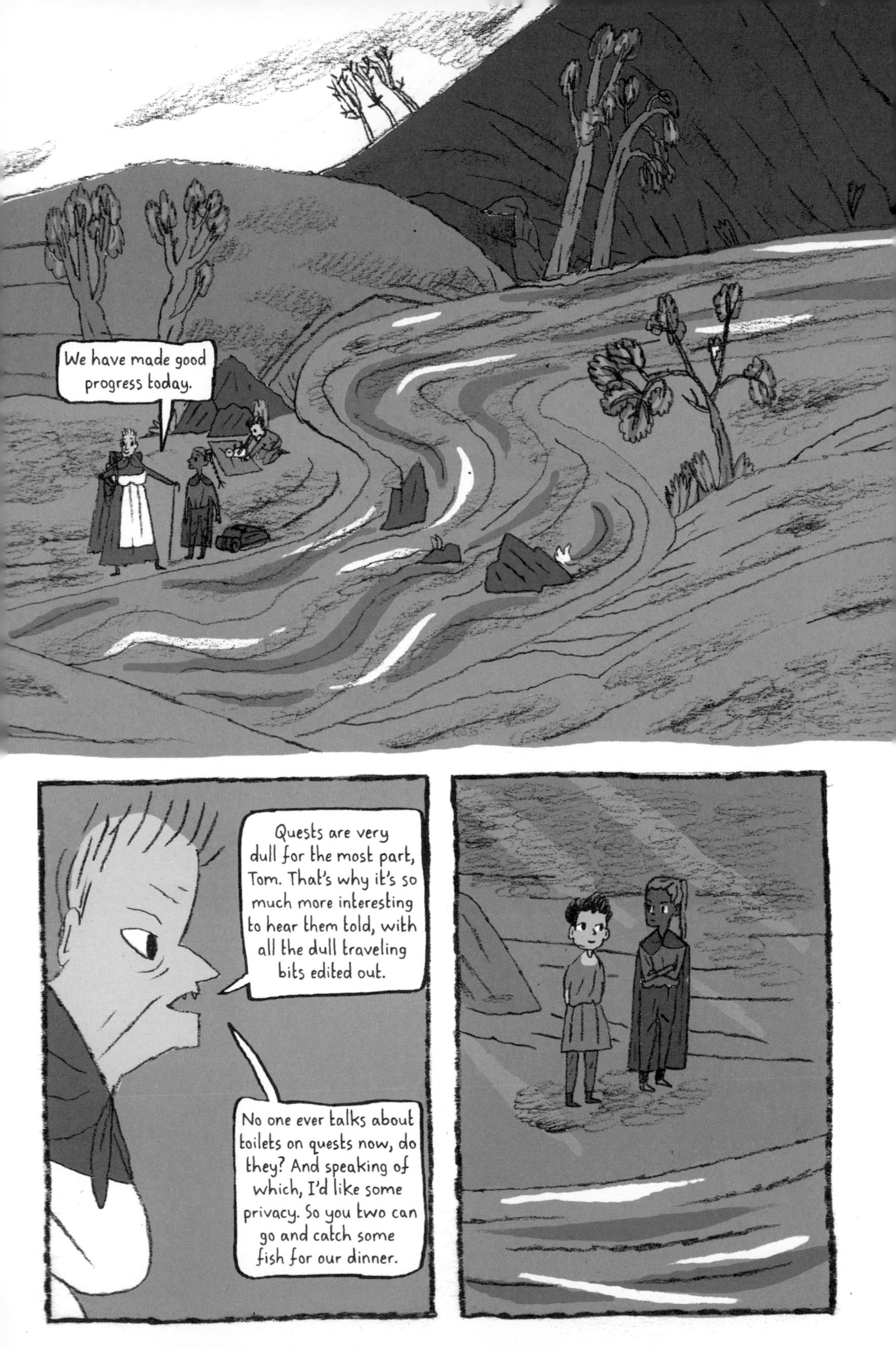

We have made good progress today.
Quests are very dull for the most part, Tom. That's why it's so much more interesting to hear them told, with all the dull traveling bits edited out.
No one ever talks about toilets on quests now, do they? And speaking of which, I'd like some privacy. So you two can go and catch some fish for our dinner.

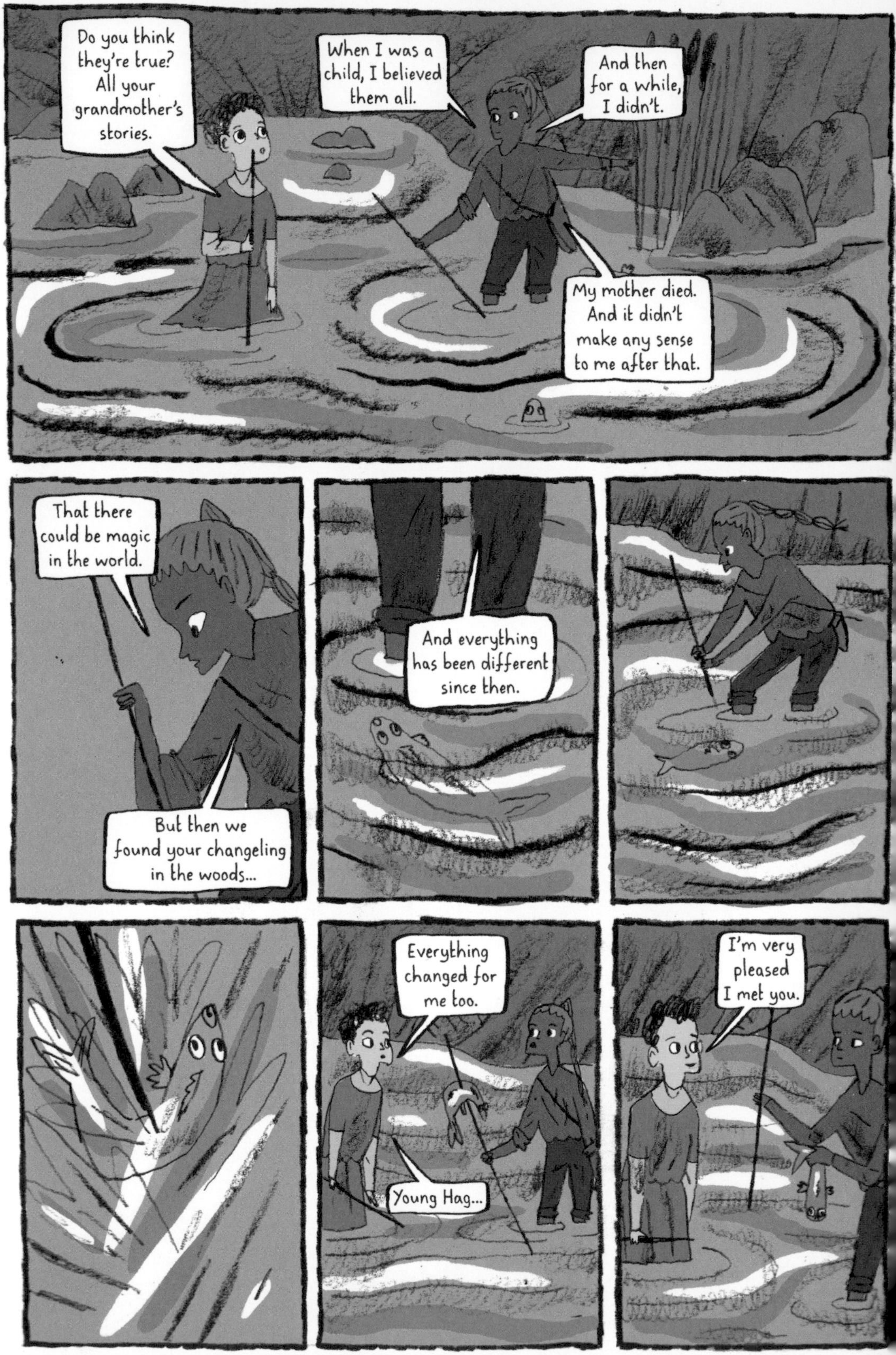
Do you think they're true? All your grandmother's stories.
When I was a child, I believed them all.
And then for a while, I didn't.
My mother died. And it didn't make any sense to me after that.
That there could be magic in the world.
But then we found your changeling in the woods...
And everything has been different since then.
Everything changed for me too.
Young Hag...
I'm very pleased I met you.

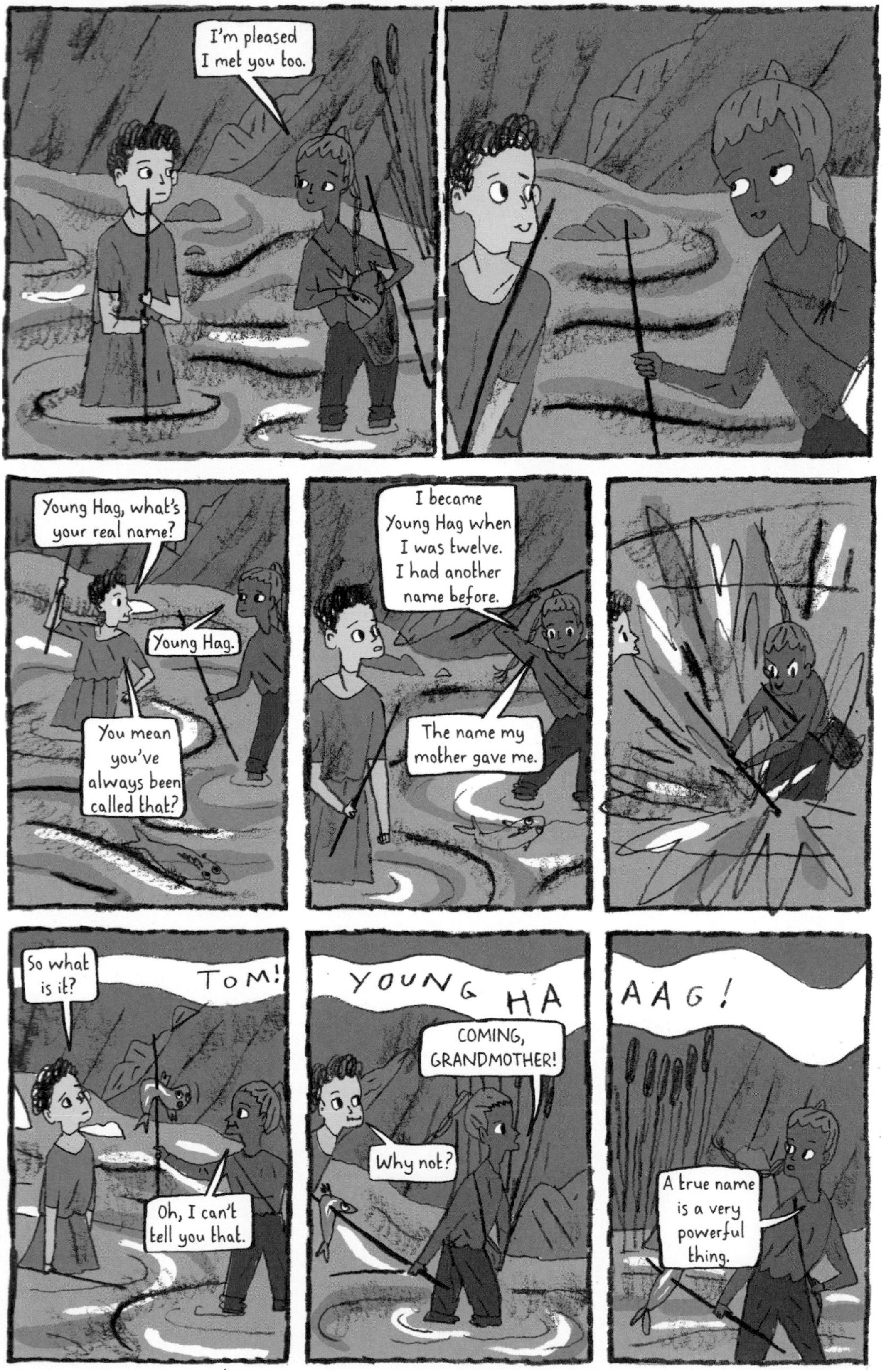
I'm pleased I met you too.
Young Hag, what's your real name?
Young Hag.
You mean you've always been called that?
I became Young Hag when I was twelve. I had another name before.
The name my mother gave me.
So what is it?
TOM!
Oh, I can't tell you that.
YOUNG HA
COMING, GRANDMOTHER!
Why not?
AAG!
A true name is a very powerful thing.

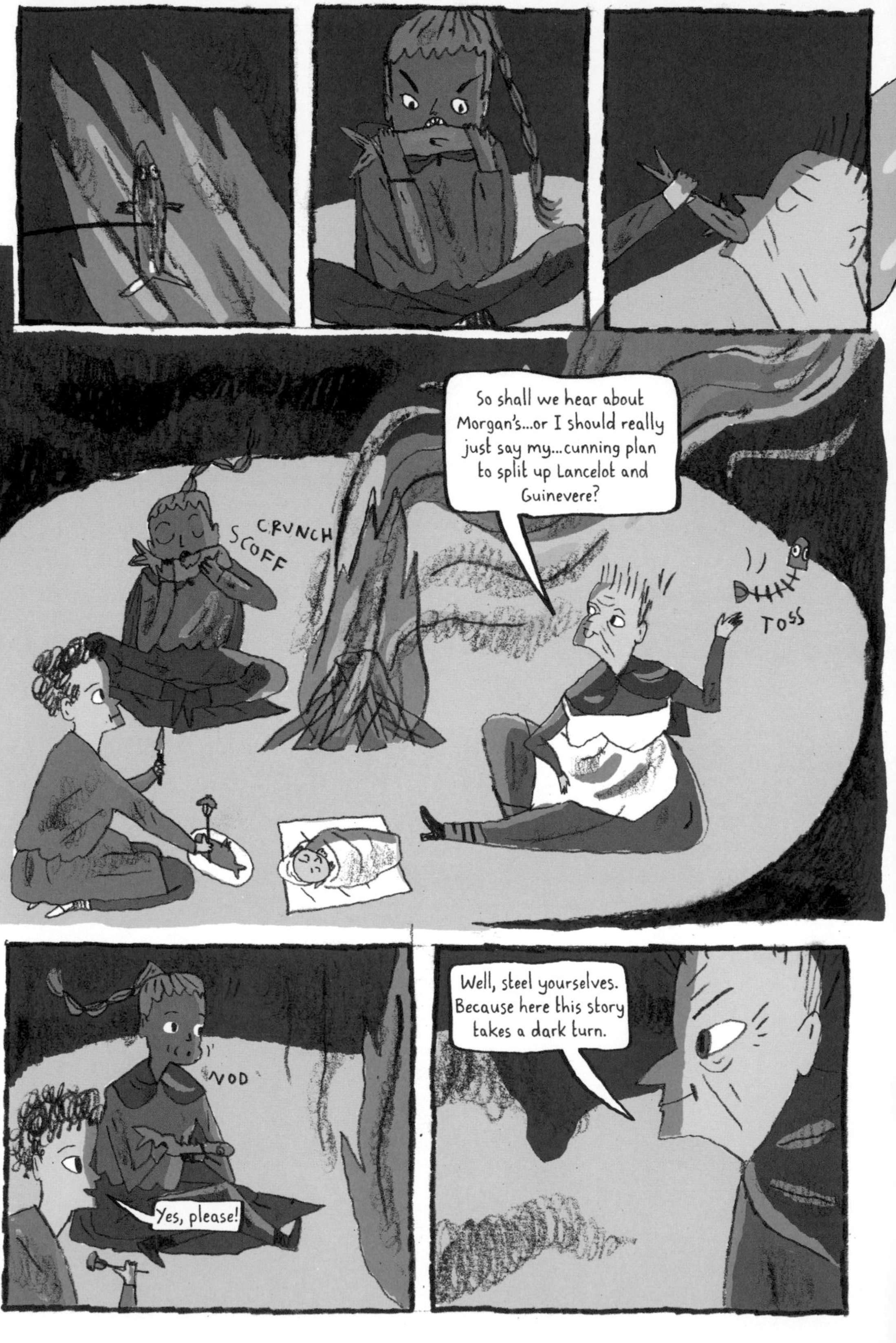
CRUNCH
SCOFF
So shall we hear about Morgan's...or I should really just say my...cunning plan to split up Lancelot and Guinevere?
TOSS
NOD
Yes, please!
Well, steel yourselves. Because here this story takes a dark turn.

The Story of Lancelot & Elaine

It was questing season! The Knights of the Round Table were leaving Camelot to seek adventure and gallantry.

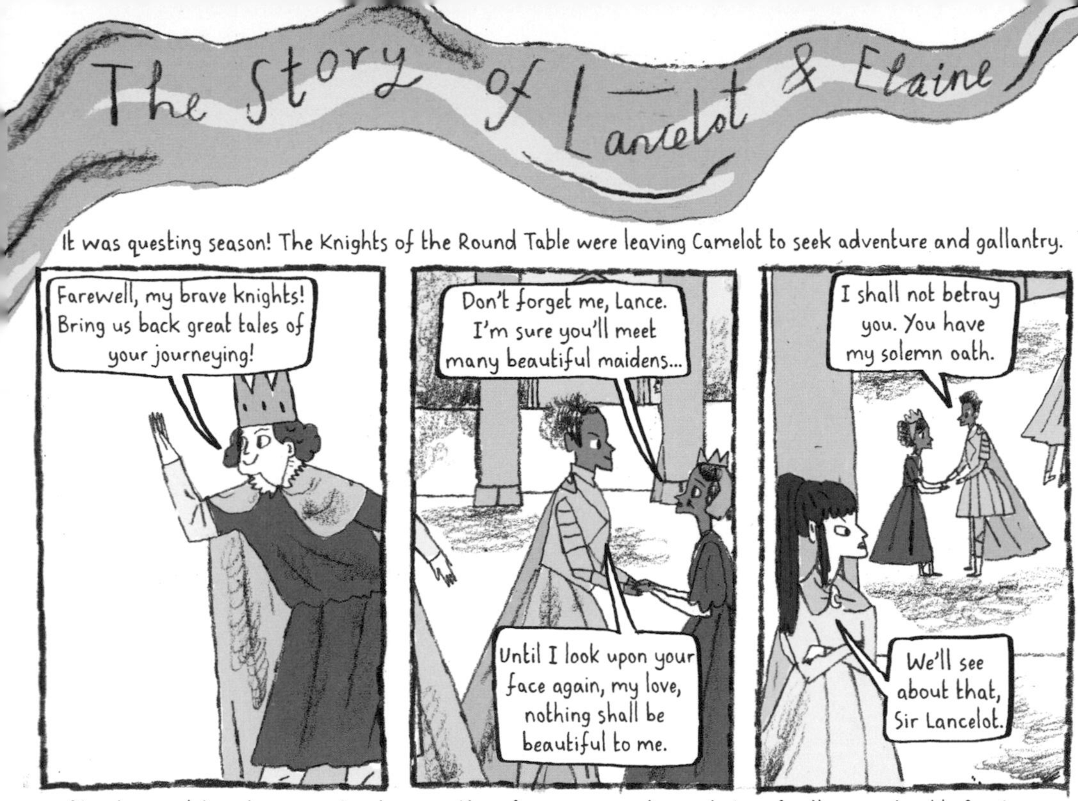
Farewell, my brave knights! Bring us back great tales of your journeying!
Don't forget me, Lance. I'm sure you'll meet many beautiful maidens...
Until I look upon your face again, my love, nothing shall be beautiful to me.
I shall not betray you. You have my solemn oath.
We'll see about that, Sir Lancelot.

Off rode Lancelot, seeking an adventure worthy of Guinevere and a good story for the Round Table feasts. He had not been riding for long when he saw a castle on a high hill, from which great plumes of smoke were billowing.

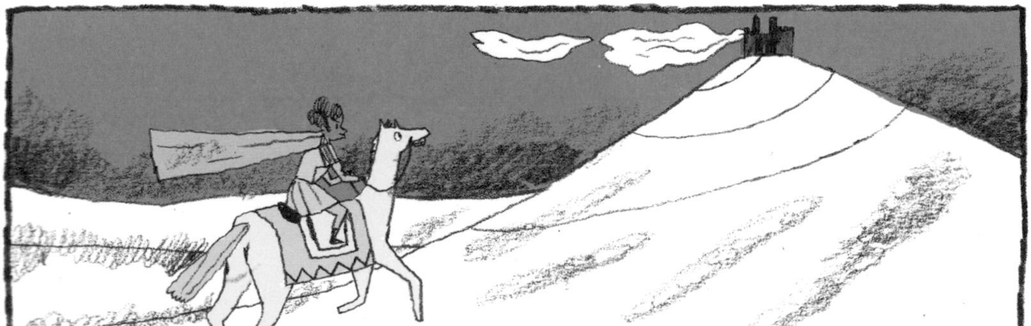

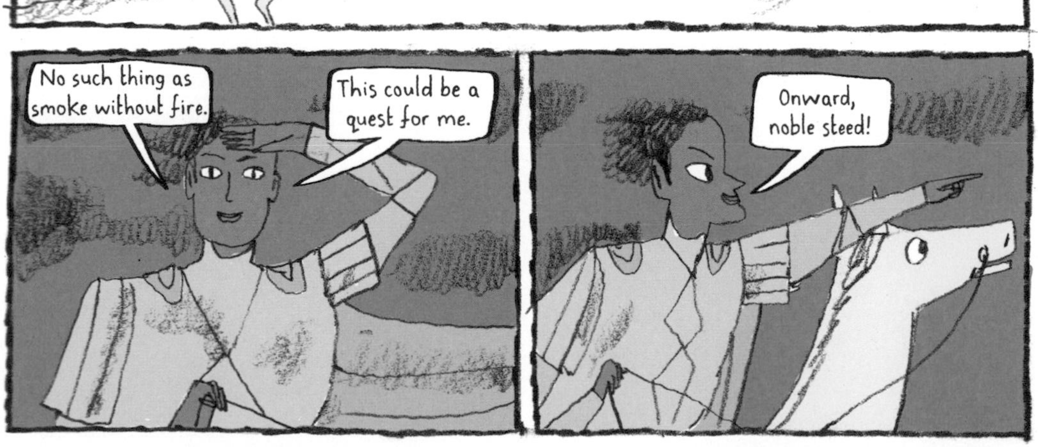
No such thing as smoke without fire.
This could be a quest for me.
Onward, noble steed!

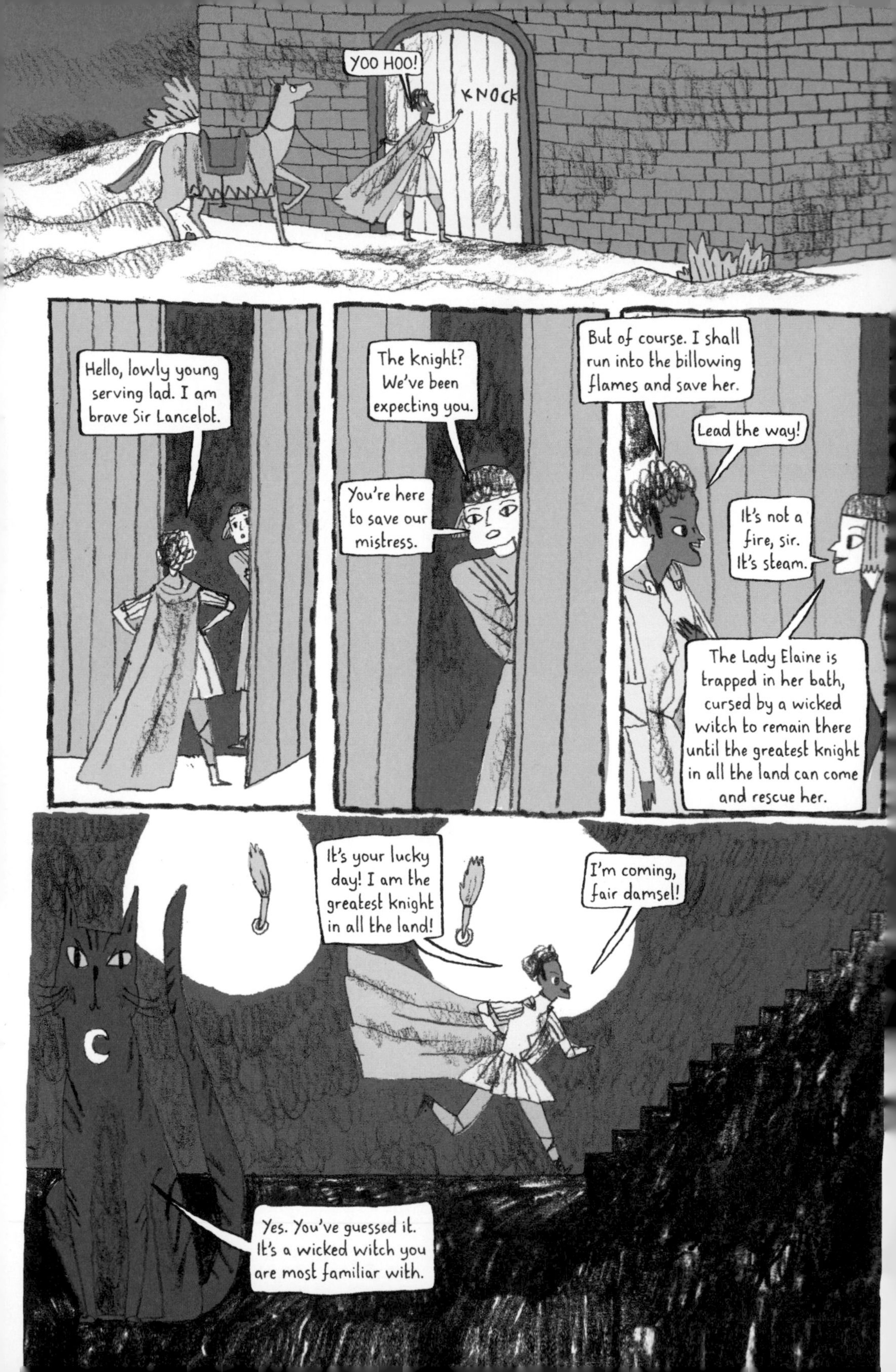
YOO HOO!
KNOCK
Hello, lowly young serving lad. I am brave Sir Lancelot.
The knight? We've been expecting you.
You're here to save our mistress.
But of course. I shall run into the billowing flames and save her.
Lead the way!
It's not a fire, sir. It's steam.
The Lady Elaine is trapped in her bath, cursed by a wicked witch to remain there until the greatest knight in all the land can come and rescue her.
It's your lucky day! I am the greatest knight in all the land!
I'm coming, fair damsel!
Yes. You've guessed it. It's a wicked witch you are most familiar with.

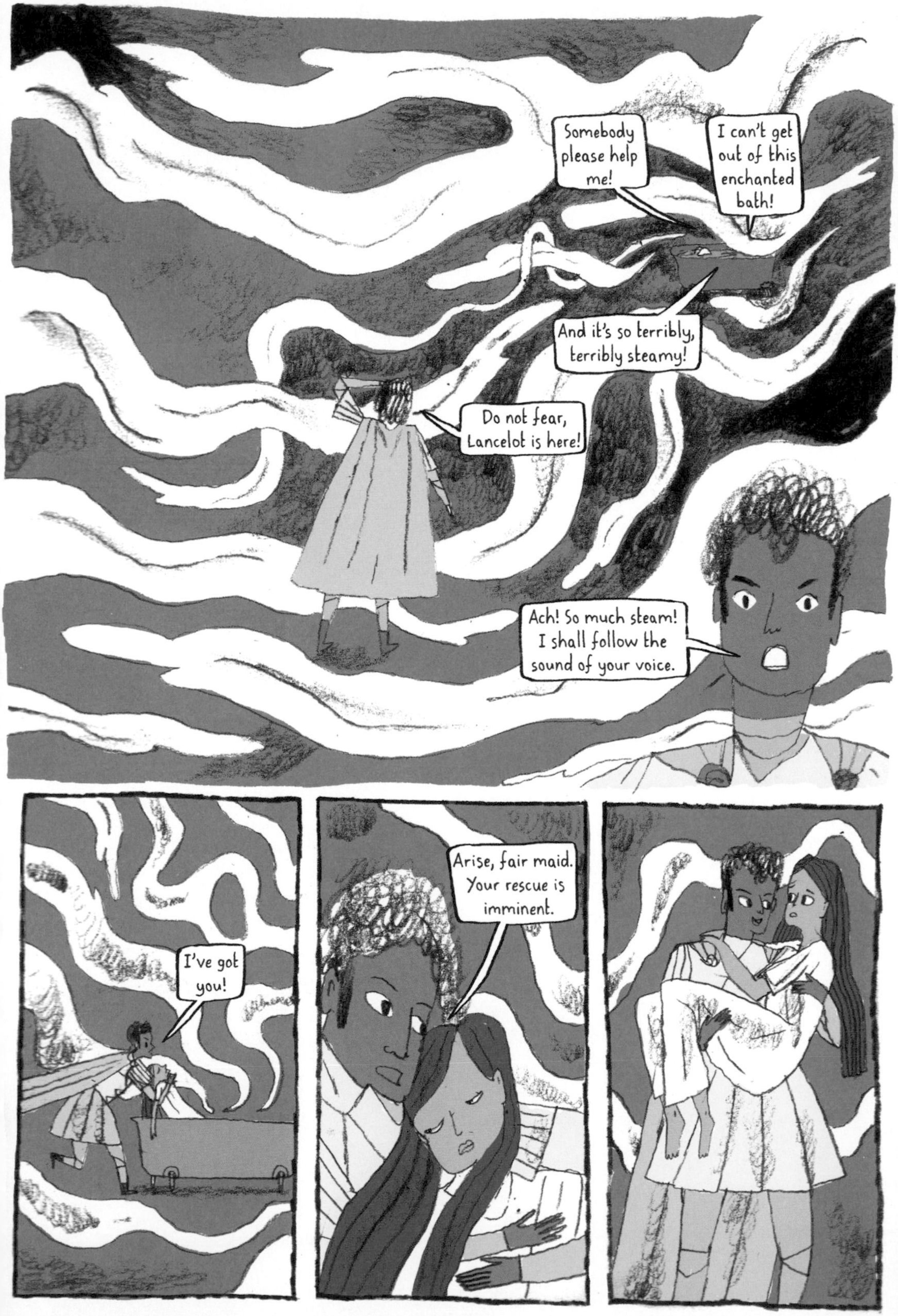
Somebody please help me!
I can't get out of this enchanted bath!
And it's so terribly, terribly steamy!
Do not fear, Lancelot is here!
Ach! So much steam! I shall follow the sound of your voice.
I've got you!
Arise, fair maid. Your rescue is imminent.

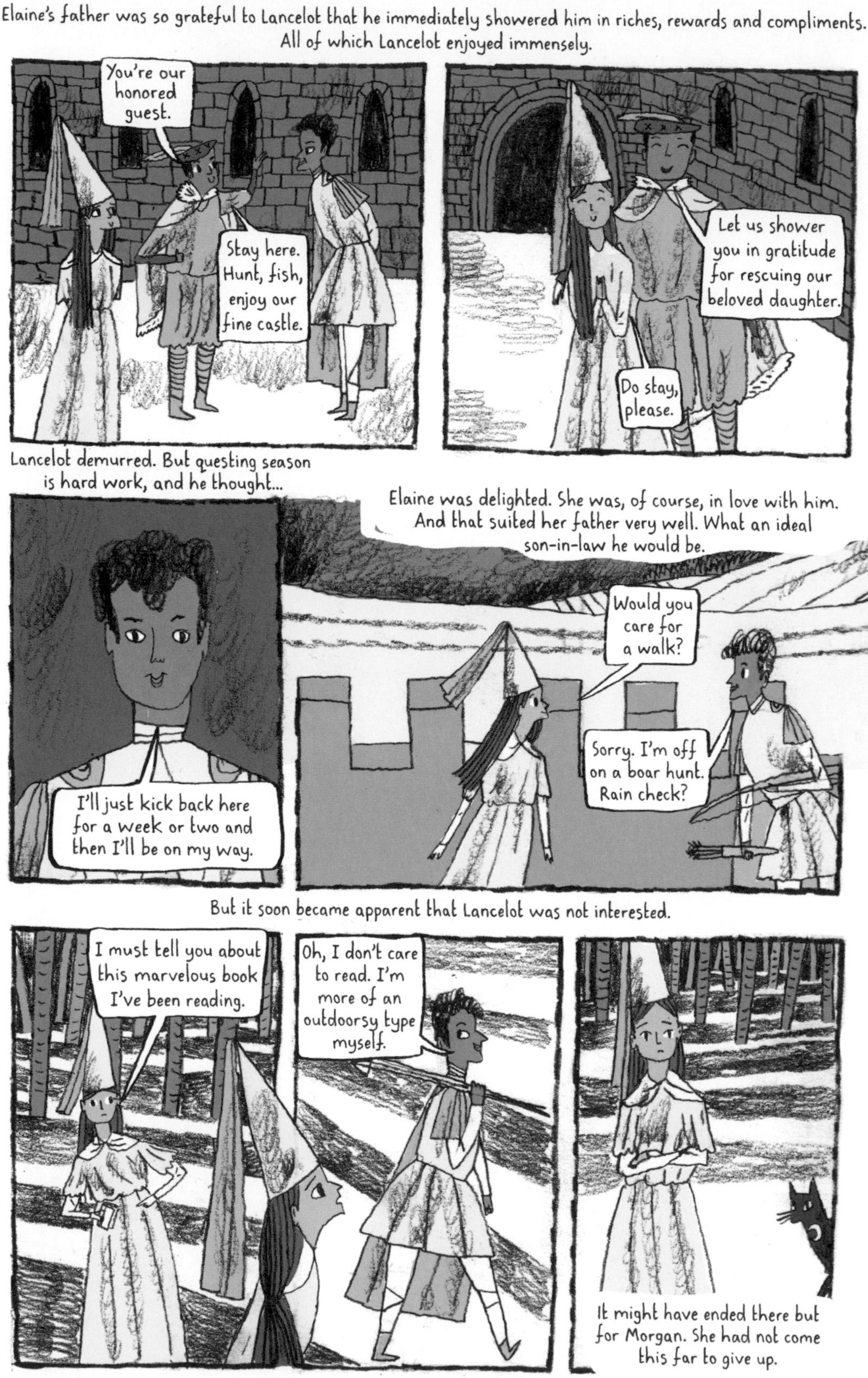
Elaine's father was so grateful to Lancelot that he immediately showered him in riches, rewards and compliments. All of which Lancelot enjoyed immensely.
You're our honored guest.
Stay here. Hunt, fish, enjoy our fine castle.
Let us shower you in gratitude for rescuing our beloved daughter.
Do stay, please.
Lancelot demurred. But questing season is hard work, and he thought...
I'll just kick back here for a week or two and then I'll be on my way.
Elaine was delighted. She was, of course, in love with him. And that suited her father very well. What an ideal son-in-law he would be.
Would you care for a walk?
Sorry. I'm off on a boar hunt. Rain check?
But it soon became apparent that Lancelot was not interested.
I must tell you about this marvelous book I've been reading.
Oh, I don't care to read. I'm more of an outdoorsy type myself.
It might have ended there but for Morgan. She had not come this far to give up.

Did you just talk? Are you a talking cat?

Why are you crying?

I'm a handsome prince, transformed into a cat by the same witch who trapped you in that bath.

Why are you crying? You're free of your enchantment and you were rescued by the dashing Lance.

I'm crying because I love him. But he's not interested in me at all.

I think perhaps he's in love with someone else.

You're right. But the other woman is married. He can never have her.

You must help him forget her. You alone can mend his broken heart, Elaine.

How? Tell me how!

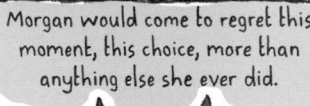

Take this ring. Wear it tonight and go to the bedchamber of Lancelot.

He will admit you. In the morning he will see you in the sunlight and know you for his love.

Will we really?

You will be married and have many fine sons.

Your first son will be conceived tonight.

Morgan would come to regret this moment, this choice, more than anything else she ever did.

But on that day, in the sunlit garden, she felt only the satisfaction of a plan coming together. And the rush of the magic of a spell well done.

Elaine did as Morgan had told her. The ring's magic did not change her appearance, nor give her any extra beauty. But it gave her a boldness and a glow. As for Lancelot, for all his splendor, he was a weak man, and Morgan knew this well. It took only a little persuasion from that magic ring to make him forget his vow to Guinevere.

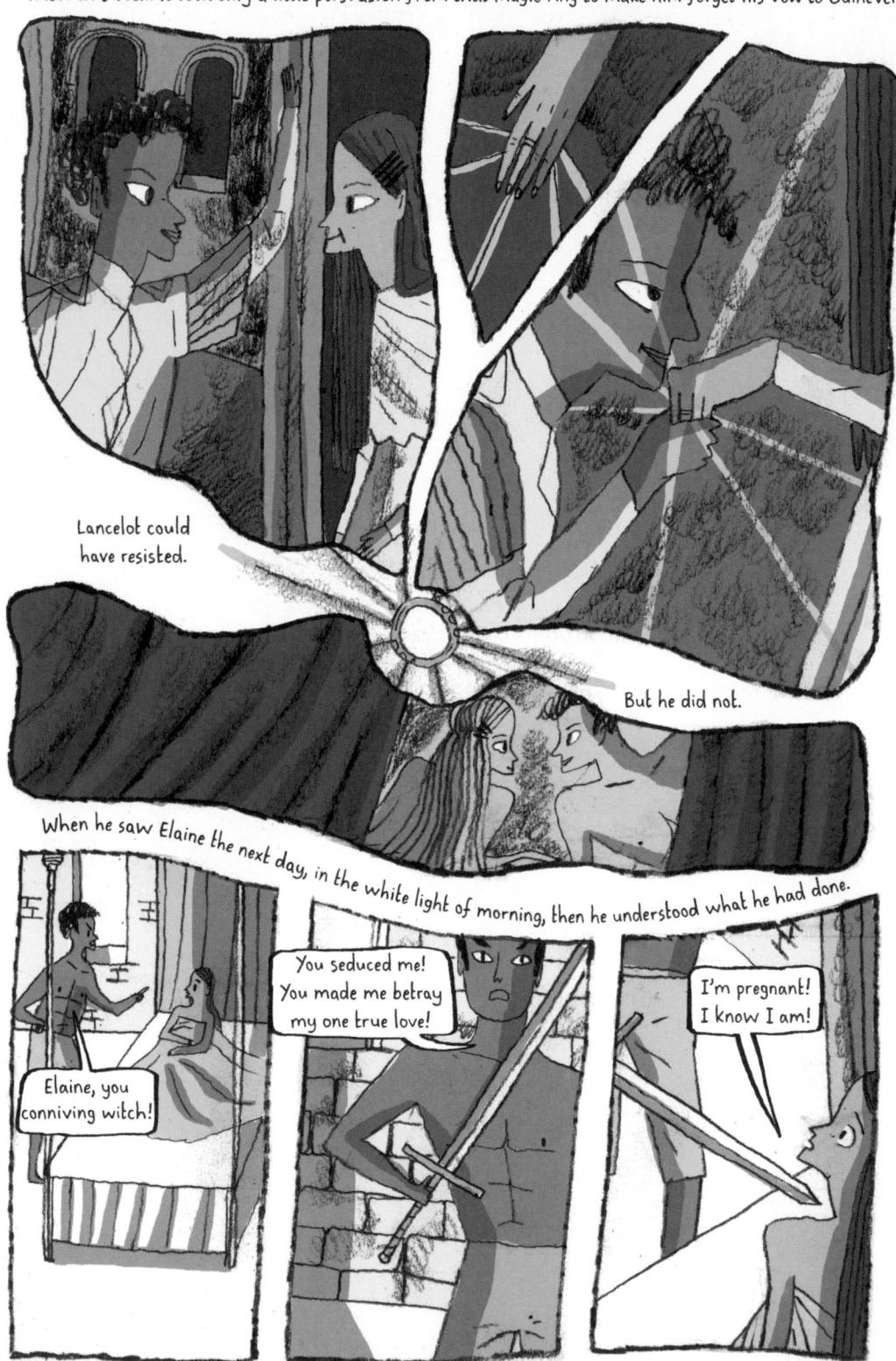

Lancelot could have resisted.

But he did not.

When he saw Elaine the next day, in the white light of morning, then he understood what he had done.

You seduced me! You made me betray my one true love!

Elaine, you conniving witch!

I'm pregnant! I know I am!

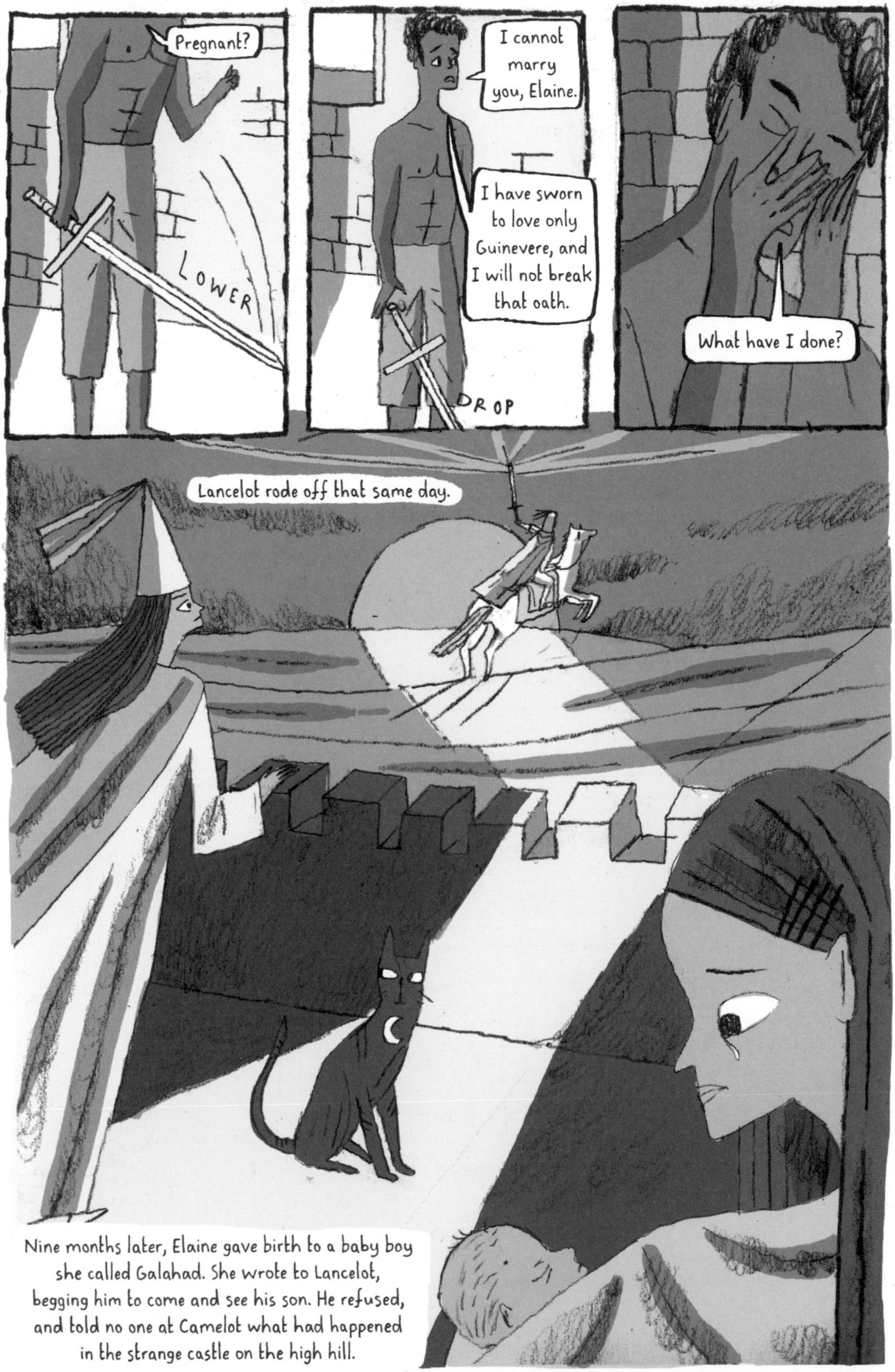
Pregnant?
LOWER
I cannot marry you, Elaine.
I have sworn to love only Guinevere, and I will not break that oath.
DROP
What have I done?
Lancelot rode off that same day.
Nine months later, Elaine gave birth to a baby boy she called Galahad. She wrote to Lancelot, begging him to come and see his son. He refused, and told no one at Camelot what had happened in the strange castle on the high hill.

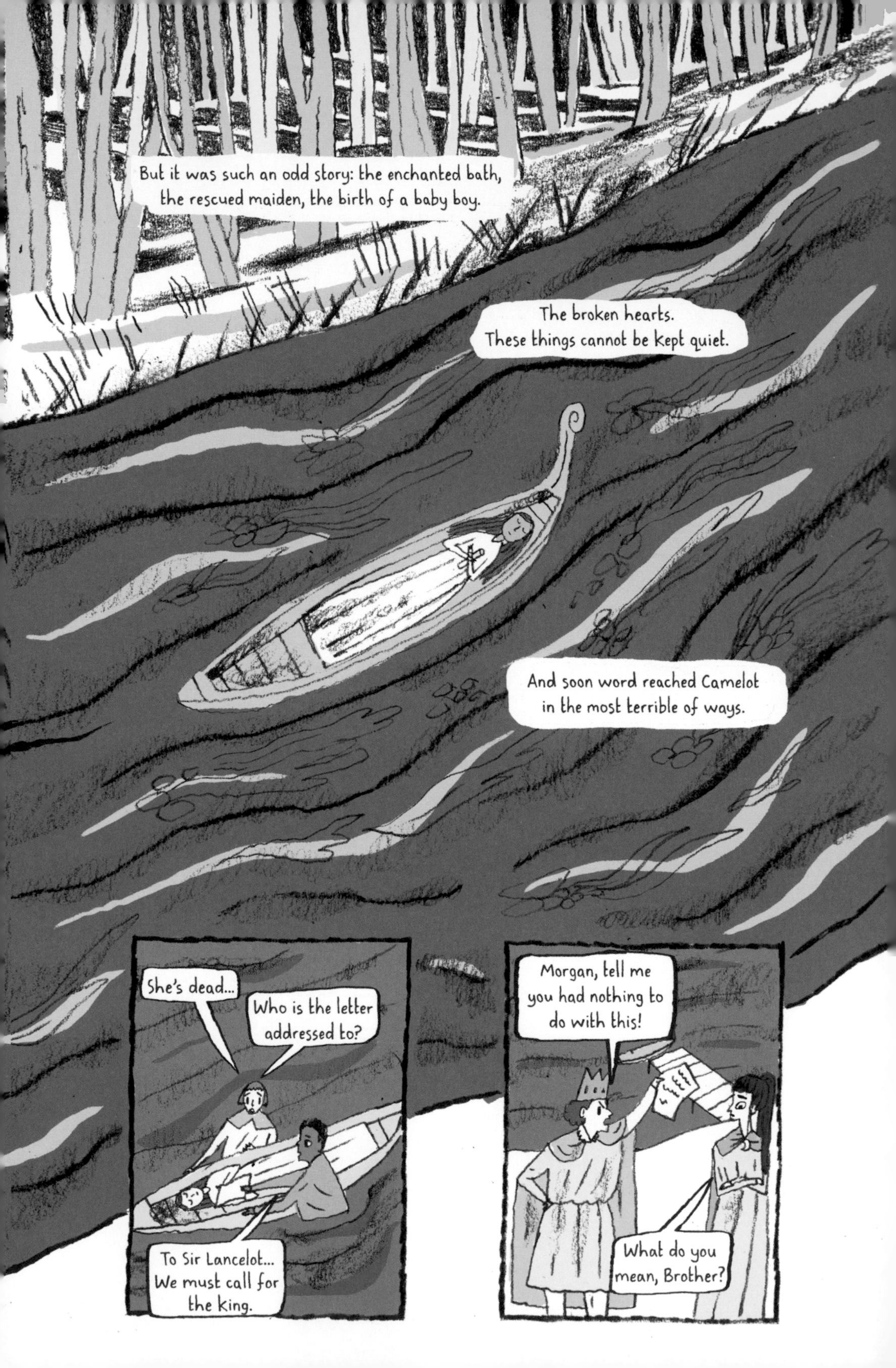
But it was such an odd story: the enchanted bath, the rescued maiden, the birth of a baby boy.
The broken hearts. These things cannot be kept quiet.
And soon word reached Camelot in the most terrible of ways.
She's dead...
Who is the letter addressed to?
To Sir Lancelot... We must call for the king.
Morgan, tell me you had nothing to do with this!
What do you mean, Brother?

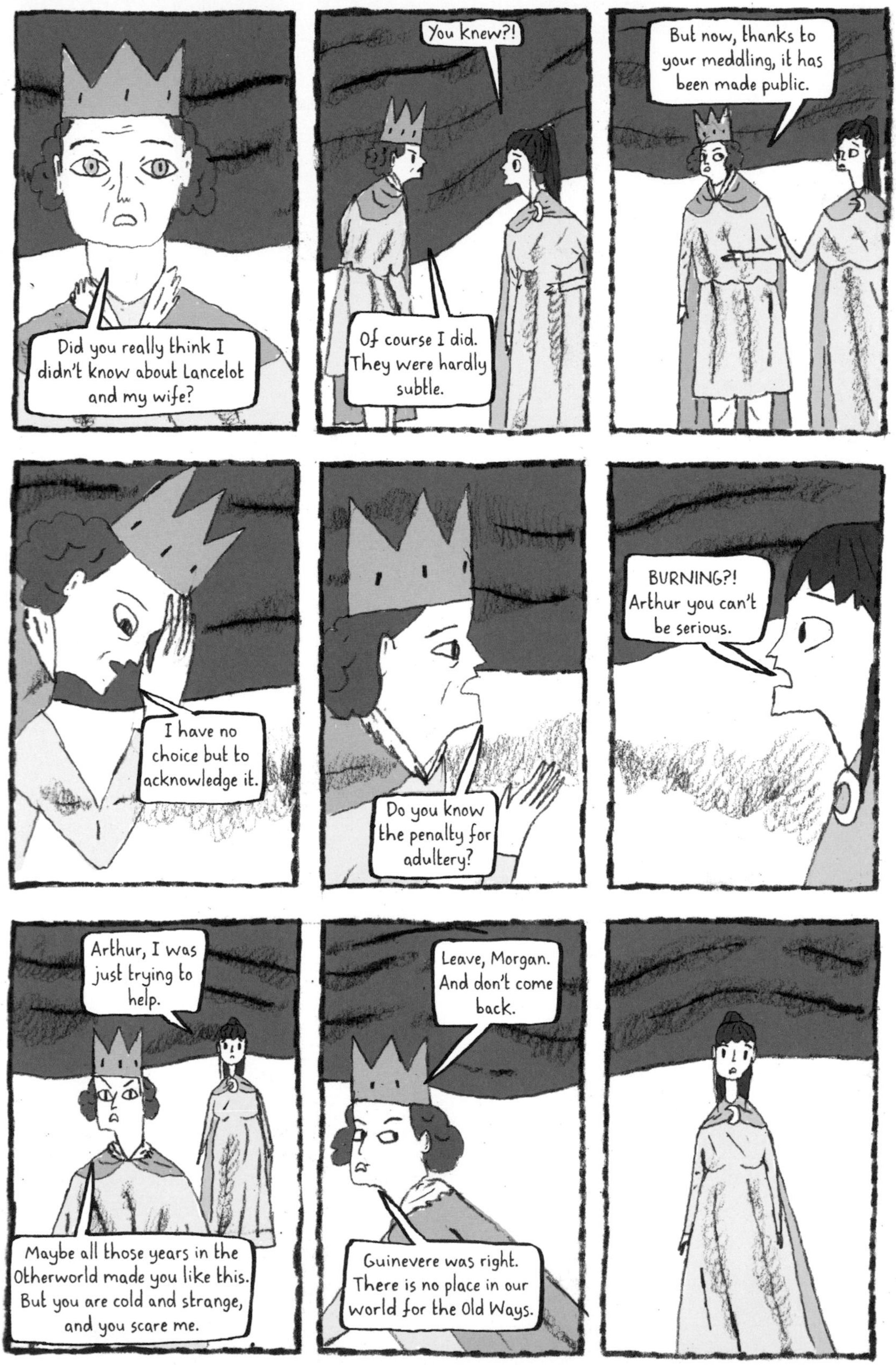
Did you really think I didn't know about Lancelot and my wife?
You knew?!
Of course I did. They were hardly subtle.
But now, thanks to your meddling, it has been made public.
I have no choice but to acknowledge it.
Do you know the penalty for adultery?
BURNING?! Arthur you can't be serious.
Arthur, I was just trying to help.
Maybe all those years in the Otherworld made you like this. But you are cold and strange, and you scare me.
Leave, Morgan. And don't come back.
Guinevere was right. There is no place in our world for the Old Ways.

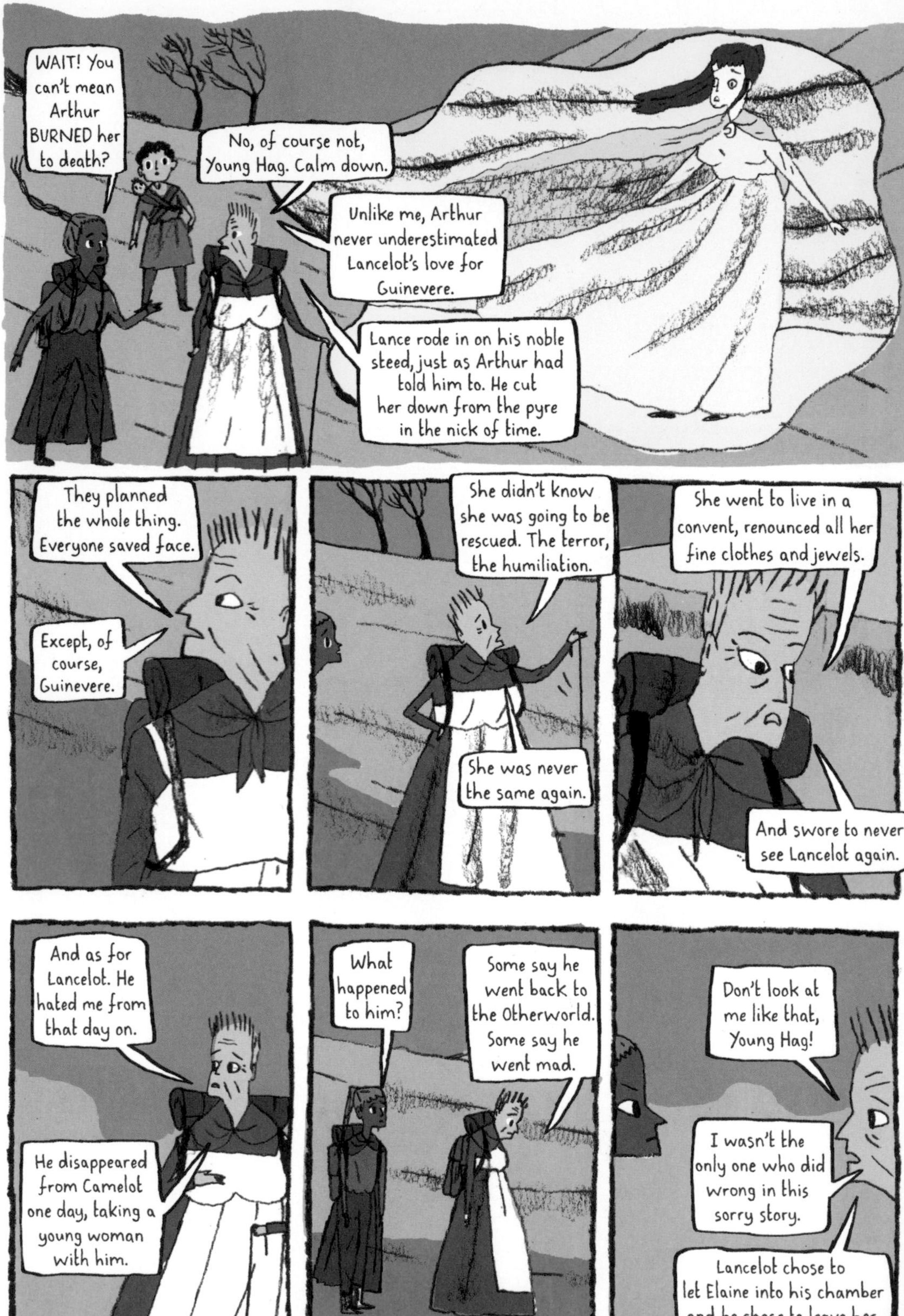
WAIT! You can't mean Arthur BURNED her to death?
No, of course not, Young Hag. Calm down.
Unlike me, Arthur never underestimated Lancelot's love for Guinevere.
Lance rode in on his noble steed, just as Arthur had told him to. He cut her down from the pyre in the nick of time.
They planned the whole thing. Everyone saved face.
Except, of course, Guinevere.
She didn't know she was going to be rescued. The terror, the humiliation.
She was never the same again.
She went to live in a convent, renounced all her fine clothes and jewels.
And swore to never see Lancelot again.
And as for Lancelot. He hated me from that day on.
He disappeared from Camelot one day, taking a young woman with him.
What happened to him?
Some say he went back to the Otherworld. Some say he went mad.
Don't look at me like that, Young Hag!
I wasn't the only one who did wrong in this sorry story.
Lancelot chose to let Elaine into his chamber and he chose to leave her.

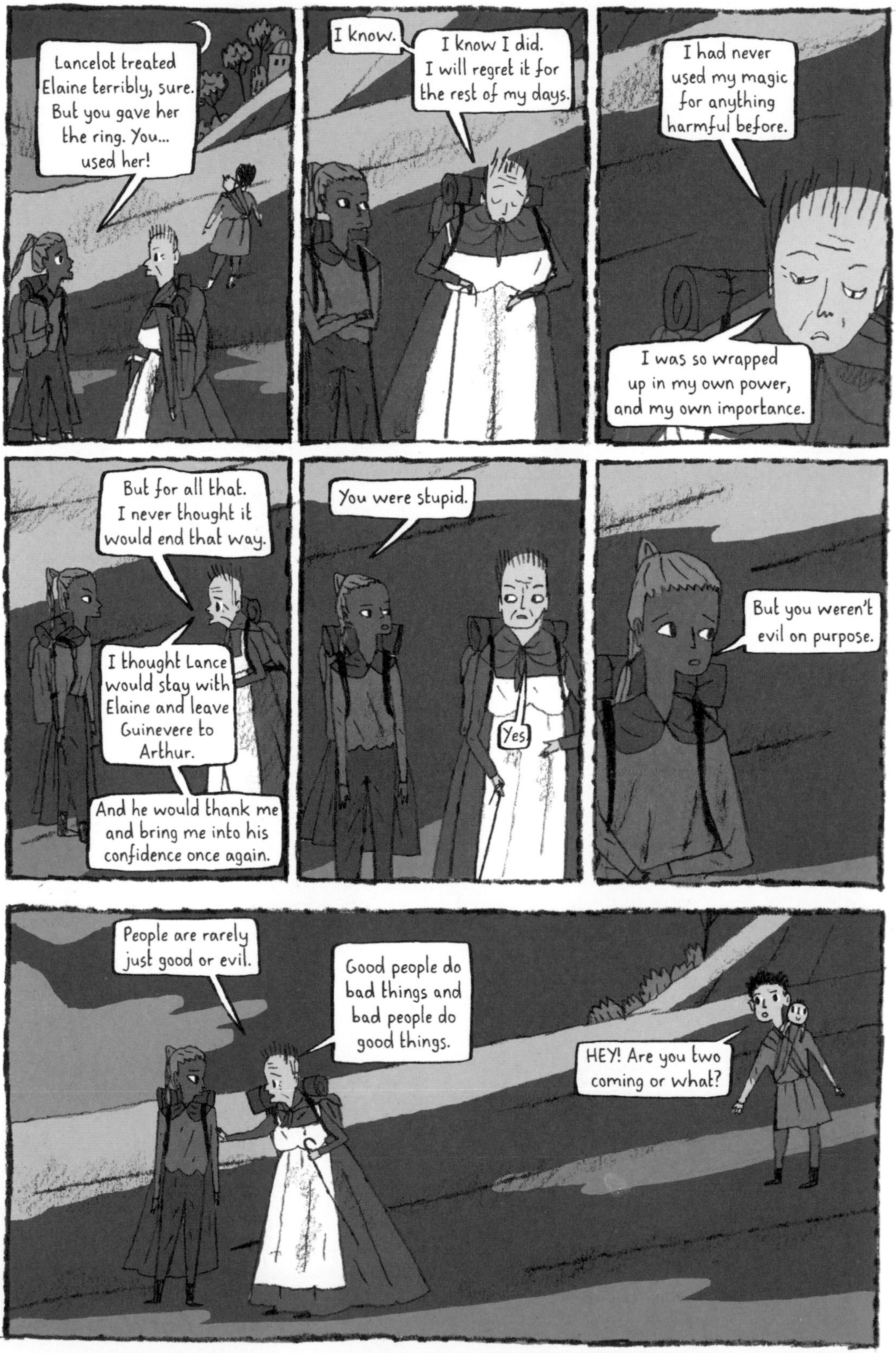

Lancelot treated Elaine terribly, sure. But you gave her the ring. You... used her!
I know.
I know I did. I will regret it for the rest of my days.
I had never used my magic for anything harmful before.
I was so wrapped up in my own power, and my own importance.
But for all that. I never thought it would end that way.
I thought Lance would stay with Elaine and leave Guinevere to Arthur.
And he would thank me and bring me into his confidence once again.
You were stupid.
Yes.
But you weren't evil on purpose.
People are rarely just good or evil.
Good people do bad things and bad people do good things.
HEY! Are you two coming or what?

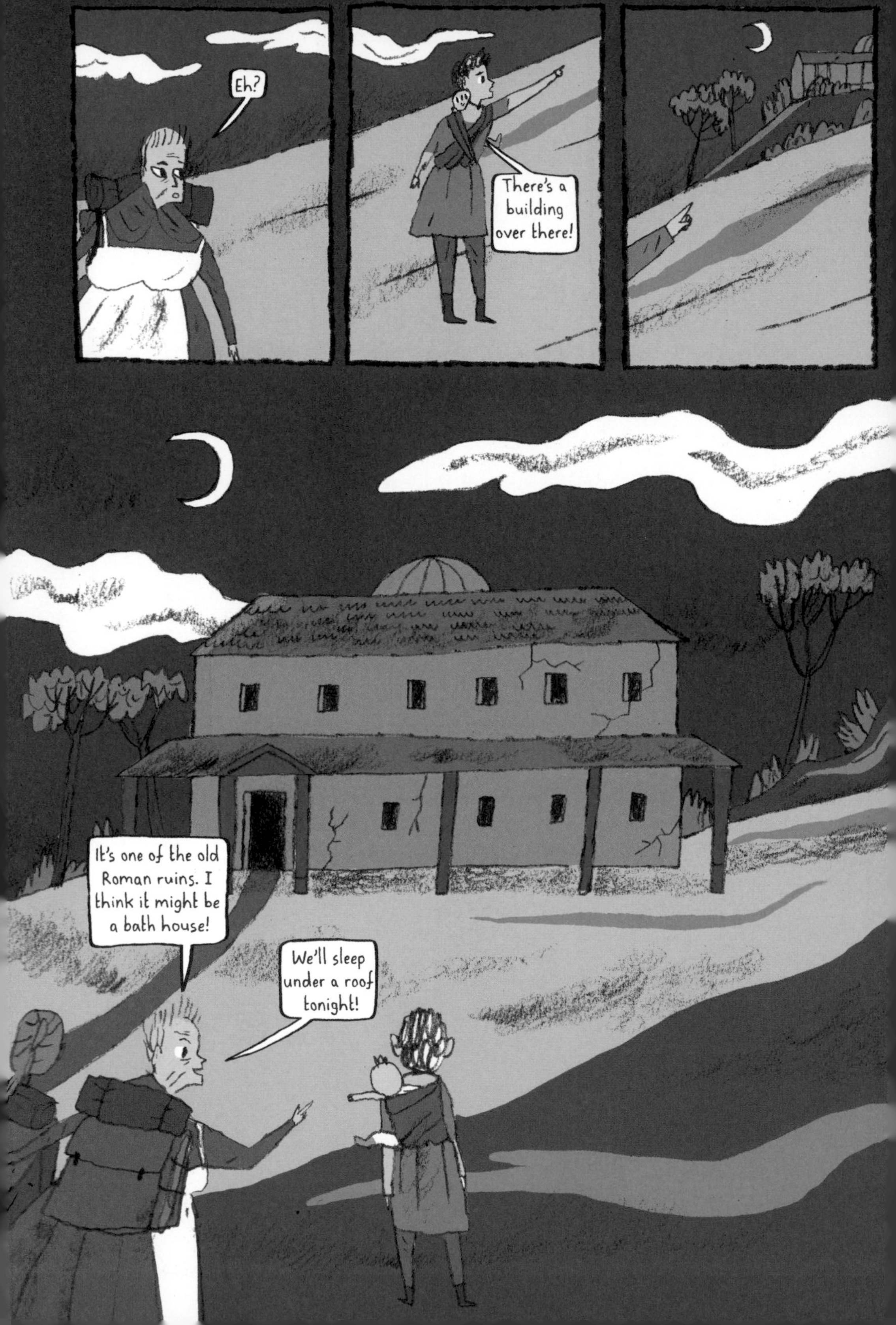
Eh?
There's a building over there!
It's one of the old Roman ruins. I think it might be a bath house!
We'll sleep under a roof tonight!

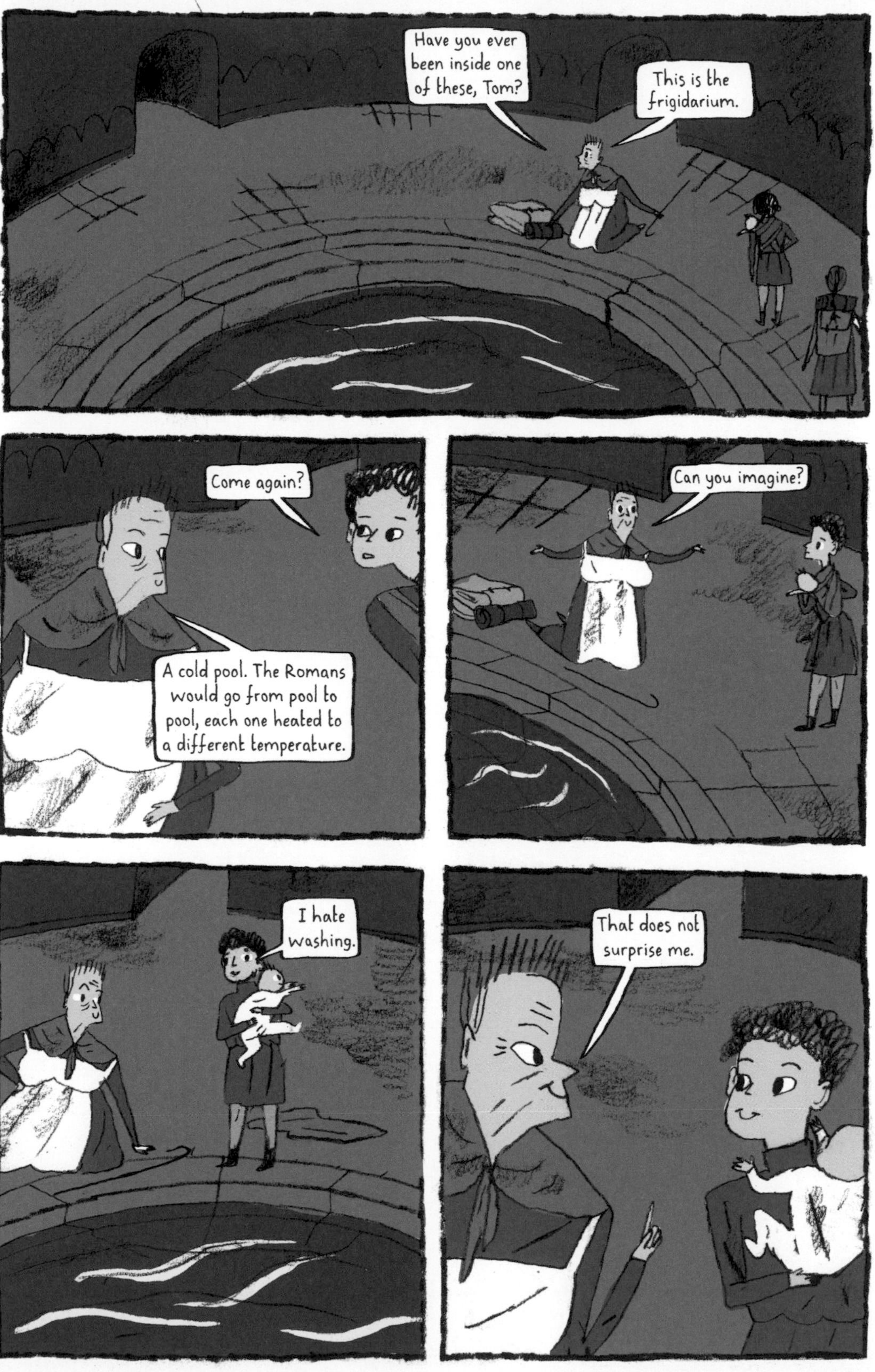
Have you ever been inside one of these, Tom?
This is the frigidarium.
Come again?
A cold pool. The Romans would go from pool to pool, each one heated to a different temperature.
Can you imagine?
I hate washing.
That does not surprise me.

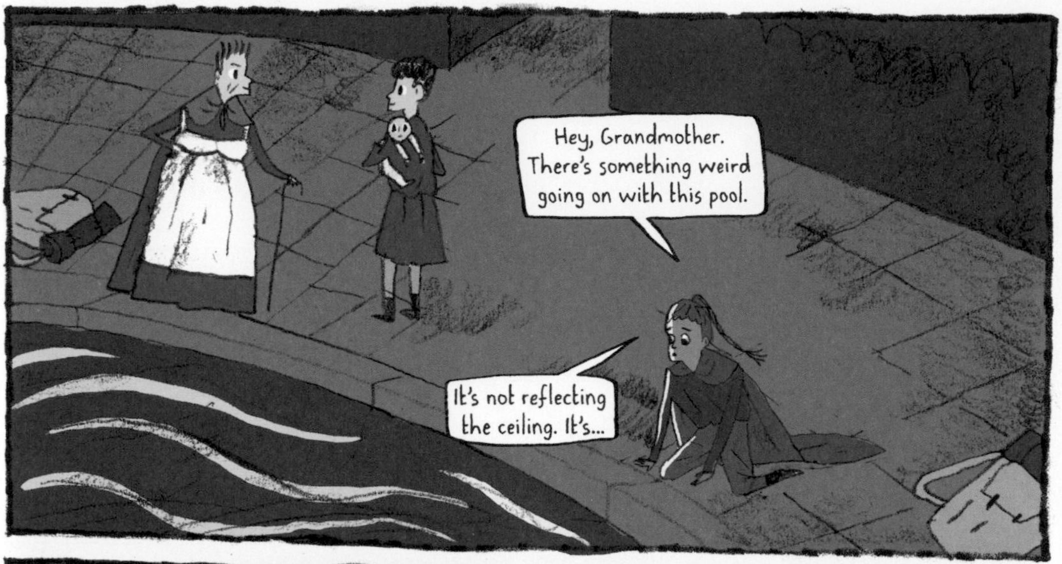
Hey, Grandmother. There's something weird going on with this pool.
It's not reflecting the ceiling. It's...

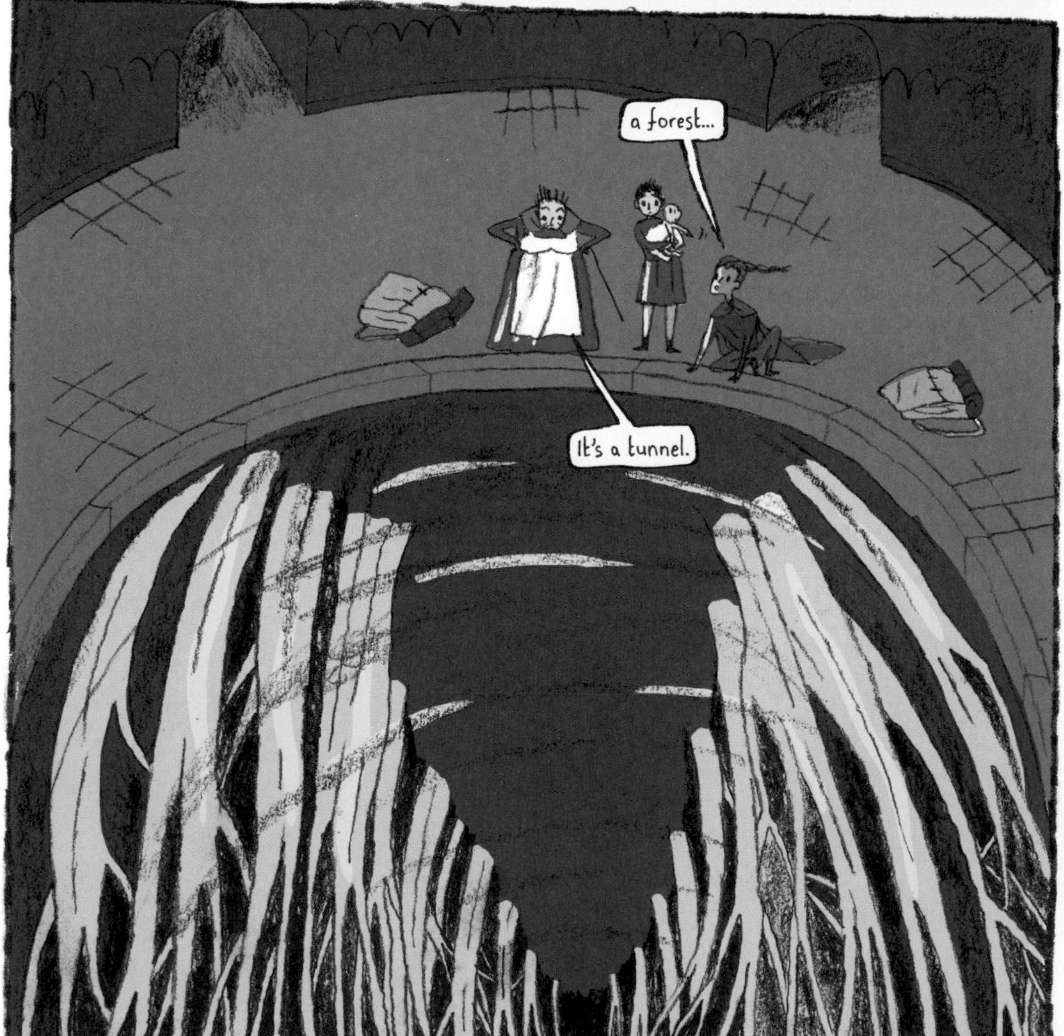
a forest...
It's a tunnel.

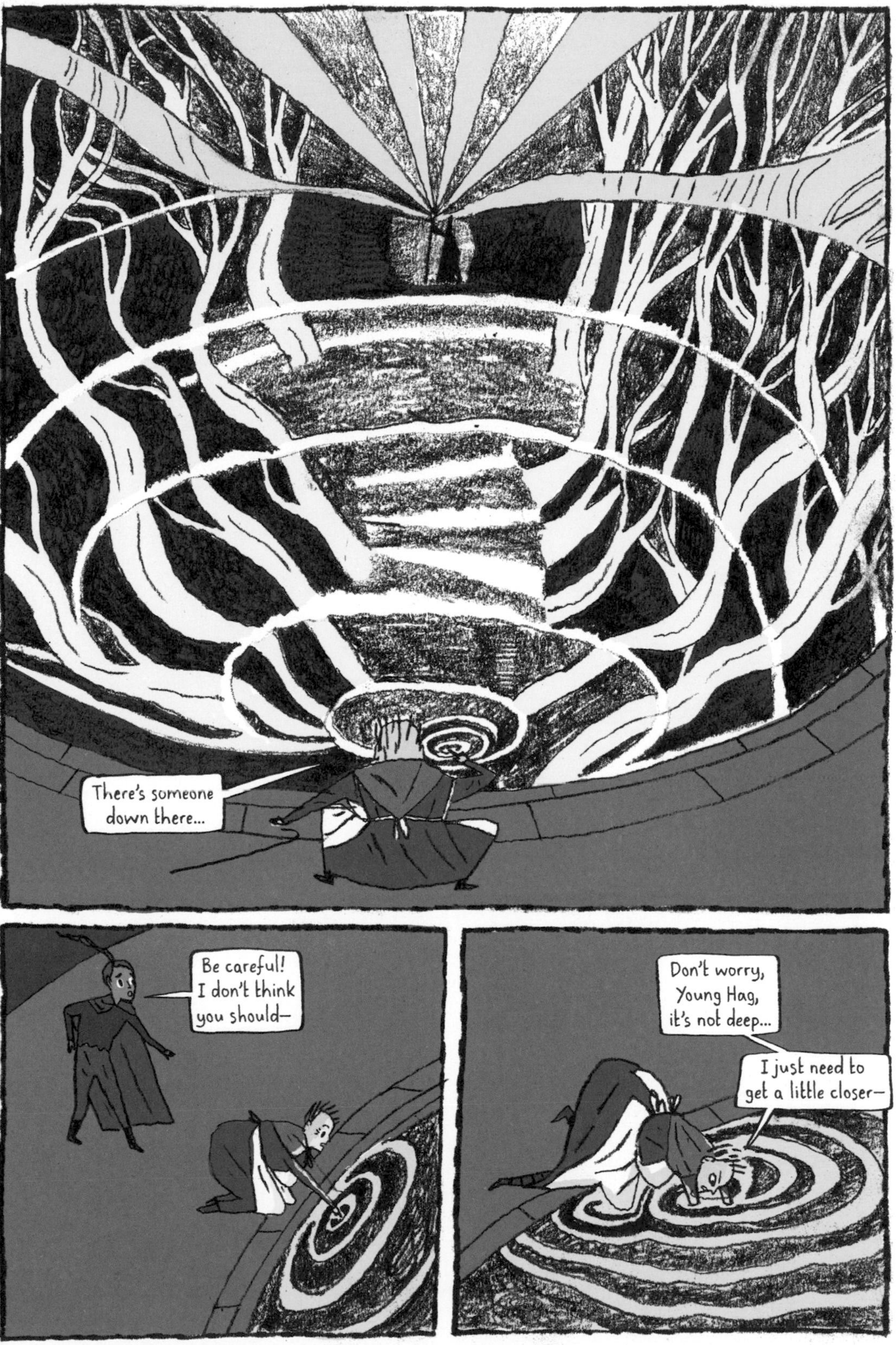

There's someone down there...
Be careful! I don't think you should—
Don't worry, Young Hag, it's not deep...
I just need to get a little closer—

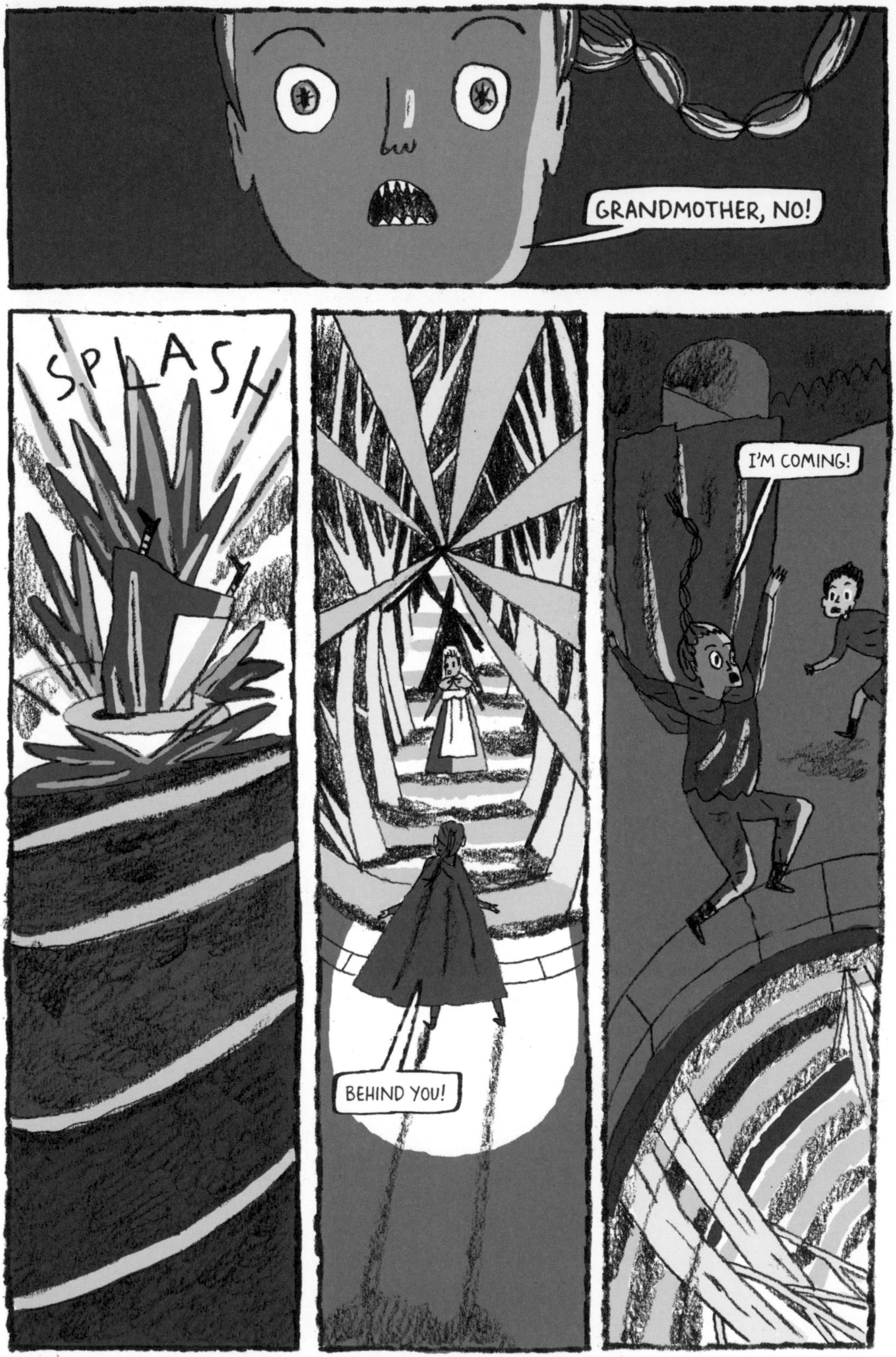
GRANDMOTHER, NO!
SPLASH
BEHIND YOU!
I'M COMING!

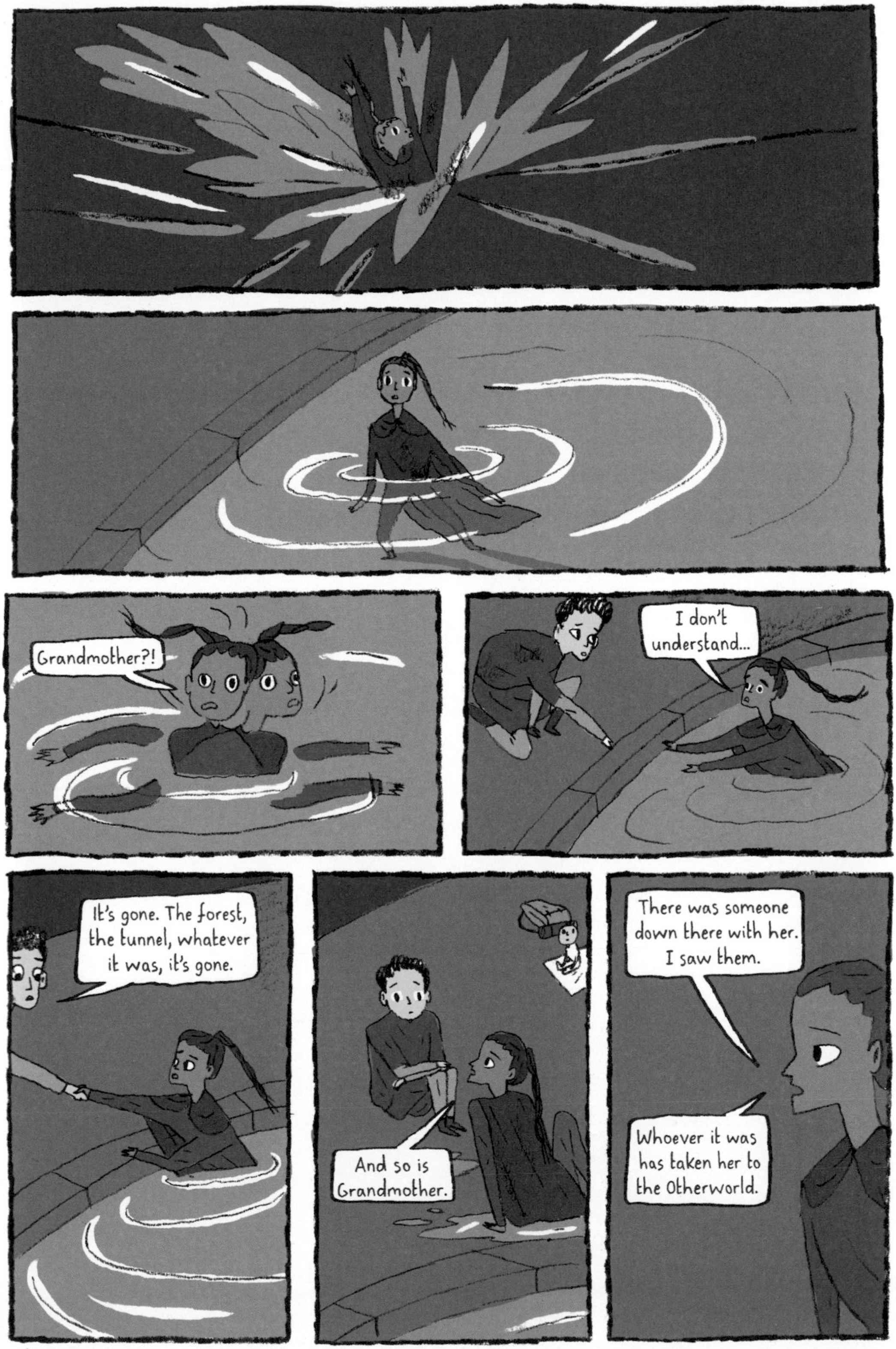
Grandmother?!
I don't understand...
It's gone. The forest, the tunnel, whatever it was, it's gone.
And so is Grandmother.
There was someone down there with her. I saw them.
Whoever it was has taken her to the Otherworld.

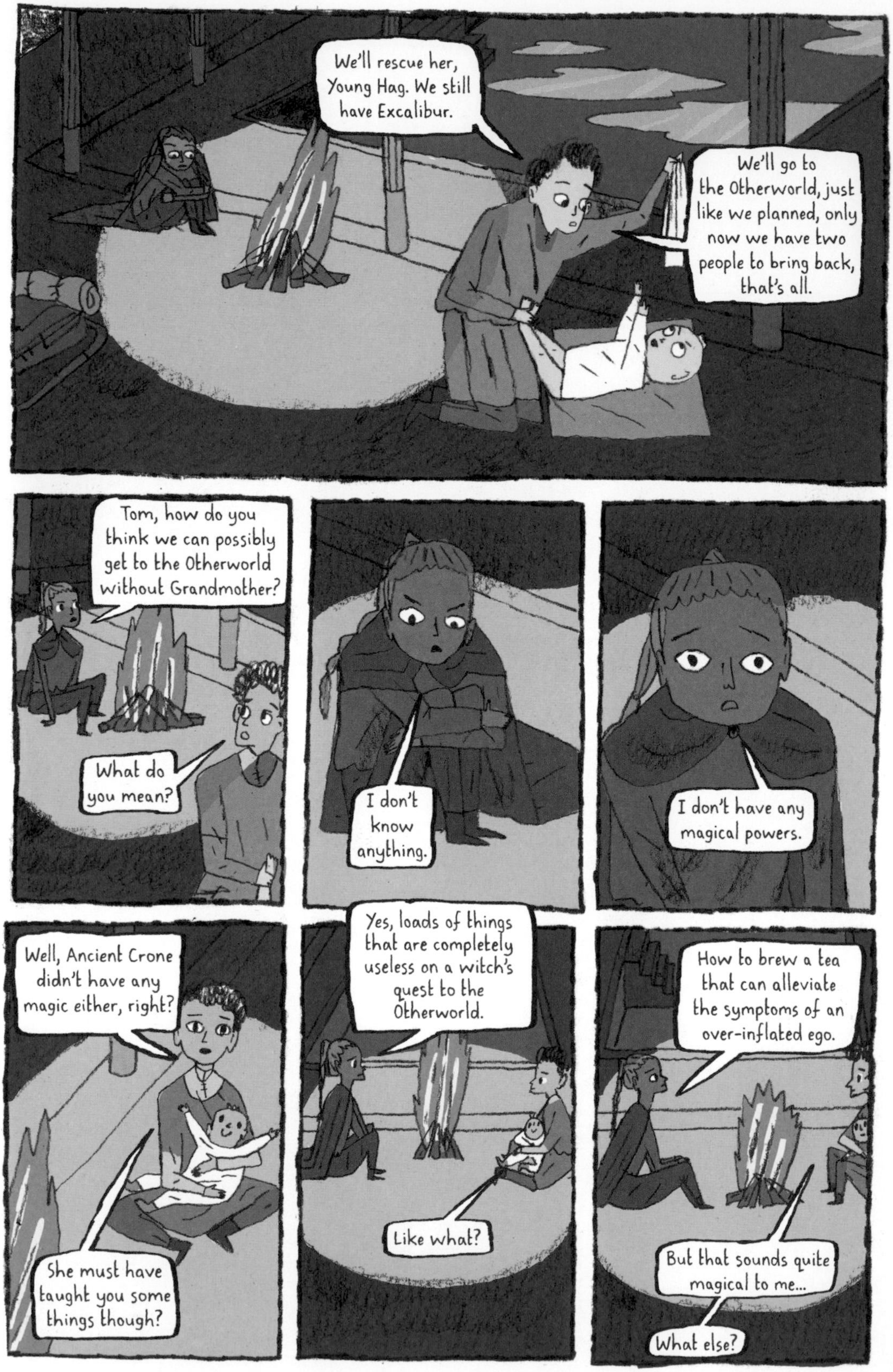
We'll rescue her, Young Hag. We still have Excalibur.
We'll go to the Otherworld, just like we planned, only now we have two people to bring back, that's all.
Tom, how do you think we can possibly get to the Otherworld without Grandmother?
What do you mean?
I don't know anything.
I don't have any magical powers.
Well, Ancient Crone didn't have any magic either, right?
She must have taught you some things though?
Yes, loads of things that are completely useless on a witch's quest to the Otherworld.
Like what?
How to brew a tea that can alleviate the symptoms of an over-inflated ego.
But that sounds quite magical to me...
What else?

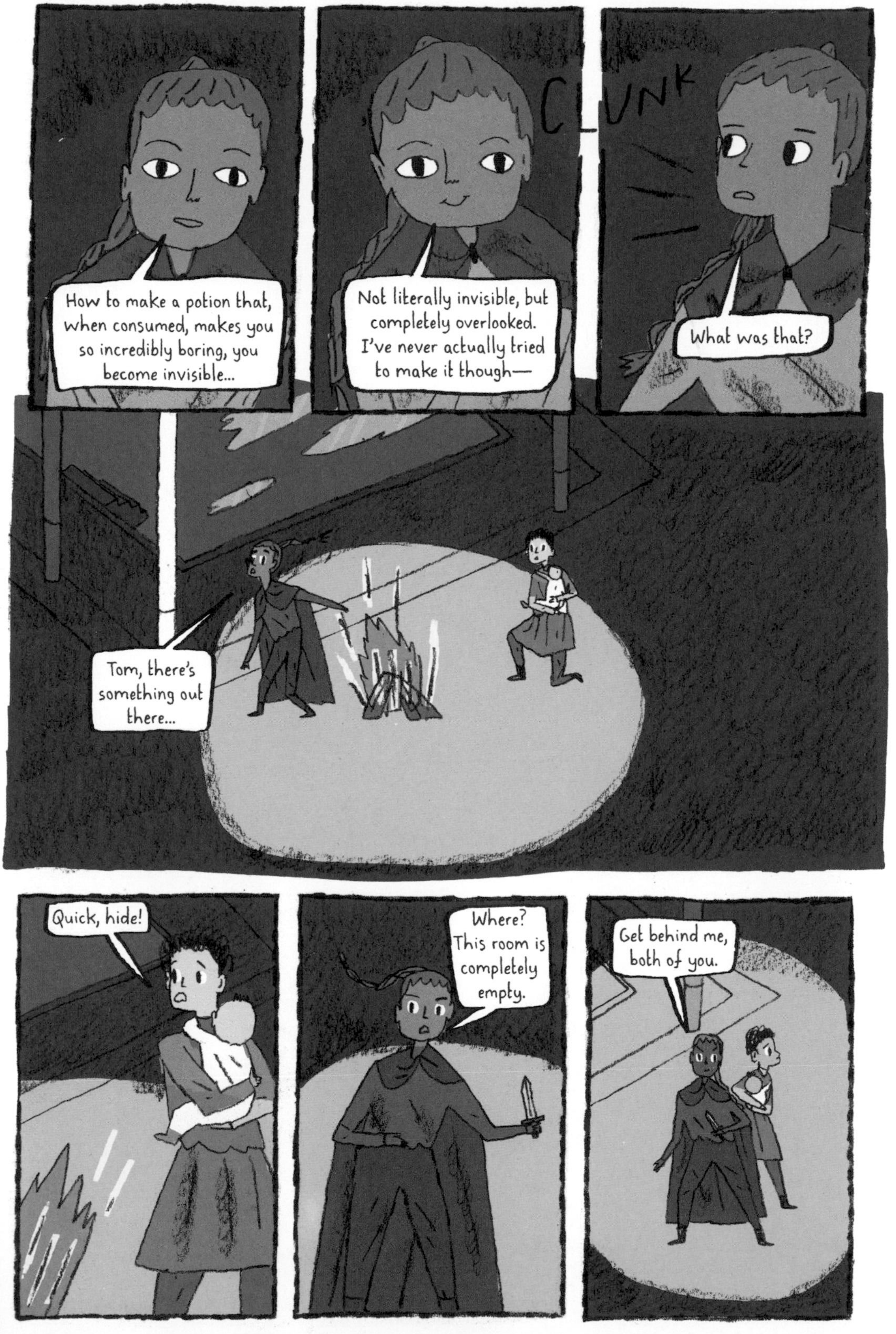
How to make a potion that, when consumed, makes you so incredibly boring, you become invisible...
Not literally invisible, but completely overlooked. I've never actually tried to make it though—
CLUNK
What was that?
Tom, there's something out there...
Quick, hide!
Where? This room is completely empty.
Get behind me, both of you.

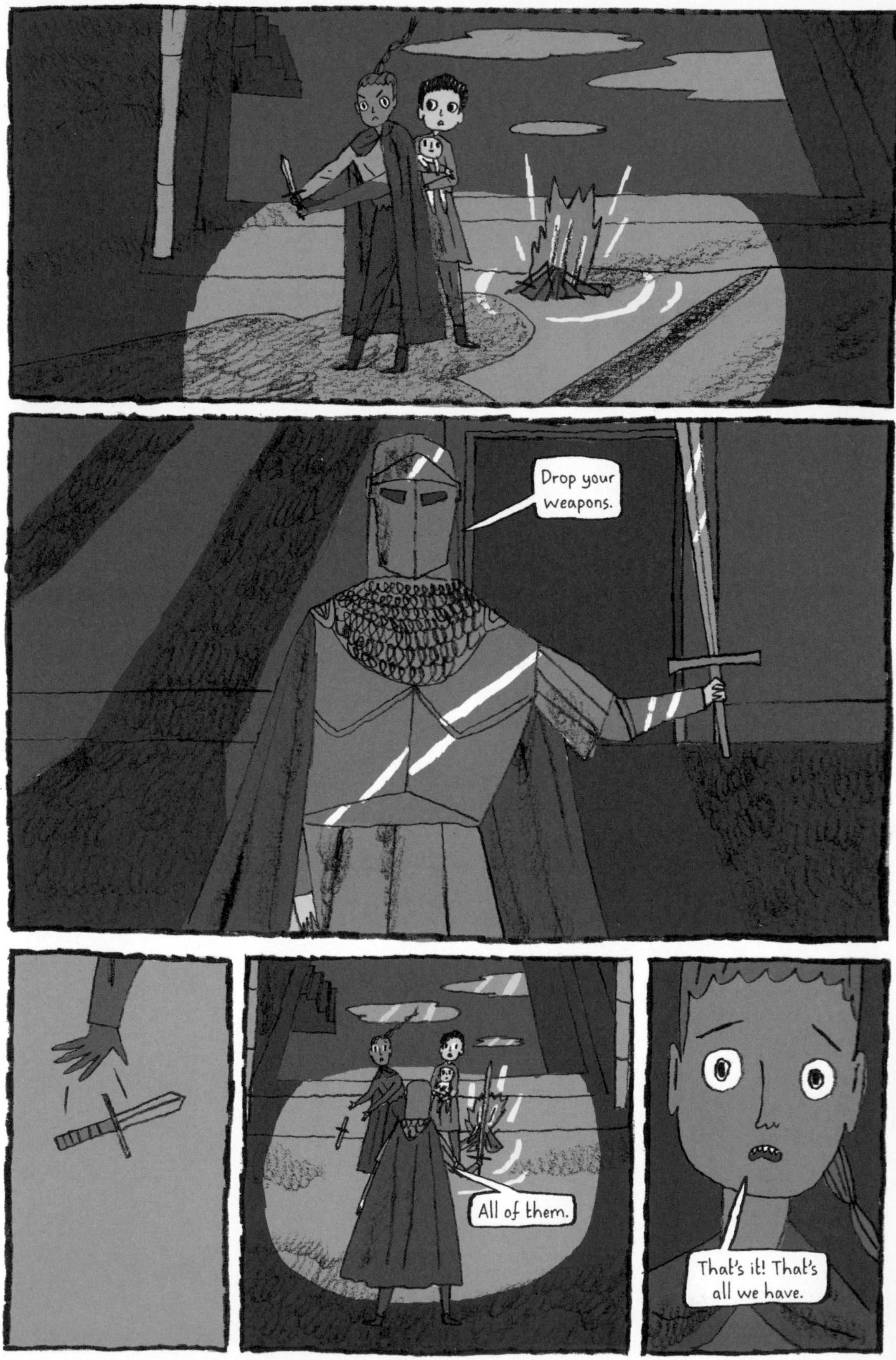
Drop your weapons.
All of them.
That's it! That's all we have.

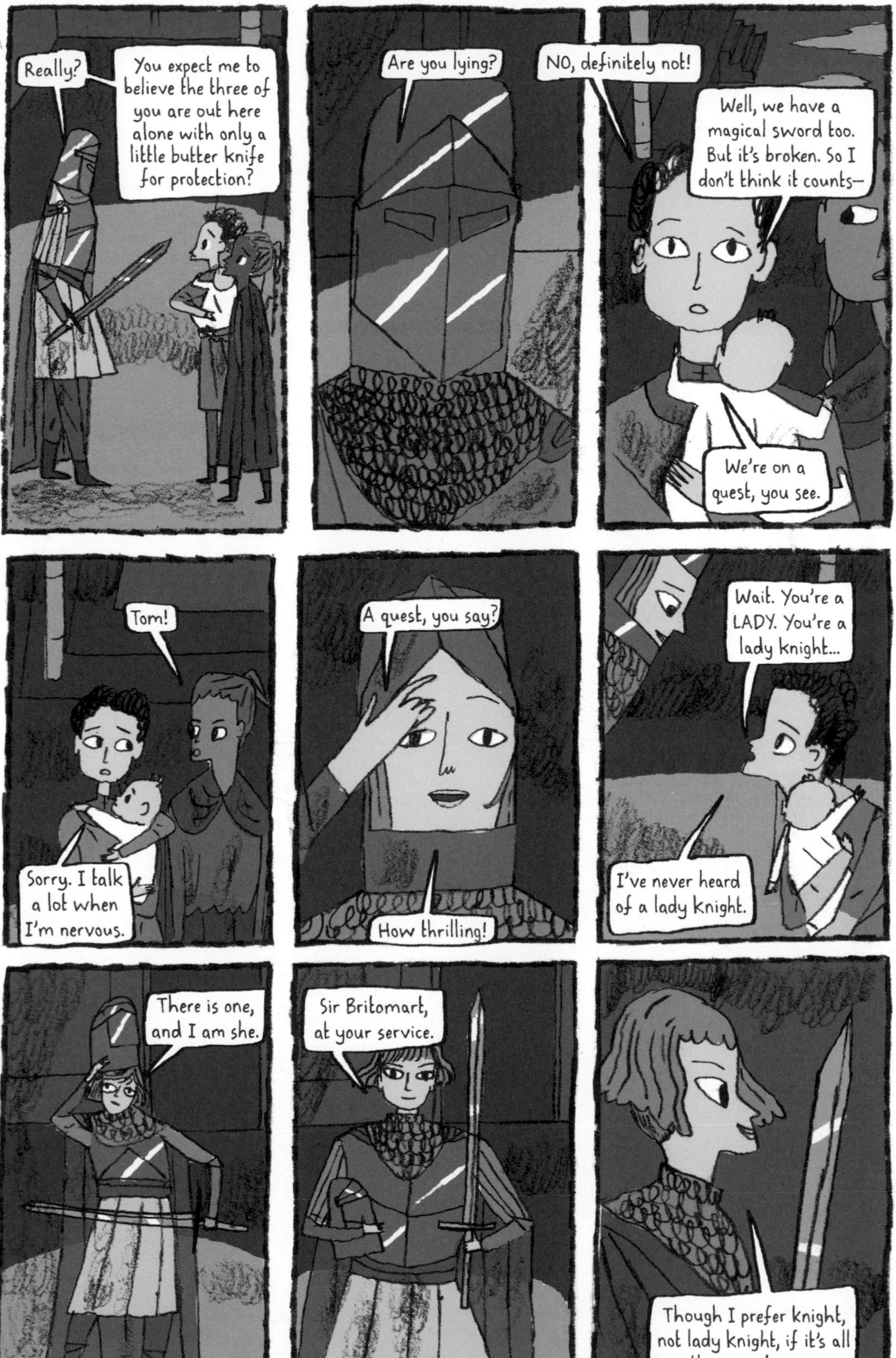
Really?
You expect me to believe the three of you are out here alone with only a little butter knife for protection?
Are you lying?
NO, definitely not!
Well, we have a magical sword too. But it's broken. So I don't think it counts—
We're on a quest, you see.
Tom!
Sorry. I talk a lot when I'm nervous.
A quest, you say?
How thrilling!
Wait. You're a LADY. You're a lady knight...
I've never heard of a lady knight.
There is one, and I am she.
Sir Britomart, at your service.
Though I prefer knight, not lady knight, if it's all the same to you.

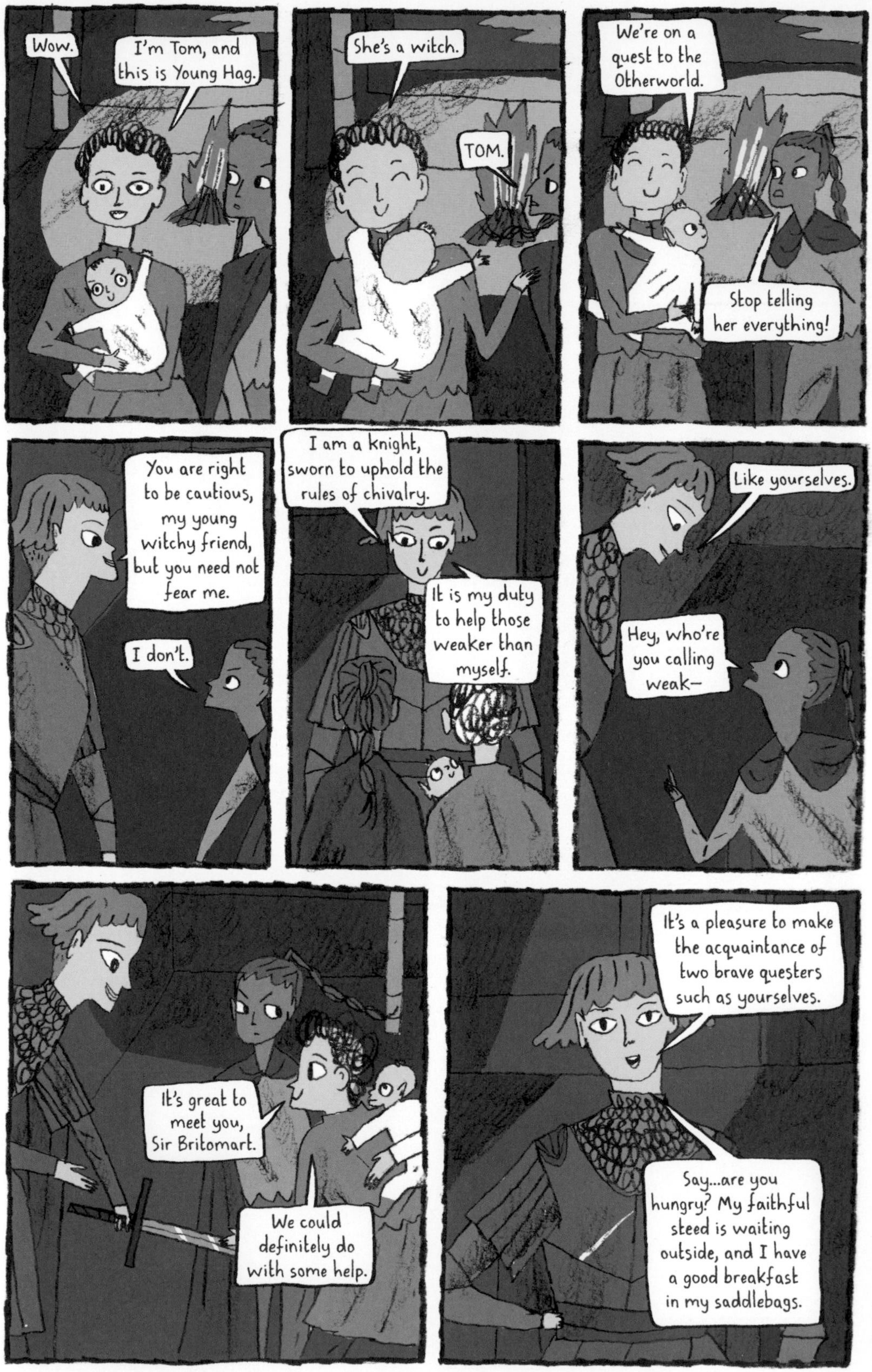
Wow.
I'm Tom, and this is Young Hag.
She's a witch.
TOM.
We're on a quest to the Otherworld.
Stop telling her everything!
You are right to be cautious, my young witchy friend, but you need not fear me.
I don't.
I am a knight, sworn to uphold the rules of chivalry.
It is my duty to help those weaker than myself.
Like yourselves.
Hey, who're you calling weak—
It's great to meet you, Sir Britomart.
We could definitely do with some help.
It's a pleasure to make the acquaintance of two brave questers such as yourselves.
Say...are you hungry? My faithful steed is waiting outside, and I have a good breakfast in my saddlebags.

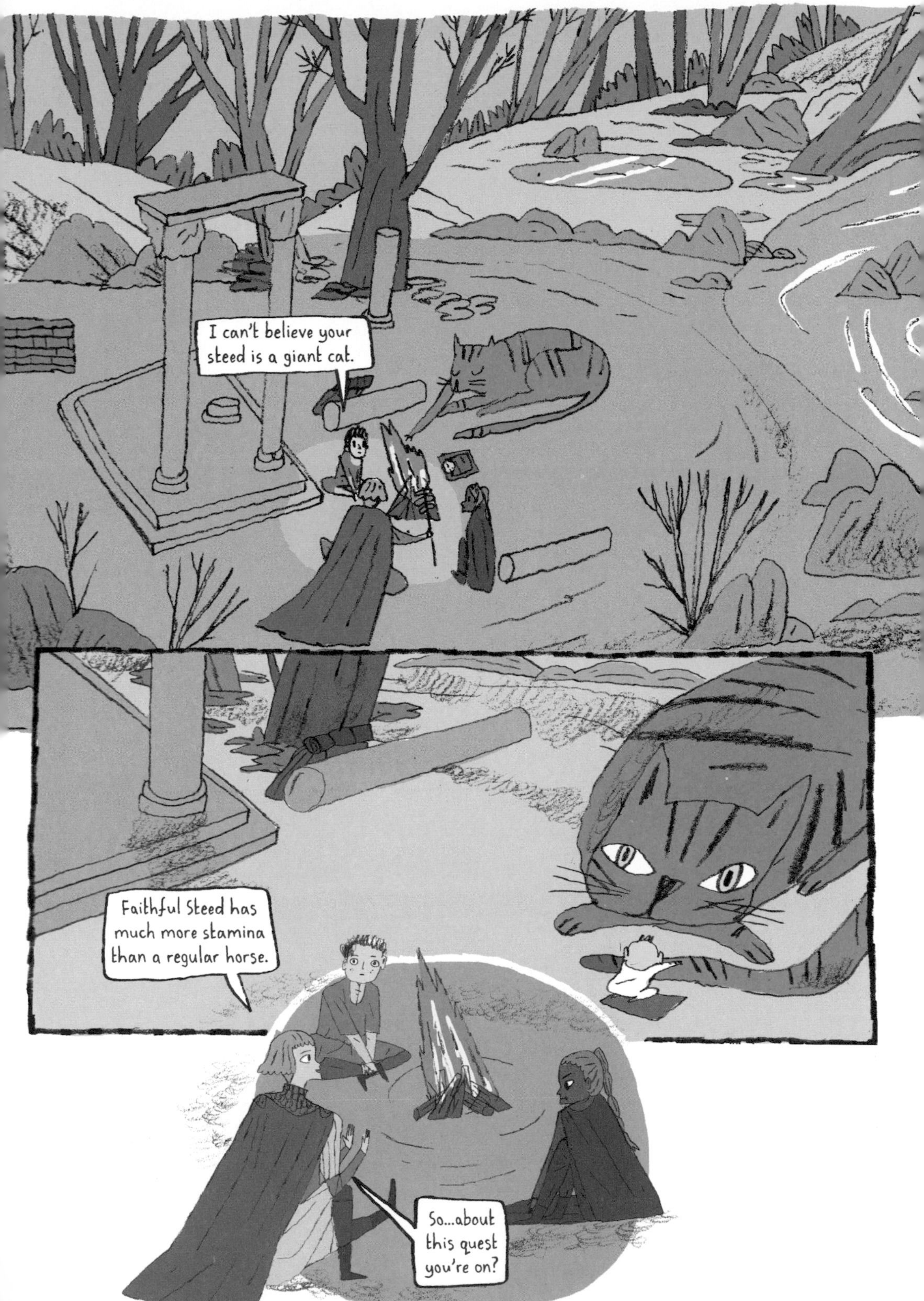
I can't believe your steed is a giant cat.
Faithful Steed has much more stamina than a regular horse.
So...about this quest you're on?

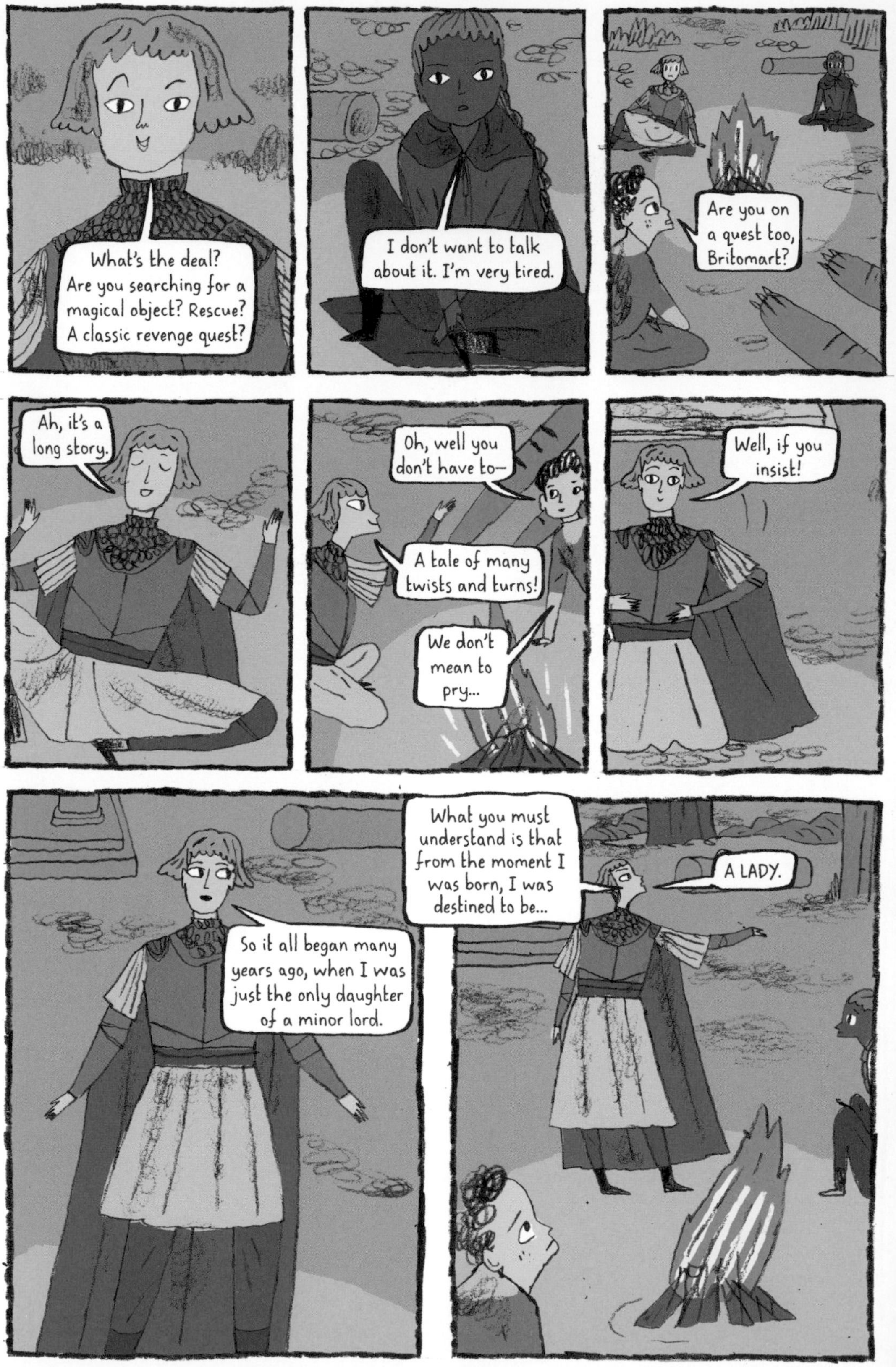
What's the deal? Are you searching for a magical object? Rescue? A classic revenge quest?
I don't want to talk about it. I'm very tired.
Are you on a quest too, Britomart?
Ah, it's a long story.
Oh, well you don't have to—
A tale of many twists and turns!
We don't mean to pry...
Well, if you insist!
So it all began many years ago, when I was just the only daughter of a minor lord.
What you must understand is that from the moment I was born, I was destined to be...
A LADY.

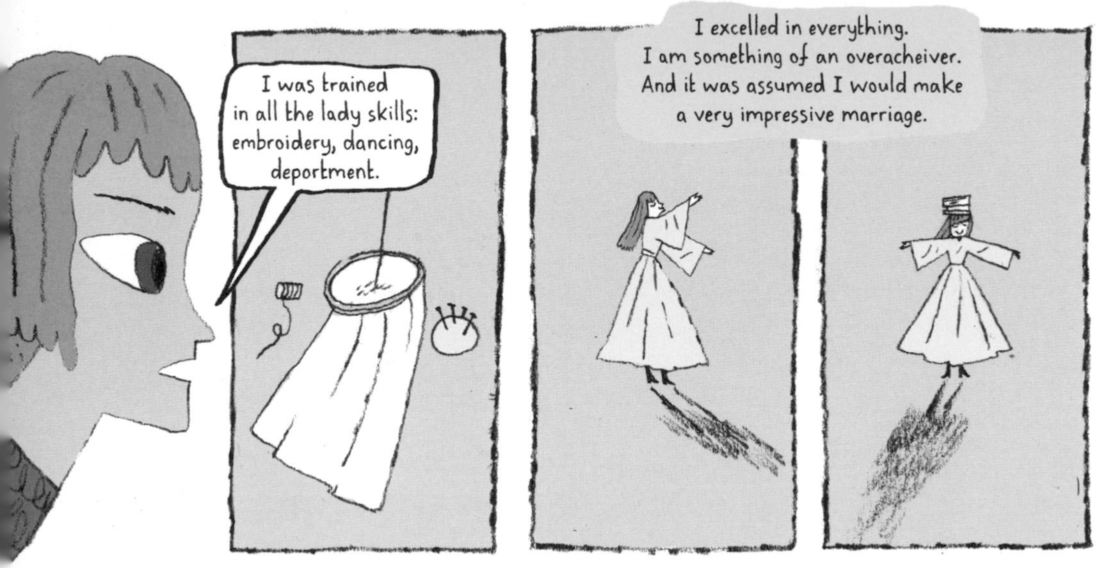
I was trained in all the lady skills: embroidery, dancing, deportment.
I excelled in everything. I am something of an overacheiver. And it was assumed I would make a very impressive marriage.

But when I was around ten or eleven, I began to grow at an alarming rate. Soon I was taller than my father.

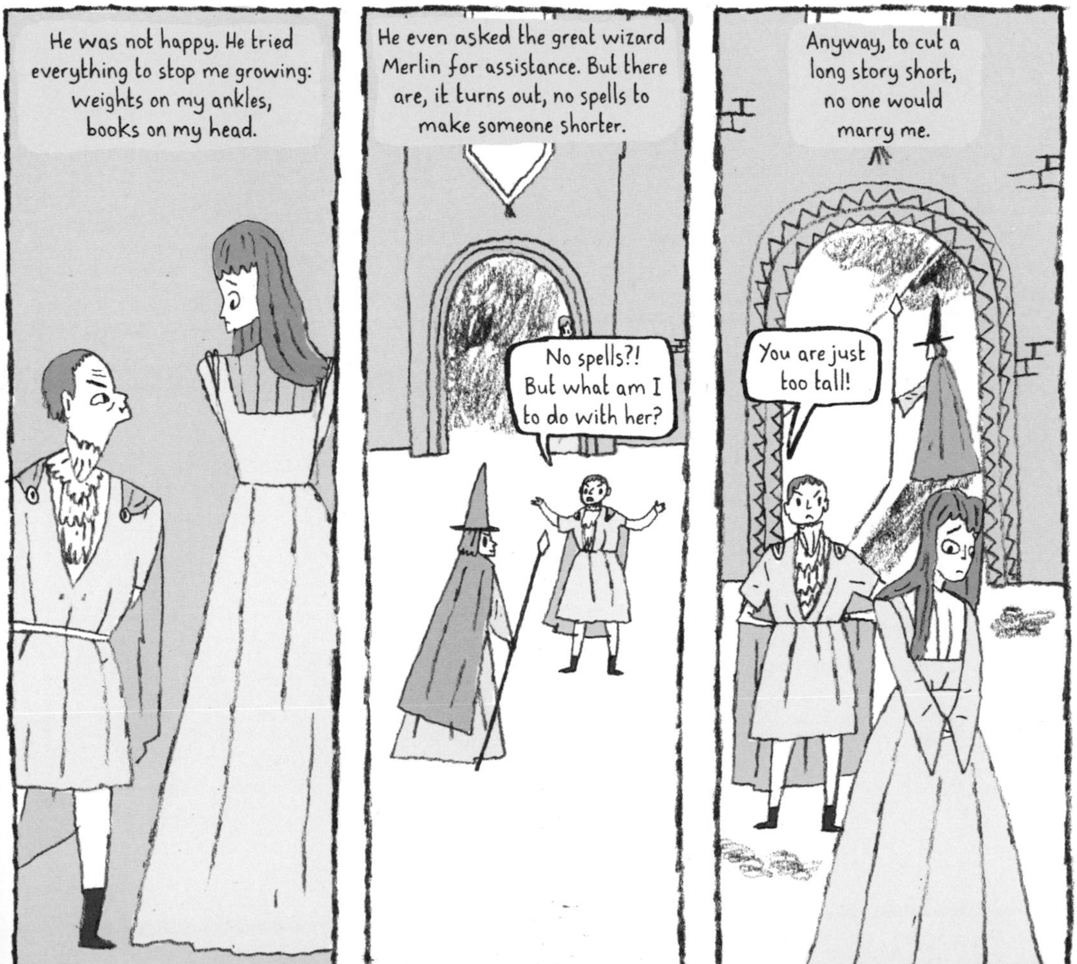
He was not happy. He tried everything to stop me growing: weights on my ankles, books on my head.
He even asked the great wizard Merlin for assistance. But there are, it turns out, no spells to make someone shorter.
No spells?! But what am I to do with her?
Anyway, to cut a long story short, no one would marry me.
You are just too tall!

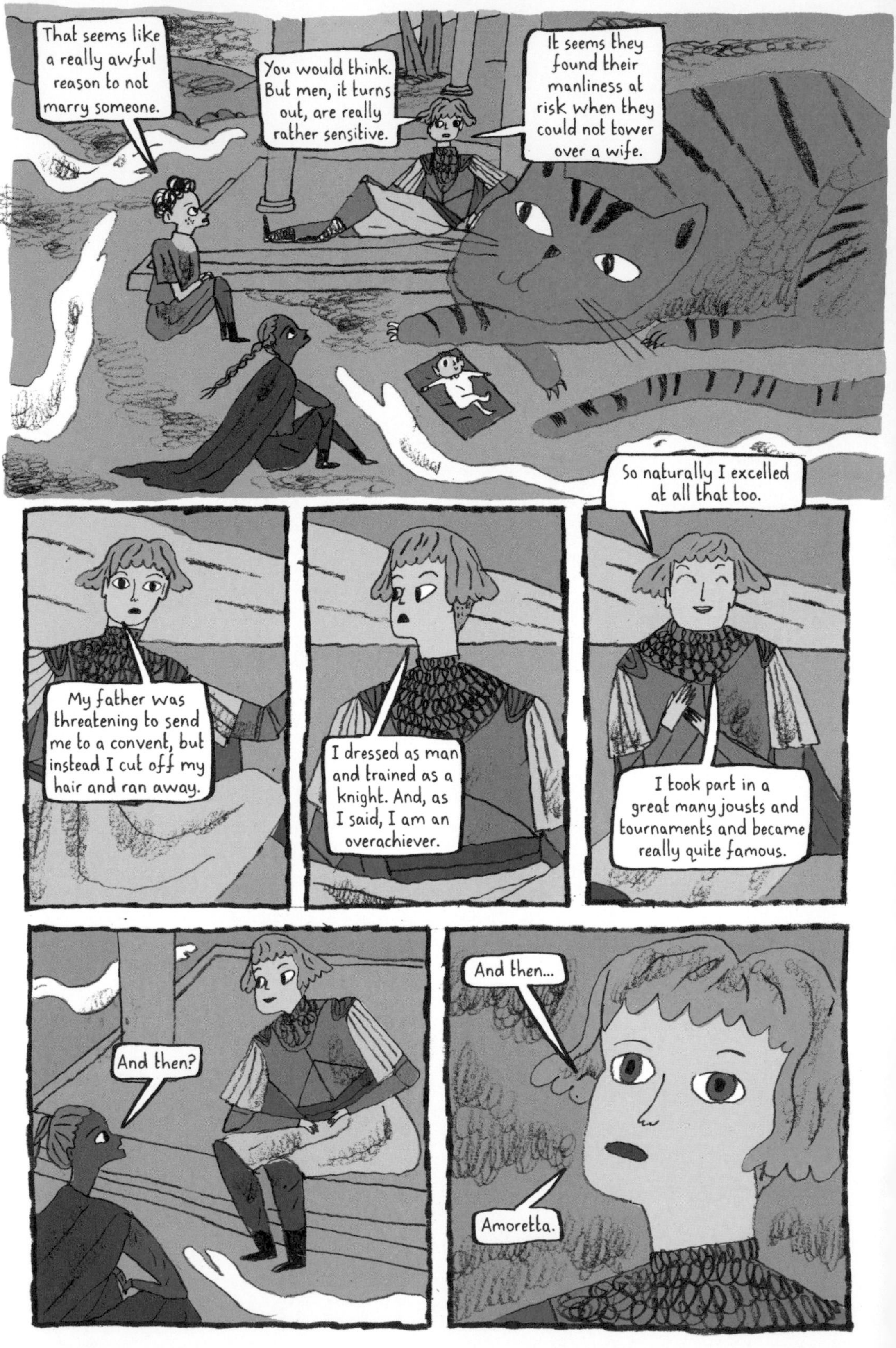
That seems like a really awful reason to not marry someone.
You would think. But men, it turns out, are really rather sensitive.
It seems they found their manliness at risk when they could not tower over a wife.
My father was threatening to send me to a convent, but instead I cut off my hair and ran away.
I dressed as man and trained as a knight. And, as I said, I am an overachiever.
So naturally I excelled at all that too.
I took part in a great many jousts and tournaments and became really quite famous.
And then?
And then...
Amoretta.

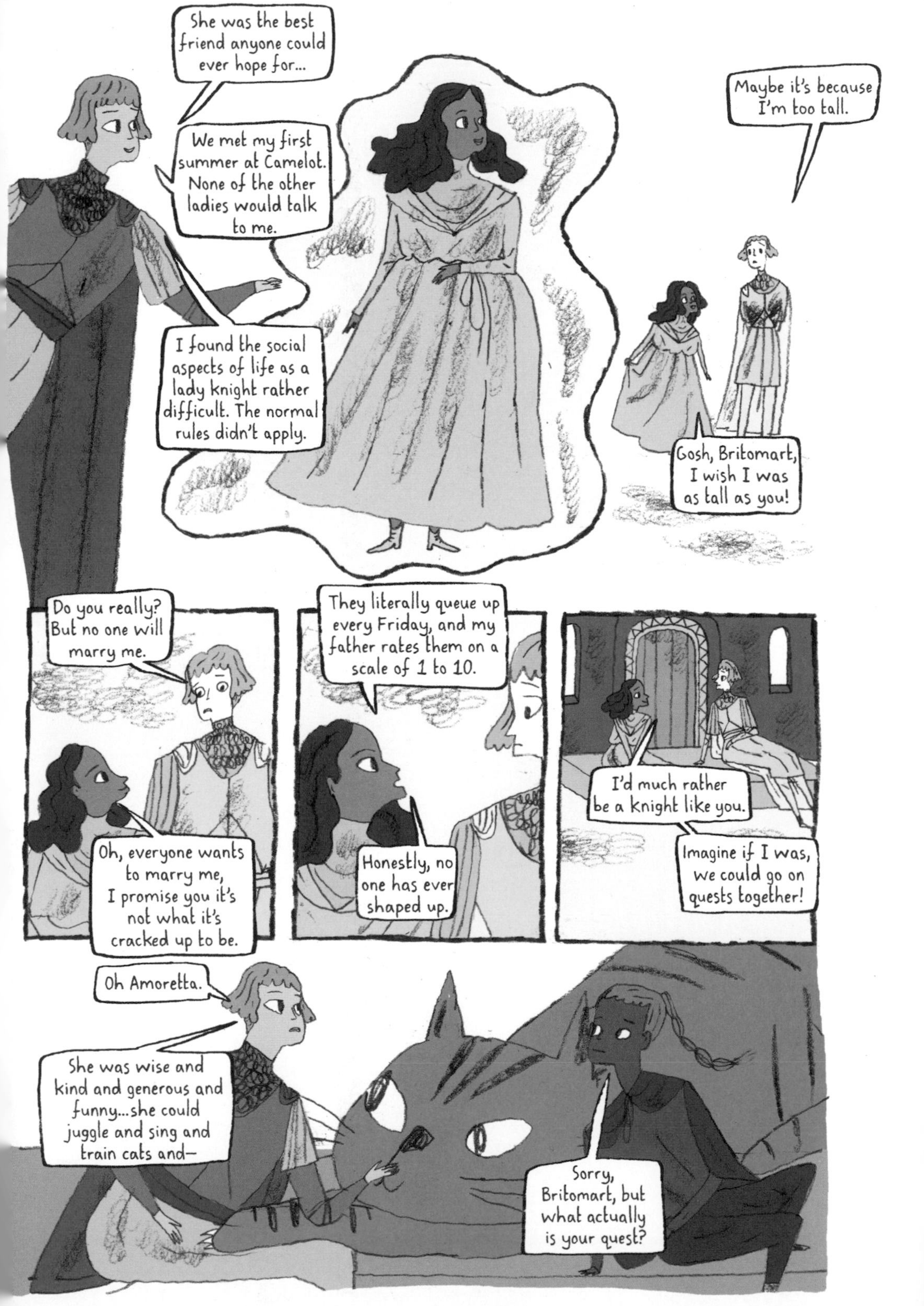
She was the best friend anyone could ever hope for...
We met my first summer at Camelot. None of the other ladies would talk to me.
I found the social aspects of life as a lady knight rather difficult. The normal rules didn't apply.
Maybe it's because I'm too tall.
Gosh, Britomart, I wish I was as tall as you!
Do you really? But no one will marry me.
Oh, everyone wants to marry me, I promise you it's not what it's cracked up to be.
They literally queue up every Friday, and my father rates them on a scale of 1 to 10.
Honestly, no one has ever shaped up.
I'd much rather be a knight like you.
Imagine if I was, we could go on quests together!
Oh Amoretta.
She was wise and kind and generous and funny...she could juggle and sing and train cats and—
Sorry, Britomart, but what actually is your quest?

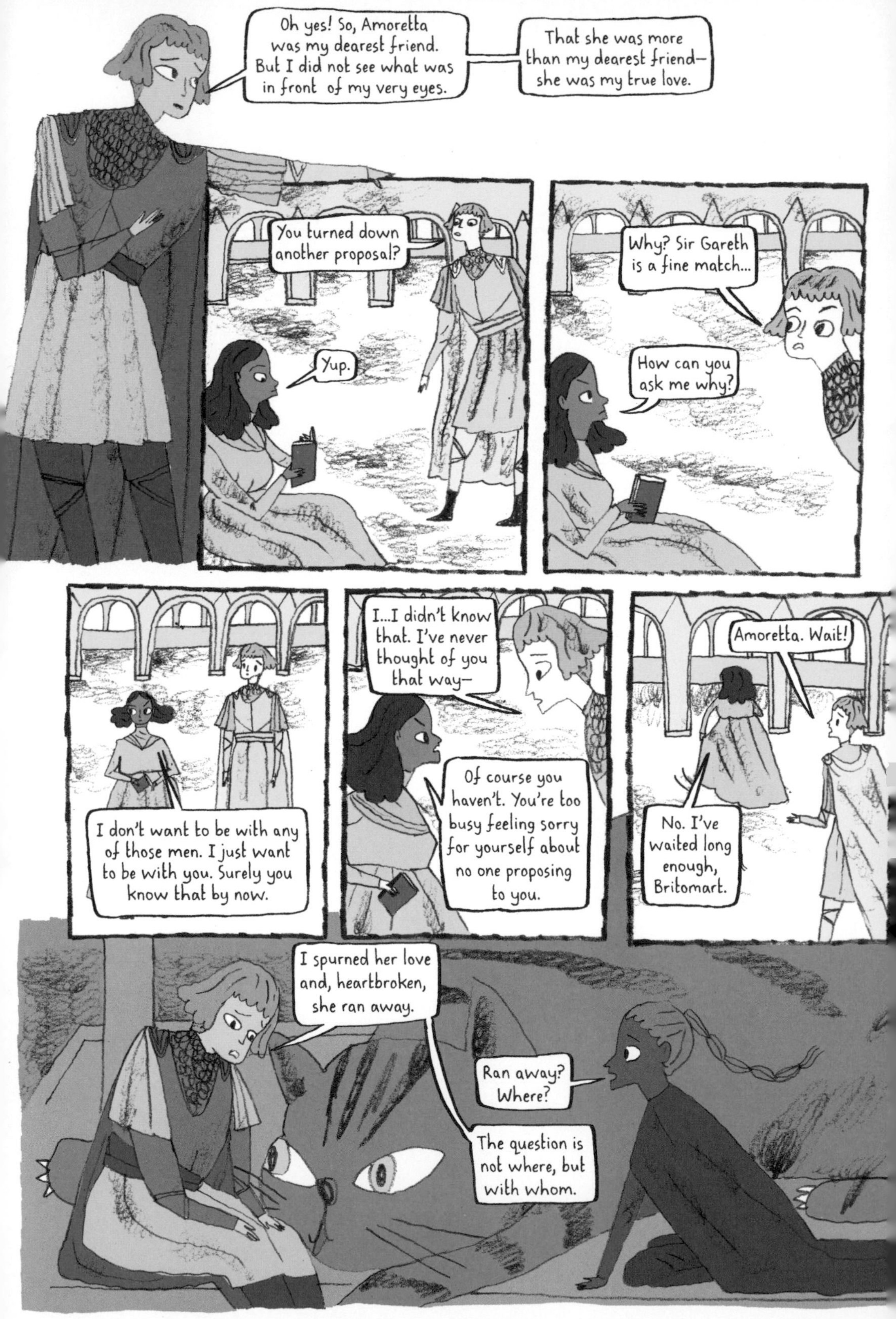
Oh yes! So, Amoretta was my dearest friend. But I did not see what was in front of my very eyes.
That she was more than my dearest friend— she was my true love.
You turned down another proposal?
Yup.
Why? Sir Gareth is a fine match...
How can you ask me why?
I don't want to be with any of those men. I just want to be with you. Surely you know that by now.
I...I didn't know that. I've never thought of you that way—
Of course you haven't. You're too busy feeling sorry for yourself about no one proposing to you.
Amoretta. Wait!
No. I've waited long enough, Britomart.
I spurned her love and, heartbroken, she ran away.
Ran away? Where?
The question is not where, but with whom.

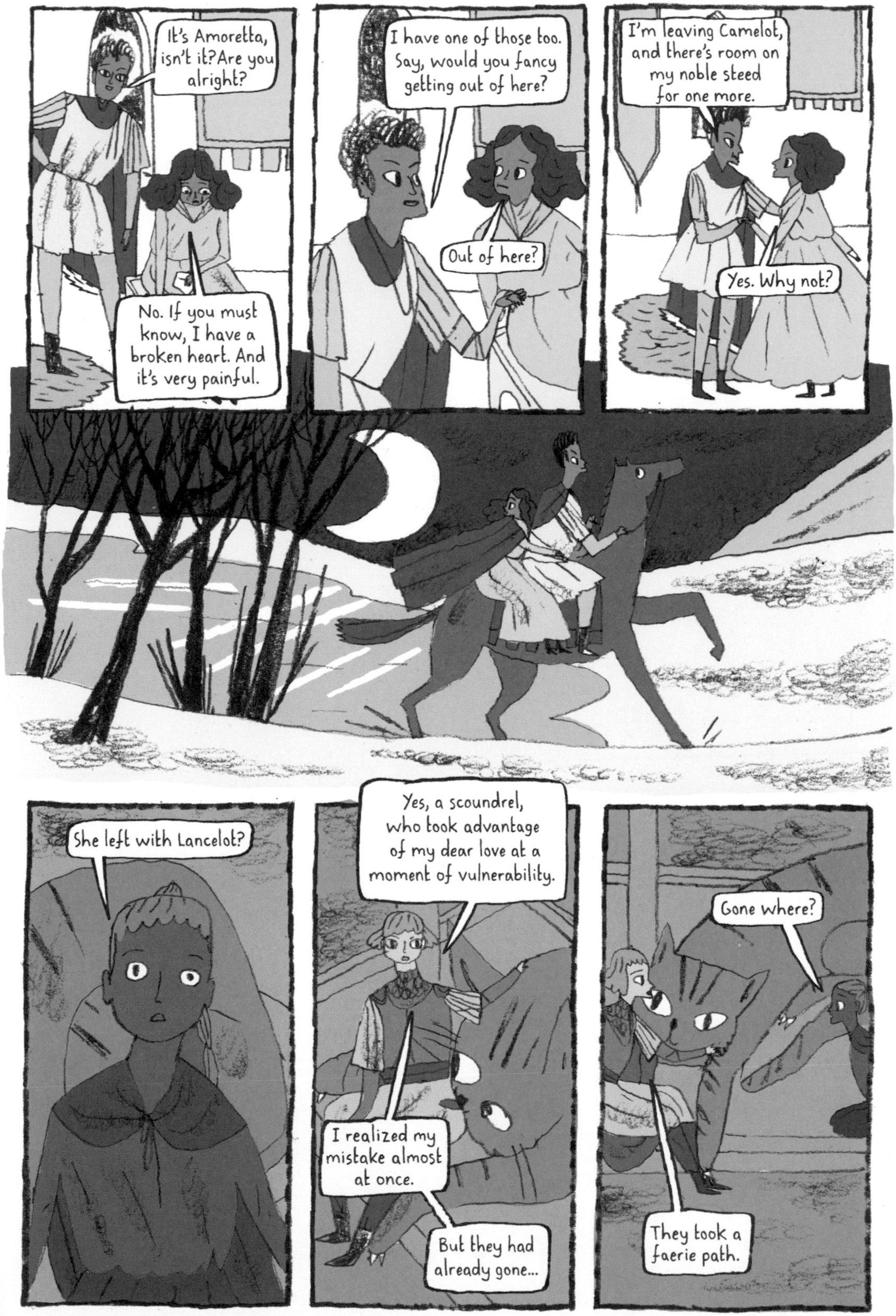
It's Amoretta, isn't it? Are you alright?
No. If you must know, I have a broken heart. And it's very painful.
I have one of those too. Say, would you fancy getting out of here?
Out of here?
I'm leaving Camelot, and there's room on my noble steed for one more.
Yes. Why not?
She left with Lancelot?
Yes, a scoundrel, who took advantage of my dear love at a moment of vulnerability.
I realized my mistake almost at once.
But they had already gone...
Gone where?
They took a faerie path.

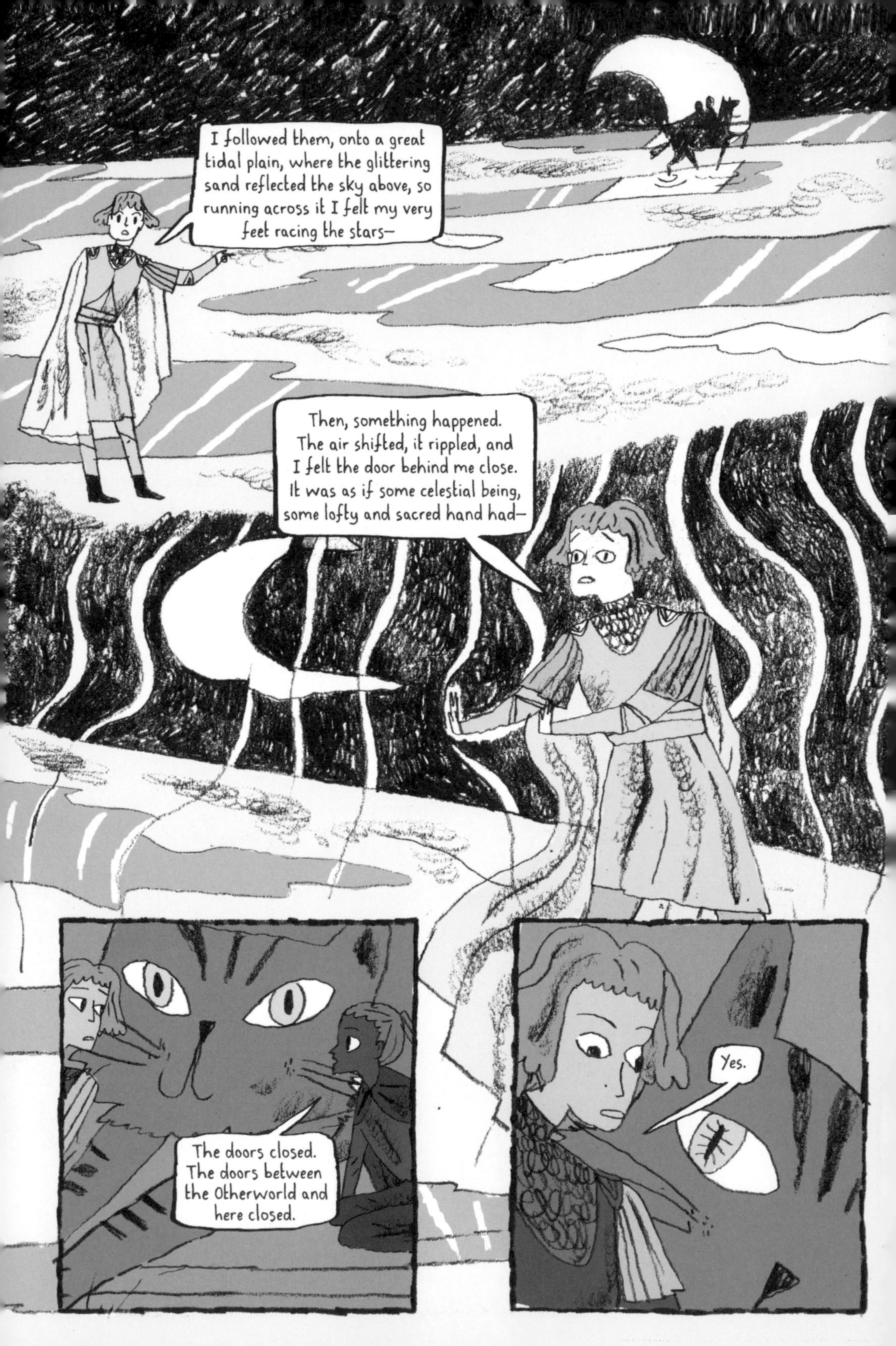
I followed them, onto a great tidal plain, where the glittering sand reflected the sky above, so running across it I felt my very feet racing the stars—
Then, something happened. The air shifted, it rippled, and I felt the door behind me close. It was as if some celestial being, some lofty and sacred hand had—
The doors closed. The doors between the Otherworld and here closed.
Yes.

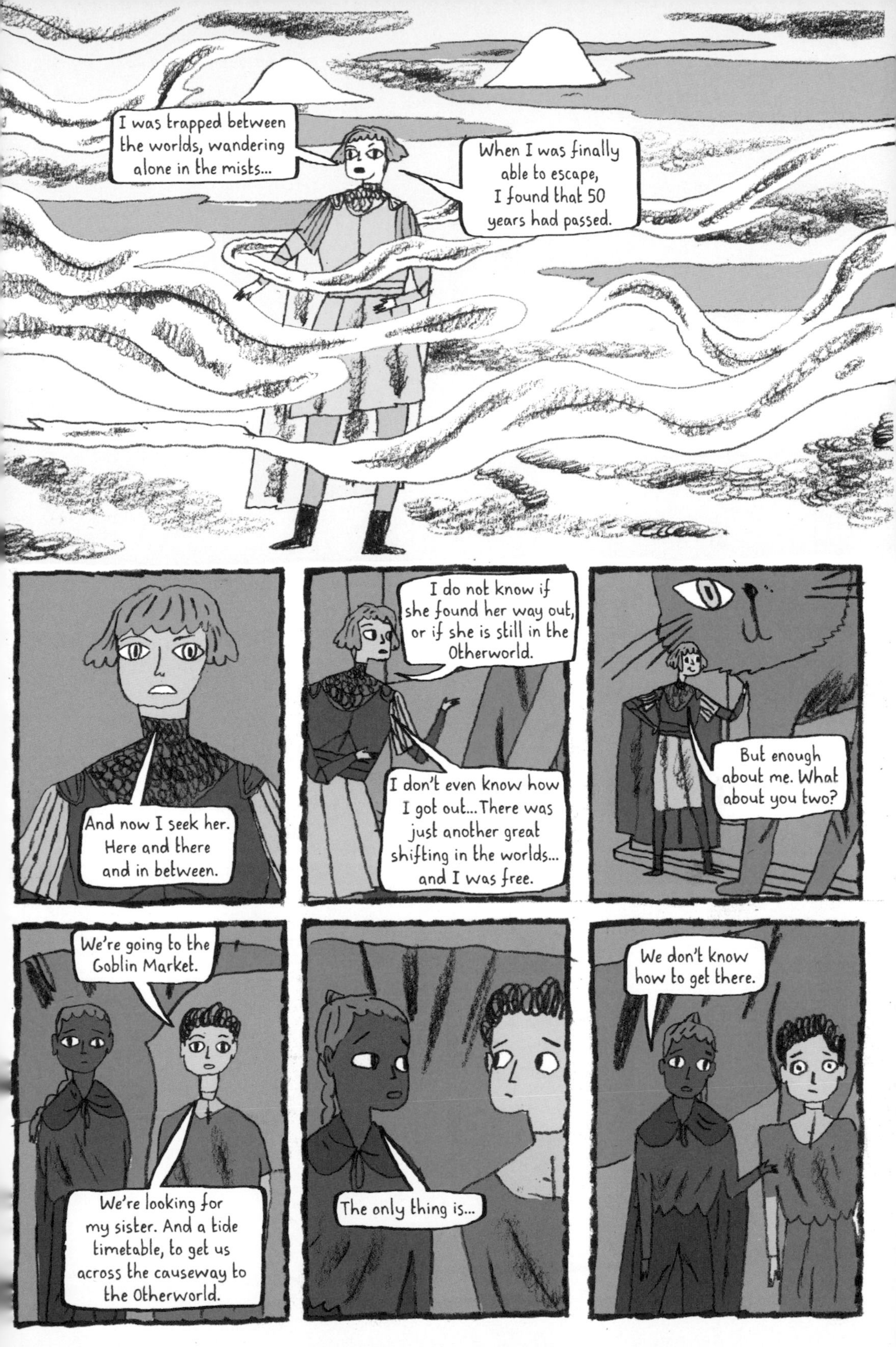
I was trapped between the worlds, wandering alone in the mists...
When I was finally able to escape, I found that 50 years had passed.
And now I seek her. Here and there and in between.
I do not know if she found her way out, or if she is still in the Otherworld.
I don't even know how I got out... There was just another great shifting in the worlds... and I was free.
But enough about me. What about you two?
We're going to the Goblin Market.
We're looking for my sister. And a tide timetable, to get us across the causeway to the Otherworld.
The only thing is...
We don't know how to get there.

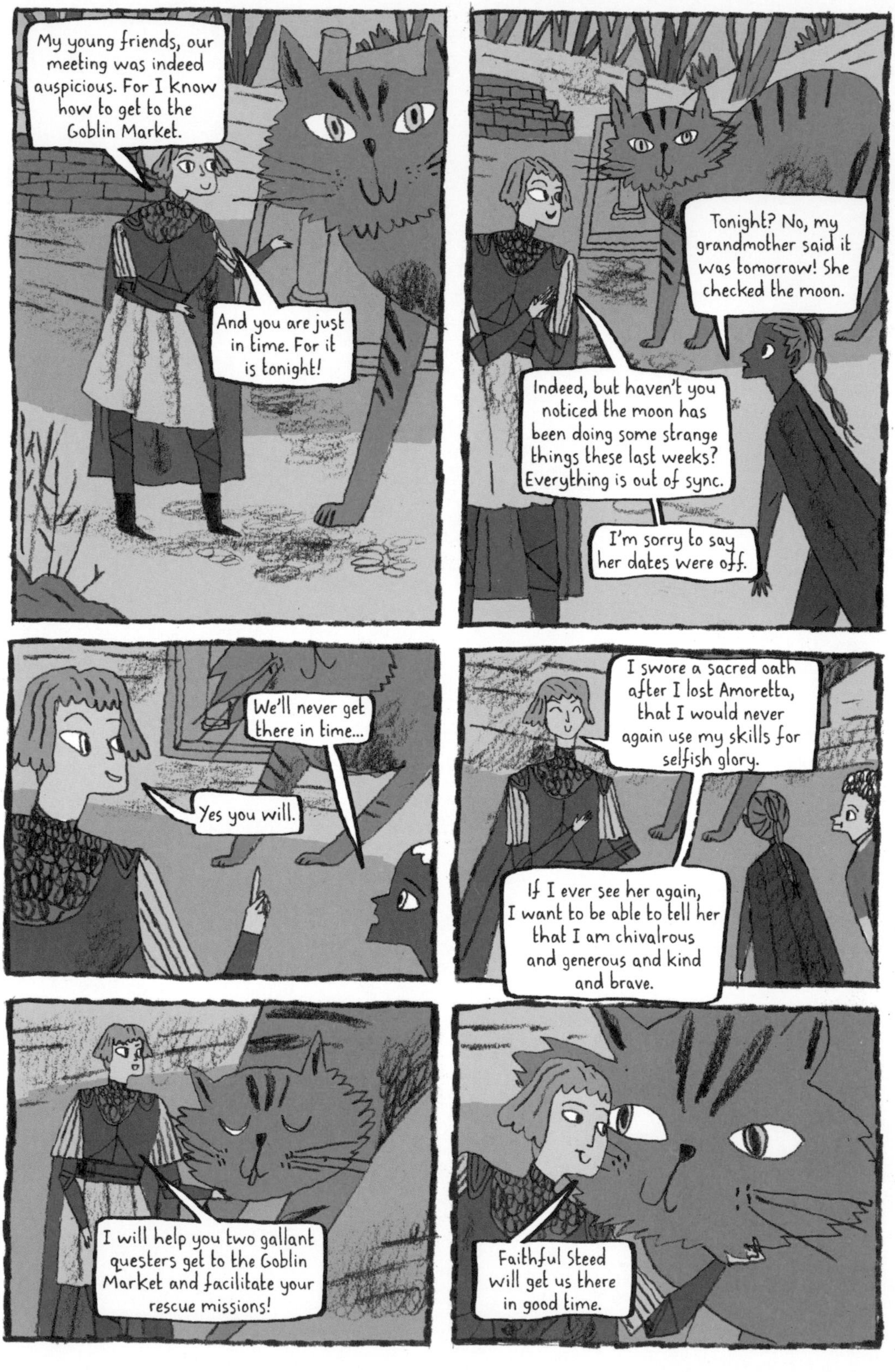
My young friends, our meeting was indeed auspicious. For I know how to get to the Goblin Market.
And you are just in time. For it is tonight!
Tonight? No, my grandmother said it was tomorrow! She checked the moon.
Indeed, but haven't you noticed the moon has been doing some strange things these last weeks? Everything is out of sync.
I'm sorry to say her dates were off.
We'll never get there in time...
Yes you will.
I swore a sacred oath after I lost Amoretta, that I would never again use my skills for selfish glory.
If I ever see her again, I want to be able to tell her that I am chivalrous and generous and kind and brave.
I will help you two gallant questers get to the Goblin Market and facilitate your rescue missions!
Faithful Steed will get us there in good time.

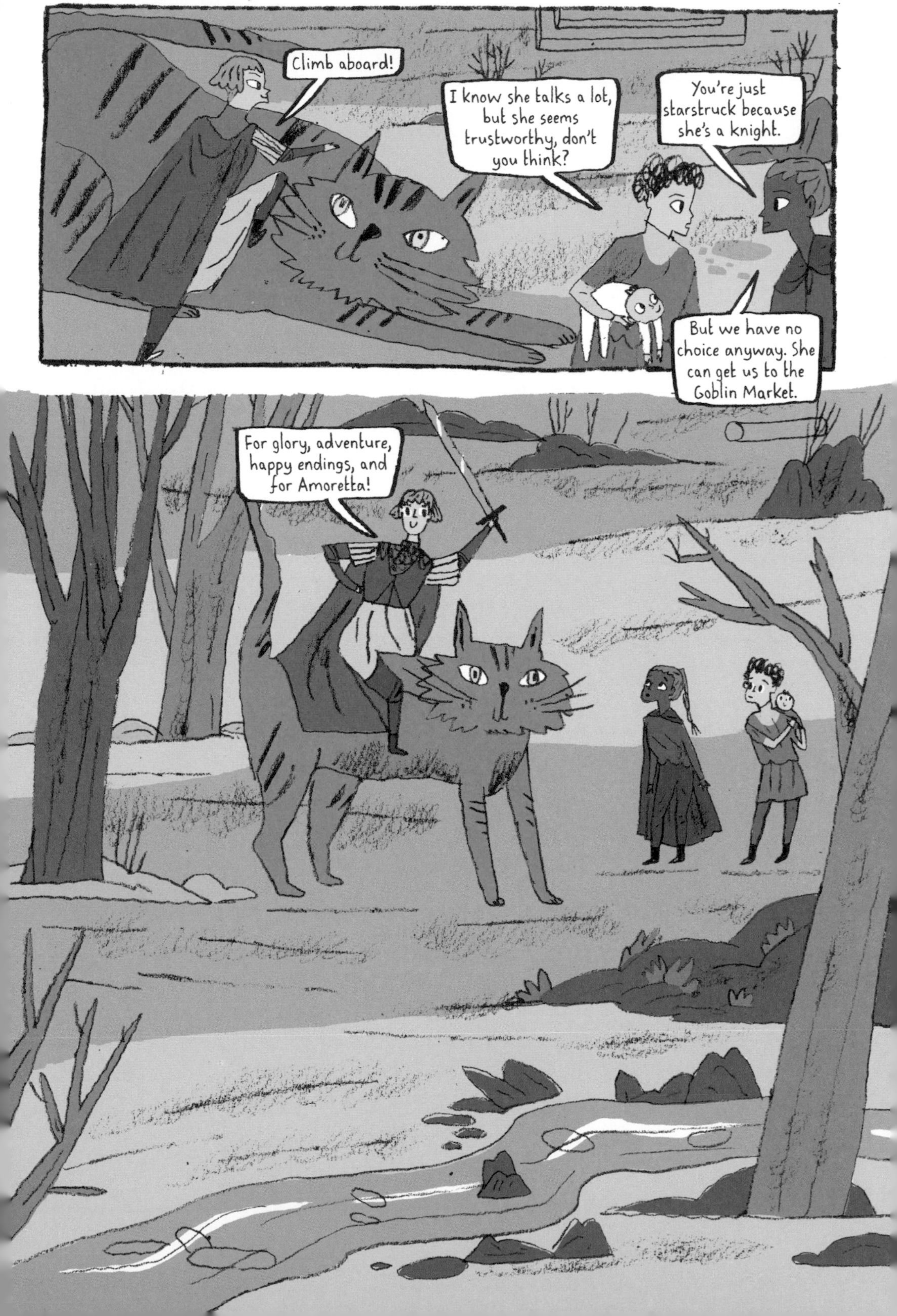
Climb aboard!
I know she talks a lot, but she seems trustworthy, don't you think?
You're just starstruck because she's a knight.
But we have no choice anyway. She can get us to the Goblin Market.
For glory, adventure, happy endings, and for Amoretta!

PART THE FOURTH

The Goblin Market

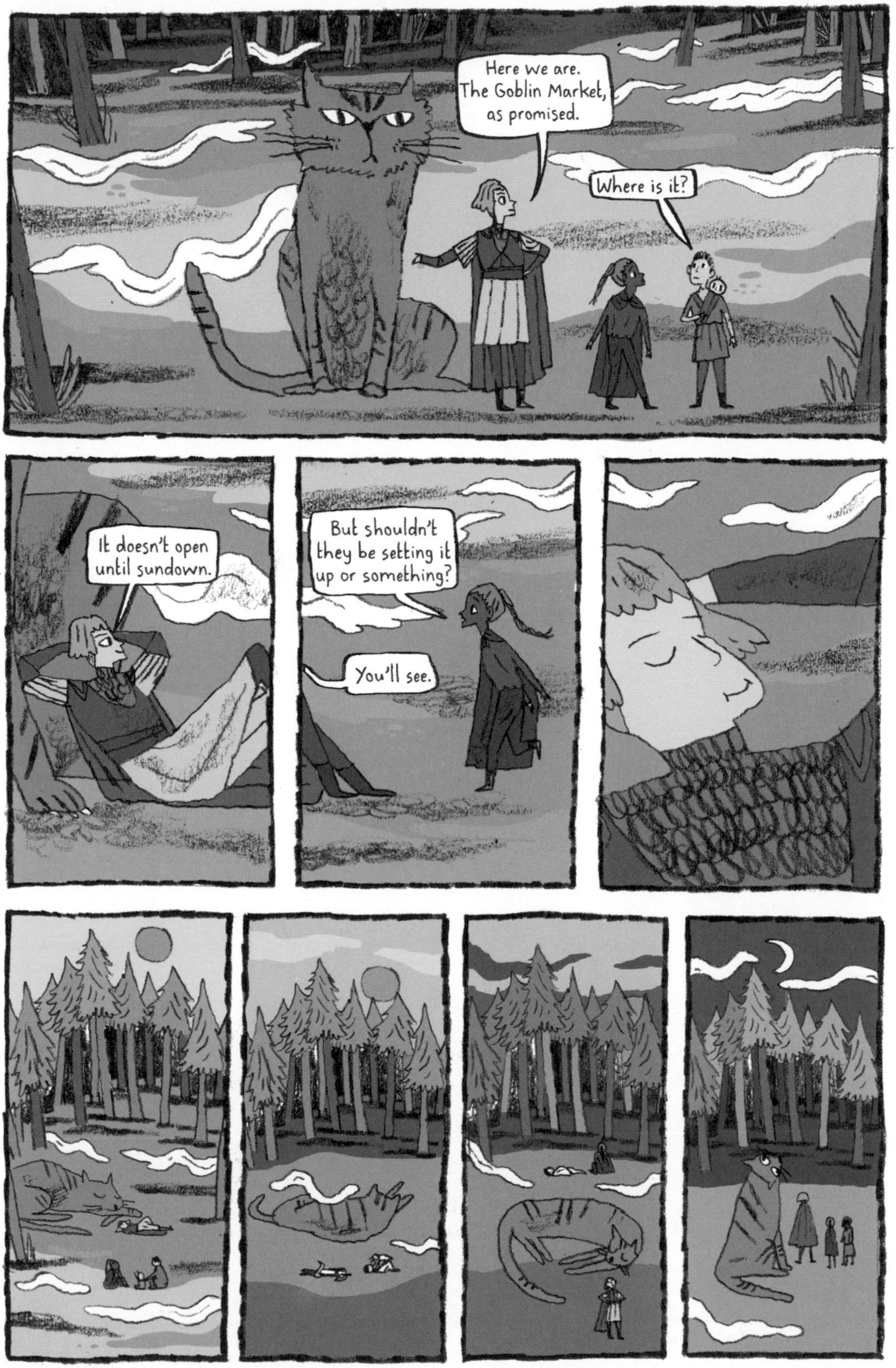
Here we are. The Goblin Market, as promised.
Where is it?
It doesn't open until sundown.
But shouldn't they be setting it up or something?
You'll see.

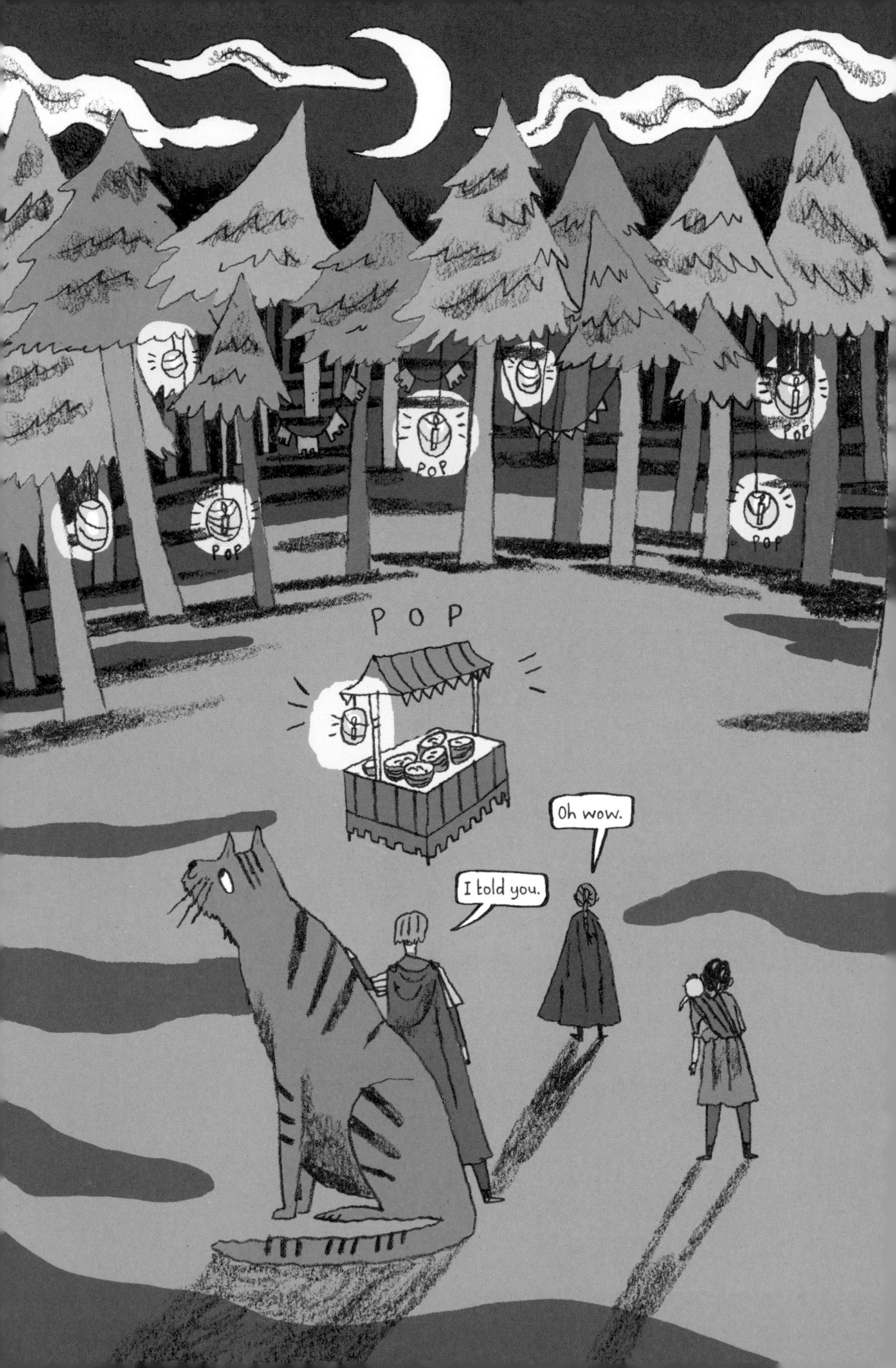

POP
POP
POP
POP
POP
POP
Oh wow.
I told you.

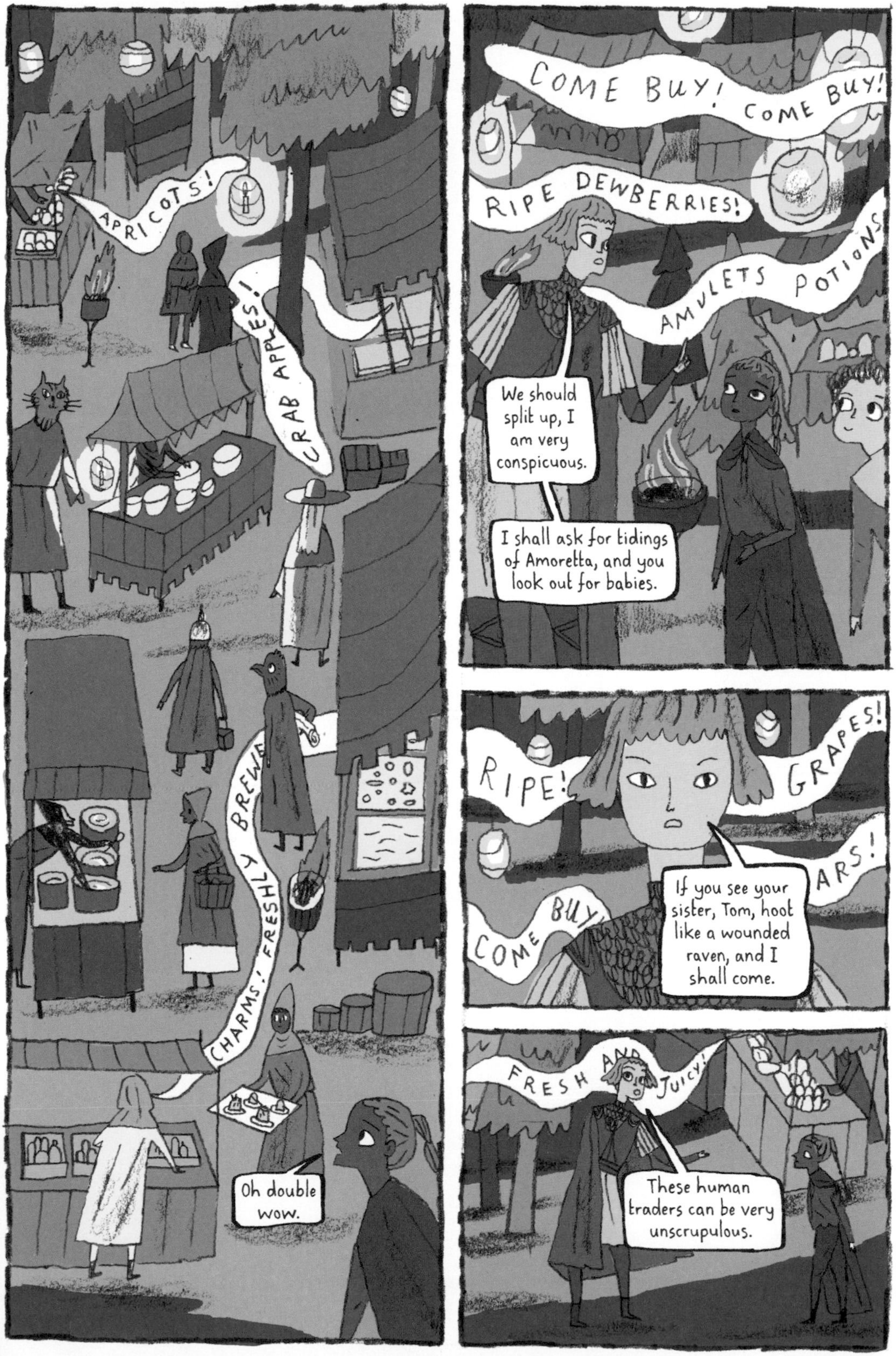
APRICOTS!
CRAB APPLES!
CHARMS! FRESHLY BREWE
Oh double wow.
COME BUY! COME BUY!
RIPE DEWBERRIES!
AMULETS POTIONS
We should split up, I am very conspicuous.
I shall ask for tidings of Amoretta, and you look out for babies.
RIPE! GRAPES!
ARS!
COME BUY
If you see your sister, Tom, hoot like a wounded raven, and I shall come.
FRESH AND JUICY!
These human traders can be very unscrupulous.

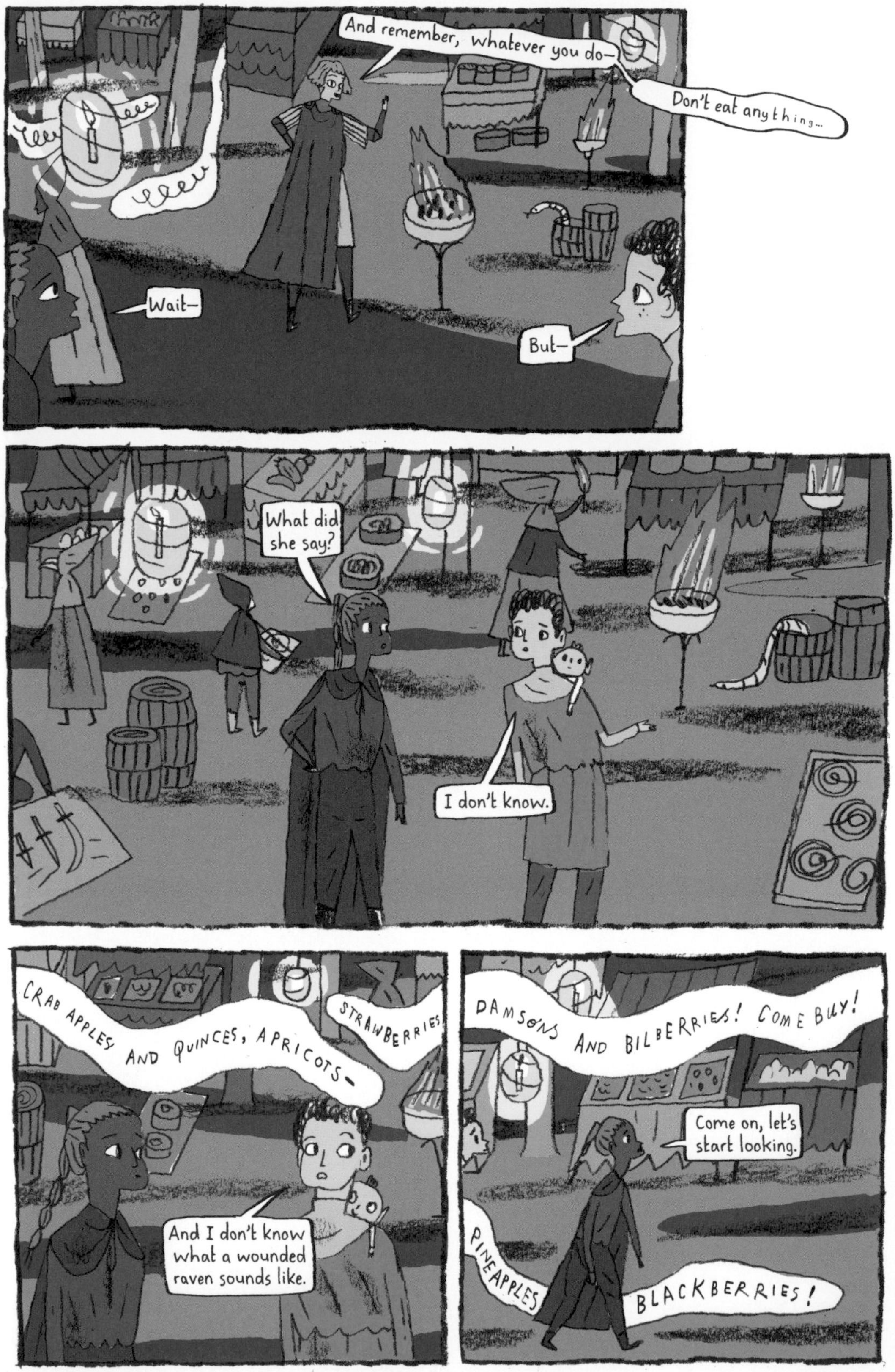
And remember, whatever you do—
Don't eat anything...
Wait—
But—
What did she say?
I don't know.
CRAB APPLES AND QUINCES, APRICOTS—
STRAWBERRIES
And I don't know what a wounded raven sounds like.
DAMSONS AND BILBERRIES! COME BUY!
Come on, let's start looking.
PINEAPPLES
BLACKBERRIES!

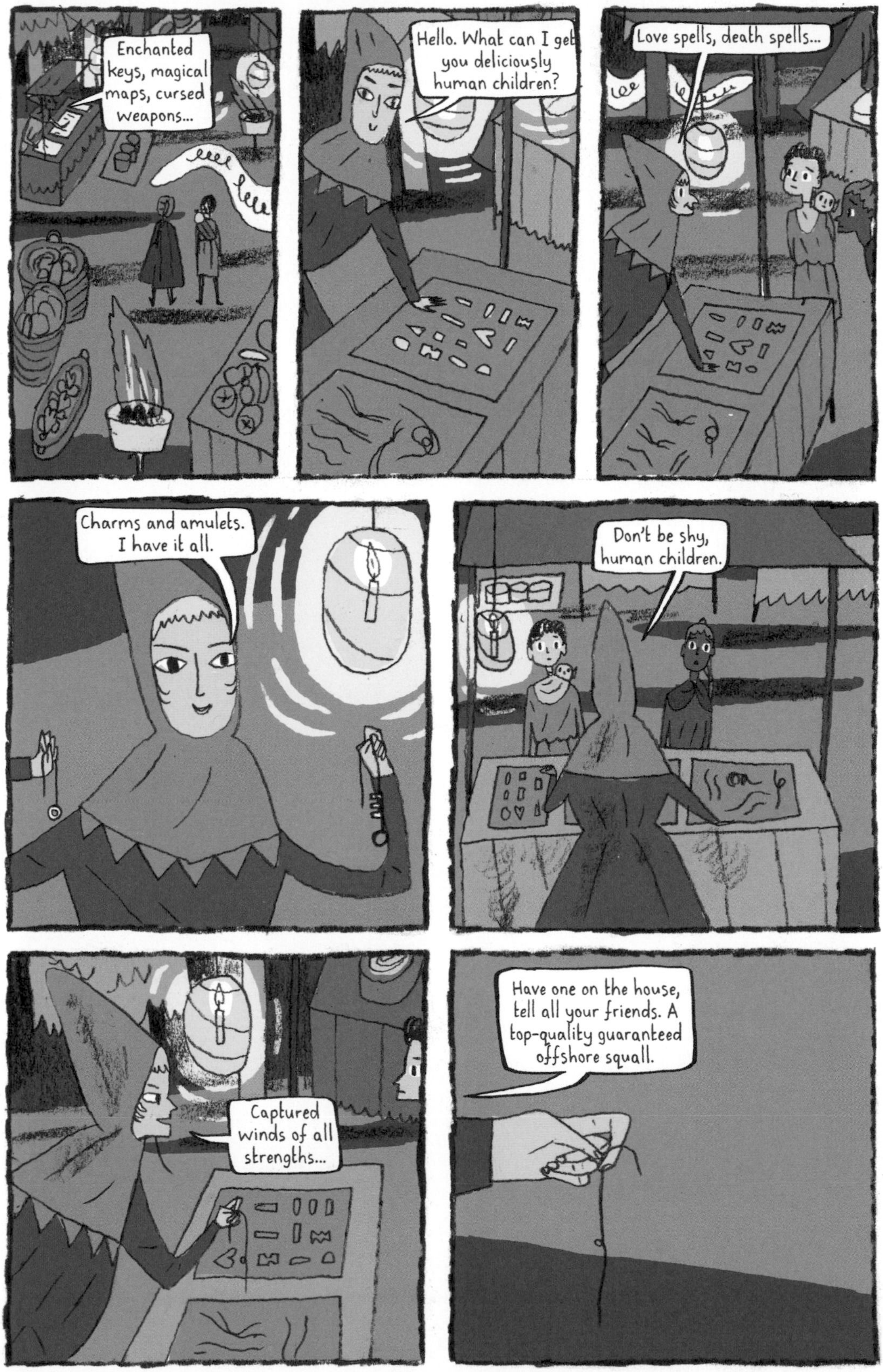
Enchanted keys, magical maps, cursed weapons...
Hello. What can I get you deliciously human children?
Love spells, death spells...
Charms and amulets. I have it all.
Don't be shy, human children.
Captured winds of all strengths...
Have one on the house, tell all your friends. A top-quality guaranteed offshore squall.

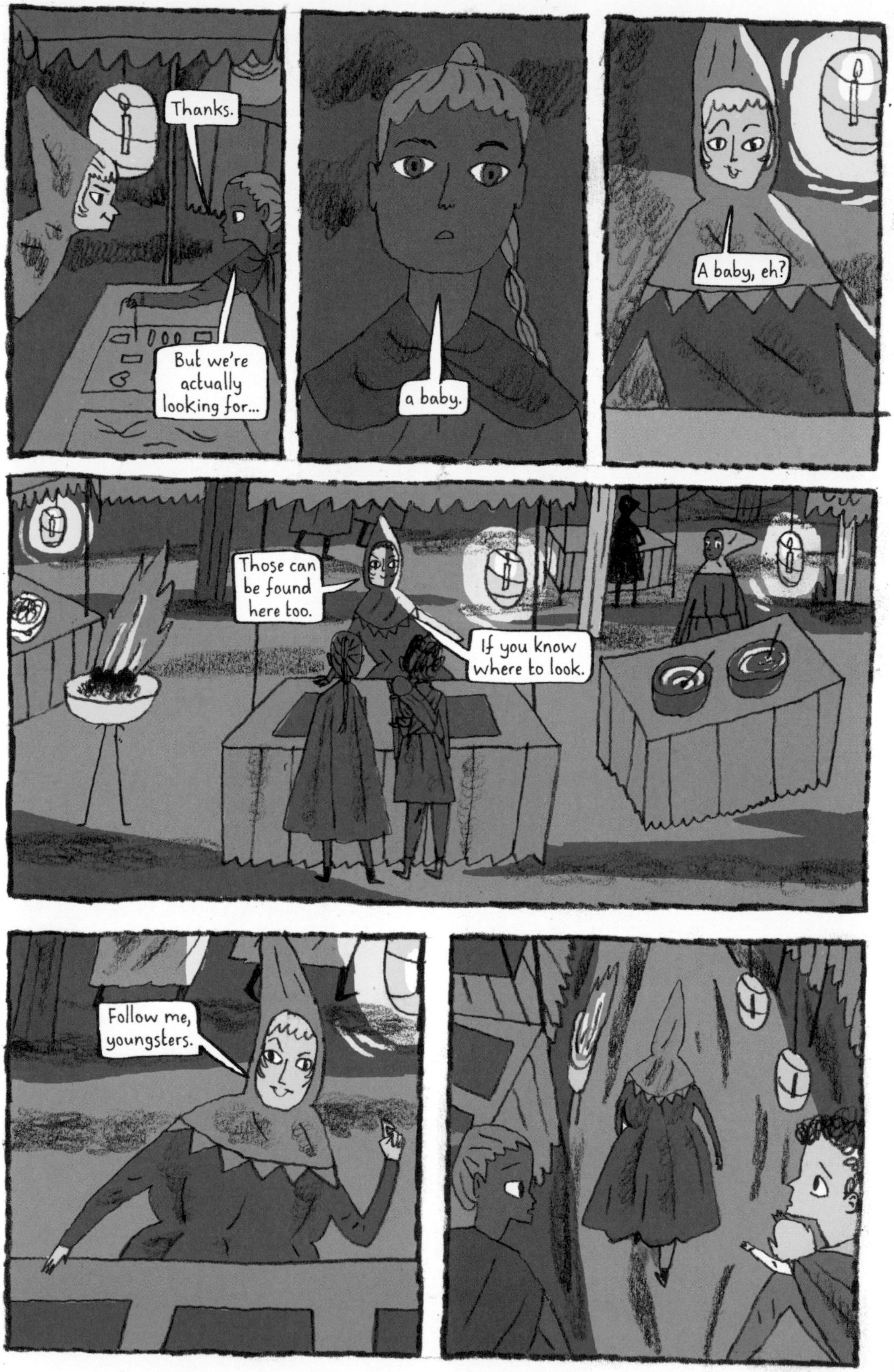
Thanks.
But we're actually looking for...
a baby.
A baby, eh?
Those can be found here too.
If you know where to look.
Follow me, youngsters.

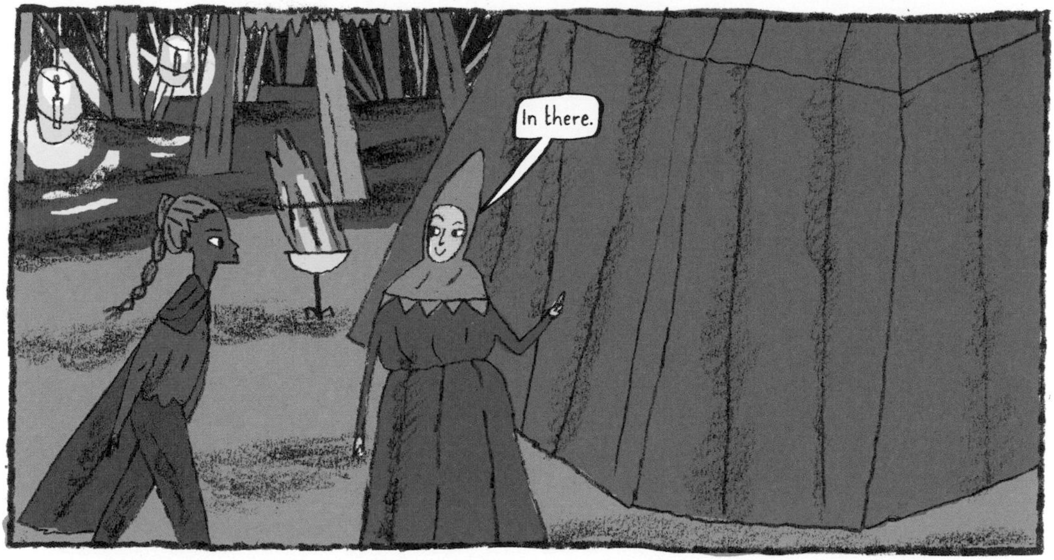
In there.

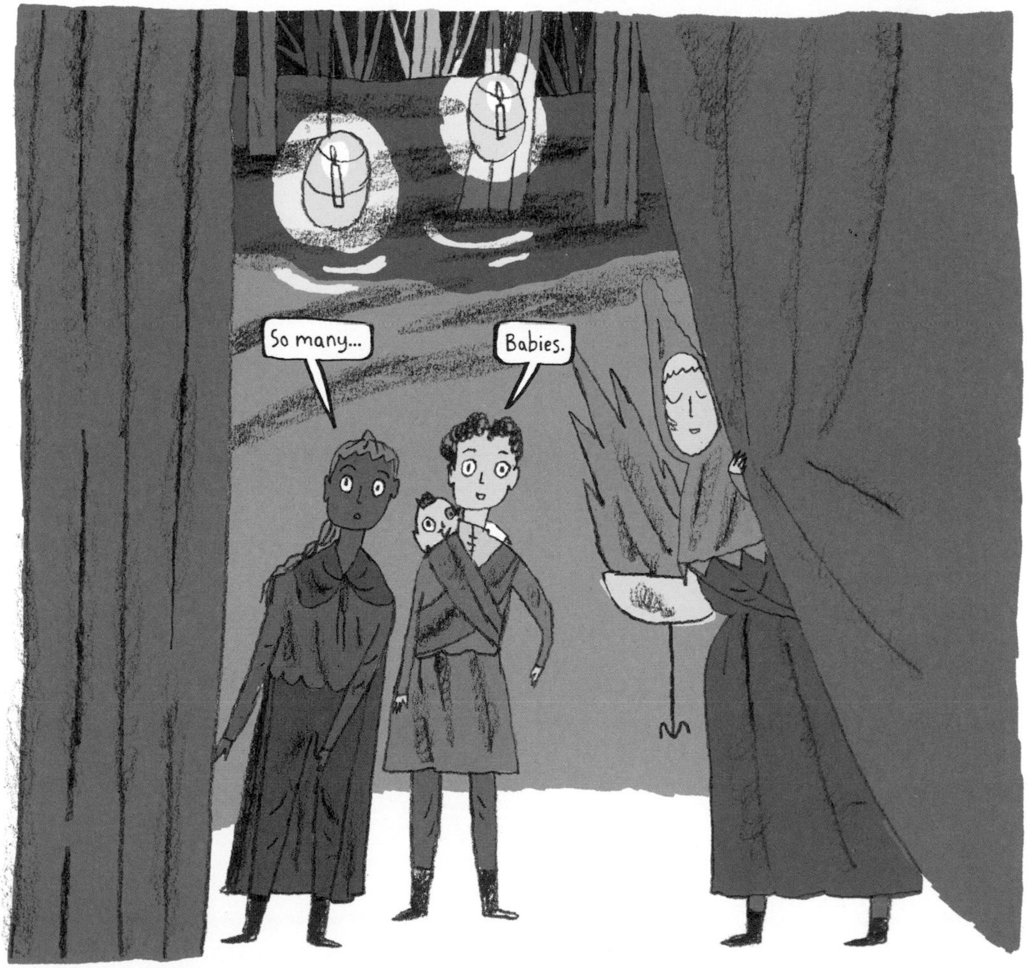
So many...
Babies.

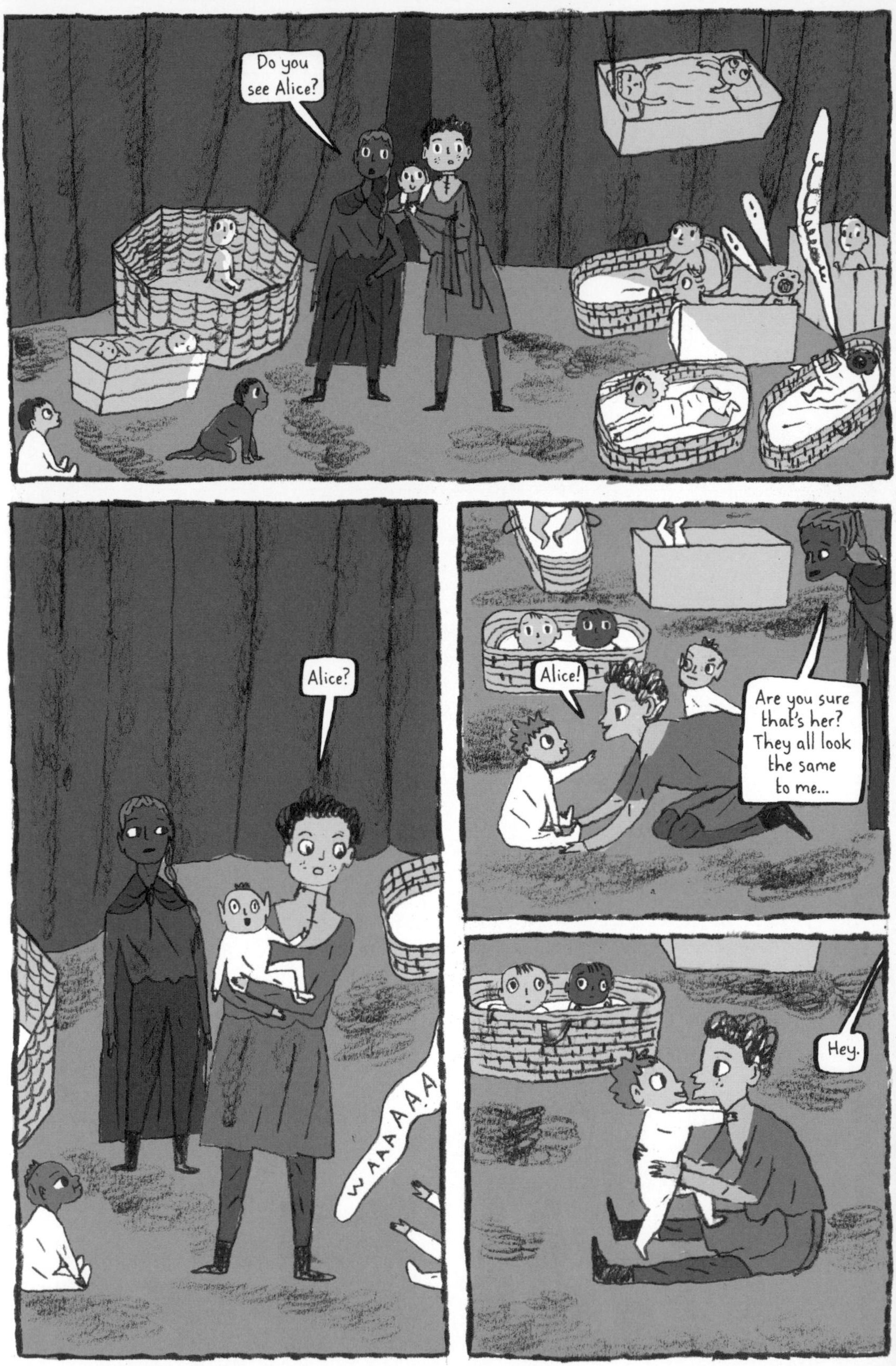
Do you see Alice?
Alice?
WAAAAAA
Alice!
Are you sure that's her? They all look the same to me...
Hey.

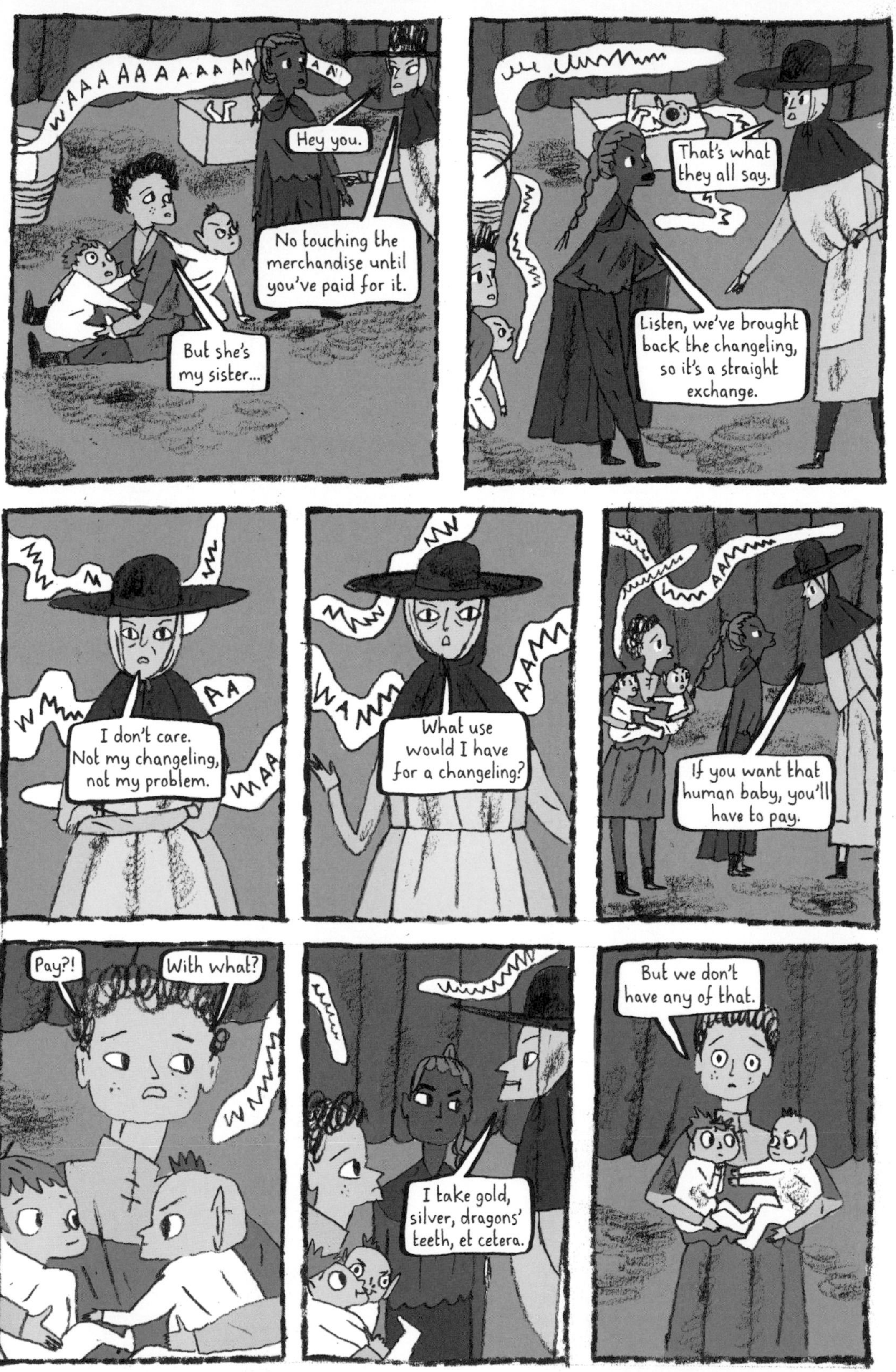
WAAAAAAAAAAAAA
Hey you.
No touching the merchandise until you've paid for it.
But she's my sister...
That's what they all say.
Listen, we've brought back the changeling, so it's a straight exchange.
I don't care. Not my changeling, not my problem.
What use would I have for a changeling?
If you want that human baby, you'll have to pay.
Pay?!
With what?
I take gold, silver, dragons' teeth, et cetera.
But we don't have any of that.

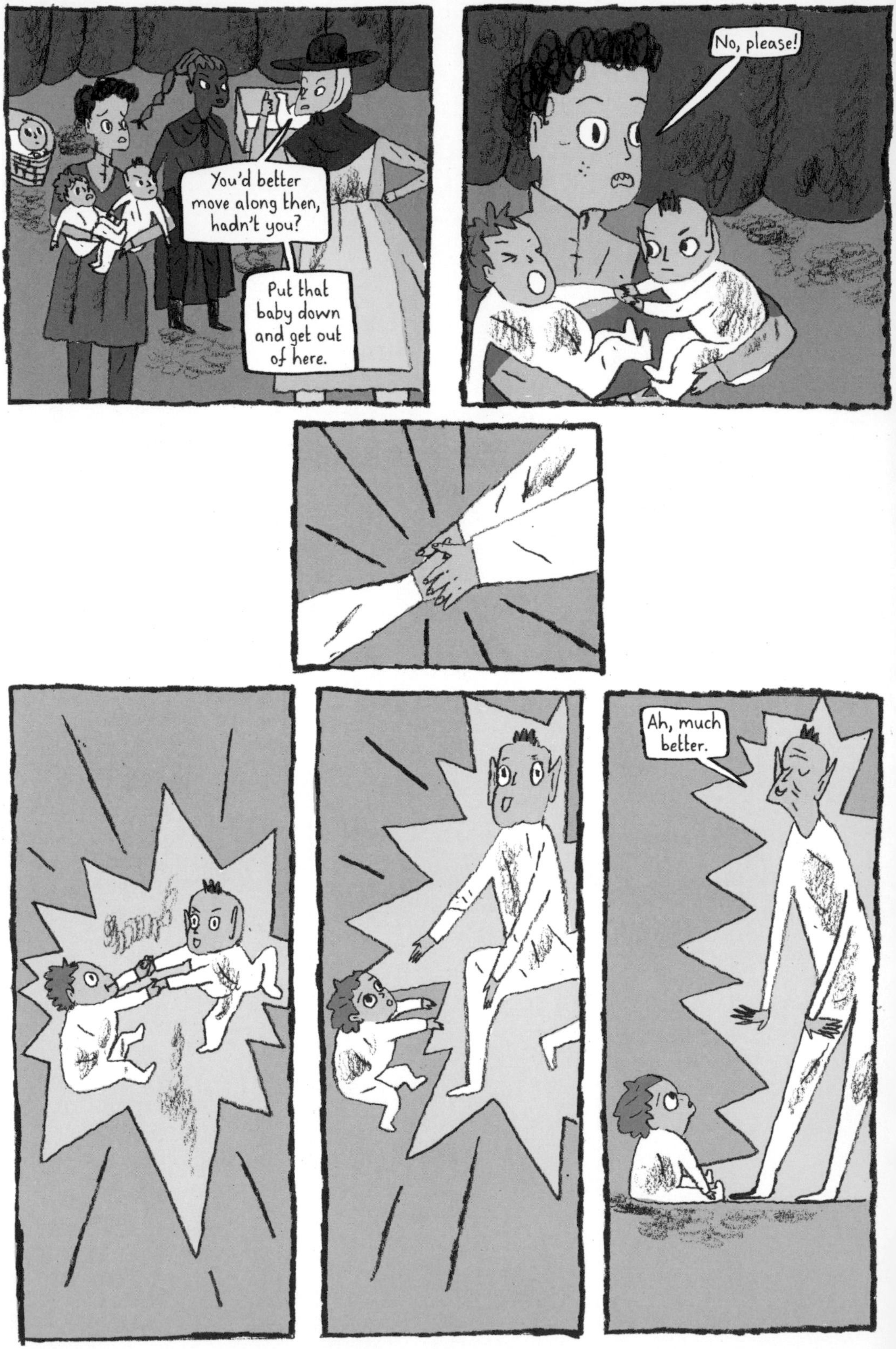
You'd better move along then, hadn't you?
Put that baby down and get out of here.
No, please!
Ah, much better.

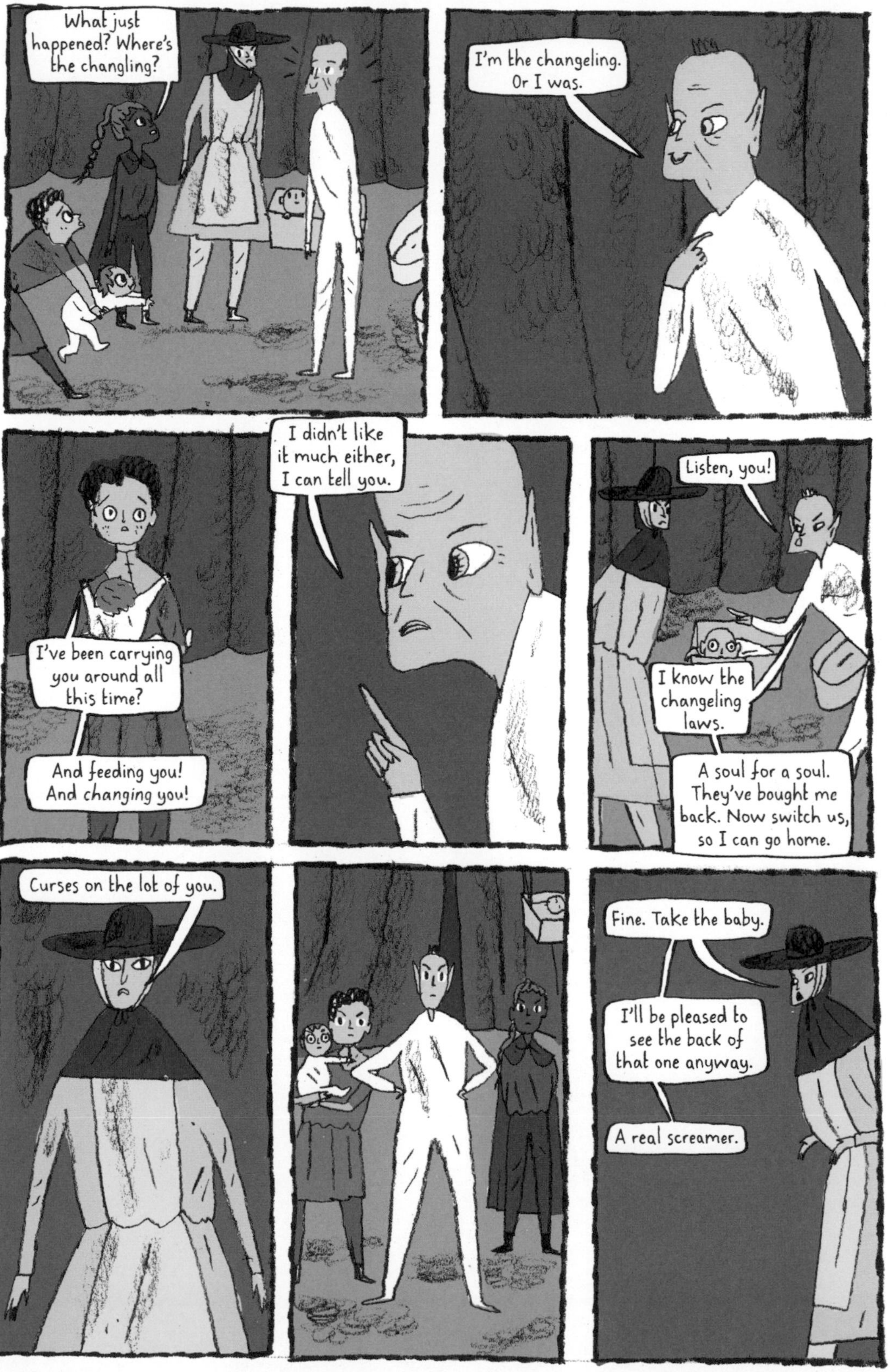

What just happened? Where's the changling?
I'm the changeling. Or I was.
I've been carrying you around all this time?
And feeding you! And changing you!
I didn't like it much either, I can tell you.
Listen, you!
I know the changeling laws.
A soul for a soul. They've bought me back. Now switch us, so I can go home.
Curses on the lot of you.
Fine. Take the baby.
I'll be pleased to see the back of that one anyway.
A real screamer.

What about all these other babies? We can't just leave them...

Well, unless you've got a dozen other changelings hidden in your pocket, you'll have to.

Not a changeling...

But I do have—

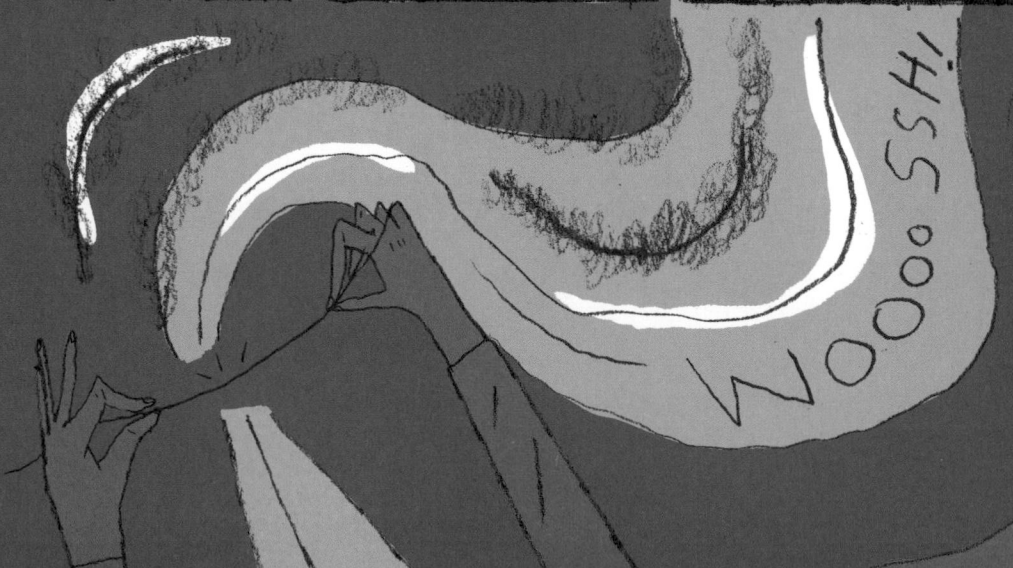

WOOooSSH!

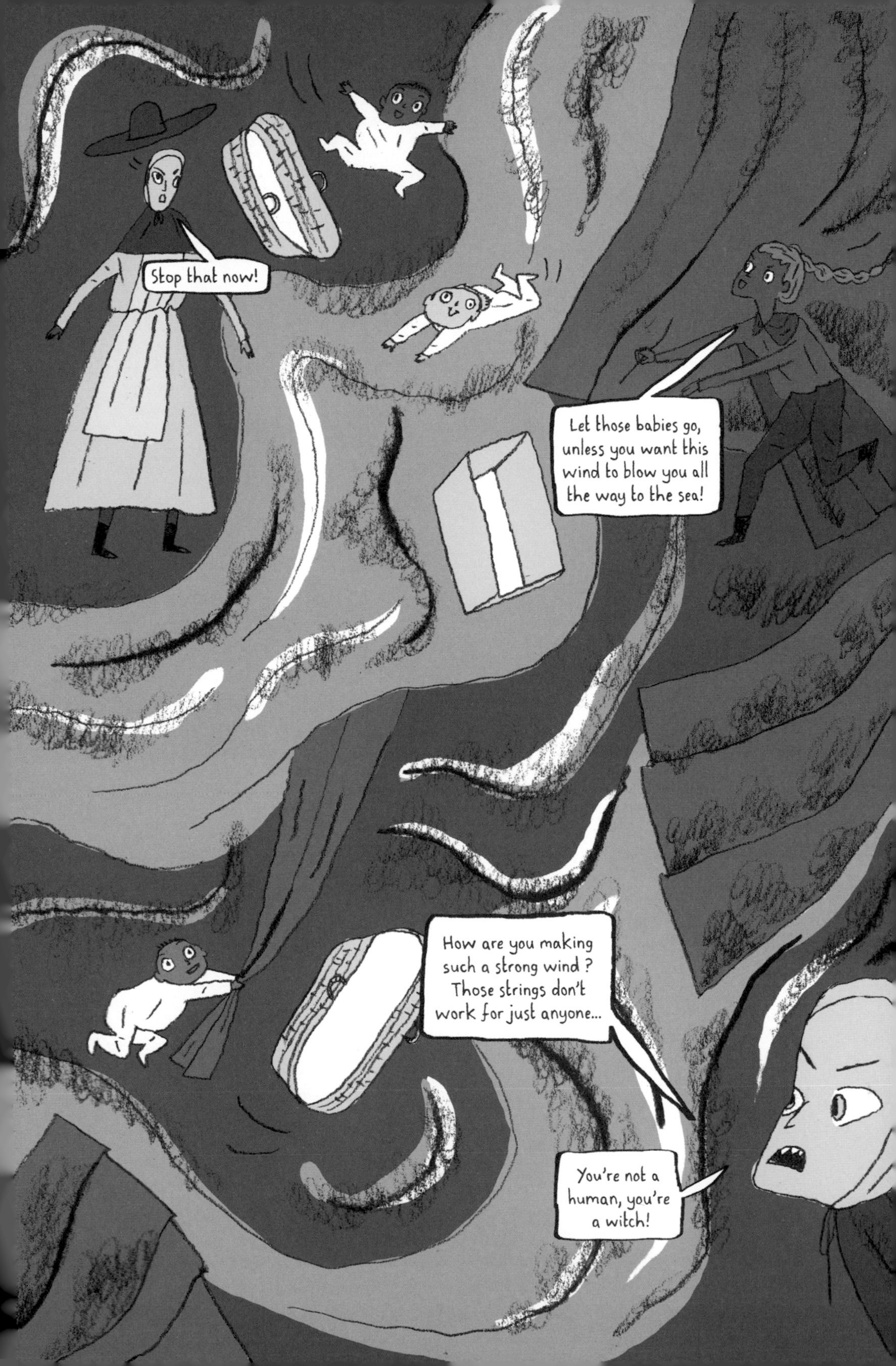
Stop that now!
Let those babies go, unless you want this wind to blow you all the way to the sea!
How are you making such a strong wind? Those strings don't work for just anyone...
You're not a human, you're a witch!

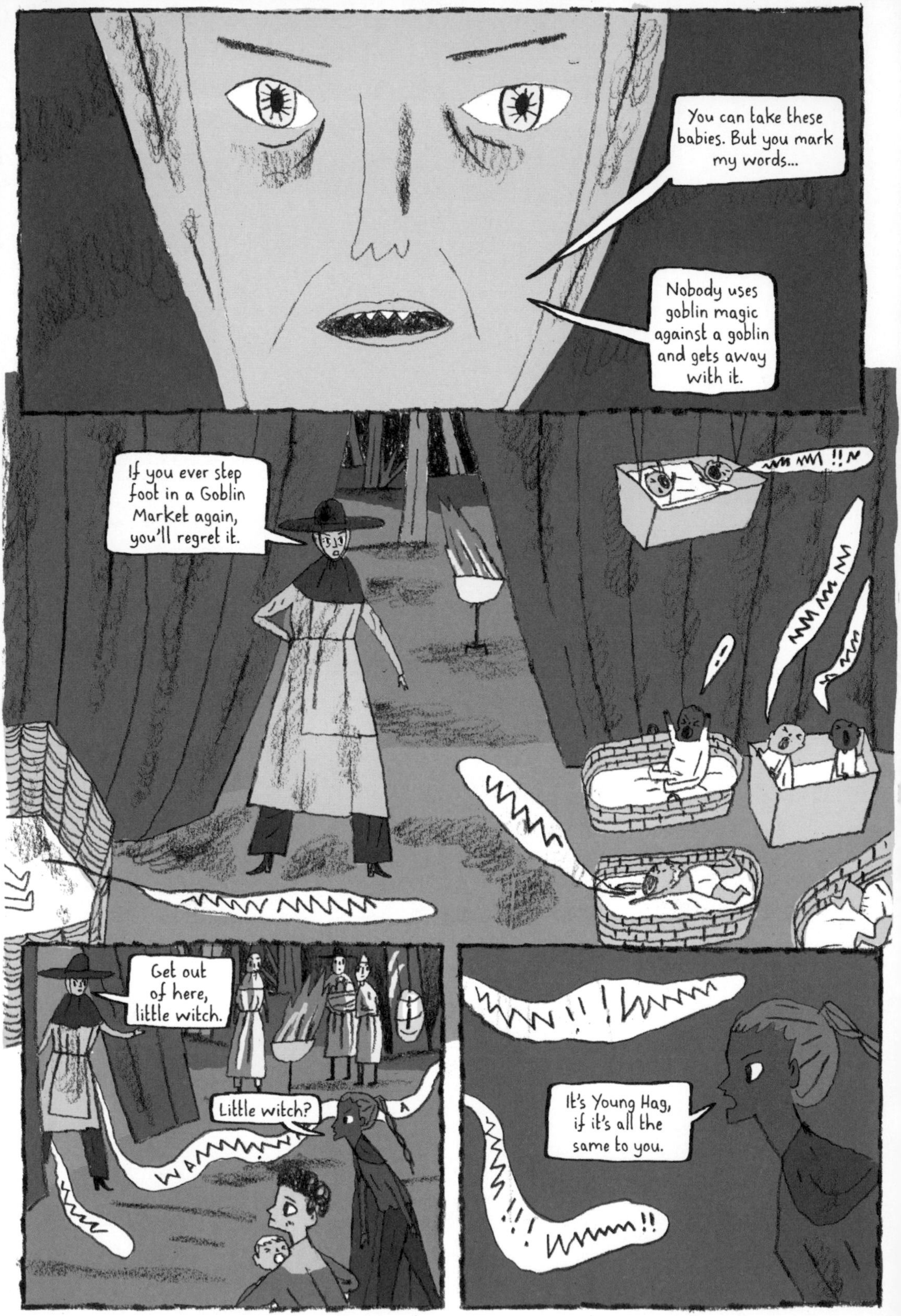
You can take these babies. But you mark my words...
Nobody uses goblin magic against a goblin and gets away with it.
If you ever step foot in a Goblin Market again, you'll regret it.
WAAAH!!
Get out of here, little witch.
Little witch?
It's Young Hag, if it's all the same to you.

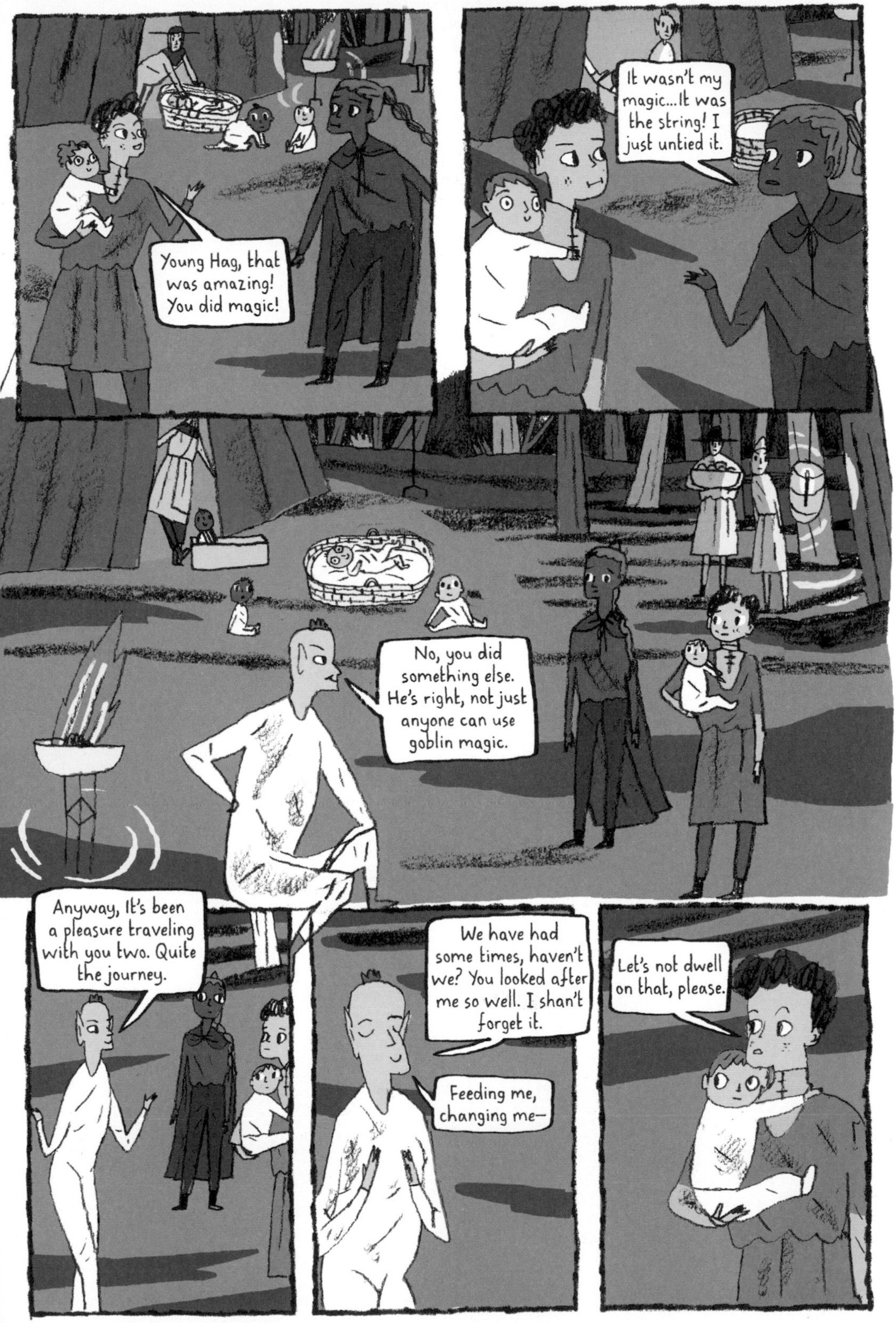
Young Hag, that was amazing! You did magic!
It wasn't my magic...It was the string! I just untied it.
No, you did something else. He's right, not just anyone can use goblin magic.
Anyway, It's been a pleasure traveling with you two. Quite the journey.
We have had some times, haven't we? You looked after me so well. I shan't forget it.
Feeding me, changing me—
Let's not dwell on that, please.

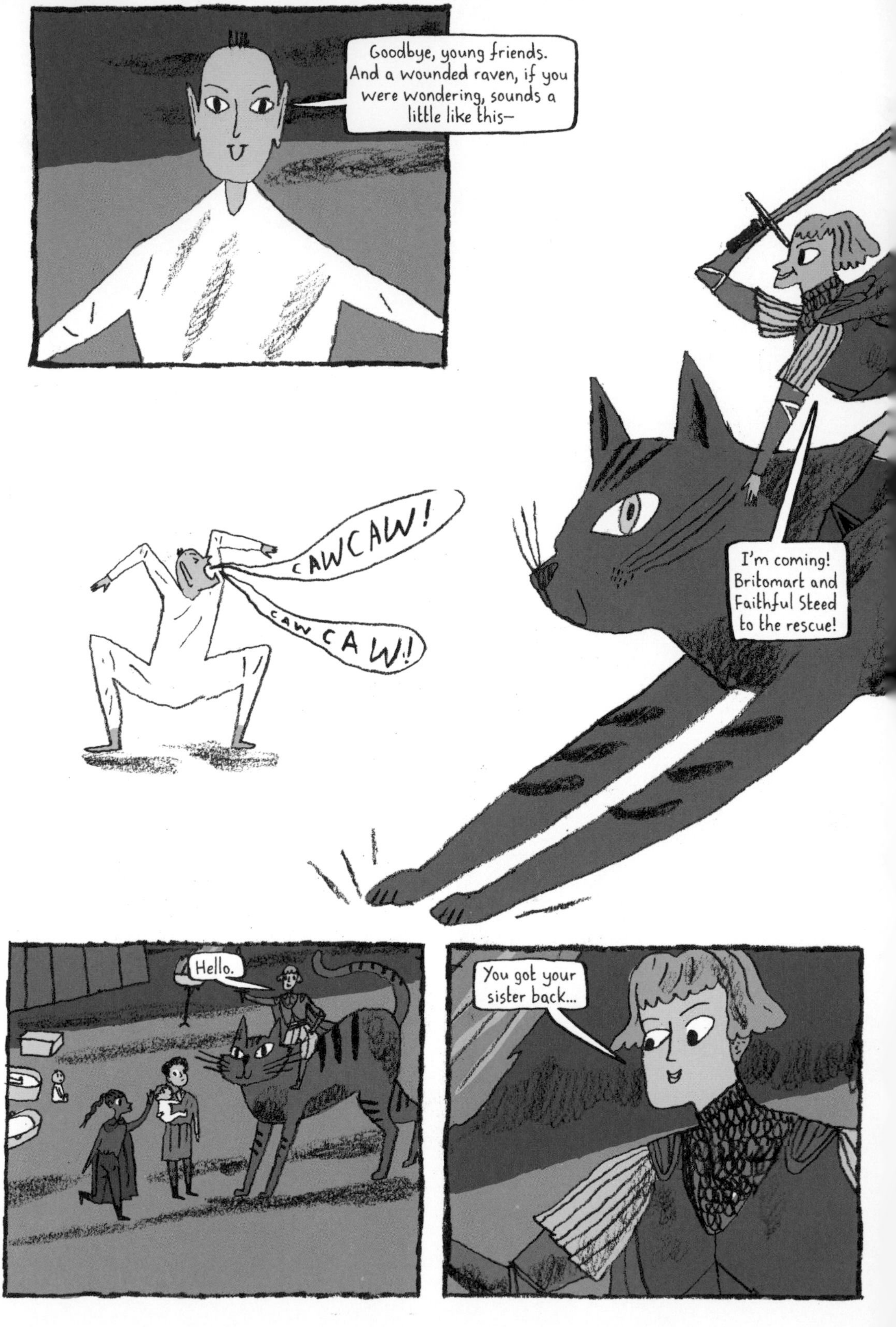
Goodbye, young friends. And a wounded raven, if you were wondering, sounds a little like this—
CAWCAW!
CAWCAW!
I'm coming! Britomart and Faithful Steed to the rescue!
Hello.
You got your sister back...

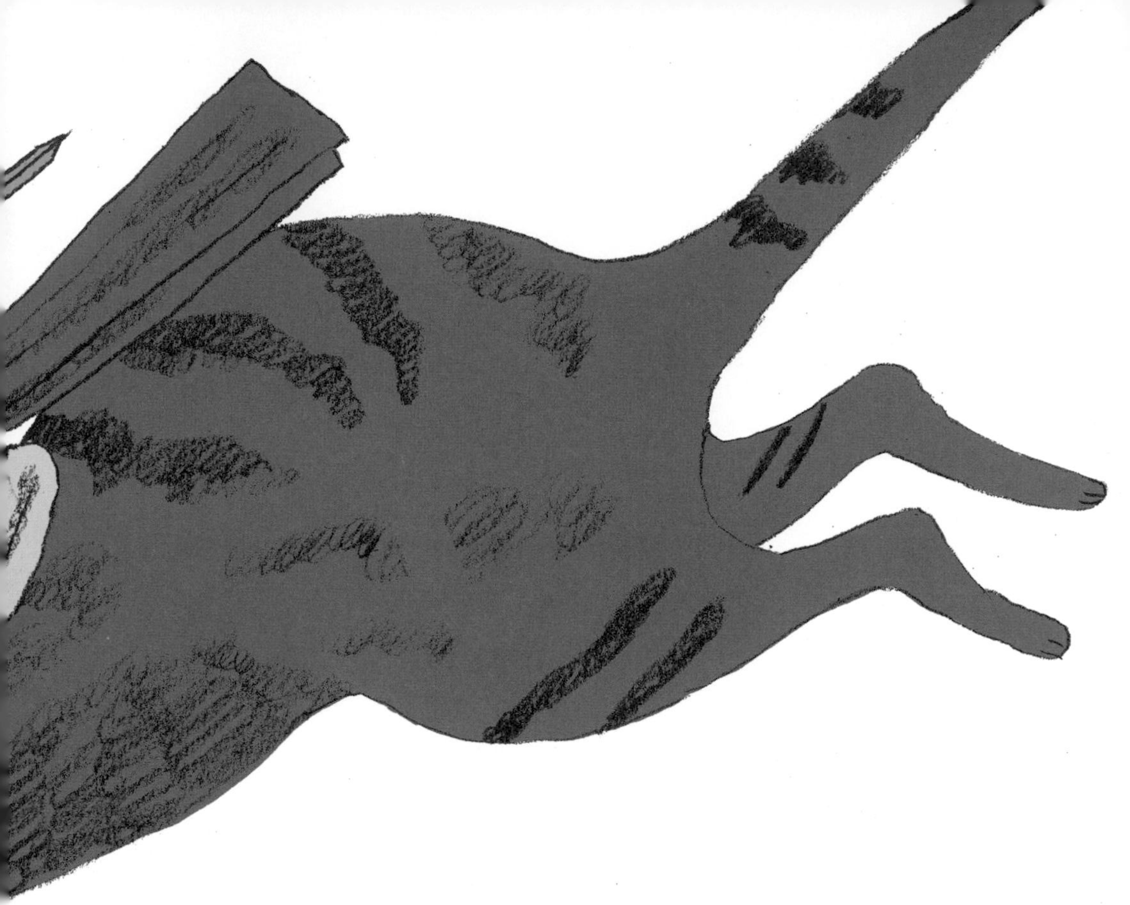

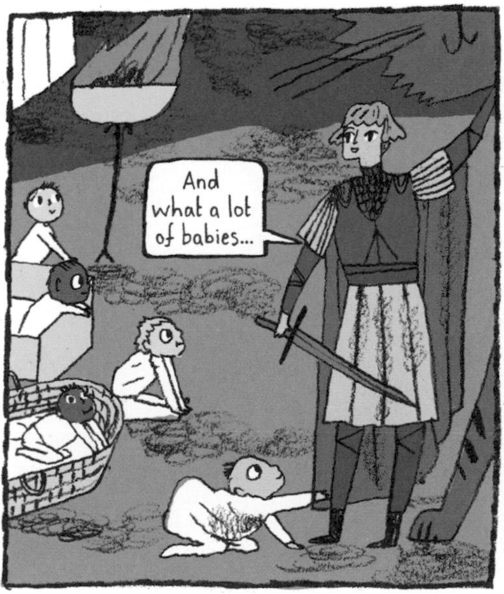
And what a lot of babies...

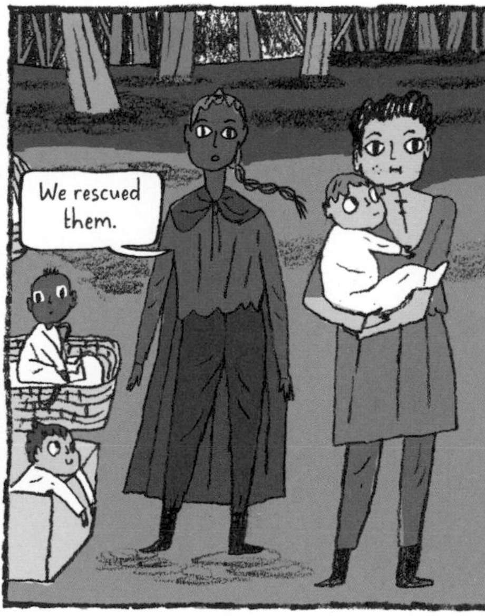
We rescued them.

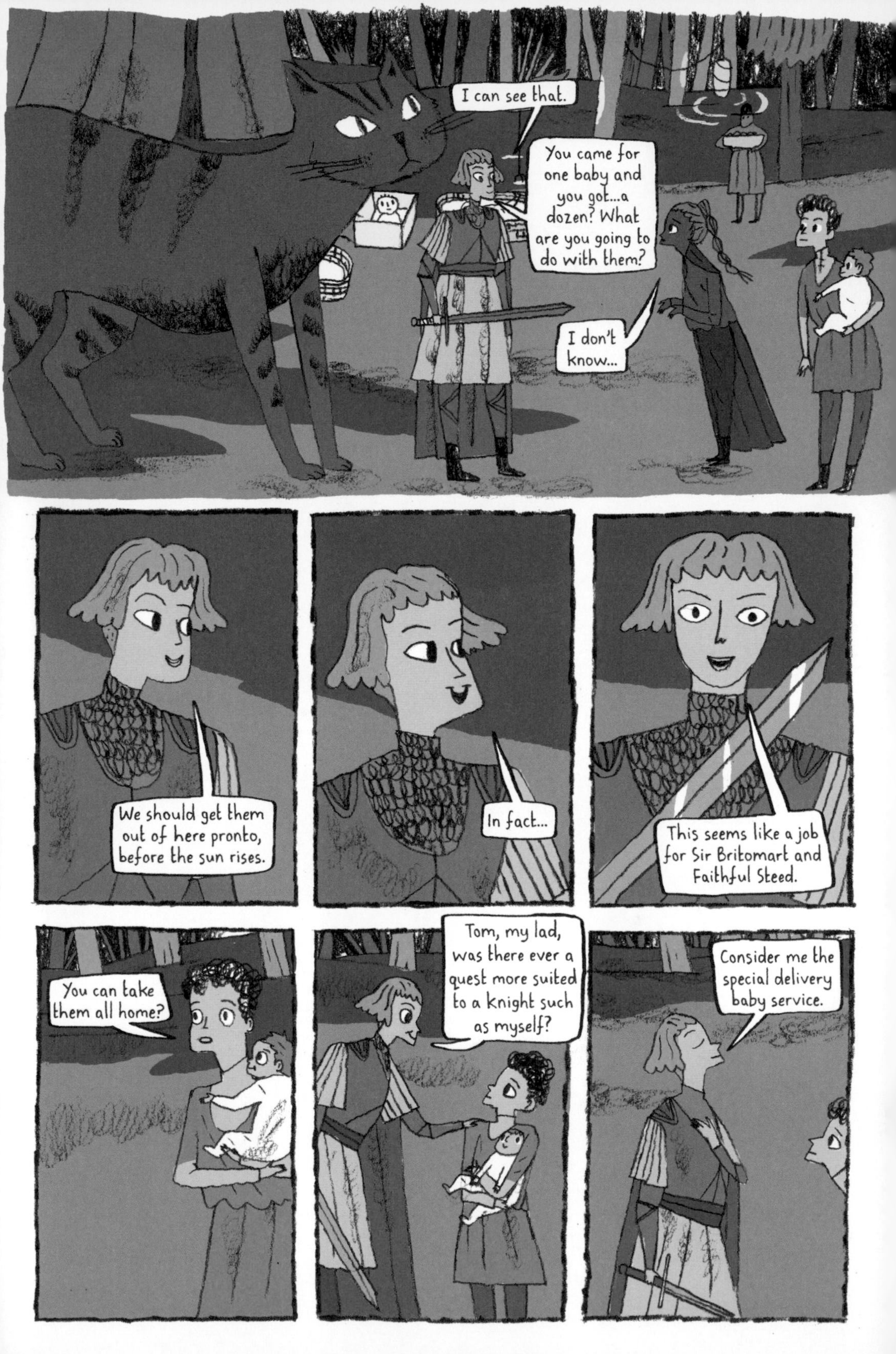
I can see that.
You came for one baby and you got...a dozen? What are you going to do with them?
I don't know...
We should get them out of here pronto, before the sun rises.
In fact...
This seems like a job for Sir Britomart and Faithful Steed.
You can take them all home?
Tom, my lad, was there ever a quest more suited to a knight such as myself?
Consider me the special delivery baby service.

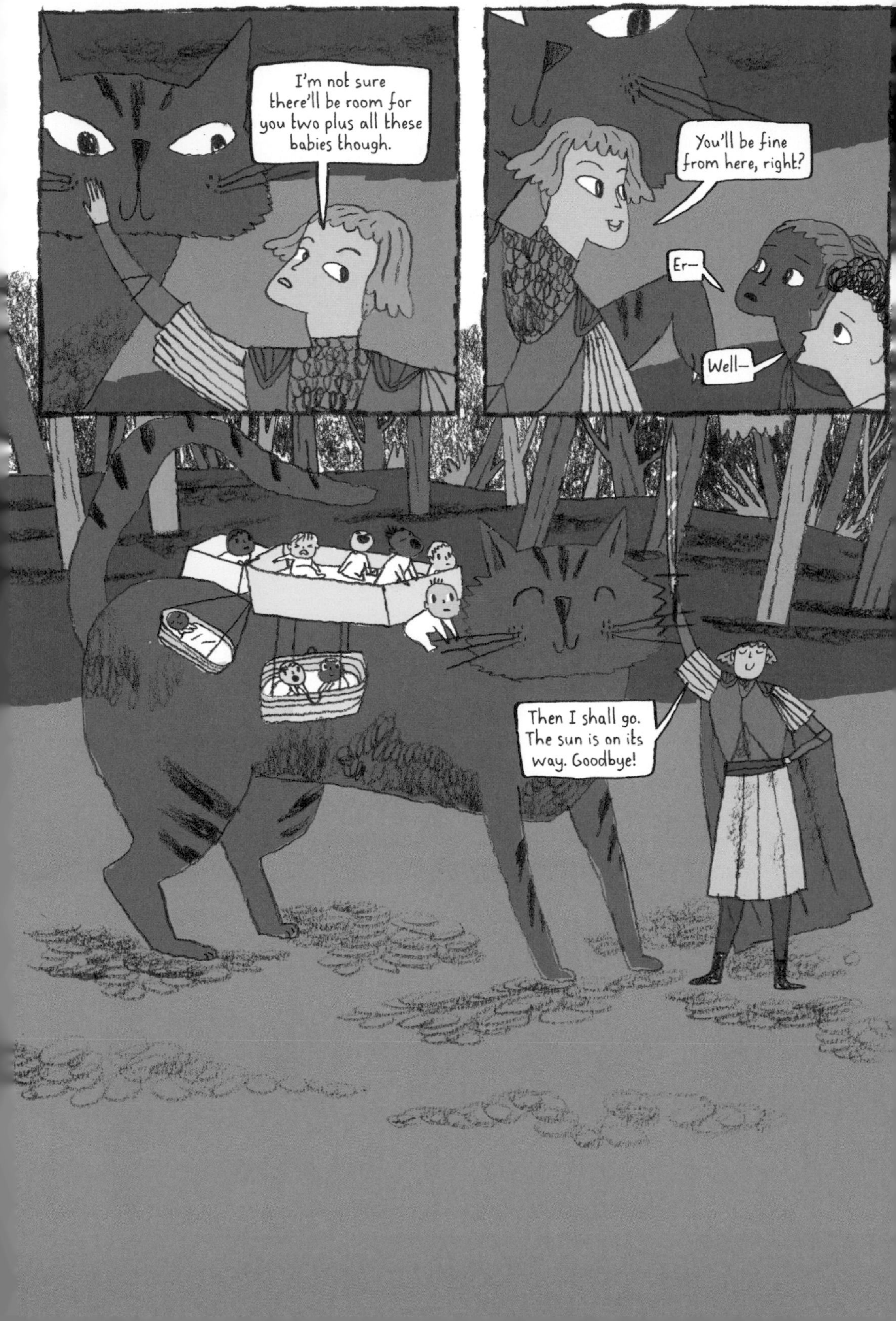
I'm not sure there'll be room for you two plus all these babies though.
You'll be fine from here, right?
Er–
Well–
Then I shall go. The sun is on its way. Goodbye!

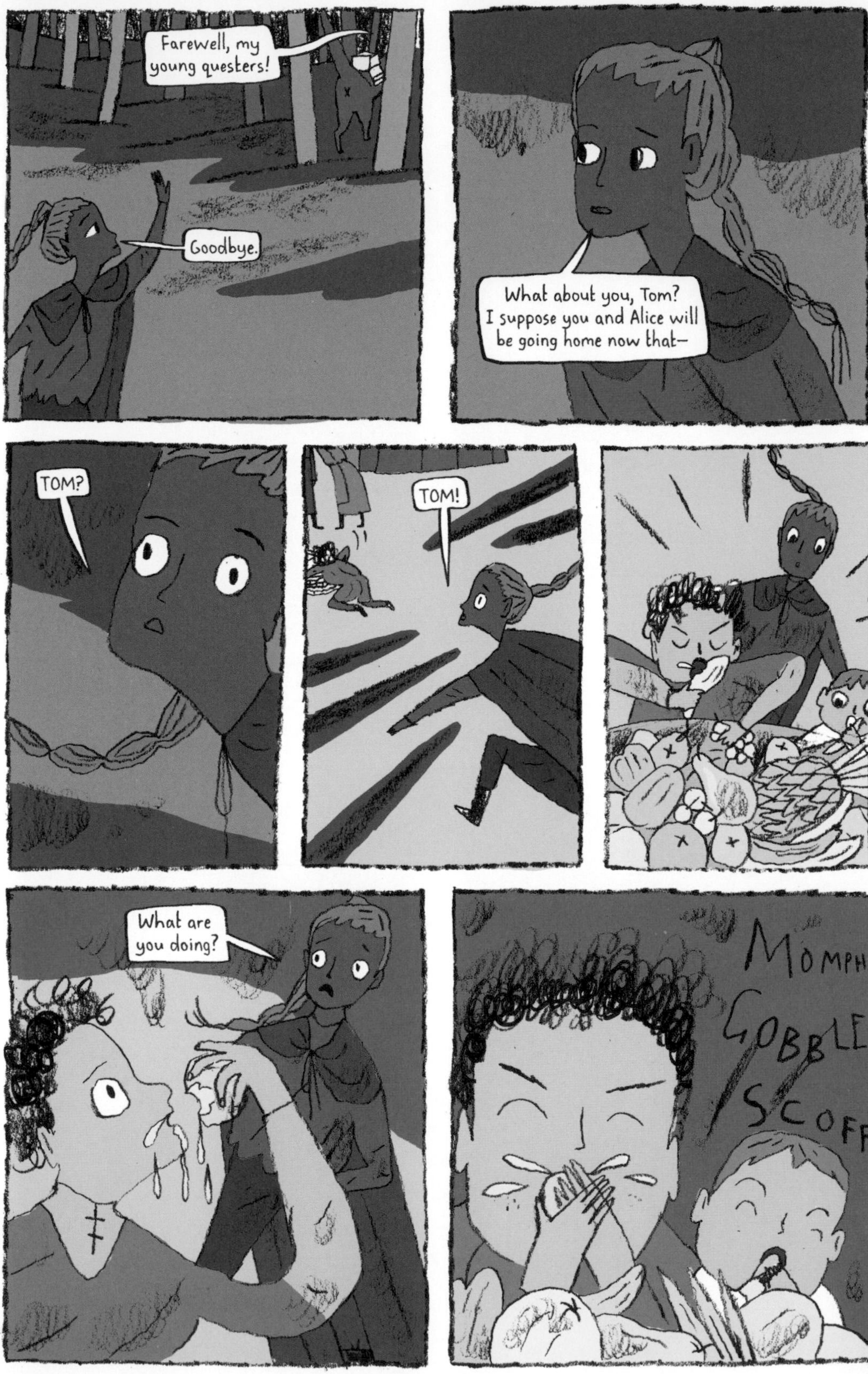
Farewell, my young questers!
Goodbye.
What about you, Tom? I suppose you and Alice will be going home now that—
TOM?
TOM!
What are you doing?
MOMPH
GOBBLE
SCOFF

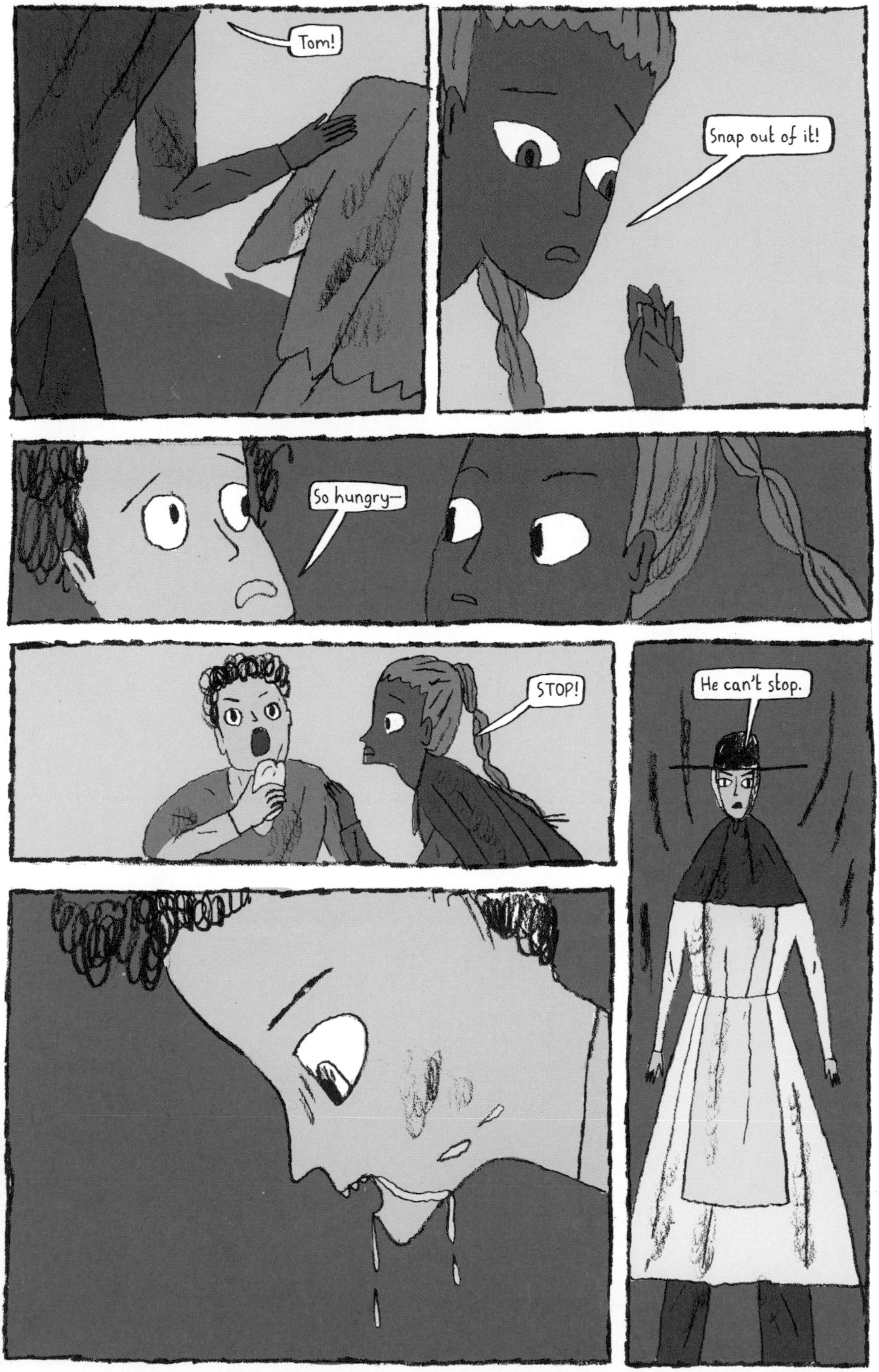
Tom!
Snap out of it!
So hungry—
STOP!
He can't stop.

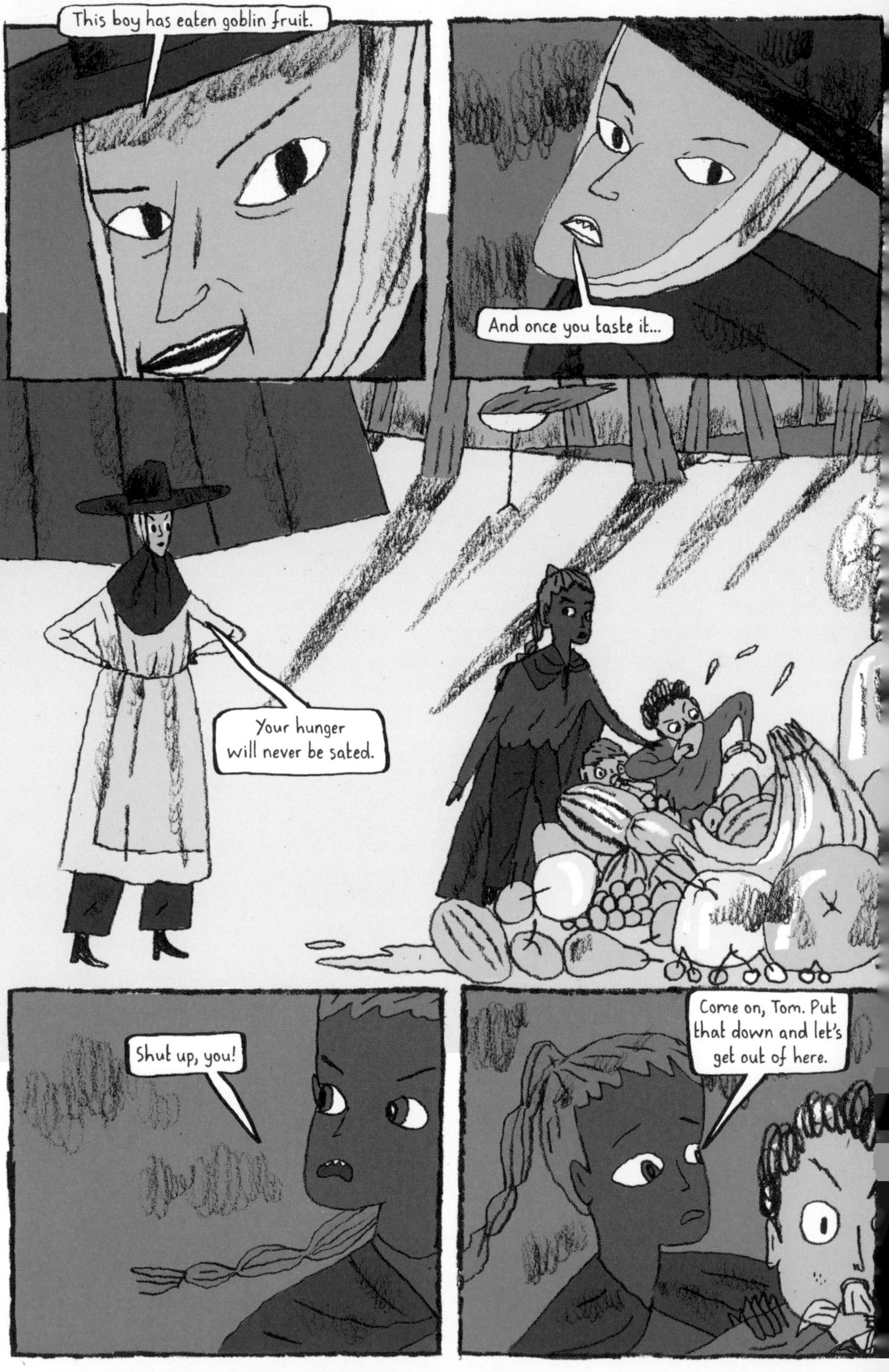

This boy has eaten goblin fruit.
And once you taste it...
Your hunger will never be sated.
Shut up, you!
Come on, Tom. Put that down and let's get out of here.

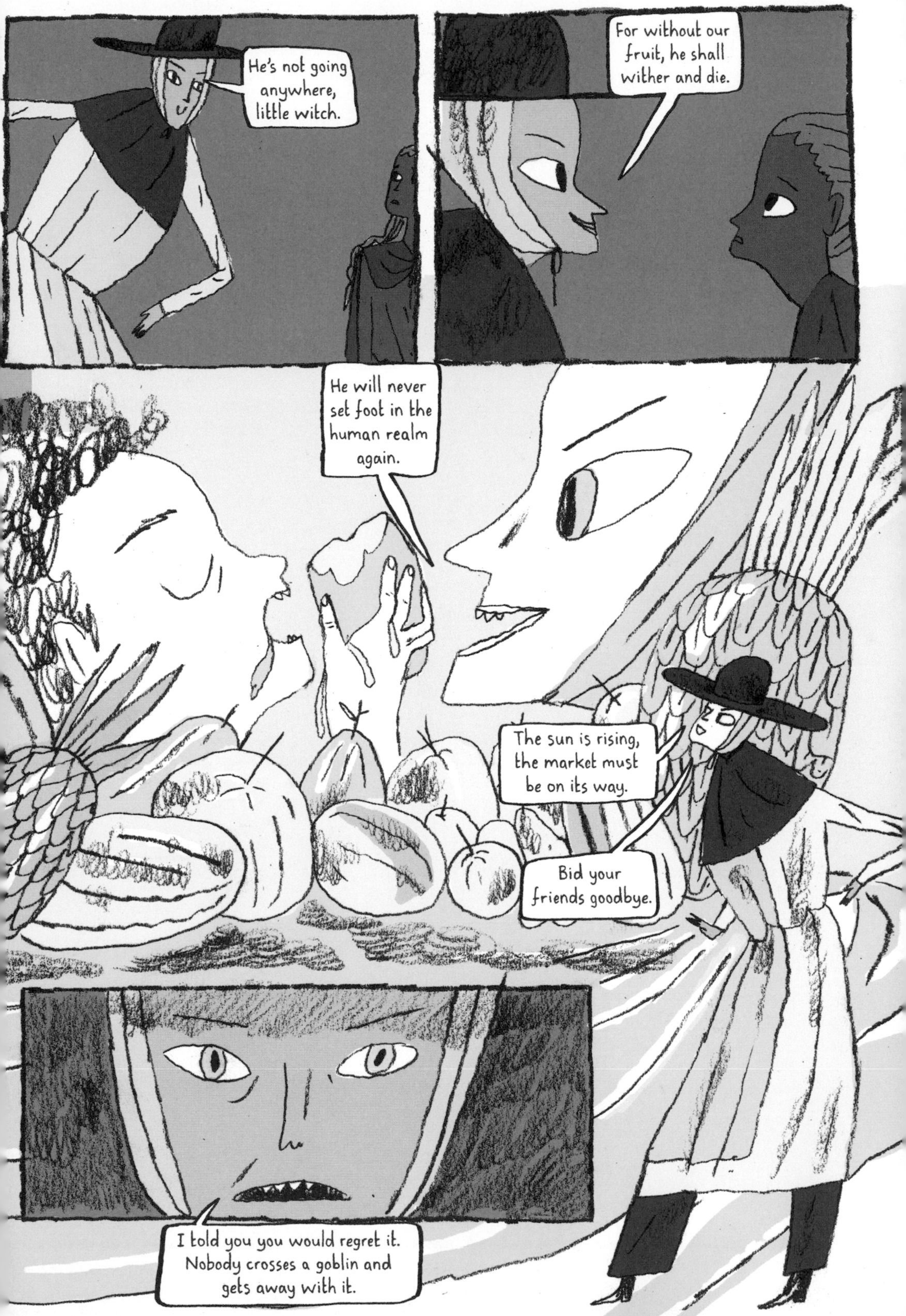

He's not going anywhere, little witch.
For without our fruit, he shall wither and die.
He will never set foot in the human realm again.
The sun is rising, the market must be on its way.
Bid your friends goodbye.
I told you you would regret it. Nobody crosses a goblin and gets away with it.

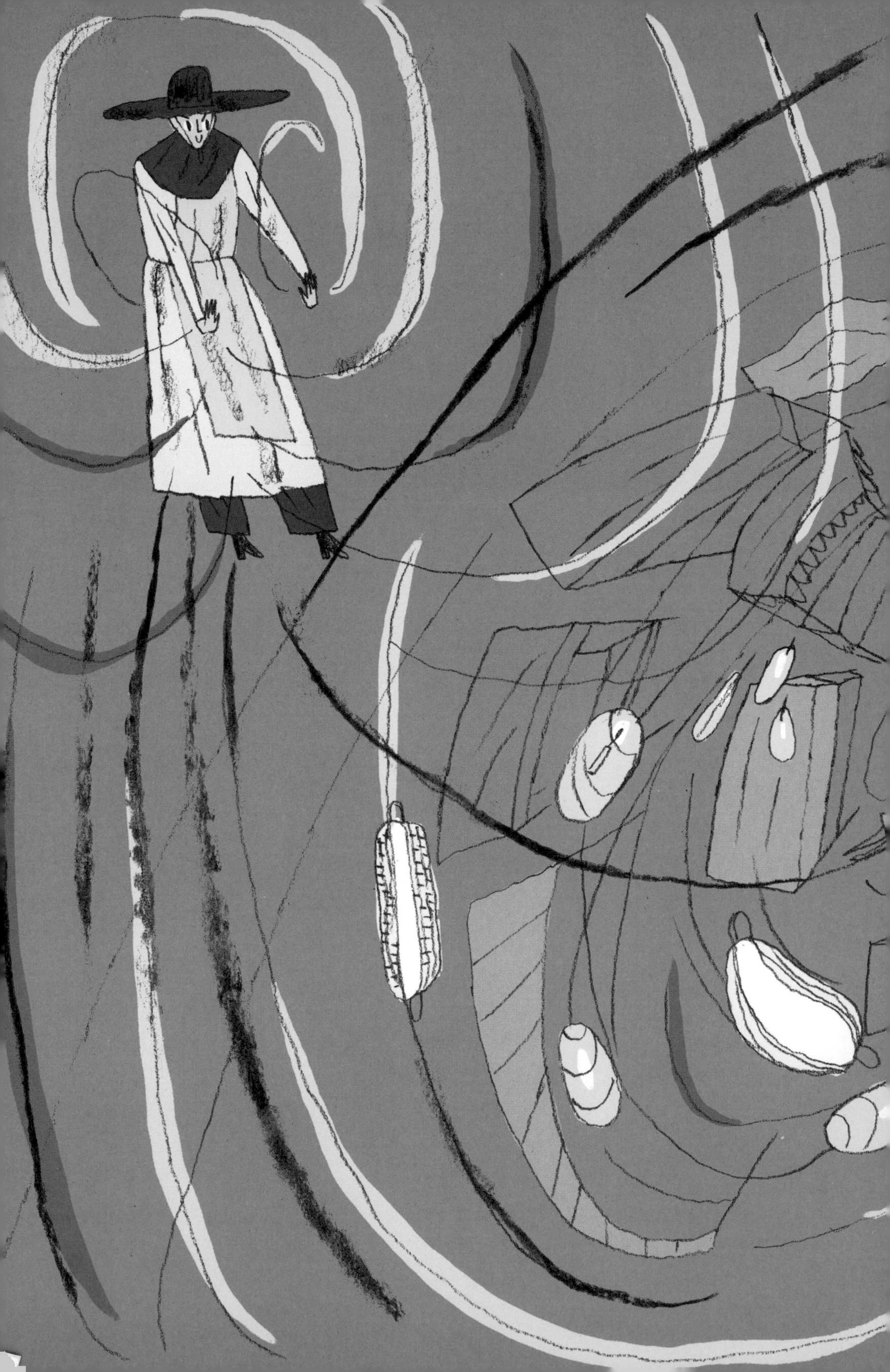

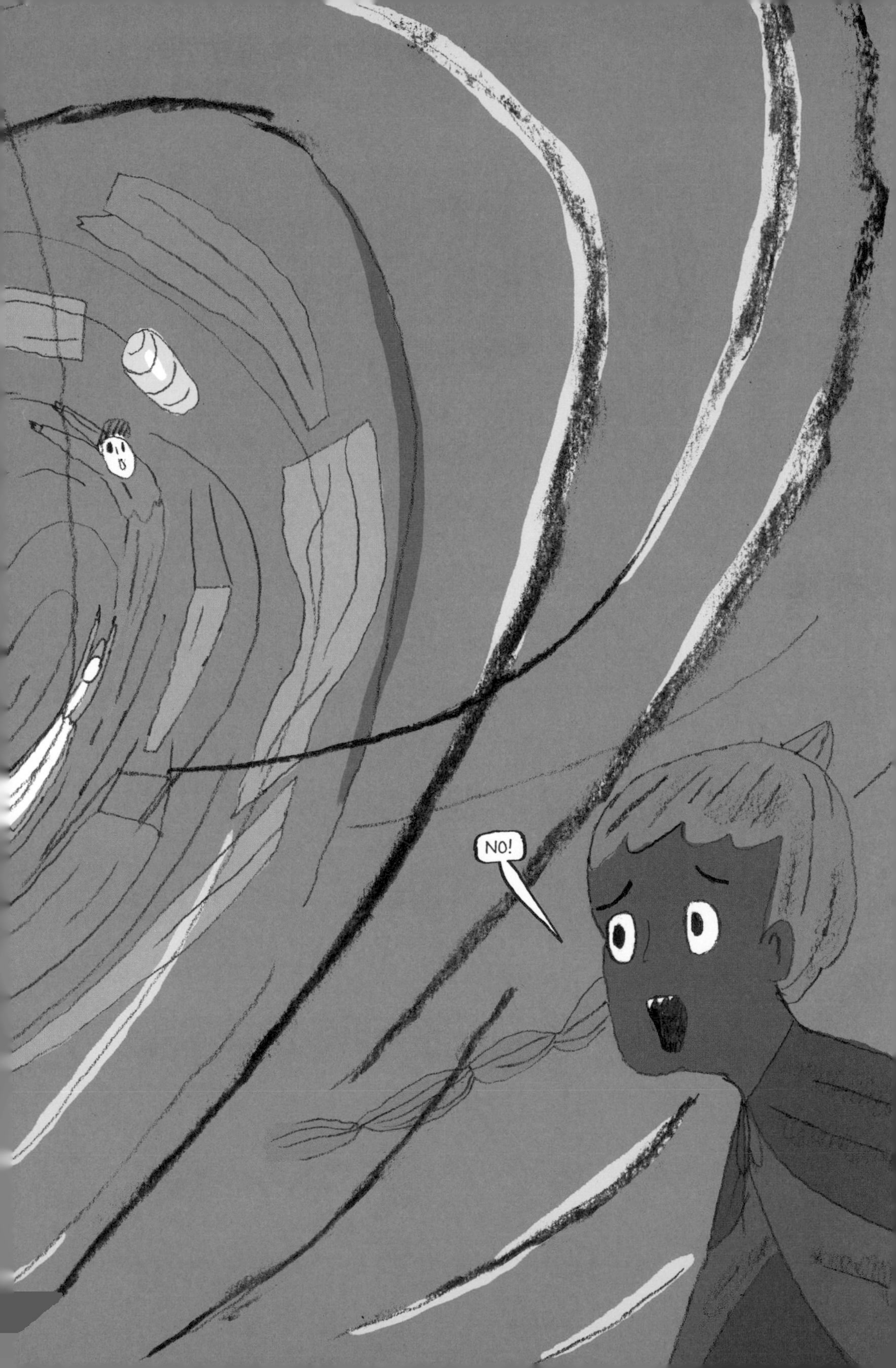
NO!

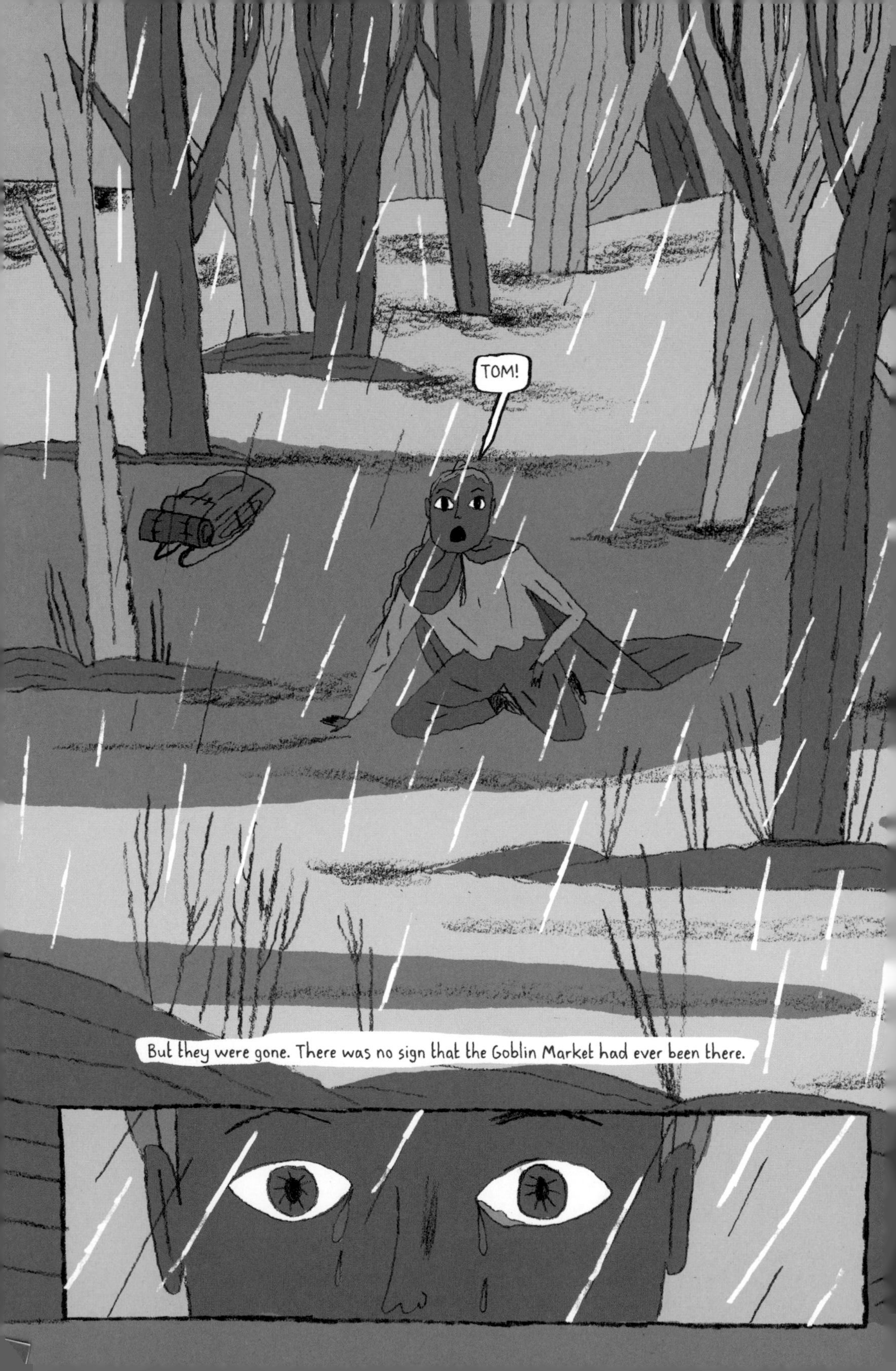
TOM!
But they were gone. There was no sign that the Goblin Market had ever been there.

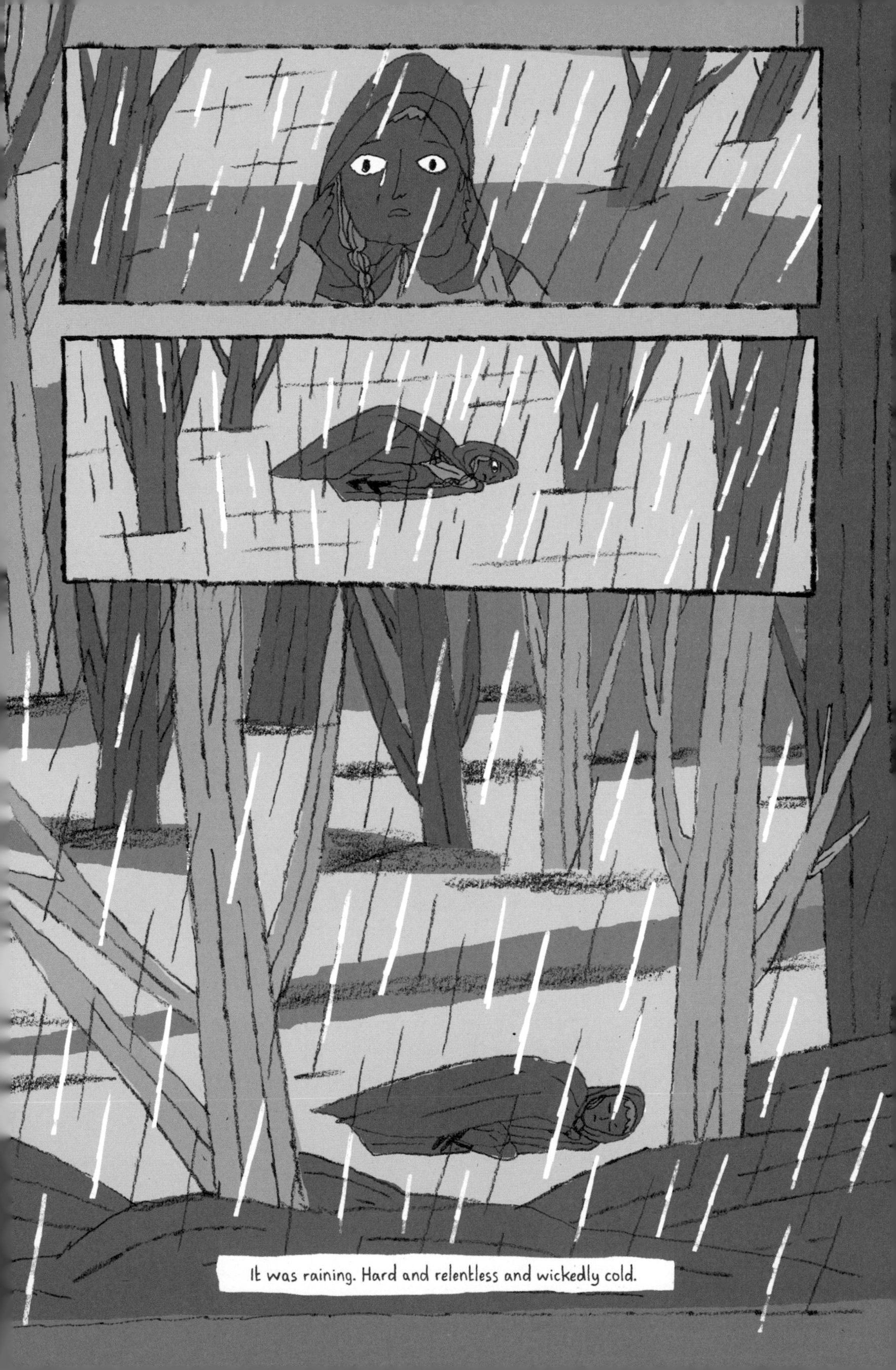
It was raining. Hard and relentless and wickedly cold.

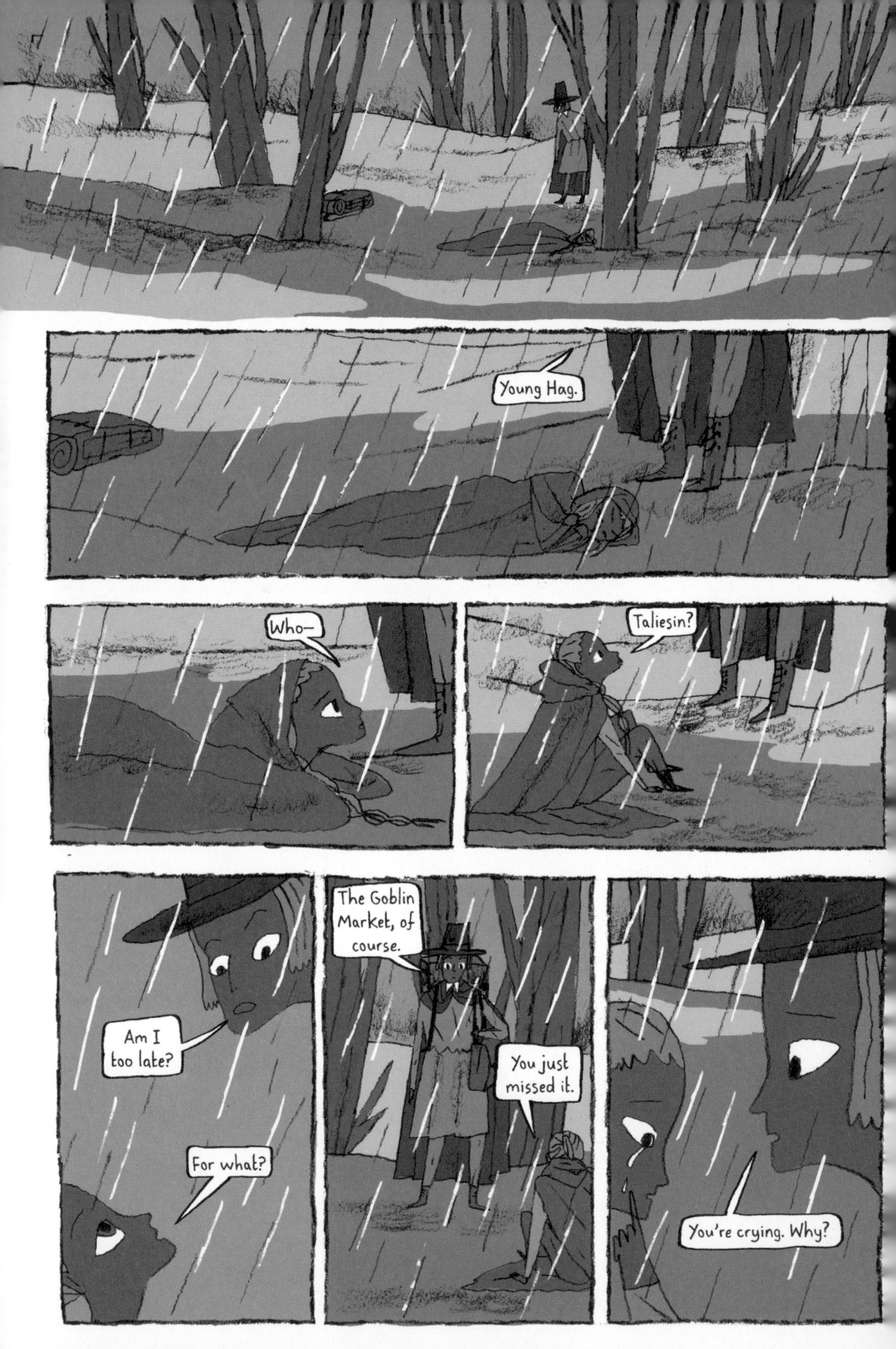
Young Hag.
Who–
Taliesin?
Am I too late?
For what?
The Goblin Market, of course.
You just missed it.
You're crying. Why?

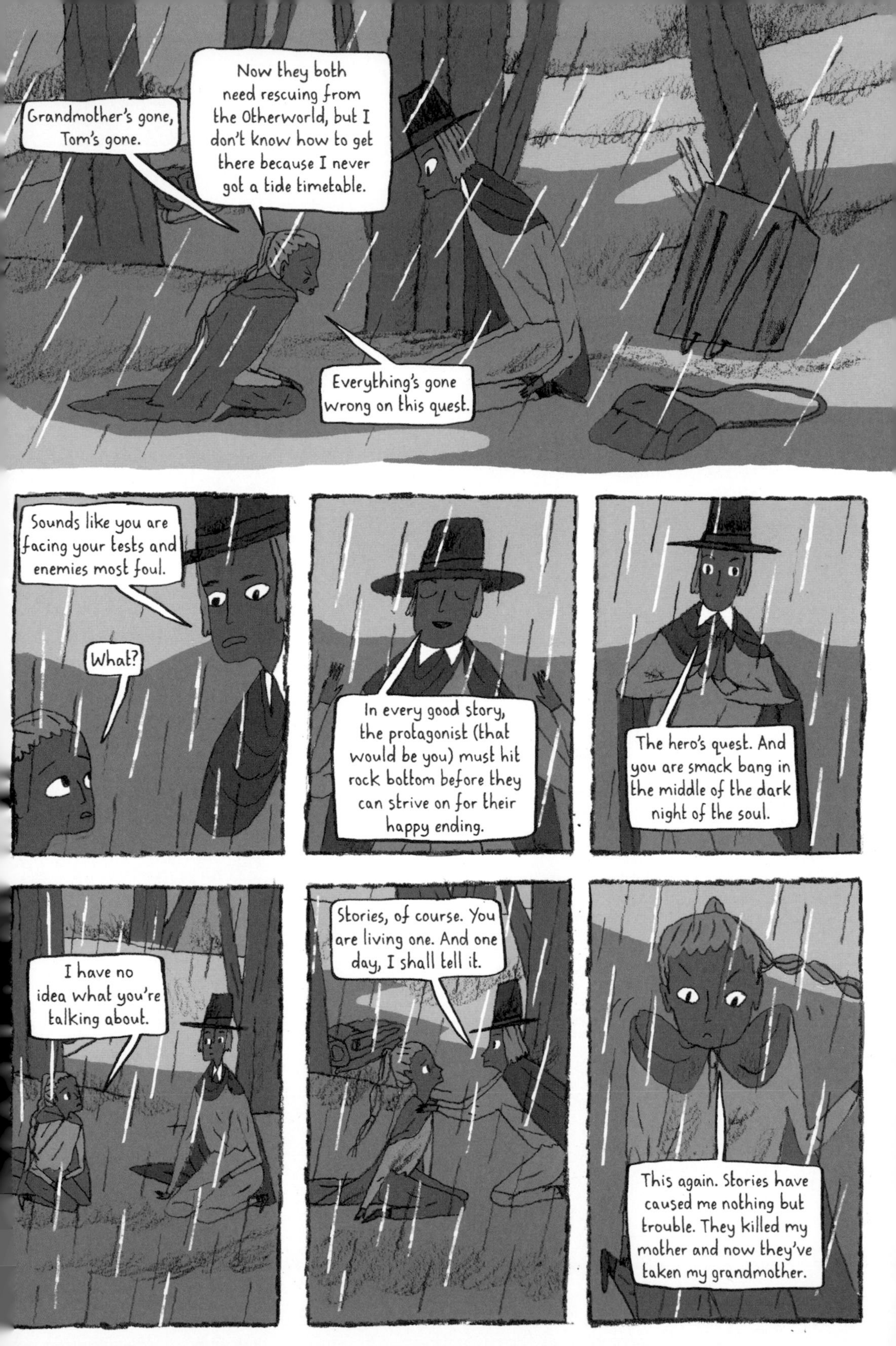
Grandmother's gone, Tom's gone.
Now they both need rescuing from the Otherworld, but I don't know how to get there because I never got a tide timetable.
Everything's gone wrong on this quest.
Sounds like you are facing your tests and enemies most foul.
What?
In every good story, the protagonist (that would be you) must hit rock bottom before they can strive on for their happy ending.
The hero's quest. And you are smack bang in the middle of the dark night of the soul.
I have no idea what you're talking about.
Stories, of course. You are living one. And one day, I shall tell it.
This again. Stories have caused me nothing but trouble. They killed my mother and now they've taken my grandmother.

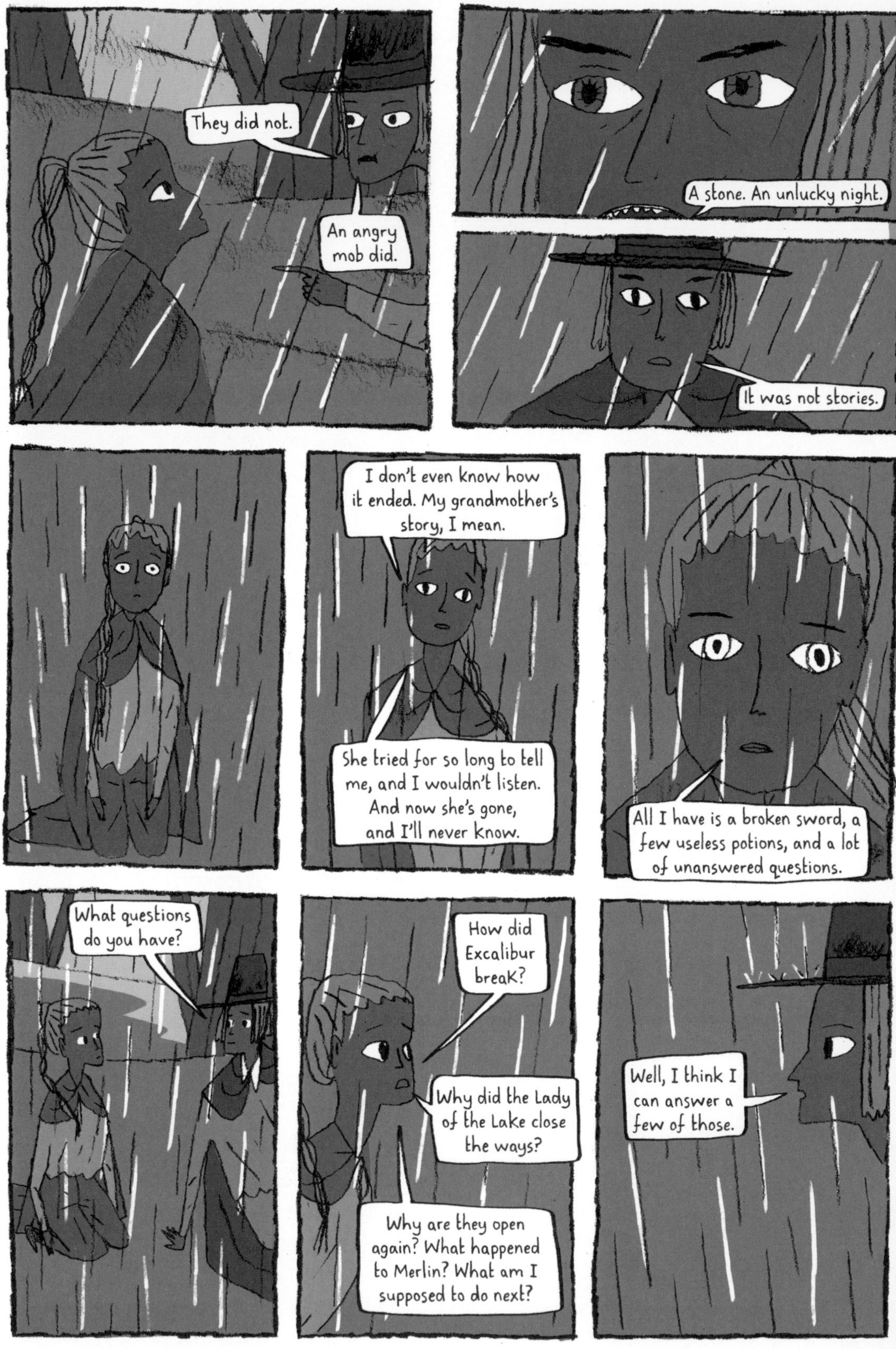
They did not.
An angry mob did.
A stone. An unlucky night.
It was not stories.
I don't even know how it ended. My grandmother's story, I mean.
She tried for so long to tell me, and I wouldn't listen. And now she's gone, and I'll never know.
All I have is a broken sword, a few useless potions, and a lot of unanswered questions.
What questions do you have?
How did Excalibur break?
Why did the Lady of the Lake close the ways?
Why are they open again? What happened to Merlin? What am I supposed to do next?
Well, I think I can answer a few of those.

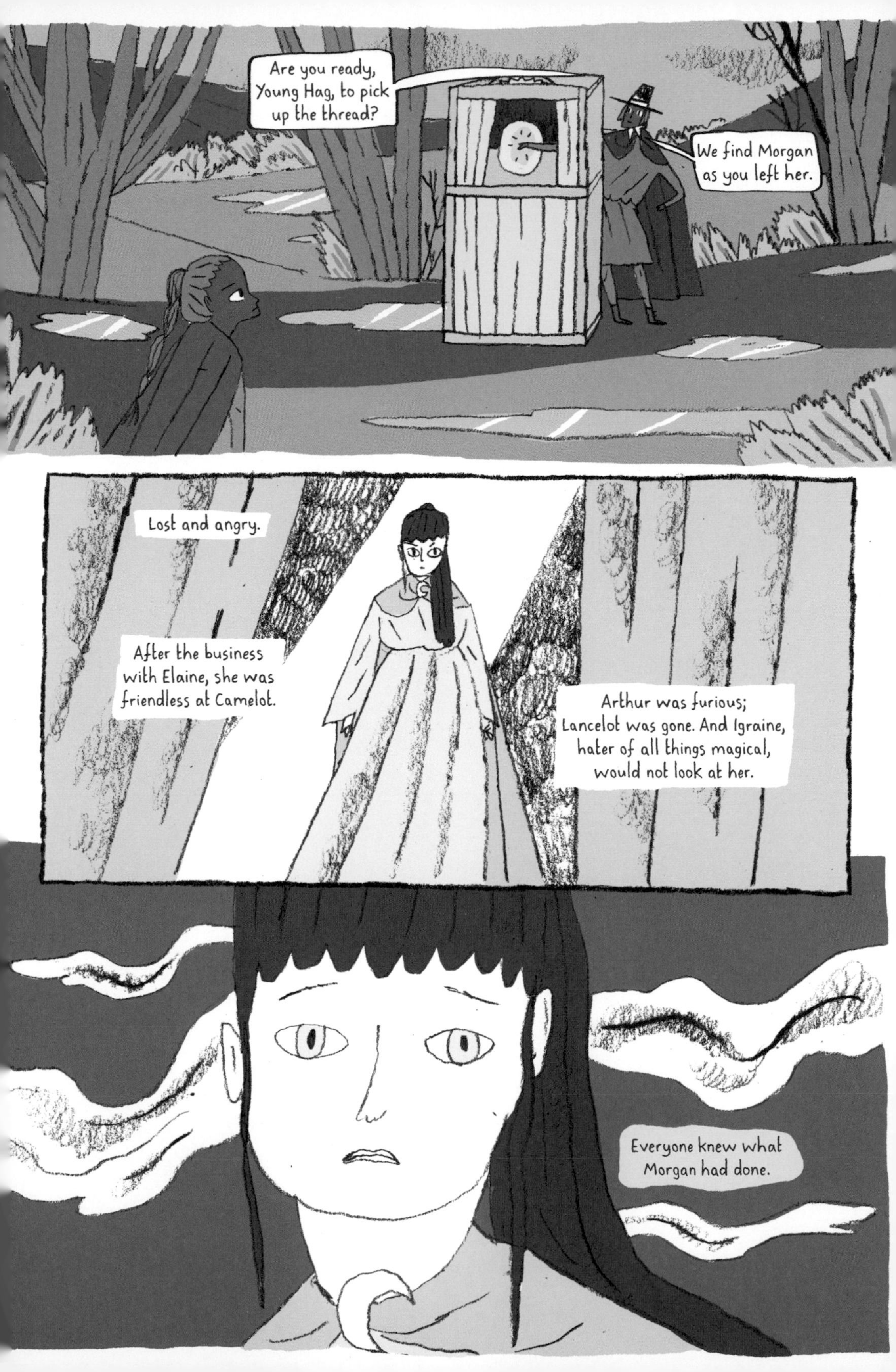
Are you ready, Young Hag, to pick up the thread?
We find Morgan as you left her.
Lost and angry.
After the business with Elaine, she was friendless at Camelot.
Arthur was furious; Lancelot was gone. And Igraine, hater of all things magical, would not look at her.
Everyone knew what Morgan had done.

Things were not going well. With Guinevere and Lancelot gone, Arthur was unmoored, and all around him plots were swirling to unseat him.

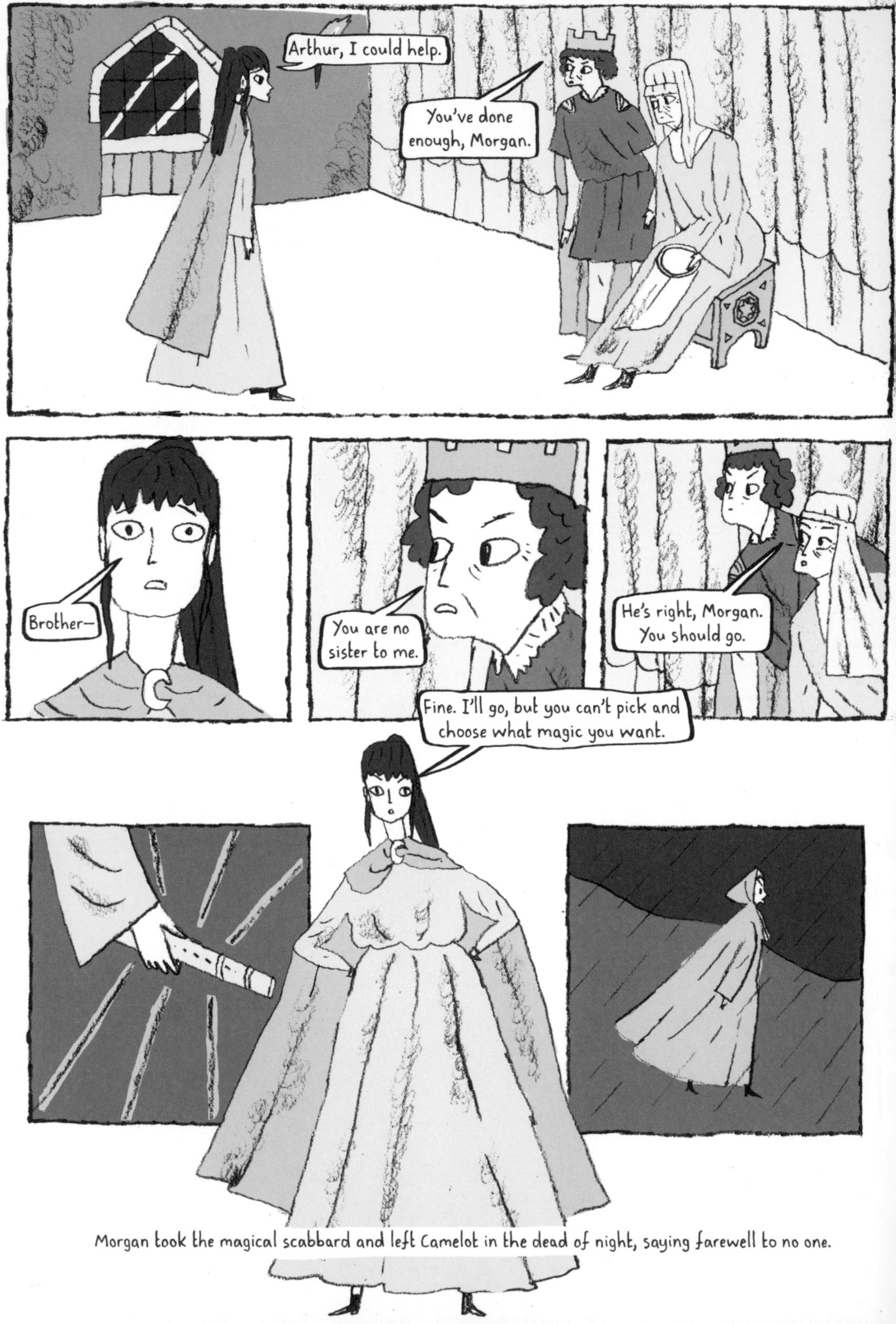

Arthur, I could help.
You've done enough, Morgan.
Brother—
You are no sister to me.
He's right, Morgan. You should go.
Fine. I'll go, but you can't pick and choose what magic you want.

Morgan took the magical scabbard and left Camelot in the dead of night, saying farewell to no one.

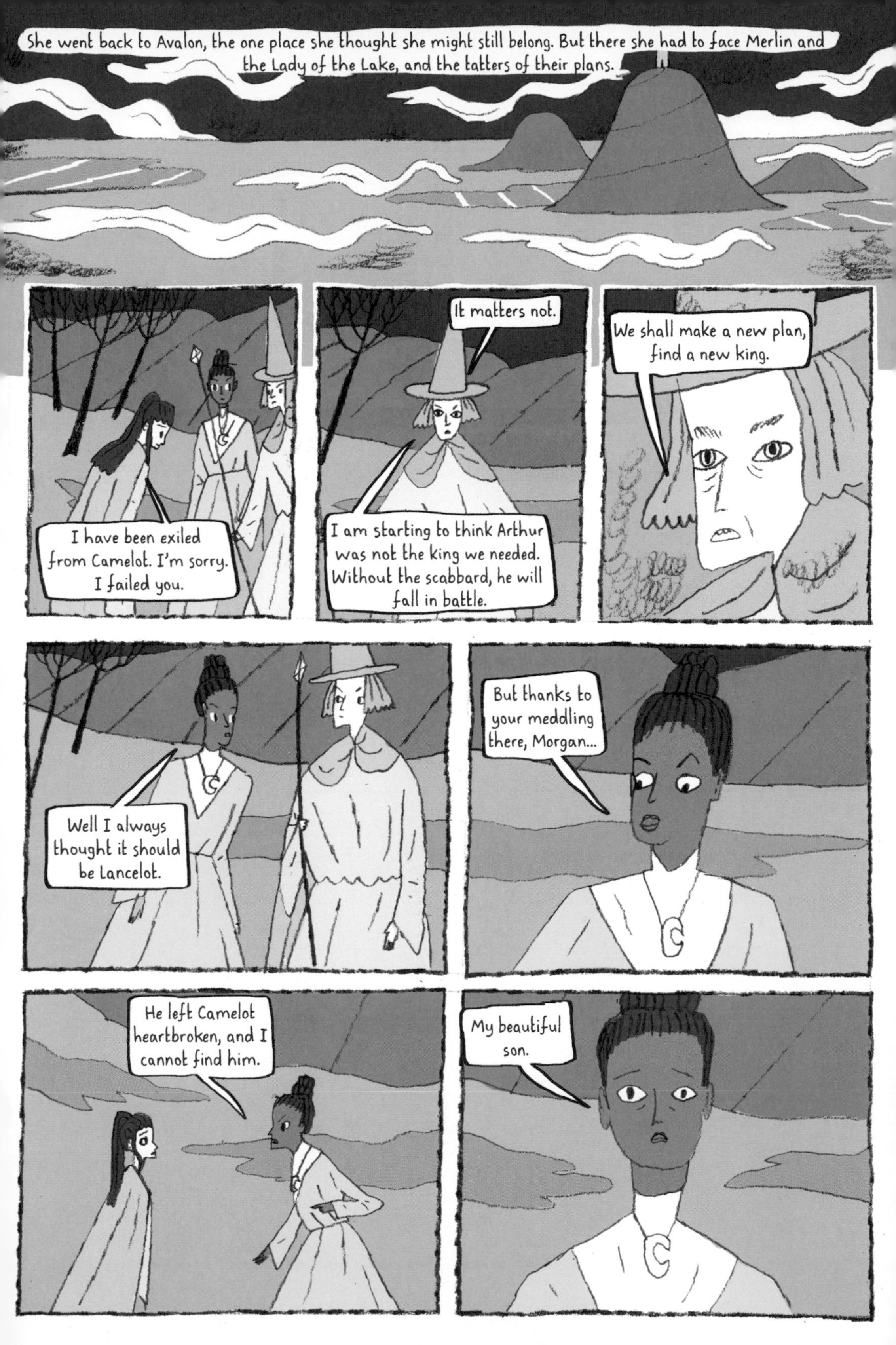

She went back to Avalon, the one place she thought she might still belong. But there she had to face Merlin and the Lady of the Lake, and the tatters of their plans.
I have been exiled from Camelot. I'm sorry. I failed you.
It matters not.
I am starting to think Arthur was not the king we needed. Without the scabbard, he will fall in battle.
We shall make a new plan, find a new king.
Well I always thought it should be Lancelot.
But thanks to your meddling there, Morgan...
He left Camelot heartbroken, and I cannot find him.
My beautiful son.

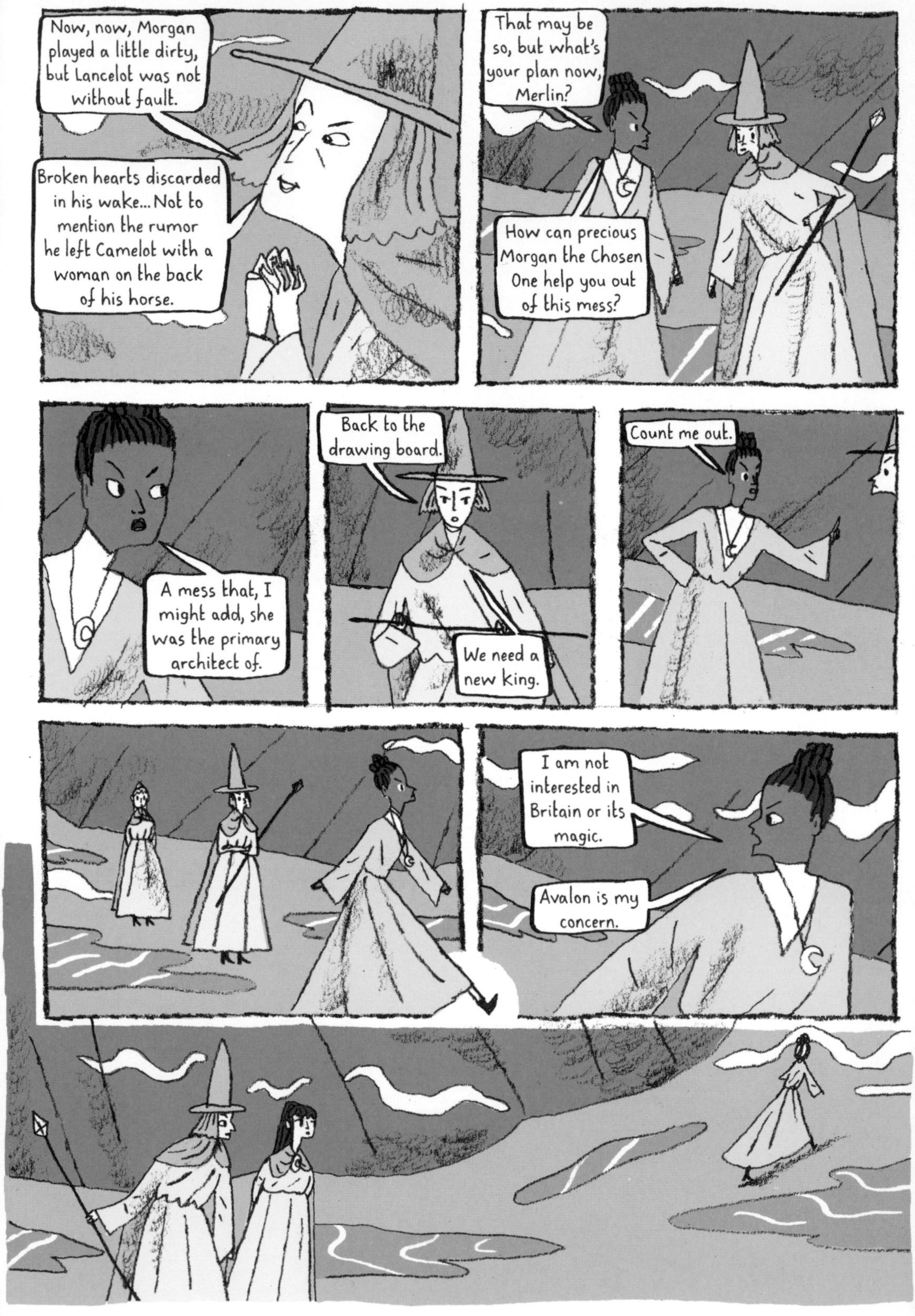
Now, now, Morgan played a little dirty, but Lancelot was not without fault.
Broken hearts discarded in his wake... Not to mention the rumor he left Camelot with a woman on the back of his horse.
That may be so, but what's your plan now, Merlin?
How can precious Morgan the Chosen One help you out of this mess?
A mess that, I might add, she was the primary architect of.
Back to the drawing board.
We need a new king.
Count me out.
I am not interested in Britain or its magic.
Avalon is my concern.

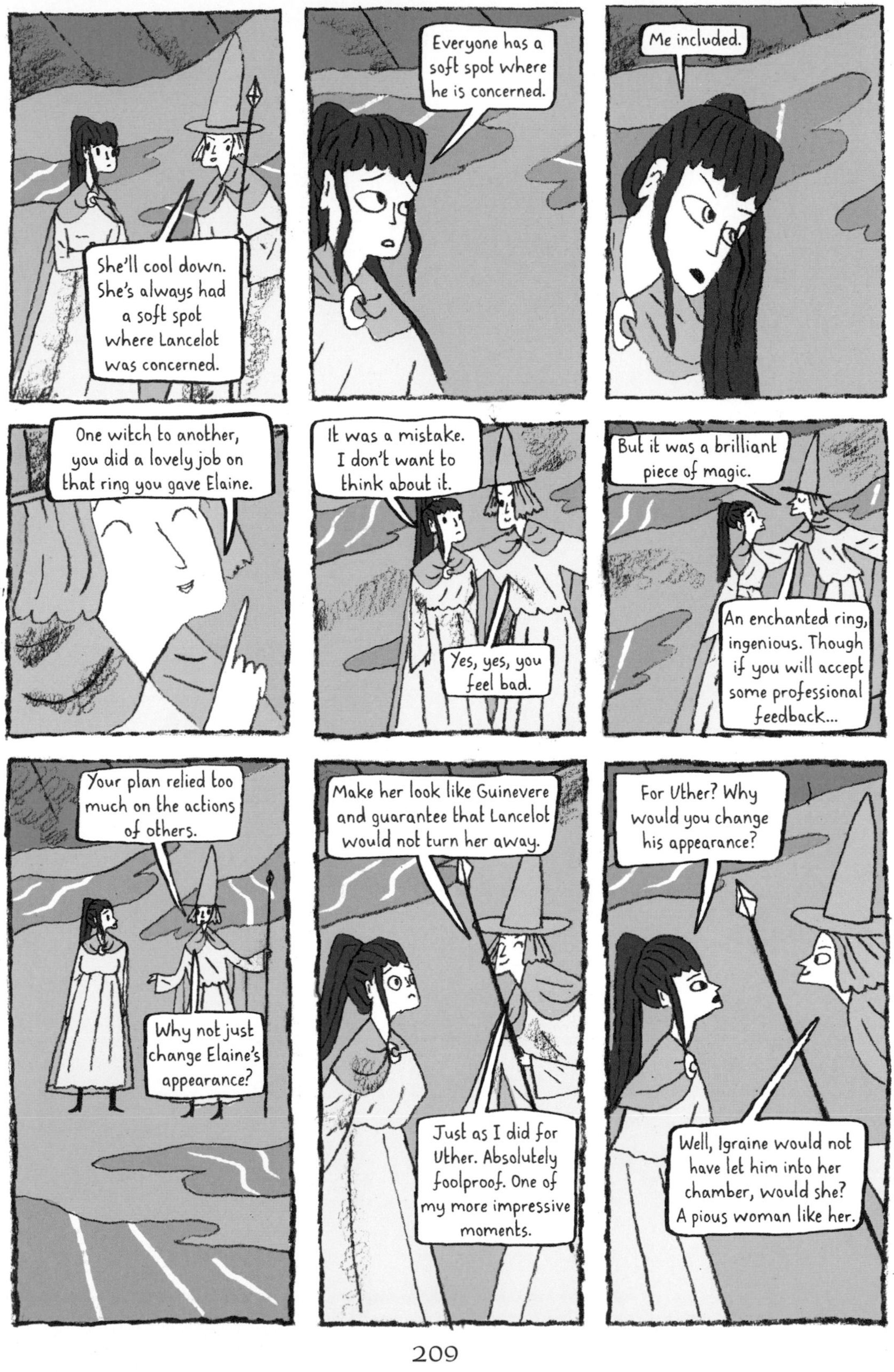
She'll cool down. She's always had a soft spot where Lancelot was concerned.
Everyone has a soft spot where he is concerned.
Me included.
One witch to another, you did a lovely job on that ring you gave Elaine.
It was a mistake. I don't want to think about it.
Yes, yes, you feel bad.
But it was a brilliant piece of magic.
An enchanted ring, ingenious. Though if you will accept some professional feedback...
Your plan relied too much on the actions of others.
Why not just change Elaine's appearance?
Make her look like Guinevere and guarantee that Lancelot would not turn her away.
Just as I did for Uther. Absolutely foolproof. One of my more impressive moments.
For Uther? Why would you change his appearance?
Well, Igraine would not have let him into her chamber, would she? A pious woman like her.

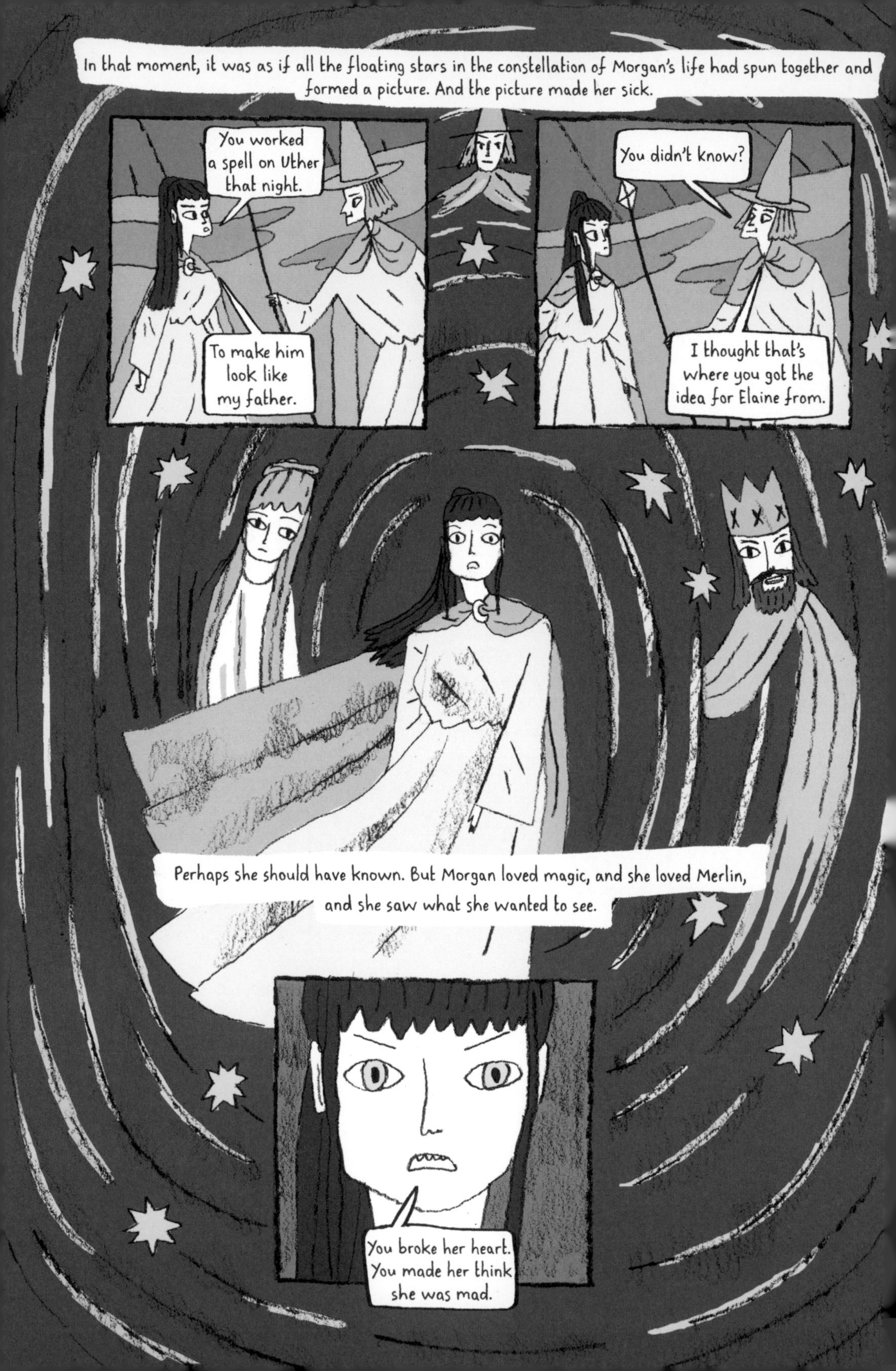
In that moment, it was as if all the floating stars in the constellation of Morgan's life had spun together and formed a picture. And the picture made her sick.
You worked a spell on Uther that night.
To make him look like my father.
You didn't know?
I thought that's where you got the idea for Elaine from.
Perhaps she should have known. But Morgan loved magic, and she loved Merlin, and she saw what she wanted to see.
You broke her heart. You made her think she was mad.

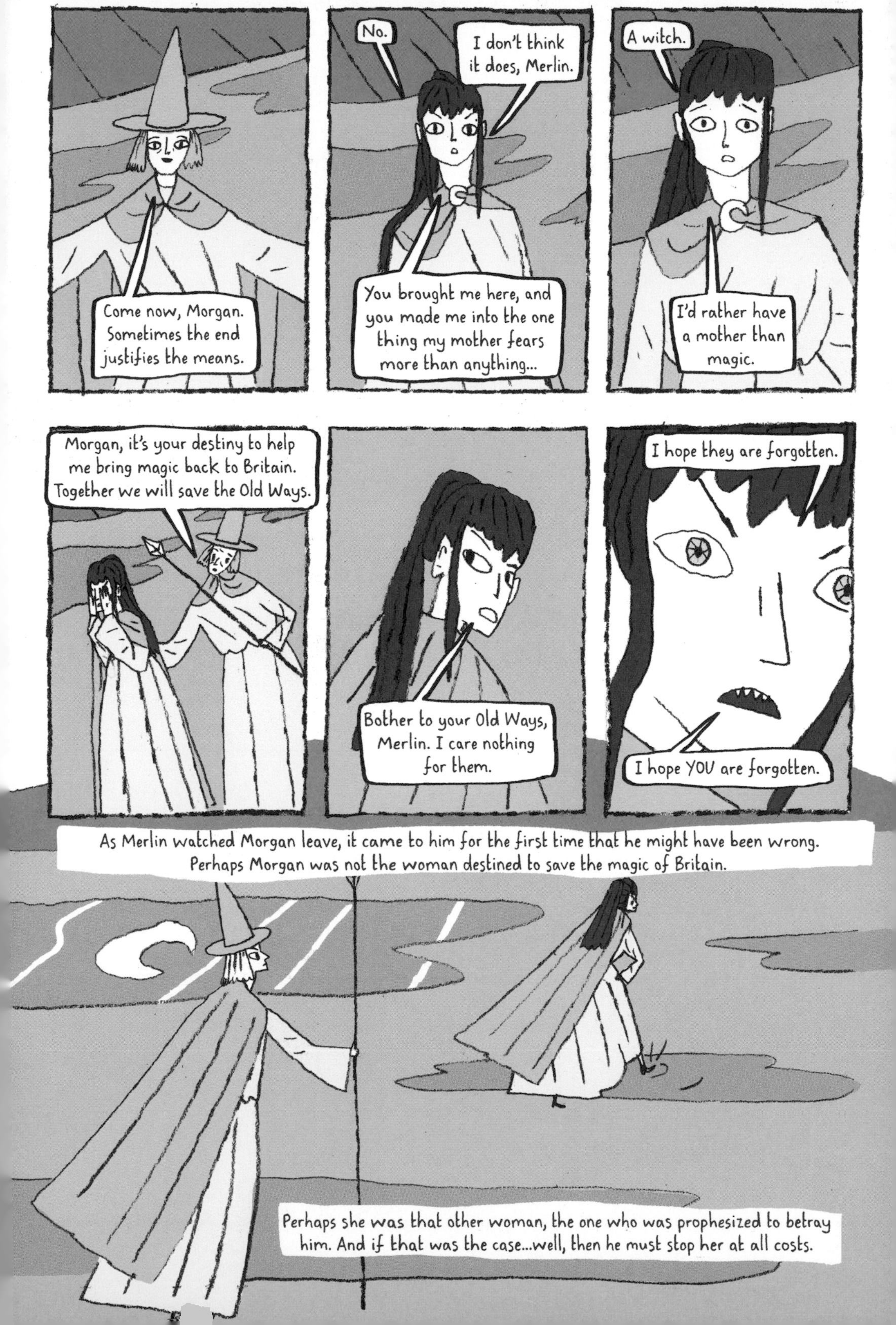
Come now, Morgan. Sometimes the end justifies the means.
No.
I don't think it does, Merlin.
You brought me here, and you made me into the one thing my mother fears more than anything...
A witch.
I'd rather have a mother than magic.
Morgan, it's your destiny to help me bring magic back to Britain. Together we will save the Old Ways.
Bother to your Old Ways, Merlin. I care nothing for them.
I hope they are forgotten.
I hope YOU are forgotten.
As Merlin watched Morgan leave, it came to him for the first time that he might have been wrong. Perhaps Morgan was not the woman destined to save the magic of Britain.
Perhaps she was that other woman, the one who was prophesized to betray him. And if that was the case...well, then he must stop her at all costs.

Meanwhile, Arthur's reign came to a tragic end. A battle, in the driving snow. Another rebellion to be quashed. Arthur fighting to the death. And without Merlin or the magical scabbard, there was nothing and no one left to protect him.

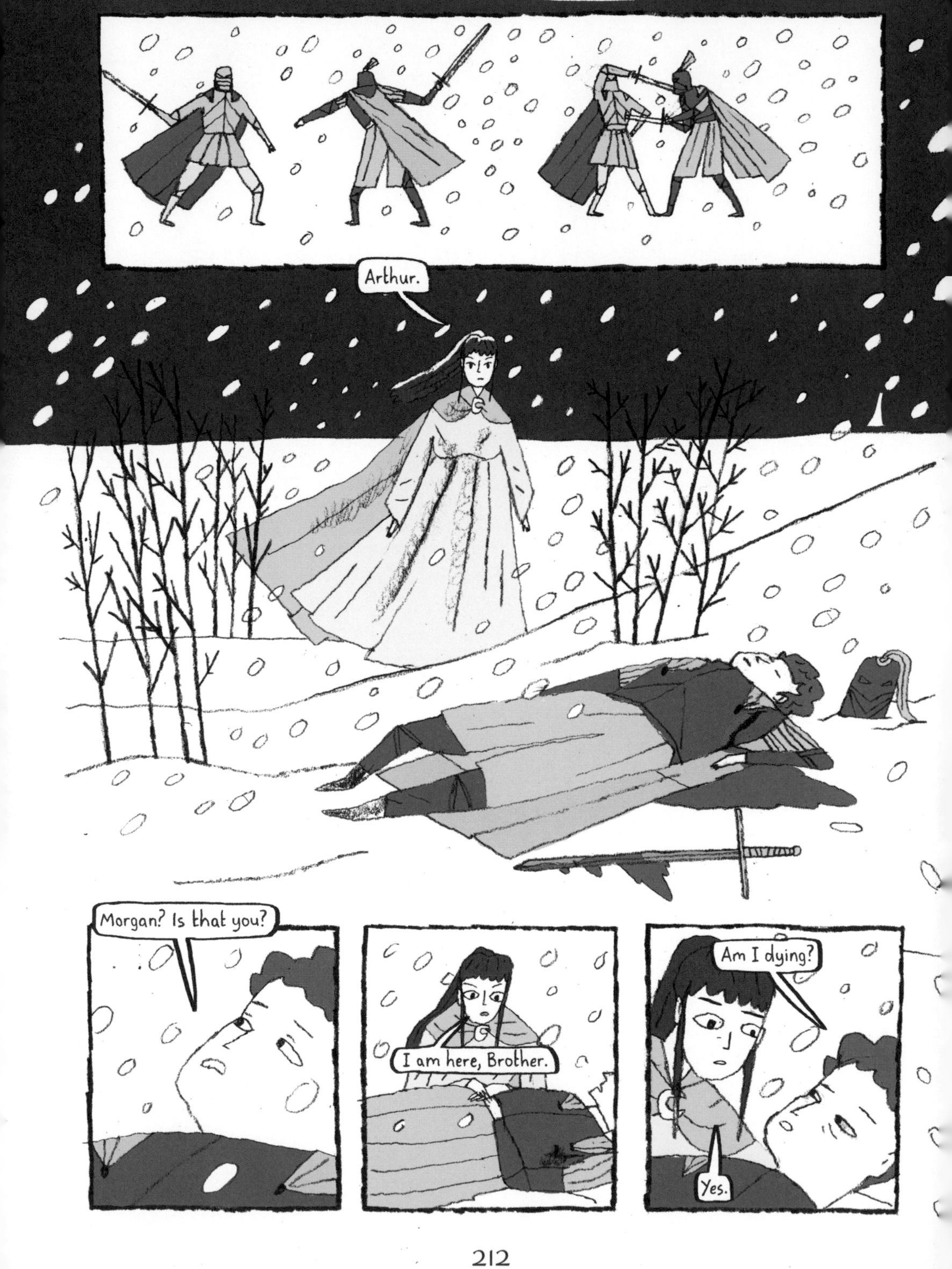

Arthur.
Morgan? Is that you?
I am here, Brother.
Am I dying?
Yes.

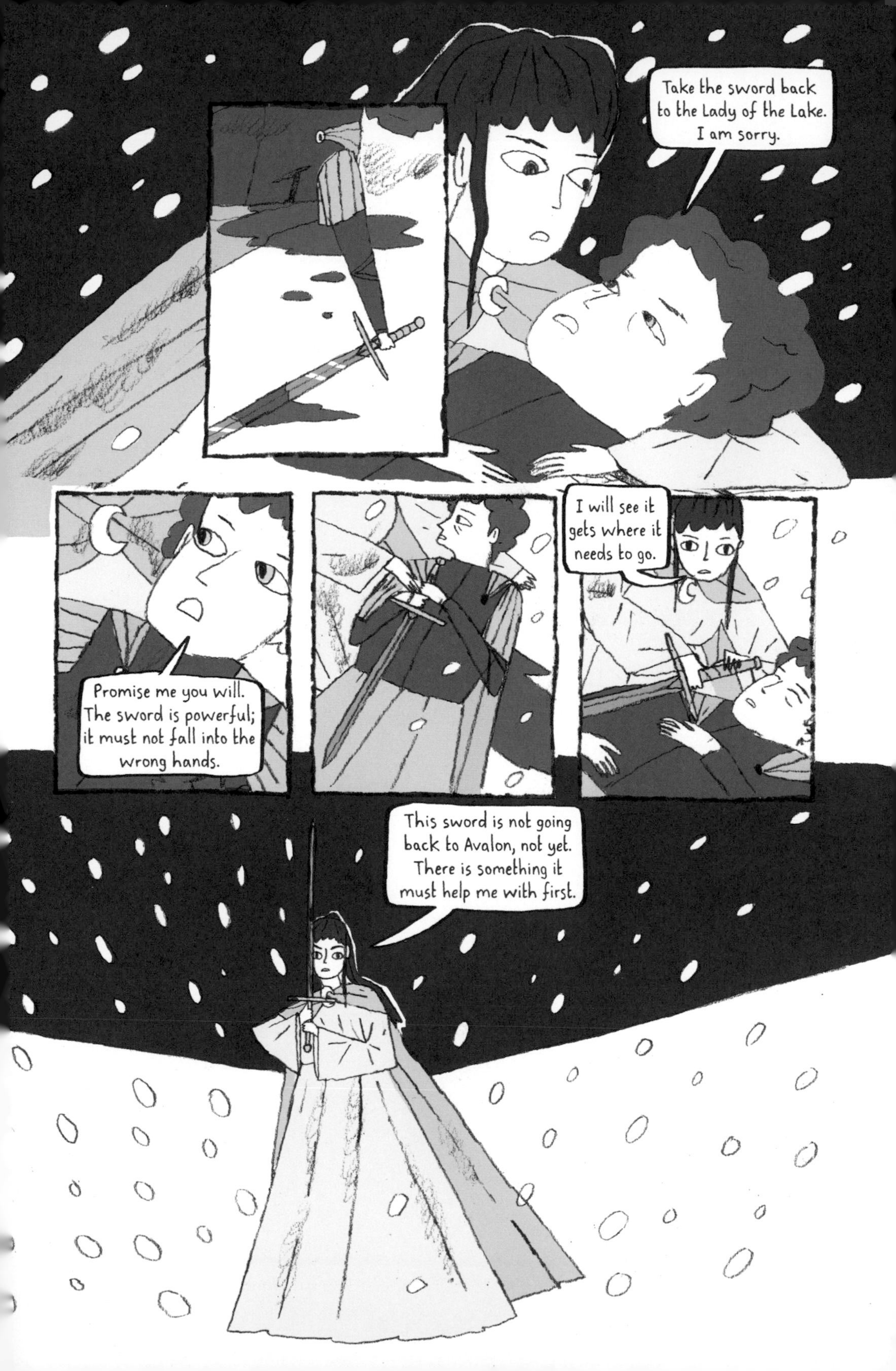
Take the sword back to the Lady of the Lake. I am sorry.
Promise me you will. The sword is powerful; it must not fall into the wrong hands.
I will see it gets where it needs to go.
This sword is not going back to Avalon, not yet. There is something it must help me with first.

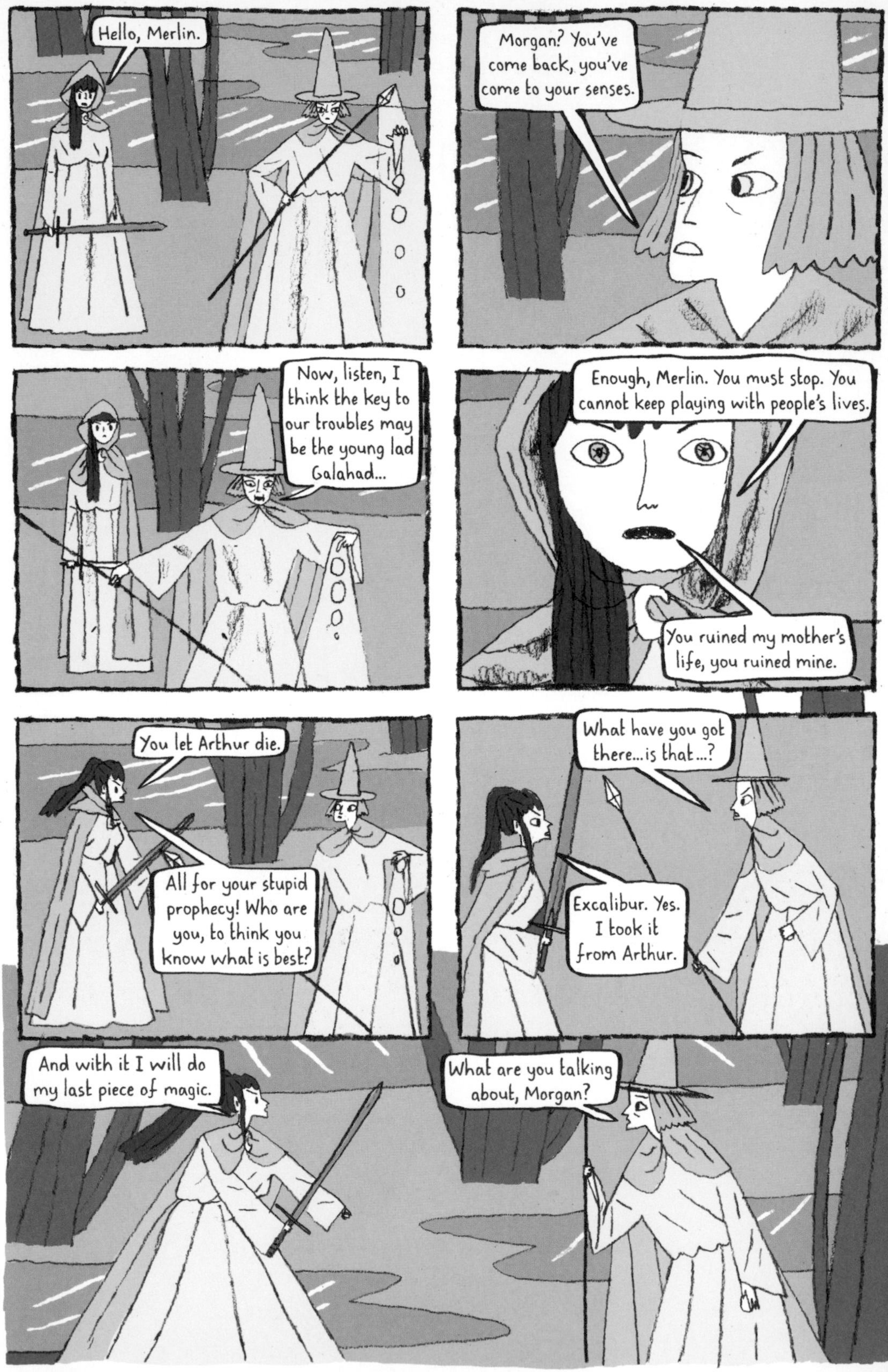

Hello, Merlin.
Morgan? You've come back, you've come to your senses.
Now, listen, I think the key to our troubles may be the young lad Galahad...
Enough, Merlin. You must stop. You cannot keep playing with people's lives.
You ruined my mother's life, you ruined mine.
You let Arthur die.
All for your stupid prophecy! Who are you, to think you know what is best?
What have you got there...is that...?
Excalibur. Yes. I took it from Arthur.
And with it I will do my last piece of magic.
What are you talking about, Morgan?

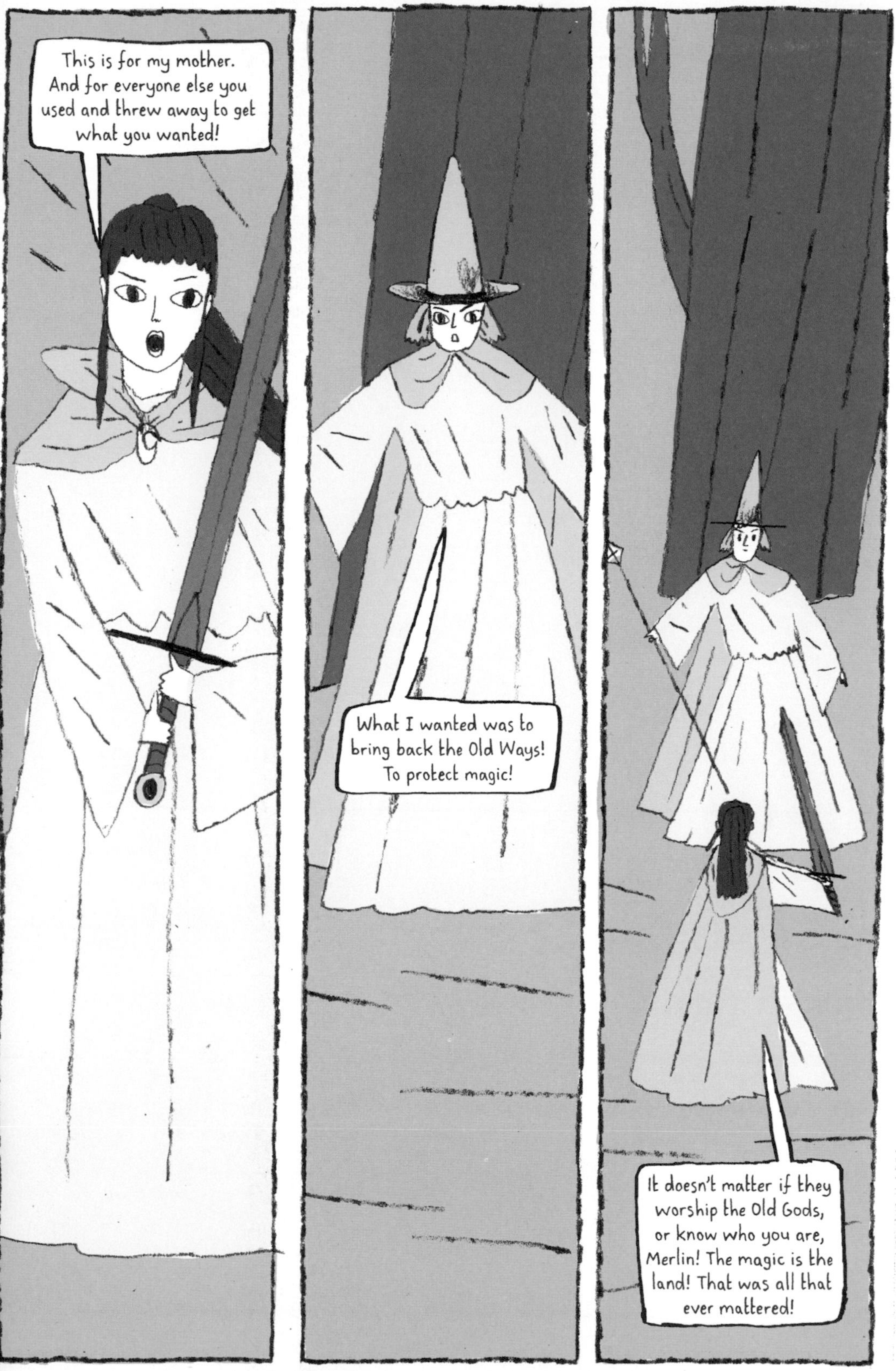
This is for my mother. And for everyone else you used and threw away to get what you wanted!
What I wanted was to bring back the Old Ways! To protect magic!
It doesn't matter if they worship the Old Gods, or know who you are, Merlin! The magic is the land! That was all that ever mattered!

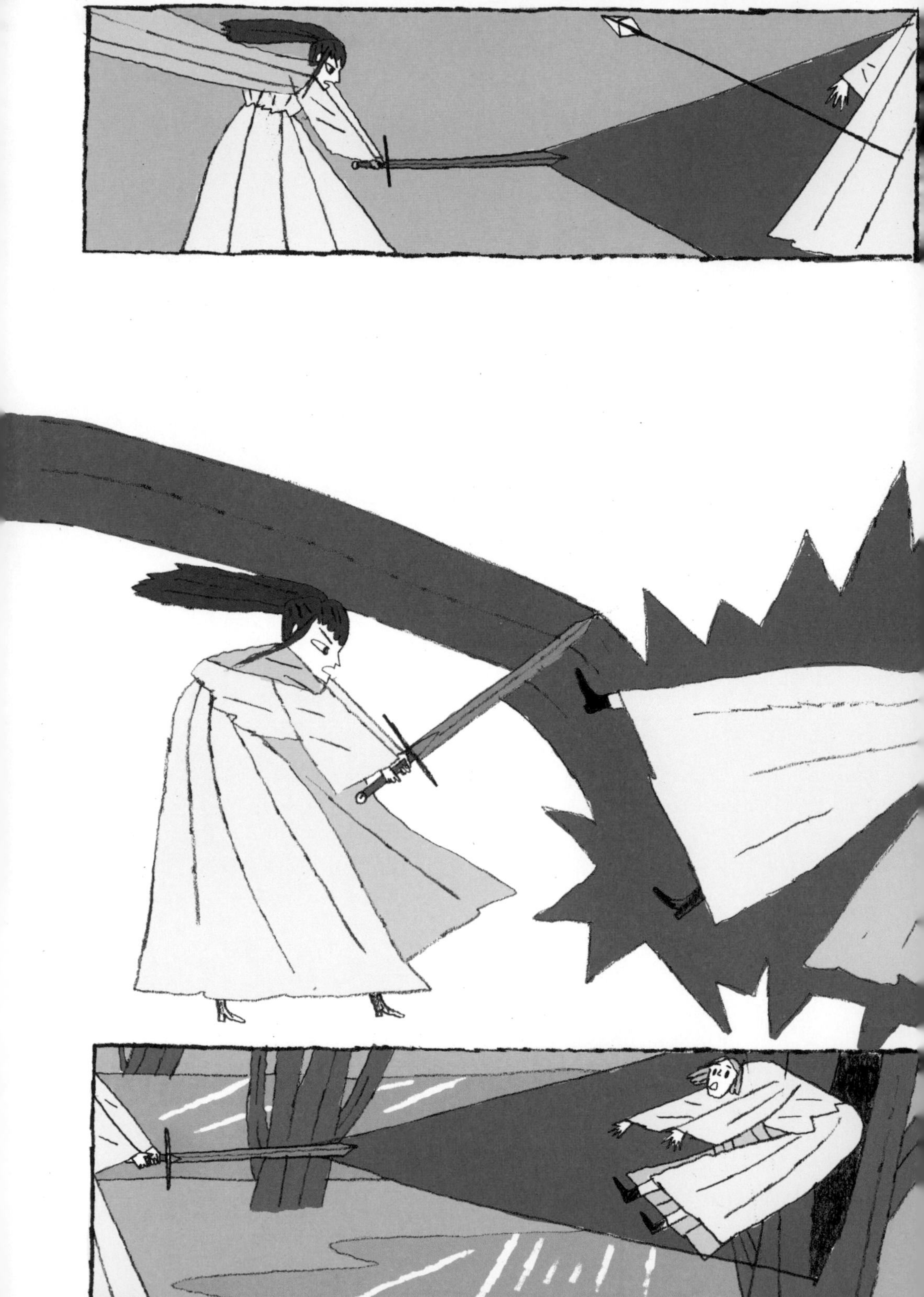

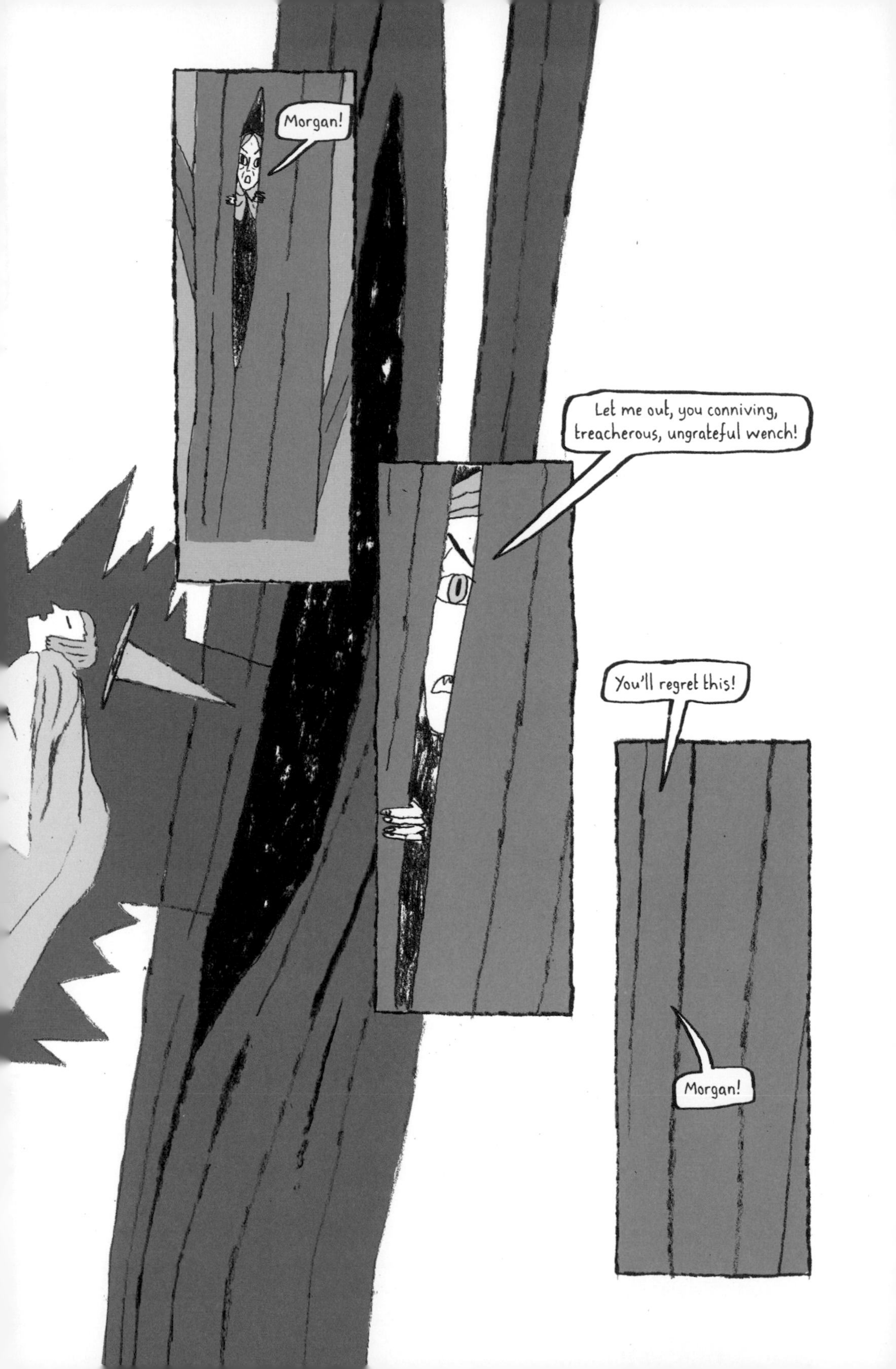
Morgan!
Let me out, you conniving, treacherous, ungrateful wench!
You'll regret this!
Morgan!

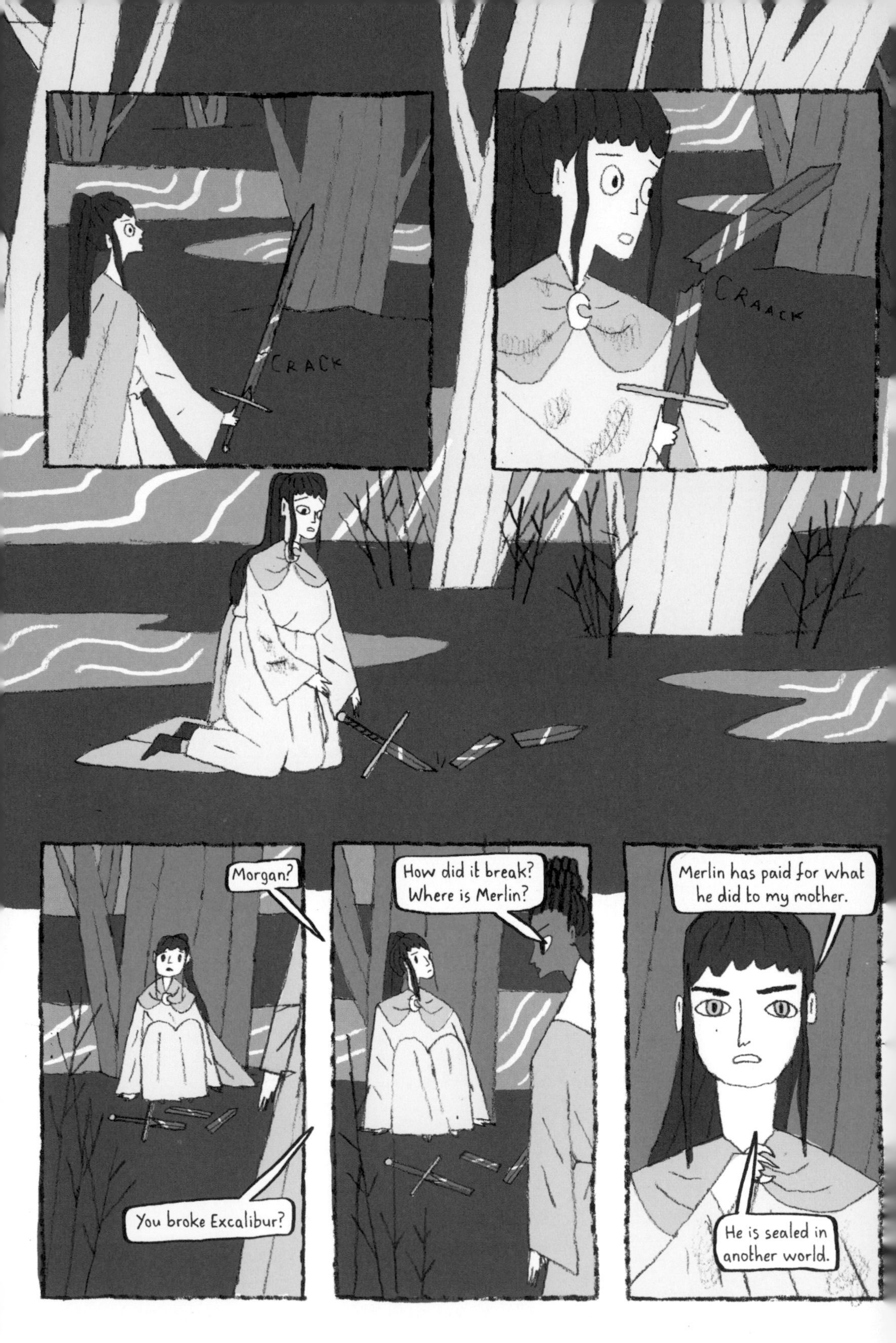
CRACK
CRAAACK
Morgan?
You broke Excalibur?
How did it break?
Where is Merlin?
Merlin has paid for what he did to my mother.
He is sealed in another world.

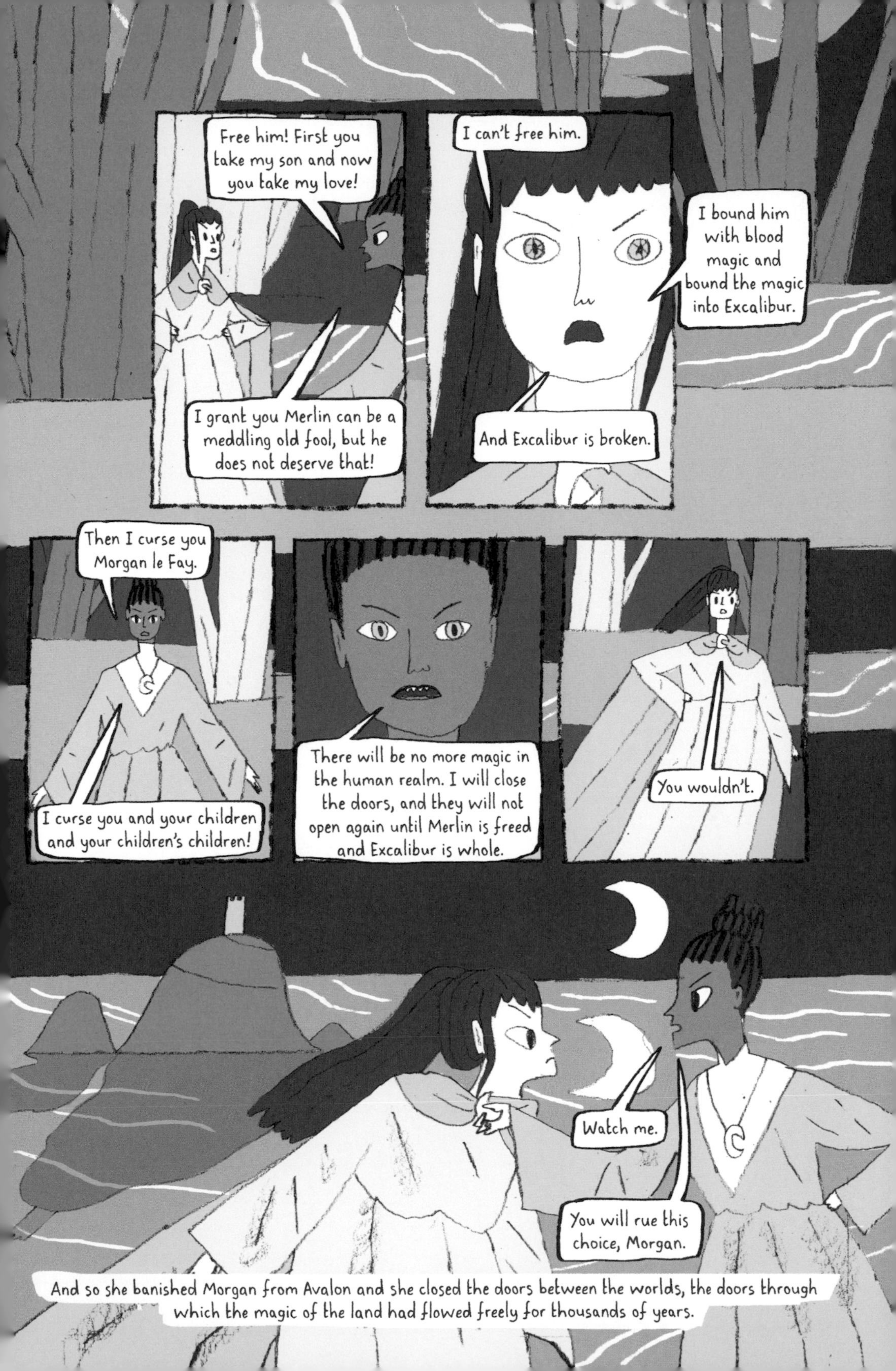
Free him! First you take my son and now you take my love!
I grant you Merlin can be a meddling old fool, but he does not deserve that!
I can't free him.
I bound him with blood magic and bound the magic into Excalibur.
And Excalibur is broken.
Then I curse you Morgan le Fay.
I curse you and your children and your children's children!
There will be no more magic in the human realm. I will close the doors, and they will not open again until Merlin is freed and Excalibur is whole.
You wouldn't.
Watch me.
You will rue this choice, Morgan.
And so she banished Morgan from Avalon and she closed the doors between the worlds, the doors through which the magic of the land had flowed freely for thousands of years.

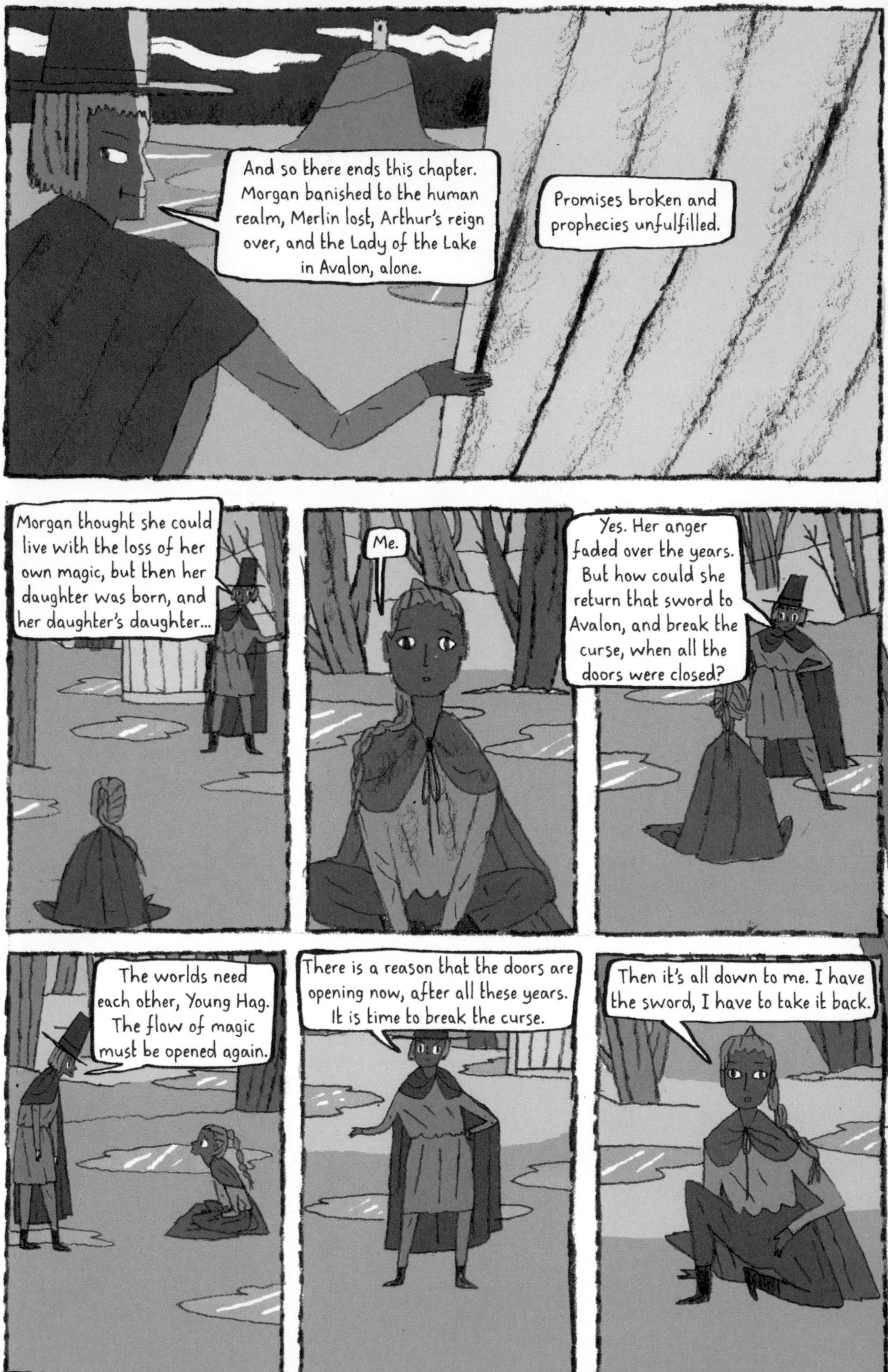
And so there ends this chapter. Morgan banished to the human realm, Merlin lost, Arthur's reign over, and the Lady of the Lake in Avalon, alone.
Promises broken and prophecies unfulfilled.
Morgan thought she could live with the loss of her own magic, but then her daughter was born, and her daughter's daughter...
Me.
Yes. Her anger faded over the years. But how could she return that sword to Avalon, and break the curse, when all the doors were closed?
The worlds need each other, Young Hag. The flow of magic must be opened again.
There is a reason that the doors are opening now, after all these years. It is time to break the curse.
Then it's all down to me. I have the sword, I have to take it back.

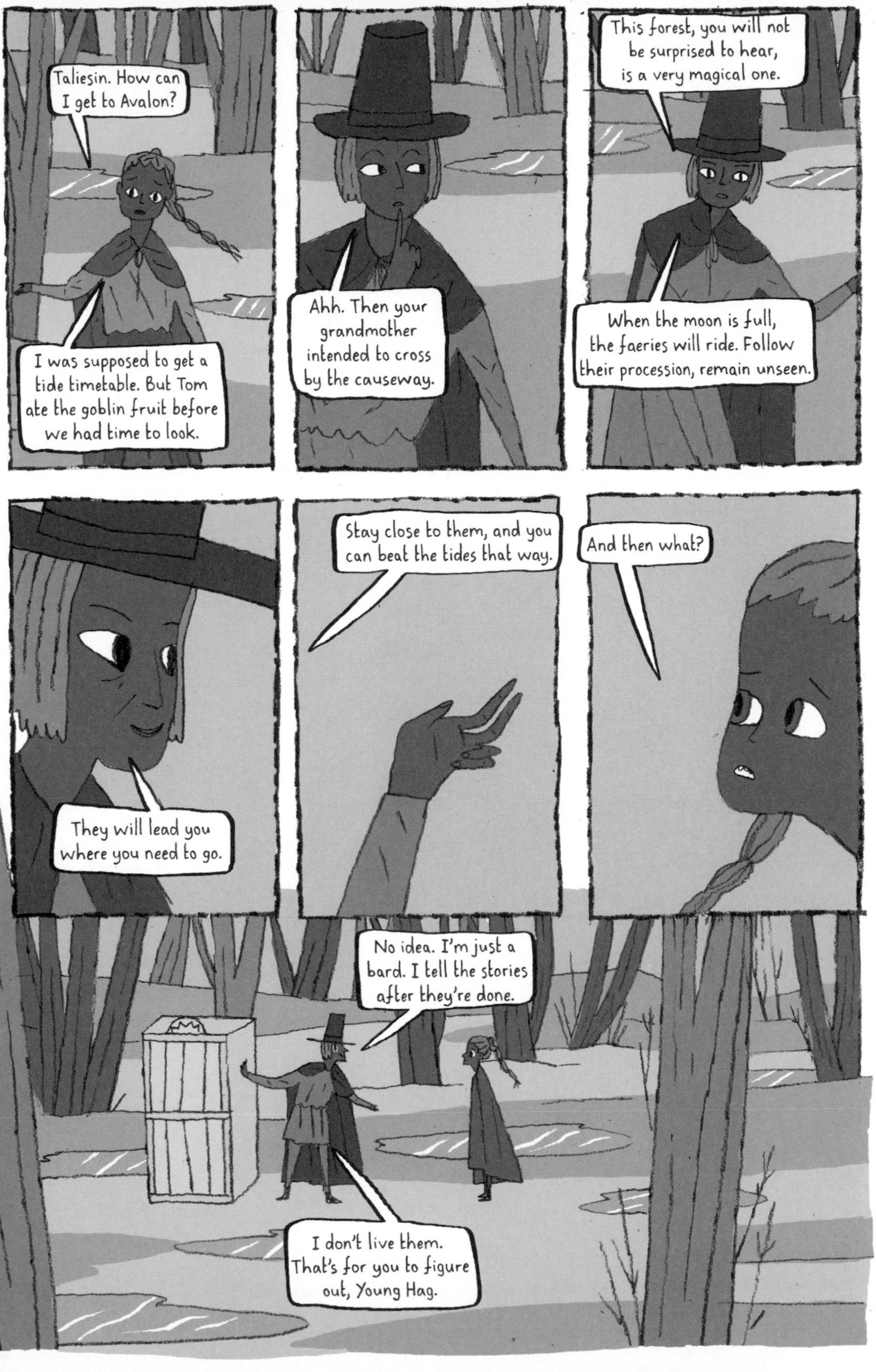
Taliesin. How can I get to Avalon?
I was supposed to get a tide timetable. But Tom ate the goblin fruit before we had time to look.
Ahh. Then your grandmother intended to cross by the causeway.
This forest, you will not be surprised to hear, is a very magical one.
When the moon is full, the faeries will ride. Follow their procession, remain unseen.
They will lead you where you need to go.
Stay close to them, and you can beat the tides that way.
And then what?
No idea. I'm just a bard. I tell the stories after they're done.
I don't live them. That's for you to figure out, Young Hag.

PART THE FIFTH

The Otherworld

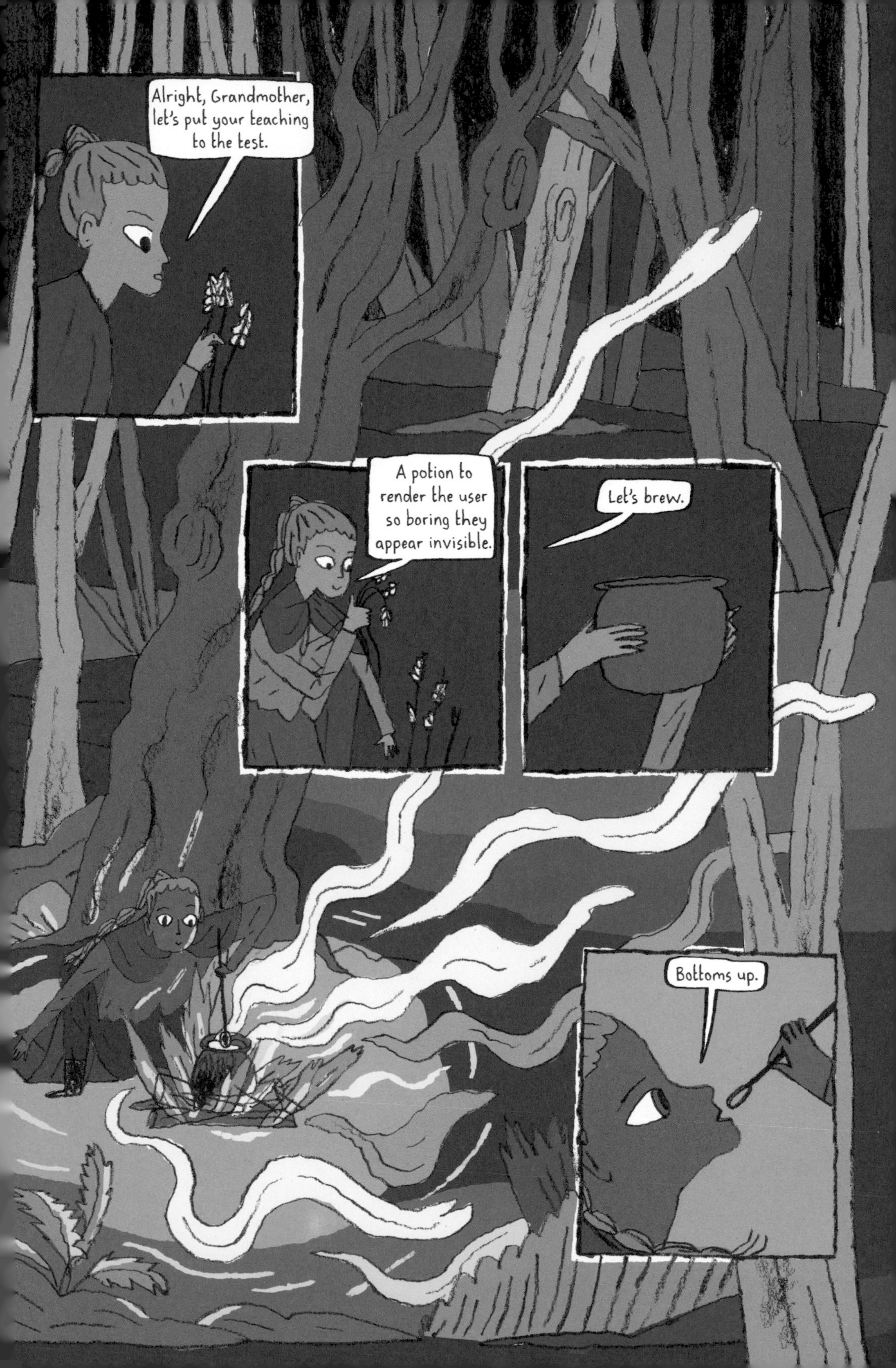
Alright, Grandmother, let's put your teaching to the test.
A potion to render the user so boring they appear invisible.
Let's brew.
Bottoms up.

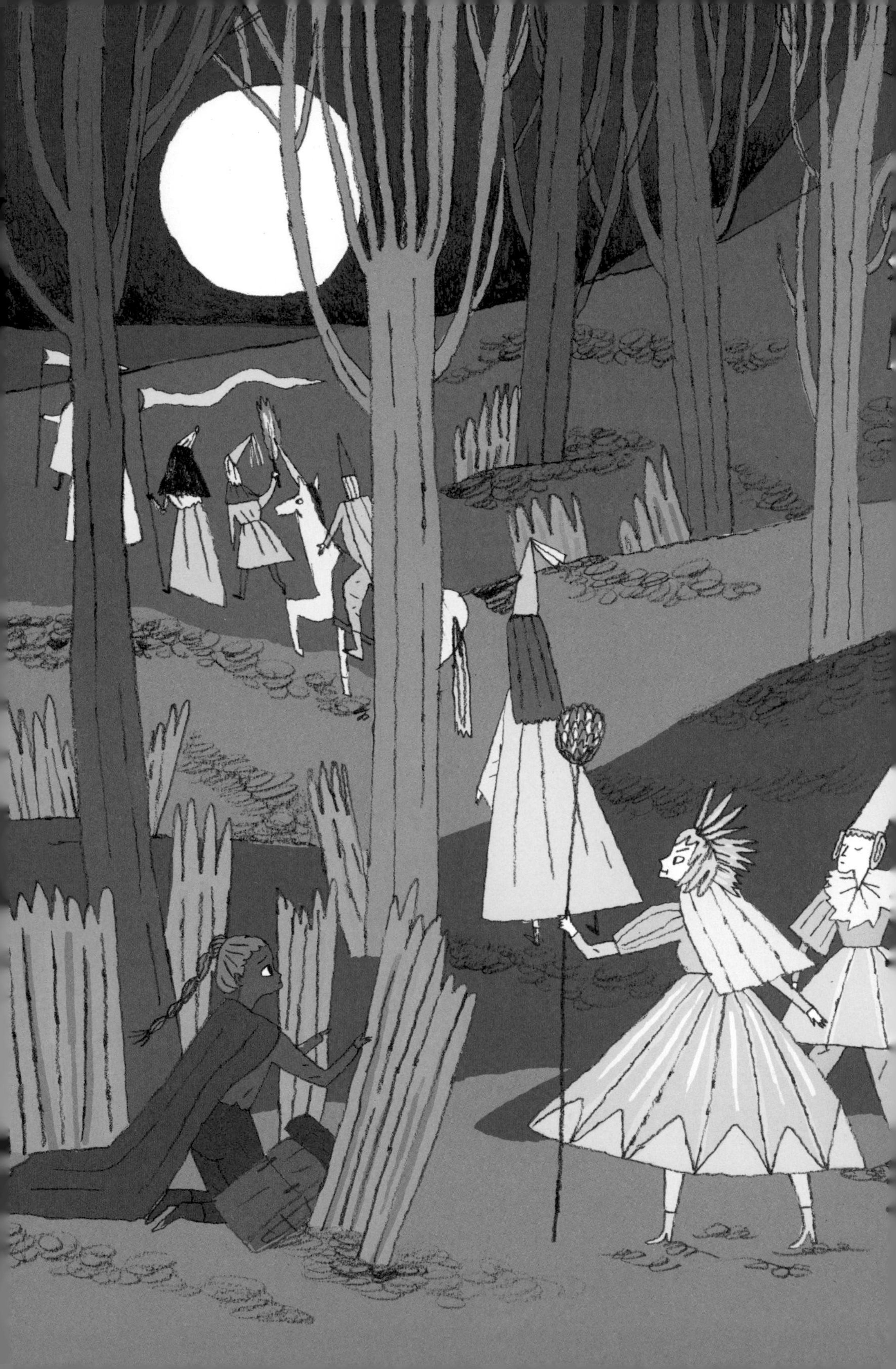

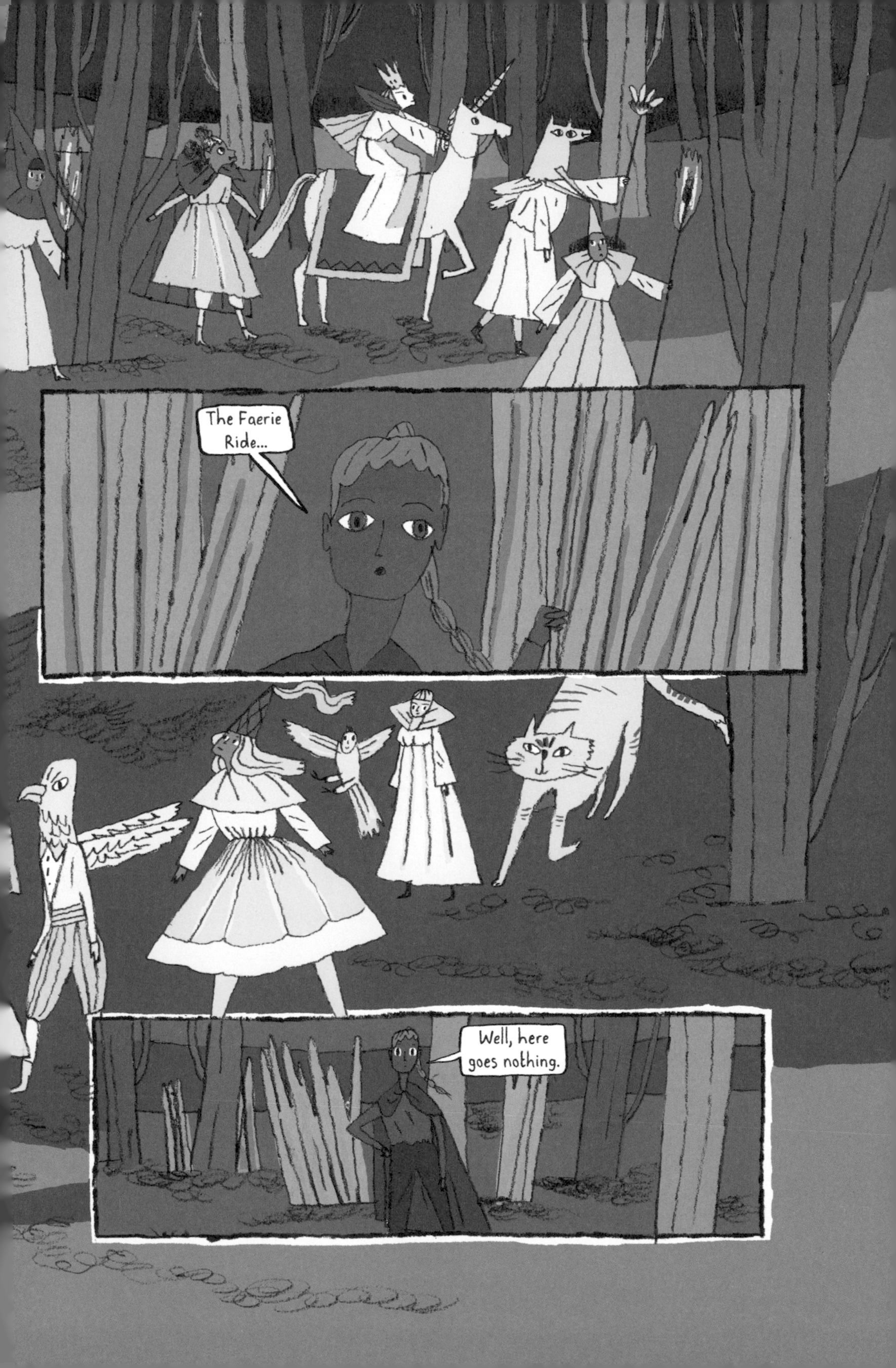
The Faerie Ride...
Well, here goes nothing.

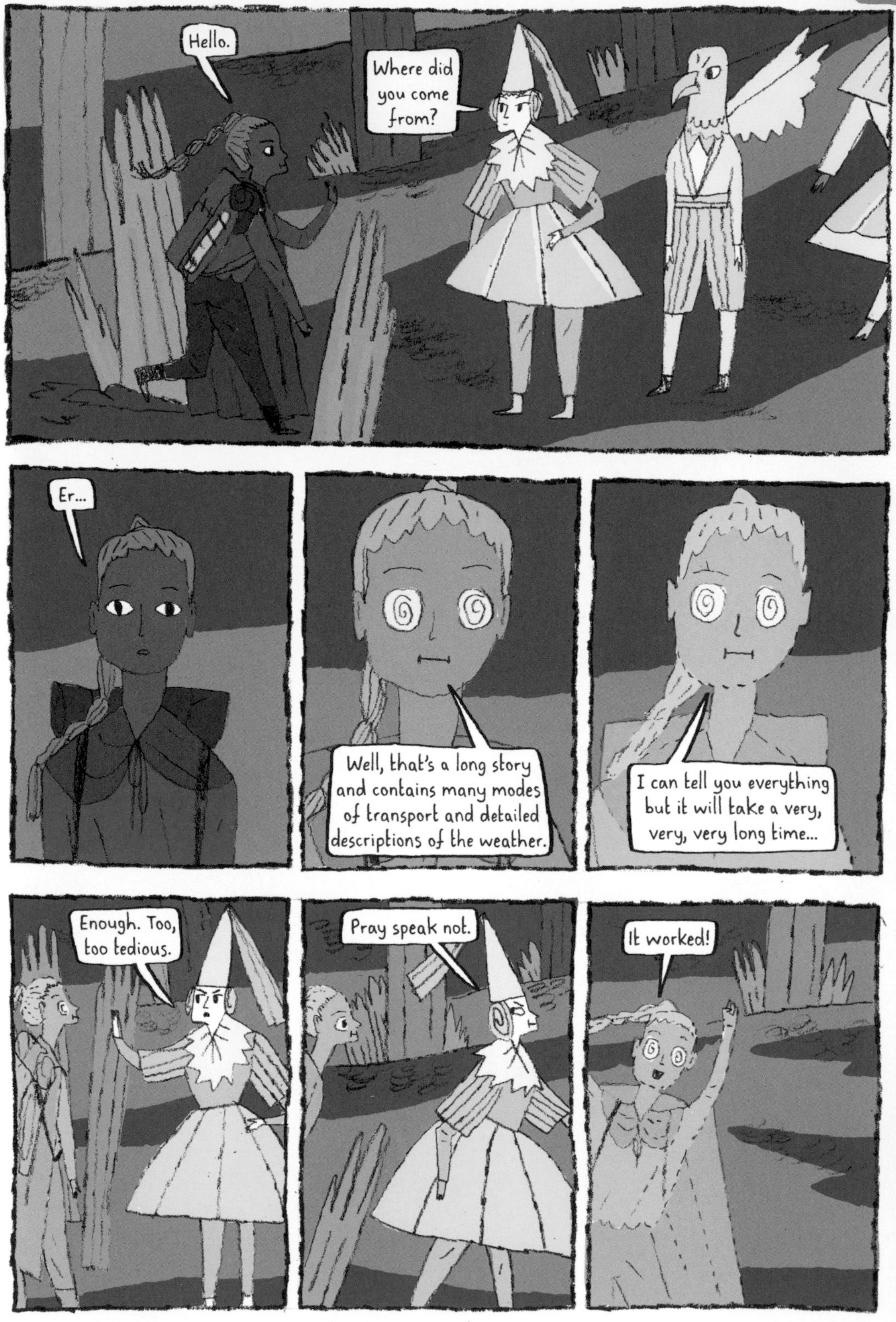
Hello.
Where did you come from?
Er...
Well, that's a long story and contains many modes of transport and detailed descriptions of the weather.
I can tell you everything but it will take a very, very, very long time...
Enough. Too, too tedious.
Pray speak not.
It worked!

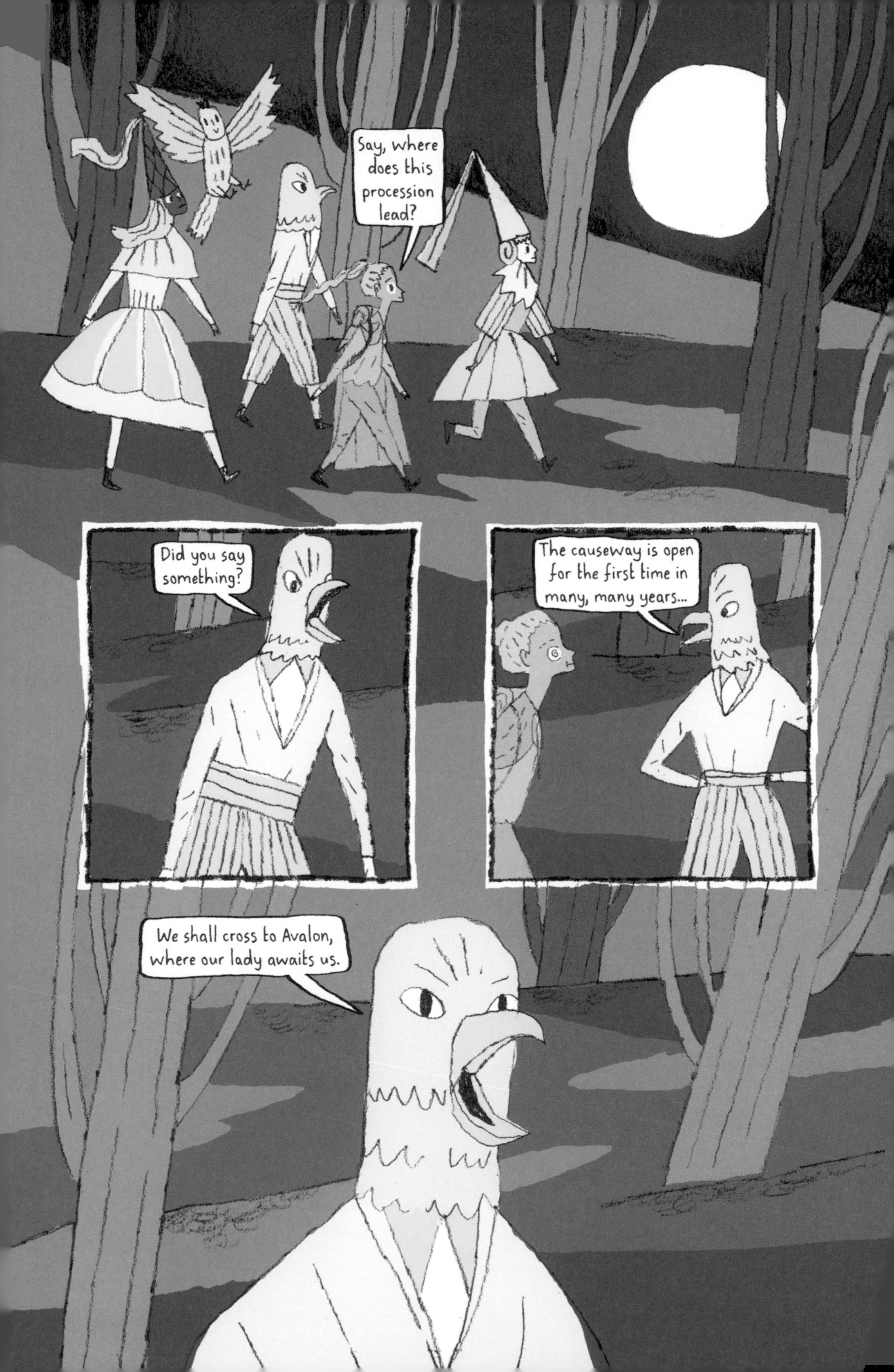
Say, where does this procession lead?
Did you say something?
The causeway is open for the first time in many, many years...
We shall cross to Avalon, where our lady awaits us.

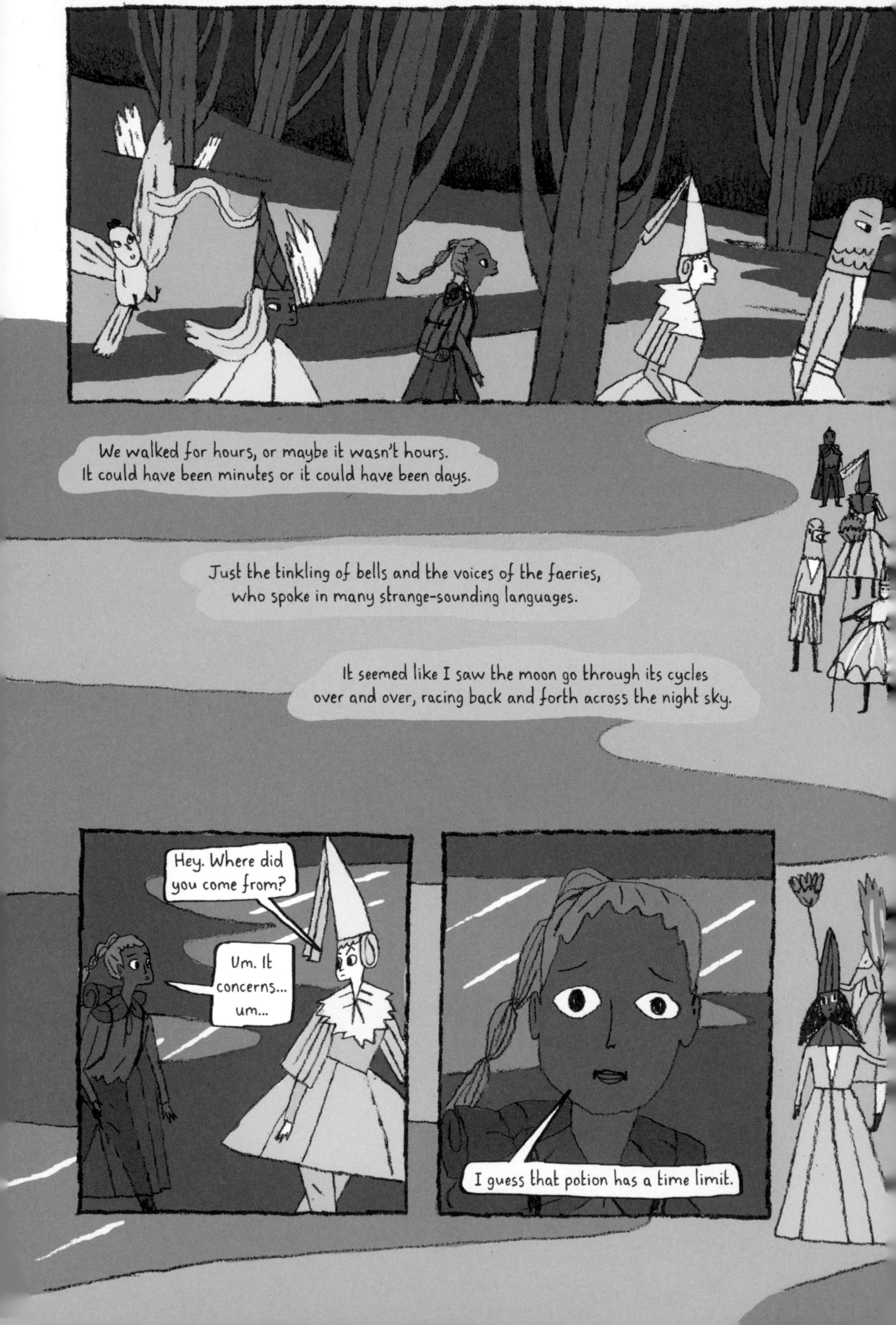
We walked for hours, or maybe it wasn't hours.
It could have been minutes or it could have been days.
Just the tinkling of bells and the voices of the faeries,
who spoke in many strange-sounding languages.
It seemed like I saw the moon go through its cycles
over and over, racing back and forth across the night sky.
Hey. Where did you come from?
Um. It concerns... um...
I guess that potion has a time limit.

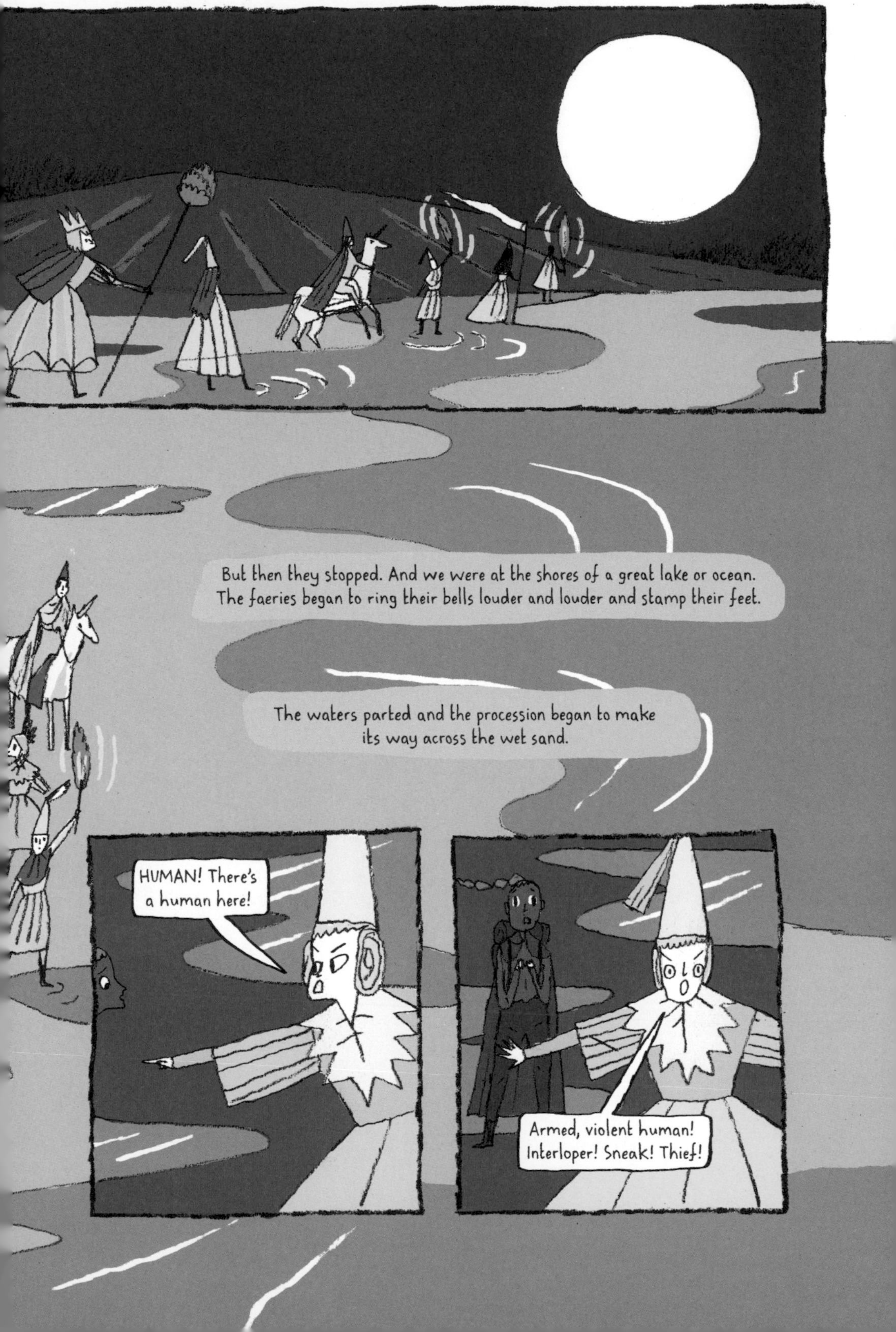

But then they stopped. And we were at the shores of a great lake or ocean. The faeries began to ring their bells louder and louder and stamp their feet.
The waters parted and the procession began to make its way across the wet sand.
HUMAN! There's a human here!
Armed, violent human! Interloper! Sneak! Thief!

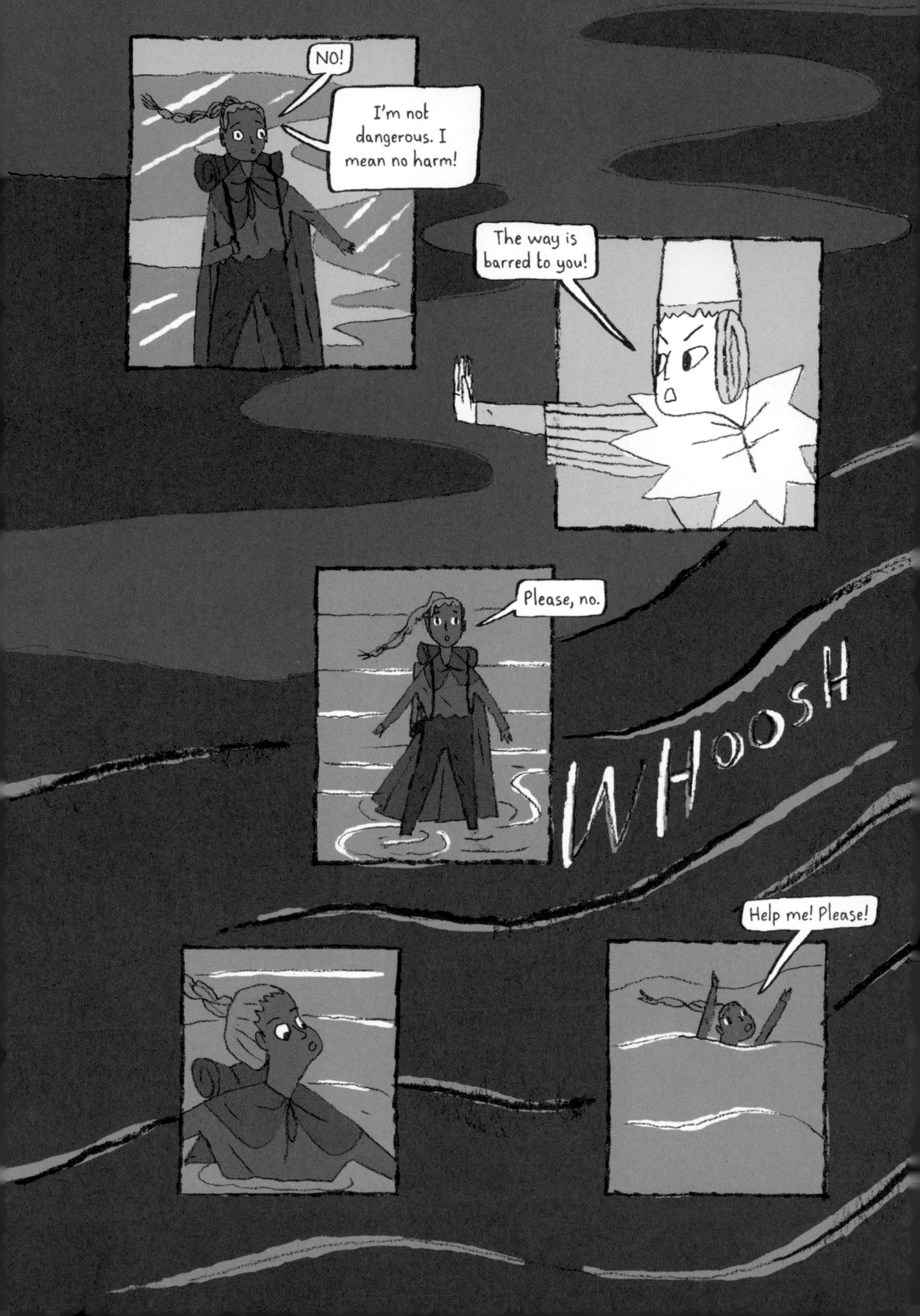
NO!
I'm not dangerous. I mean no harm!
The way is barred to you!
Please, no.
WHOOSH
Help me! Please!

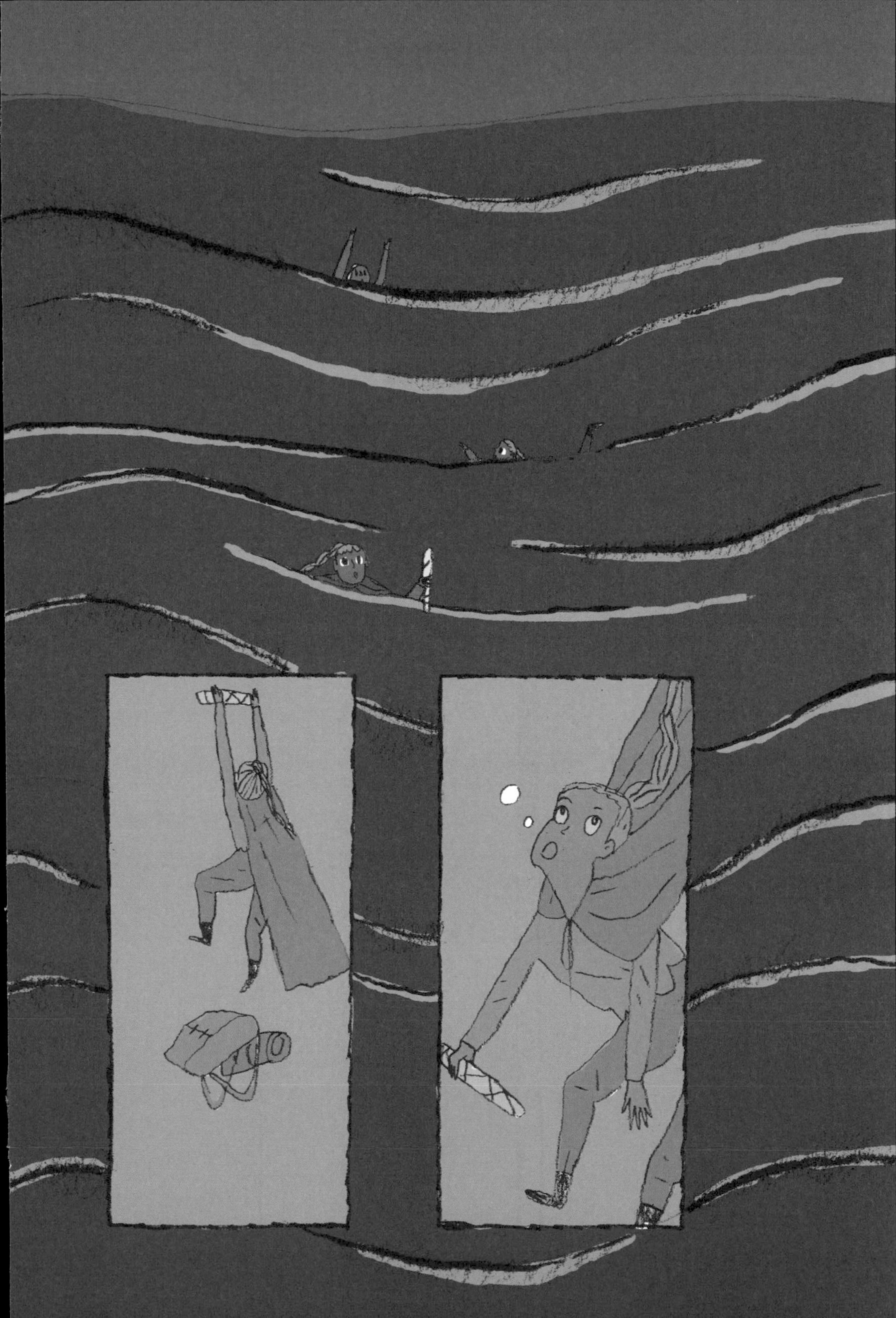

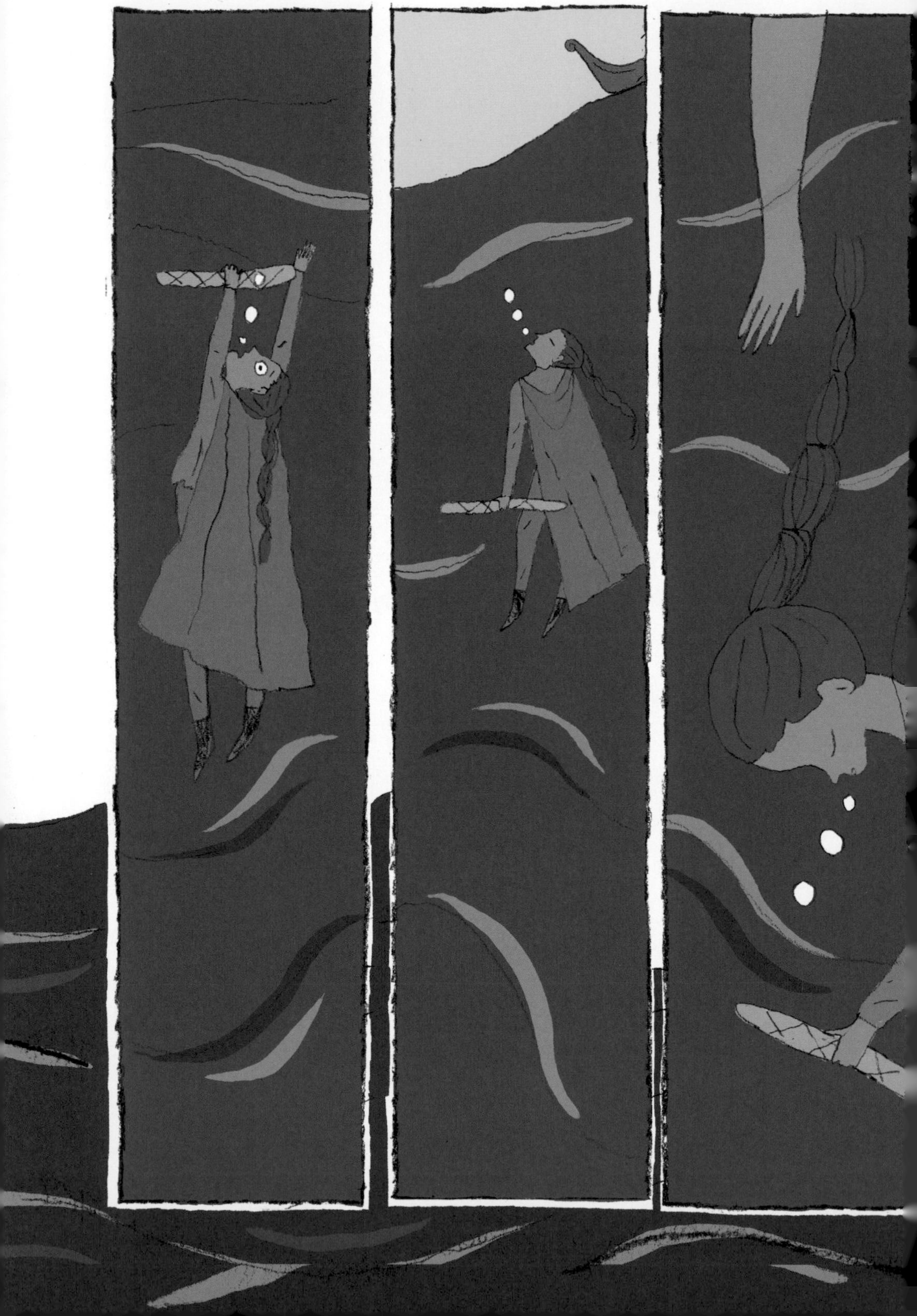

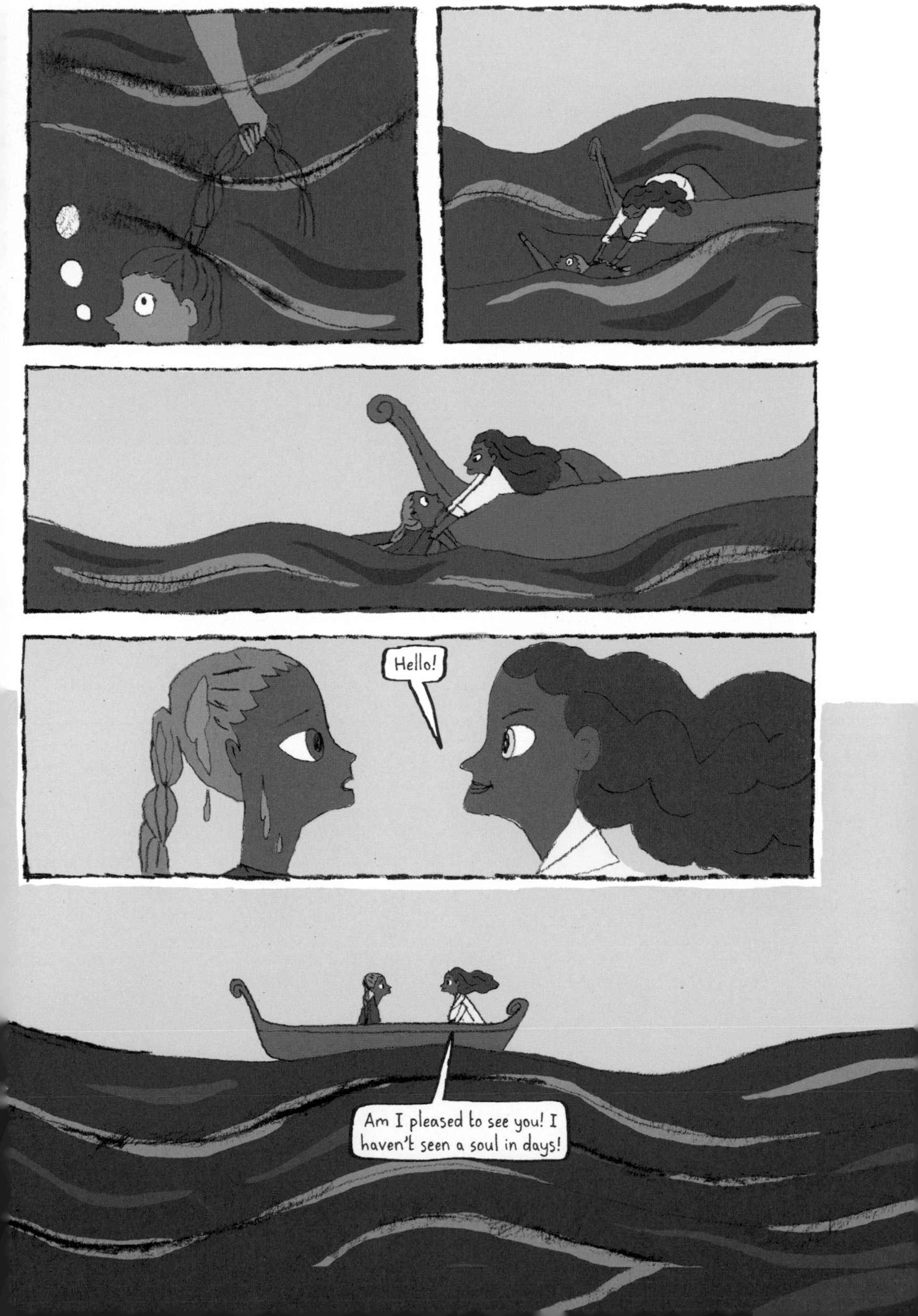

Hello!
Am I pleased to see you! I haven't seen a soul in days!

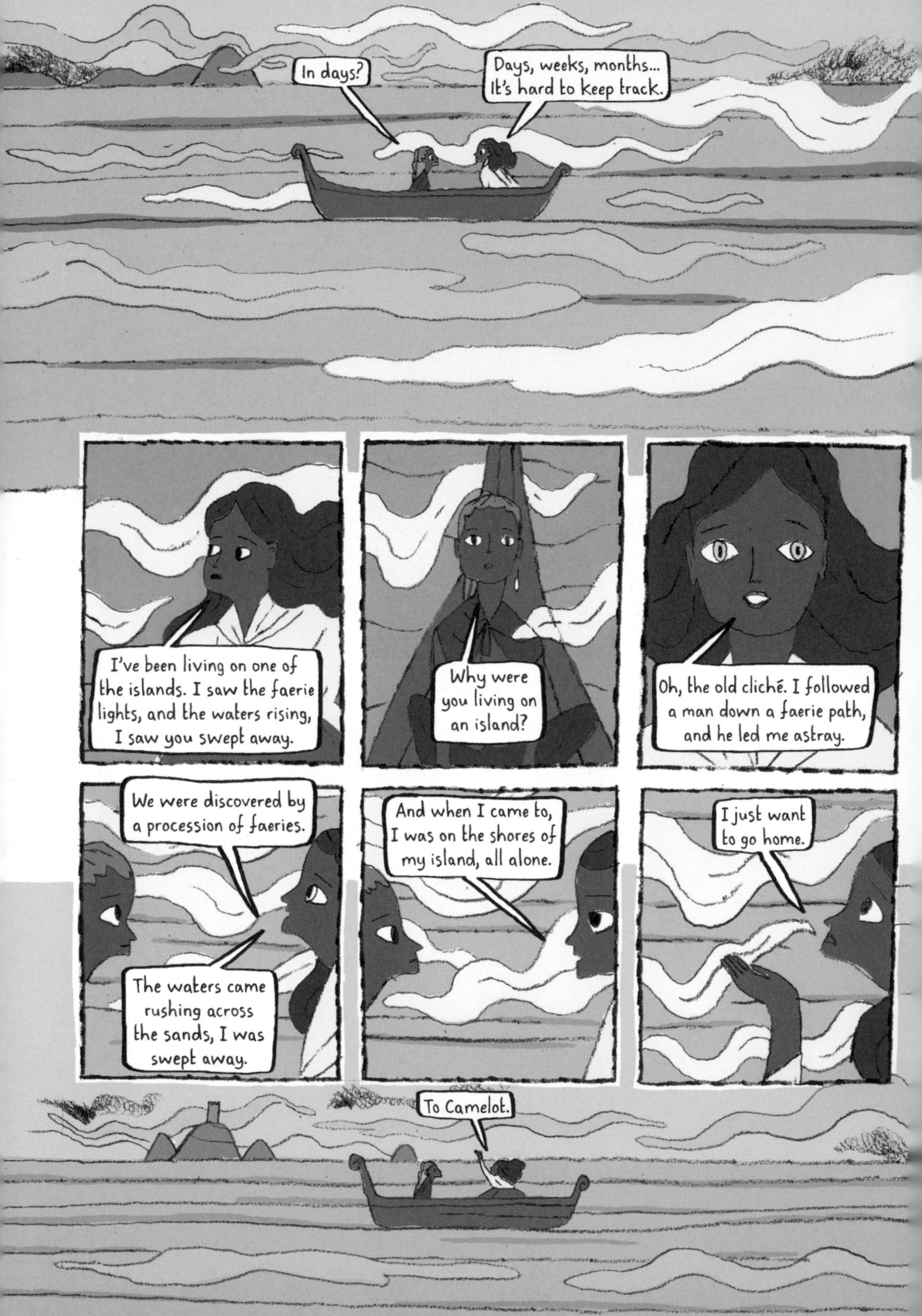
In days?
Days, weeks, months... It's hard to keep track.
I've been living on one of the islands. I saw the faerie lights, and the waters rising, I saw you swept away.
Why were you living on an island?
Oh, the old cliché. I followed a man down a faerie path, and he led me astray.
We were discovered by a procession of faeries.
The waters came rushing across the sands, I was swept away.
And when I came to, I was on the shores of my island, all alone.
I just want to go home.
To Camelot.

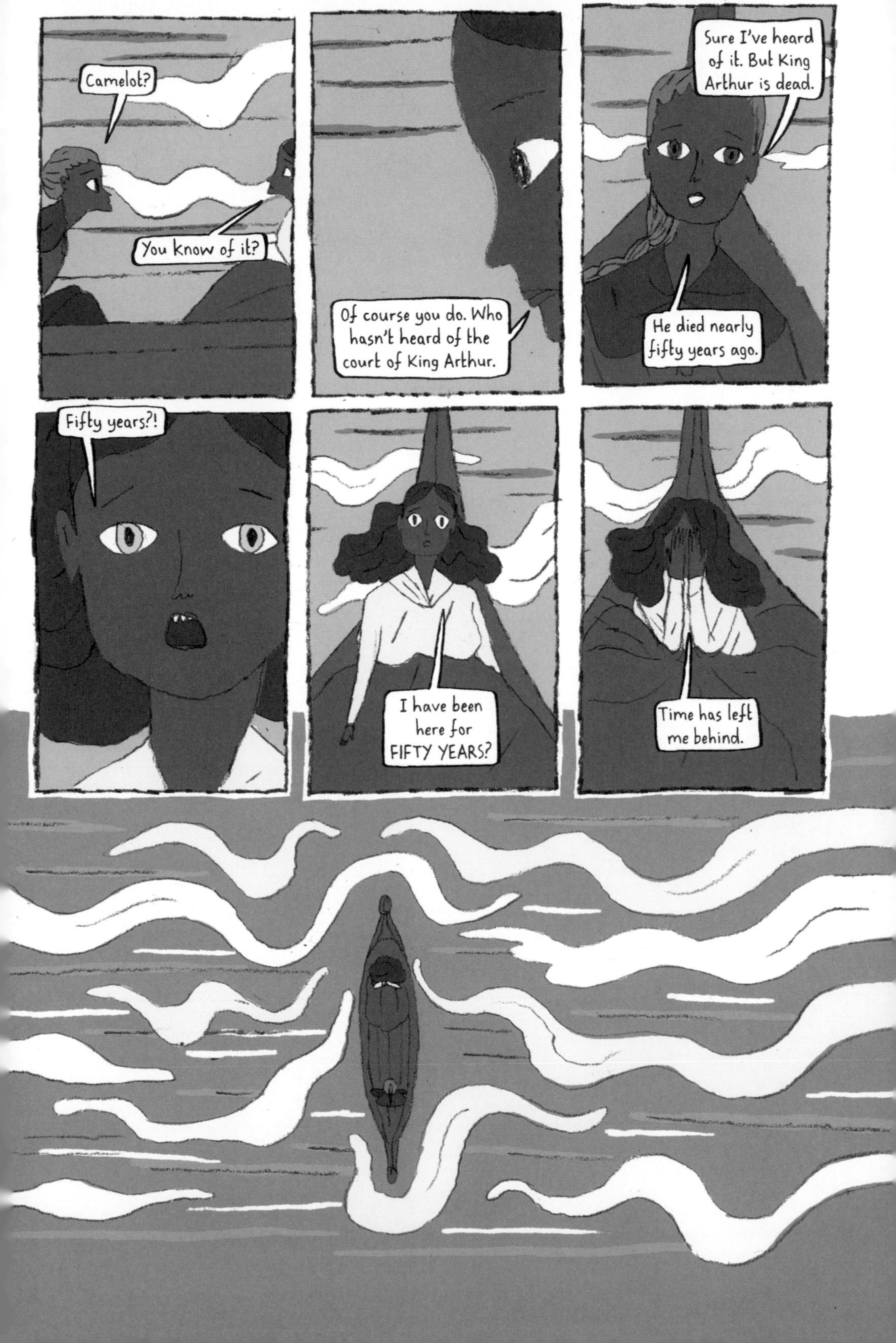
Camelot?
You know of it?
Of course you do. Who hasn't heard of the court of King Arthur.
Sure I've heard of it. But King Arthur is dead.
He died nearly fifty years ago.
Fifty years?!
I have been here for FIFTY YEARS?
Time has left me behind.

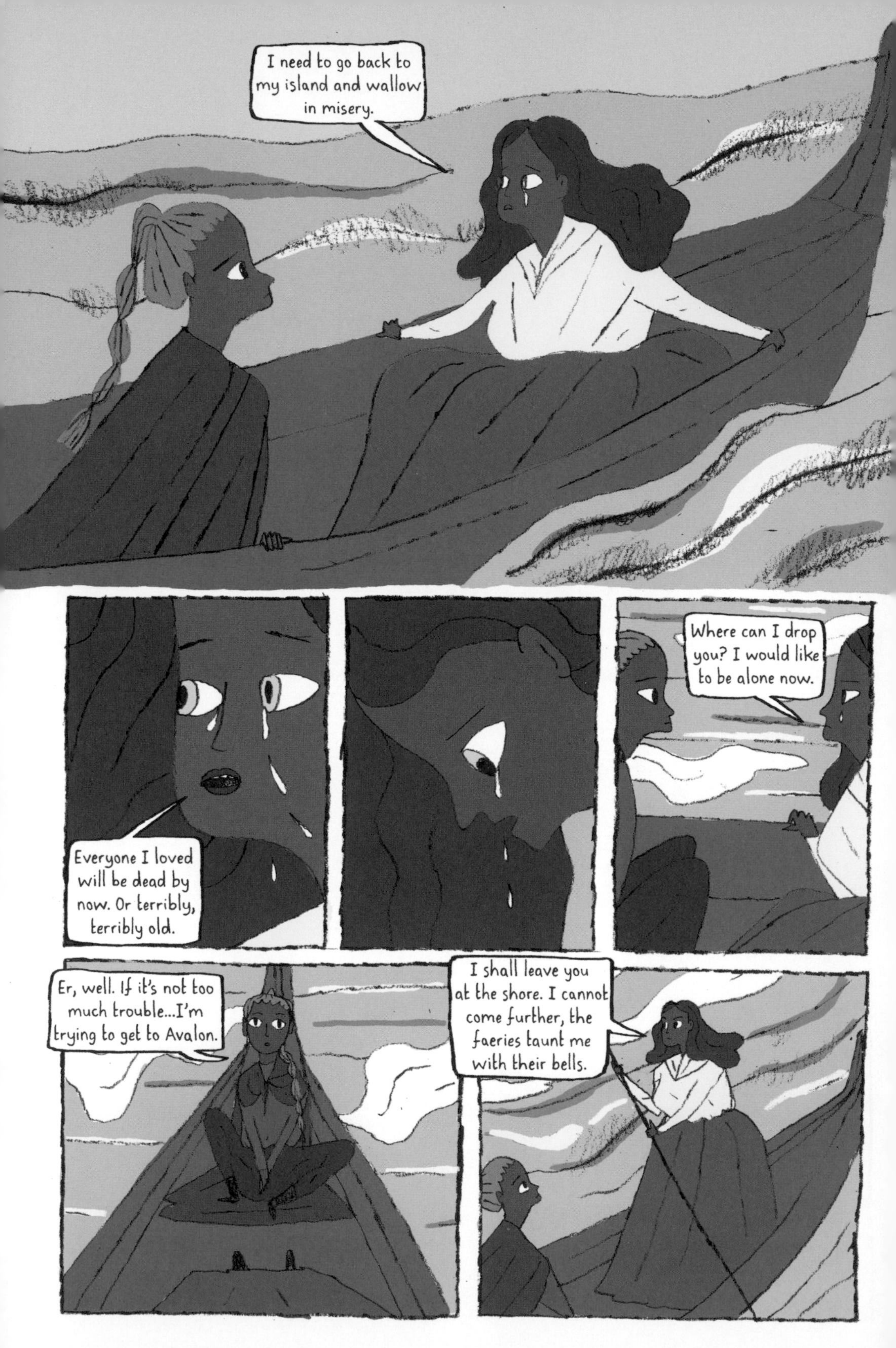
I need to go back to my island and wallow in misery.
Everyone I loved will be dead by now. Or terribly, terribly old.
Where can I drop you? I would like to be alone now.
Er, well. If it's not too much trouble...I'm trying to get to Avalon.
I shall leave you at the shore. I cannot come further, the faeries taunt me with their bells.

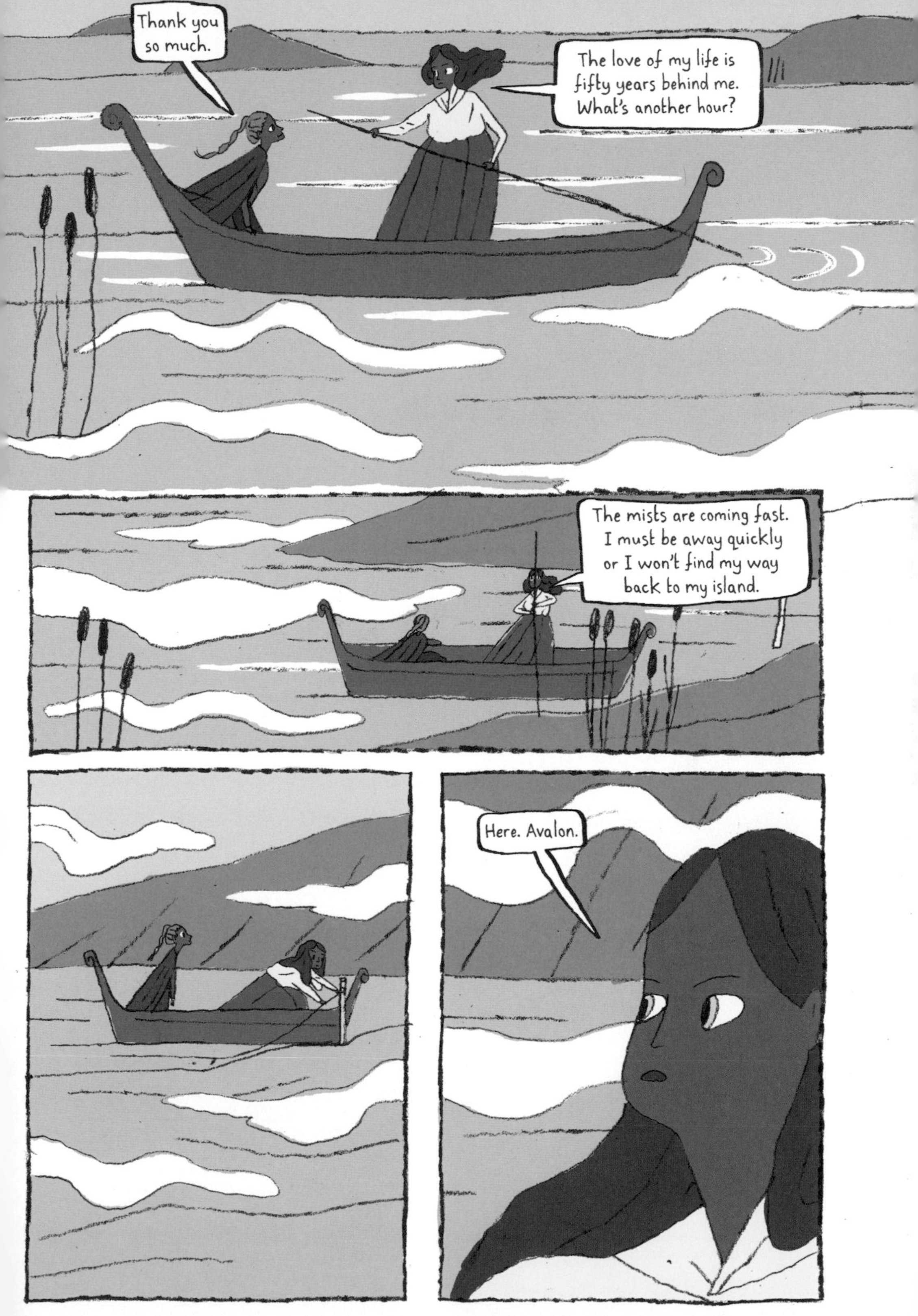
Thank you so much.
The love of my life is fifty years behind me. What's another hour?
The mists are coming fast. I must be away quickly or I won't find my way back to my island.
Here. Avalon.

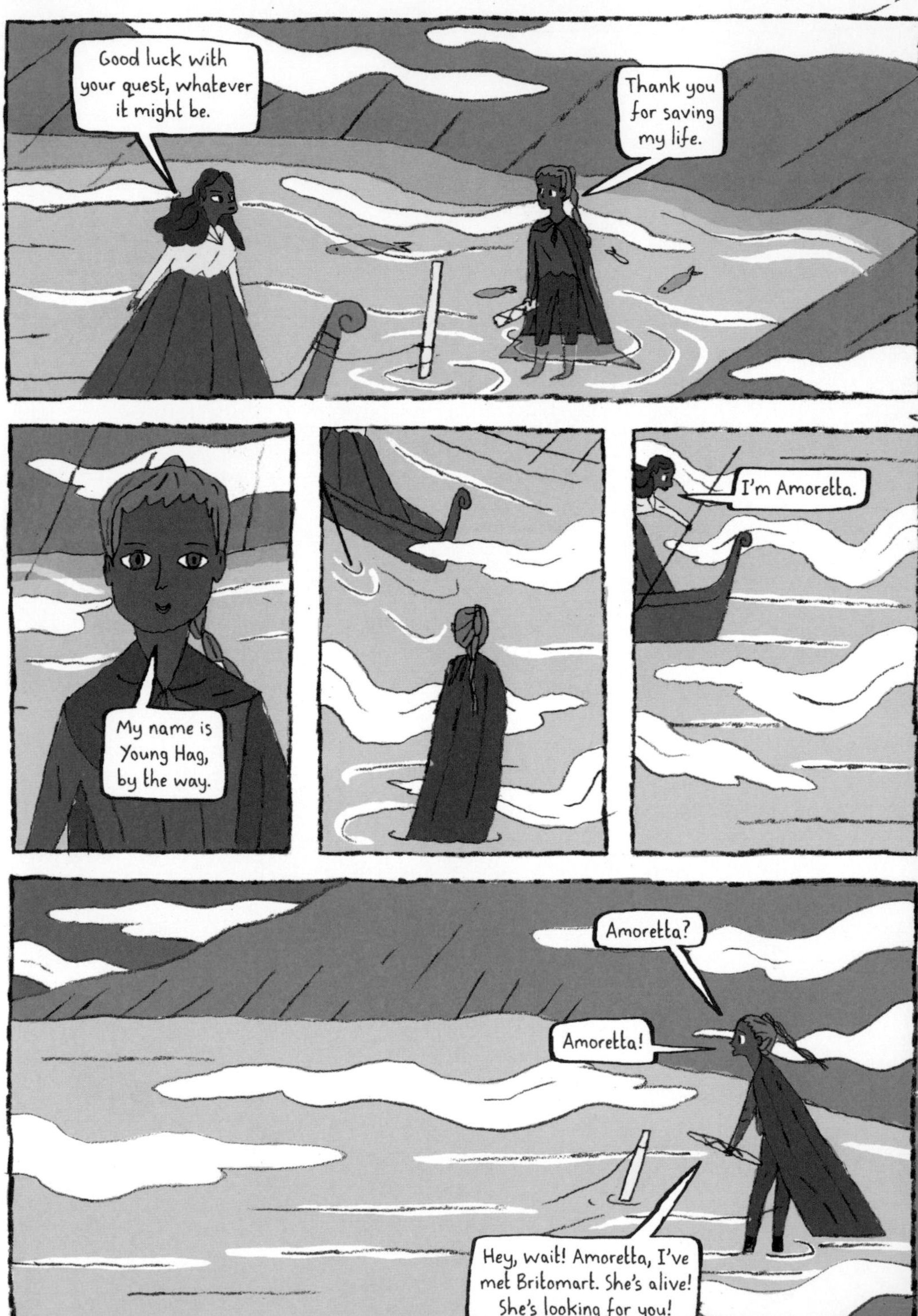
Good luck with your quest, whatever it might be.
Thank you for saving my life.
My name is Young Hag, by the way.
I'm Amoretta.
Amoretta?
Amoretta!
Hey, wait! Amoretta, I've met Britomart. She's alive! She's looking for you!

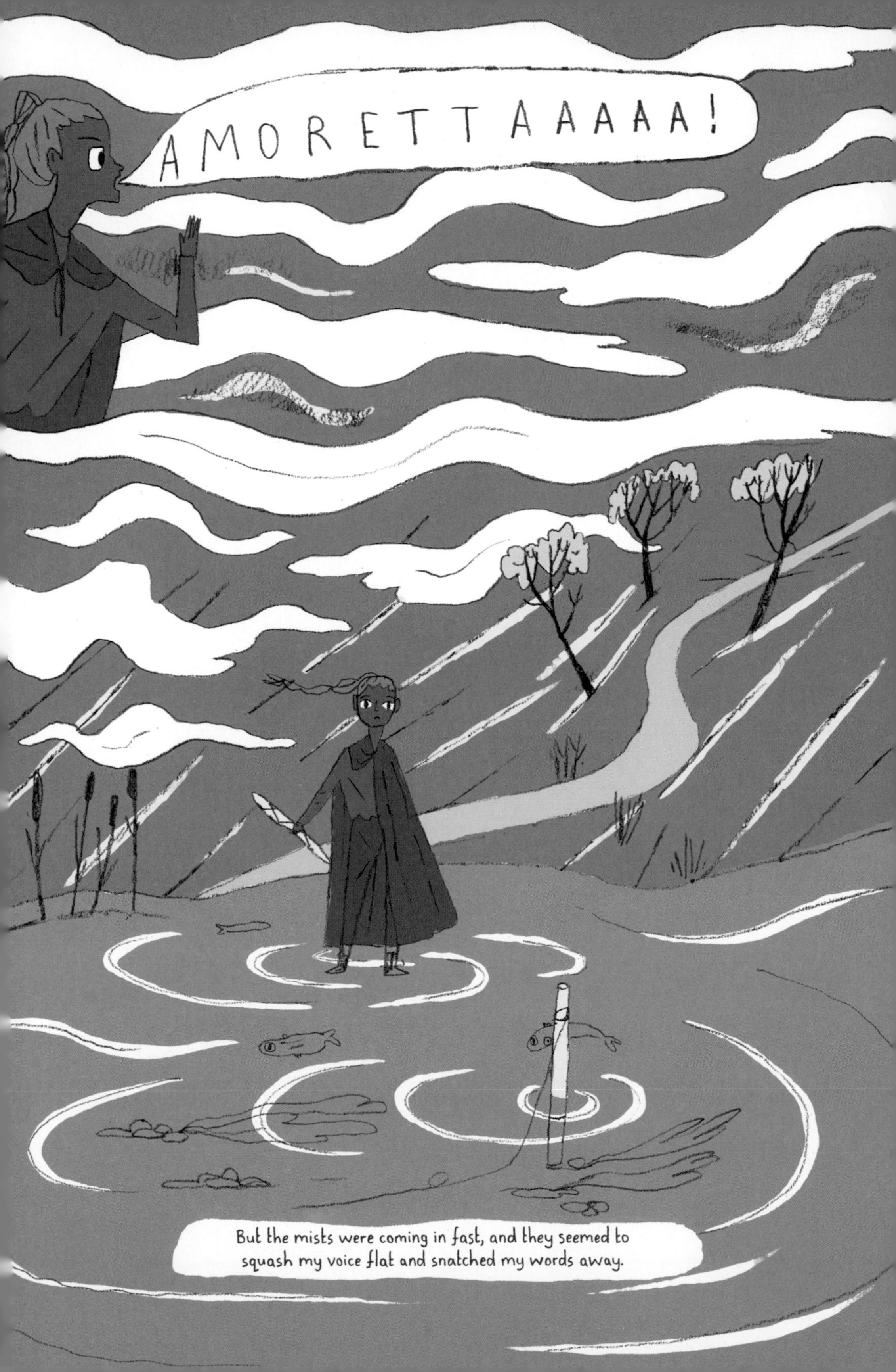
AMORETTAAAAA!
But the mists were coming in fast, and they seemed to squash my voice flat and snatched my words away.

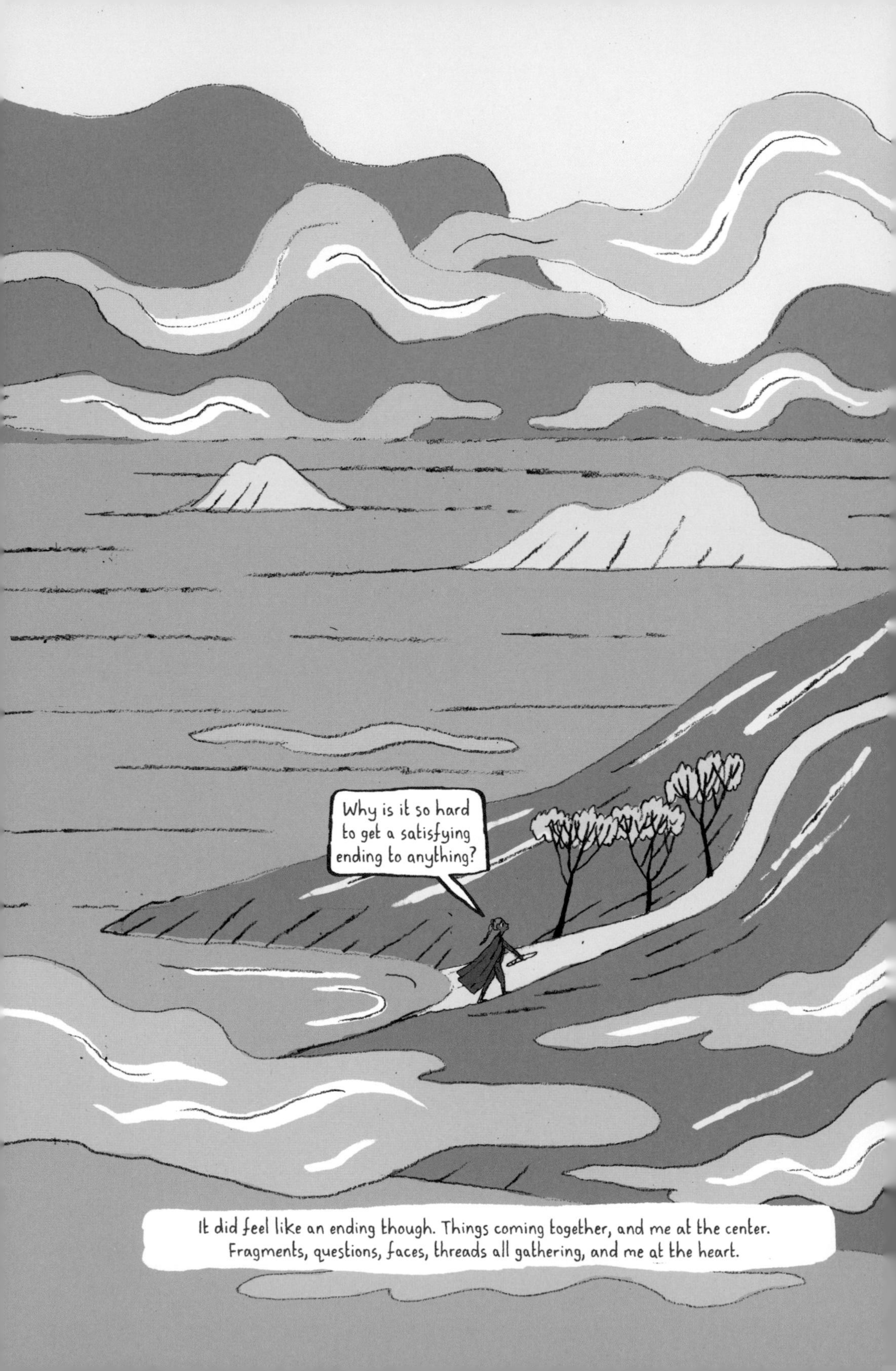
Why is it so hard to get a satisfying ending to anything?
It did feel like an ending though. Things coming together, and me at the center. Fragments, questions, faces, threads all gathering, and me at the heart.

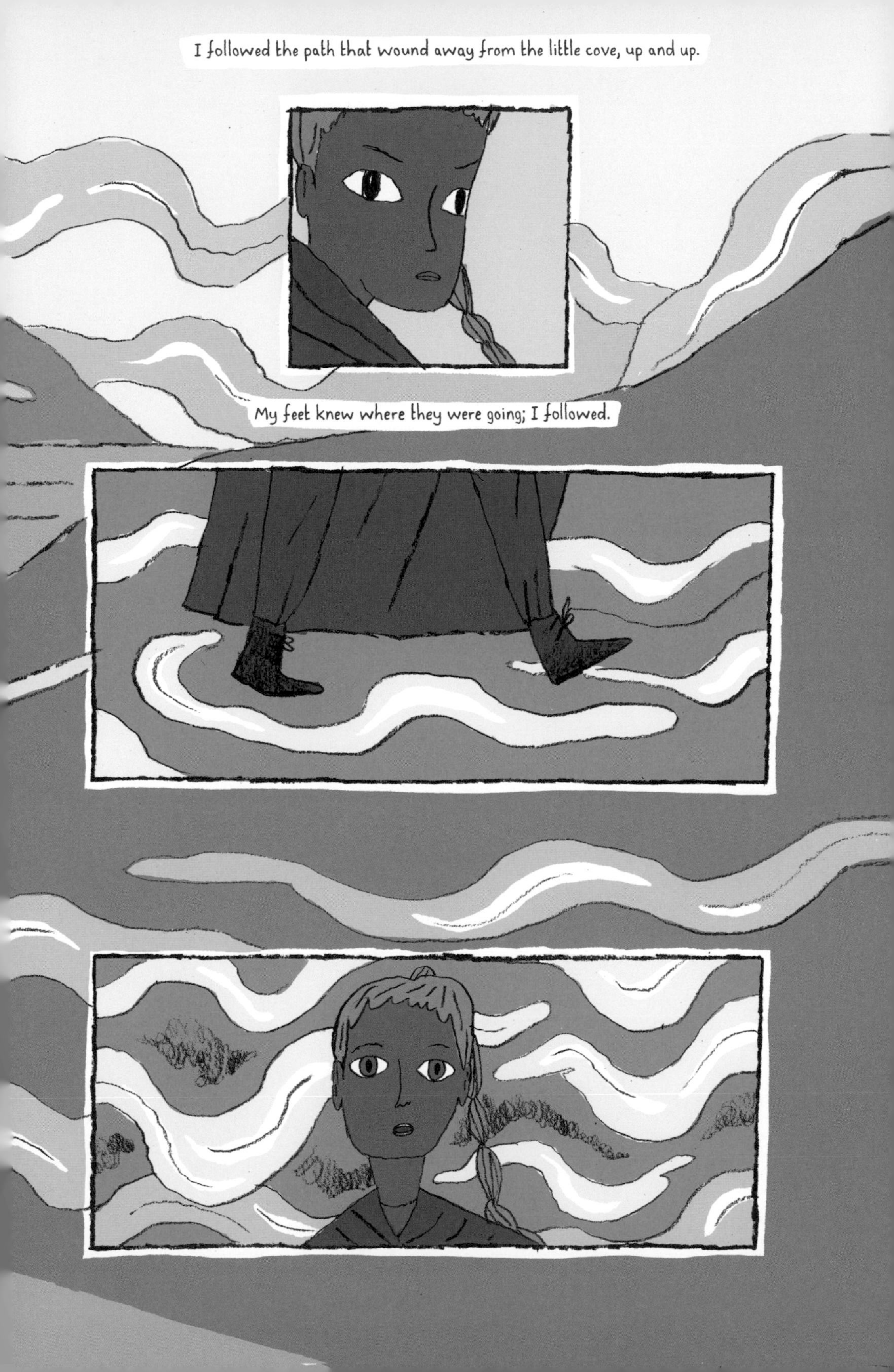
I followed the path that wound away from the little cove, up and up.
My feet knew where they were going; I followed.

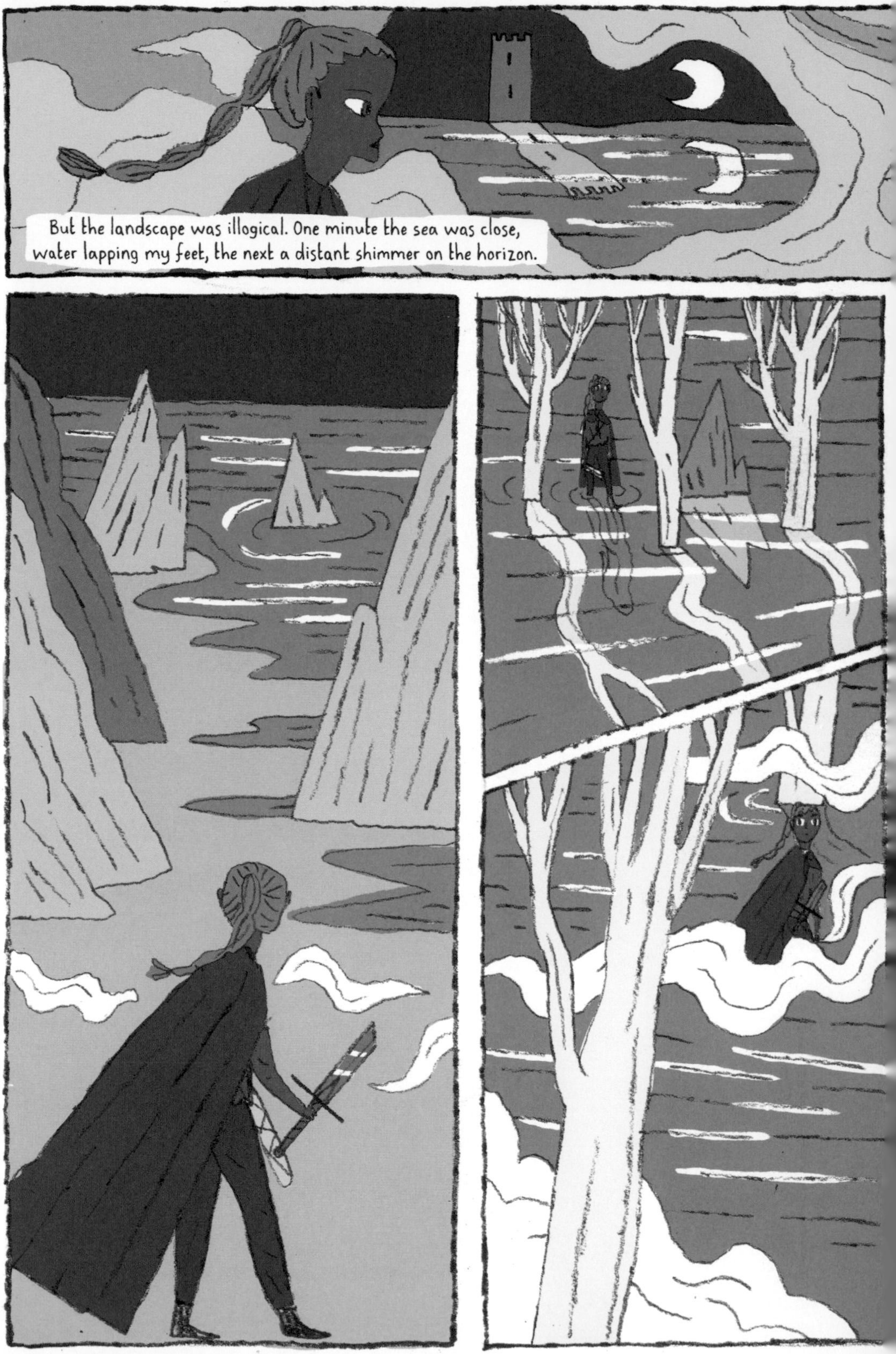
But the landscape was illogical. One minute the sea was close, water lapping my feet, the next a distant shimmer on the horizon.

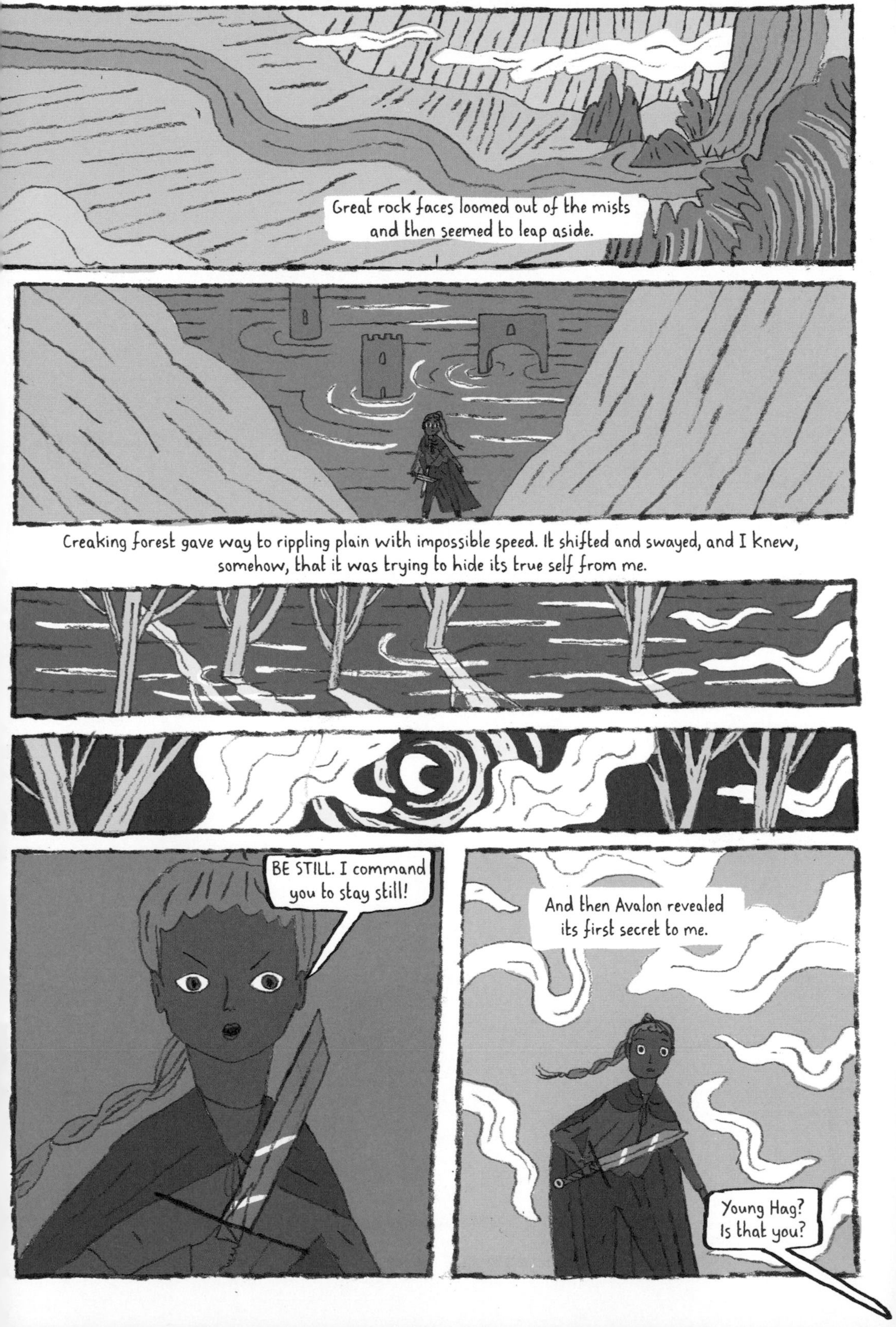
Great rock faces loomed out of the mists and then seemed to leap aside.
Creaking forest gave way to rippling plain with impossible speed. It shifted and swayed, and I knew, somehow, that it was trying to hide its true self from me.
BE STILL. I command you to stay still!
And then Avalon revealed its first secret to me.
Young Hag? Is that you?

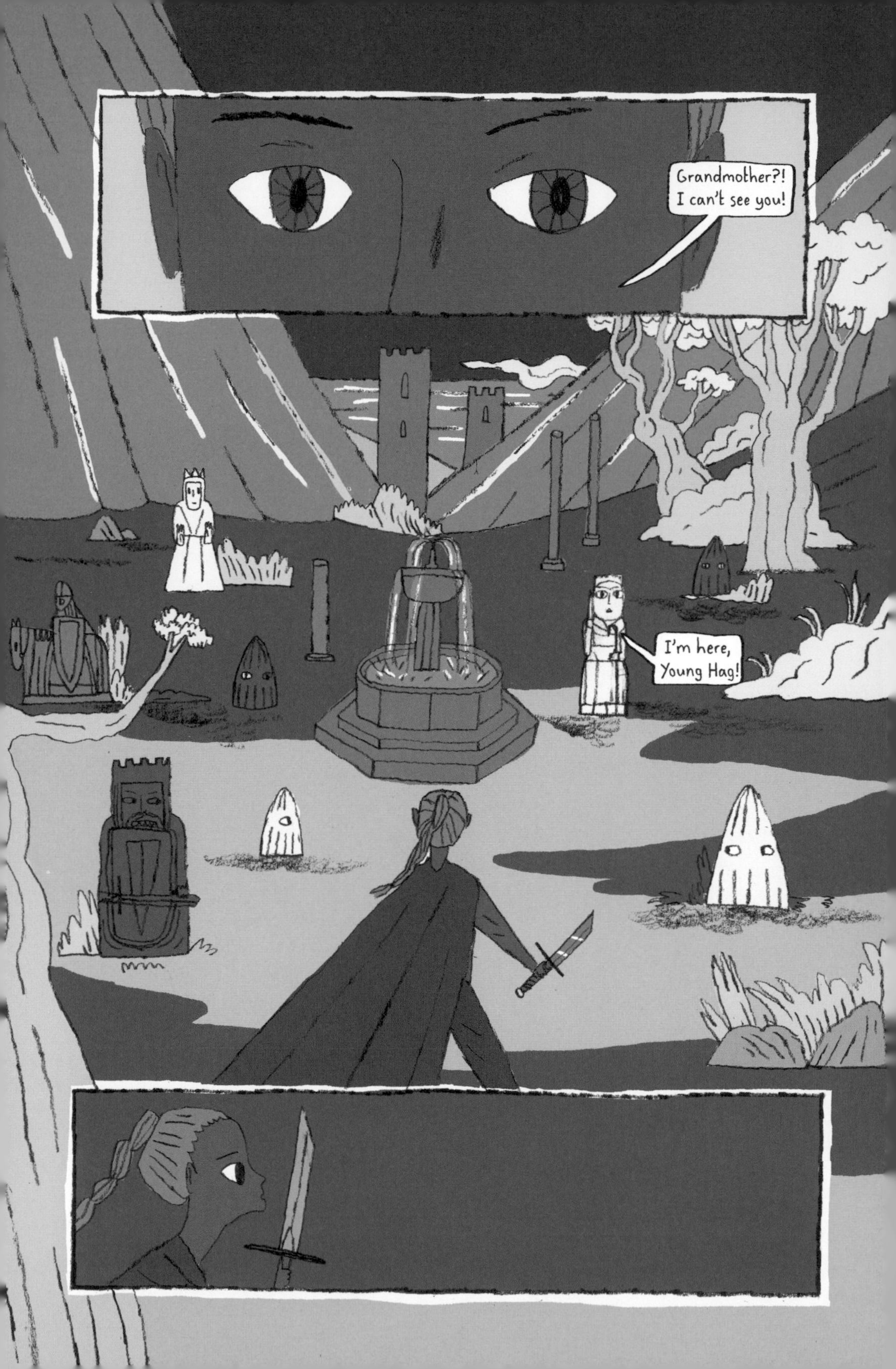
Grandmother?! I can't see you!
I'm here, Young Hag!

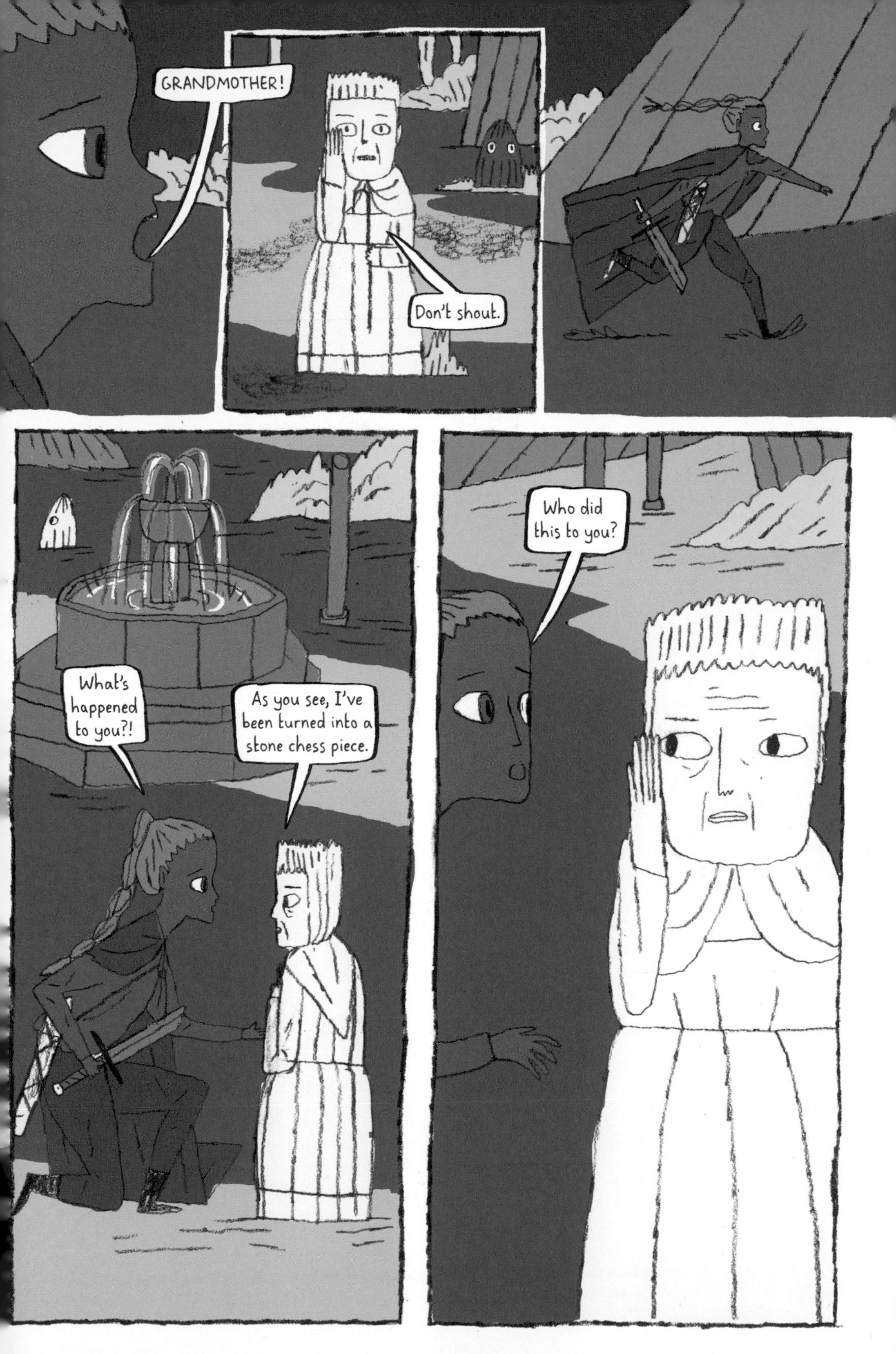
GRANDMOTHER!
Don't shout.
What's happened to you?!
As you see, I've been turned into a stone chess piece.
Who did this to you?

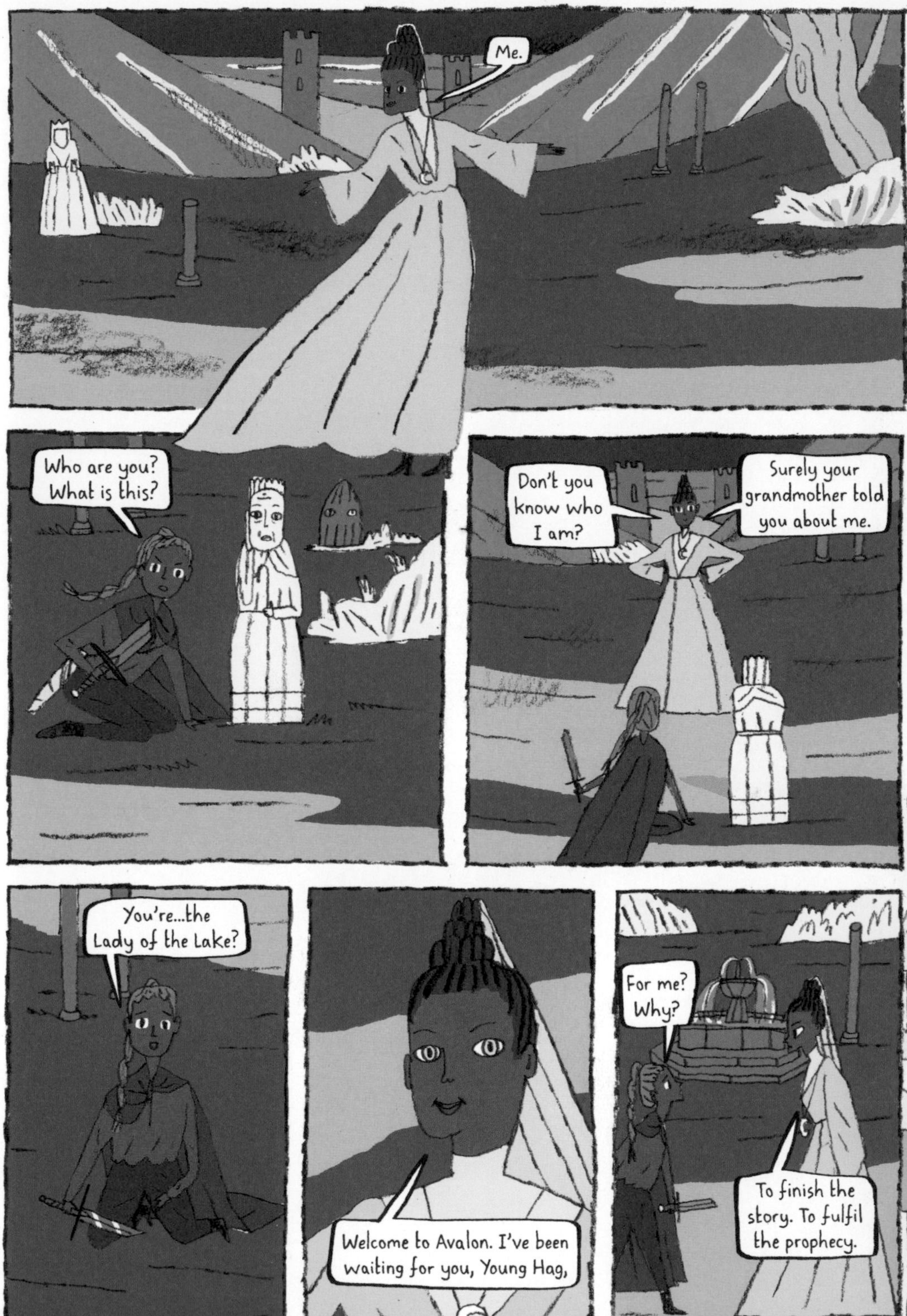
Me.
Who are you?
What is this?
Don't you know who I am?
Surely your grandmother told you about me.
You're...the Lady of the Lake?
Welcome to Avalon. I've been waiting for you, Young Hag,
For me? Why?
To finish the story. To fulfil the prophecy.

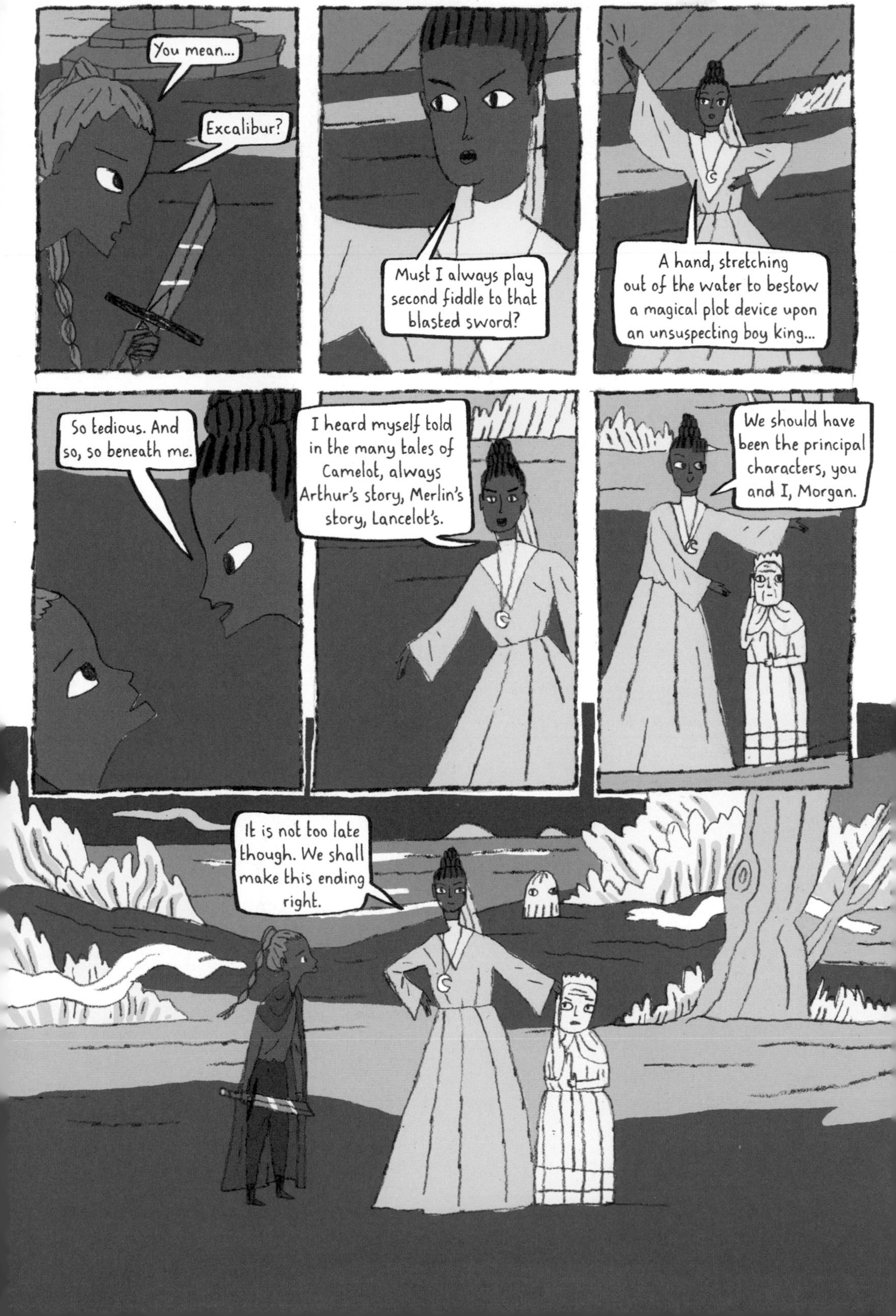
You mean...
Excalibur?
Must I always play second fiddle to that blasted sword?
A hand, stretching out of the water to bestow a magical plot device upon an unsuspecting boy king...
So tedious. And so, so beneath me.
I heard myself told in the many tales of Camelot, always Arthur's story, Merlin's story, Lancelot's.
We should have been the principal characters, you and I, Morgan.
It is not too late though. We shall make this ending right.

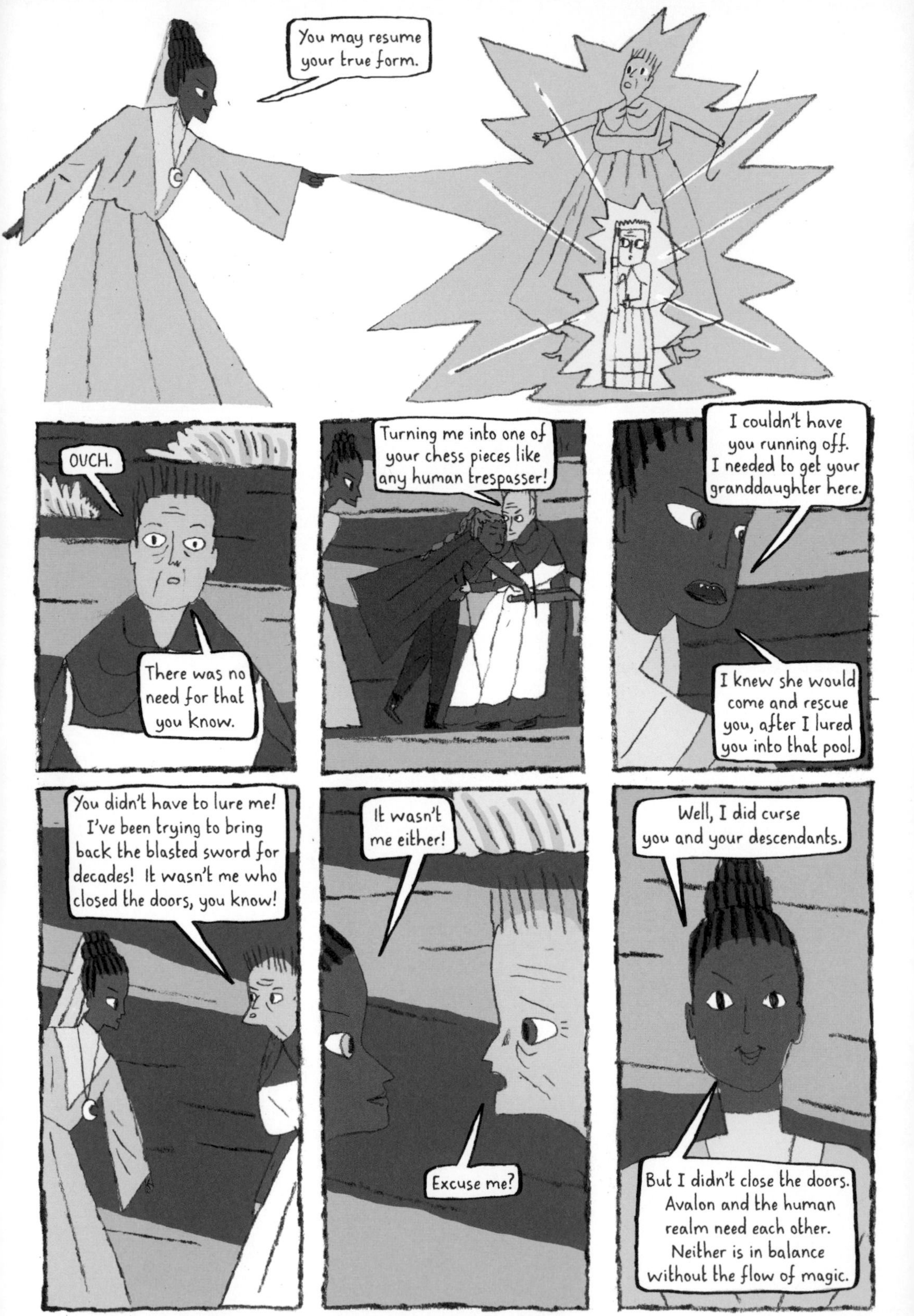

You may resume your true form.
OUCH.
There was no need for that you know.
Turning me into one of your chess pieces like any human trespasser!
I couldn't have you running off. I needed to get your granddaughter here.
I knew she would come and rescue you, after I lured you into that pool.
You didn't have to lure me! I've been trying to bring back the blasted sword for decades! It wasn't me who closed the doors, you know!
It wasn't me either!
Excuse me?
Well, I did curse you and your descendants.
But I didn't close the doors. Avalon and the human realm need each other. Neither is in balance without the flow of magic.

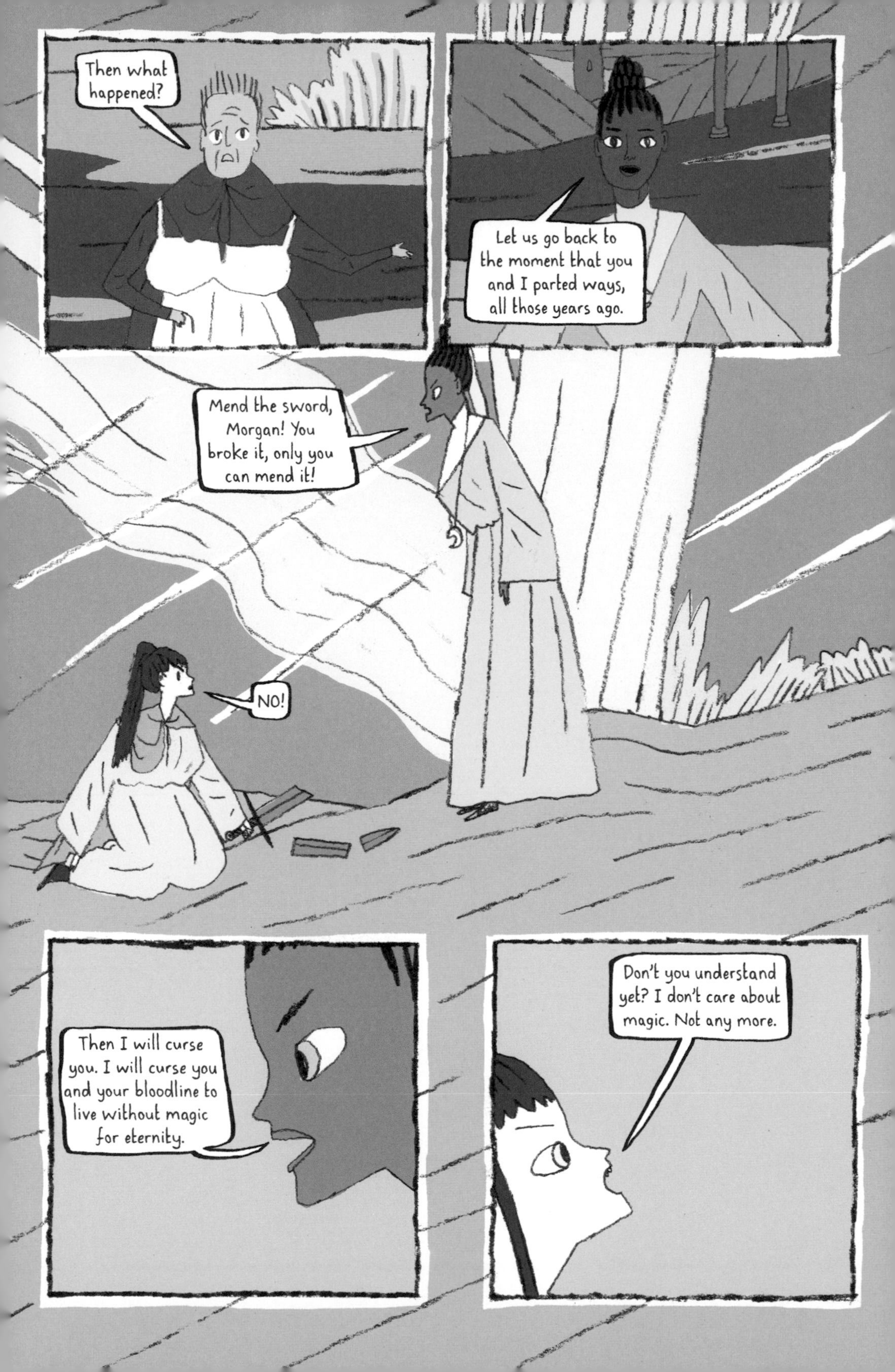
Then what happened?
Let us go back to the moment that you and I parted ways, all those years ago.
Mend the sword, Morgan! You broke it, only you can mend it!
NO!
Then I will curse you. I will curse you and your bloodline to live without magic for eternity.
Don't you understand yet? I don't care about magic. Not any more.

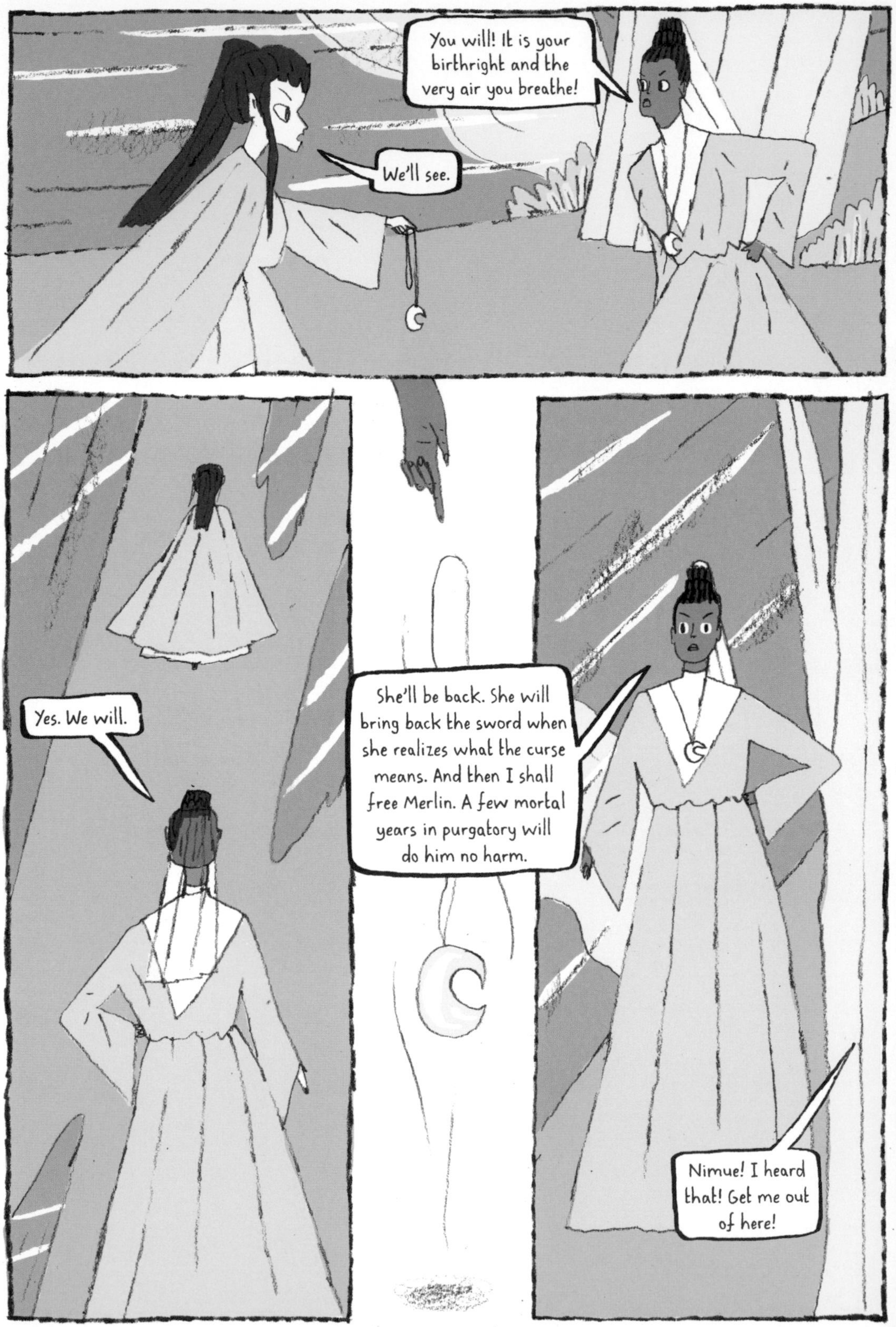

You will! It is your birthright and the very air you breathe!
We'll see.
Yes. We will.
She'll be back. She will bring back the sword when she realizes what the curse means. And then I shall free Merlin. A few mortal years in purgatory will do him no harm.
Nimue! I heard that! Get me out of here!

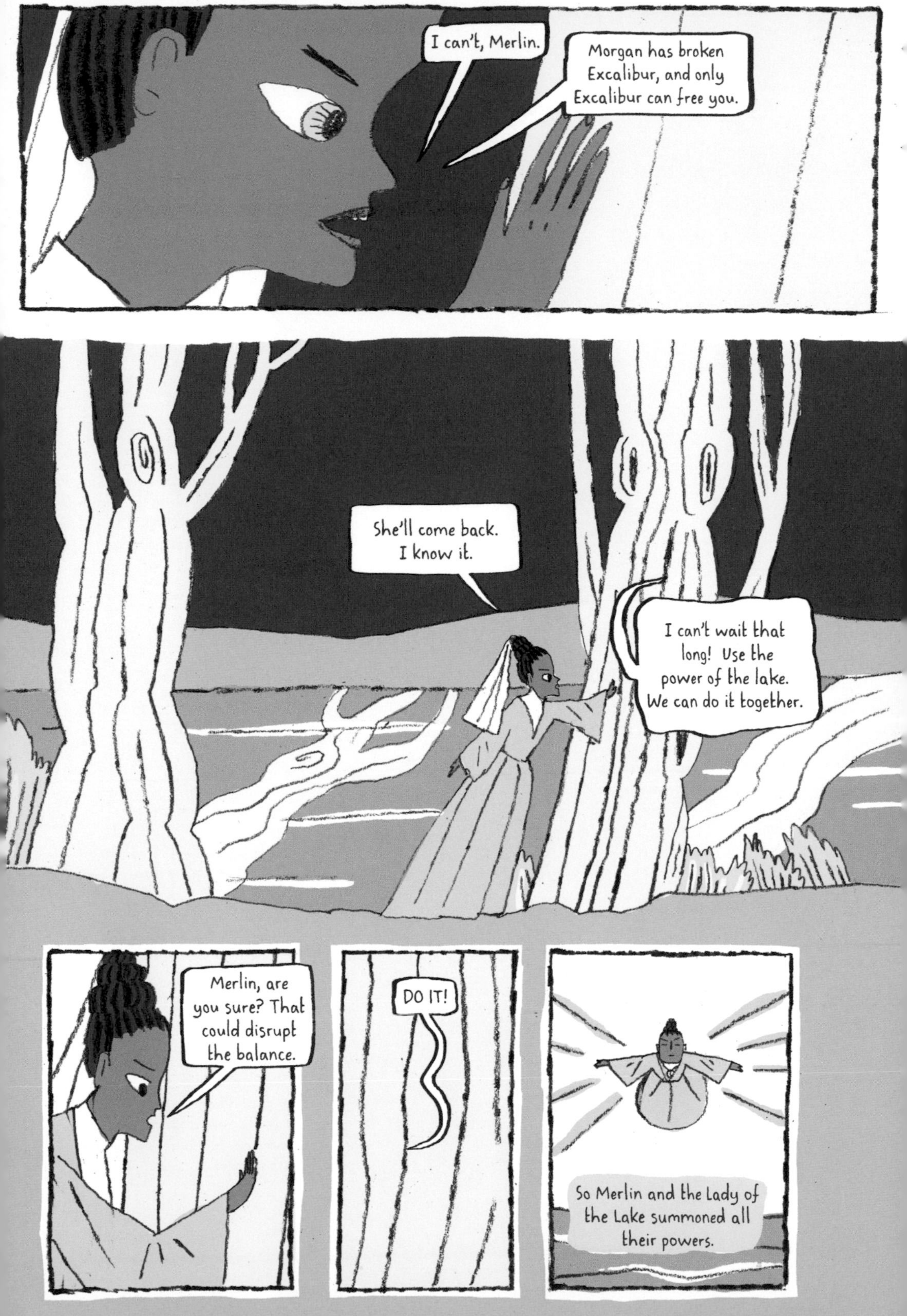
I can't, Merlin.
Morgan has broken Excalibur, and only Excalibur can free you.
She'll come back. I know it.
I can't wait that long! Use the power of the lake. We can do it together.
Merlin, are you sure? That could disrupt the balance.
DO IT!
So Merlin and the Lady of the Lake summoned all their powers.

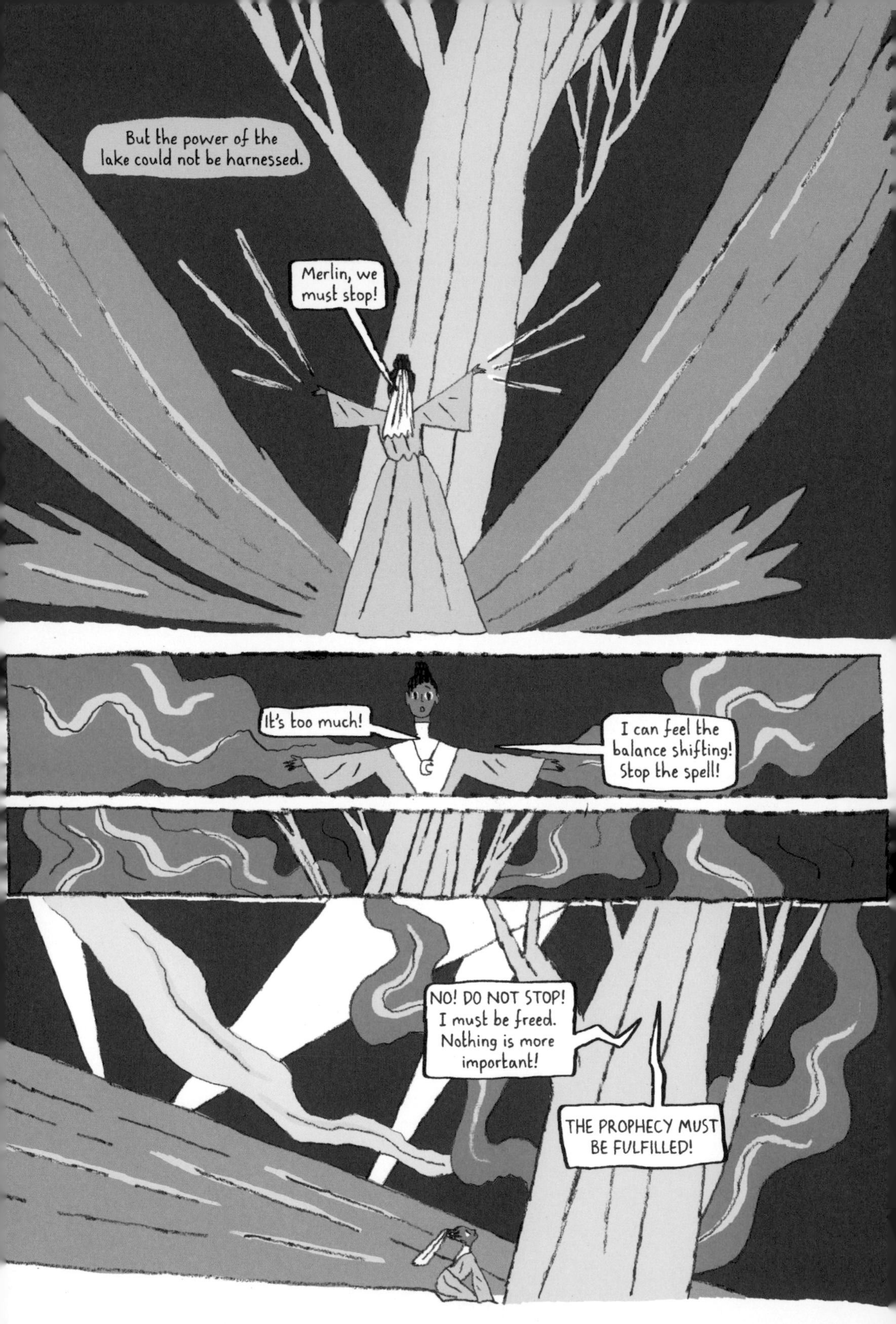
But the power of the lake could not be harnessed.
Merlin, we must stop!
It's too much!
I can feel the balance shifting! Stop the spell!
NO! DO NOT STOP! I must be freed. Nothing is more important!
THE PROPHECY MUST BE FULFILLED!

She stopped the spell. But it was too late. The power had closed the ways between the worlds. And Merlin was trapped between them, another lost soul wandering in the mists.

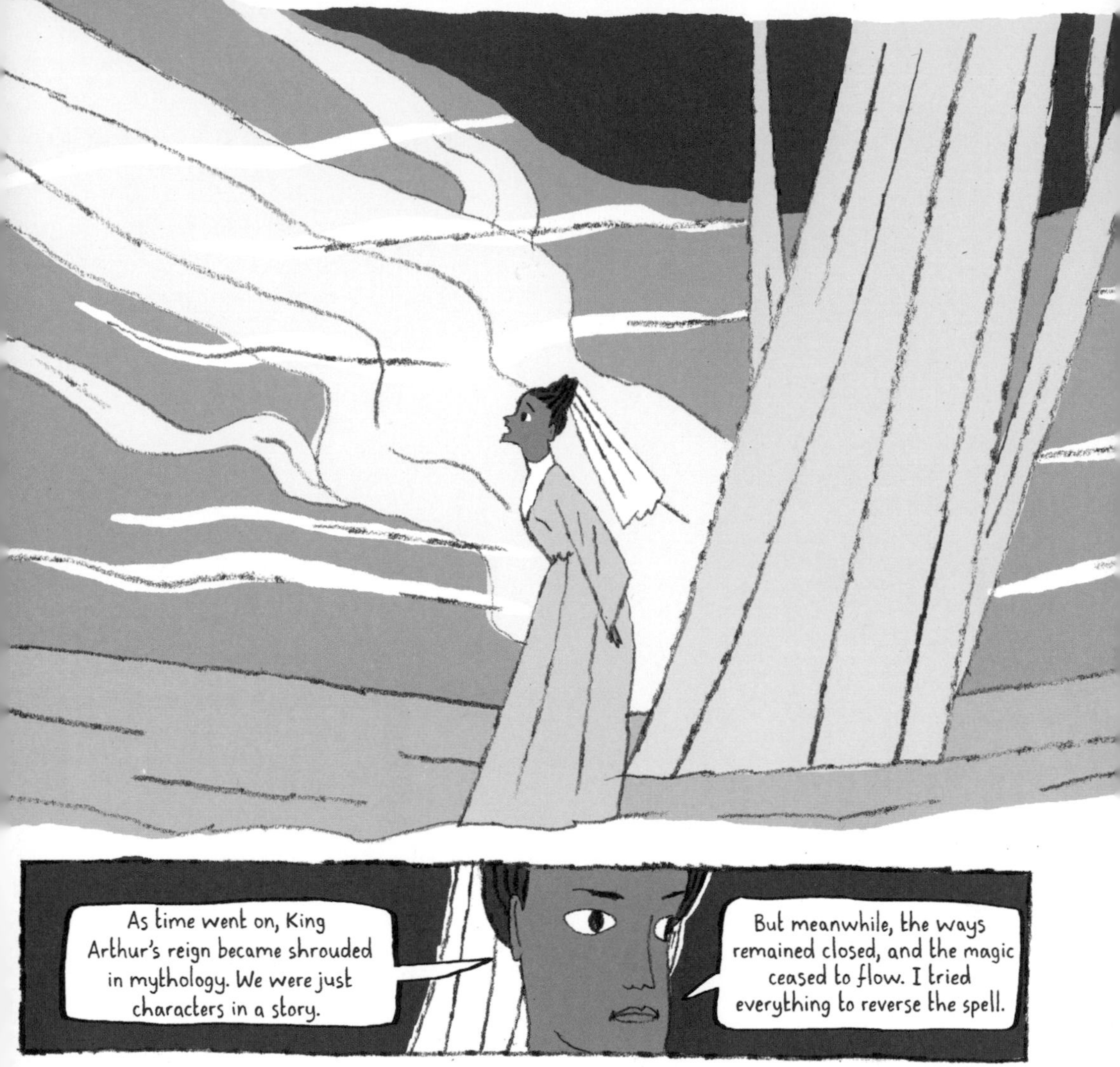

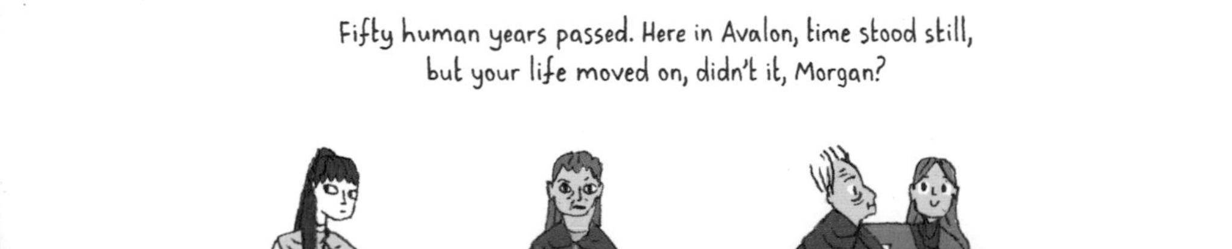
As time went on, King Arthur's reign became shrouded in mythology. We were just characters in a story.
But meanwhile, the ways remained closed, and the magic ceased to flow. I tried everything to reverse the spell.

Fifty human years passed. Here in Avalon, time stood still, but your life moved on, didn't it, Morgan?

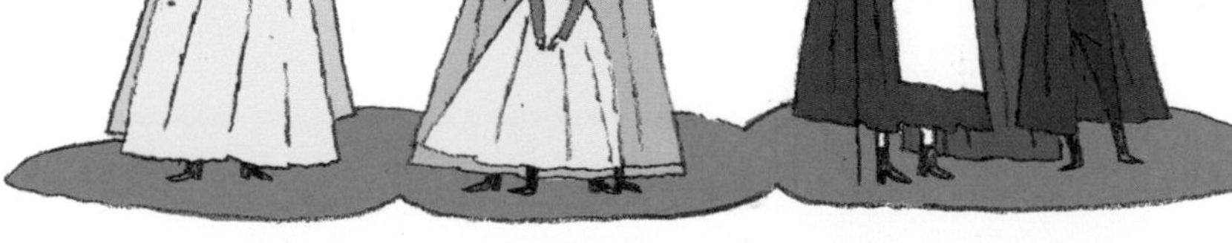

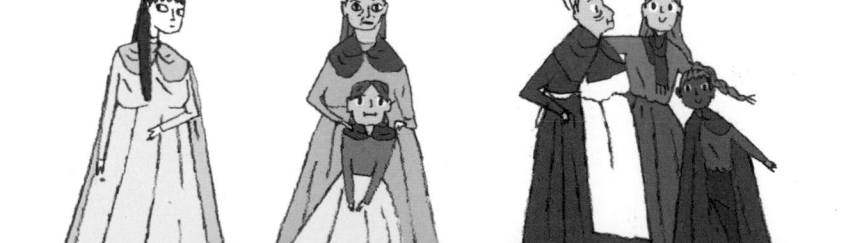

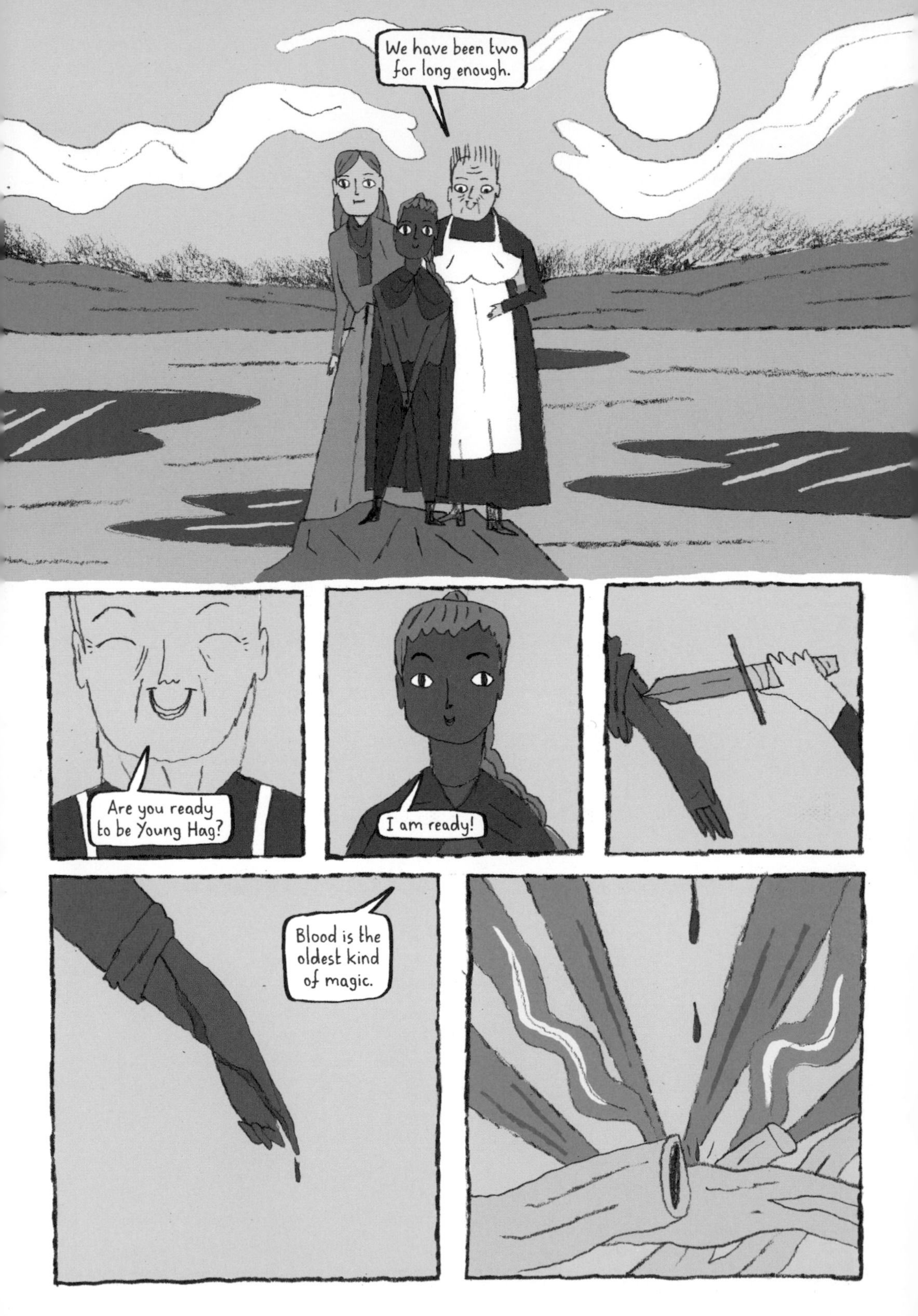
We have been two for long enough.
Are you ready to be Young Hag?
I am ready!
Blood is the oldest kind of magic.

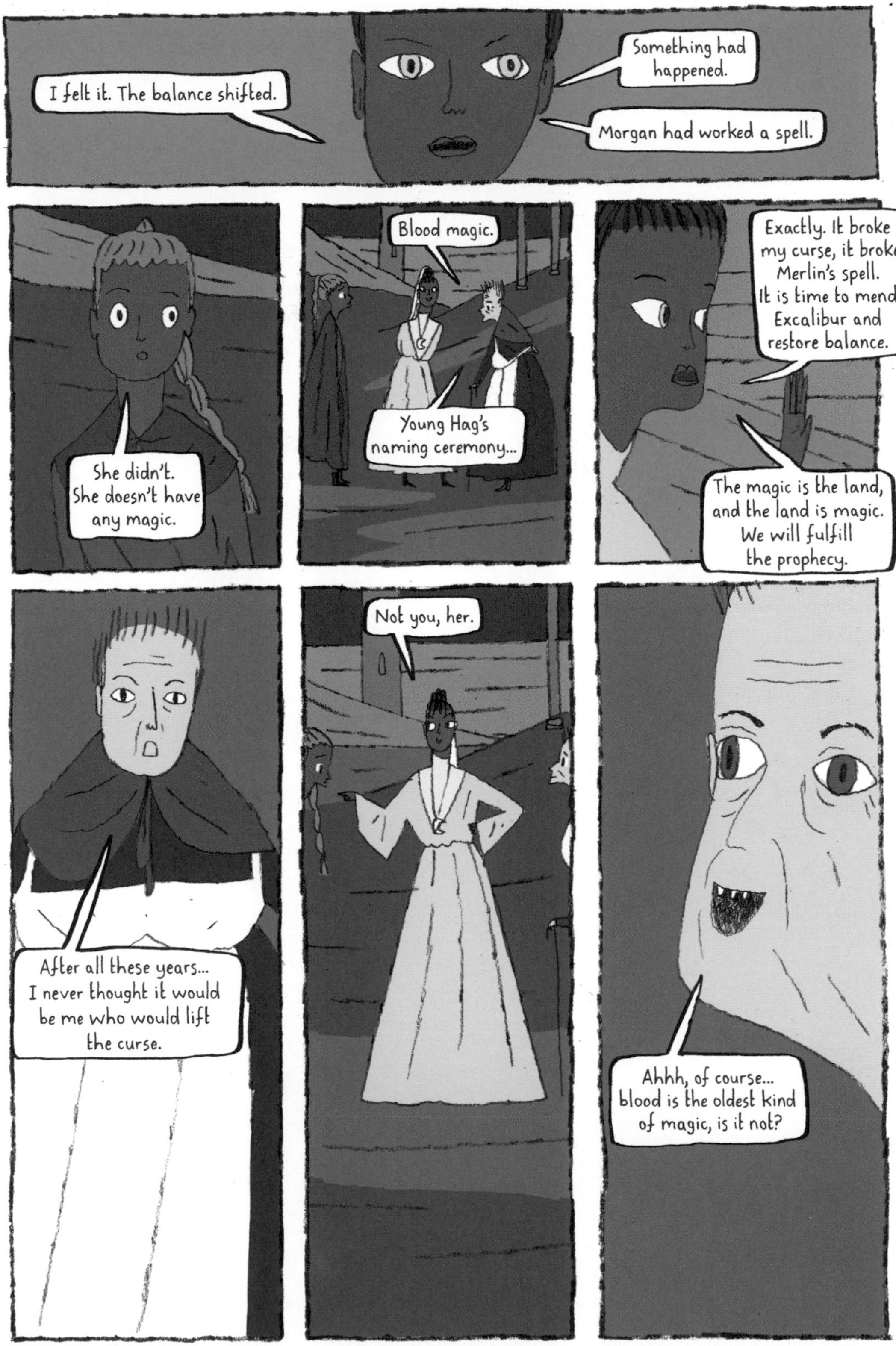
I felt it. The balance shifted.
Something had happened.
Morgan had worked a spell.
She didn't. She doesn't have any magic.
Blood magic.
Young Hag's naming ceremony...
Exactly. It broke my curse, it broke Merlin's spell. It is time to mend Excalibur and restore balance.
The magic is the land, and the land is magic. We will fulfill the prophecy.
After all these years... I never thought it would be me who would lift the curse.
Not you, her.
Ahhh, of course... blood is the oldest kind of magic, is it not?

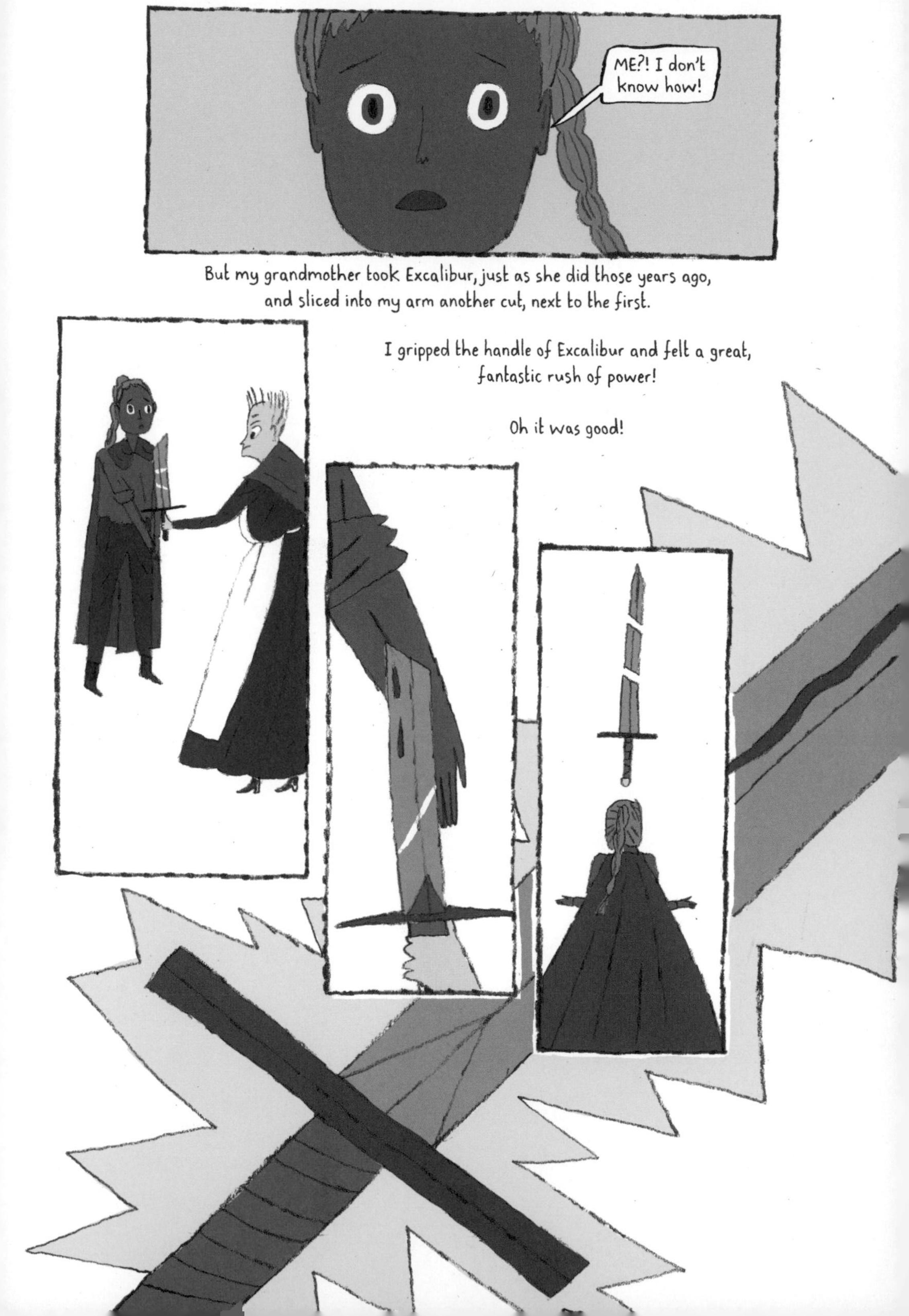
ME?! I don't know how!
But my grandmother took Excalibur, just as she did those years ago, and sliced into my arm another cut, next to the first.
I gripped the handle of Excalibur and felt a great, fantastic rush of power!
Oh it was good!

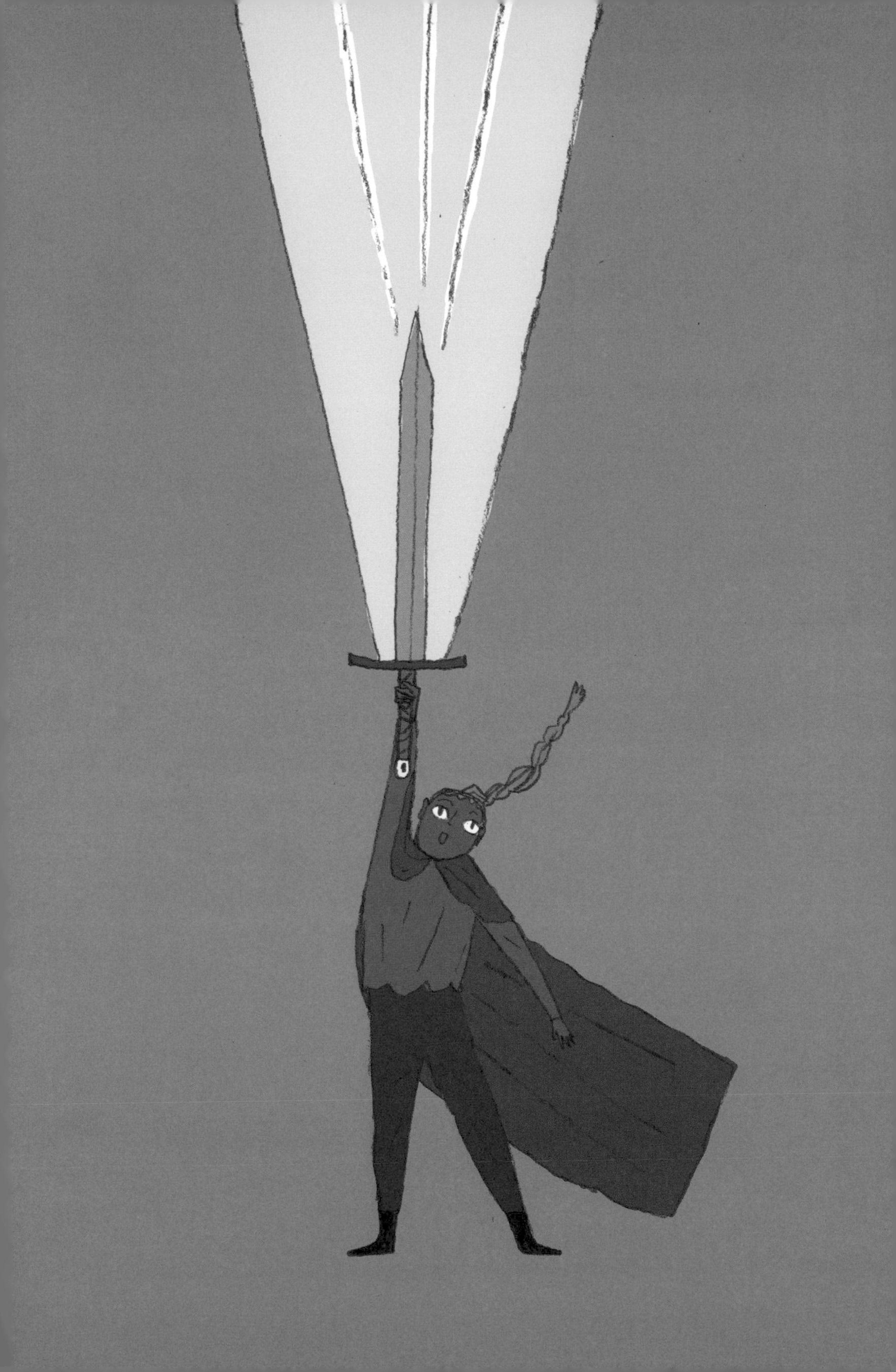

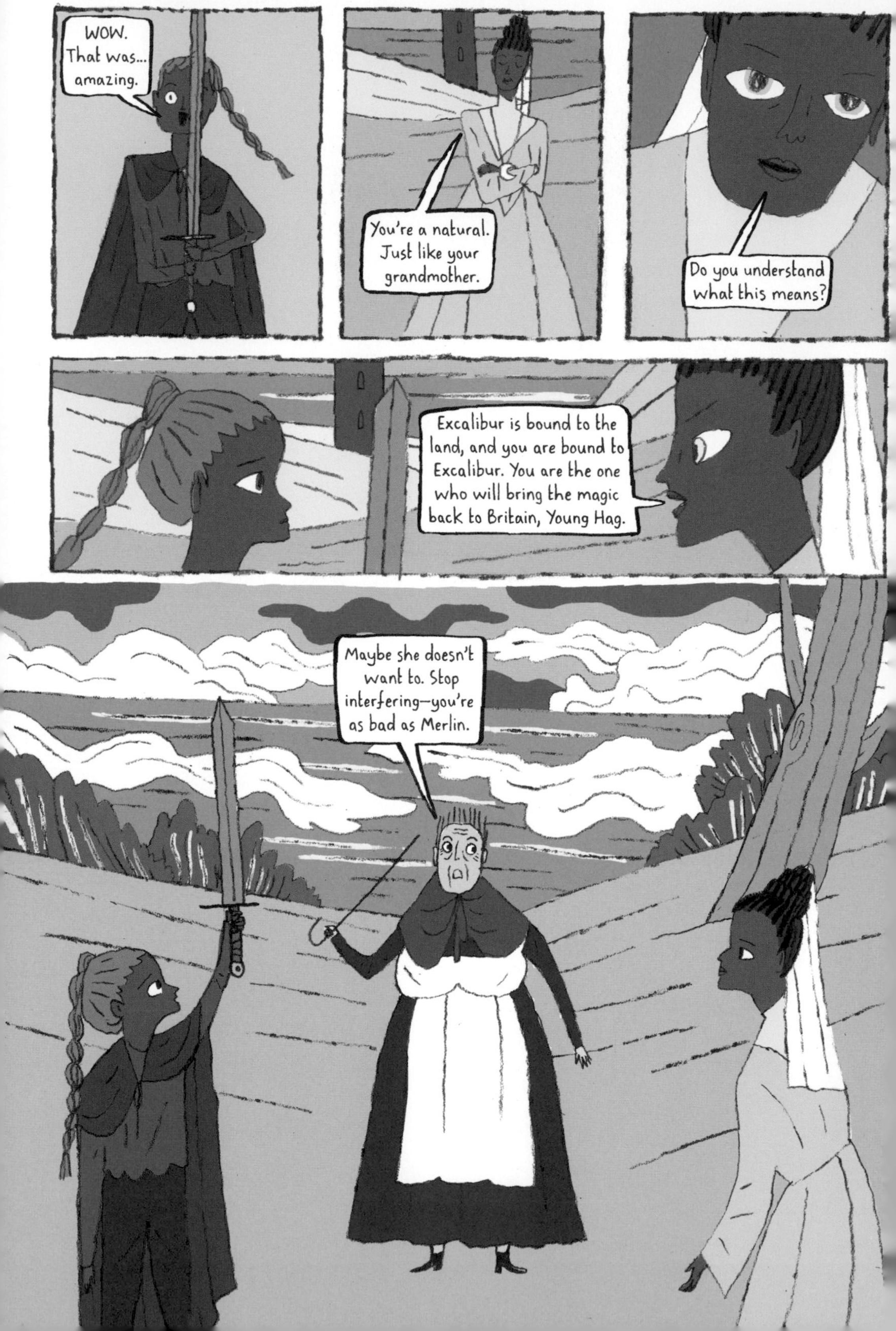
WOW. That was... amazing.
You're a natural. Just like your grandmother.
Do you understand what this means?
Excalibur is bound to the land, and you are bound to Excalibur. You are the one who will bring the magic back to Britain, Young Hag.
Maybe she doesn't want to. Stop interfering—you're as bad as Merlin.

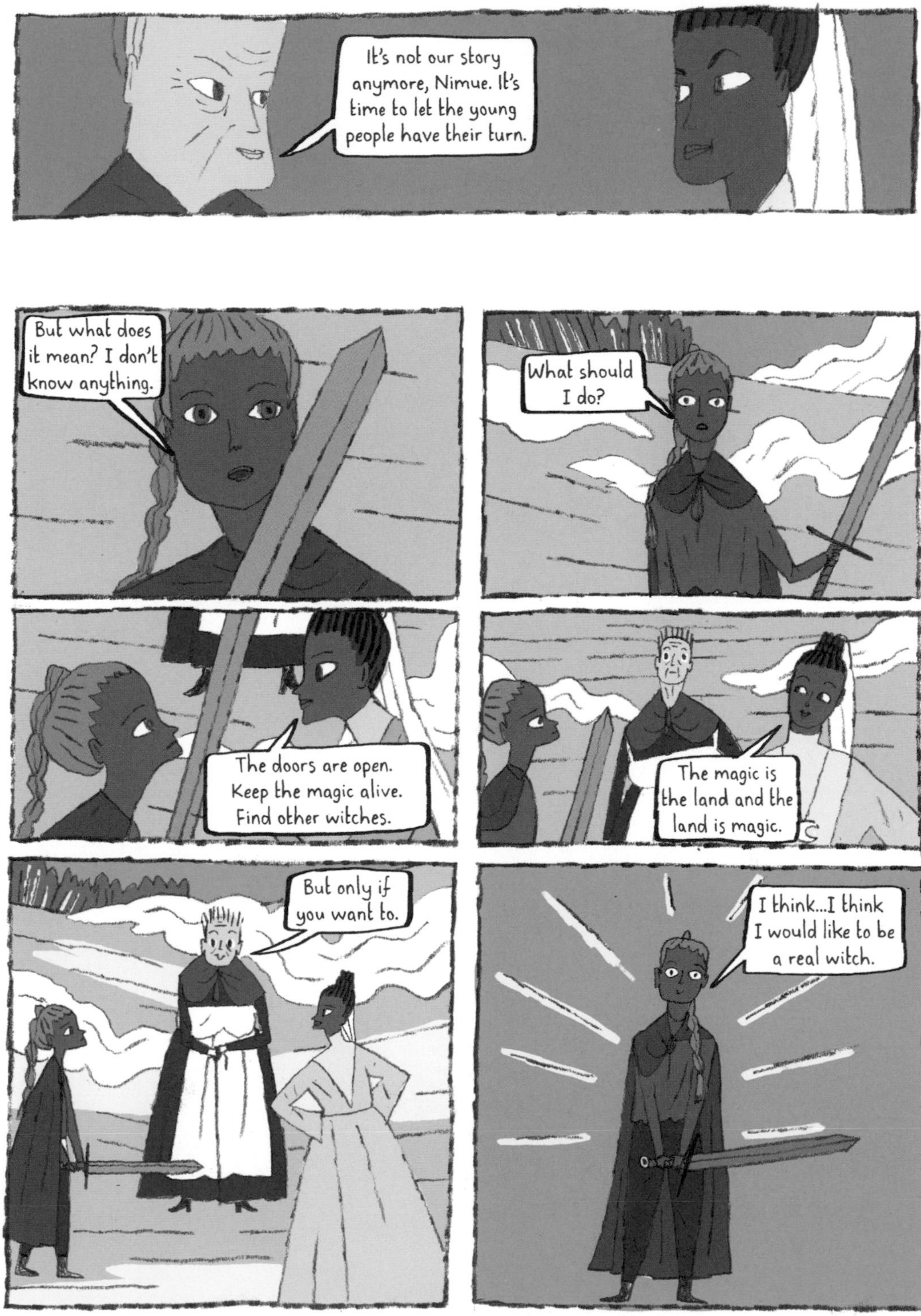
It's not our story anymore, Nimue. It's time to let the young people have their turn.
But what does it mean? I don't know anything.
What should I do?
The doors are open. Keep the magic alive. Find other witches.
The magic is the land and the land is magic.
But only if you want to.
I think...I think I would like to be a real witch.

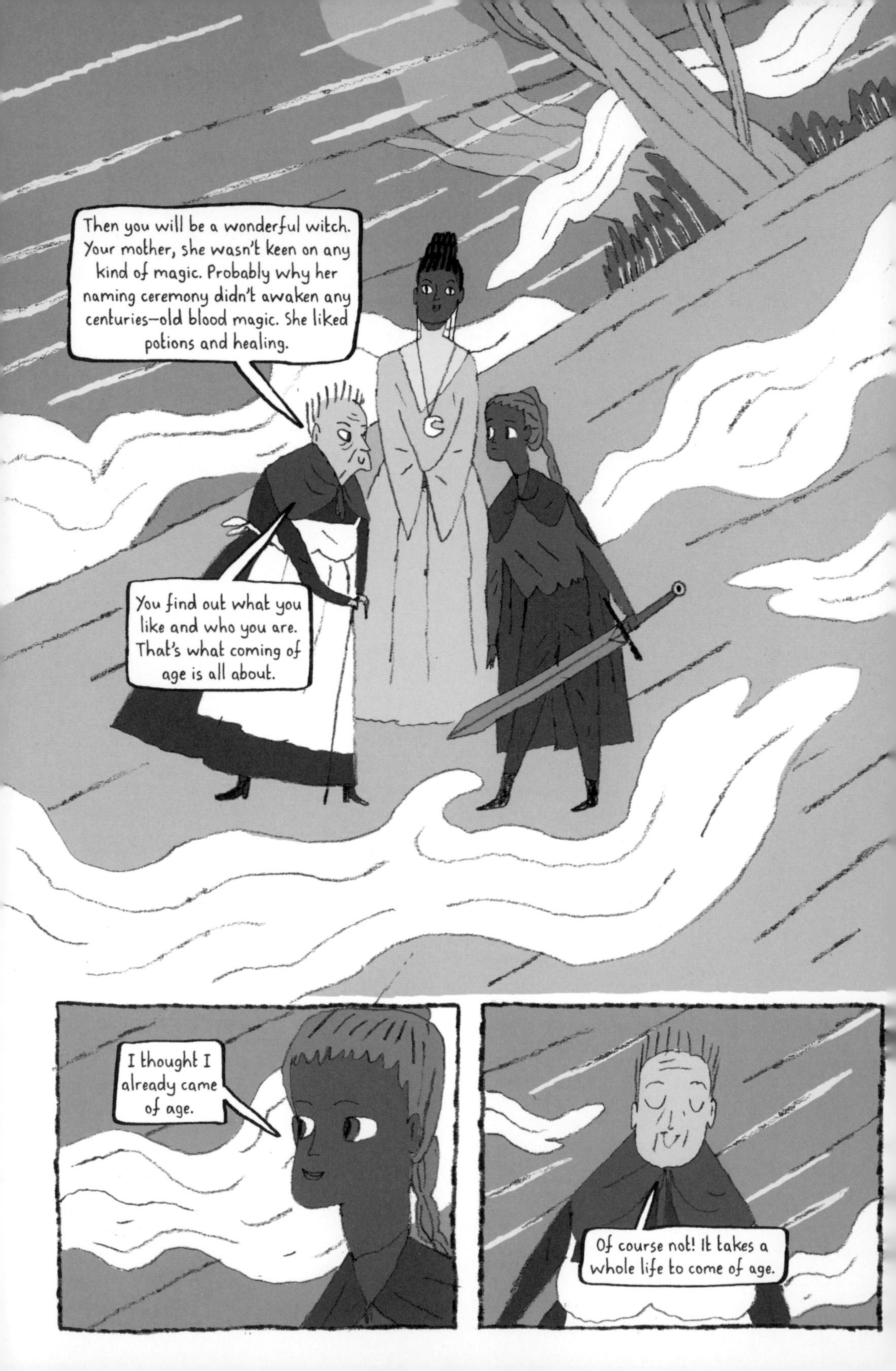

Then you will be a wonderful witch. Your mother, she wasn't keen on any kind of magic. Probably why her naming ceremony didn't awaken any centuries—old blood magic. She liked potions and healing.
You find out what you like and who you are. That's what coming of age is all about.
I thought I already came of age.
Of course not! It takes a whole life to come of age.

PART THE SIXTH

SIXTH

Endings &
Beginnings

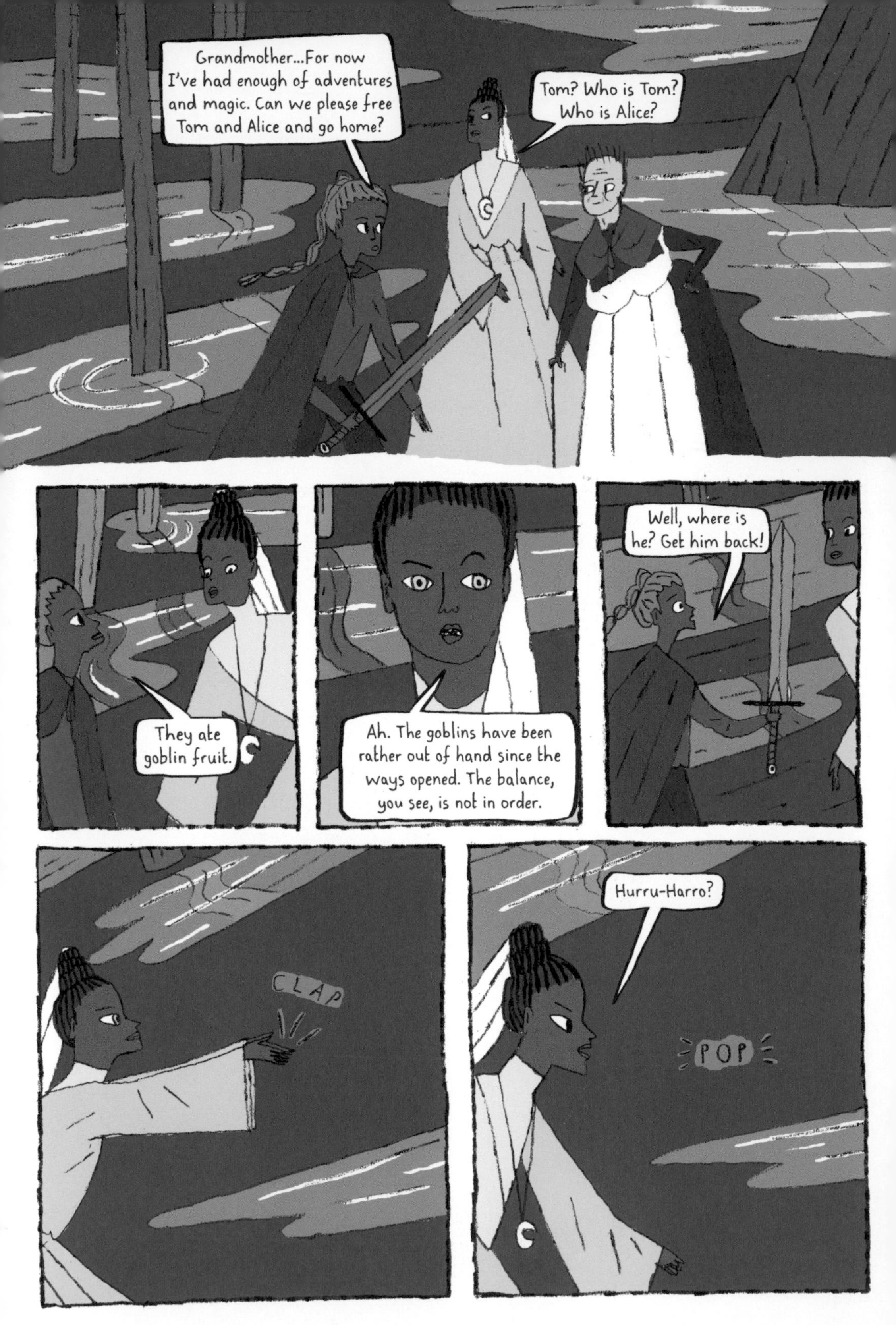
Grandmother...For now I've had enough of adventures and magic. Can we please free Tom and Alice and go home?
Tom? Who is Tom? Who is Alice?
They ate goblin fruit.
Ah. The goblins have been rather out of hand since the ways opened. The balance, you see, is not in order.
Well, where is he? Get him back!
CLAP
Hurru-Harro?
POP

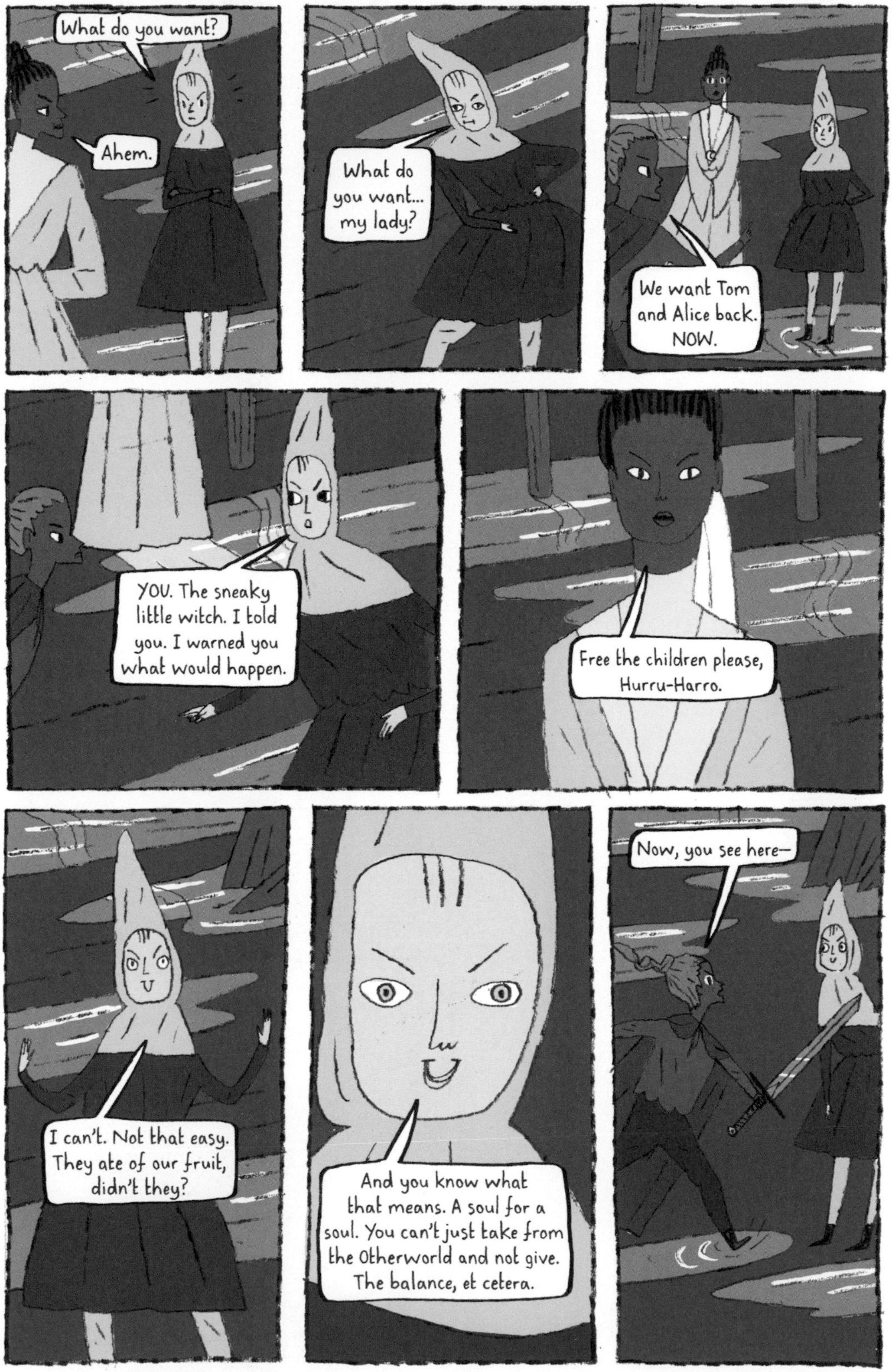
What do you want?
Ahem.
What do you want... my lady?
We want Tom and Alice back. NOW.
YOU. The sneaky little witch. I told you. I warned you what would happen.
Free the children please, Hurru-Harro.
I can't. Not that easy. They ate of our fruit, didn't they?
And you know what that means. A soul for a soul. You can't just take from the Otherworld and not give. The balance, et cetera.
Now, you see here—

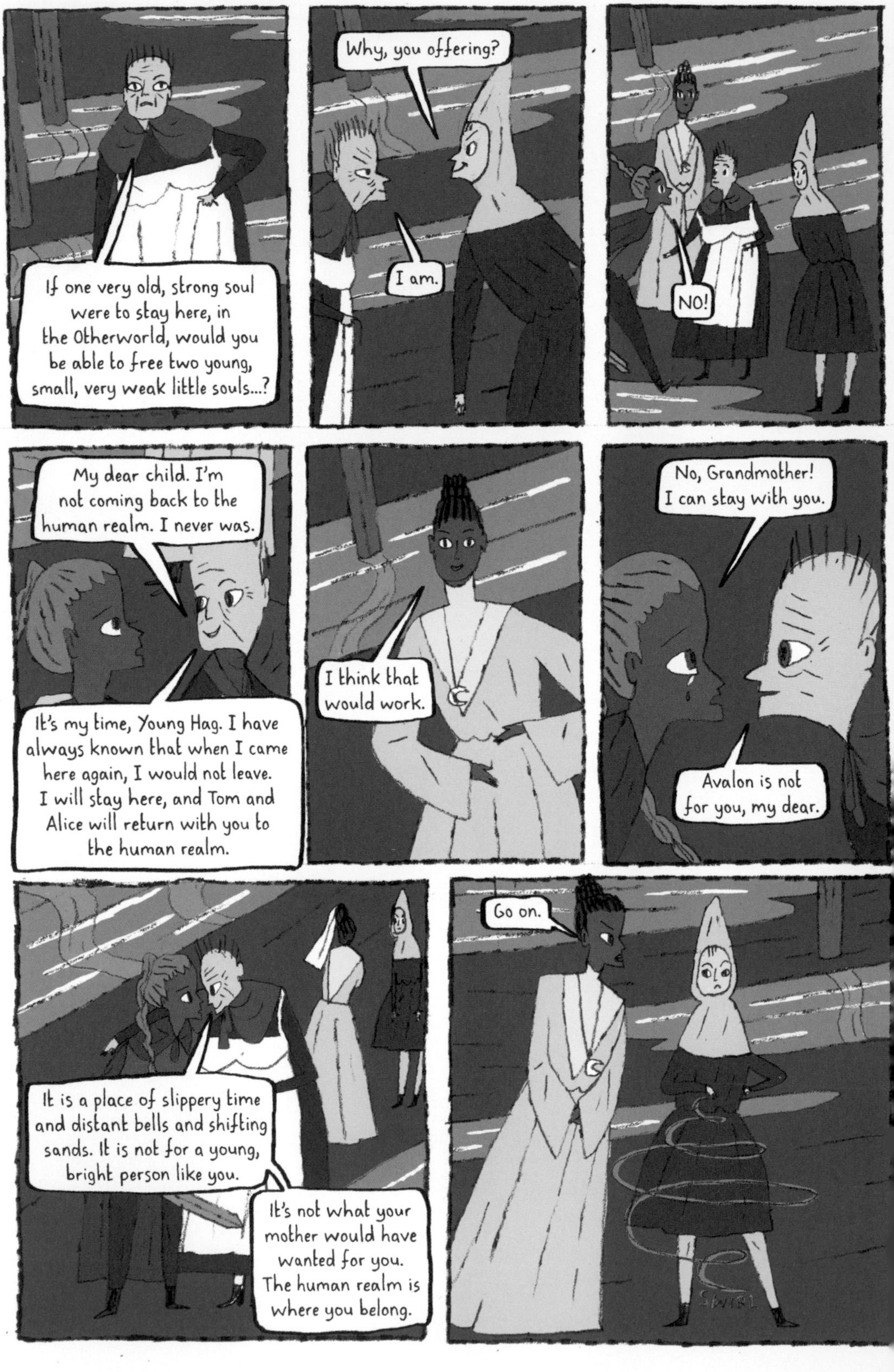
If one very old, strong soul were to stay here, in the Otherworld, would you be able to free two young, small, very weak little souls...?
Why, you offering?
I am.
NO!
My dear child. I'm not coming back to the human realm. I never was.
It's my time, Young Hag. I have always known that when I came here again, I would not leave. I will stay here, and Tom and Alice will return with you to the human realm.
I think that would work.
No, Grandmother! I can stay with you.
Avalon is not for you, my dear.
It is a place of slippery time and distant bells and shifting sands. It is not for a young, bright person like you.
It's not what your mother would have wanted for you. The human realm is where you belong.
Go on.
SWIRL

The human world is full of feelings: love and pain and anger and joy! Things are so muted here, so muffled. I want you to feel all the wonderful things of life. Go and explore it.

I'm scared. I don't have anyone there, not without you. I'll be alone.

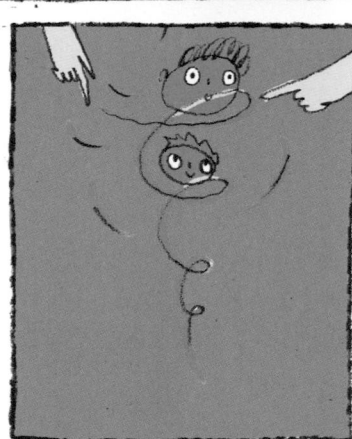

You won't be alone, Young Hag.

TOM! Alice! You're alright?

Yes. But what happened? The last thing I remember is the Goblin Market...

It's a very long story...

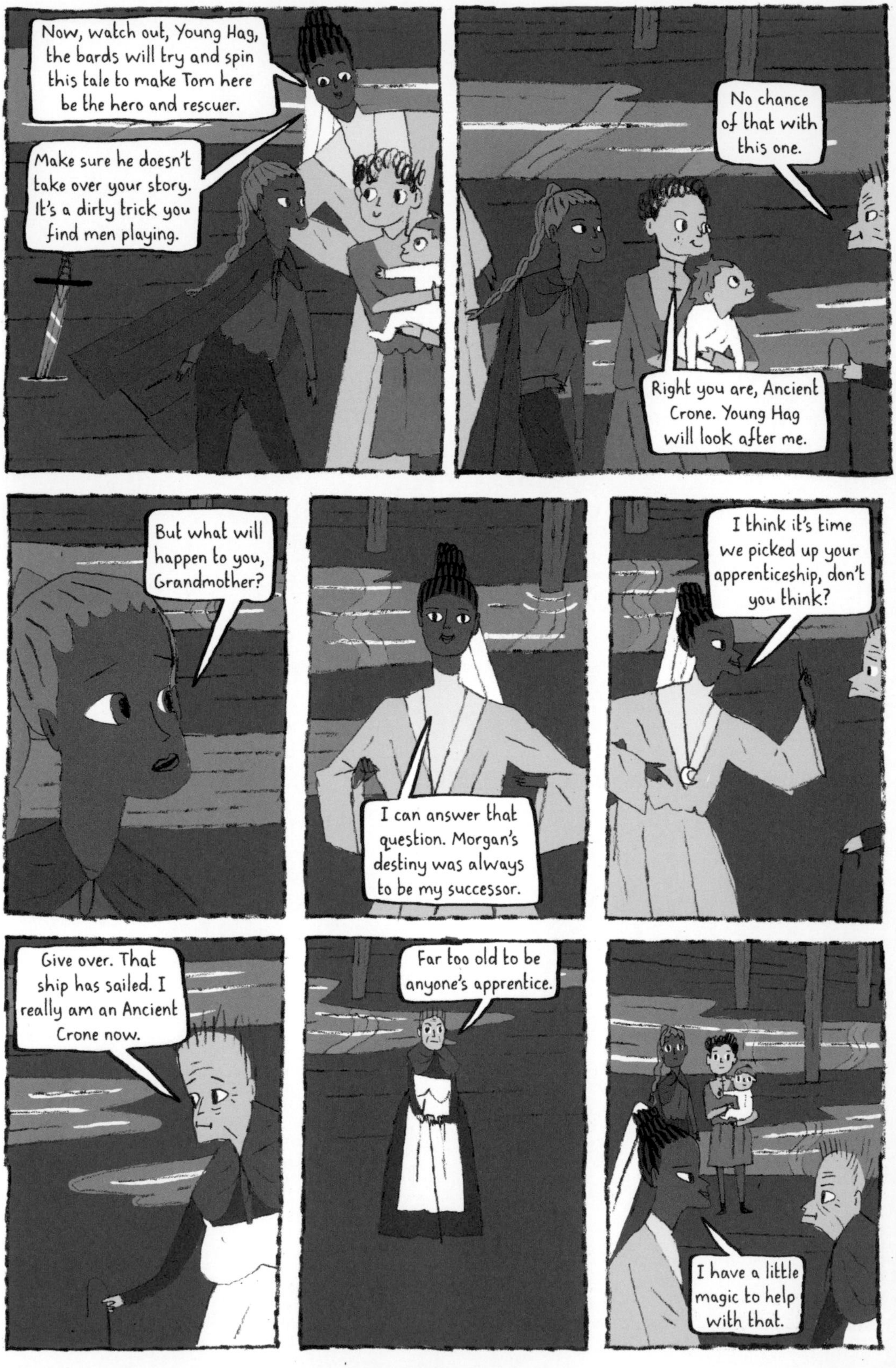

Now, watch out, Young Hag, the bards will try and spin this tale to make Tom here be the hero and rescuer.
Make sure he doesn't take over your story. It's a dirty trick you find men playing.
No chance of that with this one.
Right you are, Ancient Crone. Young Hag will look after me.
But what will happen to you, Grandmother?
I can answer that question. Morgan's destiny was always to be my successor.
I think it's time we picked up your apprenticeship, don't you think?
Give over. That ship has sailed. I really am an Ancient Crone now.
Far too old to be anyone's apprentice.
I have a little magic to help with that.

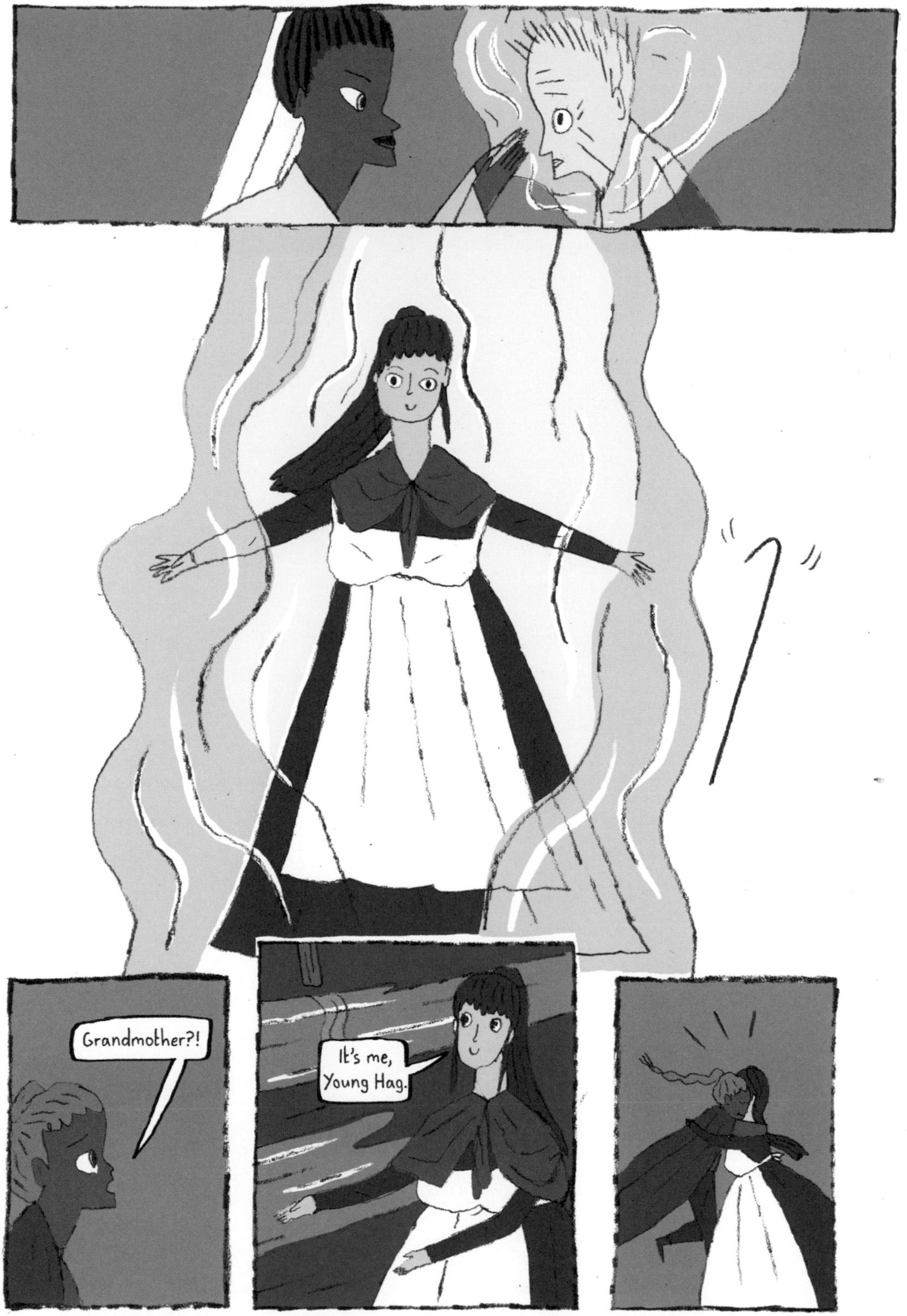
Grandmother?!
It's me,
Young Hag.

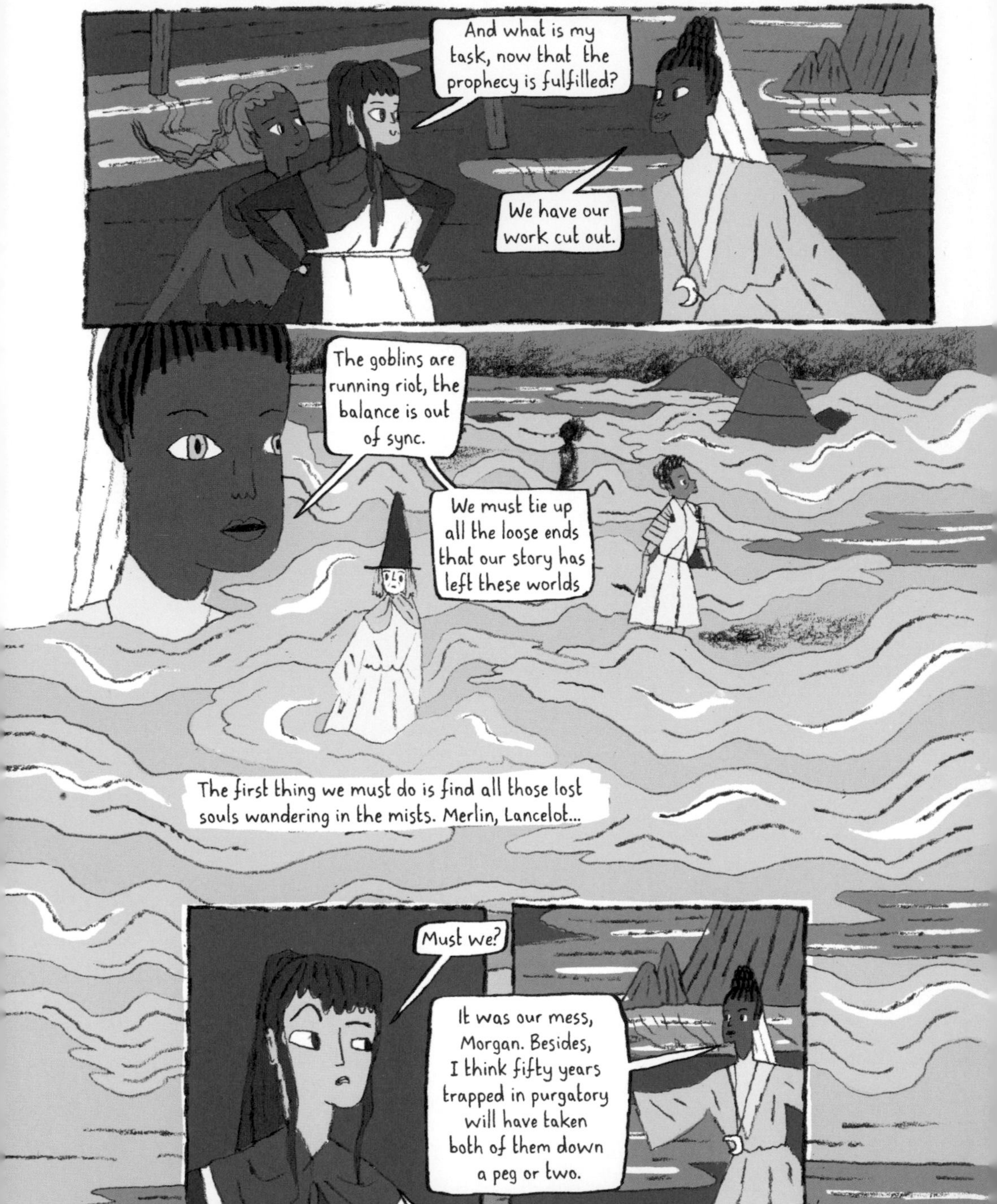
And what is my task, now that the prophecy is fulfilled?
We have our work cut out.
The goblins are running riot, the balance is out of sync.
We must tie up all the loose ends that our story has left these worlds
The first thing we must do is find all those lost souls wandering in the mists. Merlin, Lancelot...
Must we?
It was our mess, Morgan. Besides, I think fifty years trapped in purgatory will have taken both of them down a peg or two.
I wouldn't count on it.

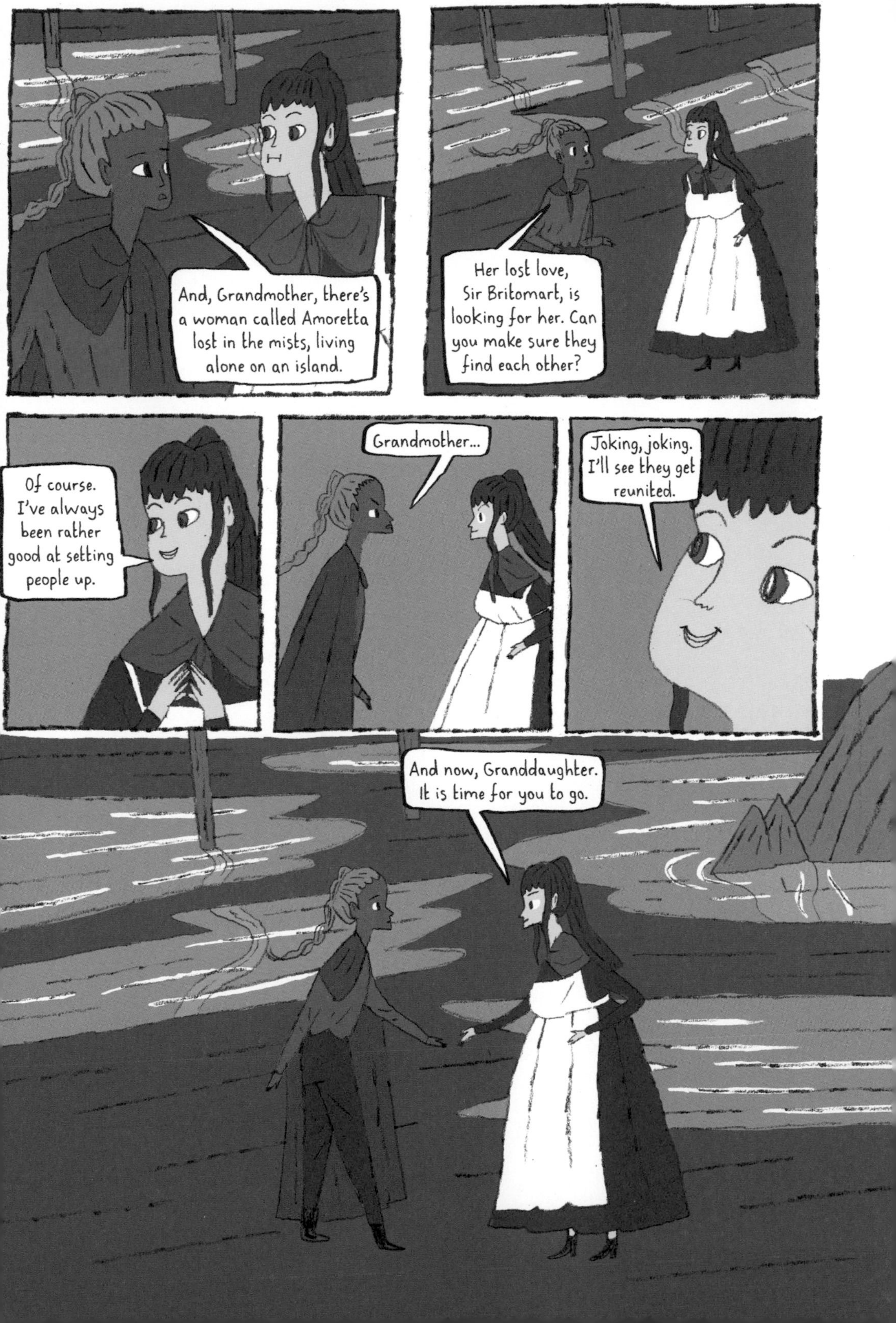
And, Grandmother, there's a woman called Amoretta lost in the mists, living alone on an island.
Her lost love, Sir Britomart, is looking for her. Can you make sure they find each other?
Of course. I've always been rather good at setting people up.
Grandmother...
Joking, joking. I'll see they get reunited.
And now, Granddaughter. It is time for you to go.

You three look after each other.
But shouldn't you teach me some more magic, before we leave?
You'll work it out just fine. I'm sure of it.
You know so much already.
Can I come and visit?

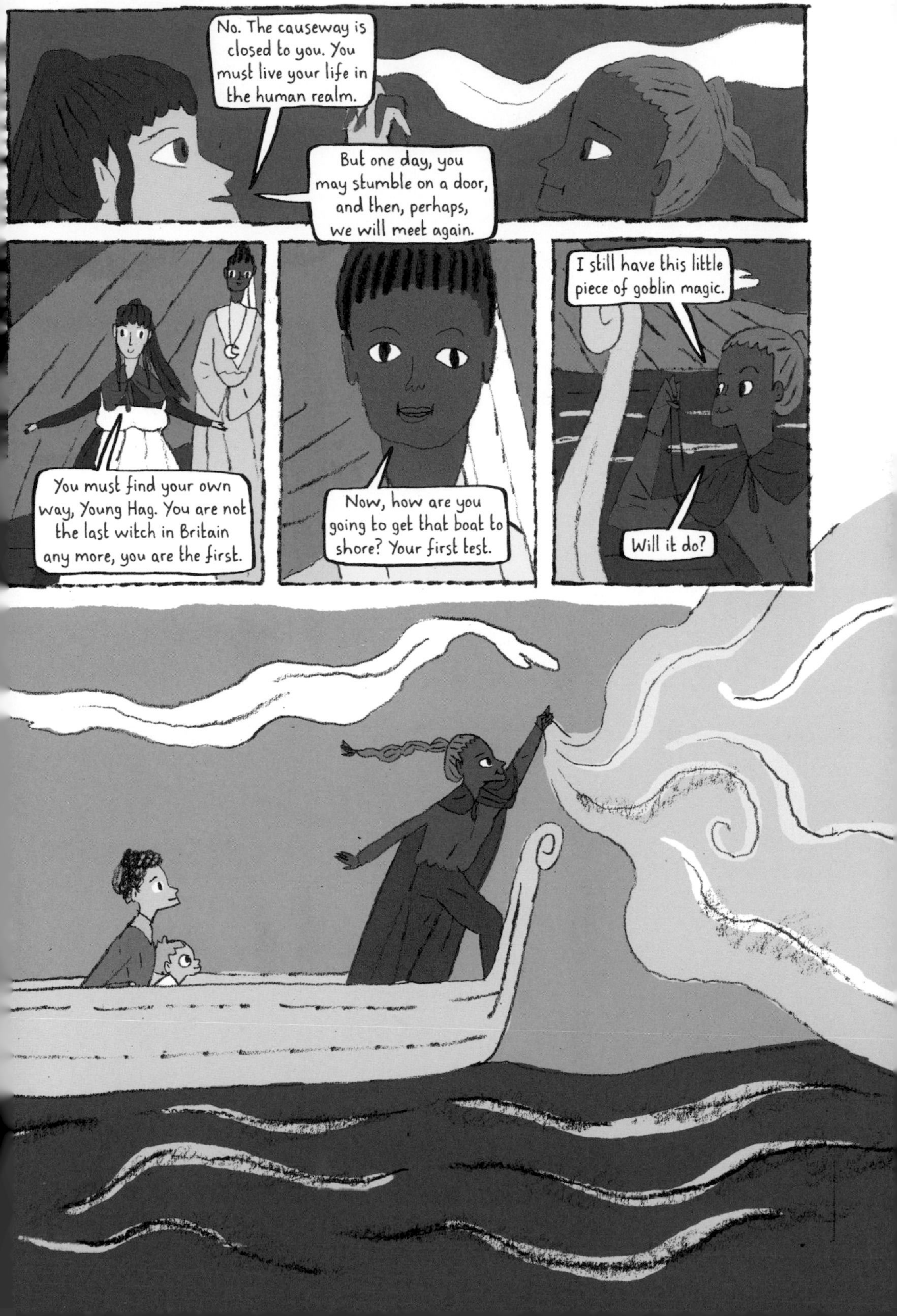
No. The causeway is closed to you. You must live your life in the human realm.
But one day, you may stumble on a door, and then, perhaps, we will meet again.
You must find your own way, Young Hag. You are not the last witch in Britain any more, you are the first.
Now, how are you going to get that boat to shore? Your first test.
I still have this little piece of goblin magic.
Will it do?

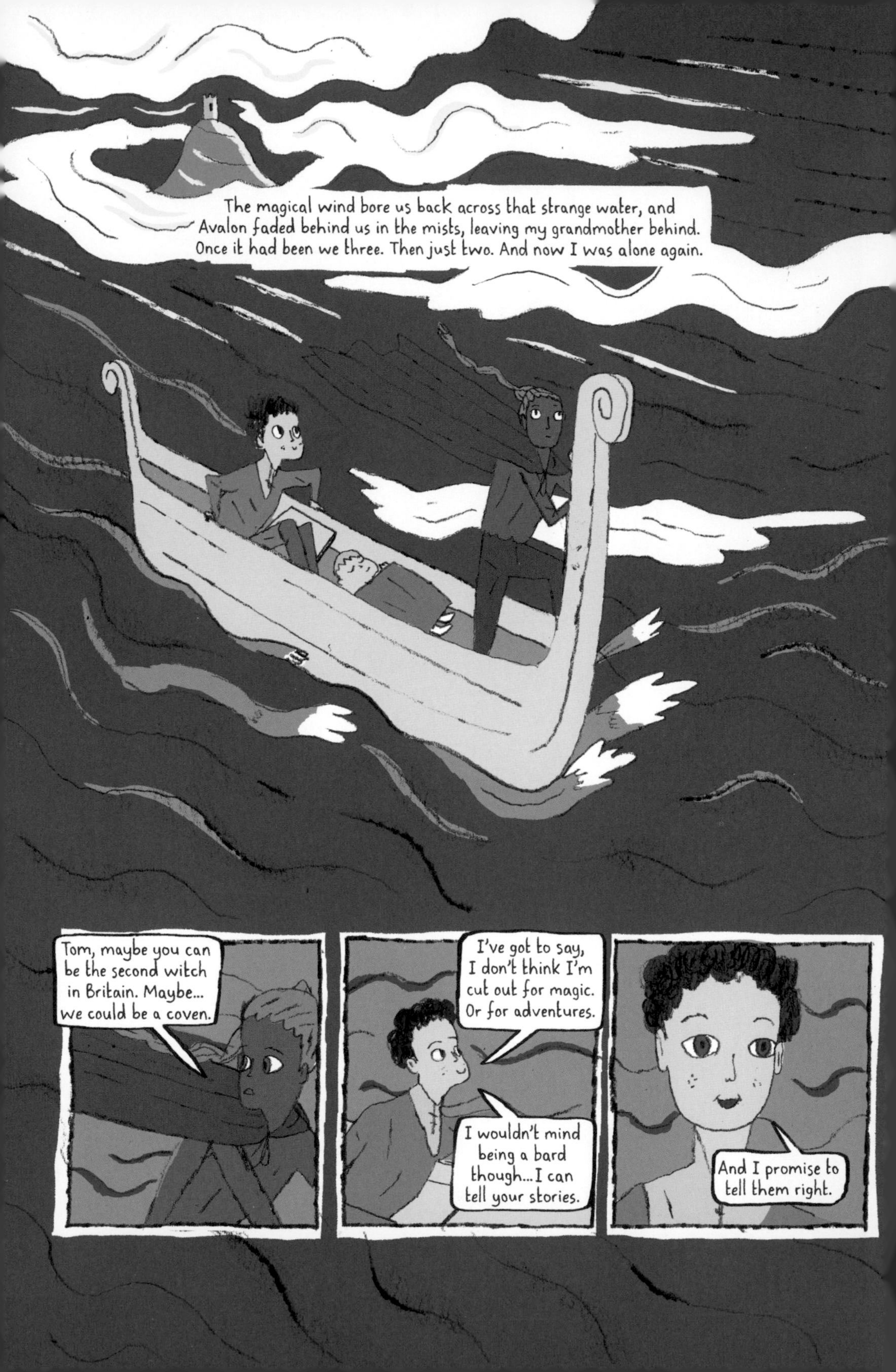
The magical wind bore us back across that strange water, and Avalon faded behind us in the mists, leaving my grandmother behind. Once it had been we three. Then just two. And now I was alone again.
Tom, maybe you can be the second witch in Britain. Maybe... we could be a coven.
I've got to say, I don't think I'm cut out for magic. Or for adventures.
I wouldn't mind being a bard though... I can tell your stories.
And I promise to tell them right.

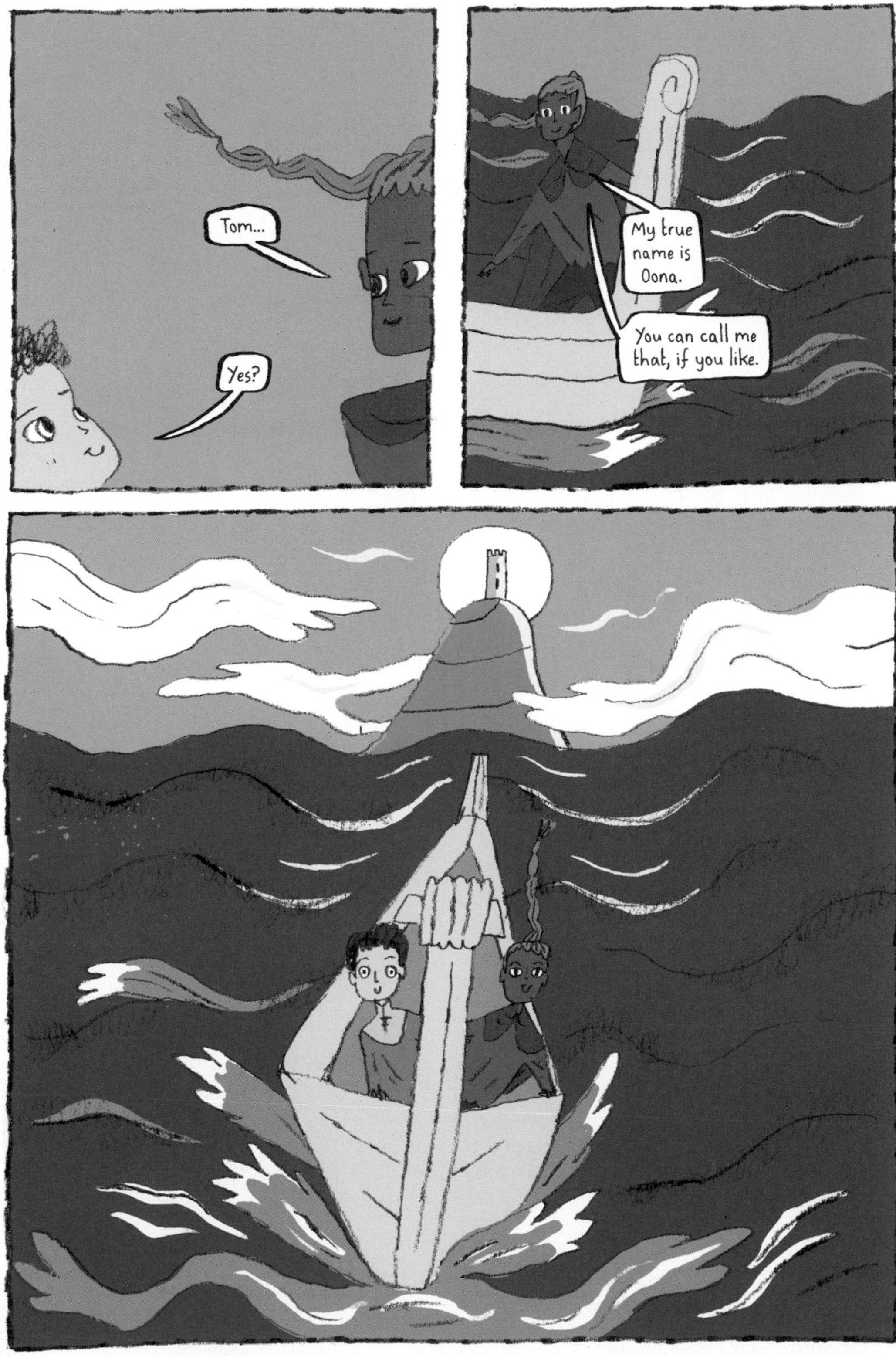
Tom...
Yes?
My true name is Oona.
You can call me that, if you like.

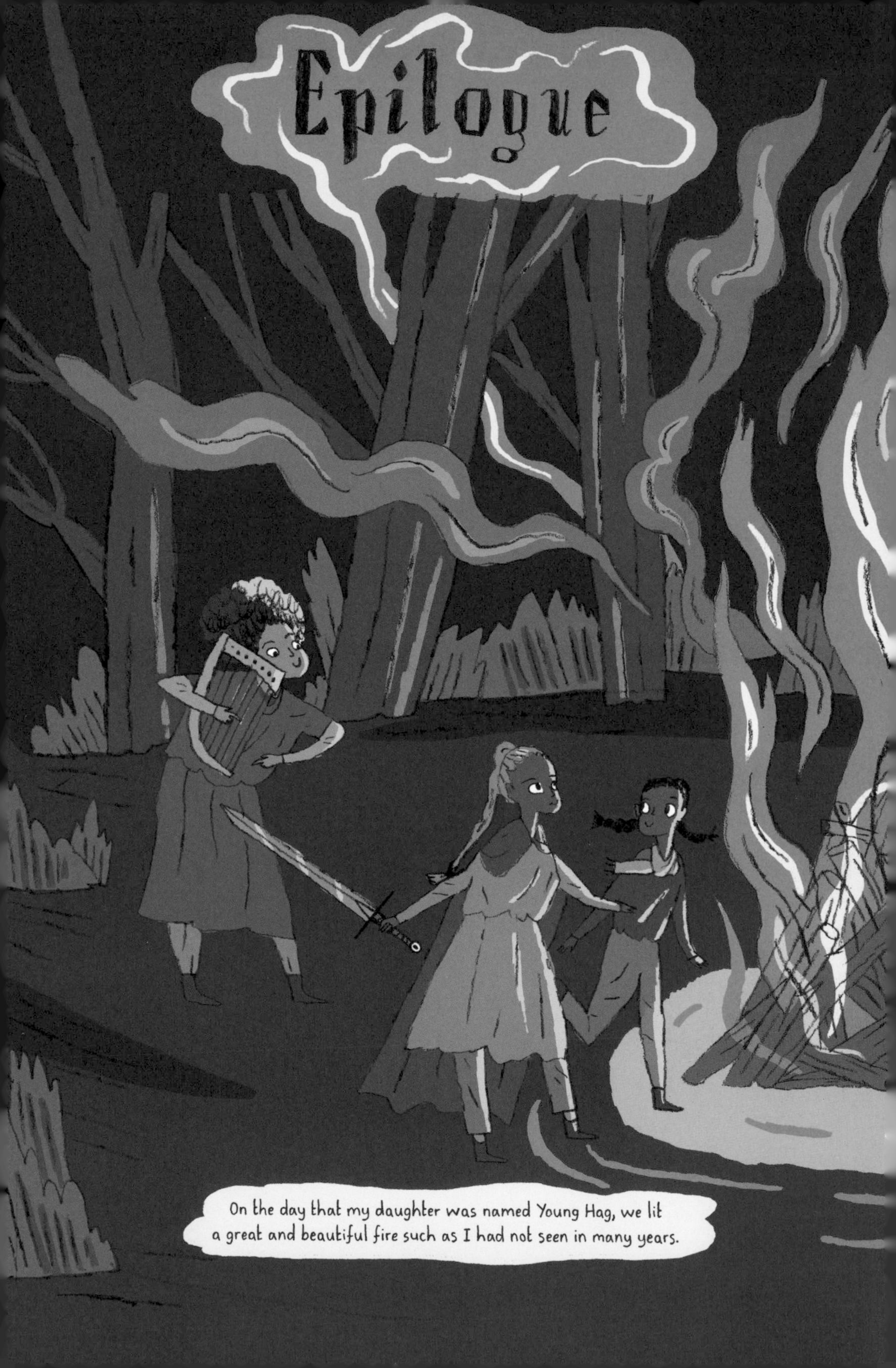
Epilogue
On the day that my daughter was named Young Hag, we lit a great and beautiful fire such as I had not seen in many years.

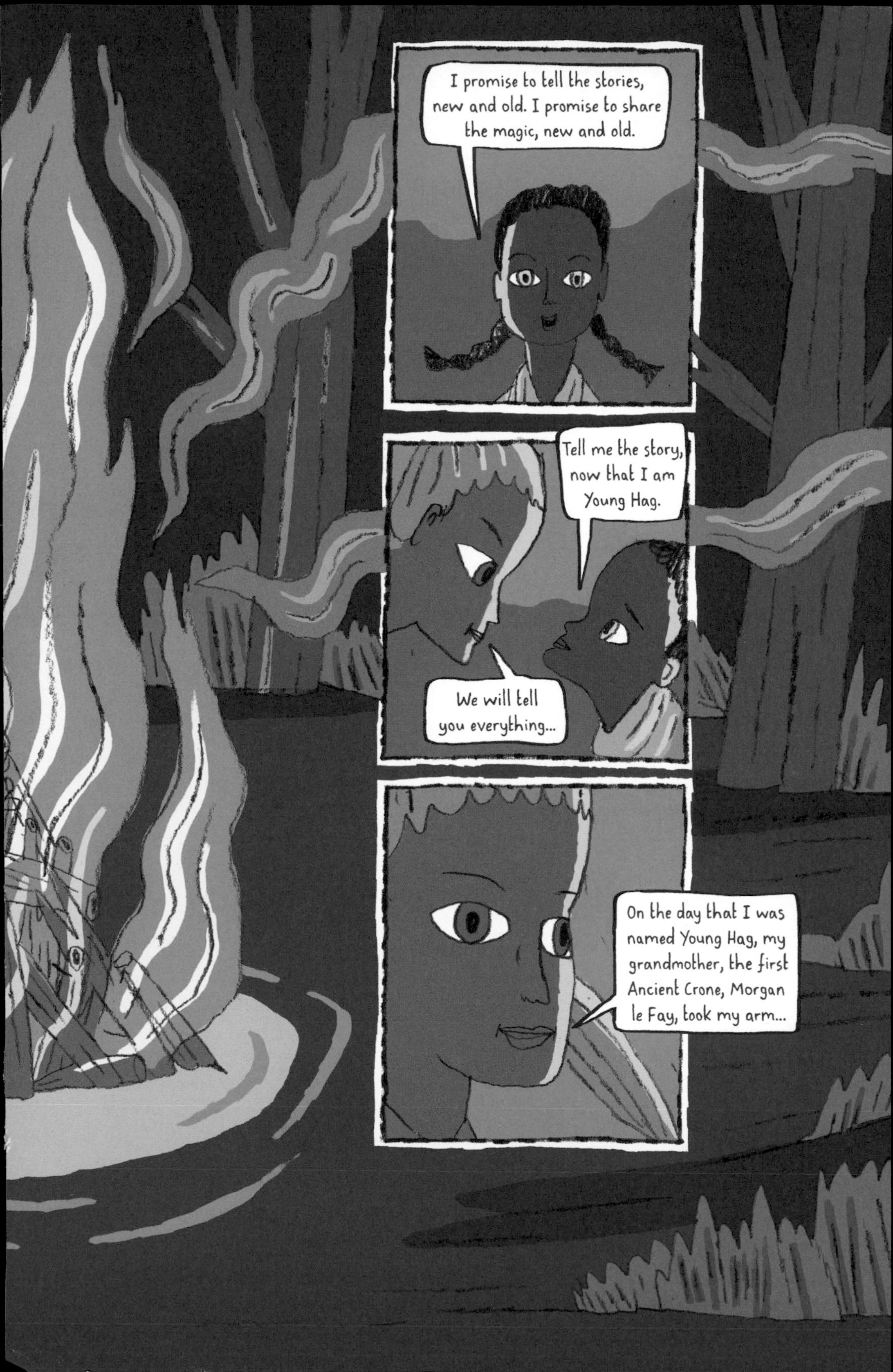
I promise to tell the stories, new and old. I promise to share the magic, new and old.
Tell me the story, now that I am Young Hag.
We will tell you everything...
On the day that I was named Young Hag, my grandmother, the first Ancient Crone, Morgan le Fay, took my arm...

For those of you familiar with the famous legends of King Arthur and his Round Table, you will recognize many characters and plotlines here in this book. There are also many things I've left out.

But stories of Camelot have been changed and retold many times over the centuries, and like the bards that came before, I've put my own spin on it.

Morgan le Fay is a contentious figure, who over the years has been a witch, a savior, a seductress, a villain and a hero. She's a slippery character and appears in many guises in the hundreds of retellings of these tales. In some versions, she and the Lady of the Lake are one and the same. If you have enjoyed meeting them, you can seek them out again in many forms.

Young Hag, on the other hand, can only be found within the pages of this book. There is no account of whether Morgan had a daughter, let alone a granddaughter. Her story stops for the most part with Arthur's death. But I like to imagine she kept on living.

ACKNOWLEDGMENTS

Thank you to my marvelous agent, Seth Fishman, and everyone at Abrams who has worked so hard on this book with me. To early readers Mairin O'Hagan, Ricky Miller, Imogen Greenberg, and Rachel Morris. And to Gordon and Frieda.

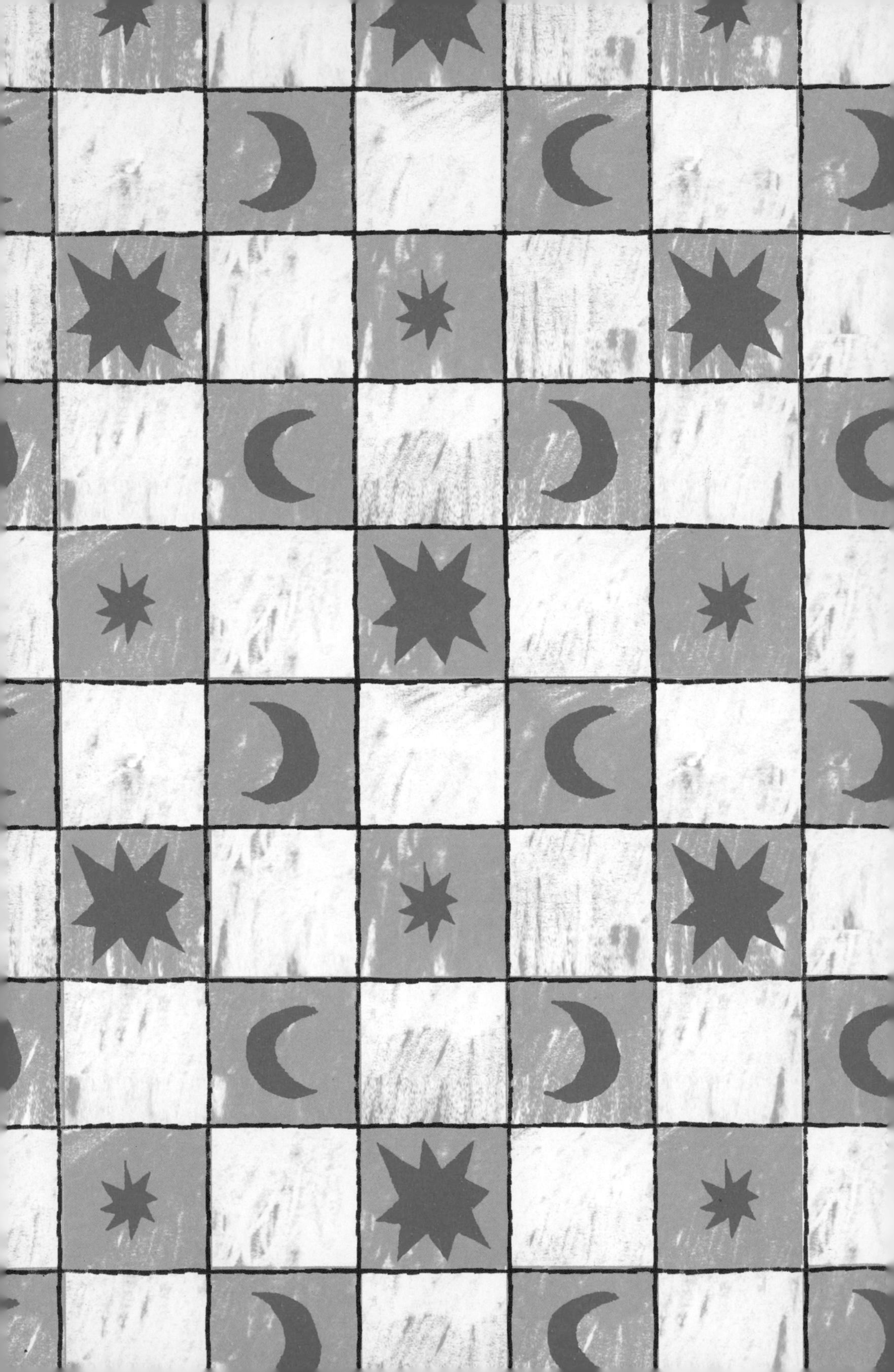